Alasdair felt a flo... Zandakar would push R... and berate and cuff her on the side of her head until she was ready to meet and defeat the dukes. He need never say another word on it. Zandakar would say it all.

He will earn her wrath and our marriage will be safe.

It occurred to him, then, so his hot blood turned cold, that he wasn't doubting Zandakar's intentions. Wasn't doubting the man would do everything in his power to keep Rhian alive and victorious. He was trusting her life to Zandakar's bloodsoaked hands . . . without a moment's hesitation.

Because he loves her. This murderous man is in love with my wife. I wonder what it says about me, that I'll use his love like a weapon to shield her. That I'll use him until he's all used up.

It didn't matter. All that mattered was that Rhian prevailed.

"Come then, Zandakar," he said, and moved to the chamber door. "Let us find Rhian a sword worthy of her, so she might take her place in history."

Praise for Karen Miller

"Adventure, magic, friendship, love, and a battle of good versus evil—I can see this tale becoming a classic."

—Scifichick.com on *The Awakened Mage*

"A skillfully created world of ritual and tradition provides a stunning backdrop for her exciting adventures."

—*Romantic Times* on *Empress*

Books by Karen Miller

Kingmaker, Kingbreaker

The Innocent Mage
The Awakened Mage

The Godspeaker Trilogy

Empress
The Riven Kingdom
Hammer of God

Writing as K. E. Mills

The Rogue Agent Trilogy

The Accidental Sorcerer

HAMMER OF GOD

GODSPEAKER: BOOK THREE

KAREN MILLER

orbit

www.orbitbooks.net

New York   London

Copyright © 2008 by Karen Miller
Excerpt from *The Accidental Sorcerer* copyright © 2008 by Karen Miller
All rights reserved. Except as permitted under the U.S. Copyright Act of 1976, no part of this publication may be reproduced, distributed, or transmitted in any form or by any means, or stored in a data base or retrieval system, without the prior written permission of the publisher.

Map by Mark Timmony

Orbit
Hachette Book Group
237 Park Avenue
New York, NY 10017
Visit our Web site at www.orbitbooks.net

Orbit is an imprint of Hachette Book Group, Inc. The Orbit name and logo is a trademark of Little, Brown Book Group Ltd.

Printed in the United States of America

Originally published in paperback by HarperCollins*Publishers* Australia Pty Limited: 2008
First Orbit edition in the USA: January 2009

10 9 8 7 6 5 4 3 2 1

For Elaine, whose friendship kept me going when the going got really tough.

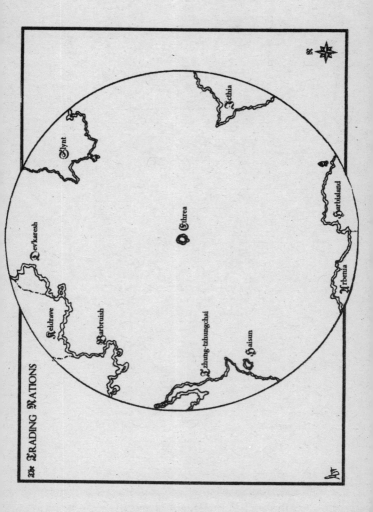

The Trading Nations

HAMMER
OF GOD

PART ONE

CHAPTER ONE

"Dmitrak."

Dmitrak kept his gaze pinned to the conquered harbour of Jatharuj, where the warships of Mijak clustered thicker than ticks on a goat. It was the time for highsun sacrifice. Ant-people swarmed down there, gathering for blood, his warriors and his slaves and all the godspeakers the empress insisted must remain. The township was over-ripe and full to bursting. Half its surviving original inhabitants had been sent to other conquered settlements, just to make room for Mijak's warhost.

My warhost. I am their warlord, they belong to me.

He did not turn. "Vortka high godspeaker."

"Warlord, you are absent from sacrifice."

He shrugged. "So are you."

A sigh. "Dmitrak . . ."

"Did the empress send you?"

"The god sends me, Dmitrak."

"Too busy to come itself, high godspeaker?"

"Dmitrak!" Vortka's voice grated with displeasure. "You desire another tasking, is that why you spit your words in the god's eye, do you think the god is blinded by words?"

Dmitrak swung round sharply enough that the silver godbells in his scarlet godbraids woke from slumber, clamouring his anger. "I am weary of taskings, Vortka. I will have no more of them."

"It is not your place to decide who is tasked, warlord," the old man said, severe. "It is not your place to say 'I will not come to sacrifice'. You are the warlord. Your place is at the altar when the god receives its blood."

He turned back to the wide, shallow harbour and the wider ocean beyond it. *Yes, I am the warlord. I am the god's hammer, I can strike down a godspeaker if I wish. Be careful, old man.* "My place is where I say it is."

"Your place is where the god puts you, Dmitrak," said Vortka, his voice cold. "By its want, you are its hammer. For as long as the god sees you and no longer than that."

Old man. Old fool. Like the empress he clung to the hope that one day the god's other hammer would return.

"Zandakar is gone, Vortka. Zandakar is most likely dead. I am the only hammer in the world."

He almost choked on the name, to say it aloud. Thinking the name made the world shimmer red. Rage shivered a harsh keening from his godbells. His skin felt hot, his blood surged hot in his veins.

He was my brother; he turned his face from me. How dare he do that? How dare he dare?

So much time gone by, and still he could weep and kill to think of Zandakar.

"He loved you, Dmitrak," Vortka said. His voice was cracked and chasmed with pain. "Your brother loved you. How can you doubt it? The world saw his love. He loved you in the god's eye."

Why would Vortka say such a thing, did he think talk of Zandakar would please Dmitrak warlord? He had never said such a thing before, they had never talked of Zandakar. Nobody dared talk of Zandakar in his hearing.

You defend him, Vortka? You defend him to the man he wronged most? Tcha, you are blind, you tell yourself lies.

Vortka's defence of treacherous Zandakar pricked him to speak, when silence would be better. "He loved his stinking piebald bitch more."

"And for that you tried to kill him?" said Vortka, angry again. "Aieee, warlord, you do not understand. A man may love a brother and also a wife. Even if—" He sighed, a sound of sorrow. "Even if the wife was a mistake. He loved that wrong woman, he did not stop loving you. He begged I never tell the empress you attempted his life, he spoke of you every highsun he was kept by my hand. Grieving and desolate, sometimes close to losing his mind, still he thought of you. Warlord, you should have a softer heart."

Dmitrak raised his right arm, let his gold-and-crystal fingers fist. Summoned the power so the crimson stones glowed. "*You* should guard your old man's tongue, I will burn it in your mouth if you do not take my advice."

"Dmitrak . . ."

Vortka sounded sorry again. Sorry, but beneath the regret a thread of fear. *Good.*

"You cannot hate forever," said the foolish old man. "Hate will shrivel your heart, it will poison your godspark."

Dmitrak grimaced into the wind. The high godspeaker was wrong, hate was more potent than the date wine of Icthia. Hate filled a man's belly, it strengthened his bones.

"Tcha, Vortka, you are stupid. The god hates. The god hates its enemies and tasks me to smite them, the god hates demons and weaklings. I am its hammer born to break them apart."

"The god hates its enemies, yes," agreed Vortka. "If we see the god in our hearts we must hate its enemies also, this is a true thing. Dmitrak, Zandakar was never your enemy."

Zandakar again! Was the old man eager to lose his tongue? "Did I ask you to come here and grind your teeth on that name? I think I did not, Vortka. I think you think I will not smite you. I will."

"You smite where the god wills, you smite nowhere else," said Vortka, once more severe. "You are warlord, you have power, you have less power than the god. I am Vortka high godspeaker, I am in the god's eye. You will not smite me, Dmitrak."

He looked over his shoulder. "No? Then why are you afraid?"

Vortka met his stare, unblinking. "Why are you, if Zandakar is gone?"

A hot pain stabbed through him. Sometimes at night, if he was not sated with female flesh or date wine, he dreamed of his brother, of the days when they were friends. He remembered laughter and horse races and the feel of a strong, warm hand on the back of his neck. Sometimes he woke from those dreams wet with tears.

Weak men weep, I am not weak. I am Dmitrak warlord, the god's hammer, doom of demons.

He shifted till he stood sideways to the harbour. "When does the god say we must sail from Jatharuj to this island called *Ethrea*?"

"Not yet," said Vortka.

Not yet. Always the same answer. "The slave sailors talk of trade winds, they say the trade winds are weak. They should not be weak. What does the god say to you in the godpool, Vortka? Why do the trade winds lose their strength? We cannot sail to this *Ethrea* if the winds are too weak to fill our sails. The slaves cannot row there, they will die in their chains."

"The godpool is godspeaker business, Dmitrak," said Vortka. "It is not for you to ask or me to answer."

And what did that mean? Did Vortka not know? Did the god not tell him why the winds had grown weak?

If Zandakar had asked him, Vortka would answer.

"My warhost grows restive, high godspeaker," he said, thrusting aside the sour thought. "Icthia is conquered. The lands behind it are conquered. The world lies in front of us, out *there*—" He waved an arm at the gently seething ocean. "My warhost trains newsun to lowsun, it knows these boats, Vortka, it knows how to sail. We are in the world to kill demons for the god, there are demons in Ethrea. *Why are we still here?*"

Vortka's godbraids were as silver as his godbells, they were weighted with amulets so his head was heavy to turn. His scorpion pectoral clasped ribs bare of flesh. He was an old man, older than the empress, but an agelessness was in him, as though he could never die.

He would die if I killed him, if the hammer struck him he would die.

Vortka's sunken eyes were bright with anger. "Dmitrak, you tempt the god to a great smiting. You are its hammer, you make no demands. The warhost is in Jatharuj until the god says it is not. Do you say to me *you* will tell the god what it desires?" His hand lashed out. "*Tcha*! You sinning boy!"

Dmitrak stared at him, his face stinging from the blow. He did not need to look to know his gauntlet had caught fire, that power pulsed from his blood to the red stones, making them glow, waking in them their yearning for death.

Why can he strike me when I cannot strike back?

Suddenly he was a child again, cowering before the empress his mother, stinging from her careless blows because he danced too slowly in the *hotas*, because he slumped astride his pony, because – because—

Because I am Dmitrak, I am not Zandakar.

"Dmitrak . . ."

The rage had died from Vortka's lined face, the heat in his dark eyes had cooled to – to – *pity*.

"You are the god's hammer, you are in the god's eye," said Vortka. "You serve the god, you serve it well, do not tempt it to smiting. Do not let anger lead you astray, Dmitrak. The empress needs you. She will not admit it."

Aieee god, the scorpion pain inside him. *I am a man grown, I need no bitch empress to need me.* He let the gauntlet cool, pulled the burning power back into himself. *I need no brother, I need no-one. I am the hammer.*

"Dmitrak warlord," said Vortka. "The warhost

looks to you, you are its father and its mother and its brother. You must come to sacrifice, you must kneel for tasking, you must be Mijak's warlord as Raklion was warlord before you."

He felt his lips thin to a sneer. "Not Zandakar?"

"Zandakar . . ." Vortka looked away, to the ocean, to the horizon at its distant edge. A terrible suffering was in his old face. "Your brother lost his way, Dmitrak. He was a great warlord until he was not, and when he was not the god smote him for his sinning. There is no mercy in it for the weakness of men. Sinning men die, how many times have I seen this? Sinning men are broken, the god hammers them to pieces. Are you stupid, Dmitrak? Do you think the god will not hammer you?"

If he said *no* Vortka would strike him again. Vortka was not Nagarak, fierce tales of Nagarak lived long after his death, but still Vortka was fierce in his own way. He was fierce for the empress, he breathed the air for her and for Mijak.

He will choose her over me, he will never see she is used up. He is blinded by Hekat. He is blinded by love. Does he think I am blind, I cannot see it? Zandakar blinded, Vortka blinded, love is a blinding thing. I keep my eyes.

"When have I not served the god, Vortka?" he demanded. "Cities are rubble because I serve the god. Blood flows like rivers because I serve the god. My blood boils and burns me because I serve the god. I sweat newsun to lowsun because I serve the god. I live in its eye, the god is all that I see. But you stand there and say I do not serve it? *Tcha!*"

Vortka looked at him steadily, hands relaxed by his

sides. In the bright sunshine his stone scorpion pectoral glowed. "You do not serve the god if you keep from sacrifice, Dmitrak. You do not serve the god if you say 'I will not be tasked'. Pain keeps your heart pure. Pain purges your godspark of sin. Pain keeps you in the god's eye, it sees your pain and knows your obedience. In your cries it hears your love."

He had cried in tasking so often the god should be dead of his love by now. He had been tasked from small boyhood more times than he could count. Breathe too deeply, too often, the empress sent him for tasking. Dance too swiftly, too slowly, the empress sent him for tasking. Speak too loudly . . . speak at all . . . the empress sent him for tasking.

If I had died in the godhouse she would not have shed a tear.

That should not matter, he should not care if she cared. Yet he did care and it burned him, as the god's power burned him when he set his gauntlet on fire.

"When you kneel for tasking," said Vortka, "your warhost sees you serve the god, your warriors know their warlord is seen, they know their warlord is in the god's eye. Can you look in *my* eye, Dmitrak, and tell me it does not matter?"

Aieee, tcha, it mattered. It mattered but he hated it. "If they are truly my warriors they know I am their warlord, they know the god sees me," he retorted. "Am I a child or a slave to be beaten, Vortka? I think I am not. Task the empress, not me."

"The god tasks the empress every day, Dmitrak," said Vortka. "That is the god's business and mine, you have your own business to think of. The warhost will not linger in Jatharuj forever. Do you wish to sail to Ethrea with your godspark in doubt?"

When he was a child the godspeakers tasked him, not kindly, but knowing he was a child. He was a man now, he was the warlord, he was the god's hammer. The godspeakers thought he would not break.

Every tasking he feared to prove them wrong.

He turned away from Vortka and stared at the clustering boats, at the sunlit water, at the ant-people scattering. Highsun sacrifice was done. Now the iron tang of fresh blood was on the salty breeze. His warhost would be looking for him, with fingers of light to fill there must be training, they could not stand idle. The empress was right about that much at least.

Vortka was right also, though it galled him to think it. *The warhost is a beast, it must stay tamed to my fist.* It must have faith in him, believe in him. It must believe, never doubt, he was in the god's eye. He turned back. "No, high godspeaker," he admitted, grudging. "I would not sail to Ethrea with my godspark in doubt."

"Then you will come to lowsun sacrifice, warlord," said Vortka, in the voice he used for the god's pronouncements. "And after you have drunk blood for the god you will kneel for the godspeakers to task you. You are the god's hope against the demons infesting the world. You are the empress's hope. You must not fail."

He stared down his nose at the high godspeaker. "Fail? I am Dmitrak warlord, I am the god's hammer. Where Zandakar lost his way *I* have stayed strong."

Vortka nodded again, his expression cautious.

"You have." Like a fish in muddy water, pity stirred again in his eyes. "But true strength lies in knowing when to bend before you break, warlord. You have pride, it has saved you, it might not save you forever."

Why do you care, high godspeaker? You love Zandakar, you love Hekat. You do not love me.

He frowned. "Yes, Vortka."

Vortka looked around the bare hilltop where they stood. Now his expression was puzzled, as though he searched for something. The sky was above them, the harbour below. Beyond them stretched the ocean, blue and deep, the greatest test the god had sent its chosen people. What was a desert of sand when the world contained deserts of water to drown them?

"What do you do here, Dmitrak warlord?" said Vortka, almost whispering. "Why do you so often come to stand on this hill?"

It was far from the township. It was dry land, no water. The breeze was cool, it soothed his skin. It made his godbells sing like sweet birds. Until recently the empress came here, this hilltop pleased her, but she came no more. The walk was too tiring. She needed to rest.

But I can stand here, Vortka. I can stand where she wants to stand, I can see what she cannot see. What I have here she wants, she cannot have it, I win.

I win, Vortka. Why else would I come?

He smiled. "I will come to lowsun sacrifice, Vortka. I am the warlord, I give you my word. When sacrifice is finished I will kneel for your godspeakers, I will permit them to task me. I am the god's hammer. I serve the god."

In silence Vortka stared at him. Not pity in his eyes, not puzzlement or caution or glorious fear.

His eyes are blank. I do not trust blank eyes.

"The god see you, warlord," said Vortka high god-speaker. "The god see Mijak in the world."

He walked away. Disquieted, Dmitrak watched until the old man disappeared from sight down the side of the steep hill. Then he swung back to the harbour, the blue water, the wet desert he must cross for the god. In the pit of his belly, a clutch of fear. Ruthlessly he killed it.

I am the warlord, what is fear to me? It is nothing, it is unknown, fear belongs to my enemies. I am not afraid.

Down in the township was a pen full of old slaves, sick slaves, crippled slaves who could no longer work. The empress desired them, their blood held great power, but he would take them first. He would deny them to her. She said the warhost must not be idle, it would not be idle, his warriors would sharpen their snakeblades on the bones of useless slaves. Warriors whose blades did not drink blood often were warriors whose godsparks withered in the sun.

How can she smite me? In her own words I am right.

Already he could feel his snakeblade biting flesh, breaking bone. He could smell the nectar of fresh blood, taste it spraying hot and iron on his tongue, his thirsty skin. He could hear the chanting of his warhost, see the empress's chagrined face, knowing she had lost to him, knowing he was right.

The hilltop breeze strengthened, his godbells sang in the ringing silence. They sang to his glory, they sang to Dmitrak warlord, Dmitrak god hammer, Dmitrak warrior of the world.

He threw back his head. He laughed, and laughed.

Returned to the township, Vortka barely noticed the godspeakers bowing to him, the warriors punching their fists to their chests, the fear in the slaves as they flung themselves face-down on the sand, the grass, the pavestones. He scarcely smelled the fresh sacrifice, the salt in the rising breeze, he paid no attention to the coins in the godbowls before this street's godposts. He hurried to his godhouse in search of the god.

Although it sat above the township, the godhouse of Jatharuj did not dominate like the godhouse atop Raklion's Pinnacle. Before Mijak came to cleanse the town, the building was the home of an official. He was dead now, his bones bleached in the sun. A godpost towered on the godhouse roof, it cast a long shadow down the Jatharuj hillside. Inside the godhouse the soft furnishings of Jatharuj were stripped away, broken up and burned, they did not please the god. The room for bathing in the house was turned into a godpool, its blood collected at sacrifices and stored in stone cisterns deep beneath the hot ground.

Vortka summoned three novices as he entered the godhouse. "Fill the godpool," he told them. "I will seek the god now."

Waiting for them to complete their task, he stood on the balcony at the front of the godhouse. In some small way it reminded him of Hekat's palace balcony in Et-Raklion. The view, perhaps, or the clean air. The sense of height and freedom. In Et-Raklion the palace was surrounded by a sea of green, fields and vine-yards and open land. Here the sea was blue, it was an ocean, it stretched even further than the green lands of Et-Raklion. He missed Et-Raklion.

He stared at the harbour but instead of seeing the warhost's crowding war galleys he saw instead Dmitrak. He saw the warlord's angry face.

Aieee, god, he disturbs me. He is a boy in a man's body, his godspark is scarred. When I praise him he suspects me, when I chide him he wants me dead. Somehow I must reach him. How can I reach him? He lives alone in his heart. Without Zandakar he is lost.

A dreadful thought, since Zandakar was gone. Dmitrak called him likely dead and it was likely, though Hekat clung to hope. Hekat clung to Zandakar so tight she did not see the son in front of her.

She has never seen him, save for something to hate. Every highsun she hates him, every highsun his scars thicken but they do not keep him from pain. Aieee, god, this is a tangle, did you mean this? Is this right?

After the godpool he must go to the empress. If Dmitrak was angry, Hekat was raging. The trade winds were slothful, he could not tell her why. She was threatening a slaughter like the slaughter in that desert behind them, the one that had drunk her first human blood. He watched his fingers tighten on the balcony railing, in his mind's eye the ocean turned stinking and scarlet.

How I wish she had never learned the power of human blood. Why did you show her, god? It is a dreadful thing.

Doubtless that thought was dreadful too, but how could he help it? To sacrifice animals, that was one thing. That was proper, they lived that they might die. But to butcher humans, even slaves, even those blighted godsparks not living in the god's eye, to slaughter them when they were not criminals . . . Mijak was in the world for the god. What purpose was served in killing when the god needed living men and women to praise it?

If Zandakar were here he could stop her sacrificing humans, her love for him was the only soft thing in her. Zandakar . . . Zandakar . . . why did you stray?

Grief was a snakeblade lodged in his heart. Every time he thought of his son it twisted and he bled inside, bled tears, bled despair, bled fear they would never meet again.

If he was dead I would feel it, surely. If my son was dead the god would tell me in my cut and bleeding heart.

"High godspeaker?" said Anchiko novice, behind him. "The godpool is filled."

He waited a moment before turning, so the breeze could dry his face. "Good. Return to your duties."

Anchiko bowed and withdrew. Vortka watched him retreat down the godhouse corridor, his rough-spun robe splashed scarlet in places.

I was that young once, I was that fearful of my fearsome high godspeaker. I am not Nagarak, I do not grow fat on the fear of novices, yet they fear me anyway. I never dreamed this would be me, I never asked for this power. Seasons pass, so many seasons, and I find myself understanding it less and less.

Perhaps in the godpool he would receive an answer.

The novices were well trained, all was ready for him in the tiled room given over to the god. It was fortunate the Jatharuj official had been a man fond of his luxuries. The sunken bath was profligate, large enough for five grown men. Small for a godpool, though, mean compared to the godpool in the god-house on Raklion's Pinnacle, but for his purpose it sufficed.

The air in the tiled room hung heavy with the scent of blood. He stripped to his skin, laying his stone scorpion pectoral carefully on the tiled floor. It had not woken for so many seasons, every highsun he prayed it would not wake again.

The blood in the godpool was cool and cloying, teetering on the edge of turning rotten. This Icthia was not like Et-Raklion, where the godhouse farms bred countless sacred beasts for sacrifice. There was less blood here, it had to be hoarded, kept until it reached the point of reeking. He felt his skin cringe at its touch. The stench clogged his nose and mouth, coated his tongue with nausea. As it closed over his head a sob caught in his throat.

Forgive me, god, forgive this sinning man in your eye.

In the dark redness of the godpool, where he could not walk properly but only crawl, he opened his heart and his mind to the god.

We are trapped in Icthia, god, we are trapped in Jatharuj. Is this your doing or do demons rise against you? We sit in your eye, we wait for your desire, what is your want? Is Hekat right, must we sacrifice more

*slaves to break the demons' hold on the trade winds?
Or do you keep them from us for some other purpose? I am here, god, in the godpool, Vortka high
godspeaker, your servant in the world. I seek to know
your will, speak to me that I might obey you, I have
obeyed you all my life.*

His snakeblade heart remained silent. He felt tears
well behind his closed eyelids, felt them swell in his
chest and make his heart throb with pain.

*Why are you silent, god? Have I displeased you?
Did I sin, saving Zandakar? Should I have let
Dmitrak kill him?*

His lips were pressed tight against the stinking
blood, he sobbed in his throat but did not let the
sound escape. How could he have done that, how
could he have given his son to Nagarak's blighted son
for killing?

*Peace, Vortka. You did not sin. Zandakar lives, he
is meant to live. Tell no-one, his life is in your hands.*

He did sob then, and the rancid blood poured into
his mouth. Choking, his belly heaving, he struggled to
stay with the god, to hear its faint voice.

*No more human sacrifice, Vortka. The wind is the
wind, it will come when it comes. Be patient. Be
guided. Your heart knows the true path.*

He did burst free of the godpool then, it was burst
free or drown. Flailing, coughing, he clung to the
bath's tiled sides, retching.

The godpool door opened and a novice looked in.
"High godspeaker? High godspeaker!"

They were listening, outside this tiled room? When
he told them to leave him they lingered? They
disobeyed?

"Did I ask for your presence?" he growled. "I think I did not!"

It was a different novice, not Anchiko, it was a girl, her name was – was – *Rinka*. "Forgive me, high godspeaker," she whispered. "I was passing, I heard a sound."

Exhausted, he clung to the dark blue tiles. His bones ached, his muscles trembled, his heart beat like a worn-out drum. The sacred blood dripped slowly, its stink would linger many highsuns. Whispering faintly, the god's voice.

Your heart knows the true path.

And yet he felt as ignorant as any novice.

Rinka's dark eyes were wide and frightened, she knelt at the godpool's edge and stared at him. "Vortka high godspeaker, should I send for a healer?"

A healer? No. He was healed already, the snake-blade pain was gone from his heart. *Zandakar lives.* "I have no need of healing, novice," he said. His voice was a harsh wheeze. "You may assist me, I must speak with the empress. I must cleanse myself and dress in fresh robes. Help me out."

So long ago Hekat rode his body, she rode him to spilling seed and together they made Zandakar. That Vortka's body was young and strong, it stirred at young Hekat's touch, it yearned for sensation. Now he stood naked beneath the water sluicing from the spigot in the corner, Rinka's young touch swished him free of blood and he felt nothing. He was a stone man, unstirred.

In his hating eyes Dmitrak calls me an old man, he is right. I am old. I am withered. I am shrunken for the god. Does it matter? I think it does not. Zandakar lives.

"High godspeaker?" said Rinka, hesitating.

He pretended his tears were water from the spigot, he pretended he did not want to sob out his joy. "You may leave me," he said. "Return to your tasks."

She did not want to leave him, her eyes were full of worry, but he was the high godspeaker. To disobey was to die. So she left and closed the door behind her.

He was alone, he let himself sag against the cool tiles. *I am the high godspeaker, the god has spoken in the godpool. Now I must tell Hekat she cannot summon the trade winds. Aieee, god. The tasks you set.*

It was not one of Hekat's good days, Vortka saw that immediately. Good days came to Hekat more rarely with each passing fat godmoon.

"What do you want?" she demanded, propped on her cushioned divan. "Do I need more healing, Vortka? I think I do not."

Zandakar lives. Tell no-one. She would not be surprised to hear it, she never believed their son was dead. But the god was the god, he kept that news to himself.

"Empress," he said, and gently closed the chamber door. For her palace she had taken the home of a Jatharuj merchant, a rich man with much coin to spend on comfort and lavish display. His coin had not saved his life, of course, his bones bleached too, his blood was long since spilled to serve the god.

The palace's balcony doors stood wide open to let in the fresh salt air. He breathed in its sweetness, willing the godpool's stink to fade. Smiling, he crossed the soft carpet to reach Hekat, took her hand in his and kissed its knuckles. Gold bracelets chimed on her wrist. Her bony wrist, so fleshless, with only half of the strength he remembered remaining.

"Tcha," she said, as though he'd displeased her, but that was for show, for habit, she was pleased. "You came to kiss me, Vortka? We are long past that."

So many godmoons they had walked through life together, he did not ask if he could sit. He pulled a cushioned stool closer and lowered his skinny haunches to its soft comfort. "I have been in the god-pool."

Her face had shrunk to scars and eyes. Every curve and edge of her skull was visible beneath her taut scarred skin, her blue eyes were fading, her plump lips were grown thin. Pain lived inside her, his desperate healing could not chase it away. Her godbraids were a torment, too heavy for her head. She refused to lighten them by a single amulet, by one solitary godbell. She was the empress, her godbraids praised the god.

"In the godpool," she echoed. Now her blue eyes were hungry. She leaned forward, fingers clenching. "The god spoke? What did it say?"

He took a deep breath, braced himself for her fury. "It said there must be no human sacrifice for the trade winds. The trade winds will come in their time, and not before."

"Tcha!" she spat, she drummed her heels on the wide divan. "You misheard it, Vortka! I will swim in the godpool, the god speaks to me as well as you."

"I did not mishear it, Hekat, I heard it well

enough," he replied. "And you are too frail to swim in the godpool."

She threw a cushion at him. "Too frail? *Too frail?* Who are you to tell an empress she is too frail?"

He took her hand again, it was like holding a bird's claw. "You know who I am, I am Vortka, your dear friend. I am Mijak's high godspeaker, I tell you the truth. Always the truth, though you seldom wish to hear it."

"Tcha," she said, and tugged her hand free. "Because your truths are soft, they do not please me. I wish to sail!"

"And we will sail, Hekat. When the winds come, we will sail."

"Why do they not come, Vortka?" she said, pettish. "Are your godspeakers grown weak in their faith?"

He shook his head, smiling again. Smiling though his healed heart pained him. *You were so beautiful, Hekat, time has not been kind.* "You know they are strong. You know I train them well."

"Then where are the trade winds? Why are my warships becalmed?"

He sighed. "Hekat, we do not need to know the god's purpose to know its will. There are reasons the winds are slow, I cannot tell you what they are. I am the god's high godspeaker, I am not the god."

She snorted. "Do I need you to tell me that? I think I do not!"

"Hekat . . ." For the third time he took her hand in his, folded her fingers to his palm. "You need me to be your friend, I am your friend, I will be your friend no matter what you say or do."

For a heartbeat her eyes were brilliant, then she killed soft emotion. It was her way. "Vortka, we must have the trade winds. Are you certain you heard the god right?"

He nodded. "I am certain."

"Aieee, tcha," she said, and let her head fall back. "Can the god be wrong? I think it cannot. We will wait, high godspeaker. We will wait and pray."

His relief was so great it was like pain. But beneath relief churned sorrow. She had surrendered too easily, she did not fight him long enough.

She is weary. She is worn out. Send the trade winds soon, god.

CHAPTER TWO

Edward, Duke of Morvell, cleared his throat. "I'm sorry, Majesty, but Damwin and Kyrin leave you no choice. You'll have to fight them."

Rhian stood at her privy council chamber window, back turned to her councillors, and felt her fingers curl into fists. She had such a fondness for her staunch and stalwart supporter, but even so . . .

Don't tell me what I have to do, Edward. You know such intransigent talk sours my temper.

Instead of answering, she stared down at bustling Kingseat harbour. She had a perfect view from within the castle, so high above the town. Even though it was early, yet before nine of the clock, the harbour's blue waters were clogged with vessels coming and going, loading and unloading their various cargos. As though no danger loomed in the east. As though life in its sweet safety would never change.

But it will. Life as we know it will soon be torn asunder, if the witchmen of Tzhung-tzhungchai can be believed.

She had no reason to doubt them. It was seductive wishful thinking, no more, that enticed her to hope calamity was not come upon them, that war on a scale unimaginable did not hold its foul breath, waiting to exhale and spit death on them all.

As if I needed more proof, with Zandakar locked in a dungeon beneath my feet.

A mistake, to think of Zandakar. Her eyes burned, the distant harbour prismed, as the pain of betrayal seared anew.

He should've told me who he really was. What his people are planning. He should've trusted me. I thought we were friends.

Thrusting pain aside, she turned. Let her gaze first touch upon Alasdair, silent at the table. His expression was sober, serious, most kingly indeed, but her heart beat just a little bit faster as his eyes warmed.

My husband. My husband.

But she kept her own face as well-schooled as his. In this council chamber she was queen, and he was only a councillor. Let one man think Alasdair guided her steps, ruled from the shadows . . .

Edward was frowning. "Majesty—"

"Yes, Edward," she snapped. "I heard you."

"And what I said is not to your liking, I'm well aware of that," he said, sighing. "But my duty isn't to tell you what you want to hear. My best service lies in telling you what's needful. And so I tell you now, knowing full well you're likely to sharpen your tongue on me for saying it: Damwin and Kyrin *must* be confronted. It's been nearly two weeks since you were crowned and they have yet to pledge fealty. Their recalcitrant defiance keeps Ethrea in a turmoil."

"Edward's right," said Alasdair. "Every one of us here knows it, you best of all."

"I don't dispute Damwin and Kyrin must be dealt with, and soon," she said, keeping her voice level and low. "But, Edward . . . *gentlemen* . . . I haven't changed my mind regarding how I shall rule. I *will* not pit Ethrean against Ethrean in bloody combat. There must be another way."

Her privy councillors exchanged purse-lipped looks. "If there is, Majesty," said Rudi, glowering, "we can't think of one. More to the point, neither can you."

No she couldn't, and not for want of trying. And she'd happily admit it, if only Rudi weren't so bullish in his manner. Her Duke of Arbat could pass comment on the weather and make it sound like a declaration of war.

"At this rate it's going to take a miracle to bring them to heel," Rudi added. Then he looked at Helfred, expectant.

Ethrea's prolate sighed and examined his bitten fingernails. When Rudi opened his mouth to say something else, Rhian held up a hand and shook her head at him. There was no use prodding her former chaplain; he would answer in his own time and not before.

Prodding only produced a tedious lecture, as long ago she'd learned to her chagrin.

Unlike his late and unlamented uncle Marlan, Prolate Helfred dressed like a plain venerable in a dark blue woollen robe and open leather sandals. The only concession he made to his exalted status was the newly-made heavy gold ring of office on the second finger of his left hand, containing a splinter of one of the arrows that had slain Rollin. Even his prayer beads were the same battered old wooden ones he'd prayed and complained over on their circuitous journey from the clerica at Todding to duchy Linfoi and home at last to Kingseat.

He has no vanity. No ambition beyond serving God to the best of his ability. He is that rare thing, a good man . . . and still he drives me to distraction.

Helfred's silence dragged on. And since they couldn't sit here forever, waiting for him to pronounce, she decided to risk a lecture. "Helfred? Has our age of miracles passed? Or can God intervene in the matter of Damwin and Kyrin?"

Helfred stirred and lifted his gaze. "I was never privy to miracles, Majesty, as you well know. For an answer to that question you must seek out your toymaker."

Dexterity. Again, that searing stab of betrayal. *He should've told me about Zandakar, he had no business holding his tongue.* "I think not," she said shortly. "I think I will exhaust all other possibilities first. Unless you tell me I must?"

"No," said Helfred, after another, shorter silence. "I am not moved to instruct you so. Majesty, you are the queen. God has placed you upon Ethrea's throne for his purpose, and the welfare of all who dwell here. The matters of men must be dealt with by men." He smiled briefly. "And women. The dukes Damwin and Kyrin are your disobedient subjects. It is your business to chastise them as you see fit."

"And chastise them you must," said Adric, seated beside his father Rudi and just as bullish. "They make a mockery of crown and council every minute they draw breath in defiance of your rule."

She exchanged a glance with Alasdair then turned back to the window so she could battle her temper without councillor witness. More and more she regretted elevating Rudi to the dukedom of Kingseat. He was headstrong, he was prickly, he refused to guard his tongue. *I made a mistake . . .*

"Adric makes a good point," said Alasdair, mildly. He almost never lost his temper. "Intemperately, but . . . it is a good point. A pinprick turns to a festering wound without physicking. And the people of Hartshorn and Meercheq duchies deserve better than these disobedient lords."

"I do know that," Rhian said, again staring down at the harbour. Emperor Han's swift, sleek peacock-blue hulled imperial vessel still rode at anchor along one of the ambassadorial piers, its two gold-painted sails furled and its crimson pennants becalmed. When he intended to leave Ethrea for Tzhung-tzhungchai she had no idea. She hadn't seen him since her hastily arranged coronation, when he had smiled and bowed and terrified the minor ambassadors to stuttering incoherence. Nor had she laid eyes on his witchmen. They kept to themselves within the walls of the ambassadorial residence.

And if I never see them again I'll die thrilled beyond words.

"Knowledge without action is folly," said Rudi. "Your Majesty."

She turned on them. "And what action would you have me take, Rudi? Would you have me gather every last man and boy in duchy Kingseat's garrison, thrust a sword into their right hands and a pikestaff in their left and send them into Hartshorn and Meercheq with orders to maim and kill as their fancy takes them? Is *that* what you would have me do nine days after Helfred anointed me queen?"

Rudi's swarthy face reddened. "I'd have you be less tender of your womanly scruples and more manly in your care for the crown. Like a woman you cling to the thought that a smile will solve a multitude of sorrows. But these feisty dukes aren't little boys with scraped knees, Majesty. They're men and you have gouged gaping wounds in their pride. There aren't smiles enough beneath the sun to heal the hurts you've lately dealt them. If they refuse to kneel and pledge you their fealty then their lives *must* be made forfeit . . . and the lives of any man, woman or child who is foolish enough to follow their treasonous example."

Rhian felt her heart thud, her head swim. "*Children*, Your Grace? You would have me slaughter *children* to retain power? My God, you'd make of me another Marlan. No, a ruler *worse* than Marlan. At least he never stooped to killing babies!" She glared at Edward. "Is this your remedy also? If so, I am shocked. I took you for a kindlier man."

"No," said Edward, distressed. "I did not mean—"

"Didn't you?" she retorted. "You said I had to fight them, Edward. What else did you mean but that I must seal my coronation with a kiss of blood?"

"Blood does not necessarily follow," Edward replied. "If you but threaten to bring steel against these stubborn dukes should they refuse to yield, then—"

"Oh, *Edward*. Whatever I threaten I must be prepared to carry out!"

"Yes, you must," said Adric. "Without the tempering of mercy."

Rhian swept her council with a cold look. "My lords, if you feel so inclined you may indeed blame 'womanly scruples' for my reluctance to plunge Ethrea into civil war. For myself, I prefer to think of it as statecraft. I very much doubt if the late king would've rushed to send soldiers into Hartshorn and Meercheq. I also doubt you'd have called him *womanly* for preferring to find a less violent solution to this problem."

And *that* observation struck home, as well it might.

"There is nothing wrong with being a woman, gentlemen," she continued, still cold. "Being female doesn't make me weak. If it did, would God have seen fit to put me on the throne? Helfred?"

Helfred looked up. "Majesty, you are where God intends you to be."

"But not yet doing what God intends you to do," said Rudi, stubborn to the last. "If you won't send soldiers against Kyrin and Damwin, what *will* you do to end their defiance?"

"That's a fair question," said Alasdair. "And we must have an answer."

Rhian bit her lip. Was she the only one who could hear the tension in his voice? They'd not discussed this. Some things – like planning for the coronation, or the day-to-day grindstone of the kingdom's business – she happily talked over with him at night, in bed, pillowed on his chest. But not this. It was too important. Touched too closely on her fragile sovereignty. It hurt him, she knew that, but it couldn't be helped.

As she stared them down, the dukes of her council and her prolate and her husband the king, words she'd tried hard to forget echoed loudly in her mind. The words Zandakar had spoken to her as she stood over dead Ven'Martin, the knife that killed him in her hand.

You want be queen? This is queen. To kill bad men and be wei yatzhay.

She had rejected his assertion then. She rejected it now. She would not be a queen of blood and steel.

Not unless Damwin and Kyrin back me hard against a wall.

"I'll give them a final chance to come to their senses," she said. "If this must end in violence I won't let history show I refused these foolish men every hope possible of averting disaster. Helfred . . ."

"Majesty?"

"Will you and the Court Ecclesiastica act as my emissaries? Will you travel with all solemn ceremony to the duchies of Hartshorn and Meercheq and use every persuasion in your power so their dukes might see reason?"

Helfred smoothed his prayer beads through his fingers. "Of course."

Bless you. "I'll have letters drawn up for you to present to the dukes in person."

"Letters saying what?" demanded Adric. "And promising what retribution should they fail to recognise Ethrea's lawful queen and council?"

Rhian looked at him in silence for a moment, then nodded at the venerable whom Helfred had granted her as secretary for both private and council matters. Middle-aged, pedantic and a swift scribe, he was faithfully recording every comment in a secretive church notation that later was translated into legible Ethrean.

"You would have me dictate to you my royal correspondence, Adric? Perhaps you tire already of ducal duties. Do you wish to take Ven'Cedwin's place? It can be arranged."

She spoke sweetly enough but her threat was plain. Adric darted a glance at his father, temper mottling his high, sharp cheekbones. Rudi said nothing but his eyebrows lowered in a warning frown.

Yes indeed, Adric, do have a care. My patience is rubbed precarious thin.

"Majesty," said Helfred, releasing his prayer beads. "The Church stands behind you without reservation. Defiance of you is tantamount to defiance of God. It won't be tolerated."

He reminded her of Marlan when he spoke like that. The others heard it, too. Spines straightened, jaws tightened. Knuckles whitened in suddenly clenched fists.

"I think we've had enough of interdict for the time being, Helfred," she said quietly.

Helfred's eyebrows rose. Despite their recent hardships he remained a soft man in his body, but something in his eyes had changed. He was tempered now. His soul was steel. "Majesty, it's not the Crown's place to stand between a man and his soul. That is the Church's domain. God has put us there, and there shall we be until God decrees otherwise."

She wasn't about to engage in a theosophical debate with him. Not with the rest of the council listening. And especially not when she needed him to act as go-between with the dukes. "Prolate, I don't mean to usurp your proper authority. Of course your province is the spiritual well being of every Ethrean, no matter how high or low his station. I merely seek to remind you that this kingdom is newly healed. Scratching open those wounds can't serve any good purpose."

"This kingdom isn't healed at all," said Edward. "And won't be until these laggard duchies are shepherded to obedience."

She could have shouted. Banged a fist on the council table. Reprimanded Edward for his tone of voice. But she was tired, and worried, and she wanted this meeting done with. Needed some small time in solitude, in fresh air, so she could think clearly about what must come next without their burdensome gazes and warlike expectations. Because when the matter of the dukes was dealt with, there was Mijak . . .

She felt herself shiver, felt the nape of her neck crawl. *I'm not ready. I can't do this. God, why did you choose me? I think you've made a mistake.*

"Edward," said Alasdair, looking at her. Knowing her fear. "Her Majesty needs no instruction. She was tutored by a king."

Edward nodded, saying nothing. But she thought she could hear his thoughts, and those of Rudi and Adric.

Perhaps she was, but she has yet to show us.

Which wasn't fair or right and God curse them for their short, mean memories. Hadn't she fought for her crown? Stood against Marlan? Stood against all of them until they saw reason?

With Dexterity's help. Now I'm alone, without convenient miracles. Now I'm a girl on a man's throne, hesitant to force my authority down anyone's throat with the tip of a blade. Does that make me weak? Was Zandakar right after all?

Zandakar . . . fighting . . . protecting her people . . . winning against the dukes . . . the old days of Ethrea . . .

"Rhian?" said Alasdair, suspicious. "What are you thinking?"

She didn't answer. An idea was forming, outrageous and unlikely. But no more unlikely than an Ethrean queen. She wasn't yet ready to talk about it in council.

I have to get out of here . . .

She clasped her hands before her, chin lifted, eyes wide and carefully noncommittal. All her secrets hidden from the men who would rule her, if they could, even if only with the best of intentions. "My lords, we are agreed that the matter of Kyrin and Damwin must be promptly decided. They have tried our patience to its final length and can no longer be permitted to flout the Crown. Prolate Helfred, you and your Court Ecclesiastica must be ready to depart Kingseat at first light tomorrow. My missive to these egregious dukes shall be placed in your hands before you leave, and we will have further speech on how you should deport yourself while meeting with them."

Helfred nodded. "Your Majesty."

"Edward, Rudi . . ." She made herself smile, though a part of her still fumed at them. "Your care for my stewardship of Ethrea does not go unappreciated. Nor is it taken for granted that you stay here in the capital to give me wise counsel when your duchies cry out for their ducal lords. As soon as matters are more settled here I hope to let you return home, if that's your wish. Or, if you prefer to remain on the privy council, that is equally agreeable to me."

Edward and Rudi exchanged ruefully resigned glances. "Majesty, we serve at your pleasure," Edward replied. "For so long as you have need of two old men, we will remain."

She nodded, then turned to Adric. "Your Grace, I take comfort in the presence of youth on this council. Don't despair if all seems overwhelming to you now. Time will season you, I have no doubt."

"Majesty," said Adric. He almost sounded sulky. He was such a young man. He would do well to learn from Alasdair how dukes behaved in private and public.

"Gentlemen, you are excused."

The council meeting broke up. Ven'Cedwin nodded respectfully to Helfred as he methodically salted his ink-wet parchment. Helfred spared Rhian a small, approving nod and took himself off. She wasn't sure whether to be pleased or irritated. Somehow, in some strange way, regardless of how the world tossed and turned the pair of them, a part of her would always be the princess, Rhian, and a part of him would stay plain Chaplain Helfred. They didn't speak of that, they just knew it. She wondered if he found it as bemusing as she did.

The dukes departed, and finally Ven'Cedwin, and it was just herself and Alasdair in the small, high room she'd taken as her privy council chamber. That other room, where Marlan had held sway, was locked and bolted and would not be used again so long as she ruled in Ethrea.

Alasdair shook his head at her. "One of these days you're going to sit down through a privy council meeting. You're queen whether you're on your feet or your arse, you know."

She gave him a look. "I'm not certain it's proper to use words like 'arse' to your sovereign."

Eyes glinting, he pushed away from the council table and joined her in front of the window. Kissed the tip of her nose, and then her lips, lightly. "Neither am I. Do you care?"

She rested her hand flat to his chest. "Not in here, Alasdair. Never in here."

The playful, loving light in his face dimmed. He stepped back. "Majesty."

It nearly broke her bones not to throw her arms around him. "Alasdair, please. Don't be like that. In every other room in this castle, in every room of every house in this kingdom, I can forget who I am. What I am. But if I forget that in here, in my privy council

chamber, if I once let the woman rule the queen . . ."
She shook her head. "I can't. You mustn't ask me."

He clasped his strong, gently ruthless hands behind
his back. "Edward's right, you know. You will have
to fight them. You'll have to surrender this fantasy,
that men like Damwin and Kyrin will see reason if
only you give them a little more time." He laughed,
unamused. "Even this ploy with Helfred. It won't
succeed. Do you truly think they'll kiss the hem of his
robe weeping penitent tears, and ride back to
Kingseat with him so they can pledge their public loyalty to you?"

She folded her arms. "No. Of course I don't."

"Then why—"

"Because it gives me some time, Alasdair! Time to
think, time to prepare myself for what has to be done!
Just because I recognise a harsh reality doesn't mean
I'm ready to embrace it like a lover!"

Breathing hard she stared at him, willing him to
understand. After a moment he nodded. "I can see
you'd want time. Sound decisions are rarely made in
haste."

And what did that mean? Was there a secret message coded into his seemingly harmless statement?
She'd shown up on his doorstep, a fugitive exile, and
they'd hastily married. Did he regret the decision? A
duke in his own duchy was like a little king. Did
Alasdair wish he'd remained in Linfoi, a duke, instead
of condemning himself to a life as her consort, a life
in her shadow, a life in which his crown would never
be the same as hers?

*Don't think about that now. You can't afford to
think about that.*

"What are you going to do, Rhian?" he said. "When Damwin and Kyrin push you to that last step, and you know they will. They're not sensible men. What in God's name are you going to do?"

"You know what I'll do," she said, suddenly so tired. Tears were too close. "I'll fight them, Alasdair. I have no other choice."

"I could fight them for you," he said. "I could be your king consort commander. I could . . ." And then he sighed. His plain, bony, beautiful face was sad. "Except I can't."

She'd never dreamed it would be so hard. Could be so hurtful. He *doesn't deserve this. It isn't fair.* "No," she whispered. "At least . . . not yet. One day you'll fight my battles for me, Alasdair, and nobody will think it makes me weak. But that day is a long way off. I need you, my love. You know how I need you. But for now the world must believe I need no man."

He nodded. "I know."

"I want to walk alone a while. When I'm ready I'll find you, and you can tell me where my thinking shows itself too womanly. Would you go to Ven'Cedwin, and let him know I'll need him after noon? Perhaps we could compose the dukes' letters together. If you're not taken up with other commitments."

He offered her a brief bow. "Majesty, I am, as always, your obedient servant."

There were times . . . last night, for instance, in their marriage bed . . . when he said such things and made of them a loving tease.

And then there are times he makes of them a fist, and strikes me with it.

"Thank you," she said quietly. "I'll find you later."

She was barely aware of the servants and courtiers who acknowledged her passing as she left the castle. They bowed, she nodded, no words were exchanged. She refused a cloying coterie of attendants and discouraged hangers-on at court. If she wanted company she called for it, otherwise everyone knew she was to be left alone.

The weight of their gazes as she walked by was as heavy as any crown devised.

Outside, in the privy gardens overlooking Kingseat township and the harbour, the sunshine was mellow. Warm as a mother's breath against her skin. Rhian let her fingertips touch drooping, perfumed blossoms. Resisted what she knew she must consider and flirted, for a little while, with memories of simpler, happier times.

And then she stopped, because she was no longer alone. The eldritch sense that had served her all her life told her who it was. Without looking over her shoulder she said, "Emperor Han. I know for certain this time there was no invitation."

The emperor laughed. "I took it for granted you would be pleased to see me."

"Did you indeed?" she said, and turned to confront him. "Well. That was very presumptuous of you."

He bowed. "It was, Queen Rhian."

Head to toe he was dressed in black silk: high-throated, long-sleeved tunic, narrow trousers. His long black hair was tied back from his extraordinary, ageless face. His dark brown eyes were watchful and amused. He wore no jewellery, no trappings of power . . . but even a blind man would not mistake him for a commoner.

She considered him. "How did you gain access to my privy gardens?"

"Does it matter? I am here."

"Are you an emperor or a witchman?"

His eyebrows rose two beautiful black arches. "Perhaps I am both."

"And perhaps you could answer me like an honest man, instead of playing silly word games!"

That surprised him. "You are bold, Queen of Ethrea."

"And also quite busy. Was there something you wanted, Han? Or are you simply bored, and seeking a diversion?"

He hadn't given her leave to address him as an intimate. She'd committed a breach of protocol.

So we stand evenly matched. Witching himself here was just as rude. If that's what he did, and I can't think of another explanation. He's hardly inconspicuous.

Instead of answering, Han looked her up and down. His dark eyes gleamed, but whether in appreciation or condemnation she couldn't tell.

"I have known many queens, many empresses, many . . ." He smiled. "Women. Do you dress like a man in the hope other men will accept your rule, or is it that being a woman isn't enough for you?"

She looked down at her not-very-queenly clothing: leather huntsman's leggings, a leather jerkin, silk shirt. On her feet, leather low-heeled half-boots. Strapped to her left hip, a knife once cherished by her brother, Ranald. Its hand-polished hilt was set with tigereye, his birthstone. Her fingers often found it, and touched it, remembering.

"Han," she said, looking up again, "you must think me witless if you believe I believe you're here to comment on my choice of attire. What do you want?"

He plucked a fragile pink ifrala blossom from a nearby flowerbed and held it to his nose, delicate as any lady-in-waiting. Breathing deeply he smiled. "Your mother had a sweet touch in her garden, Rhian. I remember she made ifrala perfume every spring."

She blinked. "You knew my mother?"

"Briefly." He opened his fingers and let the blossom drift to the grass. "Rhian, why have you not convened a meeting of the trading nations? Do you think this *Mijak* will change its mind? Or, like a little girl, do you hope that if you close your eyes tight the spirits and demons will not see you in the dark?"

Spirits and demons. *There are no such things.* "If you're so certain I'm wrong in waiting, Han, why haven't *you* summoned the trading nations yourself?"

"If I were the ruler of Ethrea, I would."

She folded her arms. "Why should I trust you, Han? Why should I trust your witch-man Sun-dao? I don't know you. I only know your reputation, and the reputation of mighty Tzhung-tzhungchai. You swallow nations as I swallow a plum. Perhaps I'm the pit you think to spit out in the dirt."

"Rhian, Rhian . . ." Han sounded sorrowful. "Don't disappoint me. The Tzhung empire has swallowed no-one for nearly two hundred years. You know that. And you know my witch-man speaks the truth. The truth rots in your dungeons. It yearns for the light. It dreams of a dead wife. Zandakar is the key to defeating Mijak. How long will you leave him a prisoner when your life, and my life, and as many lives as there are stars at night, depend upon him? How long will you deny the only truth that can save us?"

"Zandakar is my concern, not yours," she said, turning away.

Han sighed. "Before Mijak is tamed you must tame your disobedient dukes. The dukes are why you do not convene the trading nations. Until they are tamed your crown is in danger. Zandakar is also the key to their downfall, and you know it. There is so little time until there is no time at all, Rhian. Will you let pain and pride waste these brief moments?"

"Be quiet!" she snapped, spinning round. "Who are you to come here uninvited and tell me how I should rule and who I should see? If time is so brief, if I am so helpless, take your Tzhung warfleet and sink Mijak on your own!"

Han smiled. His eyes were flat and black as obsidian. "If the wind desired it, girl, then so it would be and my empire would flood with the grateful tears of the saved. The wind does not. It blows me to you."

"I never asked it to! I never asked for this!"

"The wind does not care," said Han. "And neither do I. Deal with your dukes, Rhian."

Still fuming, she glared at him. "How?"

"You ask for my help?"

"I ask for your opinion! My father taught me there's no shame in seeking counsel of a wise man.

You're an emperor. I assume you've had some experience of – of – uncooperative vassals."

His cold eyes warmed with amusement. "Yes."

"Well, then?"

"Rhian, there is nothing I can tell you that you don't already know. The wind has made you a warrior. No breathing man can fight the wind."

Perhaps that's true. But this breathing woman can certainly try.

"You can," said Han. "But you won't."

Was he inside her mind now? Or was her face less schooled than she liked to imagine? He infuriated and frightened her like no-one else she knew. "I don't want to shed their blood, Han."

He shrugged. "Want means nothing. Need is all."

Tears burned her eyes, then, because she knew he was right. Hand on her knife-hilt, she blinked them away.

"Go," said the Emperor of Tzhung-tzhungchai. "Do what you must, Rhian. Do it quickly. And when you are done, I will be waiting."

CHAPTER THREE

The prison cell was too small for *hotas*, but Zandakar tried to dance them anyway. There was nothing else for him to do. No-one to talk to, he was the castle's only prisoner. Sometimes the guards watched him when they weren't gambling for coins, they watched him with their unfriendly eyes, their eyes with promises in them. They would hurt him if he danced too close.

His cell was made of three stone walls and one of iron bars, a ceiling and a floor. No windows. No fresh air. No light, except for a burning lamp hung on a hook outside the bars where his fingers could not reach it. A bucket for piss and shit which his guards did not empty as often as they could. A wooden bench for sleeping. They gaye him one blanket, but only because they had to. The guards of this castle did not like him, it was in their silent stares and their fingers on their clubs how much they longed to beat him. Hurt him. Avenge the wrong he had done their queen.

Aieee, god. A dog in this Ethrea lives better. When I was Vortka's prisoner I was treated like a man. Will I rot down here, will I die in this dark?

He had been in his cell twelve highsuns. The guards did not tell him that, he counted time in his head. He visited Mijak in his memory, laughed with

Lilit, rode with Dimmi, danced the *hotas* with his mother.

Sometimes he dreamed of her, of Hekat. He dreamed she had found him, dreamed that she loved him, dreamed there never was blood and pain and misery between them.

Stupid dreams, Zandakar. Zandakar, you are stupid.

His knuckles on both hands were scraped raw where he had struck his stone prison walls trying to dance his *hotas*. His blood was on the walls of this place, in the rank air his hisses of pain. Once he would never have noticed such small hurts, now he felt as though his body was flayed. Everything hurt him. The world was a scorpion wheel, he could not escape. Crippled, he danced his crippled *hotas*, remembering Mijak and its wide open skies. The chanting of his warhost. The power in his blade.

Along the prison corridor he heard a door open. His gambling guards scrambled to their feet, small coins clinking to the flagstones.

"Majesty!"

"Your Majesty!"

Rhian.

He stumbled sideways out of his *hota*, one shoulder striking the nearest stone wall.

Rhian.

She stared at him through his cell's iron bars, her blue eyes shining like chips of ice. Her lips were straight and thinly pressed, no smile to see Zandakar, no pleasure to be here.

"Open the cell door, Evley," she said to the older of his two guards.

Both men gaped at her. "Majesty?" said Evley. He had enough years to be her father. Like a father, he was concerned. "Majesty, I—"

"*Evley.*"

The guard Evley fumbled a key into the lock and turned it. Then he hauled the heavy iron-barred door open.

Rhian's chin came up, her eyes so blue, so cold. "Zandakar. With me."

He followed her out of his lightless stone prison, down the corridor, through the door at its end, up stone stairs and more stone stairs into the light.

It hurt his eyes, he welcomed the pain. Sun on his underground skin, hot like the god's wrath. Grass beneath his bare feet, birdsong in his empty ears. Breathing was hard. Believing was harder.

I do not think I will be free for long.

She had brought him to a garden beside the tall stone castle. There was salt in the breeze blowing into his face, the sweet scent of flowers, the ache of regrets. They were alone.

Hands fisted on her slender hips, sheathed in leather like the finest snakeblade, Rhian looked at him. "Why is your hair blue?"

Bemused, he stared back at her. Why was his hair blue? Why did it matter?

"We're told your brother's hair is blood red," she said impatiently. "And your warriors' hair is black. Why are they different, Zandakar? What does it mean?"

"Ask *chalava*," he said. "I *wei* know."

"Were you born with blue hair? Was your brother born with red?"

He folded his arms. "You free me to talk hair, Rhian?"

"I haven't freed you."

Aieee, the god see him. She was still so angry. He could not tell her his truth, that the colour of his hair changed the first time he killed with the god's power. She feared him too much as it was. But he could not lie to her, not outright. Lies were poison. He could stand between the truth and a lie, that would keep him in her company for now, for a little while.

"My hair born black," he said. "*Chalava* make hair blue when it make me *chalava-hagra*." He frowned. "I think you say hammer."

"Yes, Zandakar," said Rhian. "I know what you are."

There was a knife on her left hip. He nodded at it. "You dance your *hotas*? You *wei* forget?"

"No. I dance them."

"Show me."

"What?" She half-turned from him, the heel of one hand pressing to her forehead. "Zandakar—"

"*Show me.*"

She turned back. In her eyes he saw her hunger, saw how she missed the glory of *hotas* with a fellow warrior. They were only complete if they were not danced alone.

I miss dancing them with Rhian. Aieee, god, I miss Rhian.

She unsheathed her knife. On the green grass, beneath the blue sky, his dirty blue godtouched hair combed by the salt breeze and without his own blade, he danced the *hotas* with Rhian and felt the scorpion wheel world fade away. She was the falcon, the sandcat, the scorpion. He was her shadow, her mirror, her foe. In her eyes all the pain he had caused her, in her blade the desire for his blood.

Twelve highsuns in captivity, his muscles were sluggish. Her blade did not touch him but many times it came close. Her angry eyes laughed, then, her teeth bared in a smile. She had not lied, she did not forget her *hotas*. She was Queen of Ethrea and did not forget to dance. Lithe and supple, flowing like water, like liquid gold, she gifted him with every dance he had taught her. She tasked him with every light blow of her fist. No tasking on the godhouse scorpion wheel had ever hurt his flesh so much.

Distracted by sorrow, by the pain in her because of him, he let her leap behind him. Her leg scythed out, catching him hard behind the knees. He fell to the green grass and then she was on him, thighs straddling his heaving chest, knees clamped to his ribs, one hand fisted in his hair. She was straining his head back, her sharp blade pressed against his bared throat. Was that sweat on her face or was his queen weeping?

He waited, waited, for her blade to drink his blood.

On a wild cry she released him. Her knife sank point-first into the soft ground and she sprang to her feet. Her eyes as she stared down at him were violent with pain.

"Why didn't you tell me? Why did you lie?"

"You lost in my land. In Mijak," he said, meeting her tempestuous gaze. "You afraid. Alone. You have killing secrets. What you tell me, king of my land?"

"You could've trusted me, Zandakar. I trusted you."

He smiled. "You learn my secret, Rhian. You put me in prison."

"I put you in prison because – because – *tcha*!" She bent and snatched her knife out of the ground, then stepped away from him. Her knuckles on the knife-hilt were white. "You made me a fool before Emperor Han!"

Emperor Han. The tall amber-skinned man. His servants were demons, they summoned the wind.

"Emperor Han is *gajka*?"

She dragged a sleeved forearm over her face. "I don't know what he is, Zandakar. I don't know what *you* are."

Cautiously, he sat up. "*Gajka*, Rhian. Friend."

Instead of answering she wiped the dirt and grass from her knife and thrust it back in its sheath. "Have you heard of Tzhung-tzhungchai?"

He shook his head. "This is land of Emperor Han?"

"His empire. *Zho*."

"I *wei* hear of Tzhung-tzhungchai."

Her gaze slid to him, sideways. "Well, he's heard of you. And not only recently. He says there is mention of Mijak in the Imperial Library, in books written hundreds of years ago. I thought Tzhung-tzhungchai was the oldest empire in the world. Now it seems Mijak is older. Did you know that? Do you know your own history?"

"*Wei. Wei* learn history in Mijak. Learn *chalava*. Learn *hotas*. Learn to lead *chotzaka*."

"*Chotzaka*? That's your word for army?"

He shrugged. "I think *zho*."

Pacing now, she tugged her fingers through her curling hair, grown long enough almost to be god-braided. Tiny little spiky braids, like those of a child. But she was not a child. She was a woman, with a man in her bed. She was a queen. Life and death were in her eyes.

"Han says Mijak was once a mighty empire. And then overnight it simply . . . disappeared. Your people were never heard from again. Not until now. You don't know what happened?"

"*Wei. Yatzhay.*"

"Han doesn't know either."

Han, she called him, and yet they were not friends. Or perhaps they were and she did not wish to tell him. If he asked her he thought she would not say. So he asked another question, asked what had eaten at him in the night, in the dark.

"Dexterity, Rhian. He lives?"

She stopped pacing, glared down at him. "*Zho*. Of course. What do you take me for?" Then she shook her head. "Zandakar, I don't wish to speak of Dexterity. He is one man. I have a kingdom to care for."

She had a kingdom to care for and yet she was here. He uncoiled himself from the grass to stand before her. "You come to me. Why?"

"Some on my council say you should be put to death," she said, fisted hands on her hips, a fighting challenge in her eyes.

It did not surprise him. *For certain Alasdair king would deal the killing blow himself. The dukes have no love for me, they would smile to see me die.* Who did that leave to speak for his life? Only one he could think of. "Helfred?"

"*Tcha*, Helfred," she said, impatience and reluctant admiration in her voice. Aieee, god, how he had missed that. "Who else is such a thorn in my side? As prolate, he says you are an instrument of God. He says God has brought you to us and God must use you as he sees fit."

"You say?"

"The dukes Damwin and Kyrin refuse to accept I am their queen."

He knew that. The guards enjoyed gossip as much as gambling. They spoke of Rhian's coronation, of the joyful shouting in the streets. They spoke of the dukes who had been there, and the dukes who defied her, staying away. Damwin and Kyrin, who had not fallen as Marlan fell. That made the guards angry. They were simple men. They loved Rhian, their queen.

"Rhian, *wei* let these dukes live."

"Helfred travels to them tomorrow," she said, her voice cold. "He'll take with him a letter, in which I shall command them to yield."

"Helfred. Then Ethrea god will smite them?"

"Why do you say that?" she demanded. "Why do you think God must want to hurt, to kill?"

He shrugged. "Raklion *chotzu*. *Chalava* say to him, you are Mijak *chotzu*. *Chalava-chaka* of other *chotzu*, they defy *chalava*. Nagarak *chalava-chaka*, he smites them for *chalava*."

"Raklion? Who—"

"*Adda*. I think you say *father*."

"Your father?"

"*Zho.*"

"So. Your father's *chalava-chaka*, his holy man, yes? – killed anyone who disagreed with him? And that is acceptable in Mijak?" Frowning, she shook her head. "Well, it certainly explains things."

Why did she not understand? "Helfred is *chalava-chaka* for Rhian, *zho*? He is *chalava-chaka* for Ethrea god."

"And so it must follow that Helfred will strike the dukes dead in God's name?"

"Ethrea god smite Marlan."

He watched the memory of Ethrea's burning high godspeaker shift over her face, shadow-swift and unwelcome. "That was different," she muttered. "I don't know what that was." She shivered. "And where is your father in all this, Zandakar?"

"Dead."

Her gaze softened. "*Yatzhay.*"

"Rhian . . ." He wanted to touch her, to shake her until she saw he was right. "You *wei* let Damwin and Kyrin live."

She took a step back. "Truly, Zandakar, your people are barbaric. I think all you must care about is killing and blood."

Barbaric. He did not know that word but he could guess what it meant. Anger burned him. "Rhian stupid if she let dukes live. Arrow in the body, make poison, *kill*, does Rhian leave it there?"

"You think I believe you care for me?" she said, her eyes and voice hot now. "You lied to me, Zandakar. You are in *prison* because of me. I *would* be stupid if I thought you cared!"

He exhaled a deep and shuddering breath. "My wife Lilit, beautiful like Rhian. Hair. Eyes. She—"

"She died, I know," said Rhian impatiently. "Your mother killed her. It was terrible. I know. You've suffered. But—"

"*Wei* let Yuma and Dimmi hurt you, Rhian," he said. "I see you, I see Lilit. I see Na'ha'leima. I see Targa and Zree." His fist struck his heart. "Dead people, Rhian. Many many dead people."

Her eyes were full of tears. "People you killed, Zandakar. People you murdered. So much blood on your hands. Do you think I want to be like *you*?"

He did touch her then. Fingertips to her cheek snatched swiftly away. "Mijak coming, Rhian. You *wei* fight Mijak and dukes."

"I know that," she whispered. "I'm not stupid. Why else have I come to you?"

His heart lifted. "Rhian want Zandakar to kill dukes?"

"*Zandakar*, for the love of *Rollin*!" She punched him with her small, hard fist. "*Wei.*" Then she shook her head again. "Though you'd do it if I asked you. Strange man, you are a mystery."

He looked at her steadily, not quite convinced. "Rhian will fight dukes? Rhian will kill them?"

"You doubt I can do it?" she retorted. "You doubt I can kill a man? You have a short memory, Zandakar."

No. His memory was as long as shadows in the desert. He wished he could forget. Wished he could touch Rhian and take away her pain. "You *wei* want to kill that *chalava-chaka*."

"No, I did not," she said. "Yet Ven'Martin is dead.

When I close my eyes at night his dying face is the last thing I see." She stared at him, eyes hollow, thin lines pinched round her mouth. "What do you see, Zandakar, when you close *your* eyes?"

Lilit. His butchered son. The butchered sons and daughters of the cities he had razed. That dead baby, killed by Vanikil shell-leader. In his dreams he heard it wail.

"You see your dead too, don't you?" Rhian demanded. "They haunt you as mine haunts me. Don't try to deny it, Zandakar. I can see it in your eyes. You see them. You hear them. You're never alone."

He nodded, reluctant. "*Zho.*"

"Why did you stop, Zandakar?" she whispered. "Why did you turn your back on your killing god?"

So many godmoons had waxed and waned since Na'ha'leima, sometimes he wondered if that time was a dream, if the voice in his heart had spoken at all. Vortka had not believed in it and Vortka heard the god best of any man he knew.

"I *wei* turn my back on *chalava*," he said. "*Chalava* say *wei* kill. I *wei* kill."

"Told you to stop killing and not your brother? Your mother? It makes no sense to me, Zandakar. Why would your god do that?"

"*Wei* question *chalava*, Rhian," he said. "*Chalava* is *chalava*."

That made her stare. "You never question God? Never shake your fist at heaven and demand 'Why me?' Is your god so cruel, then? Does he have no mercy, no compassion, no love for those who kneel before him?"

He could not answer. He remembered the godpool,

remembered warmth and a sweet voice, heavy with sorrow as he swam in the blood.

Zandakar, my son, my son. I am with you, though the road is long and steep and strewn with stones. All that will come to pass must come to pass. Grieve, weep, endure, surrender. I will be with you, unto the end.

That was the voice he had heard in Na'ha'leima, the voice that urged him to kill no more. He had not heard it before the godpool, he had not heard it since leaving Na'ha'leima. Was that voice the god or was it a demon? He did not know. He was lost in Ethrea, he was too far from home. If the god was with him here he was deaf, dumb and blind to it.

I am alone.

Rhian still marvelled. "Not a day goes by that I don't ask God what he thinks he's doing. He hasn't answered yet. Perhaps he's hoping I'll go away, or lose my voice."

Aieee, tcha, these people of Ethrea with their soft god who did not smite them for their wicked tongues. When Mijak's god came for them they would burn like dry reeds in a fire. Cold in the sunlight, he looked at Rhian's lovely face.

She will burn if I do not save her. How can I save her? I am nothing now.

He said the only thing he could think of, the one thing she could not seem to remember. "You queen, Rhian."

She spared him a sour glance. "Yes, yes, for my sins I am queen. And if I hadn't sought the crown, if I'd done what Papa and Marlan wanted . . ." She curled her fingers round the hilt of her knife.

"Ven'Martin would be living, not rotting in the ground. It doesn't matter that he was wrong in attempting my life. I pushed him to his sinful action. His death lies at my door and I have but one remedy for it, Zandakar. If his death is to mean something I must be more than a queen. I must be a *great* queen. I must save my kingdom from your brother and mother and bloodthirsty god. But before I can do that . . ." For the second time she slid her knife from its sheath and stared at its polished blade glinting in the sun. "I must save my kingdom from itself."

There was such pain in her face, her eyes, her voice. The knife blade trembled. "Rhian," he said, "*you queen.*"

"I know that," she said, her gaze still fixed on her knife. "And I remember what you told me in Old Scooton. The dukes are bad men. For Ethrea's sake I must see them thrown down or I'll be a bad queen."

Rhian was strong, she was a bold strong woman, but at the core of her strength beat a heart that felt so many things. He loved her for it. Would he love her if she was like the empress his mother, joyful at the thought of shedding blood?

I think I would not.

"Rhian has soldiers," he said gently.

She nodded. "Yes. But the people of those duchies have done no wrong. The dukes' soldiers are blameless too, they but follow their lords. It's the dukes who sin here, against me and my crown."

"You smite, *zho*?"

She glanced at him, her beautiful face grim with purpose. "*Zho.*"

He wanted to laugh, he was so pleased. "Good, Rhian."

"Good? *Tcha*!" She thrust her blade back into its sheath. "It's not, but I don't have a choice. We have a law in Ethrea. It's not been used in centuries, but it still holds. I can challenge the dukes to judicial combat and prove my right to rule on their bodies. If I defeat them, by law the matter is settled and can never be challenged again."

He felt his heart thud. "Dukes try to kill Rhian."

"Yes. Well." She tried to smile. "It seems you've discovered the flaw in my plan."

"Alasdair king knows you will do this?"

She stared at the castle walls as though she could see through them to the man she had married. "Not yet."

And when she told him he would not be pleased. Ethrean men did not see women as warriors.

"Rhian is sure dukes will fight?"

She smiled, unamused. "Pride will prevent them from declining to meet me. If they refuse, even using the excuse that no man of honour would draw steel on a woman, too many would taunt them and say they refused out of fear. Besides . . ." She shrugged. "These are arrogant men. It won't occur to them they could lose."

"Rhian could lose."

She shifted her gaze, her eyes bleakly upon him. "Yes. But I won't. Not with you to teach me. I need your help to prepare, Zandakar. I have no idea how to dance the *hotas* against men who have trained with longswords."

He felt the world go still and quiet. "Rhian would

let Zandakar out of prison? Trust him with a blade? A sword?"

"If I do, will you swear on Lilit's soul that you *can* be trusted?"

He held out his hand. "Rhian – your blade."

After a moment's hesitation she gave it to him. Pushing back the stained and stinking rag of his sleeve, before she could stop him he drew the sharp knife through the meat of his forearm. Pain burned. Bright red blood welled and dripped to the ground.

"*Zandakar!*" she shouted, and snatched the knife from his fingers. "Are you *mad?*"

It was the cleanest pain he had felt for so long. He watched his blood splatter and pool on the grass. "Blood for Ethrea. Blood for Rhian." He pressed a clenched fist hard against his heart, pumping his blood to the grass at her feet. "You trust Zandakar."

"I trust you're a *fool*," she retorted, pulling a kerchief from inside her leather jerkin. "I trust you're a man, and like a man you—"

A shout, and the sound of running feet. He turned and she turned with him, her hand pressing linen against the wound in his arm. His prison guards charged towards them, Evley and the youth named Blay. Their swords glittered in the sunlight and his death was in their faces.

Rhian stepped forward, her hands upheld. "Halt! *Halt*, I tell you! There's no danger here. Put up your swords and explain yourselves. Evley?"

The guard Evley grabbed at the younger man and they stumbled to a standstill. Their swords remained unsheathed, but pointed to the grass. "Majesty, we heard you shout."

"And you took that as a command to interrupt my privy business?"

The guard Evley paled. "No, Your Majesty, I—"

"You took it upon yourself to hover in the shadows, as though I were a green girl in need of protection," Rhian snapped. "You are presumptuous, Evley. Return to the garrison and inform Commander Idson of my displeasure. Blay!"

The young guard flinched. "Majesty," he whispered.

"Run to Ursa. Tell her I'm bringing her a patient. Well, why are you still standing there? I told you to *run*!"

The guards withdrew. Zandakar watched Rhian drop to the grass and wipe her knife free of his blood. When it was clean she rose to stare him coldly in the face. "Fool. How could you think I have a care for such pointless grand gestures?"

Her accusation was more painful than the blade-cut. "I swear blood to you, Rhian. My life for your life."

She shoved her knife back into its sheath. "Yes. But couldn't you have sworn blood to me without bleeding?" She reached for his arm a second time. "Show me."

Without blood, without pain, his oath would mean nothing. To swear in blood was to swear in the heart. *She is not Mijaki, she cannot know this.*

"It'll need stitches," said Rhian, and roughly bound his forearm with her linen kerchief. "Come. Ursa's waiting."

She led him into the castle, along many corridors, past shocked staring servants who bowed their heads as he and Rhian approached, then whispered and pointed in their wake. He knew he was filthy, he knew his flesh stank. He knew to these people of Ethrea he was a strange and frightening creature. It did not matter. He was Rhian's creature while she had need of him. He was the god's creature too, though it seemed the god had no need of him at all.

They made their way to the far side of the castle, to a chamber at the end of one short corridor. The corridor's windows showed more gardens and a courtyard and a wagon unloading wooden crates and parcels wrapped in canvas. Rhian pushed the chamber's door open and swept inside. The room was small, lined with wide benches and empty shelves. Shiny metal hooks hung from beams in the ceiling. The centre space was taken up by a large wooden table. Ursa stood behind it, unpacking a crate full of stoppered clay pots. She looked up and nodded, she was not a woman intimidated by power.

"Majesty. I got your message." Hands on her hips, she shifted her grey gaze. "Zandakar."

She did not like him, it did not matter. "Ursa."

The physick frowned at the bloodstained linen round his arm. "I never liked knives. This is what happens when idiots play with knives."

"He did it on purpose," said Rhian, and closed the chamber door. "I need him healed enough for sword-play, Ursa."

Ursa's eyebrows lifted, disapproving. "You've released him?"

"Am I required to explain myself to you?" said Rhian sharply. "Stitch his wound, Ursa. Give him whatever drugs he needs so we can train in the hour before sunset."

"*Hotas*," said Ursa. Her lips thinned, her brows lowered. "Majesty—"

"The answer to my question, Ursa, is *no*," said Rhian. "I am *not* required to explain myself to you. Do as I've asked." She turned. "Zandakar, you'll remain here until someone comes for you. When they come, obey their instructions. I'll see you again before dusk."

He pressed a fist to his heart. "Rhian."

"Well, well, well," said Ursa as the door closed behind Rhian. Her eyes were unfriendly, there was no warmth in her. "I thought we'd seen the last of you."

He shrugged. "Rhian did this, I *wei* ask."

"Then Rhian's a fool, and you can tell her I said so."

"Ursa . . ." He stood adrift in the chamber as the physick rummaged in her familiar battered leather bag. The sight of it, a reminder of their days on the road, the times she had smiled at him and he had helped with her physicking, the other times she had healed him, those memories made him breathe deeply and sigh. "You live in castle?"

She glanced up. "No. I'm appointed Rhian's royal physick, and so I must keep a chamber here and be ready should she need me. I also take care of the castle staff. But I'm keeping my old practice. Bamfield's got it well in hand, and—" She slapped a hand to the table. "And why I'm telling you this I'm sure I don't know. Give me your arm and let's get this business done with."

"Ursa," he said as she physicked him with skill but little tenderness. "Dexterity . . ."

Fiercely she glared at him. "No. You've done that silly man enough harm already. If I have my way you'll not lay eyes on him again. I thought Rhian had taken care of that, locking you in prison where you belong. Now it seems she's let you out and I'm sure she thinks she knows what she's about. She's queen, she'll do as she does with no nevermind from me. But Jones is all I have of family and you won't get a chance to hurt him again. Not while God's left breath in my body. So you be quiet now and let me stitch this cut, for there's not a thing you can say to me that I have a care to hear."

He was a man grown, he had no fear of ageing women. Yet in her eyes he saw the fury of Nagarak and it chilled the hot blood seeping from his wound.

"*Yatzhay*, Ursa," he said softly. "Zandakar *yatzhay*."

She did not answer, not even to scold him with her eyes. He did as she said, he let her stitch him in silence. Never in his life had someone sewed his flesh like leather. The pain burned, he welcomed it.

Aieee, Dexterity. Are you tasked because of me?

He wanted to ask Ursa, he wanted to know what he had done. But he knew she would not answer. He sat in silence, and wept in his heart.

CHAPTER FOUR

Alasdair waited for Rhian in the privy state chamber, where she preferred to conduct matters of the realm in peace and quiet. In the past, tradition had surrounded Ethrea's monarch with the trappings of pomp and ceremony, with attendants and secretaries and under-secretaries and gentlemen of the chamber and any number of hopeful courtiers eager for notice and advancement. King Eberg had lived his royal life in such a bright and busy light. On coming to the capital as his duchy's representative on the council, Alasdair had found such crowding odd and not much to his liking. His father, though Linfoi's duke at that time, had never been one for toadies and flatterers or any kind of retinue. He'd trusted his own judgement, never requiring echoes to convince himself he was right . . . or as a reminder that he was indeed a duke.

Rhian was like him in that.

And I admire it. Although it might be nice if even once she consulted with me, her husband and king, before making a decision that will affect us both.

Anger burned dull beneath his ribs, lacking only the sight of her to fan it into full flame.

Zandakar.

In the antechamber beyond this small and cosy room waited Ven'Cedwin, ready to transcribe her final letter of appeal and command to the dukes of Hartshorn and Meercheq. He found it hard to comprehend that Kyrin and Damwin could continue so stubborn. Please God Helfred would bring them to a sense of their futility before their defiance led to bloodshed.

But I doubt it.

He'd left the chamber's door open. Through it he heard a sound in the antechamber, the whispered creaking of a hinge, the turning of a handle. Heard Ven'Cedwin get to his feet.

"Your Majesty."

"Ven'Cedwin?" Rhian sounded distracted, and surprised. "I didn't think you were sent for yet. I'm not ready for the writing of the dukes' letters."

Alasdair moved from the curtained window to the doorway and looked into the antechamber. "Since this is a matter of urgency, Rhian, I thought it best he be waiting close by. Especially since you are so busy, with other weighty matters on your mind . . ."

He saw in her face that she realised what he meant. Her eyes, which could burn so warm, lost their light. Lips tightened, jaw set, she nodded. "Indeed." She turned. "Ven'Cedwin, His Majesty and I have some small matters to discuss before I'll be ready to dictate the dukes' letters. Have you yet broken your midday fast?"

"I have not, Majesty."

She smiled. "Then by all means excuse yourself to the buttery, and be certain of a hearty meal. One hour should see me ready to begin." She nodded at his leather box of inks, pens and papers on the floor beside his chair. "Leave your tools here, I'll keep them safe."

Ven'Cedwin bowed. "Majesty." Turning, he bowed again. "King Alasdair."

As the antechamber door closed behind the venerable, Rhian pressed a hand to her eyes. "Don't shout at me, Alasdair. I had no choice."

"No *choice* but to let Zandakar out of his cell? How is that, Rhian? What possible use can he be to you now?"

She stared at him, her dulled eyes hurt. "Are you setting spies to watch for me, Alasdair?"

"Don't be stupid," he snapped. "Did you think no-one would comment as you paraded him through the palace covered in blood?"

"He wasn't *covered in blood*, he cut his arm. I took him to Ursa."

"Cut his arm how? Did he attack you? Were you forced to defend yourself?"

With a sigh Rhian dropped into the nearest chair. "No, of course he didn't attack me. If you must know he cut himself, Alasdair. Swearing a blood oath that he'd serve me unto death."

"Rhian . . ." Fighting the urge to take her by the shoulders and shake until all her bones rattled, he stepped out of the doorway. "A queen can't afford *sentiment*. The man is an enemy. Rollin save us, he's the son of the woman bent on our destruction!"

"Zandakar's not responsible for his mother and brother," she replied. "Any more than Helfred was responsible for his uncle. We are born as we're born, Alasdair. What counts is what we do, not how our relatives conduct themselves. Should Ludo run amok in Linfoi tomorrow, am I supposed to hold *you* accountable?"

The idea of Ludo running amok almost made him smile; the weight of a ducal chain had anchored his cousin almost to immobility. *But I have no doubt the shock of it will wear off. I should see him married soon, to complete his unlikely transformation.* "No. Of course not."

"Well, then," said Rhian, as though the matter were settled.

"Rhian, Ludo is not Zandakar and you know it," he replied, forcing a mildness he did not feel. "For one thing, Ludo's never killed a man in his life while Zandakar—"

"Has killed thousands, *I know*," said Rhian, allowing temper free rein. "There's no need to remind me. Alasdair, it's because he's killed that I need him now."

He moved to the antechamber's other empty chair and sat, his heart pounding. He so mistrusted the thoughts shifting behind her eyes. "Why?"

"Oh, Alasdair. When I said I had no choice but to fight the dukes, what do you think I meant?"

She can't. She can't. She's barely left her girlhood behind. "You mean to challenge them to judicial combat."

She smiled. "I should've known you'd guess."

Dear God, judicial combat. No quarter, no mercy. No verdict without a death . . .

"Rhian—"

Pushing out of her chair she dropped to one knee on the floor before him and took his suddenly cold hands in hers. "My love, I must. If it comes to it, I must. There is still some little hope that Helfred's stern warnings will bring Kyrin and Damwin to their senses, but . . ."

"Helfred's not his uncle," he said. "He lacks Marlan's natural intimidation."

"Perhaps." She smiled again, wryly. "Although I think Helfred might surprise. Would God have chosen him if he weren't more than he seems?"

He let his thumb rub the back of her hand. "Rhian, I'm not comfortable with so much talk of God. Ethrea has managed well enough these past centuries without such heady divine interventions. I mistrust these signs and omens now."

"Don't let Helfred hear you say so," she told him. "I doubt he'd take it kindly, especially from a king. Besides, how can you doubt what happened? Like it or not, Alasdair, you were there. You saw Dexterity burn, the child return to life. Marlan. You heard Helfred chosen prolate."

He pulled his hands free of her. "What I saw and heard, Rhian, and what those events mean have yet to be reconciled. All this talk of men chosen by God . . . you of all people should see where lies the danger! Let a man believe himself chosen of God and it seems to me all common sense flies out the window. Yes, and goodness too. Marlan—"

"Revealed himself Godless in the end," she said sharply, standing. "He was a wicked man, and was harshly punished for his sins."

"Rhian . . ." He stood too and did take her by the shoulders, not to shake her but to move her aside so he could pace out his fear and temper round the confines of the antechamber. "I never knew you to be so pious."

"I'm not *pious*," she protested. "But I can't deny what I've seen! I can't turn my back on what I've been told!"

"You've been told *you're* God's chosen," he said, and felt his guts tighten with fright. "That's a heady brew, Rhian. Men thrice your age might well be thrown off stride." He stopped pacing and faced her, let her see his fear for her writ plain in his eyes. "Do you think you're invincible? Do you think that because it seems you've been chosen to—"

"*Seems?*" Her chin came up and her eyes glinted, dangerously. "Are you doubting my part in this now, Alasdair?"

No. But I'm wishing some other princess had been chosen. "What I'm trying to say, my love, is that if you're not careful this choosing could lull you into over-confidence. Could beguile you into believing you're more than flesh and blood, that no harm can come to you no matter how you risk yourself. That you'd even think of fighting Damwin and Kyrin . . . Rollin's mercy, can you believe I'll stand by and watch you throw yourself onto their swords?"

Slowly she walked to him, and slowly she framed his face with her hands. Hands that were callused from the hilt of her knife and the hour upon hour she spent dancing Zandakar's hotas. Hands that only last night had—

"I believe you know I must end their defiance," she said softly, distracting him. "Every day that passes without they bend their knee to my authority is a day that lends weight to the muttering of the ambassadors."

He took her wrists and loosened her clasping

hands. There was a dried bloodstain on the cuff of her silk shirt. Zandakar's oath. A pity he hadn't sworn it in heart's blood. "You can't make decisions based upon opinions held by men who have no sway here."

"But they do have sway, Alasdair," she insisted. "They talk amongst themselves, they strike bargains, sign treaties, shift alliances as their masters dictate. They have lives and purposes beyond our influence. They are men of power. And somehow I must convince them to defer to me. To follow my leadership against Mijak. What hope do I have of that if they see I can't discipline two errant dukes? And if Emperor Han suspects I'm not strong enough to do this . . ."

"Han," he spat, and turned away. "I don't trust him. I don't trust his witch-men. I am not a pious man and even I see there is the stench of unsavoury practice upon them."

"It's true," Rhian said after a moment. "The witch-men of Tzhung-tzhungchai aren't . . . comfortable. They dabble in things we don't understand. But I have to trust there's a purpose to their presence, Alasdair. I have to trust I can trust Tzhung's emperor, at least for now."

"And I think you place too much trust in trust," he retorted, turning back. "And not enough in the world we see and touch without miracles."

"Alasdair . . ." Rhian folded her arms, growing impatient. "I'm not talking of miracles now. I'm talking of cold hard reality, of consequences that will follow if I don't face the truth. A horde of brutal warriors is poised to sweep across Ethrea – and after Ethrea, the rest of the world. Perhaps Arbenia and

Harbisland and the others already suspect trouble
stirs in the east, or it could be that Han and I are the
only rulers who know. But even if we are, Mijak
won't stay secret forever. And when the trading nations' ambassadors learn the truth, they must believe
I can stand against the coming darkness. If they don't,
if they see me weak against two mere dukes, I fear
they'll join together and wrest Ethrea from my grasp,
all in the name of self-preservation."

"I understand that," he said, his throat tight.
"What I don't understand is why you must be the one
to risk your life against Damwin and Kyrin. I'm your
king consort, Rhian. There's no shame in sending me
against them in your stead. Not even Emperor Han
fights with his own blade. He has warriors who shed
blood in his name. Let me be your warrior. Don't risk
Ethrea for your pride."

"Alasdair, Alasdair . . ." Again Rhian approached
him. "That's unfair. When was I ever a prideful
woman?"

He couldn't help it: he laughed. "Rhian!"

"All right," she conceded with a reluctant smile.
"I'm proud, but not in that way. This has nothing to
do with wanting to prove myself a dashing hero, it's
about proving myself more than an upstart miss.
And—"

"What?" he said, when she didn't finish the
thought. "Rhian, what?"

She laid a palm flat to his velvet-covered chest,
frowning. "I'll prick your pride if I say it," she murmured. "Haven't we enough strife between us?"

She didn't have to say more. He knew what she

meant. "You think I can't defeat the dukes, where you can."

"Alasdair . . ." She sighed. "If it were a public jousting, a play to entertain and amuse, with blunted swords and padding aplenty I have no doubt you'd trounce the pair of them handily. No doubt. But this bout will be to the death."

"And I've never drawn a sword in anger, or in the need to defend my life." *I've never killed.* "Still, neither have the dukes, Rhian. They and I are evenly matched on that score."

"Perhaps. But they've had more years to play with swords than you," she said. "And I know for a fact both Damwin and Kyrin take their swordplay most serious. Papa could never best them in the annual joustings. But even if you're right and you're their equal, and more than their equal, here's the bitter truth. You and Damwin and Kyrin have had fencing masters to school you. Your form may be perfect, your touch with a blade a thing of beauty . . . but you only ever danced for show. Whereas I have had a warrior train me, a man steeped in blood from the moment of his birth. Every time I dance with him it is to make of myself a better killing queen. And if I'm to win the ambassadors to my cause I must show them my cold, killing face. Mine, Alasdair. For it's my lead they must follow in the fight against Mijak."

Her eyes were devoid of light and warmth and even the smallest hint of love. She was gone far away from him, to a dark place he didn't envy, to the dark place where Zandakar lived . . . and she lived with him.

"I'll not dissuade you, then?" he said. To his own

ears his voice sounded dry and defeated. "Nothing I say can turn you from this path?"

She laid two fingers across his lips. "If anyone could, Alasdair, it would be you. I swear it. And only because I love you, and know you love me, and know you understand what's at stake here, do I dare spurn your offer." She stood on tiptoes and kissed him, the lightest touch of lips to lips. "Don't think for a moment I don't know what this costs you. Don't think I don't live forever in your debt."

He stepped back. "If you wish to insult me continue this talk of debts, Rhian. I wasn't blind when I wed you. I wasn't ignorant when Helfred crowned me King Consort of Ethrea. From that moment I was destined to live in your shadow. I *know* that, and accept it. But *you* must accept that at times, though shouldered willingly, the burden is cruel . . . and I won't always spare you its cost to me."

"That's fair," she whispered. "And more than fair. It's right."

"Yes. It is." He ran an unsteady hand over his face. "So this is why you've released Zandakar? So he can help you prepare to fight the dukes?"

She nodded. "They'll use their longswords. I'm used to dancing with a dagger. I must find a bigger blade and learn how to dance with it and I haven't much time. He's the only one who can school me, Alasdair. This isn't a matter of want, but of need."

"I grant you that," he said, grudging. "But can't he school you out of his cell? Must he be housed in the castle like an honoured guest? Like a friend?"

"You know?" Her eyebrows pinched. "It seems

my royal servants haven't enough work, so much time is spared to them for tattling and gossip."

He snorted. "Don't change the subject."

"Zandakar will remain on the top floor of the east wing," she said. "One corridor leads to his chamber, and a full skein of guards will keep him snugly within. He'll not tread a foot anywhere without an armed escort. He's still a prisoner, Alasdair. A gilded cage is still a cage. But since he'll be helping to keep me alive it would be churlish not to remove him from the dungeons."

Yet again she was right, though it seared him to admit it. "I see you've thought it all to a careful conclusion."

"I think I have," she agreed. "And I'd be happier about it if I thought you were with me. I know you'll say you are with your public face but between us, in private . . ." Her voice caught a little. "Alasdair, we can't always be at odds."

"We're not," he said, and kissed her forehead. "That I don't like a thing isn't the same as saying I can't see the right of it. Do you have a date in mind for this judicial confrontation?"

"I thought Tassifer's Feastday," she said, trying to smile. "Given it celebrates a triumph of justice over persecution."

"And that gives you time enough to learn from Zandakar what you must learn, to prevail?"

She shrugged. "It'll have to."

Rollin's mercy, how it galled him that he couldn't take this burden from her shoulders. "Very well. You'll dictate the dukes' letters to Ven'Cedwin now?"

"As soon as he's done in the buttery, yes."

"Then I might leave you to that," he said. "You don't need me to put words in your mouth. I have business of my own to truck with. Do we dine alone or on state business tonight?"

"I'd rather we dined alone," she said, pulling a face. Diverted from protest, as he'd intended. "But I think Edward, Rudi and Adric would feel better if they broke bread at our table."

Adric. "Our new duke of Kingseat makes me nervous, Rhian. He lacks . . . polish."

She shrugged. "I know. I've been thinking the same thing." Her eyes lit with sudden mischief. "In fact, I've been thinking he'd benefit greatly from a mentor. A personage with gentility and self-control, who well understands how to be a man of power without forever shouting about it to everyone within earshot. Can you suggest a candidate?"

As ever, he was warmed and softened by her compliment. "If I can think of one I'll be sure to steer them together." He kissed her again, on the lips this time, with enough passion to reassure her – and himself – that disaster hadn't claimed them yet.

Rhian returned his kiss eagerly. "I think we must make sure of an early supper," she whispered against him. "After all, Edward and Rudi are senior in their years. Late nights can hardly be good for them."

"I agree," he said, grinning, then withdrew before she could think to ask him what business he had and where he would go next.

As he stepped into the corridor beyond the antechamber he saw Ven'Cedwin approaching, prayer beads swinging from his belt and a well-fed look upon his plump face. The venerable stopped and bowed. "Your Majesty."

"The queen awaits you, Ven'Cedwin. Make sure to draft these letters in your most elegant hand," he said. "The dukes must not find fault in the manner of their chiding."

Ven'Cedwin's lips quirked in a discreet smile. "Indeed they must not, Your Majesty. I take your excellent advice to heart."

Leaving the venerable and Rhian to their exacting duty, Alasdair headed to the east wing and Zandakar, his gilded prisoner.

The skein of guards lined the corridor end to end, as Rhian had promised. Each man's hand held a pikestaff, each man's side was graced with a sword. The senior officer, his name was . . . was Rigert, bowed when he reached them.

"Your Majesty."

He nodded at the closed chamber door. "Zandakar's within?"

"Majesty, he is."

"And you know his life is forfeit should he behave untoward?"

Rigert's eyes flickered. "Her Majesty has not said so."

"You may take it I speak for the queen in this, Sergeant. Should Zandakar give you any cause to doubt him, stab first and question after. He's not a man to be taken lightly, is that clear?"

"Majesty," said Rigert. "I know enough of him to know he's a feisty one, right enough. My half-brother Ansard's in the pay of Duke Edward. Ansard was one picked by this Zandakar to help guard the queen on the road from Linfoi. You can trust I'll not blink if it comes to putting him down."

Alasdair clapped the man's shoulder. "Trust I'll hold you to that, Rigert." *And make you sorry if you fail.* But that thought he kept to himself. It was the kind of blustering thing Adric would say.

Zandakar was indeed within the east wing chamber. His hair seemed new-washed, inhumanly blue and bright in the sunlight filtering through the castle's mullioned windows. His ill-fitting attire – linen shirt, leather leggings – was clearly borrowed. He was barefoot. Doubtless Rhian had already ordered the castle tailor and bootmaker to appropriately clothe him. Standing with his back to the wall he watched warily as the chamber door was closed.

"Alasdair king," he said. "You want?"

"Yes, Zandakar, I want," he said curtly. "Rhian has told me she's released you from prison that you might help her chastise the dukes. You're willing to do this?"

Zandakar nodded. "*Zho.*"

"Why?"

"Rhian will fight dukes. Rhian must train or she dies."

"But that's what you want, isn't it?" he demanded. "Rhian's death? My death? The death of every Ethrean in this kingdom? Isn't that why you've come here? To make us trust you, to reveal to you our soft bellies? So you can send word to your warriors of Mijak and—"

"*Wei!*" said Zandakar, his face twisting. "You fool king. You think this? Ask Dexterity, he knows, he—"

"I don't need conversation with a toymaker," he

snapped. "A man who put *you*, a stranger, before his loyalty to the queen."

With a hard-breathing effort, Zandakar relaxed. "*Wei* want Rhian dead. *Wei* want Mijak take Ethrea. I fight for Rhian, for Ethrea." He held up his left arm. Beneath the loose long sleeve was the bulk of a bandage. "I blood oath this truth."

More than anything in the world Alasdair wanted to see a lie in Zandakar's intimidating blue eyes. Wanted to hear a lie in his voice, read a lie in his body. But he couldn't. For reasons he couldn't bring himself to examine too closely – *she's my wife, my wife, you had your own, leave mine to me* – Zandakar had turned his back on his own people and instead thrown in his lot with Ethrea and the perilled world.

"Can you promise you'll keep her alive? When she fights Damwin and Kyrin, you can be certain she'll emerge victorious?"

Fear . . . regret . . . frustration: they burned together in Zandakar's pale eyes. "*Wei*."

"You say no. Yet you must understand that if you fail her I'll carve your heart from your chest myself."

Zandakar smiled. "*Wei*, Alasdair king. I fail Rhian, *I* carve heart out first."

He believed it. God help him, he believed this unwanted man. Some of the taut fear in his belly eased. Breathing more freely, he nodded. "All right."

"Alasdair king, she must have good blade."

He nodded. "Yes. I know. It's why I'm here, Zandakar. I've come to take you to the armoury, so you can choose the right sword for her. One she can dance with in her *hotas* and slice through Damwin and Kyrin's treacherous throats."

"*Zho*," said Zandakar, his eyes fierce with satisfaction. "*Zho*."

"Zandakar . . ." Alasdair stared at the man. It sickened him to be discussing Rhian in such a fashion, but this warrior of Mijak might be the only thing standing between her and death. "She can't hesitate when she's fighting them. If she hesitates she's lost, and we'll all be lost with her. She's not like you, the thought of killing doesn't delight. *She's* not been steeped in blood from the moment of her birth. But if she's not prepared to gut Damwin and Kyrin like the cur dogs they are – if her heart isn't hardened to the task . . ."

Worse than discussing her was the sympathy in Zandakar's eyes. "*Zho*, Alasdair king. Rhian be killing hard or Rhian be dead. She *wei* dead." His clenched fist struck his chest. "My oath."

"You don't have much time to school her to it," he said. "And even though she knows full well what's at stake, she'll fight you every step of the way. The thought of killing again appals her – can you begin to understand that?"

Zandakar nodded. "*Zho*," he said, then shrugged. "*Wei* matter. I train, she learn, she be hard. Rhian hate me, *wei* matter. She live."

Alasdair felt a flood of relief, and was ashamed. Zandakar would push Rhian, Zandakar would bully and berate and cuff her on the side of her head until she was ready to meet and defeat the dukes. He need never say another word on it. Zandakar would say it all.

He will earn her wrath and our marriage will be safe.

It occurred to him, then, so his hot blood turned cold, that he wasn't doubting Zandakar's intentions. Wasn't doubting the man would do everything in his power to keep Rhian alive and victorious. He was trusting her life to Zandakar's bloodsoaked hands . . . without a moment's hesitation.

Because he loves her. This murderous man is in love with my wife. I wonder what it says about me, that I'll use his love like a weapon to shield her. That I'll use him until he's all used up.

It didn't matter. All that mattered was that Rhian prevailed.

"Come then, Zandakar," he said, and moved to the chamber door. "Let us find Rhian a sword worthy of her, so she might take her place in history."

Rhian took the completed ducal letters to Helfred herself. Ven'Cedwin had protested, saying it wasn't seemly for Her Majesty to stoop to such errand-running when he was here, but she put paid to his lecture with a smiling dismissal. Helfred still managed to drive her to distraction but he was Ethrea's prolate and her spiritual guide. No matter the irritation, she needed to speak with him.

He'd kept the same office in the prolate's palace his uncle Marlan had occupied. A statement, perhaps, that while the man might change the position was unchanging.

"Majesty!" he said, surprised, standing behind his desk as she was ushered into the warmly wood-panelled chamber. "Was I expecting you?"

"No, Your Eminence."

He nodded at his venerable assistant and waited

for the door to close, leaving them alone. "Is something wrong, Rhian?"

She laid the letters on his desk and sat in the austere wooden guest chair. "Read those, Helfred, then you can tell me."

Eyebrows lifted, he sat again and pulled the carefully scribed parchments towards him. When he'd read them both he looked up. "Judicial combat. Is this wise?"

She shrugged. "Probably not. But they leave me no choice, Helfred. Or can you think of some other way to persuade them to recant their defiance? If so, I'll happily hear it."

"I wish I could," he murmured, and tapped a finger to the letters. "Alas, these dukes are proving most recalcitrant. I fear even the threat of interdict won't change them."

"Then I have no other recourse, do I?" She shifted in her chair, resentful. "And the law provides me with this weapon against them."

Helfred leaned back in his chair and steepled his fingers. The light from the window showed her that newfound steel in his eyes. "True."

"But you don't approve, do you?" she said. "What, do you think that in challenging them, that if I raise my sword with the *intent* of taking life, I'm made a murderer if they fall?" She felt her skin shrink and crawl. Remembered Ven'Martin and his blood on her hands. "Is that what you think?"

"I did not say so, Rhian."

"But I think you're thinking it," she persisted. "After all, don't you call Zandakar a murderer for slaying those footpads in Arbat?"

Frowning, Helfred released a soft, slow sigh. "I think perhaps I was less . . . comprehending . . . then. Life is rarely so simple, Rhian, as each day in this palace teaches me. God knows you've resisted violence at every turn. No-one could accuse you of rushing to justice with a sword. I certainly don't, if my opinion carries any weight."

It did, though she'd walk on burning coals before admitting it. "You can be sure someone will accuse me, if I kill Damwin and Kyrin."

"Given the state of our perilous world, Rhian, you'll more likely be criticised if you don't use force against the dukes," said Helfred. "The nations who trade with us don't see the sword as a sin. Majesty, Ethrea sits in the centre of a maelstrom, on the brink of the greatest storm the civilised world has ever known and God himself has told us you must fight the threatening darkness. Until this domestic crisis is resolved you cannot do what God decrees." Helfred's unsteepled fingers found his prayer beads. They clicked loudly in the quiet. "What happens with the dukes is for the dukes to decide. They will recognise your authority or they will pay the price."

She felt her belly churn queasily. Imagined Damwin and Kyrin dead, like Ven'Martin. "And so will I, Helfred. Don't forget that. So will I."

"Yes," he agreed. "That's the price *you* pay, for pursuing a crown."

"Helfred, I never *pursued* the crown!" she snapped, and pushed to her feet. "At least – yes, I did, but not for personal glory, if that's what you imply!"

"Glory? No," Helfred agreed. "But there was

pride, Rhian. In being Eberg's daughter. In being of royal blood. In the House of Harvell."

Her pride, again. She could feel her cheeks burning. This wasn't her chamber to pace at will, but she paced anyway. "Perhaps," she admitted. "To start with. But not now. Now this is about keeping Ethrea safe. A kingdom divided can't stand against Mijak, but Damwin and Kyrin won't hear that. They refuse to believe we're in danger. All they can think of is themselves. *They're* the ones consumed by dreams of glory, Helfred, not me. All *I'm* consumed with is the desire to survive! I don't want to challenge them. I don't want to kill them. But if I have to, I will. For Ethrea, I will."

"I know," said Helfred quietly. "Pride isn't always a bad thing, Rhian. Sometimes it's all that keeps us going in the face of fearful odds and dread terror."

Surprised, she halted by the guest chair and gripped its carved wooden back. She hadn't expected him to understand that. "Yes. Sometimes." She let out a shaky breath. "Helfred, take your time travelling to the dukes. Don't be sluggardly but . . . don't hurry, either. I need some little breathing space, so Zandakar can school me in meeting and defeating these men with their longswords."

He nodded. "As you wish, Your Majesty. And as I travel I'll say a goodly prayer, that Zandakar's schooling achieves its end." Steel flashed in his eyes again. "These dukes have been disobedient long enough."

CHAPTER FIVE

"**W**ei!" Zandakar shouted. "Rhian *hushla*, you wish to die?"

Sweat-soaked and panting in the mid-afternoon sun, stippled with blood on her cheek and throat and on her arms where Zandakar's longsword had nicked her flesh to make a point, Rhian held up a hand, halting their *hotas*.

Zandakar glowered at her, barely out of breath. She glowered back, gasping for air.

I hate him. How I hate him. He'd never held a longsword until the day before yesterday and yet he wields it like he burst from his mother's womb brandishing the thing.

"What?" she demanded. Her right arm ached ferociously; the shortsword he and Alasdair had chosen for her from the armoury – *and why was I not included in that decision?* – had more than twice the length of the dagger she was used to and felt horribly unwieldy. *I'll never be able to fight with this. God, I've signed my own death warrant.* "What did I do wrong this time?"

They were sparring in the castle's tiltyard, next to the stables, where once her brothers and her father had crossed swords in training, never thinking a sword would be needed for war. She'd sparred here

too, but only with a light foil. Well-bred young ladies
had no need for hammered steel.

Or so they thought. My, how times change.

Zandakar reached out and slapped her left flank
with the flat of his blade. Even through huntsman's
leathers the blow hurt. She bit her lip, refusing to give
him the satisfaction of a wince.

"Rhian put weight wrong, put weight forward,"
he said. "Weight on back foot, *hushla*. So you dance
hota like *this*." With effortless grace he leapt straight
up in the air and flipped his tall body over and backwards. Even as his right foot touched the ground his
left leg caught her hard behind the knees so she fell
flat-backed to the ground. Before the air had escaped
her lungs in a wheezing groan his sword-tip was
pressed into the base of her throat. "*Zho?*"

"Zho," she said, glaring, and looked sideways to
where Adric and a handful of courtiers and the soldiers who guarded Zandakar were dangled over the
tiltyard fence. It was politic to let them linger, watching her, watching Zandakar, but she still didn't like it.

Zandakar stepped back, withdrawing his sword,
and she flipped to her feet. Every muscle in her body
was screaming.

"Rhian put weight forward, invite dukes to kill
her," he said. His blue eyes burned with frustration.

"I know that!" she snarled. "But this shortsword,
the weight throws my balance off. I'm used to a dagger, you know I am. I've only just learned to dance
the *hotas* with a knife, Zandakar, don't bully me
because—"

He slapped her face. "*Tcha! Hatz'i'tuk!* Rhian
wei—"

Cheek burning she whirled, her shortsword extended, her body moving to block his.

"Stand down, Sergeant!" she commanded. "*And* your men."

Rigert halted three paces distant, his own sword out and death in his eyes. His two subordinates crowded behind him, just as keen to see Zandakar spitted.

"Majesty, he assaulted you!"

"No, he did not," she said. "We're training. It's his way." She glanced over her shoulder. "I was in the wrong, and should've kept my mouth shut. *Yatzhay*, Zandakar."

Baffled, Rigert stared at her. "Majesty . . . Majesty, he should not be so close to you with a naked blade."

"No? Then how would you suggest he trains me, Sergeant? By writing me helpful notes and throwing them at my feet as I cross swords with the dukes?"

Rigert didn't care for her sarcasm. Lips thinned, eyes resentful, he put back his shoulders. "His Majesty has charged me—"

"*I* have charged you, Sergeant," she snapped. *How long, God, how long, before they see the crown first and my sex last*? "I've made it clear you'll not interfere without my express invitation. Must I find another sergeant who can follow my commands?"

Slowly Rigert's sword-point dipped towards the ground. "No, Your Majesty."

She nodded. "Good. Then remove to your post, unless you're after a haircut . . . or worse." She turned her back on him, letting him know she took obedience for granted, and met Zandakar's unblink-

ing gaze. His anger had faded. Now he looked at her
with grim amusement.

"We dance now, *zho*?"

She nodded again. "*Zho*. We dance."

This time she didn't fail. She kept her weight back,
she flipped herself up and over with the shortsword
balanced and even managed to touch its point to his
heart. His teeth flashed, smiling, and when he cuffed
her again it was with pleased approval.

"Your Majesty! Your Majesty!"

Running with fresh sweat, her muscles pleading for
mercy, she turned. "Who hails me?"

One of the castle message boys, his brown eyes astonished in his thin, freckled face. There were so many
boys like him; they leapt about the place like fleas. Neat
in castle livery, blue velvet banded with black, a flat-
brimmed blue cap on his close-cropped head, he panted
to a halt before her, flourished a bow and clasped his hands
behind his back. His wide-eyed gaze kept darting past
her to Zandakar.

"Majesty," he said in his young boy's piping voice,
"and it pleases the king to say that word is come from
the prolate. You would do the king great honour to
meet with him and your council for to discuss these
important matters of state."

Rhian smiled. *Dear God, what a mouthful. He
looks too young to understand a half of it.* "Thank
you—"

A tide of red obliterated the boy's freckles.
"Nosher, Majesty." It came out a strangled whisper.

"Nosher?" She laughed. "That's the name you
were born with?"

"No, Majesty. Me mam, she calls me Gib."

"Well, Gib, that's a message well delivered," she said. "Off you go now. Mind your duties." As the boy scuttled out of the tiltyard she looked over at Adric. "Your Grace! It seems we're needed in privy council. I'll see you within. Do not tarry for me." Adric nodded and withdrew, the courtiers following, and she turned to Zandakar. "That's it for today. I'm sorry, this summons doubtless means you'll be penned in your chamber until tomorrow. Come sunrise we'll dance again."

He shrugged. "Rhian *hushla*. Rhian say."

"Thank you for your training, Zandakar. I will be better tomorrow. Sergeant Rigert!"

Rigert came running. "Majesty?"

"Escort Zandakar to his apartments."

He bowed. "Yes, Your Majesty."

"And, Rigert?" She smiled, not comfortably. "Let him not trip or slip or accidentally hit his face on a fist between here and the castle. What is done here is done on my command."

Rigert looked down. "Yes, Majesty."

She hurried to the council chamber, not bothering to pause to make a swift toilet. Let her council see her sweaty, bloody, dressed in battered leathers with a shortsword at her hip. Let them lose as swiftly as possible their comfortable idea of what *womanly* meant.

Though they support me whole-heartedly, still they have a lot to learn.

Alasdair's eyebrows shot up when he saw her, but to his credit he made no comment. Edward, though, so old-fashioned, so chivalrous, couldn't help himself. "Majesty. Let us send for the physick! This is wrong, this is monstrous wrong, that you should be wounded unto bleeding!"

"Heed the Duke of Morvell," said Rudi. "And do reconsider this martial fervour." He peered more closely. "Your cheek is bruised."

"Zandakar struck her," said Adric, making mischief. "So hard I thought Rigert was like to spit him on the spot."

Ignoring him, taking her seat, she looked at Alasdair. "I deserved it. What's amiss? What has Helfred said?"

Alasdair was displeased, she could see that in his eyes. But he didn't task her, knowing to hold his tongue until they were private. Instead he looked at Ven'Cedwin, patiently standing behind a chair. In the venerable's ink-stained hand was a half-sheet of parchment.

"That's from Helfred? Let me see it."

"Majesty," said Ven'Cedwin, and gave her the letter.

It was addressed to her, but clearly Alasdair had read it. She didn't mind. It seemed a small thing, to give him access to state letters. Eased, she thought, the constant sting of her precedence. Helfred had written the missive himself, she'd know his self-conscious penmanship anywhere. She read it swiftly as her council sat at the table.

Kyrin and Damwin were informed of her decree. Both were furious and refused to reveal their intent, but he was certain they would obey and come to Kingseat Castle to face judicial combat. She had, he assured her, emphatically pricked their hot ducal pride. Which was of course precisely as she'd intended. One way or the other the dukes would be prostrate before her.

In obeisance or in death. The choice will be theirs.

He had been forced to make changes in both venerable houses, Helfred continued. Alas for the weakness of avaricious men who had long forgotten where their true loyalties belonged. But that was Church business and she need not concern herself. He was returning to Kingseat with the Court Ecclesiastica so they might preside over the upcoming business with the dukes.

"I see by your expression, Majesty, the dukes haven't come to their senses," said Rudi. "A pity."

She laid Helfred's letter carefully on the table. "A great pity, Rudi."

"Majesty," said Alasdair, his eyes eloquent, his voice scrupulously noncommittal. "We have five days until Tassifer's Feast."

Oh God. Five days. Could Zandakar teach her enough to survive a double duel in only five more days, when so much else in the kingdom claimed her attention?

I should've said the Fast of Wilmot. That would've given me four extra days. In nine days I could learn almost twice as much, be twice as ready for judicial combat.

But that would give Mijak an extra four days, when she didn't know how close its warriors were or how soon their sails would appear on her horizon.

They could appear tomorrow. We could be lost so soon.

Except she refused to believe that. If Mijak appeared tomorrow, defeat was inevitable. Why then would God have chosen her if that was the case?

We have time. I have time. I have to believe that.

"Five days, yes," she said, nodding. "They will suffice."

"It's not likely Damwin and Kyrin will change their minds at the last gasp," said Edward. "Stupid, stubborn fools that they are. Where shall you hold the judicial combat?"

"Here," she said. "In the castle grounds."

"Witnesses?" asked Rudi. "Aside from ourselves and the Court Ecclesiastica, that is."

"Duke Ludo will arrive from Linfoi in the next day or two," said Alasdair. "And I believe the leaders of Ethrea's venerable houses and clericas are also summoned."

Ven'Cedwin glanced up from his swift note-taking. "That is correct, Your Majesty," he murmured. "His Eminence saw to their notification before he departed."

"Prominent townsfolk should also attend," said Edward. "Representatives of the greater families in the other duchies. Perhaps even a smattering of the common people. If this is to be done, it cannot be done in secret."

Rhian stirred. "Nor can it be treated like a public entertainment. If I must judicially slaughter these men I'd prefer it be done in a sober, serious fashion."

"I doubt Edward's suggesting sideshows and food-sellers," said Alasdair. "But he's right that this cannot be done circumspect, either. Judicial combat is lawful. These dukes are in the wrong. If we attempt to hide the proceedings we risk giving the impression we're somehow shamed by our actions."

He was right. She just wished he wasn't. She nodded. "A fair point."

Edward cleared his throat. "And what of the ambassadors? What of Emperor Han?"

"What of them?" she said, staring. "Domestic Ethrean matters are Ethrea's concern. There's no need for them to attend the proceedings. They'll hear about them, and that will suffice."

Edward and Rudi exchanged troubled glances. "Forgive me, Majesty, but I don't think it will," said Rudi.

"There is . . . talk," Edward said, uncomfortable. "Servants chatter to servants, word reaches our ears. Not every ambassadorial comment remains private."

"Or flattering?" she added. Edward opened his mouth to reply, but she shook her head. "No, don't bother, I can guess the kind of things they've been saying."

"They have scant respect for women rulers, Majesty," said Adric, clearly his father's confidant and eager to assert his meagre authority. "It's hard to believe they'll tell their masters to follow you into battle. Not unless they've seen with their own eyes that you're not frightened of blood."

She felt her fingers try to clench. *I might not like him overmuch, but it doesn't mean he can't be right.* She wanted to shout, *Emperor Han will follow me. Emperor Han knows who I am in this. He'll champion my cause.* But what was the use? She couldn't ask Han of Tzhung-tzhungchai to speak for her. Ethrea could never once be seen as the emperor's lap-dog. If she was to convince the ambassadors to convince their masters that she was fit to take the lead in the fight against Mijak, perhaps Edward and the others were right. Perhaps the ambassadors should be invited to witness the judicial combat.

But how little do I care for the idea of asking the world into Ethrea's kitchen, so it might see how we bake our cakes.

"Rudi, I take it you agree with Edward? You think Han and the ambassadors should be invited as witnesses?"

He nodded. "Reluctantly, yes."

"Adric?"

"Certainly! Once they've seen—"

"Thank you." She looked at Alasdair. "And you?"

His eyes were apologetic. "I wish I could say no, but . . ."

"I see." She stood. "Gentlemen, I stink like a cowherd. While I bathe I'll consider your suggestion. If I can bring myself to agree I'll send word to let you know. In the meantime please continue with your planning of the . . . event . . . and I'll hear your thoughts tomorrow."

She left them to their organising, and closed the chamber door behind her.

God help me. God help me. Will this get any easier?

Since she had no intention of conducting further public business, after her bath Rhian dressed in one of her old blue linen gowns. With its sleeves unlaced and set aside she sat on her bed to dab some of Ursa's fierce ointment on her swordcuts. When Alasdair at last returned from the privy council chamber and found her cursing under her breath, he plucked the jar of ointment from her fingers.

"Let me." The wool-and-feather mattress sagged as he sat beside her. "I think Zandakar thinks to make of you a colander."

She winced at the ointment's burn. "No. If I'm cut the fault is mine, for not being fast enough." She gasped a little as his fingers found the deepest wound.

"It's painful?"

"Not at all," she said, frowning. "A delightful tickle. I'm struggling not to laugh."

Turning her hand over, Alasdair kissed its palm. "Sorry."

Love for him came in a wave so strong, so overwhelming, for a moment she could neither see nor breathe. This quiet intimacy, this small precious heartbeat of time snatched from the chaos that was their lives since Linfoi . . . it stung tears to her eyes. So much had changed since Ranald and Simon were brought home, fever-struck, that often she felt a stranger in her own skin. Brothers dead. Father dead. Marlan seeking to control her, destroy her. Miracles and madness. Her world ripped apart and remade before her eyes. So often it seemed she would never catch her breath. So often it seemed she'd never recognise herself again.

Quiet moments like this helped keep hysterics at bay.

Alasdair glanced up. "What?"

"Nothing," she said, and had to clear her throat. "You never mentioned you thought I should make an audience of the ambassadors."

"Edward and Rudi only broached the subject with me yesterday. I wanted to think about it. I wanted to see if you'd mention it first."

"And I didn't. In truth . . ."

"In truth, it never occurred to you?" he said, and shook his head. "It should have."

She pulled her arm free of him. "Really?"

"Really," he said. With her hurts not all tended he put the jar aside, slid off the bed and moved to the chamber window. Dusk was falling. The chamber's lanterns seemed to burn a little brighter as the light beyond the panes of glass slowly faded.

Staring at his broad shoulders, his straight spine, at his rich blue velvet doublet, she pulled a face. "You're right. It should have. Papa would scold me if he was here."

Alasdair turned. "You can't think of everything. It's a wonder you can think of *anything*, beyond trying to stay alive."

He was afraid for her. So afraid. *I'm afraid for myself*. She reached for the ointment and continued physicking herself. "Edward might he wrong. The dukes might yet surrender without combat, Alasdair."

"You know they won't," he said, his expression bleak. "They've come too far now to turn back."

And so had she. Her only way was forward, through rivers of ducal blood. "If I invite outsiders I turn law into spectacle."

"And if you don't, you lose an important chance to impress on the ambassadors your fitness to rule," Alasdair countered gently. "Adric's right. What is it to Harbisland or Arbenia that Ethrea's God declared you should lead them to war? They worship in their own way. Our way means naught to them. But they do respect a wielded sword."

Regrettably it was true. Nor was it something a ruler of unwarlike Ethrea had been forced to consider for hundreds of years. *So protected, we've been. Swaddled in peace like an infant, untouched by the squabbles elsewhere in the world. And now it seems our protection was mere gossamer. Almost illusion. We are vulnerable in ways we never imagined.*

"I'll have to invite them, won't I?" she said, and sighed. "Arbenia. Harbisland. The rest of them."

"And Han."

She jammed the cork stopper back in Ursa's jar of ointment. "Yes. He'll have to come."

Alasdair leaned against the embrasure. "You don't like him."

"He frightens me." She shivered. "It all frightens me, Alasdair. I can admit it to you, in here, while we're alone."

He returned to her, and gathered her into his arms. "With me, in here, while we're alone, you don't have to be brave. What else am I for, if not to give you strength when you feel weak?"

She buried her face in his velvet-covered chest. "Well . . . you're very good at pulling off my boots."

He laughed, and she laughed with him, and for a moment, so briefly, fear retreated.

"Come," he said, and kissed her hair. "Let's eat and retire early. The world can mind itself for one night."

*　　　*　　　*

Ludo arrived just before noon the next day, while she and the privy council were hammering out the final details of the judicial combat and its staging in the castle grounds. He was shown to the council chamber and admitted at once.

"Ludo!" said Rhian, greeting him with a sisterly kiss on each cheek. "Welcome back to Kingseat. Not so long since we saw you last, at the coronation, and still it feels an age. Your journey was uneventful?"

He bowed, and kissed her hand. "Tolerably so, Majesty. Travel on water refuses to agree with my vitals. And . . . there were some dark looks from the riverbanks as the barge passed between Hartshorn and Meercheq."

"It's to be expected," she said quietly, with a glance at Alasdair. "Some foolish people model themselves on their disobedient dukes. How is Henrik?"

Ludo, so handsome and stylish and vibrant with life, wilted a little. "Father minds the duchy for me, Majesty. He is well enough, all in all. The tonics your physick Ursa sends help him a great deal, but . . ."

But Marlan had broken him, and he'd never fully mend.

She squeezed his arm. "He's ever in our thoughts, Ludo. Whatever the crown can do, you've only to ask."

"I know," he said, his voice hoarse. "And he sends you his dearest regards." He turned. "And you, Alasdair. Your Majesty."

She indicated the table. "Sit. Speak for duchy Linfoi as we discuss matters of state. Since you're yet to nominate a voice for this council . . ."

"I am thinking on it," he said, taking the only

spare seat, beside Ven'Cedwin. "It's not a decision I'd choose to rush, Your Majesty."

She nodded. "You and Alasdair can discuss it over dinner. For now let us consider the wider needs of Ethrea."

When the council meeting ended, she left Alasdair and Ludo to their reunion and returned to the tiltyard with Zandakar for more training. She was definitely getting stronger, faster, more skilled with the short-sword, but she couldn't escape the unpalatable truth. Time was running out. Tassifer's Feast drew closer, and with it the most fateful meeting of her life.

The next day, over Alasdair's objections, she abandoned leadership of the council to him entirely. Until the day of the judicial combat she would do nothing but train with Zandakar, sunup to sundown.

"You'll work yourself to skin and bone!" Alasdair protested that night. "You'll be so exhausted he'll kill you by mistake!"

Thrumming with pain, so weary she could weep, she lowered herself into the oak tub of water prepared for her. "No, he won't," she said, wincing. "He's going to keep me alive." And when Alasdair tried to argue further, added, "*Please*. No more. I have to do this, and you know it. Keep Ludo company. I must be a poor host."

Helfred returned to Kingseat with the Court Ecclesiastica the following morning. She spared him a scant half hour from her training so he could tell her of the changes he'd wrought in the venerable houses of Meercheq and Hartshorn, and to repeat his assertions that the dukes would come to fight. She thanked him for his services, bade him to rest, then afterwards talk with Alasdair of other arrangements for the combat. He agreed without demur. On her sinewy, warlike appearance he passed no word of comment. Which was wise of him, for she surely would've said something rash.

With Helfred settled, she returned to her *hotas*.

Under the privy council's guidance, and with the efforts of so many clerks and privy secretaries, the kingdom continued to prosper. No whispers of Mijak had been heard yet around the harbour or in the taverns of Kingseat, a good thing for which she was most grateful. Save for the mutterings in Hartshorn and Meercheq, and reports from their ducal households of frantic sword practice and declarations of defiance, no disturbances were reported in the kingdom. With Helfred's venerables and chaplains preaching peace and the wisdom of obedience, the upheaval caused by Marlan seemed mostly subsided.

Alasdair and Helfred crafted the invitations to the ambassadors and Emperor Han. Rhian signed them, and sealed them, and returned to her *hotas*. Edward and Rudi drew up plans for the creation of the judicial combat arena. Rhian approved them, and returned to her *hotas*.

Sunrise by sunrise, Tassifer's Feast approached.

Her last training session in the tiltyard, late in the afternoon, was witnessed by the privy council and Ludo and Ursa and what seemed like a quarter of Commander Idson's garrison and half the castle's courtiers and staff. When it was finished Zandakar pressed his fist to his chest. His eyes were glowing with savage pride.

"You ready, Rhian *hushla*. You dance *hotas* like a queen."

He was bleeding in a dozen places where her short-sword had caught him. She bled as well, but not as much as the first time they trained in this fashion.

Sword sheathed by her side, she returned his salute. "Zandakar—" She bit her lip. "I won't see you again until this is over. Thank you."

He bowed his head. "Rhian is welcome."

As she walked from the tiltyard those watching her began to applaud. Hands clapped, feet stamped, a few voices called out.

"God bless Her Majesty! God bless our warrior queen!"

She felt tired, yet triumphant. Afraid, yet strangely at peace. She acknowledged her enthusiastic people with a smile, then beckoned to Ursa.

"See to Zandakar. I hurt him."

Ursa frowned. "I should see to you—"

"He barely touched me, Ursa. See to Zandakar," she said again. "How else can I reward him?"

As Ursa withdrew, unhappy, Alasdair joined her. Leaving the chattering, excited crowd behind they walked towards the nearest castle entrance. Off to the right, castle servants put the finishing touches to the raised timber gallery of seats for the guests invited to witness the next day's judicial combat. Hammers banged. Workers shouted. Groundsmen prowled the lawn with heavy rollers, flattening the turf so a combatant might not trip on a tussock and so present his or her throat to a sword by mistake.

"Kyrin, Damwin and their retinues have arrived in

Kingseat," Alasdair told her quietly. "Word came while you were training."

A mingling of sweat and blood trickled down her face. Zandakar's longsword had nicked her left cheekbone; she could feel the puffy swelling round the cut. "Do they lodge separately or together?"

"Separately. Damwin's in his township residence. Kyrin's with his cousin, Hadin."

She nodded. "Very well. Can you see a herald is sent to them, with strict instructions for the morrow?"

"Of course." His fingers brushed her leather-sleeved arm. "You wish to be alone now?"

Desperately. The thought of what she'd soon face was overwhelming. She made herself smile at him. "I'm sorry. I do."

"Bathe. Rest. We'll share a quiet supper," he said. "Then an early night."

She closed her fingers round his wrist and held on tight, just for a moment. "That sounds perfect."

And it was, in its peaceful way. They dined privily, no servants attending, no other company but their own. Spoke not a word about Mijak, or Zandakar, or the dukes, and how she must defeat them. Instead they spoke of the future, of a royal progress around Ethrea, of sailing to other lands and seeing things wild and new. And then, dinner consumed, they retired to bed and consumed each other. Haunted but not speaking the truth: *tonight might be our last.*

But afterwards, though Alasdair slept, Rhian stared at the ceiling. Sleep eluded her. Fears crowded in. So she slipped unnoticed from their bed, pulled on a linen shirt and woollen hose, slid her shortsword from its sheath and padded barefoot to the castle's Long Gallery where she could settle her nerves with one last dance. The castle guards bowed when they saw her. Alasdair insisted they patrol the castle corridors, fearing the dukes might attempt to emulate Marlan and send a murdering dagger against her. She wasn't worried, but surrendered to his fears. It was easier than arguing.

Feet and hands thudding on the gallery's parquetry floor, her breathing steady and rhythmical, she danced the *hotas* in candlelight and silence, through shadows and soft flame. With their forms and discipline now second nature, she found her thoughts drifting towards her dead father.

Papa, can you see me? Could you see me in the tiltyard? It appears I've become a warrior queen . . .

The thought was enough to make her smile, even though fear gibbered and nibbled around her edges. *Warrior queen.* Ranald and Simon would laugh themselves blue-faced at the notion.

If I weren't so frightened I might laugh at it myself. By this time tomorrow I could be dead . . .

She'd already signed her writ of succession, naming Alasdair Ethrea's king without encumbrance. The privy council and Helfred had witnessed her declaration, and her prolate now held it safe in Church keeping.

By this time tomorrow . . .

Shaking herself free of such unhelpful morbid fancies, she blotted sweat from her face and prepared for another tumbling pass down the gallery. It would have to be the last one. She was exhausted, and the next day would start hideously early with a full

Litany in the castle's chapel. She had no hope of evading it. Try, and she'd turn Helfred into a warrior prolate.

Rollin save me. There's a dreadful thought.

Tumble . . . leap . . . cartwheel . . . stab here . . . slash there . . . hamstrings – elbows – belly – throat – another leap . . . and another . . . with Zandakar's impatient voice ringing in her ears.

Rhian wei defend. Rhian defend, Rhian die. Attack, attack, like striking snake, attack. Speed, Rhian. Wei time duke touch you. Faster. Faster. Cut him. Duke die.

It was the heart of the *hotas*: no defence. Attacking only, with blinding speed and ruthless disregard for self. As a creed it called to something within her, released some inner wildness, unshackled a part of her that until she met Zandakar she'd only ever glimpsed.

A part of her that Alasdair didn't understand.

Reaching the end of the gallery she plundered the last of her physical reserves and danced all the way back again, punishing herself, pushing herself to her scarlet limit and beyond. There was pain, she ignored it. Lungs and muscles burned, she let them. Blinded by sweat, deafened by the waterfall thunder of blood through her veins, she reached for the dregs of her strength and poured them into the *hotas*.

Her last lethal cartwheel ended with her dropping to the floor, first to knees, then to hands, her shortsword clattering disregarded beside her. Head hanging, sweat pooling on the polished parquetry, she gasped and sobbed and prayed she was good enough to prevail. Good enough not to die.

When she looked up, Emperor Han stood before her.

CHAPTER SIX

He nodded, almost a bow. "Your Majesty."

"*Han* . . ." She sat back on her heels, panting, too perplexed to feel angry. "If I tell you to stop doing this I don't suppose you'll oblige?"

As before, the emperor's long black hair was pulled back from his marvellous face. Instead of black silk he wore multi-coloured brocade, gold and crimson and emerald and blue. Silver thread sparkled in the waning candlelight. His dark eyes were hooded, something unreadable in their depths.

"What is that fighting style called, that you do?"

Games, games. Always games with the Tzhung. Letting her hands rest comfortably on her thighs, she shrugged. "*Hotas.*"

"Mijaki?"

"That's right."

"And you think to defeat your dukes with the warfare of Mijak?"

Another shrug. "I think it's the only kind of warfare I know. My father never taught me how to wield a longsword."

Han smiled. She noticed for the first time his white teeth were slightly crooked. "The quaint customs of Ethrea," he said, faintly insulting. "No army to speak of, yet your noblemen play with their longswords and dream of the dead days killed by your holy man Rollin."

"Would you rather we had killed each other instead?" she countered, then frowned. "Yes. Of course you would. Then Tzhung-tzhungchai could've overrun this island as it's overrun so many other helpless lands. I wonder if that's not what you're hoping for now. I wonder if you expect me to die tomorrow, so you can consume Ethrea like a pickled egg."

If Han was surprised by her acumen, or affronted by her accusation, if he felt anything at all, it was impossible to say. His amber face was untouched by emotion, his eyes flat and black. He regarded her steadily, no tension to be seen in his lean, elegant body. "Do you think you will die, Majesty?"

Her shortsword was within easy grasp, but if she reached for it she'd give him something she never wanted him to have. "No."

This time he laughed. The sound was shockingly pleasant. "Brave Queen of Ethrea, your God chose well when he chose you."

Calling upon every discipline Zandakar had instilled in her, she rose in a smooth single motion to her feet. The shortsword stayed on the ground but she still had a dagger strapped to her hip.

I'm tired of his games. I'm bored by men thinking I'm the pawn on their chess board.

"What do you want, Han? Why do you keep coming here?"

His eyebrows lifted, as though she'd asked a silly question. As though the answers should be obvious.

"Curiosity, Rhian. I wanted to know how you fared, the night before your fateful encounters."

"I'm touched," she said, letting a little of insult show in her own voice. "And I can't help but notice you failed to answer my previous question."

"Do I think you'll die?" His eyes widened. "Of course. All mortals die, Rhian. Some sooner than others, some smiling, some with a scream. But they all die."

She looked at him in silence. *They*, he'd said. Not *we*. And what did *that* mean? *He's trying to unsettle me. He thinks I can be twisted round his fingers like a strand of silk.*

"Do you think I'll die tomorrow?"

Han clasped his hands placidly before him. "Sundao has asked the wind that very question."

"And did the wind answer him?"

"The wind always answers Sun-dao."

She felt her heart thud. *Don't ask, don't ask . . .* but she couldn't help herself. "What did it say?"

Instead of answering, Han unclasped his hands and reached out to the nearest tall candle in its wrought-iron holder. The mellow flame flared blue. Leapt from its wick to the tip of his finger where it danced like a firefly. Like magic. Like sorcery. Rhian stared, her heart pounding.

I thought such things were nursery tales and superstition. And then I met this emperor and his witchmen and now I'm not so sure.

She smiled. "Very clever. Might I invite you to the next birthday gathering of my flower children? I can't imagine a better entertainment."

Han's smile this time was less attractive. Was it her

imagination or did she feel a whisper of cold air stroking her skin?

"If I tell you the wind says you will die, Rhian, perhaps you will stay in your bed and not fight," he said softly. "That would not bode well for the world. If I tell you the wind says you will live, perhaps you will laugh at these dukes instead of minding your sword strokes. Perhaps then they will stab you and not the desired reverse."

She felt a flutter of heat in the pit of her stomach. *This is my castle. Mine. And you weren't invited.* "Have you come to taunt me with riddles and half-truths?"

For the first time since they'd met, she sensed disquiet in him. A baffled irritation that not even his formidable self-control could stifle.

"You are the riddle here, Rhian. I am the emperor of an ancient people, master of more lives than you can know. Men breathe for my pleasure . . ." He pinched his fingers together and the dancing blue flame was extinguished. "Men die on my whim. What are you by comparison? A little girl in wool and linen, amusing herself with the tricks of a barbarian race, a race that drinks blood, bathes in blood, will turn the seas to blood if the wind cannot blow them back behind their deserts."

She refused to be intimidated by this man. "I must be something more than a little girl, Han, if the wind blows in my direction and not yours."

His face turned ugly then, just for an instant. Beneath the smooth urbanity roiled such resentment. "Sun-dao says this is so." He smiled, his eyes savage. "Sun-dao says many things."

She lifted her chin. "I'm not Tzhung, Emperor Han. I have no care for what some tricksy man claims to hear in a passing breeze."

"So you say, little queen," said Emperor Han. "I wonder if you will say the same once the wind has finished blowing through your stone castle and into every Ethrean life."

A sudden gust of air swirled the length of the gallery. It snuffed out the candles, plunging her into darkness. But she didn't need light to know that Emperor Han was gone.

Trembling, and resenting that, she picked up her shortsword. She was far too weary to sharpen and polish it now, and that wasn't a task she wished to pass to the armoury. Before she led her court to hear Litany in the morning she would tend her sword. It would do her good. The task was like a meditation, calming and helping her to focus.

And God knows I need focus. I need faith that God hasn't made a mistake.

Carrying her shortsword she left the Long Gallery. The guards waiting outside leapt to attention as she emerged. She bade them good night and returned to her apartments, uncomfortably aware that they trailed her discreetly. Oh, how she resented that. Resented being hemmed about, considered unsafe in her own home.

Alasdair was awake and waiting for her, a lamp lit, his eyes so troubled. "Are you mad?"

Carefully she laid her sword on their chamber's padded settle and began the limbering stretches she would have done had Han not imposed himself upon her. Her cooled muscles creaked and groaned in protest. "I couldn't sleep."

"Then you should've asked for a soothing tea," he retorted. "*Look* at you, Rhian. You're so used up you can barely stand. You were awake before cock crow and it's past midnight now. In scant hours you face Kyrin and Damwin. You should've spent the afternoon resting but no, you had to train another session with Zandakar. And now you're training *again*?"

"Not for very long," she protested. "I told you, I couldn't sleep. Dancing the *hotas* settles my mind."

"You could've woken me. We could've—"

"Both suffered my restlessness? That's not the act of a loving wife."

He sighed. Smiled. Reached out his hand. "Come to bed. You need to sleep." In his eyes, the dreadful words still unspoken. *This could be our last night. Come to bed. Come to me.*

She stripped off her shirt and hose and joined him beneath the covers. Lost a little more sleep soon after . . . but considered the sacrifice well made.

Late the next morning, after preparing her shortsword in the armoury and enduring Helfred's wellmeant sermonising, she stood naked in her chamber and watched as Dinsy fussed over the clothing made specially for this occasion.

Dinsy was the only personal servant she'd recalled after taking back her castle from Marlan. The other ladies-in-waiting, sent home during the recent upheavals, remained with their families. She'd have to bring back some of them at least, for politics' sake, but for now she had neither desire nor need for female fripperies about her. No intelligent woman required fourteen other women to help her through the day. Dinsy was enough . . . and at times like this more than enough.

"Deary me, Majesty," Dinsy fretted. "I don't know what your dear mother would say and that's a fact. I can't think that outlandish costume's proper. You should be in a dress. You're a *queen*, Majesty, not a *huntsman*."

She shook her head. "Wrong, Dinsy. Today I'm both."

The doublet and leggings were of thin, supple black leather, cut and stitched to fit her form and move with her like an extra skin. No braiding, no jewelling, no ornamentation of any kind. Only her House badge on the doublet's left breast, above her heart: the triple pointed gold crown, threaded round with a spray of snowdrops, pierced by a single blood-red rose.

On seeing that Alasdair had frowned. "*What, you think you should present the dukes with a target?*"

But this was no fencing match, where a foil might pierce with exquisite precision. The dukes with their longswords would strive to cut off her head.

Of course, my crown makes that a target too.

Although today that was a simple, slender gold circlet laced with sapphires, rubies and amethysts: her royal colours. One of her mother's dragon-eye ruby earrings had been unset from its hook and strung on a gold chain. She'd wear it round her neck, beneath a white silk shirt and the black leather doublet. On her right forefinger her father's personal ring, heavy gold set with a cabochon emerald. In her left ear, Ranald's favourite pearl-and-pewter stud. On the little finger of her left hand, Simon's majority ring: obsidian carved with a stooping falcon.

My family, dancing into battle with me.

Though mollified, Dinsy was tut-tutting under her breath. "Well, Your Majesty, I suppose if you must fight these dreadful dukes you can't do it properly in a dress."

"No, I really can't."

"No," said Dinsy, mournful. Then her eyes filled with tears. "Oh, Majesty," she whispered. "This is dreadful. I'm so afraid for you."

Not as afraid as I am for myself. She clasped Dinsy's hand and squeezed it, briefly. "There's no need to be. I'm well trained. My cause is just. Right will prevail, you can depend upon that."

Dinsy gulped. "Yes, Majesty."

"*Yes*. Now help me dress, for pity's sake, before I catch cold."

Dexterity knew, of course he knew, the importance of this day. How could he not, with all his neighbours a-twitter? With the air of Kingseat itself flying thick with rumour? Rhian intends to slay Damwin and Kyrin both . . . no, no, she's going to offer them exile . . . no, no, life in prison . . . no, no, the crown.

As if she'd offer one of them her crown, after all we went through together to win it.

Other, darker whispers spread less harmless gossip. He'd heard them in the harbour tavern where once he'd drunk a slow pint of cider in a dark corner, a shapeless hat pulled low to shade his eyes and hide his face. She's in league with the Tzhung emperor, wasn't he seen at the palace? She's thrown in with foreign sorcerers, you saw that man with blue hair. You heard what happened to Marlan. Wasn't there a toymaker? What was his name? Something peculiar happened to him, didn't it?

"Jones!" a familiar voice called. "Jones, are you out here?"

Surprised, Dexterity thrust aside his disturbing thoughts, put down the puppet's arm he was whittling and sat back on his bench beneath the hasaba tree. With summer drawing to an end its scented blossoms were spent, their petals drifted to the ground.

"Here, Ursa," he replied. "At the bottom of the garden."

She stumped through the unkempt grass towards him, remarkably well-dressed for her. But of course she would be, today of all days. She was Rhian's royal physick now. She'd be on show with the rest of the court. She'd be needed, surely, given what was about to happen. He felt his mouth dry and his palms slick with sweat, thinking of it.

Oh, Hettie. It's monstrous. How could you let things come to this?

Hettie didn't answer. He'd not heard or seen her for so long. He thought he was abandoned, and had almost resigned himself. So many had turned their backs on him. Why not Hettie, too?

"Jones," said Ursa severely. "You're scruffy and ill-kempt and so is your garden. I think it's time you roused yourself from this slough of self-pity and put yourself to better use."

He indicated his whittling knife and the partially carved puppet's arm beside him. "I'm working, Ursa."

Hands fisted on her hips, she shook her head. "On the outside, maybe. But on the inside you're sulking."

"Ursa . . ." He closed his eyes and tilted his face to the sun. "Must we have this argument again? You side with Rhian. You think I betrayed her. We don't agree, but we've argued that to death, too. If you've come to poke at me, then I'll ask you to leave. I'm weary of arguments. I'd like to sit in the sun and finish my puppet, if you please. It might fetch a few piggets at the next harbour market and I sorely need the income, with my shop closed for business and the castle denied me."

Disgruntled, Ursa dropped to the other end of the bench. "Aren't you even going to ask me how she does?"

"Why should I? I doubt she asks after me."

And yes, it was a petulant answer. Didn't he have the right to feel petulant? Hard done by? Unfairly chastised? She wouldn't be queen if it weren't for him.

"No, she doesn't," said Ursa quietly. "But she would, if that Havrell pride of hers would take off its spurs and stop its pricking."

"I'll ask you how Zandakar does," he replied, still too raw and smarting to talk more of Rhian. "When will she relent and let him out of his cell? She owes her life to him, Ursa, twice. Is she so mean and short of memory that she'd keep him locked away in the dark until he dies?"

Ursa was staring. "Is it that long since I've come to see you?"

He felt the corners of his mouth pull down. So bitter he knew his face had grown, these past weeks, he no longer cared to look in a mirror. "He's dead then, is he? She finally let the council persuade her?"

"Not on that," said Ursa. "Zandakar is free, Jones. Well . . ." She sighed. "Not free, as such, but let out of his prison cell. He's kept close in the castle now. Fed, clothed, guarded, but left alone. He's been training Rhian with a sword."

"Ah." Dexterity felt a pang run through his chest, as though her words were a sharp blade. "She still has some use for *him*, then. He's not discarded."

"Oh, *Jones*," said Ursa, and banged a fist on his knee. "See past your bruised pride, will you? I've come to tell you how things stand. And there's no point sitting there with a face like to sour milk, pretending you don't care or have no interest in Rhian's doings for we both know that's a lie. *And* we know she could be dead by sunset. I've come to see if you've a message for her." She cleared her throat. "Could be I might pass it along, just in case things do fall out that way."

"She'll not be dead by sunset," he replied, with far more confidence than he felt. "Why would we have been put to so much trouble and effort only to see Rhian cut down now?"

"I admit," Ursa said after a moment, "it doesn't seem to make much sense. But sometimes life doesn't, Jones. And if we think we've been working on the side of God in this, who's to say those heathen Mijaki warriors and their bloodthirsty holy men aren't working just as hard for evil? If the Tzhung witchmen can see them, perhaps they can see us. Perhaps even now they're harnessing demons to make sure Rhian fails against the dukes!"

Dexterity had to shift on his bench a little, and stare. "Ursa? In all the years I've known you I've never heard you so superstitious! What would Helfred say if he could hear you?"

"Nothing flattering," she muttered. Her cheeks were pink. "And I'm not *superstitious*, Jones. I'm just – I think—" She folded her arms. "God protect us all, you saw those Tzhung witch-men! Are you telling me you danced into that heathen Sun-dao's embrace willingly?"

Dexterity flinched, remembering how it felt to be turned into a puppet. How his body had been plucked from a chair and whirled across the castle chamber like so much leaf litter. The sorcerer's power could have crushed him, smeared him bug-like on the floor. Worst of all he remembered feeling a familiar echo in that power. A taste, a touch, a flavour not unknown.

He hadn't told Ursa that. He hadn't told anyone. That was a question he was saving for Hettie . . . in the unlikely event that Hettie came back.

"Well, Jones?" said Ursa. "Don't just sit there with that fish look on your face!"

He shrugged. "I don't know what to say, Ursa. I'm not in this now. I've been shoved out of the chamber and the door's shut fast in my face. If you say Zandakar's freed from his prison, I'm pleased to hear it. You could – you could give him my regards if you happen to cross paths."

"He asks after you," she said. Her face was unhappy. "He's worried, and wants to see you. Of course I've told him that's not possible. Even if he wasn't trailed by a dozen guards every step he takes, well . . ."

"You sound sorry for him," he said. "I thought you'd hardened your heart to Zandakar."

Ursa stood as though he'd jabbed her with a pin. Pacing a small distance from the bench, she thrust her hands into her tunic pockets and kept her back to him. Her shoulders were slumped, but hinting of the defensive.

"After all those weeks on the road with Helfred," he added, "Rollin's *Admonitions* are fairly dinned into my memory. *Beware of judgement on a man who has strayed, or who never knew what it is to be in God's sight. For surely the righteous know how easily we come to straying, and how much God loves a compassionate heart.* I think that's how it goes. If Zandakar has done grievous wrong in his life – and I won't deny it, Hettie showed me what he's done – then I promise you he regrets it. Or aren't I someone to be believed any more?"

Ursa scuffed her toe at the ragged grass. "You sound like our prolate."

"Now there's an insult. I've never been a tedious prosy a day in my life."

She glanced over her shoulder. "He's not as prosy as he was. Marlan's death changed him."

Another memory he wished would die. Not that he'd killed the man. He'd just been there when it happened. Still . . . in the time that had passed since Marlan's immolation he'd woken more than once in the small of the night, sweating and stricken and in despair.

"I'm sorry," said Ursa, awkward. "Didn't mean to stir up that business."

He shrugged. "Never mind. It wasn't your doing, Ursa. Everything then was a madness, I think."

Slowly she sat beside him again. "I've mended my fair share of sailors," she said after a moment. "Some of them black-hearted ruffians and no mistake, with the fresh blood of murder on their hands. I don't know why one life taken shocks me less than thousands killed, Jones, but it does and I can't pretend otherwise. And I can't see how one or two good deeds afterwards can wash an ocean of spilled blood from a man's soul." Then she sighed, and shook her head. "But I know Zandakar would die for Rhian. It's all very confusing."

Love often was. "Has he had enough time with her, Ursa? Are her *hotas* skilled enough to defeat Damwin and Kyrin?" *Please, Hettie, please. Let that much be true.*

"How should I know?" she retorted. "I fight my battles with a poultice, not a sword." Then she sniffed. "But having said that, I did watch her training yesterday. She looked fierce to me. And Zandakar seemed pleased enough. He didn't slap her at least, and you'll recall he slapped her often on the road from Linfoi."

He recalled everything that had happened on the road from Linfoi. On the whole, he wished he didn't. "If you're to preside as physick at this duel, Ursa, you'll have to go."

She stood. "Rhian won't ignore you forever, Jones. Let this business of the dukes be put behind her and then you'll see. She's young. She's not cruel. You'll get your life back."

She sounded surer than he felt. Instead of answering, he picked up his whittling knife and half-carved puppet.

Ursa started to leave, then hesitated. "No message for her, Jones?"

He looked to his whittling. "Whatever you tell her, Ursa, let that be enough. If it's words from me that Rhian wants she can summon me to the castle and hear them for herself."

"Rollin save me," said Ursa, hissing. "You're a mirksome stubborn man."

And if he was, what of it? But as Ursa stamped back up the garden he felt a burning sting in his eyes.

Take care of Rhian, Hettie. Don't you dare let those dukes kill her. Don't you dare let all we've done come to naught.

Rhian stood on her castle battlements, a lively breeze ruffling her crown-confined hair, and looked down upon the Great Lawn, transformed into a judicial tiltyard. The chosen witnesses would sit opposite each other in the two large stands built specially for the purpose. The third enclosing side of the tiltyard was the carpeted royal dais, its back to the castle wall. Upon it would sit Alasdair, the privy council and the Court Ecclesiastica. The fourth side contained no seating; the ducal challengers would join them from that direction, and afterwards Commander Idson and a handpicked skein of guards would stand sentinel there in case of . . . incident.

Less than an hour before the appointed time, and

the first witnesses were arriving. From their attire Rhian judged them to be her ordinary subjects, chosen by lotteries held in their duchy venerable houses. Chattering like magpies, they obeyed the directions of the royal stewards and took the seats apportioned to them. She supposed it wasn't surprising they should feel a certain excitement: Ethrea's last judicial trial by combat had taken place more than three centuries ago. In that case history showed that the challenger – a Duke of Arbat, though not one of Rudi's direct ancestors – had emerged victorious, his dishonoured wife avenged, and the new Duke of Morvell had buried his older brother without much show of regret.

They were less civilised times. I wonder if I do the right thing in resurrecting them.

Which was a singularly foolish thing to think. It was far too late to turn back now.

Oddly, she didn't feel nervous. She didn't feel anything. Her body was numb, her imagination snared to immobility like a fly drowned in treacle. In a matter of hours she might be dead, or so badly maimed she'd wish for death to claim her. Or she might be twice more a killer.

It's in God's hands, Helfred says. Strange. While I fought to become queen I grew so used to God speaking through Dexterity. It was like God travelled with me . . . but now he's gone.

And so had Dexterity. That she could remedy, of course. The power was hers, to summon or send away on a whim.

Why is it easier to forgive Zandakar than him?

Impatiently she shook her head. Let her survive

this day's madness and perhaps she'd give the conundrum more thought. Perhaps she'd summon Dexterity and they'd find their way back to that friendship born on the road.

Far below her some merchants and noblemen arrived. Two most venerables. Three dames. One of them was Dame Cecily from the clerica at Todding.

Rhian felt her throat close, remembering the clerica. Remembering Marlan, and the brutality he'd visited on her there. Felt a tingle in the scars she'd carry to her grave. After much prayerful consideration Helfred had left Cecily in authority, though with a heavy burden of meditation and common service. She had attended Ethrea's queen and king consort's hastily convened coronation, but been denied speech with her new sovereign.

I'm not even certain if I'll speak with her today.

More senior clergy, merchants and nobles presented themselves. Swiftly the temporary tiltyard's seating filled. Liveried message boys began scurrying about the stands, plying the witnesses with wine and cider.

The first ambassadors arrived and were shown to their reserved seats: Gutten of Arbenia and Voolksyn of Harbisland. Their nations' joint history was pocked with dispute and disarray, although at the moment they were happily treated. Indeed, the men seemed positively spritely with good cheer. Should she be concerned? Possibly. No, probably. Assuming she survived, she'd be sure to discuss it with her council.

A gaggle of ambassadors from the minor nations arrived next: Dev'Karesh, Haisun, Slynt and Barbruish. She suspected they clotted together to create an illusion of strength against Harbisland and Arbenia, who – like Tzhung-tzhungchai – never hesitated to impose their mighty wills upon lesser principalities.

A handful more nobles and the ambassadors of Icthia and Keldrave joined the throng. The witness stands were practically full. And then it seemed to Rhian that the world stopped, and every person in it held his breath. Silence ruled. All heads turned, each avid gaze trained upon the same place.

Han.

Ambassador Lai walked three self-effacing steps behind his emperor, dressed in crimson and gold with much jade dangling about him. By contrast Han looked carved from amber and basalt, as though he shouted *Let lesser men dress gaudily, like peacocks. I am Han. I am my own decoration.*

As he followed a servant to his reserved seat Han looked up, unerring. Rhian felt the force of his regard like a hot sun. Standing straight and unsupported she stared back at him, unflinching. Then he looked away again, so easily she might have been a shadow of a woman, not flesh and blood and bone. She didn't know whether to be relieved or insulted.

The sound of footsteps turned her. She felt her heart leap. "Alasdair."

Like her, like Han, Ethrea's king wore black. Velvet, though, not leather or silk. His crown was un-relieved gold etched with a wreath of snowdrops. His Havrell House badge was picked out on his breast in gold, diamonds, rubies and emeralds. Creamy-white seed pearls studded his diamond-quilted sleeves. White ruffled silk showed at throat and both wrists.

A plain black sheath housed a dagger at his hip, its hilt unjewelled but inlaid with gold wire. He wasn't handsome . . . would never be handsome . . . but he was striking. Kingship became him.

"Rhian," he said. His voice was steady, his gaze cool and unperturbed. But she knew him well, now. Beneath the calm veneer his blood ran hot with fear. "It's time."

Her earlier numbness was fading. *I'm frightened . . . I'm frightened . . .* "Are Damwin and Kyrin arrived?"

He nodded. "Idson has them and their retinues under his eye, assembled and waiting for your command that they appear. Rhian, we must go. Helfred and the others are waiting."

He was right. The sun stood almost directly overhead, beating down with a ferocity usually reserved for mid-summer. It would be hot indeed fighting for her life beneath it, dressed head to toe in leather, dancing the *hotas*. But that was her choice, and she'd not moan about it now.

They left the battlements together, made their way down the castle's spiralling stone stairs side by side, but as soon as they reached the ground he dropped behind and let her lead him to the castle's east courtyard where the royal party was gathered.

Ludo stood apart, his expression unreadable. Edward, Rudi and Adric clustered, talking in low voices. Edward was in command of her sword, holding it reverently in its scabbard as he listened to hotheaded Adric's voice rise. Ursa waited some small distance from them with her apprenticed physick, Bamfield. Each was dressed in a neat green smock, and they stood guard over a mighty leather physick's bag. Rhian eyed it askance.

Please God, let them not need to fuss overmuch with me.

Ursa saw her sideways look and nodded, salt-and-pepper eyebrows pulled low. Without saying a word she said so much that Rhian felt her throat close, her eyes burn. She let her lips frame two words: *thank you.*

Helfred and his Court Ecclesiastica, breathtaking in their church regalia, stood to one side, their heads bowed in silent prayer. Ven'Cedwin prayed with them, always a venerable before he was a privy council secretary.

Raising one hand so Alasdair would pause, she crossed the close-clipped grass to her prolate and stood obediently waiting. Almost immediately Helfred opened his eyes and raised his head.

"Your Majesty."

She nodded. "Your Eminence."

For the Litany in her chapel that morning he'd worn his usual plain dark blue habit. Since then, though, he'd seen fit to change his attire. Slowly she looked him up and down, astonished that he was in velvet and ermine and silk and brocade, gaudy as a Keldravian parrot. That the prayer beads dangling from his gold-and-jewelled belt were exquisitely enamelled in vibrant greens and aquas and crimson, that a small jewelled replica of Rollin's *Admonitions* dangled from that same extravagant belt.

"Are you a prolate or peacock?" she murmured.

His severe frown admonished her, but still she thought she caught a fleeting smile in his eyes.

"Majesty, here is no occasion for levity. We are about God's dread and sombre business."

"*Yatzhay*," she said. "It's just I'm not accustomed to seeing you so splendid."

He looked down at himself, and sighed. "I'm told the court artist, Master Hedgepoole, is in attendance. It seemed politic under those circumstances that I not give history a reason to snigger."

"Hedgepoole?" she said, startled, and glanced at Alasdair before she could stop herself. "Commemorating the day?"

His eyebrows lifted. "Judicial combat is hardly commonplace, Majesty."

"No. But—" She shook her head. "Never mind."

Placing a finger beneath her elbow, Helfred drifted her sideways, out of earshot of his most venerables and Ven'Cedwin. "It distresses you, to think of a painting on a castle wall showing you bloodied and victorious?"

"Perhaps it'll show me bloodied and dead," she replied. "Unless God has told you something he's not confided in me."

This time Helfred's anger was untempered. "For shame, Rhian. You of all people in this kingdom should know better than the mockery of God. Fie on you for an undisciplined tongue."

And that was the Helfred she remembered. "If my tongue is undisciplined, Prolate, be sure my sword is not, nor my body neither," she retorted. "Both are honed for killing. Is that something you think I wish to see celebrated in *art*?"

"No," he said quietly, after some consideration. "I think you would wish to see God's purpose and the championing of his desire, the judicious smiting of his enemies, recorded so your children's children's children might not forget this day. Don't whet that undisciplined tongue of yours on your husband's hide, Majesty. He engaged Master Hedgepoole in good faith, for you and your kingdom."

The trouble with Helfred was that even when he was pompous, he was often right. She nodded. "Your Eminence."

"Kneel, child," he said, smiling kindly. "And let me bless you before this great endeavour."

CHAPTER SEVEN

Rhian knelt before Helfred and closed her eyes. His fingertips rested lightly on her head. "God, in whose sight we labour to do good, see this woman Rhian, this queen of your choosing, and gird her with righteousness that she might prevail. Inspire her with words to soften the hearts of these disobedient dukes, Damwin and Kyrin, that no blood be spilled here today. But if they keep their hearts hardened, if they remain intransigent, impious and unrepentant, then I ask you most humbly to guide her sword, that they might fall and rise no more. And if this should pass, let all know that their blood is spilled by your desire and no shame or blame lies upon her."

Inwardly shaken, outwardly composed, Rhian got to her feet. "Thank you, Helfred."

As she returned to Alasdair and her dukes, Edward held out her sword. "Majesty."

She belted it round her hips, her fingers trembling only a little, then looked at them gravely. "Gentlemen, the hour is upon us for the doing of such deeds as are required of a queen and the men who give her wise counsel. Walk with me to the appointed place, and witness the dread workings of God's manifest will."

Man by man they assembled behind her. Alasdair first, then the rest of her dukes. Next came Helfred at the head of his Court Ecclesiastica, ten old men who so recently would have fallen like Marlan had they not in their last heartbeats of grace understood their grave mistake. Then Ven'Cedwin, who carried with him a leather satchel full of writing implements so he might capture the day in words, and lastly Ursa and her apprentice, Bamfield.

As she stepped under the stone archway framing the courtyard, Rhian turned her head to the right and looked up. Within her castle's stone walls, caged inside his comfortable chamber, was Zandakar. One of his windows overlooked the Great Lawn. It was likely he'd be watching her while she fought the dukes, if they insisted on pushing her to swordplay.

He says you are mighty, that you dance like a queen.

If she danced like a queen it was because he had taught her. She glanced over her shoulder. "Alasdair—"

"Majesty?"

"If I – Zandakar—"

His fingers touched her arm, briefly. "I'll see him safe."

There was more to say, but no time to say it. She passed beneath the stone archway and stepped onto the crimson carpet laid down upon the flagstone pathway leading to the Great Lawn, the tiltyard, God's merciless courtroom. She walked alone, though she led a procession.

Heralds in blue and black sounded their trumpets as she stepped out of the castle's shadow. The gathered murmuring witnesses fell silent, and stared as she made her way to the dais. Alasdair had seen a throne placed there for her, its timber gilded, its back and seat padded with thick crimson velvet. Set back a little, to left and right, were two lesser ornate chairs: one for himself, and one for Helfred. And then behind them, the seating for the rest of her party.

Under cover of fanfare she reached her throne. Unbelted her scabbard, unsheathed her sword. Let the scabbard fall to the carpet and sat, placing the naked blade across her thighs. It shone brilliant silver in the sunlight. She looked straight ahead, to the line of Idson's soldiers forming the fourth wall of the tiltyard. So many eyes upon her. So many avid stares. She could feel Han's brooding, ambiguous presence, and the cold reserve of Arbenia and Harbisland's ambassadors. The lesser nations' ambassadors were no less attentive. Since Han's visit to the castle there had been many attempts at bribery of her servants and courtiers, for information. She doubted all had been reported to her; inevitably coins had changed hands, and whispers. People were people, and always would be. But there was nothing to tell, beyond the presence of Zandakar, and she had never kept the blue-haired man a secret.

Let them wonder. I'll tell them what they need to know in my own time, and not before.

Alasdair and Helfred took their places. Her dukes, the Court Ecclesiastica and Ven'Cedwin settled into their seats. When the shuffling had finished she raised her hand and the fanfare of trumpets fell silent. A moment later the line of Kingseat soldiers broke in two parts and swung wide, admitting Idson, their commander, and the men he escorted.

Damwin, and Kyrin, and their permitted witnesses.

Stony silent, without difficulty keeping her face a cold mask, Rhian watched them approach. The dukes were swaggering, sauntering. Arrogance rose from them like mist off a lake. They wore their second-best doublets and hose with a minimum of jewels, shouting to the world that she wasn't worthy of their finest attire.

Or perhaps they're afraid of getting my blood all over it. For certain it doesn't occur that the blood might be their own.

Subordinate behind Idson, they halted at the foot of the dais, hands hovering near but not touching the scabbarded longswords belted at their waists. Behind them their lawful witnesses, three apiece. Kyrin had brought former privy councillor Niall, and his son Raymot, and someone she didn't recognise. Family though; they shared a nose. Damwin's witnesses were identical in kind: Lord Porpont, another deserter from the privy council, Damwin's son Davin, and an unidentified third man. All six men were unarmed as the law required, and like their dukes they were meanly dressed.

Idson swept her a deep bow, his ceremonial armour – breastplate, vambrace and greaves – glittering silver with polish and care. Her royal device was newly enamelled upon his chest.

"Your Majesty," he said loudly, "I bring before you challengers to your royal sovereignty and charge, in the name of your loyal subjects, that their grievances be heard and an end found to this discommoding matter."

The words were a pattern set down centuries ago. So was her answer, and she gave it in a clear, carrying voice. "Commander Idson, I receive from you these lawful challengers and do swear by my crown that I shall hear their grievances and find an end to the trouble that plagues us."

Idson bowed again and withdrew, taking a position to the far left of the dais beside Ursa and her goggling apprentice. On a signal, his soldiers closed the tiltyard's fourth wall. There would be no leaving this place until matters were settled.

If the air could catch fire it would burn like Marlan, so fiercely and full of hatred did Damwin and Kyrin glare at her from the grass. Her fingers wanted to tighten on the hilt of her shortsword, but she refused them permission and kept her own stare cold and still.

"Your Graces, for your lives, and for the sake of your souls, I pray you have come to tell me of your contrition, and to pledge me the fealty I am owed as your queen."

Kyrin hawked and spat. "I'm here to tell you to

fuck yourself, bitch. You're owed no fealty by me or mine. The House of Donveninger won't kneel to a woman. Women kneel before men and use their mouths to better purpose than aping noble sentiments they'll never understand."

She heard gasps from the witnesses at his casual, brutal vulgarity. All she felt was sorrow; she'd have to kill this man. His heart was granite, unsoftened by the hours of prayer poured on it by Helfred and all the children of his Church.

She looked at Damwin. "Your Grace, you need not share this foolish man's fate. I understand that the past weeks have been dismaying. Ethrea is turned on its head. A new sovereign, a new prolate, miracles from God when we are long unused to the idea of miracles." She leaned forward a little, fixed her gaze hard to Damwin's sallow, bearded face. "Don't be led like a lamb to the slaughter. There's blood between us, remember, though it's well diluted by time. I would not spill it, not for this. If you love Ethrea bend your knee and leave in peace. We can find a way to work together if we want to. Would you see your ancient House broken to ruin?"

Damwin rolled his head on his neck and shrugged his russet-velveted shoulders. "Girl, it would ruin me to swear contrary to my nature. I don't say you're a bad child, though Eberg must have run aground in your raising somewhere, that you'd think this kingdom could stomach a queen. No, I say you've received bad counsel. Linfoi seduced you to get a crown on his head and his sword between your legs. When this is done with, if you're living, I'll do my best to see you're retired to a clerica where you can spend your life praying the stains from your soul."

Rhian sat back. *Which is worse, I wonder? Kyrin's obscenities or this man's bloated complacency?* She could feel Alasdair's fury sizzling behind her. If she shifted her gaze she'd see Helfred's dumbfounded rage. The Ethreans on either side of her dais were whispering and pointing. Only the ambassadors had nothing to say. Emperor Han was silent too, though his gaze was on her like the eye of a hawk.

"Gentlemen," she said mildly, hearing Ven'Cedwin's quill skittering on his parchment as he frantically recorded this historic meeting. Catching from the corner of her eye the artist, Master Hedgepoole, seated in a cloud of charcoal dust, his fingers busy. "Your replies are disappointing. Were I the mother of sons like you and heard you address any woman so, even the meanest drab by the harbour, it would be a birch switching for you till you remembered your manners. So are all spoilt boys remedied, I'm told. My brothers, of course, the princes Ranald and Simon, never needed a birching. Their father raised them well. He raised me also, and raised me right high. His blood flows through my veins. Royal blood, and undisputed."

As the witnesses murmured she let her words sink into the dukes' fevered brains, so they might at last understand – swift or slowly – that she was not a scullery maid in the cellar of their ducal home to be bullied as it suited them and broken with a look.

"We are come to that place, Your Graces, from which there is no turning back and no mercy shown once mercy is refused." She stood, her shortsword grasped firmly in her hand. "In the sight of God, and by his manifest desiring, have I been crowned the Queen of Ethrea. Here is your last chance to kneel before me as my dukes and pledge to me your fealty and the fealty of your Houses. Your only other choice is to dispute my legality and prove the claim with your swords. Which is it to be, Your Graces? I am tired of your posturing. You waste my precious time."

Before Damwin even unhinged his jaw, Kyrin had his longsword out and brandished in her face. "I challenge! I'll carve you like a Rollin's feast pullet and set your feathers in my cap for decoration!"

She nodded, bleakly. *Of course it starts with Kyrin. Papa always said he'd bluster his way to hell.*

"Challenge is lawfully given, and lawfully received. Stand your witnesses aside, Kyrin. Damwin, you and yours stand with them." As Idson came forward to chivvy them out of the way, she looked a little sideways. "Prolate Helfred?"

On a sigh Helfred rose and preceded her down the dais steps to the immaculate, unstained grass of the Great Lawn. "Kneel, Your Grace," he said curtly. "Unless you presume to tell a man of God that he may also fuck himself?"

Rhian nearly lost her balance, coming off the last dais step. *Helfred! I never knew you had it in you!* As glowering, dangerously florid Kyrin knelt, she knelt too, an arm's length distance from him, not needing to be told. Their swords stood point-first on the ground beside them. She made certain her knuckles weren't bloodless as her hand wrapped securely round her hilt. Conquered her breathing so she did

not sigh or gasp. Instead she thought of Zandakar
and the hour upon hour of training he'd given her.

He says you are mighty, and dance like a queen.

Helfred swept the seating on both sides, and the
dais, and Damwin and the dukes' witnesses, with a
look belonging to a much older man. He was inhumanly magnificent in the bright, unclouded sunshine.
The glory of God shone in his plain, pimple-scarred
face and struck sparks from his gold prolate's ring as
he raised his left hand.

"Let no man or woman here dispute God's will.
This is a matter of judicial combat, sanctioned and
sanctified by law and Church. Whatsoever the outcome be it binding upon all parties, as though God
himself had spoken aloud. I name this challenger
Duke Kyrin of duchy Hartshorn. I name this defender
Queen Rhian of the realm. Let them prove their cases
in bloody striving: should Kyrin be victorious let him
walk unmolested from this place. Should Her Majesty
prevail let no taint of murder be upon her. God, in
your unimpeachable wisdom, grant strength to the
arm of whosoever be righteous . . . and confound the
wits of the one who is false. Let the challenge begin."

It was strange, so strange, to know these might be
her last moments. This grass the last grass she'd see.
This sky the last sky. The face of this man, who hated
her, the last face in her sight . . . when it should be the
man who loved her upon whom she closed her eyes.

Kyrin was smiling. Almost laughing as he walked
away to the centre of the tiltyard so he might be surrounded by convenient space. She made no effort to
hurry after him. Let him think he dictated proceed-

ings. Let him believe he set the pace. Who cared who began this? It only mattered who ended it.

In the back of her mind she heard Zandakar's tense voice, every instruction, every sharp word, every complaint. *Wei, Rhian. Leap higher. Turn faster. Cut deeper. You wait, you die.*

But she did have to wait, now. She carried a shortsword. Kyrin's weapon was two feet longer, a monstrous blade looking sharp enough to slice the air and leave it in ribbons. It would be foolish indeed for her to rush him, as though she was a frightened girl desperate to die at his feet.

"You're a stupid bitch, Rhian," said Kyrin, circling slowly. "If you'd married my wife's little brother you'd not be staring at a coffin now."

"Really?" She kept her gaze upon his eyes, though the look in them turned her stomach. "Forgive me if I disagree. I think once I'd birthed an heir, perhaps two, I'd have succumbed to an illness . . . or tumbled headfirst down the stairs."

A flicker in is eyes told her she'd been right in her guess. But he covered surprise quickly, still circling like a wolf. "Kneel, girl," he invited. "I'll take your head cleanly. No need to prolong this past what we both know what must be."

She kept her gaze focused, but let her mind blur a little, preparing. Let the tension leave her muscles, let them slide like warm oil, with her joints like coiled springs. *I am the falcon, I stoop, I fly. I am the swift snake, I strike and retreat.*

"You should have pledged fealty when you had the chance, Kyrin," she whispered. "Now your children are orphaned. They'll curse your name before you're cold."

With a roar he came at her . . . and she began to dance.

In the castle's armoury, where Alasdair king had taken him to find a shortsword for Rhian, Zandakar had marvelled at the heavy metal skins the people of this kingdom had once worn into battle. How did they dance with their longswords if their bodies were so weighed down? How would Rhian dance her *hotas* against the disobedient dukes if she must dress as the Ethrean warriors of old? Then Alasdair king had told him, Rhian would wear no metal skin in her trial by combat and neither would the dukes who sought to slay her.

And that was a good thing, for he did not begin to know *hotas* that a warrior could dance in a heavy metal skin.

He stood at the window of his chamber in the castle and looked down at Rhian, dancing her *hotas*. Aieee, god, she was beautiful, she danced like a sandcat, lithe and deadly, this duke would soon die.

Unless . . .

He pressed his forehead to the thick glass, cursing the pane's erratic thickness that distorted the world lying beyond. He knew why he was kept in this soft chamber, knew why guards stood sentinel outside, but how he wished he was let outside for this moment, for Rhian and her dancing against the dukes' longswords.

Tcha! What is she doing? The hotas are for dancing, yes, they are for dancing your blade into the enemy's heart! She is dancing, she is not killing. She promised Rhian would be a killing queen.

On the short grass below him Rhian danced a finger's distance from the duke's sword. He was tall and broad, thick through chest and belly in the way of some men in Ethrea. He had speed even though he was large. Speed and hate, they were a dangerous combination. Tcha, Rhian should not be playing, she should kill this man.

Alasdair king had told him all the noblemen of Ethrea learned swordplay from boyhood. They did not learn for killing, it was stupid, but this fighting duke was hot for blood, hot for Rhian dead at his feet. There was blood on him, Rhian had cut him twice, there was blood on the man's right cheek and his right arm, blood dripping from his fingers to stain the green grass red. Rhian was bleeding but only in one place, from her left shoulder where the point of his sword had pricked her. If she had not danced away from him his sword would have run her through.

The two times she had cut him Rhian could have killed him. With her shortsword she could have cut his throat or taken his head, instead of cutting his arm she could have pierced his heart, she could have killed him and that would be the end of this disobedient duke.

Instead Rhian danced her *hotas*, and wounded, and did not kill him.

Why, Rhian? You promised to live. Have I failed you, have I killed you, are you dead like Lilit because of me?

He heard himself groan, felt his throat close tight

with pain. If Rhian died because his training failed her, he would die soon after. Alasdair king had said it. Alasdair king was not a killing king but he had seen his own death in the man's brown eyes. And who could blame him?

So would I kill anyone who killed Rhian.

In the tiltyard beside the castle the duke slashed his sword double-handed side to side, seeking to cleave Rhian in two pieces. Rhian danced over the blade, like a fish leaping she arced above the steel and used her own blade to wound him a third time, to bloody his breast and belly with a slash from shoulder to hip. It could have been a killing blow, the man should be tangled in his entrails, but he remained on his feet bleeding with his longsword in his hand.

Zandakar banged his fist against the stone wall.

Rhian, Rhian! What are you doing?

He felt his other hand spread flat against the window's uneven glass, felt his heart drum hard against his ribs. Sickness was in him, a vomiting fear. Aieee, god, even so far away he could see her intent, she wanted to weaken the duke, she wanted him to see her as a killing queen who would spare him if he knelt.

You stupid Rhian, you stupid girl, this duke is a killing man, you cannot show mercy.

The duke slashed again and this time Rhian's leap was not high enough, she misjudged his reach so his sword cut across her back. Aieee, god! But she was not dead, only wounded, she was not on the ground for him to butcher. Her leather doublet was opened on a slanting line from shoulder to spine, the skin beneath it opened too, he could see blood but it must only be a shallow wound for she could breathe and leap and dance.

The god see you, Rhian! Dance your sword into him up to the hilt, you cannot let him strike you again.

Tcha, how he wished he was her warlord, so he would have the power to make her listen, make her fight as she should fight, he wished Alasdair king was her warlord and not – not – what he was. *Something I do not understand.*

Wounding her made the duke bold, made him reckless, he rushed at Rhian with his sword ready to kill. She danced free of him, her *hotas* flawless, though she was bleeding and surely in pain. Zandakar did not fear for that. She had suffered pain before, in her training from the first day he made certain to hurt her so she would know how to dance, though her bones screamed and her muscles wept and the blood in her veins was turned to fire. A warrior who could not dance in fire was swiftly dead, even breathing he was dead. It was the first thing he taught her, the first thing she had learned.

The duke attacked her again, and again his sword found her, this time her left arm. Its sleeve was leather, not metal. Blood spurted, she stumbled, Kyrin almost took her head. His whirling swordpoint found her cheek instead, and she was bleeding again.

Rhian! Rhian!

Danced swiftly backwards, out of his reach, Rhian worked her blood-slicked fingers, tested her strength in that wounded arm. Then she danced towards Kyrin . . . and as she danced, something *changed*. As the duke circled her, as she circled the duke, her head high, her sword ready, light on her feet, her steps kissing the grass, Zandakar saw within her a new and colder purpose.

Aieee, god. At last. Now she is a killing queen.

If he could see that, so far away, too far, Rhian, then must the duke see it. Something changed in him, too. His easy confidence shifted, he looked wary, his cadence altered. His sword lifted, barring his body, his steps slowed, his head sank low.

Rhian attacked.

Never had she danced the *hotas* with such speed and grace, never had he seen her leap so high or spin so fast. *Aieee, god, if she learned them when I learned them, when she was a child . . .* Her sword flashed in the sunlight, where its blade was not dulled with blood. The duke tried to defend himself, tried to kill her with his longsword, but she would not let him, she cut past and under and over his guard, she cut his flesh, she danced her sword in him and through him so he dropped his own sword on the blood-splattered grass. He was cut in so many places, his fine clothes were slashed from neck to groin. His gross flesh was showing, and the wounds she put in him slicked it white to red. The duke was a dead man standing on his feet. Then he was not even that, for he dropped to his knees, his head lolling slackly, his hands dangled by his sides.

Rhian danced her shortsword into his throat.

Joy and relief burst in him, he wanted to shout. He wanted to run to her and tell her she was a killing queen, Queen of Ethrea, she was in the god's eye.

Aieee, god, you see her. You see her and she lives. Kill me before you look away.

*   *   *

Panting, sweating, dripping blood on the grass, Rhian felt the hard tug on her shortsword as Kyrin's body began its slow fall to the ground. She tightened her grip. Watched, uninvolved, while he slid off the tempered steel and thudded on the grass. The wound in his throat was neat. Only a little blood spilled as her blade emerged. His heart had stopped pumping, which meant he really was dead. *Dead, dead, because I killed him.* The blood roaring in her ears was deafening. Or was that the shouting of the witnesses she'd called? She couldn't tell.

Sweet Rollin's sacrifice, she hurt. She *hurt*.

Footsteps behind her. She shifted her gaze. It was Helfred and Ursa, with the apprentice Bamfield close at her heels. He was carrying the heavy physick's bag. Their expressions were identical: relief and horror entwined.

On reaching her, Ursa moved to inspect her wounds. "See to Kyrin," she said. "You cannot touch me yet."

Ursa looked to Helfred. "Your Eminence?"

Helfred nodded. "Her Majesty is correct, madam. Confirm that the duke's life is extinct, and we shall see what's to be done after that."

Rhian snorted. *Of course his life is extinct. I just shoved my sword through his throat.* But there was protocol here, as there was protocol in every corner of this life she had sought. Had now half-won, with Kyrin dead.

She didn't look to where Kyrin's people and Damwin were standing but she could hear furious muttering and a man's harsh sobs. Raymot, most likely. Whatever faults Kyrin had, his son had clearly loved him. She felt a pang at that and ruthlessly crushed it.

This is not my doing. This was Kyrin's mischief. I never asked for this. If he'd knelt, he'd be alive. Please, God . . . make Damwin kneel.

She could smell her own blood, metallic tang in the warm air. She could smell the stink of Kyrin's emptied bowels and flushed bladder and could easily have vomited. She could've wept.

I did the right thing, Papa. What else could I do?

Ursa looked up from her crouch beside Kyrin. There was blood on her fingers, where she'd pressed them to his neck. "Eminence, he's dead."

Helfred sighed. "And so is justice delivered." He raised a hand, and Idson joined them. "Commander, see the duke is taken from the tiltyard to the castle chamber prepared for this purpose, and leave him there with a guard that his body might not be disturbed."

Idson bowed. "Your Eminence. And what of his party?"

"They remain," said Rhian. "Until this matter is fully dealt with."

Another bow. "Your Majesty. Your Eminence."

A small bustle, then, as four of Idson's soldiers came with a cart and loaded Kyrin and his bloodied longsword onto it. Raymot's sobs turned to wild, raving shouts. Still Rhian did not look at him, or the others, but said to Idson, "Silence him, Commander. He disturbs my peace. Then have one of your men fetch me water and some cloths. My blade is fouled. I would clean it."

Idson gave her a startled look, and did as he was told.

"Majesty," said Ursa, her own hands wiped free of Kyrin's blood and a frown on her face. "I must tend you, it's my duty as a physick."

She shook her head, which was a mistake. The swordcut in her left cheek burned like fire. "Not yet."

"Majesty—"

"Not yet."

"Might I ask why?" said Ursa, her tone icily disapproving.

Because I say so and that should be enough. But if she uttered those words aloud she'd be more than a killing queen. She'd be something monstrous. And already she stood too close to that abyss, with Kyrin dead and Damwin undealt with.

She looked at the physick. "Because the trial is not over, Ursa. So says the law. Please. You and Bamfield should return to your places."

The old woman wanted to argue, but she held her tongue. "Majesty," she said curtly, and with a jerk of her chin collected Bamfield, holding the physick bag, and marched back to the royal dais.

Helfred stood beside the cart, one hand lightly upon dead Kyrin's uncovered breast. His head was bowed. He was praying.

I should pray too, but I can't. Not here. Not now. My God, my God. I killed him. Please, please, make Damwin kneel.

Helfred kissed his thumb to his heart, then to his lips. Stepping back from the cart he nodded to Idson, who brought forward a black cloth and draped it over Kyrin's body. His soldiers took hold of the cart's shafts and began to trundle it from the tiltyard. Idson watched it go, then turned.

"Majesty?"

"A moment." She looked at Helfred, whose eyes were inexpressibly sad. "Prolate?"

He moved aside, forcing her to step with him. "What did he say to you, Rhian?"

She felt her heart skip. "What?"

"Kyrin," he said, frowning. "And don't think to deny it. I saw his lips move. We all did, on the dais. Kyrin spoke, you lost your temper, and now he's dead. Before then you merely played with him. I think you were hoping he'd come to his senses and capitulate. Am I correct?"

Of all her wounds, the one across her back was the worst. Every time she breathed she could feel her breached flesh shift and split, could feel a new trickle of blood crawl down her skin. Her beautiful leather doublet was ruined. She was nearly ruined. Tcha, a stupid mistake. She'd totally misjudged herself and come close to letting Kyrin divide her.

If Zandakar is watching he'll be cross with me for that.

She wanted to turn and look up at his window, knowing his chamber overlooked the Great Lawn. But Alasdair would see her do it, and life was complicated enough already.

"Rhian?" prompted Helfred. "Answer me."

"I thought you might ask me if I were all right," she said, flicking him a wry glance. Another soldier was approaching, carrying a wooden pail and some cloths. "I am somewhat wounded, Helfred. And then, of course, there's the matter of the man I killed. Or is that a trifle now, since he isn't the first?"

Hundreds of eyes were trained upon them. This was a place of public execution. Therefore Helfred restrained himself, mindful not only of the witnesses in the stands but also Kyrin's distraught son and Damwin, who must surely be considering what he would do next.

"Did he threaten you, Rhian?" said Helfred. "Is that why you abandoned your tactic?"

"He threatened Alasdair," she replied.

When you're dead I'll have your whipped cur to play with, bitch. He'll be begging long before I'm done. I know men who know men, who know the ways of Barbruish. What they can do with a thin knife must be heard to be believed.

Helfred released a small sigh. "If you killed Kyrin for revenge, Rhian, then—"

"Revenge?" she spat. "Helfred—" Then she fell silent, because the soldier with the water and cloths had reached them and it was time to clean her sword. "Speak to Damwin, Your Eminence," she said, beginning the task. Damn, but her back hurt, and her arm. Scouring her stained blade coaxed them both to bleeding again. "Offer him one last chance to spare himself Kyrin's fate. Perhaps, now he's seen his fellow rebel butchered, he's in a mood to reconsider."

Helfred glanced over to where Damwin and the others were standing. "It does not look likely, I'm forced to confess."

If she looked too she'd be granting Damwin some kind of victory. "Ask him, Helfred. If I must have his blood on my hands as well, then I'll have it perfectly clear that the choice was his, and his alone."

Helfred let another, smaller sigh escape him. For a moment he looked again like the chaplain he had been, beleaguered and harassed by the stubborn princess in his care. Then he nodded. "Your Majesty."

Though she now hurt abominably, her muscles seized stiff, her open wounds protesting the air, she made certain no-one watching her would think she felt anything but the sunshine. The water in the bucket turned from clear to red as the perfection of her shortsword re-emerged from the blood. Behind her, Helfred's murmur ceased.

"She is foolish, Prolate," said Damwin in his deep, clipped voice, as Raymot cursed. "You would do better if you convinced her to yield, rather than thinking I'll leave this tiltyard with Hartshorn's duke unavenged."

"*I'll* avenge him!" declared Raymot. "He's my father and she murdered him!"

Not before he tried to murder me, you sot.

Suddenly she was so terribly tired. Her sword was clean again. She wanted to throw it away. Wanted to run to Alasdair and weep on his breast.

But I'm Queen of Ethrea. Tears are for subjects, not sovereigns. At least not in public.

And there'd be no privacy now until Damwin was dealt with. Then she'd be private with Alasdair in their privy chamber . . . or private in her grave, with naught but worms for company.

She turned, her heart pounding, the stares of all the watching witnesses heavy as snow. "Your Grace the

Duke of Meercheq! Do you keep me waiting? Sir, that is churlish. No gentleman would be so base."

Damwin unsheathed his longsword, roughly shoved Helfred aside and came at her in full stride, his bearded face glowering with rage and Raymot screaming encouragement at his back. When he was four paces distant she leapt straight upwards, turned once on her hips, *blossom in a windstorm*, and sank her shortsword into his belly up to the hilt. Twisted it thrice, viciously, as Zandakar had taught her, knowing its sharp edges would spill his shit on the inside and poison him. Sever the great blood vessels and drown him within.

As he plunged to his knees she turned her back and walked away, leaving her shortsword behind, leaving him gasping his last rebellious breaths. She walked back to the royal dais and her husband Alasdair, past grieving Raymot and Damwin's shocked son Davin. Every step woke in her a louder shrieking of pain.

Silence, silence, in the tiltyard all was silence.

One glance she spared for Emperor Han, seated with his splendid ambassador. His face was expressionless, no emotion, no thoughts. Only his eyes moved, following her as she strode by.

Let him learn from this, him and his witch-men. Let them all learn, Harbisland and Arbenia and Barbruish and the rest. Tempt Rhian of Ethrea to your very great peril.

CHAPTER EIGHT

Though her legs were trembling and her heart beat fit to burst, Rhian leapt all the steps of the dais at once and raked every watching face with her eyes.

"Trial by combat is over. God has passed judgement and the dukes are dead. What becomes of the Houses of Doveninger and Marshale is not yet determined, but there will be a reckoning. How severe is left to their conduct, and their conscience. All who are here as witness on this day, in this place, at this time, you have the thanks of the House of Havrell. You have the gratitude of a queen. If I am *your* queen, my life is pledged to you. All enemies of the crown, all those who would harm Ethrea, they should know the dukes' fate awaits them." She paused a moment, so her words might be absorbed. Then she bared her teeth in a smile and looked particularly at the ambassadors. At Han, whose smooth face remained without comment. "With this tedious business brought to an end, be certain you will hear from me presently, my lord ambassadors, that we might address a matter which must concern us all."

Behind her, Alasdair softly cleared his throat. "The prolate? Perhaps he would care to speak."

She glanced at Helfred, praying for Damwin's fled soul. "Perhaps he would, but I've no interest in hearing him. He tends a great sinner, that's his duty here. I am Ethrea's authority and my voice has been heard."

"Majesty," said Alasdair. He sounded . . . restrained.

Ignoring him for the moment, and ignoring her pain, she again swept her gaze around the galleries of seats. "Solemn witnesses, your service today is concluded and you are dismissed from this judicial tiltyard. Return whence you came, and be certain to spread the word. Rhian is Queen of Ethrea without doubt or dispute. God's judgement is final, and swiftly delivered."

The heralds lifted their trumpets and blew a muted fanfare. Emperor Han was the first to leave. Of course. She turned her attention to Idson, who with his hand-picked soldiers was seeing the dead dukes' parties ushered away for her later consideration. Fingers touched her arm, and she turned. Ursa.

"*Now* am I permitted to ease your wounds, Majesty?"

Rhian stared. "Now? In public? Woman, are you mad? Attend to Damwin. I will see you in my privy chambers by and by."

Ursa withdrew, her pinched lips bloodless. Alasdair stood and moved to her side. "Rhian . . ."

"Don't touch me," she whispered. "I must stand till they're all departed, Alasdair. *I must stand*. Step away. Don't hover."

"Of course," he replied, and moved to join Ludo. Left her like a lone tree in the midst of a field.

A lone tree struck by lightning and shuddered to its

*heartwood. Dear God, don't let me faint here. Spare
me that humiliation.*

She stood until the last common person of
Kingseat had departed the tiltyard. Then she turned
on the dais and looked at the royal party, at Alasdair,
Ludo, Edward, Rudi, Adric and the Court
Ecclesiastica. At Ven'Cedwin, still writing. Saw
clearly the royal artist, Master Hedgepoole, seated on
a stool in a shadow beside the dais, hastily sweeping
his charcoal stick across a sheet of paper. A pile of papers sat beside him, scrawled over black.

Delightful.

Banishing the urge to leap beside him and tear up
all evidence of these proceedings, she wrenched her
gaze back to Alasdair and the others.

"If there is something to be said, gentlemen, you
may say it to my face here and—" A sound distracted
her, and she turned to its source. Four more soldiers
were bearing Damwin away on a second cart. He too
had been covered, but the black cloth peaked oddly
over the hilt of her sword. Almost obscene it looked,
and she nearly laughed out loud.

*Oh, God, let me leave here. I would be sick, or
weep.*

Ven'Thomas, after Helfred the most senior member of the Court Ecclesiastica, pressed his thumb to
his brocade chest and then to his lips. "Your Majesty,
God was with you. What else is there to say?"

"What else indeed?" she said thinly. "Perhaps
more prayers for their souls. They were wicked and
misguided and they distressed my kingdom. But they
are gone from us now. Their blood has washed away
their sins."

"Would you be prolate now as well as queen?" said Helfred, arriving at the foot of the dais stairs. "Leave the sermons to me, Majesty. The rest is yours, and you are welcome to it."

"Your Eminence," she said, and waited until he was on the dais beside her. "I stand corrected."

He smiled, not widely. Just a small curve of lip. "Majesty, you stand, and for that may God be praised." It was his turn, then, to sweep them all with his gaze. "You'll attend a Litany in the castle chapel for the dukes on the morrow. Litanies for their souls will be held the length and breadth of the kingdom for five days unceasing. Here was a sad lesson. Let us be certain not to forget it. Majesty, since you refuse to take counsel of your phsyick, be the Church's obedient daughter and take this counsel from your prolate instead. Your case is proven. You may now withdraw."

She could see in his eyes how much he enjoyed the chance to bully her, chaplain to princess, as once they had been. But overlaying any small appreciation was sorrow, and concern, and a sense of this most sombre occasion.

She nodded. "Your Eminence. I am before all things a dutiful daughter of the Church."

He extended his hand, that she might kiss his ring. "I have often said so, Your Majesty."

He'd said no such thing, but she didn't argue. Only kissed his ring and stepped back.

"Most Venerables, attend me," said Helfred, and he led the Court Ecclesiastica from the dais and the tiltyard. Ven'Cedwin followed, his writings complete. She looked to her council, especially Edward.

"Will you stay, my lords? Be certain all is done that must be done to see this field of combat dismantled? When I rise in the morning I'd like to see my Great Lawn again. I'd like this tiltyard to be nothing but a memory."

Edward bowed. "Majesty, give no more thought to the matter. All that should be done will be done, right gladly."

They were staring at her, all of them, even Alasdair, as though she were some bizarre creature hatched among them without warning. Because these men had been with her from the start, because they knew what they knew and had seen what they had seen and risked their lives and Houses for her, she let ceremony fall like a dress, discarded.

"What? Why do you look at me like that, gentlemen? You are men, you take the hunting field. Surely you've seen blood before."

"Yes, they've seen blood," said Alasdair as her dukes exchanged blushing glances. "But never before have they seen a warrior queen."

"And God be praised for her," said Rudi, kneeling. His peers followed suit.

"God be praised," echoed his overproud son.

"God be praised," said Edward, weeping.

"God be praised," said Ludo. There was no laughter in him.

Disconcerted, she considered them. *A warrior queen. I suppose it's kinder than the truth, a killing queen. There's some glamour in the thought of being a warrior. Killing is only another name for butchery and that leaves an aftertaste sour in the mouth.*

And then all she could think about was how much

she hurt. Only now, standing still, could she feel how far she'd pushed her body. How much she'd demanded of it, and what price she'd have to pay.

"Come," said Alasdair gently. "You've proven your point. But the ambassadors are gone now, Rhian. Emperor Han is gone. There's no shame for you to take your ease and let Ursa tend you. In fact, I insist."

For a moment she was afraid that if she tried to move she'd fall down. Her wounded, over-used body howled viciously. Were it not for these men she'd let the crowding tears fall. Then she drew in a deep breath and thrust the pain where it would not interfere.

"My lords, let us convene in the council chamber on the morrow," she said. "After Helfred's service in the chapel. We've much to discuss, not least of which is what's to be done with these Houses of Doveninger and Marshale. Bend your thoughts in that direction, and we'll thrash out a solution."

"Majesty," her dukes murmured, and stood.

"Ludo," said Alasdair, beckoning him aside. "Must you go straight back to Linfoi? Or can you tarry a while longer? We need your voice on the council."

"I'll tarry," said Ludo. "There's little happening at home right now that my father can't deal with. In truth, I think caring for the duchy is the best medicine I could find him. And if something should go wrong, it's a swift enough journey home when there's a private barge with oarsmen at my disposal."

"We return to our privy chambers," said Alasdair. "Come with us. You and I can speak at leisure while

Her Majesty is tended as she ought be." Then he frowned. "Rhian, perhaps I should send for a—"

She bared her teeth. "Suggest I be carried into the castle like an invalid and you'll be next to feel the sting of my blade. I can walk. Feel free to walk with me, if you can keep up."

Ludo grinned. "Majesty, I'd walk with you into hell." But then his amusement faded. "And I'm so sorry, that the dukes drove you to this. They were fools. Fools never prosper."

These fools didn't, that much is certain. She nodded. "Thank you, Ludo."

Before she turned to seek respite within the castle, she allowed herself one glance up to a particular east wing window. But if Zandakar was watching her she couldn't see him. The sun had shifted, and the mullioned windows' expensive glass was a blank white stare.

Gritting her teeth she made herself take one step, and another. Alasdair and Ludo walked on either side of her, close enough for catching should her body betray her at the last.

She wanted to resent it . . . but that would be foolish. And as Ludo had pointed out, fools never prospered.

Dinsy burst into tears when she saw her. "Oh, Your Majesty! Oh, sweet Rollin! Oh, Your Majesty!" That was to Alasdair. "Physick Ursa's in your privy chamber, sir, all ready. Oh look at my sweet lady, she's blood from head to toe!"

Rhian sighed. "Hush your silliness. Am I dead? I don't believe I am. Perhaps a little punctured, but hardly on the point of expiration."

Dinsy gulped, and smeared her cheeks dry. "Yes, Your Majesty."

"Alasdair," said Rhian, turning to him. "Keep Ludo entertained. I'll find you once Ursa's finished fussing."

He took her hand and kissed it, seemingly oblivious to the dried blood flaking from her skin. "All right."

His tone was light and uncloying, but she knew she wasn't the only one paying a price for this day. His eyes were dreadful.

My love, my love. I'm so sorry. I had no choice.

She touched her lips to his cheek. "Thank you."

And then Dinsy was bustling her into the privy chamber where Ursa stood frowning with her sleeves rolled up.

"You can go, girl," the phsyick told Dinsy. "I've no need for a second pair of hands."

Beseeching, Dinsy turned. "Your Majesty?"

"I'll be fine. Ursa knows me of old."

"Yes, Ursa does," said Ursa grimly, when the door was closed and they were alone. "And if you dare to tell me you're not in pain, you don't need a physick and I can be on my way, well, madam, I—"

Rhian flung up a hand. "Don't. Ursa, don't. I think scolding will kill me where Kyrin and Damwin failed."

Ursa's expression changed abruptly. "Ah, you poor child," she said softly, holding out her arms.

Rhian went to her . . . and forgot she was a queen.

She killed the dukes a hundred times that night, in her dreams. After each death they lurched to their feet and leered at her, blood pouring from the wounds she'd inflicted upon them, abuse streaming from their flaccid lips.

Bitch! Whore! Slayer of a kingdom!

In her dreams she heard herself whimper, felt Alasdair's arms gather her close. Once she dreamed his fingers tightened round her throat. She woke then, flailing, and half fell out of their bed.

Alasdair sat up. "What is it? Rhian?"

Instead of curling herself into him she slid the rest of the way from beneath the blankets and touched her feet to the floor. Movement was painful, waking her strained and overstretched muscles. The sword-cuts on her cheek, arms and back that Ursa had stitched were burning. The physick had left her a potion to drink if her discomfort grew too great, but she didn't want to swallow it. A little pain seemed a just penalty when two men were dead by her hand.

Alasdair touched his fingertips to her hip. "Rhian?"

Gritting her teeth she stood, padded over to the window and drew back the heavy curtains. Beyond the panes of glass Kingseat Harbour glittered silver beneath the moons, its surface calm, no ocean storms to fret it. There was no bustle now, in the middle of the night, all the visiting boats were asleep at their moorings. But the harbourmaster's men still patrolled in their torchlit skiffs, making certain no-one thought to disturb the peace with rowdy-making or any less harmless misbehaviour. Although she was shivering, hurting, and the dreams were still so near, she felt her lips curve in bemused affection.

Everyone thinks the king – or queen – makes

*things happen in a kingdom. It's simply not true. It's
the secretaries and their staffs who keep the wheels
turning. Without them doggedly pursuing their duties
these past weeks Ethrea would've crumbled into the
ocean. They love the kingdom as much as I. In some
ways I think it's even closer to their hearts, for their
busy fingers take its pulse every day.*

"Rhian," Alasdair said again.

"I'm all right," she said, not turning.

The blankets rustled, the bed's wood frame
creaked, and then he stood at the window behind her,
his arms gathering her close. His touch was gentle,
mindful of her wounds. "You're in pain?"

"A little. It's no great thing."

He sighed, but didn't argue. "Bad dreams?"

"Bad enough."

His lips brushed lightly over her hair, but although the gesture was loving she could feel his tension and impatience. "The dukes forced you to it. If
you hadn't taken the crown, if you'd named me king
and yourself queen consort, say, don't you think
they'd still have challenged?"

She wanted to think that, but ... "I don't know.
How much were they fighting for their own ambi-
tions, and how much were they incited by me? If
Ranald or Simon hadn't died, Alasdair ..."

His embrace tightened. "But they did. They died
and you didn't. How many times will you revisit the
unchangeable past, Rhian? You are queen. And today
you did what any monarch would do – *must* do – to
preserve the stability of the kingdom."

"You'd have killed them?" she said, turning so she

could see him properly. "If you were king and they refused to accept it?"

His bony face was obdurate in the shimmering
moonlight. "Yes. Rhian, there must be order. There
must be obedience and fealty, especially now. Ethrea's
never faced a greater danger. You did what had to be
done. God's will."

"I know," she muttered. "But it wasn't God's hand
holding the shortsword, Alasdair." *It was mine. And
I can't forget what it felt like, steel plunging through
cloth and flesh, the shock of resistance, the surrender
of life.*

He took her chin in his fingers, his grip a breath
away from painful. "Yes. You killed them. And do
you think that's the first and last unbearable thing
you'll have to do as queen? Today was nothing.
Today was cracking two fleas between your fingernails. Now make your peace with it or surrender your
crown."

"That's cruel," she whispered, and retreated to
perch on the side of their bed.

"The truth often is," he retorted. "Rhian—"

"Oh, don't you understand, Alasdair? I'm *terrified.*"

Abandoning the window he crossed the carpeted
floor to her and dropped to one knee. "Of what?"

"Of myself." She couldn't look at him. "There's
power in the *hotas*. Such a raw and blinding power.
Kyrin's death was – was untidy. But Damwin? He was
dead before my sword pierced his flesh. He was dead
because I wanted him dead and the *hotas* were in me,
rich and ripe." They'd felt glorious. *She'd felt glori-*

ous. In that single white-hot moment she'd felt as invincible as God.

And what does that make me? Am I some kind of monster, like Zandakar's mother? Like Zandakar's brother?

"You're shivering," said Alasdair. "Get back under the covers."

He helped her ease beneath the blankets, and slid beside her. His fingers laced with hers and she held on, tightly, as though he could anchor her to herself.

"Killing doesn't give you pleasure, Rhian," he said. "Zandakar may have trained you, but you're not him."

There was nothing she could say to that, so she stayed silent. Beyond the chamber window the night sky was shifting slowly towards dawn. Alasdair's breathing deepened and slowed and he drifted to sleep again, but she remained wakeful. Her mind continued to replay the moments, over and over, when her shortsword had plunged deep into Kyrin's throat and Damwin's belly.

Dear God. Now three men are dead by my hand. I've killed more men than any nobleman in Ethrea since Rollin walked among us and showed us a better way.

And before this was over, she was afraid that tally would grow.

But not too high, God. I beg you, not too high.

Dexterity woke at dawn, out of habit, but instead of getting up straight away, as he usually did, he stayed in bed and stared at the ceiling. He should get up. There were puppets to finish . . . but he didn't have the heart. *Melancholy*, Ursa called it, and prescribed a brisk walk.

She'd stopped by his cottage last night to tell him how Rhian had defeated the last two stubborn dukes. Killed them both, though not before shedding blood herself.

"I see," he'd said, as though she'd mentioned it might rain at some point, even as his heart drubbed his ribs with relief. "And was that all you wanted, to pass along gossip? Only it is quite late and I was on my way to bed."

She'd scowled, so ferocious. "Jones, I could *smack* you."

"Yes, you could," he agreed. "But you won't. Not with the high opinion you have of yourself."

And that had made her stamp out crossly, just as he'd intended. Afterwards he'd sat in his kitchen, trembling, awash with gratitude that Rhian had prevailed. Though he'd been grief-stricken too, that she'd been forced to kill the dukes.

Stupid, stupid men. As stupid as Marlan. Why was it they refused to accept what had been thrust under their proud noses? He'd not been able to find an answer last night and he couldn't find one now, curled beneath his blankets ignoring his urgent bladder.

But while he could ignore his bladder if he had to, he couldn't ignore Otto. With the sun up the donkey would surely start to heehaw any moment, demanding his breakfast oats at the top of his lungs.

It promised to be a beautiful day, warm and cloudless. He fed and watered Otto, then took a moment to admire the late summer's blue sky, still blushing pink with the risen sun. But that small pleasure faded quickly. Scant weeks ago he'd have had so much to do now, his cart to load up with supplies for his toyshop, last minute sewing for his puppets' little costumes, or careful final touches of paint – a gleam in the eye, a rose in the cheeks. Scores of customers to visit, maybe even the castle. Scant weeks ago he'd been Royal Toymaker by Appointment.

But not any more.

The blue sky overhead was empty, and so was his life. No purpose. No excitement. No—

"Oh come along, Dexie. Do stop feeling sorry for yourself. As if we've time for pouts and sulking."

Hettie. Heart thudding, he kept his gaze pinned on the blueness overhead. "On the contrary, I've lots of time for anything I like. Except the thing I want most, of course. You might've helped me with that, Hettie. It's not as if I've not done anything for you of late."

"Toys, Dexterity?" she said. "You worry about toys with the world beneath so dark a shadow?"

He unpinned his gaze from the vaulting sky and looked at her. None of her substance had returned since last he saw her. In fact, she looked even more precarious. Tattered, translucent, her yellow cotton dress frayed. As though her soul had a wasting sickness, and here was its face. He wanted to fear for her, but tasted only bitterness.

"If you'd told me helping you would make me a killer, Hettie, I'd have drowned myself in that bath before ever lifting a finger."

"You're not responsible for Marlan," she said. Her soft brown eyes were full of sorrow. "He chose his own path, Dex."

"So you're saying God killed him? I thought it was

Zandakar's people who worshipped a bloodthirsty God. Has something changed?"

She took one step towards him, her feet hidden in the garden's ragged grass. "He was a wicked man, Dex. He'd have brought Ethrea to ruin. To save himself all he had to do was kneel. His pride and greed and ambition wouldn't let him, and so he died."

"He died because he touched me! You never told me that could happen, Hettie!"

She sighed. "He didn't touch you. He touched the power of God, and the power of God rejected him. You were nothing but a vessel, Dex. Unburden yourself of guilt for his death."

He gaped at her. Nothing but a vessel? What kind of thing was *that* to say? "Don't you care I'm distressed by this?"

"Of *course* I care," she said, and took another step closer. "Dexie, I love you."

"Seems to me you've a strange way of showing it," he muttered. "All the things you've had me do, I nearly died of exhaustion from them. I was in so much pain, Hettie. For days and days even the air hurt my skin. And you never came to see if I was all right. Not once. You never came, you never tried to heal me, you—"

"You had Ursa!"

"*She's* not my wife! Where have you *been*?"

"Oh, Dex . . ." Hettie's eyes filled with tears. "I come when I can. I help you as I can. Would I have left you if I'd had a choice? I know you've suffered. I suffered with you. But I told you, didn't I, that this would be hard?"

"Telling me and living it are two different things,"

he said sullenly. "Bringing that dead boy Walder back to life, that was *joyful*. But what joy has there been since then, Hettie? And you *never* said I'd lose my livelihood over this! How am I supposed to live now? My savings are dwindling. Word's spread that I've lost the queen's approval. Who'll risk angering royalty to buy a doll? The harbour markets don't pay enough. Do I throw myself on Ursa's charity? Do I abandon the craft I've spent my life perfecting and pick up a broom for sweeping the streets? Or perhaps I should leave Ethrea altogether."

"And go where, Dex?" said Hettie. "If we fail in the coming days nowhere will be safe."

"*We*?" He stared at her, then shook his head. Stepped back. "Oh, no. No, Hettie. Not again. I'll not be bamboozled and hoodwinked again. I've lost my livelihood to this business. I won't lose my life too."

"But you will, Dex," she said. The tears were dried on her cheeks, or vanished. "You and everyone else. We have this brief moment of respite, this heartbeat of time in which to act . . . and then the storm will break. Such a storm, Dex. It will sweep the world bare. It will scour every land to bones and stone. What are your hurt feelings compared to that?"

"Nothing, it seems," he retorted. "Nothing to you or to God. And that hurts me further, Hettie. Am I a wicked man for feeling so? Am I sinful, for mourning all I've lost because I did what you begged of me without a second thought? Perhaps I am. And I'm so sorry if it seems pretty, *my love*, but if you truly ever knew me you'd know toymaking is my heart. Now my heart's torn from me and I'm *grieving*. And I think I'd rather grieve alone!"

He was nearly shouting. There were tears in his eyes, clogging his throat. Never since the day they met had he spoken to her in such a fashion. Never railed at her. Never longed to shake her. Never felt so abandoned and alone.

"I'm sorry," Hettie whispered. "Don't you think I know what I've done? Using you the way I have, don't you think I know what that's cost? Of course I know, Dexie. I knew before ever I came to you that first time, the price you'd pay for loving me like you do."

It was hard to breathe. Her words were like blows from a harbour-brawling sailor. "And you came anyway. You used me and never told me what I'd lose for loving you."

"How could I not?" she said, beseeching. "With so much at stake, so many lives in the balance, Dex. How could I not use whatever weapon came to my hand?"

"But why *you*?" he demanded. "You were never so pious when you lived in this cottage, Hettie. You went to Litany most weeks, but not always. And you never gave a thought to Church beyond that. Why is it *you* who—" And then he choked to silence, and felt himself back away. "Are you even really Hettie? Or are you something else that's dressed itself in her face, to coddle me into thinking – into doing—" He sucked in a shuddering gasp. "Are you – you're not—"

"No," said Hettie swiftly. "No, Dex. I'm not God. I swear it on every sweet night we spent together. I'm your wife. I'm Hettie."

"And why have you come back to me? There's nothing else I can do for you. Rhian's on the throne and she knows the danger we're facing from Zandakar's family. She doesn't need my help any more. She's got Emperor Han and his witch-men."

"Does she?" said Hettie. "Emperor Han is a mystery, Dex. His heart is a locked box and only he has the key to it."

He stared, suddenly sick. "Rhian's in danger from the emperor?"

"She's in danger on all sides, Dex. Winning her crown was only the start. I thought you *understood* that."

Clutching at the stubbly start of his new beard, he turned away. "I don't understand *anything*, Hettie! I used to have such a *simple* life!" He turned back. "These witch-men. What are they? What power is it they command? Are they like the priests of Mijak? Do they truck with evil and darkness? With *blood*?"

Hettie was wearing a threadbare shawl. She tightened it around her insubtantial shoulders, her golden hair lank and loose about her face. "No. But, Dex, you should be wary. The witch-men of Tzhung-tzhungchai serve their emperor first and last and always. Remember that in your dealings with them."

"Dealings?" He shook his head vehemently, remembering Sun-dao. "I'll have no more dealings with them."

"Yes you will, Dex."

"Hettie, I *won't*. I'm finished with great matters. I'm a small man. I've grown so small I'm practically invisible."

She smiled. "Oh, Dex. You were never a small man. Your heart's so big the world could fit inside it."

He folded his arms. "I tell you I'm done with advising the mighty. Rhian doesn't want me anyway. She's made that clear."

"She may not want you but she needs you. *God* needs you, Dexie. Can you turn your back on God?"

"I did it before. I can do it again."

"Oh, Dex . . ." Hettie shook her head. "Put God to one side, then. Ethrea needs you. Can you stand there and say you'll turn your back on your home? Dexie . . ." She walked to him and put her hand on his arm. Her touch was lighter than a butterfly's kiss. "I'm not God, but I serve God. I'm working for the victory of all that's good in the world. Don't tell me you'd turn your back on that, for I do know you, Dexterity Jones. That kind of callousness isn't in you."

"Maybe not," he said, blinking his stinging eyes. "But I'm weary, Hettie. I'm all used up from healing people, and burning. Isn't there someone else who can do this?"

"For your sake I wish there was. But what you've started, my love, I need you to finish."

"What *I* started?" He laughed, incredulous. "I didn't start anything, Hettie."

"Dex, you must go on."

He retreated a few steps. "And if I can't? If I won't? What then, will God strike me dead? Burn me to ashes?"

"God won't have to," Hettie whispered. "The warriors of Mijak will kill you, Dex. You and everyone else they can find."

"*Stop saying things like that*! Stop trying to frighten me into doing what you want! I tell you Rhian doesn't *need* me! She's got all those trading nations with their soldiers and their ships."

"She doesn't have them yet, Dex. She might never have them. Nothing is certain. Not even God knows the outcome of this. So much depends on . . ."

"On what?" He stared. "On *me*? *No*. I won't carry that burden, Hettie. How can I bear up under that kind of weight? You're cruel. *Cruel*. To come to me now, to say that to me? Oh, Hettie. I never knew you could be so cruel."

Her eyes were wide and wounded. "Not cruel, Dex. Desperate."

"Well I don't want you desperate, Hettie!" he retorted. "I don't want you at all. Go away! Leave me be! I'm *weary*, I tell you. I can't do this. I've had enough of doom and dismay!"

Hettie looked at him in silence . . . and in silence, sorrowful, faded away.

Unstrung, Dexterity dropped to the grass. "I'm sorry," he whispered. "I'm sorry. But please don't come back."

CHAPTER NINE

"Before we do anything else," said Edward, "we must decide how to resolve the matter of Damwin and Kyrin's Houses."

"Pull them down brick by stone," said Adric. "And raise new Houses who know where their loyalty lies."

Standing at the privy council chamber's window, the sun warm at her back, Rhian fixed him with a cool stare. "And by that you mean what, Adric? Execute everyone related to the unfortunate dukes?"

Adric flushed dark red. "I mean you can't leave them to flourish unchecked, Your Majesty."

"I don't intend to," she replied. "And neither do I intend sowing seeds of bitterness that will be harvested in bloodshed at some future time." She looked around her privy council. "Raymot and Davin aren't their fathers. They must be given the chance not to follow in those dukes' misguided footsteps."

"And if they don't take that chance?" said Rudi. "If they defy you? If, God forbid, they should challenge you to more judicial combat?"

She felt a small jolt of surprise. The thought hadn't occurred. "You think they'd be so foolish?"

"I think a hot-headed man full of grief and a misplaced sense of injustice would, yes, be so foolish, and perhaps not stop there," said Rudi, sounding regretful.

"It won't come to that," said Helfred. "Judicial combat must be sanctioned by the Church. I will not sanction it. The question of the queen's right to the crown has been asked and answered. The matter is closed."

Clearing her throat Rhian resumed her seat, carefully. "I agree. And I want this business dealt with, gentlemen, so we can turn our attention to the greater dangers facing us." She nodded to her council secretary. "Ven'Cedwin? Bid Commander Idson to join us."

"Your Majesty," said Ven'Cedwin. He put aside his inked quill and moved to open the chamber door.

"Your Majesty," said Idson, entering, and swept her a military bow. "The prisoners, as you commanded."

She'd thought at one time there'd be trouble between herself and Kingseat's garrison commander, since he'd obeyed Marlan so assiduously. But after Marlan's fall he'd begged her forgiveness on bended knee, swearing loyalty to her rule. At the council's urging she'd kept him. God knew she needed men with martial experience, and he'd not given her cause to doubt him so far.

She nodded. "Bring them in."

Idson stood aside and a skein of guards escorted Raymot of Hartshorn and Davin of Meercheq into the chamber. Raymot, a barrel-chested echo of Kyrin, snarled when he saw her.

"Murdering whore!"

"No, Idson!" said Rhian as the commander's fist

lifted to strike him, and pushed to her feet. She'd chosen less warlike attire this morning: a loose-fitting midnight blue brocade gown shot through with gold. Beneath it her stitched and bruised flesh throbbed gently, the pain not quite vanquished by Ursa's potions. Sweeping around the privy council table, refusing to let any discomfort show, she halted before the prisoners. "You are angry and grief-struck, Raymot. I understand that. And though I don't expect you to believe it, I am sorry for your loss."

Raymot spat at her feet.

"You and Davin are brought before me," she continued, ignoring his provocation, "to see how best we can put the recent past behind us."

"*Never*!" said Raymot, everything about him vicious. "I'll die before supporting a whore like you."

"Is that what you want, Raymot?" she asked him gently. "To die in rebellion against the crown?"

"You don't dare," he sneered. "Kill *two* dukes of Hartshorn within hours of each other?"

She sighed, torn between pity and anger. "You're not a duke until I say you're a duke, Raymot. And looking at you now, I've no mind to say it. Raymot Doveninger, you are disinherited and your household struck apart. Your estates are forfeit to the crown. Your wife will retire to a clerica. You shall be kept in prayerful seclusion in a venerable house. Your son shall be fostered to a House of Ethrea I can trust. Henceforth some other family shall breed dukes of Hartshorn."

The blood drained from Raymot's face. "You can't do that! With my father dead I *am* the duke! You *can't*—"

Idson unsheathed his dagger and pressed its tip to Raymot's convulsing throat. "She's your queen, fool. She can, and she has. Speak another word and I'll cut out your tongue."

No-one in the chamber disbelieved him, especially not Raymot. Rhian looked at Idson. "Return him to his chamber, Commander. Double his guard."

"Majesty," said Idson, and nodded to his men. Half the skein withdrew with Raymot sagging among them.

She considered silent Davin. As Damwin's heir he'd come to court from time to time, but she barely knew him. Eight years older than Ranald and married already, herself a mere child, there'd been not an inch of common ground between them.

"Well, Davin?"

Unlike Raymot there was no hatred in his eyes or his thin face. Because he felt none, or because he was a consummate actor? She didn't know, and held her breath.

"I have no quarrel with Your Majesty," he said quietly. "I want to be Duke of Meercheq."

She smiled. Unlike Raymot, he was no fool. "And perhaps you shall be – if you can prove your loyalty to the crown. For now, return to your chamber. We'll talk again in due course."

"You can't trust him," said Rudi as Idson and the rest of his soldiers escorted Damwin's son out. "He shows a meek face now, Majesty, but that mask will surely slip."

Rhian returned to her seat. "Don't worry. I'm far from trusting Davin. He'll remain my guest in Kingseat for some little while yet."

"Hostage to his family's good behaviour?" said Alasdair.

She nodded. "It seems the wisest course."

"It is," said Edward, approving. "But I'd send the rest of his party packing, Majesty. Porpont needs an eye kept on him, but he'll oversee duchy Meercheq well enough for now."

"An excellent suggestion. See to it, will you? And as for duchy Hartshorn . . ." She turned to Helfred. "Since the Church must be so closely involved with Kyrin's surviving family, Prolate, can I leave you to oversee the dissolving of his House?"

"You can, Majesty," said Helfred. "I suggest that Raymot begins his penance in Kingseat's venerable house. His wife I'd remove to the clerica at Todding."

"Agreed," she said. "As for what else must be done, Helfred, choose such churchmen as you can trust to be discreet, humane and impervious to the distress of all concerned."

Helfred nodded. "Of course, Your Majesty."

"What of finding a new duke for Hartshorn?" said Ludo.

"No good can come from choosing Kyrin's successor in haste," she replied. "The wrong duke would be worse than no duke at all."

"Most Venerable Robert, of the Court Ecclesiastica, is a formidable administrator, Majesty," said Helfred. "He would serve you well in duchy Hartshorn until you choose its next duke."

He made it sound such a simple thing. *No more difficult than selecting fabric for a new dress. But if I choose the wrong man, what strife will I be sowing for poor Ethrea to reap?* "Very well. I accept

Ven'Robert's assistance with thanks. Now, as to the funerals of those regrettable dukes . . ."

Kyrin and Damwin had both died as traitors, rebels to their lawful queen, but to make an example of them now, with Mijak breathing hot and bloody at their backs . . .

"Let them be laid in their family vaults with the proper rites," Alasdair suggested. "And let their foolish sins be interred with them. The dukes served your father well enough, Majesty, until events overcame their reason."

And showing mercy today would temper yesterday's brutality. She nodded. "Yes. Helfred, see to it."

"What of Davin?" said Alasdair.

She closed her eyes. If she let Damwin's son return home for the funeral would that stir up trouble? Or would trouble foment if she kept him in Kingseat?

Everywhere I turn, more questions. More decisions. Did I understand it would be like this, when I dreamed of becoming a queen?

"Denying Davin the funeral might turn him from friend to enemy," said Ludo. "If you like, Majesty, I'll escort him. He'll not make mischief under my nose."

She was about to agree when she caught sight of Adric's thunderous expression. Speaking of turning friends into enemies . . . "Ludo, you and Adric both shall escort him, and at the funeral represent the crown."

"Majesty," they murmured. Adric looked pleased, like a child in a tantrum being given a sweet.

In Alasdair's eyes she caught a gleam of approval and felt, too briefly, pleasure overwhelm her pain and fear. She stood, and started pacing the council chamber, even though movement stirred her body to greater discomfort.

"Gentlemen, we must now address the vexing question of Mijak."

Silence. Consternation. The rustling of leather and fabric as they stirred in their seats.

"Both Zandakar and Emperor Han have told us that Mijak is making its way through the world," she continued. "Once it reaches Icthia nothing but ocean stands between its warriors and this kingdom." She stopped and turned to face them. "Therefore Ethrea must prepare itself for war."

Such a small word, with so much power. She felt sick only saying it . . . the thought of *waging* it . . . dear God.

"War," murmured Edward. "It seems scarcely believable."

"*Believe it*," she said brutally. "*All* of you. Accept its inevitability so we needn't waste time debating. Our breath must be saved for deciding how we'll win."

Adric stared at Helfred. "I thought God was protecting us, Prolate. Why all the miracles if God can't protect us?"

From the look on his father's face, and Edward's, even Ludo's, he wasn't the only one asking the question. Rhian exchanged glances with Alasdair, but held her tongue. This was Helfred's business.

"The divine is ultimately unknowable, Your Grace," he said, breaking the silence. "As a man I cannot answer your question."

"Yes, but you're not just a man, are you?" Adric retorted. "You're God's Prolate. How can you sit there and declare you don't know if he can protect us?"

"Say a man is thatching his roof. Does God prevent him from slipping and falling to his death? Does God prevent a woman from dying in childbirth? Does he banish illness from the world?"

"He caused a child to rise from the dead," said Rudi. "It seems God is fickle, Your Eminence."

"*Fickle*?" said Helfred, frowning. "Be careful, Your Grace. You mock God at your peril. That child was a miracle, raised from death so Rhian – Her Majesty – might take her rightful place on the throne."

"Then why doesn't God send us another miracle?" said Adric. "The divine destruction of Mijak."

"Because," Helfred said, his frown deepening, "we are not God's puppets, but masters of our own fates. When last Ethrea seemed on the brink of destruction, God sent us Rollin to help us save ourselves. Rollin pointed the way to peace but it was up to us to achieve it. And we did. Now, as we face another great danger, God has given us Queen Rhian. But whether or not Mijak is defeated is up to us. *We* must act, not sit weeping and wailing for God to intervene."

Rhian watched the faces of her dukes as they digested Helfred's unpalatable sermon. A small part of her was amused that they were now subject to the same prosing lectures he'd inflicted upon her when he was her chaplain and she couldn't escape.

Still. Prosing or not, he's right. Not once in history has God solved a human problem. This is our world and we must save it.

"It seems to me," said Edward slowly, "that if our prolate's correct and we must stand against Mijak with men, not miracles, we'd be best served if its warriors never set foot on our soil."

Rhian nodded. "I couldn't agree more, Edward. In a perfect world we'd send an Ethrean armada against Mijak and sink its warships long before they caught sight of Kingseat Harbour."

"But our world's far from perfect," grunted Rudi. "All we've got is a handful of trading vessels."

"Which is why I must persuade the league of trading nations to form an armada on our behalf."

They all stared at her, even Alasdair. "They'll never agree to it." said Edward.

"They will if I can convince them their own lands are in danger," she replied. "Zandakar and Emperor Han will help me with that."

"You expect Arbenia and Harbisland to meekly fall in step behind the *Tzhung*?" said Rudi, incredulous. "Majesty, you're dreaming!"

"And if you tell them Zandakar's one of these murdering savages coming to kill us," added Edward, "they'll accuse us of making bargains with the enemy."

"And even if they do believe you," said Ludo, "with or without Zandakar and Emperor Han our problem's far from solved. Is there even time for an armada to be gathered? The ambassadors have broad powers but they won't speak for their masters in this. They'll have to consult with them. That'll take weeks."

"And getting each nation's agreement to your plan is only the beginning," said Alasdair. "Their warships have to reach us, and that will take more weeks. Anything could happen in that time."

She felt her heart thud. "I know."

"Then there's the matter of convincing them to work together in a single cause," said Rudi. "How can that be accomplished? Half the time they're at each other's throats!"

"I know that, too."

"Then what use is this talk of armadas?" demanded Adric. "When there seems little hope of reaching agreement?"

"What would you rather we talk of, Adric?" said Alasdair. "Your complaints that the ducal house provided you is too small?"

Adric glared. "And so it is too small! As Duke of Kingseat I am—"

"That's *enough*!" With an effort, Rhian reined in her temper. "I realise the raising of an armada faces many obstacles. So, while we're working towards that, however slowly, we must also look to raising an army to defend Ethrea."

"An army?" said Edward. "It's against the trading charter for us to raise an army."

She swallowed a scream. *God grant me patience.* "I *know*, Edward. But these are extraordinary times. If we don't revisit the terms of that charter, Ethrea will either be defenceless or forced to rely on foreign soldiers to fight for us. Are you content to leave our safety in the hands of Dev'karesh or Barbruish? I'm not."

"But that's what the charter is for, Majesty," said Rudi. "Protecting us is one of the obligations placed upon the trading nations."

"From theft and each other, Rudi," she retorted. "From piracy and pillaging. Not from a full-scale invasion by a nation of warriors with powers we can scarcely comprehend."

"True," said Alasdair. "But once you convince them we *are* in danger from Mijak, all of us, they might see our raising of an army as an attempt to take advantage of the situation."

"To what end?" she said, staring. "There's no advantage to us if the charter is broken. Every trading nation knows how much we benefit from it. And armies are expensive. Why would we pour money into that ravenous belly unless we were forced to it?"

Alasdair shrugged. "We wouldn't. But that doesn't mean a nation like Keldrave won't suspect some hidden motive."

He was right. It would. They'd all be suspicious. Ethrea sat in the midst of a tangled web, each trading nation sticky with grudges and alliances that could break from one heartbeat to the next. Still . . . "I must believe I can convince the trading nations to give us leeway," she said. "Why else has God favoured me, if I can't do even that?"

"This army," said Rudi. "You're thinking to create it from each duchy's garrison?" He pulled a face. "That's not enough soldiers to defend the kingdom."

"True. But our garrison soldiers are only the beginning, Rudi," she said. "You're forgetting the men and women of Ethrea. They can be trained to defend their home. Indeed, it's my belief they'll defend it whether they're trained or not. So I think it preferable that we give them as much help as we can, starting as soon as possible. I'd not have one Ethrean die because he or she knew too little."

"*Trained . . .*" said Alasdair, slowly. "You mean by Zandakar?"

"By men he has trained, yes," she said, and tried not to see how his eyes were now blank, his expression guarded. "I'll have Zandakar train the best of our garrisons, so they in turn can train the men below them, who will then train the people."

"What makes you think Zandakar will do it?" said Edward. "You'll be asking him to turn on his own kind to help us. I tell you straight, Majesty, I'm not inclined to trust him that far."

Ven'Cedwin's inky quill scratched busily over his parchment, a loud sound as Rhian stared in silence at her dukes. The pain behind her eyes grew with each harsh breath. "Oh, Edward. Have you forgotten so soon who my father was? I grew up learning from him every trick and trade of statecraft . . . including how to read a man."

"It's true Eberg gave you an uncommon education," said Rudi, red-faced. "But it was Ranald and Simon he had in mind for leadership."

Helfred cleared his throat. "I find this conversation pointless, my lords. I find it dangerous also. If we, this privy council, cannot hold to a woman as our sovereign lord, what hope do we have of showing example to the kingdom and the world at large? God *himself* has chosen Rhian to rule. And *still* you cavil? Are you termites, my lords, that you would eat out the very foundation of this kingdom?"

The dukes, and even Alasdair, stared at Helfred – as though for the first time they truly saw their prolate. Saw past his youth, his unfortunate complexion, his even more unfortunate family . . . saw past all that to the man himself. Then they exchanged uncomfortable glances or frowned at the table, unwilling to invite their prolate's further censure.

Rhian looked at Helfred, who met her gaze without comment. His expression was composed, but she thought she saw sympathy in his eyes. They were, after all, in similar situations. No churchman in his right mind would've imagined Helfred succeeding Marlan as Prolate of Ethrea.

In his own way, Helfred is as unlikely an ally as the Emperor Han. Truly my life has become . . . unexpected.

Hurting and weary, she returned to her seat. "Gentlemen, I know this is difficult. But the Ethrea we knew died yesterday in the tiltyard with Damwin and Kyrin. This is a new day. A new kingdom. If you don't have faith in me as your queen, how can you serve me?"

Edward sat back, his eyes narrowed. "We can't serve you if, when we question your choices, we're accused of disloyalty."

"Of course you can't," she agreed. "By all means be rigorous in your examination of any plans I might put forth. But be rigorous with hearts wholly and solely believing in me. Otherwise, truly, is there any point to this?"

"This Ethrean army," he said gruffly, after a moment. "The idea's not bad, I grant you, but like the raising of an aramda it'll take time. Not even Zandakar can create an army overnight."

"I think we have a little more time than that, Edward."

"How much more time?" said Ludo. "How soon before Mijak comes knocking on our door?"

"I don't know," she said. "No-one does. Zandakar left his people almost a year ago, and Han's witch-men can tell us only that they come."

"Er – Your Majesty?" said Ven'Cedwin, looking up from his swift scribbling. "If I might interject?"

Surprised, she considered him. For all the talking he did in council meetings, Ven'Cedwin might as well be mute. "Yes?"

"Your earlier mention of Icthia stirred my memory," said the venerable. "As you know, I've been sorting through the haphazard records kept while your late father was ailing. Did you know the current Icthian ambassador was recalled from his post almost three months ago? His replacement is now some weeks overdue."

Rhian felt her mouth dry. "No. I wasn't aware of that, Ven'Cedwin."

"It might not mean anything," said Ludo, breaking the circumspect silence. "There could be a dozen reasons why the new Icthian ambassador's been delayed."

Or it might mean that Mijak had swallowed Icthia alive and even now was sailing towards Ethrea . . .

"Rudi? You oversee the running of Kingseat Harbour. Has word reached your ears of trouble to the east?"

Rudi looked offended. "If it had, you can be sure I'd have mentioned it long before now."

She pulled a face at him, apologising. "Just to be sure, find out from the harbourmaster if he knows of any other tardy vessels. It's possible no-one's thought to be alarmed yet, if there are." She took a steadying breath. *Stay calm. Stay calm.* "As Ludo says, the Icthian ambassador's delay might mean nothing. But in case that's not so, all the more reason for us to push ahead, gentlemen, as hard and as fast as we can, using whatever tools lie within our grasp to protect Ethrea."

"It's going to be a battle, convincing the trading nations the danger from Mijak is real," said Rudi. "When we can't say for certain how soon they'll attack, or even prove their existence."

"We can prove it," she said, sounding far more confident than she felt. "We have Zandakar."

"One man isn't proof," said Edward dubiously.

"We also have Han and his witch-men."

"The trading nations fear and resent Tzhung-tzhungchai, even Harbisland and Arbenia," said Rudi. "Majesty, these are treacherous waters. There are currents and cross-currents here no monarch of Ethrea has ever had to swim."

"And since I'm young and a woman I must perforce drown?" She tilted her chin. "Nonsense. You forget the centuries of goodwill Ethrea has in its bowl. The trading nations might distrust each other, but they won't distrust us. We have never lied to them or played them false."

Alasdair sat forward, his elbows braced on the table. "Fine. Say you're right, and you do convince the ambassadors that Mijak is coming. Say they agree to this armada, or at the least to us patchworking an army together. After that you'd best leave Zandakar locked safely in prison. Let the trading nations see us so cosy with an enemy and I think it likely there'll be a revolt."

She stared at him. *Don't do this, Alasdair. Don't bring our bedroom into my council chamber.* "The ambassadors aren't stupid men. They'll recognise Zandakar's worth. Once I explain—"

"You don't know that!"

"No," she said carefully. "Not for certain. But I believe I'll convince them."

"How? Castle servants chatter as much as those who serve the ambassadors. It's likely they know already you tossed him into prison."

A swift exchange of glances around the council table. Rhian felt her face heat. "I was angry," she said stiffly. "I felt betrayed because he didn't trust me with the truth. I'm not angry now. He was frightened. Any one of us in his position would've acted the same."

"Perhaps," said Edward heavily. "But even if you can ease their fears over Zandakar, you'll never stop them mistrusting the Tzhung. Han's a law unto himself. Chances are he'll step in and try to take over. The other nations won't stand for that. *I'll* not stand for it. Ethrea's no vassal state of the Tzhung empire."

"Edward's right," said Adric. "Everyone knows the Tzhung care only for the Tzhung. I doubt you'll control him. Their emperor will never be led by a woman."

She could feel Alasdair's eyes upon her, his gaze cool and speculating. Suspicious. He didn't know about her two meetings with Han. She hadn't felt strong enough for the arguments that would surely follow.

"He'll be led by me," she said flatly. "His witch-men brought him here, to Ethrea. He knows we lie at the heart of this dilemma. He'll listen. He'll be guided."

"And if he won't?" said Alasdair as Adric sat back, silenced but dissatisfied.

"He will."

Scratch, scratch, scratch, went Ven'Cedwin's quill over a fresh sheet of parchment. Underneath it, the soft slide of velvet against leather, against wood, as the dukes shifted on their chairs.

She looked at each of them in turn. "I promise you, gentlemen, I will deal with Emperor Han. I'll deal with all of them. Edward and Rudi, first thing tomorrow visit the ambassadors in person and invite them to a special convocation here, in the castle, at noon. Don't elaborate on the purpose of the meeting. Stress only that their lives depend upon their attendance."

"Majesty," her dukes murmured.

"Helfred, I'll need you at that meeting," she continued. "The full weight of the Church must be helpful when I lay our case before the ambassadors. Once they're aware of the danger from Mijak you can turn your attention to the matters of Hartshorn and Meercheq. Ludo will assist you in the matter of the funerals."

He nodded. "Of course."

She stood. "Then, gentlemen, I believe we're done for the moment. Let us be about our business."

The chamber emptied until only she and Alasdair remained. He stayed seated, staring at his hands, as she once more began to pace. Her belly was churning, and the pain behind her eyes was monstrous. Every cut and bruise shouted. Dear God, how much she needed to lie down.

"Alasdair, I want this meeting in the Grand Ballroom. Can you see all is made ready?"

He nodded. "I can."

"Have Adric assist you. He's green and needs seasoning." She pulled a face. "I fear I was too hasty in making him Kingseat's duke. Just because no king before you has been king and duke at the same time—"

"Is there any point to you looking over your shoulder?" he said. "You made your decision. You can't unmake it now.

"Besides . . ."

"What?" she said, when he didn't continue. "Alasdair? Besides *what*?"

"At the time it seemed unlikely you'd prevail and be queen," he said reluctantly. "But you did, so we must live with that decision."

Which might well prove difficult. But if I unseat Adric I offend Rudi and make every other duke and prospective duke in the kingdom nervous. Oh, Rhian. And you pride yourself on your statecraft.

"I confess, it was . . . not well thought through," she admitted. "Though the choice did bind Rudi to me, which is important. Especially with the Mijaki coming to slaughter us all." She managed a dry laugh. "And if I don't prevail against *them*, then my choice of Kingseat's duke will be the least of our troubles."

"True," said Alasdair. He still hadn't looked at her.

"I'd value your opinion of those men eligible to be made Duke of Hartshorn," she said, after a moment. "You've mixed with them all your life, but being from Linfoi . . . their stupid prejudices . . . you have the advantage of an outsider's eye."

He nodded. "Of course."

His scrupulous politeness was unbearable. She dropped into the chair nearest to him and reached for his hands. He didn't withdraw them, but neither did his fingers clasp hers.

"You know I'm right about Zandakar," she said, holding onto him. "With what he knows of Mijak, he could make the difference between victory and defeat."

"If he tells you the truth."

"He will, Alasdair. He's not what you suspect."

A muscle leapt along his jaw. "And what's that?"

"A spy, sent by his mother and brother to help them destroy us. If he was, why wouldn't he do his best to ingratiate himself instead of making me so angry by hiding the truth?"

Alasdair looked at her. "But that's exactly what he's done, Rhian. He's ingratiated himself. He's wormed his way into your affections, earned your trust. You defend him against everyone, even me. And now you're about to defend him to the ambassadors."

She released his hands. "*Because he was sent here to help us. Because he might he all that stands between us and destruction.*"

"Or he might be the key that unlocks the door, not only to this kingdom but to all the civilised world," said Alasdair softly. "But you won't even entertain that possibility, will you?"

He'd never understand. In a thousand years she'd not make him see her side of this. To him Zandakar was the enemy, even though he admitted that without Zandakar she'd be dead.

"Alasdair, all I've done is put him in a more comfortable prison cell," she said, her hands fisted in her lap. "And I promise he'll never be alone while he remains in this kingdom. You're right, I do trust him and I don't believe I'm wrong. But I'm not stupid, either. He'll be watched. And if it seems he no longer has our best interests at heart . . ."

"Then he dies, Rhian," said Alasdair flatly. "In the moment of his treachery, he dies."

She nodded. "Yes. He dies."

Alasdair dropped his gaze again, fixing it to the polished mahogany table. She waited for him to speak, waited for him to say something, *anything*, but he seemed content to let the silence gain weight and stifle the chamber's sunlit air. She didn't need words to know what he was thinking.

"Han came to me," she said, when she couldn't bear it any longer. "Twice. In secret. The first time to tell me I had to kill the dukes. The second time . . ." She shook her head. "I don't know why he came the second time. I think I confuse him. I think he resents me. The wind – the god of the Tzhung – *someone* or *something* has told him I'm important and he has to listen to me. He doesn't like it, but he obeys. He'll not move against Ethrea, or any other nation. I know it."

Alasdair looked at her again, and this time she saw what her silence had done to him.

"I'm *sorry*!" she said, then pressed her fingers to her lips. Waited until she could speak without weeping. "I've never been a wife before! I've never worn a crown! I'm doing my best, Alasdair."

"And so am I," he said, his voice almost too low

for hearing. "But *you* must see that sometimes your best leaves a little to be desired."

"So I'm to tell you *everything*?" she retorted. "I'm not to make any choice, any decision, without first consulting you? How then does that make me the queen? Alasdair, what king in the history of Ethrea, what – what duke *ever* in the duchy of Linfoi first consulted his wife in the ruling of his lands? What man would ever dream of doing so? And if he did, and others learned of it, what respect would they have for him? *How many times must we have this wretched argument?*"

"Not once more," said Alasdair, and stood. "Not this argument, or any other. You're my sovereign queen and I've sworn you my fealty. My duty's clear, and a Linfoi holds to his word."

She looked up at him. "What did you think, Alasdair, when you married me? How did you think it would be, when I was queen? Or did you think you'd never have to face this, since I most likely wouldn't prevail? Did you think I'd most likely become your duchess in Linfoi, and then you'd be the one to decide what *I* knew?"

Alasdair ran his hand over his face, then stared through a chamber window. "Rhian . . . I tell you truly . . . I don't know *what* I was thinking."

If she reached out she could touch him, yet he was so far away. "I see."

"I should go," he said, his voice rough. "There's much to do before tomorrow."

"Yes. Go. I'll see you at dinner."

She sat in quiet despair after he left, feeling her cuts and bruises pain her. Then, when she couldn't stand the silence any longer, she went to Zandakar in his plush prison. They hadn't spoken since she'd fought the dukes . . . and she needed to see him.

He stood slowly as disapproving Sergeant Rigert closed the chamber door behind her, leaving them alone. His expression was grave. "You danced the *hotas* well, Rhian."

She shrugged. "I didn't die."

"*Wei.*" He closed the distance between them, and traced his fingertip down the line of stitches in her cheek. "Ursa says scar?"

"Most likely."

"Good," he said, and lightly slapped the side of her head. "I watch. You stupid, you *wei* kill that duke quickly."

From him she'd accept the criticism. He was her teacher. "*Yatzhay.*"

"Second kill good. Quick. Clean." His fist punched against his chest, above his heart. "You in *hota, zho?*"

And of course, he understood. She nodded. "*Zho.*"

"*Zho,*" he said again, and this time he smiled.

She mustn't stay here. There was the meeting with the ambassadors to think about, matters of state she needed to address. Letters of patent to draft, that would officially dissolve House Doveninger; Ven'Cedwin would be waiting And Zandakar—

Zandakar understands too much.

"I have to go," she said, stepping back. "Thank you, Zandakar. The things you taught me saved my life."

He nodded, still smiling. "*Zho.* When do we dance *hotas* again?"

Oh, God help her. "I don't know. I'm wounded."

"But when you heal, Rhian, then we dance. *Zho?*"

"Yes. Perhaps. Zandakar—" She took a deep breath. "Tomorrow I meet with the ambassadors, to tell them of Mijak and the danger it poses. I'll need you there to speak for me. To tell the trading nations about your people. Your mother. Your brother. How dangerous they are. Will you do that? Will you speak for me, against Mijak?"

A shadow of puzzlement crept into his eyes. "Rhian?"

"*Will you?*"

He nodded again. "*Zho.*"

"Good," she said, and left him alone.

CHAPTER TEN

The castle's Grand Ballroom was crowded with memories. Alone, for the moment, Rhian stood at its centre and gave those memories free rein. Closed her eyes and swayed, just a little, hearing the echoes of sweet music long past.

Eberg had held all his official functions in the ballroom, and from the age of twelve she had been his royal hostess at the balls, the receptions, the wooings and soothings of the contentious trading nations. She'd long ago lost count of the times she'd danced across the polished parquetry floor, beneath the frescoed ceiling's ornate chandeliers, watching herself in the full-length mirrors on the walls as she glided about the chamber in the arms of the men important enough to have been invited. The sons of ambassadors, the brothers of dukes and minor nobles and foreign princes, or the princes themselves.

From the age of twelve she'd known they thought, in their secret hearts, that if only they danced well enough they might win her in marriage and so bind Ethrea close to their cause. And because she was her father's daughter she smiled and laughed and wore her jewels and silk brocades, knowing she was beautiful and they wanted her, and never once let them see the thoughts behind her eyes.

No matter the occasion, no matter the honoured guests, she and her father had danced first, and alone. The night's guests clustered at the ballroom's edges and applauded, politely, the king and his only daughter sweeping through the music. She'd had the best of dancing masters and never once trod on his feet.

"Remember, Rhian," Papa said to her every time, serenely smiling as the world avidly watched. "Their flattery serves their own purposes, never ours. Ethrea must be forever independent. The world is a house of cards, my child. One breath too strong, or too uncautious, and see what a tumbling will come about."

"Yes, Papa," she'd always replied. "I know. I won't disappoint you."

And even though they were dancing, even though they whirled and swirled in front of all those avid eyes, he'd always kissed her forehead then. Dear God, she'd been so loved. She could feel his lips on her skin even now.

Oh, Papa. We can't be independent today. I must ask for help or see Ethrea destroyed.

. She sighed, and opened her eyes. The minstrel gallery was empty of musicians. The chandeliers remained unlit. Wrought-iron candle stands, laden with fat white candles, had been brought in to dispel the gloom. With her eyes closed she heard more than music, she heard laughter and revelry. Happier times. With her eyes closed she saw Ranald dancing with a string of beauties, Simon with the beauties' younger sisters. Saw her father, the king, charming and disarming and deflecting all manner of awkward questions.

She'd danced with Alasdair in this room.

Now I dance with the future. I dance with tens and tens of thousands of lives. I dance with death.

She'd never felt so . . . inadequate.

Dinsy had helped her dress for her meeting with the ambassadors. She wore black silk brocade shot through with restrained gold thread, and her mother's dragon-eye rubies, her talisman. The gown closed tight around her throat, around her wrists, and touched the floor when she stood. She was crowned with the circlet she'd worn to kill the dukes.

"Oh, Majesty," Dinsy had whispered. "You do look fierce."

She'd stared in her dressing room mirror and couldn't disagree. The face staring back at her was still pale, still hollow-cheeked. Still beautiful, despite Ursa's neat row of stitches. But her eyes were different. They reflected her soul, and her soul had been changed.

"That gown's loose on you now," Dinsy had

added, and tsked her disapproval. "You're too thin, Majesty. You should eat more. Or do less."

That was true too. The dress had been fashioned for the boys' funeral. She'd worn it to bury her father after them. It had seemed the best choice for her meeting with the ambassadors, given her part in Damwin and Kyrin's deaths. It made the proper comment without her having to say a word. But it was definitely loose. Dancing the *hotas* had changed her body as well as her soul. She was muscled like a whippet, lean and whipcord strong. There'd been no time for a seamstress's alterations. And since her wounded back and arm were still painful, she didn't mind.

Her mother's rubies gleamed like blood against the black. Blood was part of her life now. Perhaps she should make sure to wear a ruby always, so she'd never forget it.

A dais had been erected at the far end of the ballroom and her father's public throne placed upon it. Her throne now. Slowly, almost hesitantly, she approached it. Stepped onto the dais. Sat down, spine as straight as a pine tree. Let her hands rest on the throne's arms and resisted the urge to hold on tight.

I am here. I can do this. I must do this. Papa, help me.

Truth be told, the ballroom was too large for such an intimate gathering, but she'd wanted a feeling of space around her. Wanted its opulence to remind the ambassadors that Ethrea wasn't a pauper kingdom. Wanted them feeling a little . . . awed.

Marlan was my first great test. Damwin and Kyrin my second. Now here is my third . . .

The ballroom's doors opened a handspan, and Edward peered in. "Majesty? It's almost noon. The ambassadors will arrive shortly."

She nodded. "Of course."

Edward withdrew. A moment later the ballroom's doors were flung wide open by liveried heralds and her privy council entered. She watched their approach in the great wall mirrors, their finely-dressed figures dipping in and out of reflection. Even Helfred had changed his plain blue wool habit for something more splendid: the candlelight gleamed on dark red silk. Alasdair, magnificently sombre in black velvet, led the way.

He touched her shoulder with his fingertips as he took his place on the dais, Ludo beside him. She kept her face schooled but let her eyes smile. Despite their differences and misunderstandings, she knew she could count on him . . . and he on her.

A small desk had been set to one side of the dais, so Ven'Cedwin might record the proceedings. He took his place, piled about with sheets of blank parchment, and picked up a small knife to sharpen his quill.

Beyond the open doors, a stirring and murmur of voices. One of the heralds on duty turned to her and nodded. The ambassadors were arrived.

She glanced at her privy council. "Gentlemen. We're ready?"

"We're ready, Your Majesty," said Alasdair, scrupulously correct.

So she raised a hand to the herald and he bade the ambassadors proceed.

First to enter the ballroom was Emperor Han.

His ambassador, Lai, came three paces behind him. Behind them trailed the ambassadors of the other trading nations, their expressions pruned with displeasure that the Tzhung emperor was in their midst.

They'd come in all their finery. Yes, Istahas of Slynt was still half-naked, but his deerhide leggings were new and his torso was oiled so it gleamed in the candlelight. The others were fully clothed, silk and velvet and leather and much jewellery. An-chata of Keldrave had lost two of his pendulous wife-rings; whether the women were dead or abandoned Rhian didn't know.

Behind them, the heralds closed the ballroom doors. Rhian willed her heart to beat a little slower, and favoured her visitors with an impersonal smile as all but Han and Lai straggled to a halt and stared about them, suspicious of even those men they called friends. The Tzhung did not straggle; they stood apart, self-contained and unperturbed.

"Gentlemen. You have our thanks for attending this meeting."

Before anyone else replied, Halash of Dev'Karesh stepped forward and nodded in something approaching respectful recognition. His jaw worked rhythmically as he chewed the cloves he carried in a little leather purse dangling from his plaited leather belt. He was feet away from her and still she could smell him. She watched as the other ambassadors gave him ground, their nostrils flaring at his pungency.

"And you'll have ours, lady, when you say why you send for us."

Rhian let her eyebrows rise. "The correct form of address is 'Your Majesty'."

The Dev'karesh were a pale race. Halash's white skin burned red at her reproof. "Of course. Your Majesty."

Instead of bowing, as was customary, Arbenia's representative jabbed a pointed finger at Han. Though the weather was warm, still Gutten swathed himself in bearskin, the badge of his ruler's House. "It proves troublesome to me that Tzhung-tzhungchai's emperor stands here when my count languishes in Arbenia."

The calculated disrespect, somehow more grating than Halash's brusque manner, sent a ripple of tension through her privy councillors. She raised a hand, settling them. "Ambassador Gutten, your master is always welcome in Kingseat. Every great man and woman of the world is welcome to Ethrea."

Gutten bowed, almost insolent. "But only Emperor Han is here now. He is invited? Or he comes on a whim?"

"Emperor Han is not the topic of this meeting, sir," she said coldly.

"Then what is?" said Voolksyn of Harbisland, third of the three great trading nations. Like so many of his race he was a giant of a man, made even more impressive by his clean-shaven head, his undisciplined reddish-gold beard, his ring-choked fingers and his spotted sealskin doublet.

Beneath her black brocade finery, Rhian felt her heart beat hard again. Every one of these ambassadors, and of course Han, was old enough to be her father. Two days ago they'd watched her kill to keep the crown upon her head. Would the memory be enough to keep them here now?

Please, God, please. Let it be enough.

She looked at Voolksyn. "Nothing less than life and death."

Everyone but Han and Lai stirred and muttered at her words. Ignoring them, she let her gaze rest upon Ambassador Athnïj of Icthia. "Sir," she said, "am I misinformed, or is your tenure as the Icthian ambassador come to an end?"

Athnïj, a thin, nervy man, stepped to the foot of the dais and bowed extravagantly. Large patches of sweat marred his rust-red velvet overtunic. "Your Majesty, you are not misinformed."

She drummed her fingers on the arm of her throne. "And yet you're still here, Athnïj, long after the time Icthia's new ambassador should have reached us. What has happened to the new Icthian ambassador? Are you aware?"

Athnïj shook his head, his eyes skittish. His throat worked hard as he swallowed. "Alas."

Gutten of Arbenia was scowling. "Are *you*, Queen of Ethrea?"

Rhian sat back and considered him. "If I said I was, Ambassador Gutten. If I said I knew things that would freeze the blood in your veins . . . would you believe me? Or would you dismiss me, as Marlan and Damwin and Kyrin dismissed me, because I am young and female?"

A hurried exchange of glances between the ambassadors, then, and a smattering of whispered comment. Gutten spoke to Voolksyn, his back half-turned to the throne. Voolksyn listened, his face betraying nothing. Leelin of Haisun, a nation cousined to Tzhung-tzhungchai, tried to catch Ambassador Lai's attention, but Han's man stared at the parquetry floor. Istahas tugged at his scalp-lock and said something swift and guttural in An-chata's ready ear. The Keldravian snorted, puffy eyes narrowed, and slid his hands into his wide sleeves as tiny Lalaska of Barbruish shook his oiled ringlets and stroked his green silk stole. Istahas and Halash exchanged soft comments too. Athnij pressed his knuckles to his lips and said nothing.

Emperor Han, still standing apart, was almost smiling, as though he found this entire gathering some kind of prank or waste of time. His gaze touched Rhian's face once, then slid aside. She felt her fingers tighten.

She'd half-expected him to walk out of thin air again last night, to bewilder her with more cryptic utterances. When he didn't appear she was relieved . . . but somehow disappointed.

And does that mean I'm a fool?

"My lords!" she said, raising her voice above their mutterings.

One by one they looked at her, seemingly startled all over again that they must dance attendance upon a woman.

"Gentlemen," she continued, "I understand your dismay. We smile and we smile, we have treaties and a charter, yet none of us here believes we're all bosom friends. There are difficulties between some of you, I'm aware of that. But Ethrea is friend to every nation in this room and has been for centuries. You must know that whatever I tell you today is the truth."

Voolksyn settled his fists on his hips and jutted his beard at her. "Like your father you pour words from your mouth like syrup, queen. What do you know?"

His tone was insolent, his green gaze hostile. Her privy councillors bristled again, and for the second time she calmed them with a lifted hand.

"Ambassador Voolksyn, I know a new power rises in the far east," she said softly. "A long-dead empire crawling out of its grave. It is called Mijak, and it is soaked in blood. Already many lands have fallen to its fearsome warriors. I fear Icthia is its most recent conquest. And I believe that if we do not act now, together, Ethrea will fall . . . and after us, all of you."

As Voolksyn considered her words, Gutten stared at Han. "Who told you this? His witch-men?"

Han met Gutten's glare calmly. "Sun-dao, my most powerful witch-man, has seen in the wind the warriors of Mijak. He has seen the blood tide. He has seen the end of all things. Only a fool turns his face from the wind."

"Only a fool believes the word of Tzhung-tzhungchai," retorted Gutten. "The wind of your words would blow us on the rocks. You would wreck every nation and make the pieces Tzhung. You and this woman of Ethrea, you concoct a tale to frighten children. You and this woman plot behind closed doors and seek to swallow the world."

"Gutten speaks the truth," grunted Voolksyn. "No Emperor of Tzhung-tzhungchai has done a thing that will not serve him first."

Han smiled. "Do you insult me on your master's

behalf? Or does the Slainta of Harbisland keep a dog that barks without permission?"

"You call me dog?" Voolksyn bared his teeth, one fist rising. "Harbisland has no fear of the Tzhung! Harbisland spits on Tzhung-tzhungchai! Harbisland—"

"*Gentlemen*!" Rhian shouted, and leapt to her feet. "You stand in *my* realm, beneath *my* roof. Try my patience further and I shall see you both recalled in disgrace. I did not invite you here so you might brawl like common sailors in a harbour tavern!"

As Voolksyn stared, shocked to silence, Gutten wrapped his stubby fingers round his ornate chain of office. "So you learned of this Mijak from the Tzhung emperor."

She sat again, and took a moment to arrange her heavy skirts. "I knew of it before Emperor Han came," she said at last, her voice cool. "That is how I know he tells the truth. When he came, it was to warn me that Ethrea is in danger. He has acted as my kingdom's true friend."

"And we have not?" demanded Istahas. "Harsh words, Majesty. Friends do not say things like that to each other."

"Friends tell the truth," she said. "And the truth is we stand in grave peril. *All* of us."

"From this Mijak?" said An-chata, almost sneering.

"Yes." She folded her hands neatly in her lap. "As you know, my lords, every vessel's captain leaving Kingseat Harbour informs the harbourmaster when he anticipates his ship's return. My harbourmaster advises me no less than four vessels are late, according to their sailing documents. One belongs to Tzhung-tzhungchai. The others sail for Arbenia, Barbruish and Dev'karesh. All were bound for Icthia . . . and from Icthia they have failed to return."

The ambassadors of the nations she'd named stared at each other, then at her.

"You weren't aware of this? How can that be? You all trade with Icthia, don't you know the whereabouts of each other's—"

"They're aware, Majesty," said Han, mildly amused. "But to admit it could be seen as spying. The nations you mention aren't all treatied together."

She glared at the ambassadors. "I don't care about your treaties and intrigues, gentlemen. I care only that you realise something is *wrong*. All these ships missing, and no new Icthian ambassador! What else can it mean but Mijak has reached the far eastern coast?"

Lalaska shrugged. "Trading *is* a dangerous business. There are storms. Ships are blown off course. Sometimes they sink." He glanced up at Han. "There are pirates."

"*Gentlemen*," said Rhian, before another argument could erupt. "Of course the voyage between Ethrea and Icthia is dangerous. Every ocean voyage is dangerous. And in the past, yes, ships have been lost to storms. But this is not the storm season. Are you suggesting all these vessels are somehow blown off course in fair weather, or mysteriously sunk without trace or cause?"

Voolksyn grunted. "It is said the witch-men of Tzhung-tzhungchai control the wind."

"And sank their own ship? To what end?"

"Who knows the devious heart of Tzhung-tzhungchai?" said Gutten, glowering. "It cannot be trusted, it—"

"*Stop it*!" said Rhian, and banged her fist on the arm of her throne. At this rate she'd be bruised to the elbow. "We are gathered to talk of how we'll save ourselves from Mijak." She swallowed. "And how you can help Ethrea save itself first. For you must know that if Ethrea falls to this ravenous invader, your great nations will be ruined."

Gutten glared down his nose. "Why should we believe your words? We do not see Mijak. We never hear of Mijak. We see you with Emperor Han. You look to lie with this man of Tzhung."

Alasdair stepped forward. "Mind your tongue, Arbenia. The council will not tolerate slurs against the queen."

"Heh," said Gutten, sour with contempt. "He speaks? This man behind a woman? Is this a king?"

Rhian felt her blood scorch. Felt Alasdair's rage as he stood beside her throne. *I did this to him. He married me and that gives him to men like Gutten for baiting. I should've insisted he sat a throne beside me.* But he'd refused, quoting herself back to him. And she'd let herself be persuaded because . . . *admit it, admit it* . . . in her heart she thought that was right. Her father never once diluted his authority. Never once shared it with his queen while she lived. *And I'm my father's daughter.*

"For shame, Ambassador Gutten. You should know better," said Helfred, before she could speak. "As for Mijak, the danger is real. God himself has said it."

"Your God," said An-chata as Gutten choked on

Helfred's reprimand. "You say we are subject to the God of Ethrea?"

"No," said Rhian. "This isn't about religion, it's about death and dying. It's about saving our lives and the lives of our people." She shook her head. "My lords, this is not a new move in an old game. This is a *new* game, that we'll lose for certain if we're not careful. You demand proof that Mijak exists? I have proof." She looked over at Ven'Cedwin. "Venerable?"

Her council secretary put down his quill and went to the ballroom's doors and swung them open. A moment later Zandakar entered, escorted by Idson and six conspicuously armed soldiers. Han and the ambassadors stared as he came to a halt before the dais and punched his fist to his chest.

"Rhian *hushla*."

Ignoring him, she looked instead to the foreigners on whom so much depended. "His name is Zandakar. He is a prince of Mijak."

Consternation from all but Han and his ambassador. Gutten and Voolksyn exchanged dark looks, and Voolksyn stepped forward. "Word has reached us of the blue-haired man in your midst, Majesty. Whispers say he is dangerous with a blade."

She nodded. "He is."

"A prince of Mijak, you say?" Voolkysn's fingers twitched, as though he longed for his own knife. "Then he is the enemy. The enemy sleeps in comfort beneath your roof, queen?"

"He's not our enemy," she said swiftly. "He's pledged to aid us against the warriors of Mijak."

"So he is a traitor," said An-chata. "He betrays his

own blood. You would trust a traitor, and ask us to trust you?"

She couldn't help it. She looked at Alasdair. His eyes were on her, his expression grim. "You might call it treachery, An-chata, to see a wrong done and try to stop it," she said coldly, and looked away from her husband. "I prefer to call it noble. Gentlemen, Zandakar was disowned by his people because he refused to kill any more men, women and children whose only crime was that they were not born Mijaki. He has sworn to help me turn back the tide of blood. He has sworn to die before letting Mijak swallow one more nation. He grieves he wasn't able to save Icthia."

"You have no proof Icthia is swallowed," said Gutten. "This man with blue hair is not proof. This man is a man and can say what he likes."

Nervous Athnïj shook his head. "Majesty, I believe you. Icthia is not a silent nation. There is a reason I've heard nothing for so long. I think it must be this Mijak."

"You fool, Athnïj," said Gutten. "To fall prey to—"

"*Wei*," said Zandakar, and turned his pale blue eyes to Gutten. "You stupid man, you say *wei* Mijak, *wei* Hekat, *wei* warriors. Rhian *hushla* kill three men, *zho*? Zandakar kill three *thousand*." He held up a finger. "One day."

As the ambassadors stared, Rhian stood again. "Zandakar speaks the truth. Tens of thousands are slaughtered already, gentlemen. Slaughtered or enslaved, their cities reduced to rubble. Unless you can put your differences behind you, unless you can accept that here is a time where pettiness has no place, where we must all make a leap of faith and trust each other, we shall fall too and before Mijak is done the oceans themselves shall be turned red."

"What do you say, then?" said Leelin of Haisun. "You say we go to war for Ethrea?"

"For Ethrea and for yourselves, yes. By our charter you're pledged to protect us from harm. I say the trading nations must raise an armada and sail to defeat the warships of Mijak."

As the ambassadors shifted and muttered, she looked at Alasdair. He nodded. "Go on," he said in an undertone. "It's too late to turn back now."

"Have faith," murmured Helfred. "God is with us in this."

Heart pounding, she looked swiftly at the rest of her council. They smiled at her, even Adric. Warmed, she turned again to the ambassadors. "Gentlemen, there is more," she said loudly, and silenced them. "I ask your leave to break our charter. Ethrea would raise an army so it can defend itself should war come."

"Impossible!" protested Halash of Dev'karesh. "My chief will not hear of that."

More agitated muttering as the others agreed. Rhian lifted her hands, palm out. "Please. Be reasonable. My people have the right to defend themselves."

"And we have the right to defend ourselves from Tzhung-tzhungchai!" said An-chata.

"You are in danger from Mijak, not from the Tzhung," said Han. "Or from a little army of Ethrea. Listen to the queen. Listen to this prisoner prince of Mijak. Listen—"

"To the wind?" sneered Gutten. "To the farting of Tzhung's demon god? No. Without Arbenia and Harbisland to hold you in check *your* empire would own the world, Han. That ambition is thwarted. Now you tell these lies so you can rule us all." He swung round. "You are a girl. What do you know of men and their greed for power?"

Rhian felt another wave of heat rush through her. "You can ask me that? When you know how Marlan pursued me, would have *killed* me? When you saw me kill Damwin and Kyrin because *their* greed for power overturned their minds? *You can ask me that, Gutten*? My God, I'm almost tempted to let Mijak have you. Wouldn't that serve you right for being so short-sighted and *stupid*."

"Your Majesty—" said Helfred, sounding pained.

She lifted a clenched fist to his face. "Be quiet, Your Eminence."

She leapt down from the dais, heedless of the pains such sharp movement woke in her still-recovering body, and stormed among the gaping ambassadors. Han and Lai melted into the shadows. Zandakar, startled, would have moved to protect her but his guards took hold of him and dragged him out of the way. She barely noticed.

"Rollin's grace! How are you the best your masters can find? How am I, so newly come to power, the only one who sees clearly the danger we face? You prate to me of treaties and charters and you forget this: *Mijak has made no treaty with us*. Mijak seeks to *destroy* us. Its warriors are thralled to an evil beyond comprehension. The god they worship is a god of blood and death and they *will not stop* until we bow down before it. Instead of accusing Emperor Han you should be on your knees *thanking* him, because he has offered the might of Tzhung-tzhungchai against these demon-driven warriors of Mijak."

"The might of Tzhung-tzhungchai is used for one thing only!" Gutten shouted. "Conquest for its emperor!" He turned to his fellow-ambassadors, his eyes alive with hate and rage. "You see what this is? This is Han of Tzhung in league with Rhian of Ethrea, determined to swallow the world between them. There is no Mijak, there is no horde of warriors waiting to slaughter us. She *lies*!"

"I do *not*!" Rhian shouted back, and shoved Gutten in the chest with both fists. "You fool, is Zandakar here by *chance*? God sent him to me so I would know about Mijak and its bloodthirsty empress. God gave me miracles so I would be crowned Ethrea's queen and have the power to use Zandakar to save my kingdom from Mijak. To save *all* of us from Mijak. Tzhung isn't the enemy. Ethrea needs the Tzhung empire, it needs Arbenia and Harbisland and Keldrave and the rest of you. It will take all of us, Gutten, fighting together, to have any hope against Mijak. Do you want to die, Ambassador? Do you want the world to drown in blood?"

Silence. Every man in the room stared at her. She stared back, dizzy with shouting, desperate for their belief.

Athnïj of Icthia cleared his throat. "We heard there were miracles, or some such thing," he said diffidently. "Of course we heard. There was talk of a common man . . ."

"A toymaker," she said, abruptly exhausted. "I've

known him all my life. He raised a child from the dead. Marlan touched him, and died. God sent him dreams of Mijak so he could bear witness to the truth."

Even as Gutten turned away, his face twisted in ugly rejection, Voolksyn of Harbisland stroked his fingers down his beard. "Dreams, you say?"

She nodded. The swordcut on her back was burning, and there was a slick wetness beneath the silk brocade of her dress. In her passion, in her anger, she'd torn open Ursa's stitches. But what did it matter? There'd be more blood where that came from if she failed to win this fight.

"Dreams can be powerful," said Voolksyn. "Dreams can come from the mother."

The people of Harbisland worshipped a goddess. They called her *nanatynsala*, mother spirit of the earth. Helfred said it was more heathenish nonsense, but right now she'd take any help she could find.

"The toymaker's dreams are powerful beyond imagining," she said. "And on Eberg's grave I swear, they show him the truth."

"Voolksyn?" said Gutten, incredulous. "You cannot listen to her. This is Han, this is Tzhung, our masters will not have it!"

Voolksyn shook his head. "If she lies, the mother will break her. Queen, you say this toymaker dreams to bear witness?"

She nodded. "Yes."

"Then let him bear witness. Let him speak, and we will judge."

Rhian swallowed. *Oh, God. Dexterity* . . . "Of course. Commander Idson—"

Idson bowed. "Your Majesty?"

"Fetch Mister Jones. Bring him here, quickly."

Another bow. "Yes, Your Majesty," said Idson. And then he was gone.

She nodded at Voolksyn, turned and walked back to the dais. Kept her head high and her spine straight, even as her heart pounded painfully in her chest.

Dexterity . . . Dexterity. Please. Don't hold a grudge.

Dexterity was pottering in the vegetable patch at the bottom of the cottage's back garden when Commander Idson came for him.

"Mr. Jones?"

He turned round so fast he overbalanced and fell over, squashing a very fine tomato plant. Dripping red pulp and seeds, heart thudding, he stared at Kingseat's garrison commander. "Yes? What? What have I done wrong now?"

Commander Idson's breastplate was too bright to look at. The unclouded sun dazzled the polished steel, transforming him into a man of white fire. *Marlan, burning, mouth wide in a scream* . . . Dexterity closed his eyes and averted his face.

"I'm not privy to that information, Mister Jones," said Idson. "Her Majesty requires your presence at the castle."

He unscrewed his eyes and peered cautiously at Idson, then past him. Where were the other soldiers? They didn't usually send just one man for an arrest. Was this a trick, then? Or some cruel method of luring him into an uncautious utterance?

Carefully he stood. "I'm not dressed for royalty."

Idson looked him up and down, taking in the compost-smothered gardening clogs, the baggy trousers, the shirt that had certainly seen better days. And, of course, the remains of squashed tomato.

"Nevertheless, Mister Jones. Your presence is required."

A tiny bubble of resentment rose to his throat. "Why? I haven't done anything wrong. Unless weeding is counted a crime these days."

Commander Idson's mouth tightened. "Mister Jones, I don't care to lay hands on you, but I will if I must. Her Majesty has given me an order and I'll obey it."

"An order to escort me to the castle." He wiped his hands on his trousers; sweat was turning the dirt to mud. "What bit of the castle?"

"The Grand Ballroom," said Idson, after a moment. As though saying that much was a betrayal of state secrets.

Not the dungeons, then. She's not putting me back there, to keep company with Zandakar.

The bubble of resentment persisted. "She needs me, does she?"

"What Her Majesty needs or doesn't need is not for me to say." Idson took a suggestive step backwards. "The queen is waiting, sir."

And that was that. *The queen is waiting* . . . so who cared what a nobody toymaker might need, or how busy he might be, or what other plans he might have for the rest of his day.

I don't care what Hettie said, I'm not mixing myself up in this business again. Whatever I do it'll end up being the wrong thing and I'll find myself locked up a second time.

Even to himself he sounded sulky . . . and didn't care.

"All right," he said, grudging. "I don't suppose I've a choice."

"None, sir," said Idson.

He was perversely pleased the matter was so important, apparently, that he wasn't even to have a moment to change into clean clothes.

Even if I could change I think I'd stay like this. I think that young lady needs to know not everyone thinks the sun rises in her eyes.

Not any more, anyway.

Idson had come in a light cart pulled by a strong fast horse and driven by one of his subordinates. It had an uncovered back, which meant everyone in the street could see Mister Jones was in trouble again . . .

As the young soldier whipped up the horse and guided the cart into a swift about-face, Dexterity sat on the hard wooden seat and scowled at the curtained windows of his neighbours' cottages.

Yes, yes, I'm in trouble again . . .

Idson said not a word during the journey to the castle. Dexterity wanted to ask him about Rhian's judicial combat with the dukes, but the commander's expression was so forbidding he didn't dare. How frustrating. Ursa hadn't been precisely forthcoming with details. Even though he was still so hurt and angry, he couldn't help but feel worried too.

I remember her a little girl, trailing a lambswool-stuffed dolly behind her. Now she's killing grown men with a sword. And is that God's plan too, Hettie? A

*young girl slaughtering men old enough to be her
father?*

Not that Rhian had been given much choice. The
dukes had practically slaughtered themselves, so stubbornly had they refused to yield.

*Even so, Hettie. What has the cost been to the girl?
All very well to say they deserved it. But does she deserve a life crowded with those kind of memories?*

A pang went through him, remembering how
she'd suffered over the death of Ven'Martin. And
then he remembered he was angry and hurt, and
what Rhian might or might not be feeling was none
of his business. He folded his arms, ignoring Idson
and glaring at the back of the younger soldier's head
for the rest of the journey.

They reached the castle without incident. The cart
halted in one of the rear courtyards and Idson gestured him out. In silence he followed the commander
inside and through a maze of ground floor corridors
until they reached a set of magnificently carved,
gilded and painted double doors guarded by a full
skein of Idson's finest men. They saluted when they
saw their commander.

"The Grand Ballroom," said Idson, with a sideways glance. "Her Majesty waits within. Are you prepared, Mister Jones?"

No, of course he wasn't. But there was no point in
saying that, so he shrugged. "Yes. I suppose."

"All right then," said Idson, and nodded.

Two of his soldiers flung open the doors.

CHAPTER ELEVEN

The Grand Ballroom was breathtaking, and full of ambassadors. Well, not *full*, the hall was an enormous space that could fit three hundred dancing couples, at least. But it felt full, with all those people staring incredulously at Commander Idson and his scruffy companion.

"Dexterity!" said a guttural, familiar voice as the soldiers pulled closed the ballroom's wide doors.

Dexterity looked left and saw Zandakar. It was most disconcerting to see the Mijaki warrior dressed like an Ethrean in linen and wool. His blue hair, so long now, gleamed in the bright candlelight. He looked well-fed. Not ill-treated, despite the six soldiers flanking him. His pale blue eyes were warm with pleasure.

Despite everything, he smiled. "Zandakar."

"Mister Jones," said Idson, coldly.

Of course. Greeting anyone before making obeisance to the queen was a glaring breach of protocol.

And you know something, Hettie? I could not care less.

Idson left him to walk to the dais alone, where Rhian sat on a throne surrounded by so many important men. There was Helfred, splendid in crimson. There was Alasdair, with such dark, shadowed eyes. Ah yes, and the king's cousin Ludo, the new Duke of

Linfoi. A bright, merry young man – when he wasn't caught up in terrible happenings. Duke Edward. Duke Rudi. And Rudi's son Adric, so recently elevated.

The privy council as it is now. She's got so many courtiers to give her advice, she doesn't need me.

He felt a particular cool gaze upon him and looked sideways. *Emperor Han.* There was a man to chill a toymaker's bones. The gathered ambassadors, well, they meant little or nothing to him. But Emperor Han and his witch-men were frightful. Memory battered him, of being held in that prison cell below the castle's foundations, being confronted by Han's merciless Sun-dao. The man had winnowed his soul without hesitation or mercy.

And was that a part of your plan too, Hettie?

No doubt about it, his unkempt appearance was making an impression. On the dais the privy council frowned, to a man. The gathered ambassadors inched backwards in case his dirt was contagious.

But Rhian just waited for him to reach her on the dais. Magnificent in black brocade and those savagely carved rubies, she looked pale and exhausted and in quite a lot of pain. Was he the only one here who could see that? In their crowded weeks together he'd come to know her so well.

"Mister Jones," she said, as he reached the foot of the dais and stopped. "It seems you have been interrupted."

He bowed. "I was gardening . . . Your Majesty."

"Yes. I thought you might've been." She nodded at the dried pulp on his trousers. "Does the crown owe you a new tomato plant?"

Her humour was brittle, with anger lingering beneath it. Oh, if only they weren't in front of an audience. If only they were on the road again, in the peddler's wagon, and he could speak to her plainly, man to woman. Friend to friend. They had been friends, hadn't they?

"Majesty, Commander Idson said you wanted me."

Rhian nodded. "Yes."

He let his gaze slide sideways to Helfred. Very, very slightly Ethrea's new prolate nodded, his eyes narrowing. Dexterity read the message without difficulty. *This is important. Your hurt feelings can wait.*

One of the ambassadors, Arbenian from the gruff bearhide look of him, pushed forward. "You are the toymaker she says is touched by your God?"

She says. Well, here was a rude fellow and no mistake. Dexterity felt his spine stiffen. All very well for him to be at odds with Rhian. She was his queen and something more, besides. But what right did this *foreigner* have to be rude to Rhian under her own roof?

"Sir? I don't believe we've been introduced."

The man's eyes widened. "What?"

"Ambassador Gutten, this is Mister Dexterity Jones, House Havrell's one-time royal toymaker," said Rhian. There was the faintest breath of amusement in her voice. "Mister Jones, you are presented to His Excellency the Arbenian Ambassador. You may address him as Sere Gutten."

It came as a surprise to discover there was something . . . *liberating* . . . in having fallen so low. Dexterity shoved his dirty hands in his pockets and looked Gutten up and down, much as Idson had surveyed him in his garden. "Yes, Sere Gutten," he said, as though the Arbenian was a shopkeeper. "There was a time, in the recent past, when I was touched by the grace of God."

Another of the ambassadors stepped forward. Dexterity looked up and up into the man's broad, bearded face. His feet tried to step his body backwards but he over-ruled them. He had no intention of revealing weakness in front of Rhian. It was important that she not think him awestruck or in any way malleable.

My life's my own again and that's how it's going to stay.

"Jones?" The giant tipped his head to one side. "Voolksyn."

Huge, bald and bearded? Dressed in sealskin? This had to be the ambassador from Harbisland. Ursa said she stitched up more Harbisland sailors than any other kind. They were always finding their way into trouble. Certainly this enormous fellow was a sight to strike fear in the heart of an ordinary man.

He nodded, cautiously. "Ambassador Voolksyn."

"Her Majesty says your God speaks to you in dreams."

"Ah . . . well, yes," he replied, still cautious. "I've had some dreams, it's true." He looked at the rest of the ambassadors, searching for answers and finding none. Lastly he looked again at Rhian. "Is that why I'm here? Because I don't dream any more."

Which wasn't a lie. The last time he saw Hettie he'd been wide awake.

Rhian sat so still on her throne she might have been a carved statue. "They want to know what you know of Mijak," she said. Her voice was cool and unexcited. Whatever she was feeling was hidden deep within. "I want you to tell them about Garabatsas. I want you to tell them what Hettie's told you."

He stared at Zandakar, whose face also looked carved. The warrior wasn't in chains but the soldiers stood so close around him he might as well have been. Although six Ethrean soldiers were no match for Zandakar. If he wanted them dead they'd be dead by his bare hands. So why was he letting himself remain a prisoner? Did he think he owed Rhian his presence, unprotesting?

Perhaps he does, but I don't. I don't owe her anything.

Resentment bubbled again. He'd been sent away, he'd been put aside like a broken doll. Well then, let him *stay* put aside! People weren't puppets, they weren't to be played with like toys of wood and string and paint. He glared at Rhian, letting her see his resentment, not caring he showed an impolite face to the world.

"Dexterity . . ." Rhian almost sighed. The effort it cost her to remain upright and unaffected was palpable, at least to him. "Some of the ambassadors believe I have concocted the threat of Mijak with the aid of Emperor Han and Zandakar, so Ethrea and the empire of Tzhung-tzhungchai might dominate the world."

What? "But that's ridiculous," he said, turning. "Her Majesty has concocted nothing. Mijak is real. Its threat is real. You have living proof of it, there." He pointed to Zandakar. "Ask *him* what he knows. What he's seen." *What he's done. But I won't tell them. If they learn the half of it they'll bay for his life, and I'll not have Zandakar's blood on my hands.*

"As we have said already to your queen, one man is not a nation," said the ambassador from Keldrave. He needed no introduction, not with his ears weighed down with wiferings. "Saying Mijak is real, do words make it so? We have not heard of this place until today."

"Mijak has been sleeping for a very long time," he retorted. "Now it's woken up, which is a great pity."

"You are a little man," said another ambassador. Everything about him said he represented Slynt. "Little men want big men to raise them high." He jerked his chin at Emperor Han, so quiet while the ballroom hummed with tension. "What does Tzhung-tzhungchai promise to little men to say the things its emperor and your queen want said?"

"Tzhung-tzhungchai promised me *nothing*!" he snapped. "And even if they did offer me something I wouldn't take it. I don't like Tzhung-tzhungchai. Until the emperor came I was happy enough. Ethrea's queen trusted me and knew I would never hurt her, at least not on purpose, but Emperor Han changed that. He barged in where he wasn't wanted, him and his witch-men. Just because they'd learned a *little* of Mijak—" He held up his thumb and forefinger, pinched close. "They'd learned *this* much, no more, but they're so arrogant they thought they knew more than me. And they *didn't*."

Voolksyn narrowed his eyes. "You knew of Mijak and did not tell your queen?"

"It wasn't *time*!" he said, despairing. "Hettie said I had to keep it secret. Rhian had to be made safe on her throne first."

"Hettie?" said Voolksyn.

Dexterity pressed a hand to his forehead. *Oh dear,*

oh dear. Whyever did I come? "My wife. She died twenty years ago. She brings me messages from God. I know it sounds absurd, but I'm afraid I can't help that. Hettie showed me the destruction of Garabatsas. It was a small township in Sharvay." He looked around at the ambassadors' skeptical faces. "You must've heard of Sharvay. Even *I've* heard of Sharvay."

They nodded reluctantly. Gutten growled. "What do we care of Sharvay?"

He nearly stamped his foot. "We care because the warriors of Mijak destroyed it! As they have destroyed scores of towns and cities, as they will destroy Ethrea and all your lands if they're not stopped. It's true. I *saw* it," he added as the ambassadors glanced at each other, unconvinced. "All those poor people . . ." His voice caught in his throat. The horror of Garabatsas was never far away. "They had no hope against the warriors of Mijak. They burned alive. *All of them.* And *we* shall burn too, because the Empress of Mijak wants to conquer the world for her dreadful god. She *will* conquer the world, she and her son. If we don't work together they will. I promise."

"You promise?" said Gutten. His face was ugly with derision. "Little man? Little toymaking man?"

Dexterity stepped back a pace, then turned to stare at Rhian. "You sent for me so they could *sneer?*"

"No," she replied. The stitched cut in her cheek looked swollen. Painful. Beneath her careful mask of indifferent self-control he could see how she was struggling. "I sent for you because I need an honest man to speak for me."

Well, that was nice. A pity she hadn't remembered his honesty before she gave him to Sun-dao . . .

But that was an argument for another time.

He turned back to the ambassadors. "My lords, you'd be well advised to heed my words. I have spoken the truth here. Ethrea concocts no nefarious plans with the Tzhung, or with Mijak. Ethrea seeks to save you. *I seek* to save you, and so does Queen Rhian."

"We should believe you?" said one of the ambassadors who'd been silent till then. From Dev'karesh? He looked pale enough and he stank of cloves. That was a Dev'kareshi custom, one Ursa said gave them cankers of the mouth.

"Yes," he said, suddenly wary. "You should."

The ambassador's eyes were wide and malignant. "Burn with a miracle, to show you do not lie. Burn and we will consider Mijak and gods of blood and whether Tzhung-tzhungchai can be trusted."

He stared at the ambassador, aghast. "Just like that? I can't. I can't pull a miracle out of my pocket like a kerchief!"

More muttering, ugly now, as the trading nations' ambassadors glared. Dexterity folded his arms, forcing himself not to cringe beneath the weight of their suspicion. He looked at Emperor Han. Emperor Han looked back. Whatever he was thinking and feeling he kept locked behind his smooth amber face.

"This Jones does not burn," said Gutten, still sneering. "There is no danger. It is all lies, to break charter. Lies to destroy the trading nations."

"*That's not true!*" said Rhian, and stood. "Dexterity's miracles weren't lies! His visions – the people he healed – the child he brought back from death – these things are not *lies*, Gutten!"

"I did not see them," said Gutten, his lip curling.

"I saw them! The king saw them! God's Prolate in Ethrea saw them!" Rhian retorted. "Am I lying, Ambassador? Are these good men of my council lying? Have I suborned them? Why would I do that? Ethrea is my sacred trust. Would I risk it, would I betray every man, woman and child in my kingdom to make an alliance with Tzhung-tzhungchai?"

Gutten looked her up and down. "Yes."

"Why? Because *you* would?"

"I make no alliance with Tzhung-tzhungchai!" snarled Gutten. "I honour the treaties, I honour the charter!" He swept his arm round in a fierce arc, taking in everyone but Emperor Han and his ambassador. "*We* honour, but *you* do not! You wheedle, you plot, you want to steal what is ours!"

"*That* is the lie!" Rhian cried, and would have leapt from the dais except the king took her arm. She snatched herself free of him, searing him with a look. "You are swift to smear me, Gutten. You are quick to point an accusing finger, but I see you in corners with Voolksyn of Harbisland. What are *you* plotting? What do *your* whispers mean? Perhaps our treaties and charters are in danger from *you*!"

"Harbisland plots nothing with Arbenia!" said Voolksyn, his face darkening with displeasure.

"How do I know that?" Rhian demanded. "Must I trust your word when you won't trust mine? How am I to trust *any* of you when you're so quick to think the worst of *me*?"

Uproar then, as the ambassadors shouted and protested and turned on each other to vilify or seek support. Only Han and his ambassador kept apart, their expressions wary. Caught unprotected in the storm, Dexterity watched as Idson and his soldiers stepped forward, prepared to leave Zandakar alone. And Zandakar . . . he stood taut, ready to kill anyone who dared raise a hand to Rhian.

"Enough! *Enough*!" Rhian shouted. "My lord ambassadors, control yourselves!"

But they ignored her.

Dexterity closed his eyes. He could hear the roaring flames of Garabatsas, hear the screams and the wailing and the warriors' terrible chant. *Chalava! Chalava! Chalava zho*! Even with his eyes closed he could see the burning people, see the buildings fly apart in flames as the warrior Dmitrak, Zandakar's brother, used his dreadful gauntlet of power to reduce the township to rubble.

"Stop it," he muttered, feeling his fingers clench to fists. "Stop it. Stop it. Stop it. *Stop it*!"

As he shouted he raised his fists above his head, pain and despair and a righteous anger igniting him.

He opened his eyes, and saw he was on fire.

Oh, Hettie.

The last time he'd been a prisoner of this mystifying power, Marlan had died for touching him. How he'd screamed and screamed inside his head, screamed at Marlan *stay back, don't touch me* . . . but Marlan was never a man for listening and so he'd burned and died.

Not again, Hettie. Don't make me kill again.

In the castle's Grand Ballroom the ambassadors stumbled to a choking silence. Even Gutten of Arbenia stared, abruptly speechless.

To his great relief, this time his wits didn't desert

him as he burned. He knew who he was, and where he was, and most importantly, what he must do.

Turning his back on the dumbstruck ambassadors, he walked to Rhian on her dais.

"You're hurt, Majesty," he said. "Let me heal you."

"Please," she replied, tears glinting, and stepped down to join him on the parquetry floor.

He cupped his palm to her stitched cheek. Heat surged through him, and she gasped as her wound burned bright as a brand for one heartbeat, two heartbeats. Then it faded, Ursa's neat stitches consumed, and all that remained was her whole, healed face.

Rhian stepped back, unsteady on her feet. Her fingers came up to touch her mended flesh. "Thank you, Dexterity," she whispered.

"It's God's doing, not mine."

"And we offer him our thanks," said Helfred loudly, from the dais. "And thank you too. God bless you, Mister Jones."

Bless Hettie, more like. She'd got him mixed up in this again. Knowing he didn't want it. Knowing he'd rather be at home, weeding his tomatoes . . .

"Don't mention it, Prolate."

As suddenly as they ignited, the flames wreathing Dexterity extinguished. Relieved, and yet oddly disappointed – *Have I done enough? Can I go home now?* – he turned to see how the ambassadors reacted to his miracle.

Only Lai was unperturbed. Like his master, Emperor Han, he seemed undismayed by miracles.

The rest of the ambassadors were *most* dismayed.

To a man they were chalky-white, and sweating. Forgetting the treacherous cross-currents of their alliances and enmities, they huddled together like hens facing a fox.

Well, that's something, Hettie. At least it appears they're listening now.

"My lords, you are foolish, every one of you," he told them severely. "Rich men grown fat and complacent in the world you've created. Well, that world stands on the brink of destruction." He pointed at Zandakar. "His people are coming to wrest it from you, to bend it and break it and remake it in their cruel image. Together, God willing, we can stop them. But only if we take heed of the warnings God has sent us!"

Gutten, the boldest hen, folded his arms. Chalky-white, yes, and slicked with sweat like the others . . . but he wasn't just afraid. Bone-deep suspicion warred with his fear. He pointed at Zandakar.

"Warnings from him? Why should we believe them? You say we are complacent. You think we are *stupid*. You say he comes from Mijak but *you have no proof*."

"*Proof?*" Dexterity stared at him, stunned with disbelief. Then he lifted his healing hands and held them out. "You asked for a miracle, and God provided one. What more proof do you *need*, Sere Gutten?"

Gutten looked to the shadows, where Emperor Han stood. "The sorcery of Tzhung-tzhungchai is legend."

"*Sorcery?*" he said, almost spluttering in his outrage. "It wasn't sorcery, and it wasn't Tzhung-tzhungchai, either!"

Emperor Han came forth from his shadows. "The only sorcery here, Gutten, is the spell of lies you weave with your busy tongue."

"Mine?" Gutten's chalky-white face burned red. "The lies are *yours*. Han of Tzhung-tzhungchai is an *emperor* of lies!"

"Enough!" said Rhian. "*Both* of you, enough! I'll not have God insulted in this castle."

Han looked at her, so haughty. "You call what has happened in Ethrea the work of God. My people call it the will of the wind. The wind whispered of blood-soaked Mijak in my ear. The wind—"

"Does not blow in my court or my kingdom," said Rhian curtly, and fixed him with a brilliant blue stare. "It has blown you to us, Emperor Han, and I am grateful for your support, but this is Ethrea . . . and *I* am ruler here." She swept the gathered ambassadors with her bleak gaze. "And as Ethrea's ruler I tell you, gentlemen, there is *no* sorcery conducted in my name or for my benefit. Not by the Tzhung, not by any nation under the sun. And while I am grateful to Tzhung's emperor, you can believe that any country that fights with me against Mijak will *also* receive my heartfelt thanks. You have my word as queen, I'll be playing no favourites."

Brooding, Voolksyn of Harbisland tugged at his beard. "You show us a burning man. You show us a prince of Mijak. I cannot say it is enough for my slainta."

"Then what *is* enough?" Rhian demanded. "Your people murdered by Mijak? Your streets running with their blood?" She closed the distance between them and stared up into Voolksyn's shuttered eyes. "Are you willing to gamble I'm wrong, Ambassador? You have family in Harbisland. Are you willing to gamble *them*?"

Voolksyn bared his teeth in a snarling smile. "To reach Harbisland, first Mijak must overrun Ethrea."

She smiled back at him, just as fiercely, and punched her fist lightly against his spotted sealskin chest. "*Exactly*. Which is why you must help me." She looked around. "Why *all* of you must help me."

Gutten spat on the beautiful parquetry floor. "You think to lead the trading nations to war? You? A girl?"

"Not a girl," said Rhian. "A queen who doesn't hesitate to kill for her crown. Don't forget that, Sere Gutten. Besides, you might not all be treated with each other, but you *are* all treated with Ethrea. It's a place to start. A way to find common ground. Surely you can agree with that?"

"Heh," said Voolksyn. Was he, at least, convinced? It was impossible to say. "When does Mijak come in its warships?"

"I don't know," said Rhian. "But if I'm right and Icthia has already fallen, then surely our time is running out."

"Harbisland and Arbenia are treated beyond the Ethrean charter," said Voolksyn, turning to Gutten. "What my slainta does, your count considers."

"And you say your slainta will consider *this?*" said Gutten, disbelieving.

Voolksyn shrugged. "I say I will tell him what Queen Rhian says."

"And you'll ask him for ships to sail against Mijak?" said Rhian. "You'll ask him to agree to an Ethrean army?"

"I will ask," said Voolksyn.

"And the rest of you?" Rhian demanded of the other ambassadors. "Will you make the same requests of *your* rulers?"

Silence like a knife-edge, sharp and deadly. Dexterity watched as the ambassadors from the lesser trading nations looked to Gutten. It seemed they were too timid to do anything but follow Arbenia's lead.

God save us, Hettie. Their cowardice will kill us all.

"Sere Gutten," said Rhian, gentling her voice. Behind her softness, Dexterity thought she was raging. "Will you at least consider my request?"

"I will consider it," Gutten said at last, grudging. "But do not hold your hopes for Arbenia. My count is not ordered by Tzhung-tzhungchai, or a queen who is ordered by the Tzhung in secret."

A muscle leapt along Rhian's jaw. "I assure you of this, Ambassador. When you hear my voice, you hear *only* my voice. I am no pupper, I am a sovereign queen. And let me remind you of this, also, Sere Gutten. Ethrea stands as a bridge between every trading nation in the world. Any nation seeking to undermine it must surely do so at its peril. Be certain your count understands *that*, sir."

She was threatening him, and Gutten knew it. His florid face darkened and his brows pulled low in a scowl. "Brave words," he growled. "My count will be interested to hear them."

"And I will be interested to hear his reply," said

Rhian, so sweetly. Turning from Gutten, she considered the other ambassadors. "Gentlemen, I thank you for your attendance today. Doubtless you'll wish to convey our discussion to your rulers. Please do so, as swiftly as you can contrive. Mijak breathes down all of our necks."

As the ballroom emptied of Emperor Han and the ambassadors, all mired in their private thoughts, Rhian turned to Idson. "Commander, you and your soldiers escort Zandakar to his apartments. Zandakar—"

Zandakar stirred. "*Zho?*"

"Meet me in the tiltyard one hour before sunset. Now that Mister Jones has healed me, I'm ready to dance."

Zandakar's answering smile was brief. "*Zho*," he said again, and left with the soldiers.

Dexterity looked at Rhian. "Majesty, might I also be excused? I've gardening to finish and—"

"In a moment," she replied, and considered her privy council. "My lords, I think that went as well as we could hope for."

King Alasdair nodded. "I was surprised by Voolksyn's support."

"He's certainly a better prospect than Gutten," said Duke Rudi. "That man is trouble."

Rhian shrugged. "They're all trouble, Rudi, in their own ways."

"Even Emperor Han?" said Helfred, fingering his prayer beads.

Dexterity watched Rhian and the king exchange glances. "Especially Han," she replied.

"So all we can do now is wait and pray," said

Duke Ludo. "While their masters make up their minds to help us, or not."

"Wait, and pray, and take care of domestic matters," said Rhian. "My lords, you know what's to be done. See it done swiftly, before wider events overwhelm us."

The privy council murmured acknowledgement of her command. Ven'Cedwin at his little table gathered together all his scribbled parchments and the ballroom emptied completely. As they passed Dexterity, the king and Helfred spared him swift, difficult smiles.

And then he and Rhian faced each other, alone. The silence stretched on and on . . . full of raw and painful memories.

Rhian broke first. Arms folded, chin tilted, she looked down her nose at him. "I was angry, Dexterity."

He snorted. "I noticed, Rhian."

"Can you blame me? You *lied* to me, you—"

"Did as Hettie asked. How can you complain when that put you on your throne?" He felt the air hitch in his throat as his deepest outrage escaped him. "You gave me to Sun-dao! *A witch-man*!"

Rhian paled, then tilted her chin higher as colour flooded back into her cheeks. "If he hurt you, Mister Jones, I am truly sorry. But I had to be sure."

He folded his own arms and matched her stare for stare. "That I hadn't betrayed you? And are you? Are you quite convinced, now, that I never meant you harm?"

"Oh, Dexterity," Rhian whispered, and suddenly she was a girl again. The haughty queen had disappeared. "Of course I am. I always was, I just – I was rattled, I was overwhelmed. I'm sorry. I'm *sorry*. I was a fool to doubt you. And I *never* wanted to cause you pain."

A blind man could see her contrition was genuine. Dexterity felt the stinging hurt ease. Let his arms slowly unfold. "Yes, well," he muttered. "I doubt you've been sleeping on a bed of roses, either."

She managed an unsteady laugh. "Bed of thorns, more like. Dexterity—" She took a step closer. "Can we put this behind us? Will you stay, and be my friend again? This fight isn't over. I – I need you to stay."

He swallowed a sigh. *Oh, Hettie. Hettie. You won't let me rest, will you?* With a smile, he nodded.

"Of course I'll stay, Majesty. Where else would I go?"

PART TWO

CHAPTER TWELVE

Dining with Hekat in her palace's dayroom, Vortka picked up his cracked mutton bone and noisily sucked the marrow from it. The glutinous jelly, well-flavoured with spices, slid easily down his throat – but pleasure was fleeting.

Hekat's cooling meal remained untouched.

Leaning over to her plate he selected a choice piece of sauced meat with his bare fingers and held it out. "Eat, Hekat. You must eat."

Her gaze flickered over him like a blue flame. "Am I hungry, Vortka? I think I am not."

"Do I care, Hekat?" he retorted. "I think I do not."

Irritated amusement chased across her face. "Tcha, you are a bold man, you give your empress orders." She snatched the dripping mutton from him and pushed it between her teeth. Chewed. Swallowed. Her throat worked to get the soft meat into her belly. "You think I will not smite a bold man? I think you are wrong."

He answered her with another piece of mutton. "Smiting takes strength, Hekat. Eat more, you will have strength."

She took the meat from his fingers with her teeth this time, she bit him too and smiled to hear him cry out. "I am strong, Vortka high godspeaker," she said, capturing smears of sauce with her fingertips. "I save my appetite for the god."

He watched her suck clean her skin, remembering the she-brat in Et-Nogolor, so haughty, so self-possessed, who had given him food from her own meagre bowl. He remembered the confusion in her startling eyes, she did not know why she gave her food to a slave.

Her first time generous, she has rarely been generous since.

"The god desires its empress healthy," he said, returning to his own plate. Warm flatbread sat on a plate between them. He selected a piece and sopped up his meat's spicy sauce. "Rest and good food, the god desires you glut yourself with both, Hekat. The journey to Ethrea will be arduous, will you be weak when we see that island?"

She glowered at him from beneath lowered lashes. "I do not wonder if I will be weak, Vortka, I wonder if we will ever see it."

"We will see it," he replied. "In the god's eye, in the god's time, Mijak will see the island of Ethrea."

"Tcha." She pulled her burdened plate closer and ate savagely, tearing at the meat as though it was that island. "The god's time is slow, Vortka. How many more highsuns must I wait before the trade winds come?"

"As many as please the god, Hekat. Do you need me to tell you that?"

"*No,*" she muttered, with a poisonous look.

He poured more wine for her and held out the goblet. With a grunt she accepted it. He watched her drink deeply, swiftly. She drank more these days, he saw that but said nothing. Icthia's date wine soothed the pains that lived inside her, it made his crystal healing of her easier to bear. He did not speak of her drinking, she would strike him if he dared. If she drank too much he would speak then, let her strike him as she liked.

Slaves entered the dayroom with platters of fruit, sweet melons and tart pomegranates and honey-soaked dates. They took the emptied plates away with them, Hekat paid no attention. She stared through the open balcony doors to the harbour where the boats of Mijak's warhost danced on the water in patterns like *hotas*. Her warriors grew more skilled every highsun, boats were feared no longer, the water was no enemy to Mijak.

Perhaps this is why the god has kept the trade winds from us. Hekat is impatient, she would lead her warhost into the world and the warhost would follow for love and fear of her. But if the warhost is drowned because it is not yet ready, how then can it serve the god? It cannot. Aieee, the god see me. It knows what to do.

"Vortka," said Hekat, "how do your godspeakers progress with the warhost's horses?"

It was part of her grand plan, that her warriors must have their horses when they reached the island Ethrea and every land beyond it. How would they be warriors of Mijak if they walked on foot? But horses could not swim to Ethrea, they could not gallop across the water, they must travel with the warriors in the warhost's boats.

Captured slaves had told them how horses on boats could not be ridden after, not for many highsuns. The slaves had told them how horses could die on boats, cooped up below the timber decks, crushed into small stalls with nowhere to run. Horses were animals that died easily with nerves, what Mijaki did not know that, when horses were their lives?

Do something, Vortka, Hekat had said. *You are high godspeaker, you are a healer with your crystal. Find the way to heal a horse.*

So he and his godspeakers prayed and worked to satisfy Hekat. They were not altogether successful, many horses still died from the crystal. Some godspeakers had died, he had not told her that.

"It is a difficult task you have set, Hekat," he said.

She glared. "Do I care? I think I do not. *Give me horses for the warhost.* Will my warriors be slaves on their feet in Ethrea?"

He sighed. "Healing is not a simple thing, Hekat."

"You are not healing, Vortka. The horses are not sick. I think you must try harder."

"Harder than dying, Hekat?" He slapped his hand to the table. "*Tcha!*"

She sat straighter upon her cushioned divan, fingers drifting to curl about her snakeblade. "Who is dying? What do you keep from me?"

Aieee, the god see him, he had not meant to say it. She could goad him to hot words like no other in his life. "You need not worry, it is godspeaker business."

"*Vortka!*" It was two fingers before lowsun, that time when her strength was ebbed closest to its dregs. She did not think of that, she leapt to her feet like Hekat the knife-dancer, she clenched her fist in his face, then struck him on the cheek. "You dare to say this? You dare keep secrets from *me*?"

In her rage she was not weary, in her rage she was the Hekat who slew the warlord Bajadek. She snatched at her scorpion amulet, she shook it before his wary eyes. Her silver godbells shouted her anger.

"Shall the god task you, Vortka? Shall this scorpion sting your godspark for your sins?"

Another sharp memory: Abajai and Yagji, those greedy traders, stung to death by the god.

I grow older, I remember things, the past returns to plague me.

He stood to meet her fury. "Does the god need your amulet to task me, empress? I think it does not." His fingers drummed the scorpion pectoral clasping his chest then closed hard around hers. The scorpion amulet was cold, the god was not woken. "I breathe by the god's desire, I die when it decrees." He laid his hand against her scarred cheek and smiled. "Godspeakers dying is godspeakers' business."

She did not want to be moved by his hand on her face, she resented all human touching, all gestures of warmth. Her cold eyes showed him her resentment, showed him how she fought not to be moved by his touch. It made his heart ache.

Hekat, Hekat, will you die if I touch you? I am Vortka, you are safe with me.

She stepped back. "Why do your godspeakers die, Vortka? What have you done wrong?"

"Nothing," he told her. "I have told you already, what you ask for is difficult."

"The god asks for this," she said, her eyes slitted. "The god asks, you obey."

Aieee, the god see him. When would she listen? "Hekat, if the warhost's horses are to survive in the boats, if they are to leap strong and angry from the boats to dry land, then my godspeakers and I must *change* them from within. Do you think this is simple?"

"I think this is what the god desires you to do!"

"And I strive to do it, Hekat. But I am a man, I am only flesh and blood. The god's power is mighty, when it thunders in the blood a man's bones might melt. A godspeaker might melt, Hekat. I might melt."

"Tcha! This cannot be a concern to you, Vortka. You are *high* godspeaker."

Now he smiled at her. "And still I am a man."

"A *stupid* man," she muttered, temper easing at last. "I am the god's empress, how can I help you if you do not tell me what you do?"

How can you help me when you cannot help yourself? But he kept that thought close, frail or not she would strike him to the ground if he spoke those terrible words aloud.

"I do not think there is a way for you to help me," he said carefully. "You are a warrior, you are not a healer. This is godspeaker business."

Hekat's blue eyes widened. "And I breathe for the god." She snatched her snakeblade from her hip and slashed it through her forearm. "I *bleed* for the god. When you could not break that desert, Vortka, *I* broke it. I conquered the scorpion pit. I defeated Nagarak. I gave the god two warlords, two hammers for its fist. *I am Hekat, Empress of Mijak.* The *world* is my business, I give the world to the god."

Her blood was dripping to the blue marble floor. The cut in her arm must hurt her, she did not show her pain. Vortka sighed. "You think the god wants this, Hekat? I think it does not."

"The god wants Mijak in Ethrea, Vortka, it wants Mijak in Keldrave, in Barbruish, in Haisun. It wants Mijak in Arbenia and in Harbisland and Tzhung-tzhungchai. Where there are men in the world the god wants them kneeling before it. Godposts on every street, godhouses on every hill. The valleys must run with blood until the god is everywhere."

"But not *your* blood!" he retorted. He slid his healing crystal from its pouch, took hold of her wrist and tugged her to him. "Stupid Hekat, do you need to convince *me* you are chosen by the god? I think you do not. I think I knew it before you did."

"Tcha," she said, scornful, but did not pull away.

The god's power filled him as he healed the wound in her flesh. She still held her snakeblade, he had no fear of that. She might strike him, she might scourge him with her tongue, she would never touch him with her snakeblade. He belonged to the god as much as she, never would she tempt its smiting by harming him.

When she was whole again she looked up, grudgingly thankful. "Be as skilful with the horses, Vortka, and the god will be pleased."

"The god is already pleased," he said. "It sees how I am working for it and knows I am obedient."

"And it knows Hekat can do things that Vortka cannot," she replied, pushing her snakeblade into its sheath. "You and your godspeakers need help to change the horses. You need more power, I know where power lies."

He felt his skin chill to coldness. "No, Hekat. We need slaves as much as warriors and godspeakers."

She grimaced. "Not old ones. Not crippled ones. Not slaves that spread disease. Those slaves have one purpose, to give their blood to the god."

"Hekat . . ." He turned away from her and walked to the balcony, let the clean ocean air whip his godbells into song. "That power is unclean."

"Unclean? You can say so? Vortka, you are stupid. That power broke the desert!"

And I think it broke you, too. Ever since those thousands of dead slaves, dead by your hand, you have been different, as though something within you drowned in those wet red sands.

Another thought he must keep to himself. He had tried and tried, she would not listen when he counselled caution in this.

I think I would rather that desert had defeated us, we crossed that desert and left something precious behind.

"The god has said no human blood for sacrifice."

"No human blood for the trade winds," Hekat retorted. "I have obeyed, I do not summon the trade winds. I wait and I wait, while the trade winds do not come. This blood is for the horses, the god does not say no to that."

Vortka ground his teeth. Hekat made words a game, she made them say what she desired. If he argued with her she would close her heart to him.

I need her heart open or else I cannot help.

Hekat joined him on the balcony and tugged him round to face her. Her fingers tapped lightly on his cheek. "I am the god's chosen, I know what you need.

Come. We will walk to the slave pens, I will give you hot blood and with its power you will change the warhost's horses."

"Walk?" He shook his head. "Hekat—"

"Tcha!" she said, frowning. "I have eaten meat and fruit, I am strong for the god."

He did not argue this either, she would never listen. She stood defiant before him, dressed in an old linen training tunic, pretending she was still the Hekat who danced with her snakeblade. It was true, she did dance, some newsuns here and there, when she was not quite so frail.

But you are not invincible, Hekat. Aieee, god, help me to help her see it.

Together they walked from her small palace into the hot and blinding sun.

The slave pens were down at the harbour. Before Jatharuj fell to Mijak, they were pens for livestock. Before Mijak, the people of Jatharuj had bred goats with long curly coats, the hair was shorn for wool and sold to other godless nations and the goats were sold too. Not any more. Those goats belonged to the godhouse now, they birthed more goats for sacrifice, not wool, and the pens by the harbour held discarded human slaves.

The streets of Jatharuj were almost empty. Jatharuj slept in this hot time before lowsun, and woke to bustling and business as dusk cooled the air. There were godspeakers seeing to the god's wants, collecting coins and lesser offerings from the godbowls, making certain slaves who had permission to be outdoors did not attempt a blasphemy or dally in gossip. Three thousand Mijakis from Et-Raklion had made the long journey to Jatharuj. It was their city now, the Icthians who had owned it were dead or made slaves. Jatharuj was all Mijak, it was too important a place to be anything else. Other capitulated cities had been permitted to live in the god's eye, but not Jatharuj. Nearly all of its houses were made barracks for the warhost, most of its resources were given over to Mijak's warriors.

So many warriors, they would conquer the world.

The slaves who did walk the streets fell to the ground as Hekat approached, their scarlet godbraids bright in the sun. If they did not they were nailed to a godpost, it had only taken a handful of nailings for the slaves of Jatharuj to understand their place. The walking godspeakers did not fall to the ground, they bowed to their empress and their high godspeaker. They did not speak unless spoken to first.

Hekat was in no mood for speaking.

On the wide harbour the warhost continued to dance *hotas* with its boats. Walking with Hekat, aware of her every sharp breath, every hitch in her stride, Vortka rested his gaze upon them and marvelled at the skill.

"Dmitrak trains the warhost well," he said. "He does not let them sit idle, he does not say 'this is enough'. Look at the warships dancing, Hekat. Who would think your warriors had so lately learned to sail?"

She grunted. "Dmitrak does what he is told to do."

"He serves the god, he is fierce in his service. If you do not acknowledge that you make him weak before his warriors, Hekat."

"*My* warriors," she said, glaring sideways. "The

warhost is mine, it has been mine since Raklion stumbled. If I told it to kill him, Dmitrak would be dead."

Aieee, god, it was true. They obeyed Dmitrak, it was their blood and breath to obey, but it was Hekat they screamed for when she rallied them to war.

"He is a good warlord."

Another sideways look. "You do not love Dmitrak, why do you pour honey on him? Do you think he will be sweet to me with your honeyed words?"

"I think he is your warlord, empress."

Her face tightened, the old scars twisting. "He is Nagarak's spawn. He is nothing of mine."

They had reached the harbour and its closed city gates. The warriors on guard there bowed to their high godspeaker, then pressed their fists to their chests, smiling to see their mighty empress.

"The god sees you, Empress Hekat," the taller woman said. "The god sees you in its conquering eye."

"It sees you also, Nedajik," said Hekat. She nodded at the other guard. "It sees you, Yogili."

"It sees you, Empress Hekat," said the shorter, younger guard. "How do we serve you?"

Hekat's teeth bared. "You stand aside. The god sends us to make sacrifice."

The guard Nedajik frowned. "Sacrifice, Empress?"

"Are you stupid?" said Hekat, staring. "Sacrifice, Nedajik. Blood for the god."

Flinching, the guard Nedajik shook her head. Silver godbells sounded her dismay. "Empress, there is no blood here."

"There is blood. There are slaves, discarded for age

and other reasons. You stand aside, Nedajik, or Vortka high godspeaker will give you a slave braid."

Vortka watched the warriors exchange anguished glances. Touching his fingertips to Hekat's arm, he met her sharp look calmly. Then he turned to the guards.

"What has happened to the blood?"

"It is spilled, Vortka high godspeaker," the guard Yogili whispered.

"*Spilled*?" Hekat seized the warrior's face between her fingers. "How is it spilled? I am the empress, *I* spill blood in Mijak. *Speak*!"

"Dmitrak warlord," whispered Yogili. "He trains his warriors, he says blood must be spilled for a blade to stay sharp."

Vortka closed his eyes briefly. *Dmitrak, stupid boy, do you seek confrontation? Did your mother not tell you never again take her slaves without asking?* He could feel his heart pound behind his scorpion pectoral.

"Dmitrak warlord," said Hekat. Her voice was stony. Grating. She released her cruel hold of the warrior's face. "You Nedajik, you Yogili. Did your snake-blades drink the blood of these slaves?"

Yogili shook her head. "No, Empress. Dmitrak warlord ordered the shell-leaders to draw lots, only those warriors in the god's eye drank the slaves' blood."

Pressing her fist to her chest again, Nedajik bowed. "Empress, the warriors chosen did not know the slaves were yours." It was the closest she would tread to laying blame at Dmitrak's feet.

"Tcha!" spat Hekat. "*All* slaves are mine!" And

then she relented, and Vortka relaxed. She would not smite her warriors, she knew they were not to blame for this. He felt a wicked sense of relief. If the useless slaves were dead already, Hekat could not stain herself by spilling their blood.

"Stand aside," said Hekat, so frail, so furious. "I will see for myself what the warlord has done."

Vortka followed her as she discarded her warrior guards and walked more quickly than was wise to the pens put aside for those old sick slaves who must be kept separate.

They were empty.

Breathing harshly, Hekat looked at the pens where the slaves should be. Vortka looked too and read the story of that place. Shackles were there, abandoned like dead snakes. Emptied waste troughs were there, and troughs for the slaves' food. The salt breeze was fresh, only a faint hint of human remained where the slaves had been. Other slaves had cleaned away their memories, doubtless glad for the task. Better to clean than be cleaned up after.

"Dmitrak has done this to anger me, Vortka," said Hekat, her jaw clenched. "He is Nagarak's son, he seeks to slay me with anger."

She was so harsh, she would not be soft with this son. "Hekat, Dmitrak is the warlord. He trains his warhost as he sees fit. When you were warlord you gave your warriors slaves and criminals for their snakeblades to drink, why should Dmitrak believe this is denied him?"

"He should believe because I told him it was so! The last time he killed slaves without my permission, I told him."

He sighed. "Nearly a fat godmoon has passed since then."

"Does that matter, Vortka? I think it does not," said Hekat, stabbing him with a hot blue glare. "If I did not spend my time in that palace, away from the warhost, resting by your want, *this would not have happened*. I spend my time in that palace, the world does not see my face. Dmitrak does not see my shadow, he forgets I exist. *I exist, Vortka*. And I have rested in that palace long enough. Jatharuj is not the world. The god desires the world and I will deliver it."

Aieee, god, the iron in her voice. Vortka felt her words like fisted blows. "Yes, you will, Empress, when the time is ripe."

"Ripe?" She laughed, a bitter sound. "Vortka, it is rotten. And we will rot with it if we stay here another godmoon."

Aieee, the god see him. *The trade winds again. Can she not think of anything else?* "We will stay here as long as the god desires our staying."

"The god?" She clenched a fist. "Are we penned in this harbour like slaves by the god? I do not think so. I think we are penned in Jatharuj by demons. They must be broken. This is the desert again, Vortka, can you not see it?"

"The god has not said so."

She stared. "It has said so to me. And it looks to *me* to break these demons. You did not break those demons in the sand, I broke them." She pointed at the harbour before them, where the warhost's boats no longer danced but turned at last towards the shore.

"The ocean beyond the harbour, that is another desert. It is a desert of water and I must break it."

"Not with slaves' blood, Hekat."

"*Tcha*!" she spat. "That is not for you to say! You do not serve the god in this, you do not bring the trade winds, Vortka. You have had many godmoons and *still we are here*. So I will bring the trade winds to Jatharuj."

Vortka felt his belly knot with fear. "Hekat, you cannot. The god's words in the godpool—"

"*I am the empress*!" Her bird-claw fingers jabbed his scorpion chest. "You do not tell me *I cannot*."

Despair was a black tide closing over his head. "Hekat—"

"Dmitrak has wasted the slaves here, but no matter," she continued, ignoring him. Her silver godbells shone in the sun, the amulets in her godbraids gleamed like fresh blood. "There are always more slaves. Their blood will flow, it will drown those demons. I will summon the trade winds and we will sail from Jatharuj."

His eyes burned, he could weep. *Hekat, Hekat, will you not let me save you?*

She turned her fierce face to the open water, rested her eyes on the horizon, so distant. "Dmitrak is right, the warhost needs blood. Like its empress it has rotted here long enough. The warhost was weary, it is weary no more. Now it is hungry, it needs to be fed."

"And you will feed it in defiance of the god?" Vortka demanded, anger stirring with his fear.

"Nothing I do defies the god, Vortka," she said, suddenly serene. "I am its chosen, every breath serves it sweetly."

"Hekat!" If she was not frail he would shake her to pieces. "The god has told you, *do not sacrifice more slaves*!"

"I have thought on that in my resting, Vortka," said Hekat, coldly smiling. "I have wondered why the god would say such a thing when it knows the power human blood brings it."

He could feel his scorpion pectoral thrum in time with his heartbeat. "You think a demon spoke to me, not the god? In the *godpool*, Hekat?"

She shrugged. "Demons have power."

"You think I would not know the *difference*?"

"I think you are a man and a man may be deceived."

"And you cannot?"

She laughed again, a soft chiding sound. "I have lived in the god's eye since I was a child, Vortka, I cannot be deceived. I will bring back the trade winds, I will help you change the horses. I will lead my warhost into the world."

Where they stood, at the slave pens, they could see clearly the warhost's ships ride into their moorings like obedient stallions. They saw Dmitrak leap from the deck to the dock, his scarlet godbraids flaming under the sun. His warriors leapt after him, lithe and lethal, exultant in their skills.

"Hekat," said Vortka, watching her son, "I know you are certain, does it matter I am not?"

"It matters to you, it does not matter to me," she said. "You have doubted me often, I have never been wrong. When was I wrong, Vortka? Can you tell me? Tell me once."

He could not tell her once and she knew it. *Aieee,*

the god see me, she knows I cannot. "You are quick to dismiss me, Hekat, but if I had lost my purpose would the god see me still? I think it would not, I think Vortka would be blind in the god's seeing eye."

She laid her hand on his arm, he could feel new strength in it. "Of course you have a purpose, but it is not to thwart me. Your purpose was always to serve me, Vortka. When you serve Hekat you serve the god, has that not always been true? From the very beginning, is it not so?"

"Yes," he whispered . . . even as he heard his heart cry out *no*. Heard his heart cry out *stop her*.

"Good," she said briskly. "Vortka, this is good. Now let us greet Dmitrak, Mijak's warlord. He must answer to his empress. He has wronged her, and should know."

They skirted the empty slave pens and walked to the top of the long pier where Dmitrak's warriors clustered round him as they waited for all the returned ships to empty. When the last warrior had joined him Dmitrak turned and led his warhost away from the water. The sliding sun flashed on his gauntlet, gold-and-scarlet in the light.

The warhost saw its empress and stopped in one breath. Fists punched against horsehide chests, in one joyful voice they shouted.

"The god see Hekat! The god see her in its eye!"

Vortka, looking sidelong, saw the warm pleasure flash in Hekat's thin face. Then she settled her blue gaze on Dmitrak and that pleasure plummeted cold.

"Warlord."

Dmitrak's gauntleted fist at last kissed his breast, lightly. "Empress."

"We will talk now. Your warriors will leave us."
Her cold gaze warmed again as she smiled at them.
"The god sees them, warlord, it sees them in its satisfied eye. Go now," she told them, raising her voice. "I
will see you at sacrifice, we will serve the god together
then."

"*Empress*!" shouted the warhost, and continued
along the pier without a second look at Dmitrak.
They bowed their heads, godbells sighing, as they
passed their high godspeaker.

Vortka nodded, he needed no more than that.

The smile Hekat gave her son was full of memories
and spite. "They are mine first, Dmitrak, they are
mine always. Remember that."

Whatever dark thoughts curdled behind his eyes,
Dmitrak was too canny to let the world see them.
Instead he nodded. "You are the empress, you were
warlord many seasons." His gaze shifted. "Vortka
high godspeaker."

"Dmitrak," he said. "I am no warrior but I think
your warships danced their *hotas* well, to please the
god."

"To please me," said Dmitrak. "My warriors
please me, high godspeaker. After the empress, the
claim on them is mine."

Hekat stepped forward, eye to eye with her son.
"There were slaves in the slave pens, warlord. They
are not there now."

Dmitrak shrugged. "Old slaves. Diseased slaves.
What is their purpose but training for the warhost?"

"Whatever they are, warlord, is my place to name
it. I told you the slaves of Jatharuj belong to me."

Dmitrak shrugged again, he flirted with insolence.

"Empress, you have been long within your palace, we do not see you. Your voice is hushed, it fades with time."

She looked down. "I see your legs, warlord, the god has not cut them from your body. I hear you speaking, it has not taken your tongue. You could not walk on your legs to my palace, warlord? You could not use your tongue to ask '*May I have those slaves?*'"

Now Dmitrak scowled. "If I am the warlord then I am warlord of those slaves, Empress. Whatever my warhost needs it is my purpose to provide it, when I am in the world with my warhost do I ask you before I wield it? Do I send a warrior to ask you '*May Dmitrak warlord kill these slaves?*'"

She stepped closer again, and spread her hand on his broad chest. "Your heart beats, Dmitrak. I feel it. You live. You live because I say so. You are warlord by my will."

Dmitrak's eyes, so like Nagarak's, stared fearless at Hekat. She tried to deny it but he was her son. "And the god's hammer by its making," he replied softly. "By blood and by its purpose do you and I walk together, Hekat. There is no breaking of us. We are two, and we are one."

Seabirds cried in the silence that followed. Mooring ropes creaked, wooden hulls groaned, salt water slopped and splashed, a soothing sound.

Hekat smiled. "Until I say we are not."

Dmitrak glanced away, for a heartbeat. He lowered his head. "Empress, my warriors' snakeblades were thirsty. The warhost is becalmed here, as its warships are becalmed. There is little to do, there is much time to fill. You were once the warlord, you taught me well. Idle warriors are prey to demons."

Hekat's fingers fisted and punched his chest. "This is true, Dmitrak," she said, stepping back. "You say a true thing. So I will not smite you for the taking of those slaves. You thought of the warhost, the god sees you in its eye. Vortka—"

"Empress," he said, not looking away from Dmitrak's dark face. *What are you thinking, warlord? Are you pleased or disappointed your mother has spared you? Did you hope to provoke her, or show her your worth? You have done both, do you know it? Was that your desire?*

"You have a finger of light till lowsun, perhaps a little more. Take this warlord and with him choose three hundred slaves who will die for the god at sacrifice."

Again he felt his heart cry out. *The god said no, Hekat.* "Empress—"

Her back was to him, her clenched fist came up. If she had worn a gauntlet it would spit fire in his face. "You have known me a long time, am I known for my patience? Do I care to repeat myself? I think I do not."

Dmitrak's nostrils were flared, as though he smelled the fresh human blood already. "You will give the god slaves, Empress?"

"I will give the god trade winds, warlord," she replied. "And horses that can ride in boats."

Dmitrak frowned. "Three hundred slaves, Empress? It took thousands to break the desert."

"I know," she said. "But Jatharuj is not filled with

slaves. There are not thousands here to die in my cause. If I need more, I will send for them."

"You will not need more, Hekat," Vortka said swiftly. "We have sacred beasts in Jatharuj, their blood will serve. *You will not need more.*"

Now Hekat turned and looked at him. "I will need as many as I need. Why do you stand there? Bring me those slaves."

Vortka swallowed every protesting word he longed to speak. He had no choice, he must leave Hekat standing alone on the pier and do as she told him.

She is chosen by the god.

"Come, warlord," he said quietly. "The empress has spoken. We will obey."

Dmitrak fell into step beside him and they made their way back to the township, leaving Hekat behind them in silent communion with the god. With lowsun approaching, the day's heat falling away, Jatharuj was stirring from its slumber.

"I am surprised," said Dmitrak, after a moment. "I thought the god said—"

"Are you a godspeaker, Dmitrak?" Vortka said, glaring. "I think you are not. Concern yourself with the warhost, that is your purpose."

Dmitrak sucked in a breath between his teeth, then shrugged. "Yes, high godspeaker."

"You took those broken slaves to goad her, warlord. You took them because she said you must not."

"Did I, high godspeaker?" said Dmitrak, glancing sideways.

Vortka snorted. "You know you did." They were in public, on the streets of Jatharuj, filled now with more godspeakers and warriors and slaves who could well soon die. This was not the place for a scene between them, so he kept his voice steady and did not strike Zandakar's brother, though the temptation was great. "Dmitrak, be careful. Hekat is filled with new purpose, this once she let you be. Has the sun baked your memory, has your childhood turned to dust? You *know* her, warlord. Will Hekat be thwarted twice?"

Dmitrak smiled, a sardonic curl of his lips. "You are so afraid of her, high godspeaker. Can you hear how you are afraid? I am not. I am the god's hammer, its power is in my blood. Hekat is old, Vortka. Dmitrak is young."

He swallowed anger, and a sigh. *She is old, yes, but she is not stupid. You are stupid, warlord, to speak like this to me.* "Why do you say that? Do you think to sway me from her side?"

"Never," said Dmitrak. "Even if I wanted to, I could not do it. You are the god's chosen, as Hekat is chosen. As I am chosen. All of us chosen, Vortka, for Mijak and the god."

He was a grown man, and dangerous, and desperate to be seen in his mother's bleak eye.

But she does see you, Dmitrak. That is the problem.

He did not say so, the words would change nothing. He let his hand touch lightly to Dmitrak's shoulder. "I will not tell her what you have said. I know Mijak needs you, I see you in the god's eye. You were born for a purpose, you live that purpose now."

I wish my knowing and seeing were enough for you.

Dmitrak shrugged irritably. He did not like to be

touched. "Can she bring us the trade winds, Vortka? Can she see our horses safe on the warships?"

"I do not know," he said, but that was a lie. *She can but she should not. This is wrong, this is wrong, this is wrong* . . .

"I hope she can," said Dmitrak, his voice fat with impatience. "I am weary of Jatharuj. I wish to see the world."

CHAPTER THIRTEEN

In beautiful Tzhung he was called "Child of the Wind."

Emperor Han, the wind's child, sat cross-legged on the black marble floor of the Sighing Room and strained to understand its whispers. Lost himself in the singing of his witch-men both here and at home, joined in spirit to contain the trade winds and so thwart Mijak.

Beads of sweat trickled down his bare chest and back to soak into his black silk trousers. His hair, unbound, stirred around his face, alive in the gusts and eddies of air swirling within the Sighing Room's crimson-walled silence. Candle-shadows dipped and danced.

It was a fearsome thing, to hold back the trade winds. Indeed, it pressed the witch-men of Tzhung-tzhungchai to their limits. Once, it had seemed, there were no limits for witch-men.

But that was before Mijak.

He had brought with him to Ethrea two witch-men, and Sun-dao. Sun-dao was a witch-man, but so much more than that. His friend. His conscience. His brother-in-blood. The only man living who could call him by name.

After that first confrontation with Zandakar in the castle, and the questionings that had followed it, the two witch-men and Sun-dao had not left Ambassador Lai's residence. They lived here, unseen by the common world, and poured their strength and power into the fight against Mijak. In far away beautiful Tzhung-tzhungchai, the witch-men of the empire fought too. Tzhung-tzhungchai was neglected, they fought only this battle.

In that twilight realm of the spirit where the witch-men dwelled, where physical distance meant nothing, where all witch-men were one, Han rallied his witch-brothers. They were weary, he could feel it. He could feel their bitter, unrelenting pain. Mijak was a cruel foe.

And then, like a lightning strike, he felt a whiplash of black power sear through the souls of his witch-men. Sear through his own soul, so he cried out aloud. Echoing in his mind, the cries of his witch-men.

Mijak had spilled human blood, again.

Doubled over, his nerves screaming, Han struggled for control. Tears filled his eyes, overflowed down his cheeks. The wind's pain was in him, its grief howling through his bones. Tzhung's witch-men howled too, on the edge of his hearing. In distant Tzhung-tzhungchai they howled, and here in Ambassador

Lai's Ethrean residence, in the witch-garden, where they battled their enemy.

Han released a shuddering breath and opened his eyes. Beneath the pain his witch-senses were humming. Sun-dao approached. A moment later the Sighing Room's door slid open and Sun-dao entered swiftly, on bare feet. He slid the door closed and turned. His eyes were wide and dark with rage.

"You feel it?"

Han nodded. "Of course."

Sun-dao joined him and sank cross-legged to the cold floor, facing him. The sighing wind played with his long, plaited moustaches and rattled together their sacred bones. Together in spirit they once more sank out of the world, sank into the sighing wind, into the twilight place of the witch-man.

No peace. No tranquillity. The twilight was tortured. Mijak's black power burned like acid in the air. The witch-men of Tzhung breathed their spirits upon it, breathed it to thinness, even as they struggled to keep their desperate hold on the trade winds.

Han felt the pain of their struggle as he struggled with them, as he fought against Mijak's blood-fed dark power. He felt Sun-dao beside him and wept for his pain. The twilight filled with keening as Tzhung and Mijak fought. A wild wind raged within the red-walled Sighing Room.

Heartbeat by heartbeat, Mijak's black power retreated. Thinned to vanishing. Vanished. Gasping, groaning, Han returned to the world. Sun-dao returned with him and for a long time they sprawled side by side on the cold marble floor. The raging wind died. Slowly, raggedly, the blown-out candles reignited, shedding light.

At last Han stirred. Touched Sun-dao's arm. "You breathe?"

"I breathe," said Sun-dao, sitting up. The whites of his eyes had flooded crimson. "And you breathe. Mijak is defeated."

Han shivered. "For now."

They stared at each other, still gasping. Han felt his eyes change, even as he watched the red fade from Sun-dao's eyes.

"It is a strange thing," said Sun-dao slowly. "Mijak spilled less blood this time. Far less blood than broke us in the desert."

It was true. In that far-distant eastern desert, where the witch-men of Tzhung had for so long held back the warriors of Mijak, enough human blood was spilled to make an ocean. Hundreds of witch-men had died broken that day . . . and the witch-men of Tzhung were rare enough as it was. To lose so many with one blow . . . it was dreadful.

In the dark of night, tormented by doubts, Han wondered if Tzhung-tzhungchai would ever recover from their loss. Yet it must recover. It was his sacred duty to protect the witch-men of Tzhung. It was also his sacred duty to protect the empire.

His greatest fear was that in protecting Tzhung-tzhungchai from Mijak with his witch-men, he would kill Tzhung-tzhungchai by killing them.

"Why would Mijak spill less blood?" he said, frowning at his brother. "When it knows blood can break us?"

Sun-dao's fingers smoothed the tails of his moustaches, bumping gently over the sacred bones. "I cannot say. I cannot see. My vision clouds further with each passing day."

"They will try again," Han murmured. "But how soon?"

Sun-dao's lips thinned. "As soon as they can."

"But we hold, Sun-dao," he said, swallowing more scalding fear. "Tzhung holds against them."

"We hold for the moment," Sun-dao said bleakly. "It hurts, but we hold. But if they kill as many again as they killed in the desert, Mijak will break us a second time. The trade winds will blow and Mijak will come."

Han nodded. "I know." Around the Sighing Room, the candle flames fluttered. The blood-red walls flickered. The wind sighed its pain.

"Han . . ." Sun-dao folded his hands in his lap. "Never in our history have Tzhung's witch-men been so challenged. Your witch-men love and obey you, but love and obedience are not enough. They weaken."

And he knew that also. It broke his heart. The witch-men who survived that battle in the desert had been hurt in their spirits, wounded in their souls. Now, not fully recovered, they were again pitted against Mijak's evil. Hour by hour he could feel their strength wane. The fight against Mijak was brutal, and had lasted so long already. His witch-men suffered, faded, and he could not see the end of strife.

"Han," said Sun-dao. "The girl must be told."

The girl. Rhian. Little Queen of Ethrea, queen of a realm so small. So important. Every night the wind whispered her name in his dreams. It whispered too of Zandakar, blood-soaked fallen prince of Mijak. Rhian and Zandakar. A girl and a murderer: the wind blew him strange allies. Strange inferiors who must stand tall above him.

"How can Rhian help us?" he said. "She has no power to speak of."

Sun-dao raised a chiding finger. "You know her power, Han. She is the eye of the tempest."

Of all men breathing, my brother calls me Han. And Rhian calls me Han. This girl, this child, she sees herself my equal.

The thought was amusing. Preposterous. And yet . . . and yet . . .

"The wind has blown us to her," said Sun-dao severely. "It wishes us to work together against Mijak. Would you defy the wind?"

His head came up. "You know I would not."

"Then you must confide in the Ethrean queen," said Sun-dao, so solemn. "Tzhung-tzhungchai is not as mighty as it was. The wind knows we can no longer hope to defeat Mijak alone. Mijak will break us, Han, and sooner than we can bear. We must have help."

Yes, yes, Sun-dao was right. He was the wind's greatest witch-man. He was always right. Han pushed to his feet, anguished. To hear such a truth spoken aloud when his bones still burned with his witch-men's pain, with his own pain . . . it was hard, so hard. To be an emperor, and helpless. That was hard.

"And if I tell her our secret, Sun-dao? That we hold back the trade winds? How will that help us?"

"The girl's thought of an armada is a good

thought," said Sun-dao, standing. His face creased with the effort: he was hurting too. "But there is little time for its creation, even with the help of Tzhung-tzhungchai. Every day the ambassadors delay in agreeing to it is a day closer to Mijak's breaking of us. Rhian must be told how little time there is. She must be made to press these reluctant ambassadors. She must not scruple to use Ethrea as a weapon. Go to her now and tell her, Han. Before it is too late. Before Mijak breaks us."

He is Sun-dao, the greatest witch-man in the world. He is my brother, the better part of myself. What I must know he tells me, whether I would hear it or not. To play emperor with him is to be a great fool.

Han bowed. "I go."

Bathed and dressed in sober dark green silk, he wrapped the wind about himself and stepped into the witching twilight. Stepped out of it into early afternoon sunshine, into the castle's privy garden where Rhian fled to seek peace. Its beauty came as a startlement after the darkness of Mijak.

Ethrea's queen stood at the garden's edge, dressed in her common huntsman's leathers, staring over the busy harbour to the empty ocean beyond. Staring at the horizon. Waiting for Mijak. Her head tilted, just a little. She knew he stood behind her.

"How is it," she asked, not turning, "you always manage to find me?"

It was possible to answer without betraying Tzhung-tzhungchai. "You have a bright soul, Majesty. It is easy to find."

That made her turn. Blue eyes wide, her cheeks tinted pink, she stared. "What an extraordinary thing to say."

He smiled. "And yet it is true."

She shook her head, baffled, as he'd meant her to be. "You need something else from me, Han?"

Han. "Your help."

"My *help*?" She considered him, arms folded hard across her chest. "And how can I help the mighty Emperor of the Tzhung?"

There was a note of scornful teasing in her voice. Beneath it, suspicion. Still she was not easy about him. Too many mysteries. Too much unexplained. She was brave but he frightened her, though she would never show it. Not willingly.

He clasped his hands behind him. A salt breeze blew in his face, tugging at his hair. "The witch-men of Tzhung-tzhungchai hold back the trade winds from Icthia. Tzhung-tzhungchai keeps Mijak at bay. But my witch-men cannot fight Mijak alone forever. You must form your armada quickly, before they falter and break."

When she was angry her eyes turned the deepest blue. "Your witch-men are holding back the trade winds," she repeated, as though she could scarcely believe it. "And this was something you felt wasn't worth *mentioning*?"

"No," he said, shrugging. "At least, not until now."

She flung away from him to stare again across the harbour. "Emperor Han, your arrogance astounds me." Her voice was unsteady. "Have you no *idea* of the trouble this will cause?"

He waited until his silence made her turn back again.

"*Well?*" she demanded. "Don't you realise what you've *done?*"

"I have spent my witch-men in the service of Ethrea," he said, and let his voice chill. "The warriors of Mijak might be sailing into your harbour now if my witch-men didn't break their hearts restraining them."

Now she fisted her hands on her hips. "I take it you expect me to thank you?"

He was aware of his own anger. "Yes."

"*Han—*" She let out a sharp, impatient breath and began to speak, then stopped. Stared for a moment at the gravel-covered ground. "Yes," she said, still angry. "If your witch-men are throwing Mijak into disarray, I do thank you. But surely you see I'm in an impossible position!" Then she shook her head. "Or perhaps you don't. You're the Emperor of Tzhung-tzhungchai. Your lightest whim is imperial law. Have you ever had to wrangle with *anyone* to get your way? I can't imagine you have."

He thought of his childhood, and kept his face schooled. "What has that to do with Mijak?"

"Oh, only everything," she retorted. "Han, why didn't you tell the trading nations this? When we met in the castle to discuss the threat of Mijak, why didn't you *say?*"

"The secrets of Tzhung-tzhungchai are not for the world to know."

"But don't you see how this will look to the ambassadors?" she demanded. "I told them, I *swore* to them, that Tzhung-tzhungchai did not meddle for me.

And now you've made a *liar* of me. When they find out—" With an effort she controlled her temper. "Han, in the two days since I told them of Mijak only Voolksyn has said he's sent word to his master." She pulled a face. "Well, Athnïj has too, for all the good it'll do him or Ethrea. But the other ambassadors still haven't committed to my cause. They're waiting to see what Gutten does, and Gutten—" She bit off a curse. "Surely you understand this is only going to make things worse."

"Worse?" he said, and took a step towards her. "*Worse* is the warships of Mijak sailing into your harbour! *Worse* is the slaughter of your people in the streets. Rhian, my witch-men cannot hold back Mijak much longer. You *must* make the other nations agree to your armada before Mijak comes to Ethrea."

"How?" she said, glaring. "By snapping my fingers? Doubtless that will bring Gutten to heel!"

Gutten was a cur dog who'd do better spitted on a sword than speaking for his master the Count of Arbenia. "Rhian, I'm not ruler here. It's for you to bring the trading nations together. That is why your God chose you, yes?"

She muttered something under her breath. "We should continue this conversation with my privy council – except I hardly *have* a privy council at the moment, with Ludo and Adric at the dukes' funerals, and Edward and Rudi inspecting the kingdom's garrisons." Her eyes were bright blue again, her anger rekindled. "But Alasdair is here, at least, and Helfred. Dexterity, though he's at home taking care of personal matters. And then there's Zandakar. He—"

"No," he said. "You cannot tell the Prince of Mijak."

Her chin came up, defiant. "Why not? His heart is sworn to Ethrea."

"Exactly. Trust him with your secrets, Rhian, if that's what you wish. You will not trust him with mine."

"You say you trust me, but you won't trust who I trust?" She sneered. "What kind of trust is that, Han?"

"It is the trust of Tzhung-tzhungchai. Would you prefer I withdraw from our alliance? Would you rather my witch-men fight only for the Tzhung?"

"Of course not," she said, after a moment. "Very well. I'll not tell Zandakar."

In aggravated silence she led him from the garden into the castle, sending the first servant she saw to summon the king and the prolate to the privy council chamber.

"And the toymaker?" he enquired as he followed her up the nearest staircase.

"It'll take too long for him to come. I want this dealt with," she replied, over her shoulder.

As they waited for King Alasdair and Prolate Helfred to join them, she stood at the council chamber window, her back resolutely turned. Han sat in one of the council table's chairs, patiently silent.

Eventually the council doors opened, and King Alasdair arrived. "Rhian? What's—" And then he stopped.

Han stood. "Your Majesty."

"How . . . unexpected," said King Alasdair, sounding not at all pleased. "And yet, it seems, typical. Emperor Han, for what reason—"

Rhian turned from the window. "Do you mind if we wait for Helfred, Alasdair? This is a tale I'd prefer to tell only once."

The king nodded. "All right."

Han favoured him with a small smile. "Forgive me," he said, scrupulously polite. "If your queen is in a temper you must lay the blame at my feet."

"Have no fear," said King Alasdair, sitting. "I do."

Hiding a larger smile, Han resumed his own seat. This new-crowned king, subordinate to his queen, still had some bite. That was good. Toothless men were of no use against Mijak.

The doors opened a second time and the prolate entered. "Your Majesty? What's amiss?"

"Thank you for attending so promptly, Helfred," said Rhian. "Emperor Han brings news. I suggest you sit down, for it's like to knock you quite off balance."

Cautious, the young prolate groped for a chair. "Emperor Han. God's blessings on you."

Another smile. "And may the wind blow good fortune to you, Your Eminence."

Rhian marched around the table, kicked the chamber door shut, then began pacing. "Very well, gentlemen. Consider our discussion privy state business, and this a meeting of council."

"If it's a meeting of the council," said Helfred, "then Ven'Cedwin should—"

She raised a hand, still pacing. "No. No record. When the others return we can tell them what we've said here."

King Alasdair was frowning. "Why keep this so secret? To humour Tzhung-tzhungchai?"

"Yes."

Han met the king's hot stare and Helfred's speculative look with a bland, half-smiling gaze of his own. "Her Majesty indulges me."

"Han's witch-men are keeping Mijak's warships penned in Icthia," Rhian said baldly. "They have control of the trade winds, at least for now. But Mijak threatens to break the witch-men. Han says if we don't form the armada soon, it will be too late. And *yes*—" she added as the king began to protest. "I have pointed out the inconvenience of his silence on the matter."

"Rollin's mercy," whispered Helfred. "You can do this, Emperor Han? You can summon God's wind at will?"

If ever this little man learned what Tzhung could do, his heart would give out and he would fall dead where he stood. "It is not so simple as you make it sound, Prolate."

"Oh, Emperor Han, I don't call it simple at all!" retorted Helfred. "Indeed, I fear it skirts close to—"

"Please, Helfred!" said Rhian.

As the prolate subsided, unhappy, King Alasdair tapped his fingers on the table. "You say your witch-men are in danger, Han?"

Someone else who presumed to use his name. In Tzhung he would be executed for the liberty. *This is not Tzhung. I must remember that.* "Grave danger, Alasdair. Mijak seeks to make itself even more powerful. It spills human blood."

Silence as the Ethreans stared at him. *Human* sacrifice? said Rhian at last, her pacing abandoned. "But I thought—"

"Animals," said Helfred, his voice faint. "Zandakar has told us they sacrifice beasts. He *never*—"

"We must ask him," said Alasdair. His voice was cold, his eyes colder. "We must discover what else he *never*."

Han watched, curious, as Rhian and her king exchanged daggered looks. Then Rhian's chin lifted, her expression so defiant. "He doesn't know. I'd chance my life on it."

"You might well be chancing all our lives," said Alasdair, unconvinced.

Rhian turned away from her husband. "Han, do you know without doubt there's human blood spilled?"

An echo of pain whispered through his flesh. "Yes."

"And you're certain Tzhung's witch-men can't—"

"*Yes!*" he said. "Would I share our secrets with outsiders otherwise? Would I come to you for help if we weren't driven to our knees?"

"No," she murmured, breaking the frozen silence. "Of course you wouldn't. Han, please, promise you won't speak of this to anyone else. If there should be talk, if people tar Zandakar with this abominable brush, I fear—" She swallowed, her eyes wide. "We need him. This dreadful news can't be allowed to endanger him."

She was so sure of Zandakar, where her king clearly harboured doubts. He doubted too, but how

could he refuse her? The wind had made its choices
clear. He nodded. "I will keep my counsel."

"Thank you," she said, and seemed to breathe a
little easier. "Han, how long do we have before Mijak
defeats your witch-men? How long before the trade
winds blow again?"

"I cannot say. But you must not delay further in
bending the ambassadors to your will."

"And how am I supposed to do that without telling
them what your witch-men have been up to?" she
replied, pacing again. "And I have to hide that, Han.
No-one can know what we know of your business,
because—"

"If Gutten and the others suspect we're privy to
Tzhung's secrets where they're not, any trust they had
in us will burn like tinder," said Alasdair, and sighed.
"But without a good reason to side with us they're
more likely to dig their heels in harder, just to prove
they'll not be told."

"Precisely," said Rhian, her face and voice grim.

Han stared at her. "These nations need Ethrea,
Rhian. You threatened Gutten with that."

"And you think I should make good on my
threat?" she said, throwing him an impatient glance.
"I can't. Not yet. Not until all hope of cajoling
Arbenia's support is extinguished. The danger we face
from Mijak is far beyond the scope of the trading
charter. If I punish any of the trading nations too
swiftly I risk a revolt. And how will that help us? We
must still gain their agreement for an Ethrean army. I
don't dare threaten Ambassador Gutten until the very
last gasp."

"Still," said Alasdair, after some consideration. "It

won't hurt to recall the ambassadors to the castle. We can sound them out, gently. Nudge them towards agreement for our army at least. They have to know it won't pose a threat to their safety. We've no ships to sail to their nations, threatening an invasion of our own."

"Very true," said Prolate Helfred, stirring from his melancholy. "God knows we must do something, Your Majesties. With Mijak slaughtering innocents for their blood we can't sit idle hoping against hope the tide will turn in our favour. God expects us to act."

Rhian nodded. "Yes, Helfred. He does." She continued to pace, as though she had to move or die, her expression stricken. "It must be the peonple of Icthia being sacrificed. Rollin's mercy, I'll have to tell Athnïj." She halted, her eyes wide. "How can I? There's a chance his family's slaughtered. God help me, how can I tell that poor man . . ."

"There's no need to tell him anything yet," said King Alasdair quietly. "Not if we're keeping what more we know of Mijak a secret. Besides." He pulled a face. "In his heart I think Athnïj must suspect he'll never see his family again."

Abruptly Rhian stopped pacing and swung about. Now she looked angry. "I'm a fool, not thinking clearly. Han, if your witch-men are strong enough to hold back the trade winds, what else are they strong enough to do? Can they raise a storm and sink Mijak's warships at anchor? Can they scour the warriors of Mijak from the face of the world? What, precisely, are the limits of their power?"

Han lowered his gaze. He'd wondered how long it would be before these thoughts occurred to her.

How can I answer without betraying our perilous weakness? How can I satisfy her without breaking my sacred trust?

He looked up. "Rhian . . . if my witch-men could destroy Mijak, they would have done so already."

But by the time they'd realised the danger, Mijak had already grown too strong. Witch-men were not gods. They could not order the whole world on a whim. And now, after battling Mijak's darkness for so long, they were too exhausted. Too few. The raising of storms was a killing endeavour even when a witch-man was not already exhausted. Even in the days when Tzhung's witch-men were plentiful, such a feat would be nearly beyond them.

And we are no longer plentiful. We are stretched pitifully thin.

Rhian was staring. "I don't understand. Are you saying you won't even try?"

He felt a stirring of rage, that he must endure censure from this child. "Try? Even as you stand there, Queen of Ethrea, my witch-men spend their lives in your defence! And you dare to—"

"Please," said Alasdair, holding up a hand. "Emperor Han, please. Fighting amongst ourselves will achieve nothing. We know you're doing all that you can, and we're grateful." His gaze flickered. "Aren't we, Your Majesty?"

Rhian breathed out harshly. "Yes. Yes, of course we are." Then she pressed her fingers briefly against her eyes. "Only I fail to see how we're any further ahead. Even if by some miracle I can convince Gutten

and the others to set aside their suspicion and join
Voolksyn in aiding us, surely it's too late." She let her
hands drop to her sides. "The ships of Arbenia and
Harbisland and the other trading nations are weeks
away. What if Tzhung's witch-men can't hold out for
weeks? What if they break tonight – or tomorrow –
before even one friendly warship can reach us?"

Han sighed. *I must trust, I must trust . . . the wind
has blown me here, after all.* "You need not fear,
Rhian. Once the rulers of the trading nations have
agreed to join you against Mijak, my witch-men can
help their ships reach Ethrea in time."

"How?"

"I thought you were uncomfortable, knowing the
secrets of Tzhung-tzhungchai?" he said, mocking.

She grimaced. "I am. Forget I asked. Instead you
can suggest how I'm going to explain to Gutten and
the others what's happened to the trade winds, and
how they must act quickly before their return, without telling them the truth."

"You'll say it's a miracle," said Prolate Helfred,
stirring at last. "One that won't last for long. You'll
say God told you the armada must be formed now.
After all, to my mind the halting of the trade winds is
a miracle, and all miracles come from God. And as
God sent Zandakar to you, so has he sent the emperor." He smiled, his eyes shadowed. "So indeed
God has told you . . . after a fashion."

"Of course . . ." said Alasdair as Rhian stared at
her prolate, incredulous, "even if they believe in
Ethrean miracles, once they know the trade winds are
altered they might well claim their missing ships are
not taken by Mijak, but only stranded somewhere on

the ocean. They could claim this is a plot between Ethrea and the Tzhung."

Rhian groaned. "He's right, Han. Give Gutten the smallest excuse to doubt me and he will doubt me, and drag the others into doubt behind him. Worse than that, they might even form alliances amongst themselves and think to overthrow my kingdom."

Han shook his head. "No. They stand to lose too much. The penalties listed in the treaty charter would ruin them."

She stared at him, as though she thought he was stupid. "Han, I think you've grown sheltered in your mighty empire of Tzhung. No-one dares raise a hand to you, so you've forgotten how to fear. Remember I grew up in Ethrea, in Eberg's court. I've watched the ambassadors circle and dance and whisper in corners my whole life. If they think their nations stand to lose everything they've built here, if they believe you and I have made a secret pact that threatens their wealth and sovereignty, the charter will mean *nothing*. They'll claim we broke it first."

"And if they are so foolish as to raise arms against Ethrea," Han replied, "the Tzhung empire will protect you."

"Thereby proving to them all their suspicions," she said, smiling wryly.

"What of Dexterity?" said Prolate Helfred. "They've seen the power of God in him. How—"

"Helfred, *think*," said Rhian, impatient. "You know as well as I do that mystery, superstition and rumour surround the Tzhung. There's nothing so outlandish it can't be laid at their feet."

And that was true enough, Han silently conceded.

"If Gutten and the rest would risk the world for their greedy fears, then they are fools and deserve to die."

Prolate Helfred pushed to his feet. "Shame on you for saying so, Emperor Han. It's not your place to condemn so many souls. If God desired their destruction – or the destruction of their nations – he wouldn't have sent us Zandakar. He wouldn't have bestowed miracles upon Mister Jones. He wouldn't have called upon Queen Rhian to lead the league of trading nations against the might of Mijak and its bloodthirsty false god. We would even now be breathing our last days in blissful ignorance. We are required to save lives, sir, not pass judgement on the follies of other men."

This man, this plump little man, presumed to lecture an emperor of the Tzhung? *Nobody speaks to me like that but Sun-dao. And not even Sun-dao uses a tone so disrespectful.* Seething, Han opened his mouth to blister the upstart priest – then caught Rhian's eye. Her expression was serious, but in her eyes a sardonic gleam.

He decided upon a different attack. "I notice, Prolate, you do not count as worthy of mention Sun-dao's windblown visions. Are you a man who believes his god is the only god?"

"I believe, Emperor Han," retorted the prolate, "that God has many faces and many truths and he shares those truths among his children."

As Rhian sighed, Alasdair leaned forward. "I fear we've allowed ourselves to become distracted. Are we agreed, then, that we must recall the ambassadors and press as hard as we dare for a commitment to the armada on behalf of their masters?"

"As hard as you dare?" said Han. "No. As hard as you can." He stared at Rhian. "Haven't you heard me? There is no more time for coddling the feelings of the other trading nations. If your God has decided you *are* the one to lead us, Rhian, then you must *lead us*. You must be bold. Decisive. Only then will men follow you."

He saw a muscle leap along her jaw, saw that she heard his unspoken words quite clearly. *Only then will I follow you*. Alasdair and the prolate heard them also. The three Ethreans exchanged guarded glances.

"Your advice is . . . appreciated," Rhian said, after a moment. "I'll think on it, and decide how best to proceed. I must tread carefully where the trading nations are concerned."

He felt his anger stir again. "Rhian, I have told you how best to proceed. How can I make you see the truth more clearly? In the heartbeat that my witch-men lose their grasp upon the trade winds, Mijak will know. Don't you understand that forming the armada is but the beginning? There will be arguments about who's to lead it, arguments about how best to attack Mijak, arguments about—"

"I know!" Rhian said, nearly shouting. "How can you think I don't *know* all that, Han? I'm sleepless at nights thinking of it. When I stop and consider the task before me I could *weep*. You say I must see to the swift forming of this armada, and I'll do my best, but you must do your part too. Your witch-men *must* keep hold of the trade winds. Whatever it costs, Mijak must remain penned as long as possible."

Slowly, Han stood. "Whatever it costs? *It will cost*

witchmen their lives. You ask the Tzhung for this sacrifice, yet seem to care more for the feelings of Arbenia and Harbisland and the rest than you do for the witchmen who'll die for you, Rhian."

"That's *not* true!" Raising a hand to Alasdair and the prolate, who looked to speak in her defence, she strode around the table to face him. "But these trading nations aren't slaves or servants to obediently follow my orders. I must coax them, I must coddle them, I must keep them sweet when their very blood runs sour and that takes *time*. If we can't stop the Mijaki warships from sailing before we've cobbled together some warships of our own then this will be over before it's begun and I might as well send a letter of surrender to Zandakar's mother now. Should I do that, Han? *Is that* your advice? Do advise me, mighty emperor. *What should I do?*"

He stared into her brilliant blue eyes. *Girl, girl, you are a puzzlement to me. The wind won't say why it's blown us together. Sun-dao can't tell me. Won't tell me, perhaps. It's the same in the end. Rhian is the queen here, and Han is her consort.*

"You should do what you can, Rhian," he said, his voice low. "I will do what I can. And we must hope it's enough."

With a curt nod he left her, and her councillors. Found a stretch of corridor free of servants or courtiers, wrapped the wind about himself and returned to Lai's residence. His imperial palace in exile. It felt like an exile. He was so far from home.

Patient Sun-dao waited for him in the Sighing Room, seated cross-legged and flickered with candles.

He looked so weary. He led the fight against Mijak. Without him they would surely be lost.

"And so?" he said, his voice thin. "Will Rhian of Ethrea give us her help?"

Abruptly exhausted, Han sank to the black marble floor. "She says she'll try, Sun-dao. But I fear. Brother, I fear. She is young, she's a girl, and the ambassadors don't respect her. They don't fear her, and fear is the only thing that will bring them to heel. I begin to think we must find another way."

Sun-dao's eyebrows lifted. "Another way? *Is* there another?"

He sighed. "I don't know. But if there is . . . I will find it."

CHAPTER FOURTEEN

It was Helfred who broke the long silence after Emperor Han's abrupt departure.

"Rollin's mercy!" he declared. "If that man is not the most *arrogant*, the most *insufferable*, the most—"

"Formidable, Helfred," Rhian said, and sat down at the table. Her head was pounding. "Intimidating. Overpowering."

"And yet," said Alasdair, thoughtful, "in many ways, he's deferring to you. I find that odd."

So did she, but she wasn't about to look any gift

horse in the mouth. "So long as he continues to help us, I say let him be as odd as he likes."

"I find all this talk of witch-men most unsettling," said Helfred, and reached for his old wooden prayer beads. "How can a mortal man control the wind? It's not Godly. I fear some dark, supernatural forces are in play."

Rhian pressed her fingers to her temples, willing the pain in her head to subside. "If you wish to talk of things *unsettling*, Helfred, then we should discuss Han's news of human sacrifice."

"And what Zandakar knows of it," said Alasdair, sourly. "Though you protest his innocence, Rhian, we must make certain."

She nodded, reluctant. "Yes. We have to ask him if he knows . . ." *Oh, God. And if he does? If this is yet another lie uncovered?* "Helfred—"

Helfred stood, his prayer beads dangling, his face pale. "He's in his apartments? I'll fetch him here directly."

As Helfred closed the chamber doors behind him, softly, Rhian looked at Alasdair. "He can't know," she said, and heard the desperation in her voice. "If God's hand is in this business, Alasdair, how can—"

"It seems to me that anything is possible," said Alasdair. "After all, we've allied ourselves with Emperor Han . . . and who among us knows the truth of Tzhung-tzhungchai? What the Tzhung do within their borders, unscrutinised by the rest of the world, is a mystery."

"You think I've been naïve," she whispered. "You think I trust too easily, that I take too much on faith. From the very beginning, when I trusted Dexterity and Zandakar to help me escape the clerica, you think I've never once looked before I leapt."

His expression sombre, Alasdair considered her across the vast expanse of table between them. "I think you have the purest heart of anyone I've ever known. I think, since your father died, you've been outrunning demons without a chance to draw breath. Lurching from crisis to crisis, making desperate choices, facing dire situations no other monarch of Ethrea has ever had to face. And . . . yes. At times I think you've leapt before you looked."

It was somehow worse, that he sounded so *sad*. "I'm guided by what I believe is best for the kingdom," she replied. "If you think otherwise, Alasdair, then—"

"No," he said swiftly. "But, Rhian, things aren't so simple. Rejecting Mijak doesn't make a man good. There's more than one kind of evil in the world."

Before she could answer him, the chamber doors opened again and Helfred returned with Zandakar behind him.

"Rhian *hushla*," Zandakar said, pleased and wary at once, then nodded to Alasdair. "You need?"

She sat straight in her chair, even though her bones were aching and her head pounded without mercy. "Yes. I need. Helfred? The doors."

Helfred closed the chamber doors and took his place at the table. His prayer beads were wrapped tight around his fingers, and she had never seen him look so grave.

Zandakar stood before them, uneasy in his linen shirt and leather leggings. Beyond the chamber windows the afternoon light was beginning to wane. His blue hair shone darker, just like his eyes.

Clasping her hands in case they trembled, she met his gaze directly. "Your mother the empress is sacrificing people to your god, Zandakar. What do you know of this?"

He said nothing, at first. As though he were the Zandakar fresh off the Slynt slave ship, and had no understanding of Ethrean words. Then he stirred. "People?" His voice was husky. "*Wei* understand, Rhian *hushla*."

"Oh, I think you do, Zandakar," said Alasdair. "I think you understand full well."

"Whatever you know," Helfred added gently, "it's best that you tell us, Zandakar. These secrets aren't helpful."

Zandakar shook his head. "Secrets? Wei secrets. *Wei* people."

Alasdair slapped his hand on the table. "Zho people, Zandakar! Not cows and goats and whatever else your priests sacrifice. Now Mijak's killing *humans*, for the power in their blood. How long have you known this? How long have you been lying?"

"Please, Alasdair," Rhian murmured. "Give him a chance."

Zandakar was shaking his head. "*Wei*. *Wei*. Alasdair king is wrong. *Wei* people. Vortka – Yuma—" His voice broke, his face twisted. "People?" He turned away, his outreaching hand touching the wall, seeking support, as though he found it impossible to stand.

"King Alasdair . . ." Helfred sounded uncertain. "I

believe he didn't know. I believe his distress is genuine."

"You sound surprised, Helfred," Rhian snapped.

"I – I—" Helfred stared at his prayer beads. "I confess, I don't know what to think."

"And I confess I find your willingness to believe the worst of Zandakar without proof to be a shameful thing." Leaving Helfred to his blushes, she turned on Alasdair. "Well? Are *you* still convinced he's a party to this vile slaughter?"

"Zandakar!" said Alasdair. "Look at me. *Look at me.*"

Slowly, Zandakar pulled away from the wall and turned. His face was blank, his eyes hollow with pain. "Alasdair king."

"If I gave you a dagger, now, would you swear in your blood that your denials are the truth? That you had no knowledge of this abominable thing?"

Zandakar held out his hand. "Give me dagger. I will swear."

"You'll do no such thing!" said Rhian. "You'll go down to the tiltyard and wait there for me. We've time to dance our *hotas* before I attend this evening's Litany. Go on. I think you know the way without a gaggle of soldiers showing you."

Walking like a man bereft of hope, Zandakar obeyed.

"I'll wait with him," said Helfred. "It's plain to see this news has hurt him. Perhaps I can be of some little comfort."

With an effort, Rhian throttled her simmering temper. *Too little, too late, Helfred. Your doubts hurt him first.* "That would be charitable, Prolate."

"Indeed," said Helfred, subdued, and departed.

Which left her alone with Alasdair, again.

"No soldiers?" he demanded as the doors closed behind her prolate. "Rhian—"

"I know what I said," she replied. "But to shadow him with soldiers now, after such a showing of mistrust—"

"I'll not apologise for questioning him, Rhian," Alasdair retorted. "One of us must be prepared to suspect those we'd rather hold close to our hearts. I know you prefer not to think of betrayal. I know making such accusations offends you. But I say it's better to offend than learn too late you were wrong."

She nodded. "You're right."

"About?" he said, sitting back in his chair. He seemed to her braced for another attack.

"About me being offended," she said gently. "About needing you to be hard." She bit her lip. "It's just . . . I don't have so many friends, Alasdair, that I can discard them lightly."

"You're still convinced Zandakar's your friend?"

"I'm not convinced he isn't."

"And Emperor Han? Is he a friend too?"

Remembering Han's cold eyes, the way his gaze seemed to look right through her, she shivered. "I've no idea what Han is. All I know is I don't want him for an enemy."

He started to answer, but stopped when the chamber doors opened and a herald entered. "Majesty," he said bowing. "I bring a message."

Rhian held out her hand. "Very well."

The herald presented it and departed. She picked

apart the ribbon tying the scrolled parchment, un-rolled it and read.

"What?" said Alasdair as the chamber wheeled around her. "Rhian, what's happened?"

There were two scribbled notes, one from an apologetic chaplain called Hyse, the other—

"It's Rulf," she said dully. "He's killed himself."

Alasdair stared. "Rulf? Who's—" Then he swore. "*Lord* Rulf? Marlan's ward? The useless man he wanted to—"

"Yes." Tears were pricking her eyes. "He left a letter," she added, and held up the scrap of paper rolled inside the parchment. "He says he feared for his life after my slaying of Damwin and Kyrin. According to his parish chaplain, he drank poison."

"Rhian . . ." Alasdair reached across the table and closed his fingers over the notes, taking them from her. "You didn't kill him. You'd never have harmed him, he wasn't responsible for Marlan any more than Helfred was."

The council chamber was warm, yet she felt so cold. "I never gave him another thought," she murmured. "As soon as we were wed, and I knew I was safe from him, his welfare never once crossed my mind."

Blindly she pushed away from the table and moved dreamlike to the window. Alasdair followed, to pull her against him. She heard the notes crumple in his fist as he closed his arms tight. "Why would you? He was no-one. None of us considered him. Besides, you had more important things to occupy your thoughts."

She rested her cheek against his chest and breathed in the scent of him, so warm and reassuring. "I should've thought of him once, Alasdair. I should've thought to let him know I bore him no ill-will."

And now it was too late. Rulf was dead. He'd died in pain and fear, without reason, all because she'd been too busy to think of him.

Too busy, or too careless.

She stepped back from Alasdair, breaking his embrace. "I have to go."

"Of course," he said, expressionless. "Zandakar's waiting."

"My *hotas* are waiting," she said sharply. "I can't afford to neglect them."

He nodded. "Of course you can't."

"While I'm training, would you find Ven'Cedwin?" she said, when she could trust herself not to snap. "And craft a summons to the ambassadors? Bid them meet us here at ten of the clock tomorrow morning. We've no time to lose, now."

"Of course," he said. "Your Majesty."

"*Alasdair*—" She punched his chest lightly with her fist. "Don't be stupid."

And left him to join Zandakar before she said more that she'd regret.

Dexterity stood with Ursa and watched as Rhian and Zandakar danced their violent *hotas*. They were the only two people watching; Helfred, an unexpected attendant, had departed as soon as they arrived and Rhian dismissed the handful of courtiers who'd come to gawk.

"Brings back memories, Jones," said Ursa, then hissed as Rhian avoided the tip of Zandakar's blade by a hairsbreadth.

Draped over the castle tiltyard's railing, he nodded. It did indeed. Rhian and Zandakar broke apart, sweating and panting, and took a moment to consider their next dance.

"You finished with all your puppetry bits and bobs?" Ursa said, considering him sidelong. "Now you've been asked back to serve on the council?"

He shrugged. "For now. Just one more cartload to sell at the harbour markets tomorrow. But I'll not be abandoning my trade altogether, Ursa. Serving on council's not a full-time occupation."

"Perhaps not," she said darkly. "But waging war is. There'll be plenty for you to do once this kingdom's finally told what's what in the world."

He shifted against the splintery railings, uncomfortable. It had to happen, he knew that, but oh, how he dreaded it. Dreaded the destruction of Ethrea's peace. For so long the people of this kingdom had lived without the fear of bloodshed. They knew wars happened, of course. Kingseat's taverns were filled nightly with sailors and their gruesome tales of this battle, and that one. The tales spread.

But hearing of war and living it are two different things.

He grunted as Ursa nudged his ribs with her elbow. "You're brooding," she muttered. "Stop it. What's to come will come, Jones. Do you think you can prevent it?"

"I know I can't. I know there's things set in motion not a one of us can change," he muttered back. "And I'm sad for that, Ursa. You can't tell me not to be sad."

"Well, I *can*," she said, lifting an eyebrow at him.

"But I won't, for I'm old enough to know better than to throw good advice at a deaf man."

In the tiltyard, Rhian and Zandakar had returned to their *hotas*. Dexterity, watching closely, was struck by how Rhian had changed. She was leaner. Faster. More supple. Less predictable. On the road, while she was first learning, he'd always thought Zandakar had held himself back. Even though he was hard on her, even though he shouted and cuffed her and called her rude names in Mijaki, it seemed clear he was protecting her, too.

But not any more.

Be careful, be careful, Rhian, don't take chances.

She wasn't listening. She flirted with death.

Ursa stifled a groan, her fingers bloodless on the tiltyard rail. "I'm not sure I can keep watching, Jones."

He was risking splinters too. "She's different, isn't she, from her time on the road?" he said as Rhian turned a neat circle around her blade. "She doesn't dance these wretched *hotas* the same."

Ursa sniffed. "She's killed two men with a sword, Jones. Of course she's different."

She still wouldn't tell him what she'd seen the day Rhian had faced Damwin and Kyrin, and defeated them. He was partly relieved, partly annoyed. He wanted to know . . . and yet, he didn't.

I could always ask Rhian. But I doubt she'd tell me, either.

"Oh!" Ursa exclaimed, and pressed her hand to her mouth.

"She's all right, she's all right," he said, his heart

thundering as Rhian sprang to her feet after slipping and falling on her back.

"All right? She's bleeding!" said Ursa. "Are you blind?"

No. And she was right, Rhian was bleeding. Zandakar's blade had caught her down one arm, slicing through her linen shirt-sleeve, leaving a thin trail of blood. But she didn't cry out. She scarcely seemed to notice.

He put his hand on Ursa's shoulder, squeezing. "Don't fuss yourself, old woman. Our Rhian's in no danger."

"Old woman yourself," said Ursa, shrugging him free. "I'll give you *old woman* next time you need a posset for your innards!"

He smothered a grin in his beard, and kept his gaze on Rhian.

The only sound in the tiltyard was Rhian's breathing, and Zandakar's, deep and fast, on the very edge of laboured. Grunts, as they leapt and spun and cartwheeled and flipped. The swift thud-thud of their feet as they landed in the dirt, on the grass, the lighter patpat as their hands followed their feet.

Rhian, with a great gasp, sprang onto her extended left arm and swirled herself upwards and sideways, her right leg extending to catch Zandakar across the belly. He twisted under her foot, seemingly boneless, and his leg caught her instead in the chest. She crashed heavily, awkwardly to the trampled and sweat-stippled grass. With a shout of savage triumph he came down on top of her, straddling her torso, knife swinging round to press to her throat.

But before his blade could cut off her breathing,

hers whipped up into his face, its tip pricking the skin beside his right eye. One deep breath and she'd have him blinded . . . or worse. A thread of blood, like a tear, found its way down his cheek.

"*Setzhay*?" she demanded, the air rasping in her throat.

Zandakar's blade fell to his side. "*Setzhay, hushla*," he replied, then smiled. "Good. Good."

Dexterity let go of the breath he'd been holding, aware that beside him Ursa's face had paled to milk-white. This time he put his arm all the way round her shoulders, and she was so shaken she didn't object.

"Rollin have mercy," she murmured. "I can't come here again."

He would. Not because he enjoyed the sight of Rhian and Zandakar fighting like cat and dog, but because it was one of the few ways he knew how to show them he cared.

Zandakar hadn't moved. Neither had Rhian. Her knife-point still pricked the skin beside his eye. The trickle of blood on his cheek was drying a darker red.

She said, still breathing heavily, "Do you believe that I believe you? Do you?"

So slowly, so gently, he took her wrist in his hand and lowered her blade from his face. "*Zho*. I believe."

"This is a new thing? Since you were banished, Zandakar?"

Dexterity watched Zandakar's face twist with pain. "I think *zho*. Rhian . . ." He took a shuddering breath. "*Yatzhay*, Rhian."

"What are they talking about, Jones?" said Ursa. "What's a new thing? Why is he sorry?"

He shrugged. "I've no idea."

"Then you'd best find out, hadn't you?" she replied. "Because it's trouble, whatever else it may be."

Yes. It was trouble. There was dreadful grief in Zandakar's face, revulsion in Rhian's. And beneath the revulsion a deeper, sharper pain.

Oh dear. What's happened? Hettie, what's gone wrong now?

Rhian slapped Zandakar's thigh with the flat of her blade. "Up. I must get ready for Litany."

Elegantly uncoiling, Zandakar rose to his feet. Then he held out his hand to help Rhian onto her feet. She followed his easy movement, their gazes not shifting from each other's face.

"Speaking of trouble," said Ursa, under her breath. Then she shook herself, and turned her back to the tilt-yard. "I'm off, Jones. Physick Travvis in the township's got a bunion, so I'm taking his place at the clinic tonight. Don't blame me if I stink of regurgitated ale come the morning."

"Oh, must you go?" he said. "You're the royal physick now, Ursa. You should have a care for yourself."

"No, I should have a care for those folk less fortunate in their health," she snapped. "I never was a physick to give myself airs and graces, and I'm too old to start such nonsense now." She slapped him. "As you well know, Jones. Wash your mouth out with soap."

He watched her stamp away, muttering, and smiled. It was good to be on side with her again, that was certain. He'd missed her severely, even the rough side of her tongue. Or perhaps especially . . .

"Dexterity!"

He turned. Rhian was walking towards him, sweaty and dirty, lightly spattered with blood. Her own blade was sheathed again, and Zandakar's was in her hand. He walked behind, nicked and bloody himself here and there.

As he watched her walking, Dexterity felt his heart thud hard. Yes indeed. Oh dear. Something definitely was wrong.

When she reached him, he bowed. "Majesty. Is everything all right?"

She smiled. "Of course."

Her statecraft was flawless. Without his days on the road, learning her, he'd not have seen the truth beneath the mask. "But you're wounded."

"Wounded?" She glanced at the red-stained slash in her sleeve. "A scratch. No need for healing. And no time if there was. I have to go, I'm running late for Litany. Did you come out to stretch your legs, Mister Jones? Perhaps Zandakar would keep you company."

Her message was clear: she wanted him to spend time with Zandakar. He glanced in the warrior's face, and saw there an echo of the distress he'd witnessed earlier. *Yatzhay, Rhian.* But why was he sorry?

"Yes, indeed, Majesty," he said heartily. "I do need the fresh air. Would you walk with me, Zandakar? I'd be glad of the company."

"Of course he'll walk with you," said Rhian. "But mind you stay in the gardens, Mister Jones. The soldiers will fetch you when it's time to come in."

As he watched Rhian out of sight, he heard

Zandakar sigh. Without turning he said, "Zandakar. Why are you sorry?"

Zandakar didn't answer. "Zandakar?" he said, and did turn. "What's happened?"

The warrior's brief captivity in the castle's dungeons hadn't marked him. Not like the nobles had been marked by their stay, under Marlan. He looked strong and well and just like himself. Dexterity looked closer.

No. Not quite like himself. He's had a bad shock.

"Dexterity—" Zandakar began, then shook his head.

"Come along," he said, and patted the man's arm. "You heard Rhian. We're to stroll in the gardens."

A scattering of bees still buzzed in the fragrant flowerbeds, even though the sun was slowly sinking, dragging dusk in its wake. From the corner of his eye Dexterity caught sight of four castle soldiers, hovering discreetly beyond the garden's borders. He thought Zandakar knew they were there too, though he made no comment.

How small his life has become. Not so long ago he was a prince in his own land, commander of an army. And now he's a prisoner who must walk in a garden watched by men who'll gladly kill him if he so much as takes one wrong step.

"Zandakar," he said again, breaking the long silence. "I can see you're upset. Rhian's upset too. I wish you'd tell me what's happened."

The late afternoon air was warm and scented, almost too sweetly for comfort. Zandakar reached out his hand and trailed his fingers through a waterfall of pale yellow sassy-blossoms. Then he sighed again, deeply, a sound full of pain.

"Yuma gives humans to *chalava*."

It took him a moment to make sense of the comment. Understanding halted him dead in his tracks. "You mean – *sacrifice*? Human sacrifice in Mijak?"

Zandakar continued another few paces, then slowed. Stopped. Without looking back he nodded. "*Zho*."

Oh dear. Oh, *Hettie*. Feeling sick, Dexterity stared at Zandakar's braced, rigid shoulders. "You didn't know."

That made Zandakar turn. His ice blue eyes were too bright. "*Wei*."

"But Rhian thought you did?"

Zandakar swallowed. "*Wei*. Alasdair king."

Well of course Alasdair thought that. Alasdair would believe anything of the man who loved his wife.

"Human sacrifice?" he said, still sickened. "Oh, this is bad, Zandakar. It's – well, it's worse than barbaric." A thought occurred. "How did Rhian learn of it?"

Zandakar shrugged. "*Wei* know."

"But she's quite certain? She knows it for a fact?"

"I think *zho*."

"And you believe it," he murmured. "With no proof, you think it's true."

His face twisting, Zandakar nodded. "*Zho*."

Because you know your mother. Because you've seen what she can do, you've seen her slash your unborn child from your wife's belly. Seen your own death in her eyes.

"Zandakar . . ." Dexterity folded his arms, suddenly chilled through. "Is this *chalava*? Has your god ever asked for human blood before?"

"*Wei! Wei!*" Zandakar's fist struck his chest. "*Chalava* say *wei* kill."

To you. Not to her. "Zandakar—"

Zandakar said something swiftly in his own tongue, then, the words dressed in misery. Only one word was familiar. *Yuma.* His fist struck his chest again, surely hard enough to hurt.

Dexterity stared at him, nonplussed. *He's grieving. After all she's done, he's grieving for his mother. I don't understand it, Hettie. Why doesn't he hate her?*

"Zandakar . . ." He put a gentle, careful hand on Zandakar's shoulder. "This is dreadful news. *Yatzhay.*"

A little of the pain eased from Zandakar's face. "*Zho.* Thank you. Dexterity *gajka.*"

"*Zho,*" he said. "You mustn't forget that. Even though we've had our differences and difficulties I *am* your friend, Zandakar. You can confide in me."

Zandakar rubbed a hand across his face. The thin line of dried blood from Rhian's knife-prick flaked off his skin, to float haphazardly on a current of air. "Rhian is Dexterity *gajka*?"

He sighed. "Yes, we're friends again. She's forgiven me, it seems. I'm back on the council."

Zandakar mimicked whittling. "Toys?"

"I'm afraid they'll have to wait. But I'm sure I'll get back to my little business one of these days. Zandakar—" He took a deep breath. "I'm sorry you ended up in that prison cell. I did try to speak for you. I tried to explain. You must understand, people are frightened.

And with Emperor Han arriving unexpected like that—"

"*Zho*," said Zandakar. "I know."

Dexterity started walking again, and Zandakar fell into step beside him. "While you were in prison, nobody . . . hurt you?"

A shadow of memory chased over Zandakar's face. "Witch-men."

He felt his own memories shudder through him. The winnowing of his soul by Emperor Han's Sundao. Not a word spoken, yet all his life laid bare . . . or so it had felt at the time.

"I know. They're awful. But no-one else?"

"*Wei*," said Zandakar.

"Well that's good. That's good. And now you're free."

Zandakar glanced across the flowerbeds, to where the soldiers were lurking. "*Zho*," he said, his expression wry. "Free."

Oh dear. Change the subject. "I'm told you saved Rhian's life by teaching her how to fight Damwin and Kyrin. That was a good thing, Zandakar. That was the right thing to do."

"*Zho*."

"Did you see it? Were you there?"

"*Wei* there." Zandakar glanced up at the nearby looming castle. "In chamber. I saw from window."

"And was it – was it dreadful?"

"Dreadful?" said Zandakar slowly, as though he tasted the word. "*Wei*. Rhian stupid, she *wei* kill Kyrin quick." His face clouded with remembered anger, then his teeth bared in a smile. "She kill

Damwin quick. She kill Damwin in her *hota*. Rhian *hushla*, killing queen."

Dexterity stared at him. *I will never, never understand this man. The thought of human sacrifice torments him, and yet he is pleased by the deaths of those wretched dukes.* "Well," he said faintly. "It was a nasty business, but it's all over now."

"*Zho*," said Zandakar, then stopped and looked to where the soldiers were approaching.

"Ah," said Dexterity. "It seems our pleasant stroll is over too."

"Sir," said the sergeant, joining them with his men. "This man must be escorted inside."

"*This man* has a name!" he snapped. "I'll thank you to use it."

The sergeant's eyes narrowed. "Sir—"

"And I've got a name too. It's Dexterity Jones. I'm one of the queen's councillors, in case you weren't aware."

"Mister Jones," said the sergeant, his manner deflating considerably. "I see."

He felt slightly ashamed, puffing himself up with consequence like the worst kind of nobleman, but he couldn't bear to have Zandakar treated like a common villain.

"Dexterity," said Zandakar as the soldiers gave a little ground. "I eat now. You eat with me?"

Dexterity looked at him. Zandakar's face was schooled again, he and Rhian were equals in their discipline, but even so . . . he couldn't quite hide his loneliness.

Or perhaps it's just I know him as well as I know Rhian.

"It would be my pleasure," he replied. "Sergeant, lead on."

The castle apartments given over to Zandakar for his use were neat and pleasant, but hardly lavish. It seemed there were two rooms, a public area for sitting and dining, and a smaller room for sleeping.

Dexterity flinched at the sound of a key turning in the outer door's lock. He glanced at Zandakar, but if he heard it he gave no sign. Probably he was used to it now.

Used to being a prisoner. It may not be a dungeon cell, but that's the only difference.

"This is wrong," he said, frowning. "It's an insult. I take it the soldiers remain on the other side of the doors?"

Drifting over to the window so he could look outside, Zandakar shrugged. "*Zho.*" He sounded . . . resigned.

"Well, it's not good enough. I'll talk to Rhian, Zandakar. I'll see the soldiers sent away, I'll see that your doors are left unlocked. Rollin's mercy, you're a man, you're not some – some dangerous *animal.*"

Zandakar glanced over his shoulder. "You say?"

He took a step closer. "Rhian will listen to me."

"Rhian, *zho,*" said Zandakar, and shrugged. "Alasdair king? I think *wei.*"

"It won't be Alasdair's decision! It's for Rhian to decide how you're treated and I tell you I won't stand for you being treated like *this.*"

Slowly, Zandakar turned from the window. "You care, Dexterity. Why? I am Mijak."

"*Why?*" Dexterity found the nearest chair and dropped into it, abruptly weary. "Because it's reprehensibly immoral for us to expect you'll fight with us against your own people, against your *family*, yet continue to treat you like a pariah. Either you're one of us, or you're not. And if you're one of us, then you'll *live* like one of us. Truly free. Truly trusted. *That's* what I intend to say to Rhian."

Zandakar shook his head. "And Alasdair king? Council? Emperor of Tzhung?"

He banged his fist on the arm of his chair. "Zandakar, if God himself were here I'd say it to him!"

Now Zandakar was frowning. "*Wei* trouble, Dexterity. For you. *Wei* trouble."

"Oh, it's no trouble. I don't like to see anyone slighted. And Rhian will listen, just you wait. Like it or not, I'm more than a toymaker these days. And if I have to remind her of that, I will. Unless—" Dexterity hesitated. "Unless you don't want me to. Unless you're happy to remain here under lock, key and guard."

Zandakar sat back, relaxing a little at last, and let his gaze roam around the small apartment. "Happy?" His face settled into a sharper expression. "*Wei*."

"Then it's settled. The first chance I get, I'll have words with Her Majesty."

"Thank you," said Zandakar, again. Then he looked down at himself, sweat-stained and dirty from dancing the *hotas*. "Food soon. I bathe. You wait, *zho*?"

He nodded. "*Zho*. Of course."

Zandakar went into the second room, closing the door. Dexterity settled himself comfortably in the armchair, and at length Zandakar returned in a clean linen shirt and another pair of leather huntsman's leggings. His feet were bare. If it weren't for his blue hair, tied back now with a strip of leather, he'd look like any ordinary man.

Dexterity shook his head. *And yet he's anything but commonplace.* "Zandakar . . ." He hesitated. "When this is over, what will you do? Where will you go?"

Zandakar moved back to the window, and stared down at the Great Lawn. "If I live, Dexterity? If I *wei* die for Ethrea?"

He swallowed. "*Zho.* If you live. Will you go home?"

"Home?" said Zandakar. "Tcha. What is home?"

He didn't know how to answer that. And then he didn't have to, because the key turned in the chamber door's lock, it opened, and two soldiers entered bearing trays of steaming food. They put the trays on the small dining table, nodded warily, and withdrew.

It had been a mistake to ask that question. Thoughtlessly cruel. He stood, and dusted his hands together. "My, that smells good!" he said brightly. "Shall we eat? I'm famished."

"*Zho,*" said Zandakar, his expression cool, contained. "We eat."

CHAPTER FIFTEEN

Within days of his elevation to the prolateship, Helfred had begun conducting evening Litany in Kingseat capital's great chapel. It was important, he'd said, that the people of Kingseat quickly accept him as their new spiritual leader. The faster Marlan's memory was laid to rest, the better for everyone. So every night of the week, as darkness rolled over the harbour and the township, the chapel bells rang out and the devout of Kingseat gathered to pray.

The queen and her king consort gathered with them.

"Every night?" Rhian had protested when Helfred informed her their presence was requested. "You expect us to attend public Litany *every night*?"

"Every night that you can," said Helfred, serenely unmoved by her lack of enthusiasm. "Majesty, it is vital you set a most perfect example for your people. You are Ethrea's first queen, they must see you are a queen in whom they can repose their trust. God himself placed you on your throne. Would you deny him thanks? Is Eberg's daughter so churlish?"

She'd felt her face heat at that. "No, of course I'm not, but Helfred, *every night*?"

Not answering her immediately, he'd turned to the Living Flame of her privy chapel and contemplated its steady burning, his expression sober.

"Rhian," he'd said softly, "you are a monarch like none other in our history. Not only because you're a woman, but because of the dangers confronting us. Ethrea, having weathered one tempest, will soon face an even greater maelstrom. The peace we enjoy now is an illusion, and you know it. When the truth of Mijak is revealed you and the king must *not* be strangers to your people. Most particularly, they must know you for a faithful queen who is reconciled with God. They must know in their hearts that when they lean on you, you'll not falter."

She'd shaken her head at him. "And you think me going to Litany every night is going to achieve that?"

"Going to Litany in the town's great chapel, yes," said Helfred. "Rhian, *think*. When word spreads that you attend public Litany many folk who rarely bother will come for curiosity's sake, just to see you. So they can *say* they've seen you. Who knows? It may well be that folk from beyond our own duchy might come to see you for themselves. I pray they do, it can only be to our benefit."

"I see little benefit to being paraded like a cow at market," she'd grumbled.

Helfred had sighed. "Majesty, the benefit is clear. If we fail in our effort to sink Mijak's warships at sea, if we are forced to confront them here, in Ethrea, every man, woman and child shall be made a soldier in your army. They'll look to you for leadership and the saving of their lives – and *I* look to pave the way to their belief that you will. Once captive in the chapel, your people will have no choice but to hear my admonitions. I can quietly, discreetly, prepare them for what's to come. I can give them hope and strength and belief in God's mercy, in *you*, and remind them you're queen because of God's great grace."

The worst of it was, Helfred made sense. She'd almost heard her father's voice, whispering agreement in her ear. Was sure she could hear her brothers, sniggering. They'd always poked fun at her impatience of Church ceremony.

"All *right*," she'd said, without any grace at all. "I'll be there, *some* nights."

And Helfred had smiled.

So now here she sat in the front pew of Kingseat's great chapel with her husband, acutely aware of the crowded pews behind them, of the folk pressed close at the chapel's open doors, of even more residents and visitors collected in the township's streets waiting for a glimpse of their young queen as she returned from Litany to the castle.

Helfred, in his prolate's robe of good quality but great restraint, stood in his pulpit before the Living Flame in its magnificent gold and jewel-crusted sconce. He was flanked on either side by those members of his Court Ecclesiastica not engaged on royal business, equally magnificent in their finest attire. Their presence lent weight to his youthful, deliberately unflamboyant appearance.

Though he preaches like a man thrice his age. But then he always did, and wasn't that just one reason why he drove me to distraction?

And still did, if she were honest. But she was able to admit – if only to herself, and grudgingly – that she needed him in this fight, the greatest fight of her life.

Beside her, Alasdair shifted a little on the hard pew. Not looking at him, feeling her heart thud beneath her gown's ornately beautiful green velvet bodice, she slid her fingers over his and listened to Helfred's voice thunder beneath the rafters.

"For did not Rollin himself say, in *Admonitions 32*, '*Be sure you do not let down your guard, for evil flourishes in quiet places*,'" he preached. "'*Its seeds take root in an untilled garden. Do not think because I bring you peace today that peace tomorrow is your portion. Peace must be husbanded, for God knows there are men of the world who see peace as an enemy to be defeated. I say again, be on your guard, for who shall know when God's peace will stand threatened?*'" Hands firmly grasping the edge of his gilded wooden pulpit, Helfred swept his fierce gaze across his congregation. "Rollin wrote those words centuries ago, my children. But what is time, to the timelessness of God? We must be ever vigilant. We cannot take our island kingdom's serenity for granted."

Upright on their carved, gilded benches, the most venerables of the Court Ecclesiastica nodded their approval of his words. The congregation murmured, inspired by his passion.

"We are a blessèd people, my children," Helfred continued. "For in the midst of upheaval and despair God heard our prayers and delivered unto us a queen of might and power. The wicked fall before her like wheat before the scythe. She is young and full of fire. She is the Rollin of our age, sworn to preserve God's peace, God's garden kingdom of Ethrea. Let us pledge to be her trustworthy gardeners. Let us commit our hearts and souls to plucking out any weeds that would take root in this our glorious, peaceful home."

In the choristers' gallery above the pulpit, a lone exquisite voice rose in song.

"To those whom God has granted much bounty, much devotion is in turn required."

It was the signal that the Litany had concluded. With a gracious lifting of his hands, Helfred invited the congregation to stand and sing.

Rhian, painfully aware she had the vocal talents of a frog with a sore throat, mimed the words and basked in Alasdair's glorious tenor, which helped soothe her irritation and jittering nerves.

A queen of might and power? The Rollin of our age? Helfred, are you mad? How am I to live up to such fulsome praise?

It was the most extravagant he'd been since she'd started attending each evening's service. At first he'd hardly mentioned her, choosing instead to focus on her father's legacy of harmony and prosperity, on the good fortune of Ethrea to be a shining example of peace in the world. He'd preached the importance of friendship: husband and wife, brother and sister, neighbour and neighbour . . . nation and nation. Encouraging each night's congregation to look upon the league of trading nations as friends and brothers under the skin, people of good heart and good intent whose differences from Ethrea were far outweighed by their shared beliefs in mutual support and appreciation.

Preparing the fallow field of public opinion for the day warships of Harbisland, Arbenia and Tzhungtzhungchai are moored in our harbour. Oh, Papa. Did you ever think to see such a sight?

In the past week, though, Helfred had slowly but

surely shifted his compass until it pointed *due Rhian*. It was important, she knew, for her people to see her as some kind of invincible, God-blessed hero. Her mantle of royalty must glow so brightly that they were blinded to the truth of her youth and inexperience. They had to believe in her, be willing to lay down their lives, the fathers and sons, the wives, mothers and daughters of Kingseat, who would surely be the first at risk should the warriors of Mijak reach their shores.

Oh, God, I beg you. Don't let it come to that.

As ever when she let her thoughts touch upon Mijak, her belly churned with nausea and her palms slicked with sweat. Especially tonight, with fresh horrors newly revealed.

Human blood for sacrifice. Is there no end to Mijak's evil?

Also churning through her, Emperor Han's revelations. Just when she thought she had his measure, he found new ways to confound her.

But I have to trust him. I can't let myself be a prisoner of the childish, mistrustful past. It seems that without Han and his witch-men, the warships of Mijak would be in the harbour already. But, dear God, he frightens me.

And so did her prolate's extravagant praise. Being chosen by God didn't make her divine. Helfred of all people should understand that.

The hymn ended. Helfred descended from his pulpit and walked the tiled pathway between the chapel's pews, followed by his Court Ecclesiastica. As soon as they reached the chapel's open, ornate doors, Rhian followed with Alasdair half a pace behind her.

The crowding townsfolk on the wide, torchlit stone steps had respectfully fallen back, giving her prolate his pride of place. The most venerables stood ranged behind him, lending him their aged, solemn presence. She still found it marvellous that these old men, so united against her under Marlan, now stood shoulder to shoulder in defence of her crown. In support of Helfred, whom they had so eagerly declared anathema and would happily have seen flogged near to death.

It's extraordinary, really, what one little miracle can do.

As was by now their custom, she and Alasdair joined Helfred on the top step. Though by rights it was the prolate who should receive the congregation's respects after Litany, Helfred was only briefly acknowledged as the church slowly emptied of Kingseat's devout. Instead, again, Rhian found herself the focus of attention.

After their first attendance at the Litany, Alasdair had been uneasy, so many people crowding that close. Ven'Martin was buried but his memory lived on. He'd wanted a skein of Kingseat guards posted outside the chapel, a silent warning to anyone with ideas.

She'd over-ruled him. "Let them stand in the street at the foot of the chapel steps," she'd decreed. "That's not unseemly. But to post them a handsbreadth from me? It would send the wrong message entirely. I am Rhian of Ethrea, God's chosen queen, who slew two recalcitrant dukes with her righteous sword. How then can I stand on the chapel's steps surrounded by armed guards?"

He'd acquiesced, of course. But every time he made

a suggestion and she declined to take it, she thought she saw him drift a little further away.

Now, standing with him and Helfred, lit by rank after rank of burning torches and accepting her subjects' awed praise and thanks, smiling, smiling, frozenly smiling, she knew she'd done the right thing . . . no matter the personal cost.

She'd thought she might become used to this, to facing the people she'd sworn to defend with her blood and her life. Instead she felt the weight of that promise pressing her harder and harder against the ground. The hope in their eyes. The blind, fervent belief. The love they had for her because she was Eberg's daughter, his sole surviving child. Because she had God's favour. Because she was so young and beautiful. But how would it be when they realised their lives really were in her hands? Would they still believe in her? Would their faith remain strong?

Or will they turn against me when the first blood is spilled?

A frightening thought. She felt herself shiver.

"Rhian?" murmured Alasdair, his hand on her elbow. "You're weary. We should return to the castle."

She was more than weary, she was exhausted. The afternoon's *hotas* had been relentless. "In a moment," she said, smiling, and eased her arm free. "Let everyone come out of the chapel first."

He didn't protest, just gave the signal to their footman, waiting discreetly at the bottom of the chapel steps. As the last worshipper paid his respects their carriage drew to a halt in the street before them. She turned to Helfred.

"Your Eminence, thank you for such a rousing sermon. Surely you've given us much to think on."

"Majesty, that is always my intention," he replied, his eyebrows raised.

Young and full of fire, indeed. If you're not careful, Helfred, my fire will singe you.

She turned to the most venerables. "My lords, God's blessing and the peace of Rollin upon you."

They murmured the same to her in reply. Then it seemed she was free to depart . . . only it was swiftly apparent her people didn't wish her to leave.

"God bless you, Majesty!" a voice called from the crowd.

"Bless the memory of your father, too!"

"Aye, bless him and bless you!"

Distinct words were quickly lost in the rising tide of praise, prayer and acclaim. Helpless she stood there, awash in emotion . . . theirs and her own. This hadn't happened before. Helfred's pointed sermon had surely stirred them.

"Good people!" she cried at last, struggling to pitch her voice above the clamour. "Good people of Kingseat and Ethrea, my thanks!"

Raggedly the crowd fell silent. So many torchlit faces, staring. So much eager, breathless hunger for her words, for *her*. It almost stole her courage.

"Good people," she said again, "indeed, my thanks, and the thanks also of Alasdair, your king. My beloved husband and the strength by my side."

Another cheer went up, and more calls for God's blessings.

"You ask God to bless me," she said, "but I tell you he already has, beyond measure. I am queen of a jewelled country. My dear friends, know that you and your welfare are my first and last thought upon rising and upon closing my eyes at night. There's nothing I won't do for you. No battle I won't fight, no danger I won't face. I am my father's daughter, I'm the sister of your two grand princes, three men taken from us so untimely. I still grieve. I know you grieve with me. But I also know they want me to be strong . . . I know you need me to be strong . . . and I am. You give me strength. You heal my heart. You're my family."

The crowd's roar then threatened to crack the new night sky. Stinging with tears, abruptly overwhelmed by the past, she made her way down the steps to the carriage with Alasdair's hand warm on her back. The footman opened its door for them. Before she ducked inside, Rhian turned and raised a hand to the people clustered on the great chapel's steps and on the cobbled footpath, even spilling into the street.

"Come," said Alasdair. "You've done enough for one day."

She let him guide her into the carriage and sagged into her cushions as he sat opposite. The footman closed the doors. A moment later she heard the thud, felt the jolt, as he leapt onto his travelling step. The coachman cracked his whip and the carriage rolled forward. She closed her eyes, and still saw the crowd.

Dear God, they look at me as though I am Rollin reborn.

The clip-clop of the horses' hooves was oddly soothing as the carriage made its careful way through the most populous part of the township, heading for Kingsway which would take them back to the castle. It was expertly sprung, jouncing gently over the cobbles. A pity it couldn't jounce the memories from her mind.

"Rhian," said Alasdair. "Are you all right?"

"When I was twelve," she said, with her eyes still closed, "Papa, the boys and I attended a wedding in Meercheq. It was my first grown-up outing, and I was ever so proud of my brocade and pearls."

The dress had been one of her mother's, expertly altered to fit her girlish form. The fabric had smelled faintly of rosewater, Mama's favourite scent. She could remember that much of her long-dead mother. Queen Ilda always smelled of roses.

"Something happened at the wedding?" said Alasdair.

She rolled her head against the cushions behind her. "No. On the way home. It was autumn and the weather was still fine, so we were riding in an open carriage. I remember that journey so clearly: the sun on my face, Simon teasing Ranald over some girl who'd spent the whole wedding making sheep's eyes at him. Papa trying not to laugh." She felt her lips curve in a remembering smile. "Ranald threatening to hang Simon over the side of the carriage by his heels if he didn't shut up. Simon used to pester him unmercifully, you know."

She heard Alasdair chuckle. "I know. That never changed, even when they were grown."

He was right. It didn't. "We passed a ploughed field," she continued, and felt her smile fade. "There were pheasants in it, exploring the tilled soil for any abandoned seeds. Their plumage was brilliant. Iridescent. They were beautiful. So innocent. The field was bordered by a copse . . . and on its far side I saw a group of hunters, with their game dogs and their slingshots and their bows and arrows. I wanted to leap from the carriage and run back to warn the pheasants. I was twelve, and I knew I'd seen them in their last living moments. I knew they'd soon be dead, strung up in a larder somewhere. I wanted to cry. To scream. I was so *angry*."

"Why? Birds die so men can live, Rhian."

She opened her eyes. "I knew that, Alasdair. But I didn't *want* to know it, I *hated* knowing it, knowing those pheasants were about to die . . . when they were so innocent of the knowledge." She blinked hard. "When I stood on the chapel's steps and looked at Kingseat's people, the memory came flooding back. I was twelve years old again, helpless to save those innocent lives."

Alasdair raised her hand to his lips and kissed it. "You're not helpless, Rhian. You're not twelve. And you're not alone."

"In my head I know that. But in my heart . . ." She sighed. "When Papa died so soon after the boys, all I could think about was protecting the kingdom from Marlan. The only thing that mattered was keeping the crown, because it was my birthright and he had *no* business trying to take it. Not *him*. I was prepared to die for my cause. Now those weeks seem almost insubstantial."

In his plain, bony face, Alasdair's dark brown eyes were fierce. "They're not."

She tightened her fingers round his. "I had a dream last night. I dreamed I stood on the castle battlements looking over the water to the horizon. I saw a terrible storm approaching. I couldn't stop it, couldn't turn it back. All I could do was stand there, and wait for it to strike."

"Rhian . . ." Alasdair shifted to sit beside her. "I have bad dreams, too. Dreams that you die because I can't protect you. They're our fears talking, they're not the future. I can protect you. I *will* protect you. And you'll protect Ethrea. Yes, Mijak is a terrible storm. But we can weather it. We *will* weather it."

"Do you truly believe that?" she said eventually. "Or are you just saying so to soothe me?"

"I believe it," he said firmly. "I'll never lie to you, Rhian."

"Nor I to you. But, Alasdair, we won't win this fight without Zandakar."

He turned his head to look out of the carriage window. The last of the town's lights were slipping behind them; they'd reach the castle soon. "You're so certain of him. Despite everything you've learned of him, the slaughters and the brutality, the blood, the destroyed cities, who he *is*, who his *family* is, my God, what they're doing even now, you have no doubt he can be trusted."

How could she answer that? How could she tell him: "*From the moment Zandakar picked me up and carried me from the clerica at Todding I've felt safe with him. I've trusted him. What he's done is not who he is. Not all of who he is. Another man dwells inside him, a man yearning to be free of violence and bloodshed. Who looks to me to set him free.*"

She couldn't. Alasdair would never understand. And this fragile moment would shatter irredeemably.

"I'm certain we need him," she said, choosing her words carefully. "I have no doubt of that."

Alasdair looked at her, his eyes resigned. "Then for your sake I'll try to work with him, Rhian. But please don't ask me to befriend the man, or lose all my mistrust, or for one moment cease my scrutiny of him. As your husband – as Ethrea's king – to do less would be the worst kind of betrayal."

"I won't." She smiled, and he kissed her, and for that brief moment their world was at peace.

They returned to the castle to find that Ven'Cedwin had been admitted to the foyer of their privy apartments, and was waiting for them. He stood at their approach, his lined face creased further with concern.

Feeling her belly twist, Rhian glared at the guards . . . but in fairness knew she couldn't complain. Cedwin was a venerable, he was her secretary, they knew he had the freedom of the castle.

"What now?" she muttered, and moved forward to meet him. "Ven'Cedwin? This can't wait till the morning?"

Her secretary glanced at Alasdair, then shook his head. "Sadly I fear it cannot, Your Majesty."

"The ambassadors?" said Alasdair. "I take it you saw the letters dispatched to them?"

"Indeed, Majesty, I did," said Ven'Cedwin. "Each was delivered, and each has received a reply."

"Which I'm not going to like," said Rhian. "Am I?"

"No, Your Majesty," said Ven'Cedwin. "I feel it's likely you'll be greatly displeased."

God give me strength . . . She looked at Alasdair. "He's right. This can't wait."

Alasdair opened the door to their apartments.

"Then by all means, let us withdraw and be displeased in private."

Ven'Cedwin collected his leather satchel and followed them inside to the parlour. As he closed the door behind them, Rhian began to pace. Alasdair, frowning, stood beside the bookcase.

"Let me guess," she said, passing Ven'Cedwin in a swirl of green velvet skirt. "They decline to attend any meeting tomorrow."

Ven'Cedwin fumbled open his satchel and withdrew a sheaf of papers. "Yes, Majesty. All but one."

"Ambassador Lai."

"That's correct, Majesty."

She glanced at Alasdair, hard put not to shock Ven'Cedwin by swearing. "I do hope our friends, the ambassadors, are struck down by a sudden plague."

"A plague of excuses, perhaps," said Ven'Cedwin. He shuffled through the notes in his hand. "*A previous engagement* – that's Arbenia. *Religious observances* – that's Keldrave, Haisun, Barbruish and Slynt. Icthia claims to be unwell—"

"Now Athnïj I'm willing to believe," she said, still pacing. "If I were him I'd be sick too, knowing my homeland's been conquered by Mijak. What of Dev'karesh?"

"Dev'karesh also pleads a previous engagement."

"With Arbenia?" Alasdair snorted. "I suppose anything's possible."

Halting, Rhian whirled to face Ven'Cedwin. "Are you saying not even Voolksyn will come? I thought he supported me. He stood up to Gutten."

Ven'Cedwin shook his head. "No, Ambassador

Voolksyn has also declined. But of them all, he's the only one to give an honest answer."

She held out her hand. "Show me."

Ven'Cedwin gave her the note from Voolksyn. *Harbisland regrets absence,* it read. *Harbisland respects Ethrea but we are sovereign.*

"Well?" said Alasdair.

Rhian watched her fingers crush the note. "Harbisland doesn't care to dance to our tune." She threw the ball of paper across the room. "*Damn* them! Those arrogant, fools! Do they think this is a *game*?"

"They think they have more to fear from losing face before us, and each other, than from Mijak," said Alasdair. "The threat of Mijak's not real to them yet."

"*Not real*? My God, Alasdair! I told them. *Han* told them. *Zandakar* told them. *Dexterity* told them!"

Alasdair shrugged. "Words, Rhian. If you don't wish to believe them, words are easy to dismiss."

"What, they'll not believe the threat is real until they see themselves spitted on a Mijaki sword?"

"It would be more convincing."

"Fools!" she said again, and dropped into the nearest chair. "I can't leave it like this. I can't let them defy me so openly. If Han thinks I'm not capable of holding this alliance together—"

She didn't dare think of it. Without Han's witch-men they were doomed. If he lost faith in her he might abandon Ethrea and everyone else to Mijak. His witch-men's power might well save Tzhung-tzhungchai, if Tzhung-tzhungchai was all they had to defend.

"We have to try again," she said grimly. "I have to write another letter, I have to – to find a way to convince Gutten and Voolksyn to take me seriously. If I can convince them, the others will follow. And if I can't . . ." She heard her voice break. Saw Ven'Cedwin lower his gaze, discomfited.

"Rhian," said Alasdair, crossing to her. "I'll write the letter. Now. Ven'Cedwin and I will go to his office and we'll—"

She shook her head. "No, no, I should do this, I—"

"*Rhian*," said Alsadair, and took her cold hands in his. "You're exhausted. We'll show you the draft before it's sent out in a fair copy, I promise. But you need to stay here, you need to eat and rest."

She pulled her hands free. "You need to eat, too. You need rest. Alasdair, I'm—"

"Queen of Ethrea, I know," he said. "With a king who is telling you, *enough is enough*. Once, this once, you *will* be ruled by me."

Her eyes burned and for a moment she feared she'd weep before Ven'Cedwin.

"Very well," she said, when she could trust her voice. "Inform Ambassador Lai there's been a slight delay. Impress upon the other ambassadors my sincere need for their aid. Ask them to consider our treaty, the ties between our nations. Ask them—"

"I will," said Alasdair, and nodded to Ven'Cedwin, who collected his satchel and tactfully moved to the door. "And when the venerable and I are done, you'll see the letter. But now I want you to *rest*."

The door closed behind him and Ven'Cedwin, but instead of withdrawing to her inner chambers she continued to sit, hands loose in her lap, her aching head spun about with calamitous thoughts.

I am failing. Ethrea will be destroyed. Why won't they listen? Why won't they believe—

And then she heard raised voices beyond the parlour's closed door. Someone was challenging the guards on duty in the foyer. Groaning, she pushed out of the chair to discover who was responsible for this latest disturbance.

"Dexterity?" she said, standing in the open doorway. "What's this?"

The senior guard, Bowman, spun round. "Your Majesty! Forgive me, I tried not to disturb you but—"

She raised her hand. "It's all right, Bowman. Mister Jones is a friend, and welcome. But don't disturb me hereafter, is that clear?" She stepped back. "Come in, Dexterity. I can spare you five minutes."

"Thank you, Majesty," Dexterity said. "I'll not need longer, I hope."

"You hope?" she said, shutting the door much harder than was necessary. "Do you presume on our friendship, Mister Jones?"

Dexterity pushed his hands into his baggy jacket pockets. He looked as rumpled and unkempt as ever, and unhappy too. "Not without good cause."

"Dexterity . . ." After all they'd been through, there was little point in trying to keep up appearances. She slumped into her chair again. "What is it? Has Hettie sent you another vision?"

"No. This is about Zandakar."

Oh. Of course. "He told you? About—"

"Yes, and it's dreadful, but that's not why I'm here."

Though her bones were aching, she sat a little straighter. Temper was stirring. "Really?"

If Dexterity was chastened by the ice in her voice, he didn't show it. "Yes. Really," he replied. "I want you to let Zandakar free of this castle."

She blinked. "I beg your pardon?"

"It's not right, the way he's living here," he said, his cheeks touched with colour. "Locked up in his chamber, trammelled about with soldiers. After all he's done for you, Rhian, how can you repay him by keeping him a prisoner? Can't you see he's miserable? Like – like an eagle crammed in a cage. It's not right, I tell you. Rhian, it's *cruel*."

The accusation stole her breath. She was on her feet before she realised it, fists clenched, heart pounding. "Mister Jones, you do presume! How *dare* you—"

"How can I *not* dare?" he retorted. "Who else is there to speak for him? Aside from me he's friendless in the world. If I don't champion him, nobody will!"

"That's not true, he's not friendless!" she snapped. "*I* am his friend."

Dexterity jutted his beard at her. "Then you've a ragged way of showing it, *Majesty*! Rollin's mercy, he's sworn to shed his blood for you. For you and for Ethrea, and he's a stranger here. All that moves him is the desire to save lives."

Oh, he was unfair. He was *monstrous* unfair. "The saving of lives is all I desire, Dexterity. And one of the lives I want to save is *his*. Are you mad, to think I can leave him to wander freely about Kingseat? Looking as he does? With the skills he possesses?"

"What are you afraid of?" said Dexterity. "That he'll come to harm, or run away to sea?"

"Both, if you want the truth!" she replied, goaded. "And I'd be a poor queen if I didn't consider either possibility. He might be all that can save us from Mijak, you know that as well as I!"

"Oh, *Rhian*!" Dexterity stamped to the window, and back again. "Run away? Leave you? He'd sooner cut out his own heart!"

Silence as they stared at each other. When she found her voice, it was thinned to a whisper. "I don't know what you mean."

He snorted. "Oh yes you do, but it's neither here nor there. I've not come to talk of that, I've come to talk of giving Zandakar his freedom. Rhian, you can't ask a man to die for you, and treat him like a slave."

She stepped back. "A *slave*? Dexterity Jones—"

"A slave's what I said and a slave's what I meant," he said, caring nothing for protocol. "If you can't trust him to stay by your side unchained, what makes you think you can trust him with Ethrea?"

"That's *not* – I *don't* – how *dare* you come here and—"

"Majesty?" said a shocked voice. "Majesty, is aught amiss?"

She turned to see Dinsy, as rumpled as Dexterity, her plump cheeks flushed with sleep, standing in the parlour's other doorway.

"Oh, Majesty," said Dinsy. "Forgive me! I – I – fell to dozing and didn't realise you and His Majesty were returned from chapel."

Fell to dozing? Oh, poor Dinsy. *She looks as tired as I feel. It's no good, I must send for noble ladies to help her. She can't continue to maid me on her own.* Ignoring Dexterity, she went to the girl. "Don't cry, Dinsy, it's all right. I'm not angry. And no, there's nothing wrong. Mister Jones and I were merely — disagreeing."

Dinsy sniffed. "You were shouting, Majesty. It's a wonder the guards haven't broke in."

"I told them not to," she said. "Go back inside. I'll join you in a moment."

With a last glowering look at Dexterity, Dinsy obeyed.

"You know I'm right, Rhian," Dexterity said as soon as they were alone again. "I can see it in your face."

Drat her face. "Dexterity, it's complicated."

He stared, his eyes narrowed. "You're the queen, Rhian. It's only as complicated as you choose to make it."

"As I choose? Oh, Dexterity!" She folded her arms. "Yourself aside, my councillors don't trust him. Neither does Emperor Han. And if I let him go roaming about Kingseat I have no doubt he'd end up kidnapped by Gutten or Voolksyn or one of the others! I keep him close here for protection, can't you see that?"

"So close he's suffocating," said Dexterity. "Let him come home with me, just for a day or two. There's that much time you can spare him, isn't there?"

Well, yes. She did have a few days, especially now the ambassadors were playing their stupid games.

"Rhian," said Dexterity. Not angry now, but more serious than ever she'd seen him. "This news of Mijak. The human blood being spilled. It's crushed him. He needs some time, to ease his pain. He needs fresh air and sunshine and a change of scenery. I'll keep him safe at my cottage, you know I will."

Curious, she considered him. "I never realised you were so fond of him."

Dexterity shrugged. "Am I fond, or do I feel responsible? Could be it's a bit of both. It doesn't matter. Can he come home with me? Please?"

If she said yes, Alasdair would shout at her. Helfred would likely scold. So would the dukes, if they were here.

But Dexterity's right. I am the queen. And I owe Zandakar so much more than my life. If he needs this small favour, how can I not grant it?

"Very well," she sighed. "I'll grant you three days. I expect Edward and Rudi home from inspecting Ethrea's garrisons in that time. Once they've returned we must look at building our army, and Zandakar is central to that."

"Of course, Your Majesty," said Dexterity, widely smiling. "Three days and not a clock-tick longer, you have my word."

"I don't want him out of your sight, Dexterity. And he's not to travel beyond the home districts," she added. "You're to tell no-one who he is. If they ask, he's a servant."

He was nodding vigorously. "Yes, yes. Of course. *Thank you*, Your Majesty. You're doing the right thing."

"Let's hope so," she replied. "Now we'd best give him the good news."

CHAPTER SIXTEEN

Han wandered the paths through the main garden of Ambassador Lai's residence, listening to the windchimes singing. Breathing in the scents of his empire. Every flower around him came from somewhere in Tzhung-tzhungchai: the mountains of Tzinto, the marshes of Yeuhy, the spreading plains of Golontan. Every province represented, not a district forgotten. The sand beneath his bare feet was brought here from Tzhung's beaches and rivers, ochre and salt-white, eggshell blue and obsidian black, swept and swirled to honour the wind. If he closed his eyes, he might believe he was at home.

If I close my eyes, I will fall to sleep on my feet.

He'd spent the night in the witch-garden with Sundao and his witch-men, helping them keep the trade winds at bay. Now his bones were hollow. The early morning light stabbed pain through his head. He was hungry, thirsty, he needed to rest. But instead he prowled this garden, breathing memories and wrestling with thoughts he did not wish to share.

Beyond the high walls of the residence, Kingseat township and its harbour were stirring to life. The restless wind chimes drowned the sounds of voices, horses, carts and barrows and the ivy-covered stonework hid Kingseat from his sight, but with his witch-senses he could feel them.

All these innocent souls, whom Rhian can't protect.

A second letter had come from the castle late last night, informing his ambassador that the urgent meeting of trading nations she had requested was now postponed. Of course Lai had brought it to him at once, daring to sound the chimes at the witch-garden's gate, daring to disturb his emperor at work.

Han had not chastised him, for the letter was important, the meaning behind it clear and unwelcome: the other ambassadors had refused Rhian's summons. They resisted her authority. She could not bend them to her will.

And so was he presented with a dilemma. The wind had blown him here to seek Ethrea's help . . . or so he'd thought. But Ethrea could not help, for Rhian was helpless in the face of the other ambassadors' intransigence and ruthless self-interest.

I think we are the only hope to defeat brutal Mijak. I think there is room for but one empire in the world – and it will be the empire of the Tzhung.

The salt breeze blew, the wind chimes sang softly, melody and descant, harmony and counterpoint. Every note contained a truth. Han stood in the sunshine and let the truth blow through him, opened himself to the wisdom of the wind.

"Sun-dao," he said, when he understood what must be done. "Sun-dao, come."

A moment later Sun-dao stepped out of the twilight and joined him among the sunlit flowers.

"Han."

Han stared at his brother, stricken. The sunlight was merciless, revealing in full the cost of their battle against Mijak. "*Sun-dao* . . ."

Sun-dao smiled. "Emperor, you must not distress yourself. I am not dying. Not yet."

Turning away, Han stared at the vibrant pink blossoms on a nearby chynyi tree from Tan-tan province. "You don't amuse me, Sun-dao."

"Did you summon me for amusement?"

Sweating beneath his black silk tunic, Han turned back. "I summoned you because there is a task. But Sun-dao, I see you now and—"

"What is this task?" said Sun-dao, still smiling. "What does my emperor desire of me?"

"The wind has spoken, Sun-dao," he sighed. "It says—"

"That Rhian of Ethrea has failed," said Sun-dao. "I know."

Of course he knew. He was Sun-dao. "She has failed . . . but we have not. There is another way to defeat Mijak, Sun-dao."

"Han . . ." Sun-dao shook his head. "Do we discuss this again? The blood power of Mijak obscures all vision. I am the greatest witch-man in Tzhung and I cannot see what I must see to do what you want. I could, with great difficulty, witch my way to Icthia, yes, but—"

"And you will," he said. "But not alone."

"Not alone?" echoed Sun-dao, after a silent, staring moment. "Han, you cannot come."

Han sighed again, and tipped his face to the sun. "I know it. And even if I could, what use would I be? I can't see what must be seen, either. But, Sun-dao, you and I don't need to see. In Ethrea there is a man who can see these things for us. Who can show us the way so what must be done, can be done."

Sun-dao breathed in sharply. "*Zandakar*?"

"It's possible we misheard the wind, Sun-dao. It's possible it blew us here not for Rhian, but for her captive prince of Mijak."

"You think to trust Zandakar to kill his mother and brother?" said Sun-dao, incredulous. "You'd send him to strike off the twinned heads of Mijak so its body will die?"

Han laughed. "No. How could I? I've seen his heart, Sundao, as you have. Even as he hates what they do, weak love tells him they can still be turned from their slaughter. This prince of Mijak is a great fool."

"And yet you would trust him?"

Han rested his arm about his brother's weary shoulders. "To guide you to his murdering mother and brother once you reach Icthia, so you can kill them? Yes. I would."

Sun-dao smoothed his moustaches. "And you would tell him . . ."

"That the wind has told me he can save them, with our help. He won't refuse. He loves them too much."

Sun-dao nodded slowly. "This is true."

Turning, Han pulled Sun-dao to him in a close embrace. "But oh, my brother," he whispered. "It will be a cruel thing, witching a boat all the way to Icthia. Were you rested and unchallenged it would be cruel enough. You are neither. This battle for the trade winds—"

"Has not defeated me, Han," said Sun-dao. "You are my emperor, and this is my task. When do I go?"

For a moment he couldn't answer, struck to silence by Sun-dao's simple faith. "Soon," he said, his voice breaking. "It must be soon. After you've rested."

Sun-dao nodded. "And the trade winds?"

Han released him and stepped back. Laid a hand against his brother's thin, pain-filled face. "You will not worry," he said sternly. "I'll fight the trade winds for both of us, Sun-dao."

"You've done *what*, Jones?" demanded Ursa, standing aghast in the sunlit kitchen. "Brought Zandakar *here*? Rollin's mercy, are you out of your mind?"

Dexterity flapped a hand at his unexpected visitor. "Hush, Ursa! He's awake too, and only in the other room. Do you want to hurt his feelings?"

"I want to hurt *you*, Jones," she snapped. "What were you *thinking*? Are you going to sleep with your eyes open to make sure he doesn't bolt like a rabbit the first chance he gets?"

"He's not going to bolt. He gave Rhian his word."

"His *word*?" said Ursa, incredulous. "And what's that worth? He's a heathen warrior with blood on his hands! He shouldn't even be out of the castle dungeon."

"How can you be so harsh? After everything he's done for Rhian, how can you—"

"And after everything you've learned, Jones, after what Hettie showed you, how can *you* not see him for the danger he is?"

Bewildered, Dexterity retreated to the sink and

slumped against it. "I don't understand. You liked him well enough on the road."

Hands on her hips, eyes squinting with her displeasure, Ursa made a sharp, dismissive sound. "That was before I knew the truth of him, Jones. That was before I knew he'd murdered *children*."

"And he's sorry for that," he retorted. "Which must count for something. Think how he was raised, Ursa. From the moment of his birth Zandakar was taught to kill. He was taught to worship his god with blood and death. And now he's turned his back on that. I think it's a miracle as great as anything *I've* done, don't you?"

"Being sorry is all well and good, Jones," said Ursa, "but can his sorrow undo the destruction of cities? Can *anything* undo murder on that scale?"

Dexterity stared at the floor. They were fair questions. And of course he understood how Ursa felt. He'd felt the same way himself. With the death of Garabatsas haunting him still . . . of *course* he understood. But he still believed in Zandakar's remorse.

Does that make me a gullible fool? I hope not, for all our sakes.

"Ursa . . ." he said, gentling his voice. "I confess, when I first learned what he'd done I wanted to hate him. I wanted to leave him to starve to death, or worse. But Hettie says we need him. And doesn't Rollin expect us to find forgiveness in our hearts?"

"*Rollin?*" Now Ursa was almost spitting. "You'd quote *Rollin* to me, *you*, a man who refused to set foot in a church for twenty years? Jones, you're perilous close to hypocrisy!"

"You're *complaining*?" He straightened, offended.

"After twenty years of nagging me about not going to church you're *complaining* because I've reacquainted myself with Rollin?"

"No, Jones!" Ursa roared. "I'm complaining because when that bloodthirsty heathen *does* bolt like a rabbit it's *your* head Rhian'll have shoved on a chopping block!"

"Well, I'm sure I'm touched by your concern, Ursa, but seeing as how Zandakar *won't* be bolting you're wasting your time worrying about me and—"

"*Wei*, Dexterity. *Wei*, Ursa," said Zandakar, standing in the kitchen doorway. "*Wei* fight for me."

Dexterity threw up his hands. "See, Ursa? *Now* look what you've done!"

Instead of answering, she watched as Zandakar came into the kitchen, opened a drawer in the dresser and took out a carving knife. Gasping, she took a step back.

"*Wei*," Zandakar said, and held out the knife. "*Wei* be afraid, Ursa."

"Jones?" Her voice quavered. "Jones, what is he doing?"

"I don't know. Zandakar—"

Zandakar held up a hand, demanding quiet. Taking a step closer to Ursa, again he tried to give her the knife. Not violent, but insistent. "You take."

Eyebrows pinched she took it, reluctant. "Now what?"

His answer was to wrap his fingers round hers on the knife's old hilt, drop to his knees and press the blade's point against the hollow in the base of his throat.

"Zandakar, stop this," said Dexterity nervously. "It won't solve anything. Violence rarely does."

Zandakar ignored him, instead fixing his gaze on Ursa's alarmed face. His expression was almost tender in its concern. "You *wei* trust? You think Zandakar hurt Dexterity, hurt Rhian, hurt Ethrea?" His fingers tightened. The knife-point sank into his flesh, releasing a bright red bead of blood. "Kill now, Ursa."

"Jones, is this some kind of trick?" said Ursa.

Dexterity hesitated, then shook his head. "No, I think this is the only way he can think of to make you believe him."

"Well, it's ridiculous!" she retorted. "I'm a physick, I don't kill people. Not even when they're as wicked as Zandakar."

Oh dear. "This is silly. Ursa spoke harshly, it's true, but Zandakar – you know she's got a tart tongue. You've heard her sharpening it on my hide often enough. She didn't mean what she said. Did you, Ursa?"

"I meant every word, Jones," said Ursa. Frightened but stubborn, clinging to her principles no matter what.

"I kill, *zho*," said Zandakar, his hands and voice steady. "For Mijak. Is done. I blood oath for Rhian now."

"Which only goes to show you're fickle!" said Ursa, rallying. "Who's to say you won't change your mind again?"

"Ursa!" Dexterity protested. "He turned against Mijak because he realised the slaughter was wrong!

You can't have it both ways! How can he be wrong for killing *and* for refusing to kill any more?"

"He can be wrong a dozen ways between now and Rollin's Day, Jones! Your problem is you're a soft-hearted ninny."

Her words stung, but he pushed the pain aside. "Ursa, our queen accepts him. How can you do any less?"

"*Tcha*!" said Ursa, and blew a strand of silver hair out of her eyes. "Who's our queen, Jones? A young girl not even at her majority, dragged way past her depth and scared into desperation. *And* with her head turned by this handsome troublemaker. A bit of fancy footwork with a knife and her judgement's gone to blazes."

"But what about Hettie, Ursa? You know what she told me. What about God?"

Ursa snorted. "What about *his* god? His *chalava*? What if it starts whispering in his ear again, commanding him to kill all us heathens – starting with you!"

Zandakar's fingers tightened on the knife again. "*Wei*, Ursa. *Wei* hurt Dexterity. *Wei* hurt Rhian."

"That's what you say now, but how can I believe it?" said Ursa, a storm of conflict in her face. "You're *dangerous*, Zandakar."

Zandakar nodded. "*Zho. Yatzhay.*"

"Oh, *yatzhay, yatzhay*," she said, bitterly scornful. "You throw that word around like rice. But do you *mean* it, Zandakar? Are you *really* sorry? For *all* of it?"

Slowly, so slowly, Zandakar's eyes filled with tears. "*Zho.*"

Still racked with indecision, Ursa looked up. "Jones?"

He nodded. "*Zho*."

A riot of thoughts chased across her face. "I wonder which is worse?" she said at last. "To murder thousands of innocents and feel no remorse . . . or to murder thousands and then realise you were wrong."

"I don't know," he replied. "You'd have to ask Helfred."

Ursa sighed heavily. "*Helfred*. I suppose he's on your side?"

"Mostly he's on God's side. But he sees we need Zandakar."

"Yes, we do, Jones, but do we need him in your kitchen?"

"Ursa . . ." Dexterity tugged at his beard. "Zandakar needed to get out of the castle. It's only for a few days. And nothing will go wrong."

She shook her head. "You'd better hope not, Jones, for all our sakes." She glared down at Zandakar. "Oh, do get up. You look ridiculous, and my fingers have got cramp. If I sneeze accidentally I *will* kill you. Go on! Get up!"

Zandakar let go of the knife and stood. After tossing it in the sink, Ursa examined the small cut at the base of his throat.

"It's nothing," she muttered. "Dab some phorbia sap on it, you'll never know the skin was breached." Then she turned. "Well, since you're set on ignoring good advice and keeping him here, Jones, how are you going to amuse yourselves?"

He exchanged glances with Zandakar. "Well, today we're selling toys in the harbour market. And tomorrow I thought we'd take the donkey cart and trundle for a looksee round the home districts. Fresh air and sunshine, that's what he needs."

"That may be what *he* needs," she said. "As for what ails *you*, Jones, I'd say there's no cure!"

"See?" he said, grinning at Zandakar. "Didn't I tell you she sharpens her tongue on my hide?"

Ursa rolled her eyes. "For all the good it does me. Jones, I've got to go. Walk me to the front gate."

As they meandered down the path she said, "Well, Jones, if you're determined to take him romping in public you'd best shave his head again. That blue hair's a beacon for trouble."

Dexterity swung the gate open for her. "There's no need. Last night I made him a headwrap, like they wear in Dev'karesh. Nobody'll look twice."

"Jones, you're a cock-eyed happy hoper," said Ursa, exasperated. "Just you keep a close eye on him, d'you hear?"

He kissed her cheek. "I do. Come for dinner tonight."

"Can't. I'm spoken for."

"Tomorrow night, then. I'll make mutton stew," he promised. It was her favourite.

"All right," she said, pretending reluctance, and stomped away.

Dexterity watched her go. He still hadn't told her of Hettie's return. He'd have told her this morning, if they'd not been sidetracked by Zandakar.

But that news can wait. She's enough to feel scratchy about as it is.

He went back inside. It was time to get ready to take his last toys to the market.

*   *   *

A half hour later, seated beside Zandakar on the donkey cart as they trundled their way down to the harbour, he looked the warrior over again. Zandakar's head was wrapped in a tightly-tied square of black and yellow cotton. Not a single strand of blue hair could be seen. And he'd exchanged his linen shirt and leather leggings for the roughspun working clothes he'd worn on the road and in his prison cell. Clean but tatty, he appeared to be nothing more than a common hired hand.

"Zandakar," he said, suddenly curious, "what clothing do you wear in Mijak?"

"Horse hide," said Zandakar. "Leggings." He patted his arm. "*Wei* sleeves. Mijak hot. Much desert."

"You lived in a desert?" It was hard to imagine. No grass. How horrible . . .

Zandakar shook his head. "*Wei*. Et-Raklion *wei* desert. Et-Raklion like Ethrea." His voice had fallen to a whisper. "Et-Raklion beautiful."

Otto had fallen back to a dawdle. Dexterity slapped the reins against the donkey's rump, stirring him up, then glanced sidelong. "Do you miss Mijak?"

After a long pause, Zandakar nodded. "*Zho*. Is home, Dexterity. You leave Ethrea you miss home, *zho*?"

"And your mother? Your brother? You miss them, too?"

An even longer pause this time. Zandakar stared at his folded bands. "Before Lilit, Yuma – Yuma—" His clenched fist struck his breast. He seemed lost for more words.

He sighed. "She's your mother, Zandakar. No matter what she's done . . . that bond is hard to break."

"*Zho*," said Zandakar softly.

"And what of your brother?"

"Dmitrak," said Zandakar. His expression remained baffled. He punched his chest again. "Dimmi – Dimmi—" He unclenched his fist and instead knotted his fingers, turning them into something gnarled and twisted. "Like this, *zho*? Heart like this."

"Why? Why is he like that?"

"Yuma *wei* want," said Zandakar, shrugging. "Yuma birth Dimmi, hurt body. She hate. Always hard to Dimmi, *zho*? *Wei* smile. Dimmi try, always fail. From a baby, *zho*? From small sent to *chalava-chaka*, beat him for *chalava*." He sighed again. "Dimmi angry boy."

As a way to raise children it was abhorrent. "And you?" he said, staring. "When you were a child, were you beaten for your god?"

Zandakar nodded. "*Zho*. And as man."

"As a man?" If he didn't know better he'd have thought Zandakar was lying, or trying to see if he was indeed gullible. "Why would you permit it? You're more than capable of defending yourself. Are you saying you *wanted* them to beat you?"

A glimmer of resigned amusement in Zandakar's face. "Want? Tcha. *Wei*. It is for *chalava*."

"I don't understand, Zandakar. Explain it to me. I mean, was it just you and your brother, or is everyone in Mijak so severely treated?" *Mistreated. Abused.*

"Me. Dimmi. Raklion *chotzu*. *Chalava-hagra*. Wicked people," said Zandakar. "Pain for *chalava*. Show *chalava yatzhay*. Show *chalava* love."

Love? "Well, I'm sorry, but it sounds utterly barbaric," he retorted. "Barbaric, uncivilised and downright cruel." Which summed up Mijak quite neatly, really, now that he thought of it. "Zandakar, surely there must be better ways to worship. Ways that don't involve blood and pain?"

Zandakar didn't answer. As Otto's hooves tit-tupped along the stone-paved road leading down to Kingseat, Dexterity nodded to a few folk he knew, early risers passing on foot or in their own carts and carriages. In the distance Kingseat harbour sparkled beneath the morning sun and flashed it on the rooftops of the township. Now there was a hint of salt in the air.

In a blinding instant he saw scarlet-haired Dmitrak and his warriors running wild in the streets, hacking and slashing the people of Kingseat with their long sharp blades . . . and Zandakar's brother with his gauntlet of power, unstoppable fire lancing from his fist, smashing Ethrea's jewel of a capital to rubble and blood.

No. No. I can't let that happen . . .

"Zandakar?" he persisted, feeling the sweat of fear trickle down his spine and slick his hands on Otto's reins. "Isn't there another way?"

Zandakar stirred and looked at him. "Ethrea way, Dexterity?" He shrugged. "Ethrea way strange. Ethrea god strange. Ethrea people *wei* worship, they *wei* suffer. Ethrea god *wei* care. *Chalava* care. *Chalava* want all men worship and obey."

He had to clamp his lips together and grit his teeth to stop himself from blurting out the truth. *Chalava isn't a god, Zandakar! Mijak has no god, all it's got is mad priests drunk on human blood and dark power!*

He cleared his throat, swallowed the words he wasn't allowed to say.

"Yes, well, I'm sure there's something strange to be found in every man's religion: if you look hard enough. I suppose all I'm saying is it's possible your brother Dmitrak might be a different soul today if it hadn't been for all that beating. The angry boy grew into an angry man. And now that angry man leads an army against us."

"*Yatzhay*, Dexterity," said Zandakar, his expression turned from baffled to sorrowful. "*Yatzhay*."

"Gracious, Zandakar, it's not your fault," he said briskly.

Zandakar shook his head. "I think . . . *zho*. Raklion father. Dimmi born, he die. Dimmi born, Yuma nearly die. I am brother. I am *gajka*. Friend. *Wei gajka* but me, *zho*? I am brother, I am like father. Then I love Lilit, Dimmi think *wei* love him. Aieee, *tcha*. Dimmi hurt. I hurt him."

So families were families no matter what language they spoke. *A pity it's not more comforting to learn Mijak and Ethrea have that much in common.* "I'm sure it sounds like he had a miserable childhood but I still say that's not your fault. And whatever choices he makes as a grown man, well, they're his choices, Zandakar. Not yours."

"Choice?" Zandakar considered that. "*Wei* choice Mijak, Dexterity. *Wei* choice. Only *chalava*."

The resigned acceptance in his voice was as horrible as any revelation he'd made. Dexterity shifted on his donkey cart's hard wooden seat, deftly guiding Otto through the gradually increasing traffic as he tried to make sense of the strange man beside him.

"Zandakar, your brother murdered your wife. That was his choice, surely, a choice made out of spite and childish jealousy. Do you forgive him for it?"

"I think . . . *zho*," said Zandakar slowly. "He is Dimmi."

Dexterity felt his guts tighten. *Oh dear. If he can forgive his brother for killing his wife, if he can still love his mother after all that she's done . . . can we trust him to stay on our side? Is Ursa right, and Rhian wrong?* "And what does that mean for Ethrea, Zandakar?"

Zandakar looked at him, his pale eyes clear and unconflicted. "I fight for Ethrea, Dexterity. I fight for Rhian. *Chalava* say *wei* Mijak kill. *Chalava* is *chalava*."

Dexterity swallowed. *What is it like, I wonder, to feel faith like bedrock, to believe in a god as though it were the sun in the sky? I can hardly imagine.*

"Good," he said, and smiled, though inside he was shaking. "That's good to hear."

They reached the heart of Kingseat township soon after that, and conversation was abandoned in the tricky business of winding through the crowded streets, dodging carts and carriages and butchers' boys with trays of meat and girls with their little flower barrows and the foreign sailors taking in the sights and too much ale, even at this early hour, and the sober respectable men and women of Kingseat conducting their lives and the guards chivvying those who weren't quite so respectable.

Zandakar stared at the townsfolk and the sailors and the shopfronts and the paved streets, his dark face alight with curiosity. The smell of the harbour was stronger here. Between this building and that one, tantalising glimpses of the water and the moored trading vessels and Kingseat's fishing fleet. Masts poked above the lower roofs, romantic hints of far-flung lands.

Dexterity guided Otto down the sloping cobbled street to the harbour market gates and took his place in the long line of stall-holders waiting to be admitted. Memory stirred again, of that other lifetime. The morning he'd found Zandakar chained and dying on the Slyntian slave ship, and bought him.

If anyone had told me what that one act would unleash . . . would I have done it? Would I have dared?

Perhaps not. Perhaps that was why Hettie had kept so many secrets from him.

And now here's me keeping secrets. Are secrets contagious then, like plagues from distant shores?

It seemed they must be.

At last they were cleared to drive through to the marketplace. It was located on the far right hand side of the harbour, well away from the mooring places of the ambassadorial vessels and foreign trading ships in its middle section, and the fishing boats on the far left. As a rule, the general public weren't permitted to wander around the harbour docks for fear of accidents or unfortunate misunderstandings. There'd been plenty of both, in the old days, before the rules were changed. Any brash young men thinking to flout authority soon found themselves in a different kind of deep water . . . or, even these days if they were monstrous unlucky, the actual harbour, face-down and floating.

And if I fail there'll be a lot of Ethreans following suit . . .

Breath caught in his throat, heart beating too fast for comfort, he squeezed his eyes tight shut and willed that kind of nightmare to leave him be.

As they meandered their way in line to the market place he couldn't help looking back over his shoulder at Emperor Han's splendid vessel, still dominating the harbour. Admiring its sleek lines, its bold colours, he heard again Hettie's warning.

"Emperor Han is a mystery, Dex. His heart is a locked box and only he has the key to it . . . The witch-men of Tzhung-tzhungchai serve the emperor first and last and always. Remember that in your dealings with them."

How he wished Rhian weren't mixed up with Han. How he wished Ethrea had no need of Tzhung-tzhungchai.

"Dexterity?" said Zandakar. "Something is wrong?"

Indeed something was: he couldn't seem to stop this plague of calamitous forebodings. He banged a fist on his knee, then made himself smile. "No. No. Just wool-gathering, Zandakar."

A few minutes later he was too busy for frightening himself with imagined horrors, because it was time to set up his market stall. Pointed to their allotted space by a harbour official, they unloaded the wicker toy baskets – so much easier with two pairs of hands! – and saw Otto settled in his temporary stall. Then it was a matter of unpacking the toys, arranging them in a beguiling fashion . . . and waiting for the customers to arrive.

Kingseat's harbour markets were popular, and so were toys made by Dexterity Jones. He couldn't ask the same prices he'd asked of affluent nobles like Lady Dester, which was a pity, but he could ask enough so his labour wasn't valued at a pittance. A little over five hours after the markets opened all the toys were sold, and they were free to leave. But Zandakar seemed reluctant. From the moment they'd arrived at the harbour his attention was snared by it. Every chance he got, he stood and stared across it to the open ocean beyond its wide mouth.

"Dexterity," he said as they gathered the emptied baskets. "We look more?"

"At the harbour?" he said, surprised. "Well . . . yes. I suppose. We can't see all of it, though. We don't have the authority. Why are you interested?"

"Mijak," Zandakar said softly, so no-one standing close by could hear.

"Oh. Yes, all right," he said. "For a little while." He patted his moneybelt, tied tight around his middle. It was stuffed full of coins, satisfyingly heavy. Just to make sure, he buttoned his coat tight over it. "I want to look in on Otto first, though, make sure he's in clover. And remember, Zandakar: mouth shut. I'll do the talking if there's talking to be done."

Otto was dozing, quite happy to be left alone. So they started by wandering through the busy market, slowly but surely inching their way closer and closer to the water's blue edge, as near to the working dock as regulations allowed. For a long time Zandakar brooded at the lapping wavelets, at the ambassadors' vessels and the moored trading ships and Kingseat's fishing fleet, waiting for the next turn of tide to sail out again. Then he stared behind him at the crowding township, hugging as close as it could to the harbour's scooped hem.

"What are you thinking, Zandakar?" Dexterity asked at last, made nervous all over again by the warrior's stern expression.

Zandakar stirred from his reverie. "I think if I am Mijak *chotzu*, how I take harbour. How Dimmi will take harbour."

He shivered. Not would. *Will*. As though it were a foregone conclusion. As though Ethrea were defeated already. "And?"

Zandakar looked at him, his blue eyes bleak. "Ethrea harbour. How many?"

"Just the one. This one." At Zandakar's surprise he added, "Of course there were many more before Rollin and the charter of trading nations. It was part of the agreement, you see. Each duchy was to stop trading on its own behalf and instead send all its produce and so forth here to be stored, then transported to its various destinations by hired outside vessels. The kingdom's permitted its fishing boats and a handful of other vessels for sanctioned business. The crown has one ship, the *Queen Ilda*. And a wall was built around the entire kingdom, cutting off the other ports and helping to keep us protected from pirates and marauders and suchlike ruffians. The trading nations do their part, too. They regularly patrol the waters around Ethrea as part of the trading charter."

"Wall?" said Zandakar, frowning.

"Yes. Look." Dexterity pointed over to the right. "See the headland, there? See the stone wall? If you climbed on top of that and started walking, provided you didn't fall off or drop dead from over-exertion or find yourself arrested, you'd eventually end up back here . . . but on the opposite side of the harbour." He pointed again, to the left. "There, you see? The wall goes right round Ethrea, Zandakar. I believe we're the only entirely walled kingdom in the world. As part of their duties, the dukes maintain the section of wall that marks their sea-facing boundary. It's all very tidy. And it works remarkably well. I'm sure it will give Dmitrak great pause."

Zandakar stared at him. "*Tcha*. Stupid Dexterity. In dream you saw Dmitrak *chalava-hagra*?" He clenched his fist and extended his arm, as though he wore a gold-and-red crystal gauntlet. "You think Ethrea stone wall stand?"

Dexterity felt his spirits plummet. No, of course it wouldn't. Not against the power Dmitrak commanded.

"If you were still the *chalava-hagra*, Zandakar, how would you defeat Ethrea?"

"Dimmi has boats now?" He shrugged. "Sail round Ethrea. Destroy wall. Send warriors into duchies. Duchy soldiers die quick. Duchy soldiers . . ." He spat on the ground. "*Tcha*."

Dexterity felt ill. *I'm not a soldier, I have no knowledge of things military, but even I can see that makes perfect sense. Flood Ethrea with Mijaki warriors, crush the people in their duchies . . .* "And then you'd sail into Kingseat harbour and destroy the town?"

Zandakar nodded. "*Zho*."

"Perhaps it won't be as easy as you think for your brother to conquer us," he said, rallying. "There's the armada, remember? And if that fails, we'll have Emperor Han and his witch-men. We might even have soldiers from the other trading nations."

Again, Zandakar stared. "Mijak has *chalava*. *Chalava* has *chalava-haka* and *chalava-hagra*. *Chalava-hagra* has *chotzaka*."

He had to think for a minute, getting all the strange Mijaki words straight. God. Priests. God's hammer. Army. "How many, Zandakar? How many warriors of Mijak?"

He shrugged. "I think you say tens of thousands."

God help us . . . "And can you think of a way to defeat them?"

Another shrug. A sigh. "I try, Dexterity."

Chilled to the bone despite the bright sun and his buttoned jacket, Dexterity folded his arms and hugged his ribs tight. "Let's go home," he said, subdued. Dispirited. "Unless there's anything else here you need to see?"

There wasn't. They hitched Otto to the donkey cart and made their slow way back to the cottage, winding through Kingseat township's narrow, crowded streets so Zandakar became at least a little familiar with the place.

Home again, Zandakar spent what remained of the afternoon dancing his *hotas* with a kitchen knife, in the back garden. After that he took care of Otto while Dexterity cooked a simple dinner of braised coney and beets. Night fell. With their meal eaten and the untidiness of dinner tidied away, they sat in companionable silence in the kitchen and whittled.

As the clock struck ten a wind sprang up inside the

cottage . . . and Emperor Han's witch-man Sun-dao appeared.

CHAPTER SEVENTEEN

Dexterity leapt to his feet so fast his chair fell over and his whittling knife skittered out of his hand. Zandakar leapt up too but he didn't drop his knife. It was held before him, ready to strike.

Sun-dao looked at him. One extravagantly arched eyebrow lifted – and a cold wind lashed out, plucking the blade from Zandakar's grasp and flinging it to the other side of the kitchen. It hit the wall and dropped to the floor. The sound of its spinning was loud in the fraught silence.

Dexterity found his voice. "*Stop that*! I won't have your witch-man tricks in my home!"

Zandakar said nothing. If he was shaken by Sun-dao's action it didn't show on his face . . . but he was balanced on the balls of his feet, ready to launch into his *hotas* even though his knife was gone. His eyes were as cold as splinters of deep winter ice.

Dexterity held out a warning hand. "Peace, Zandakar. Let's not do anything hasty." He glared at Sun-dao. "What is the meaning of this? How *dare* you barge in here without so much as a by-your-leave!"

The witch-man Sun-dao bowed, his carmine-tipped fingers neatly clasped before him. The movement set his long bone-plaited moustaches to swinging. Head to toe he was dressed in black silk. The sumptuous fabric seemed to drink the kitchen's lamplight, giving it a kind of golden glow.

Or perhaps that was the Tzhung's sorcerous power.

"*Well?*" he demanded, thrusting aside the memories of their last encounter. "Are you going to stand there like a mute or are you going to answer me?"

Sun-dao's eyes were almond-shaped and black. Very little white showed. His amber skin was as smooth as a youth's, and his black hair was bound behind him. He was a good two handspans shorter than Emperor Han and much slighter of build. He looked almost frail, as though the winds he commanded could blow him away on a whim.

"Zandakar of Mijak," he said. His voice was thin and reedy, flavoured with the mystery of Tzhungtzhungchai. "You will meet with the emperor."

"Why?" said Dexterity, before Zandakar could speak. "What does Han want with him?"

"That is not your concern," said Sun-dao.

He shook his head. "Oh, it is. It's very much my concern. You see, I'm responsible for Zandakar. Her Majesty released him from the castle into my custody. Zandakar goes nowhere without me."

"You?" Sun-dao frowned. "The emperor has no need of you."

"Then we've nothing to discuss. You can go," he retorted. "And don't you think to try any of your witch-man trickery, sir. Her Majesty would be most displeased . . . and I've the feeling your emperor doesn't wish to displease her."

Sun-dao's red fingernails gleamed as his fingers tightened in annoyance. As a witch-man of Tzhung he must be more used to inspiring fear than defiance. "You will come to the emperor with Zandakar?"

"If you'll tell me what this is about . . . I'll consider it."

"You wish to stop Mijak's scorpion god?" said Sun-dao, his reedy voice tight. "You will come with me to Emperor Han."

Oh dear, oh dear. Dexterity hissed a breath between his teeth, then looked at Zandakar. "This might be important. *I'll* go. You stay here. If I don't return—"

"*No!*" said Sun-dao. His voice cracked just a little, as though his store of patience was fast running dry, and a thin edge of air stirred in the kitchen. "Both of you will come. You will come *now*."

Mouth dry, palms damp, Dexterity stared at Sun-dao. The man was a cipher, impossible to read. His face had less expression than a painted puppet. It would never surrender its secrets. *You wish to stop Mijak's scorpion god?* What kind of a question was that? Of course he wanted to stop Zandakar's *chalava*. They all wanted to stop it. But why this secrecy, why a mysterious witch-man in the night?

What does Han want of Zandakar that can't be talked of in daylight?

If they didn't go with Sun-dao, he'd never find out.

He looked at Zandakar. "I think we should go," he said quietly. "Are you willing? If you're not, then we won't."

Instead of answering, Zandakar rested his cold blue gaze on the witch-man. He'd taken off the

Dev'kareshi headwrap. In the warm kitchen lamp-light his blue hair glowed, so strange.

"This man. This Dexterity," he said. His voice was harsh. "My . . . *friend*. He is good man. You say here this Dexterity safe? You say here this emperor *wei* harm?"

Sun-dao's dark eyes glinted with a reluctant respect. "I say."

Zandakar nodded. "Tcha. We go." Then he smiled, a feral, brutal baring of teeth. "Sun-dao witch-man. You lie, I kill. Zho?"

Sun-dao laughed, and clapped his hands.

A great wind sprang up. The kitchen lamps blew out. Dexterity shouted as he felt the cottage dissolve around him, as he felt his own flesh and blood stream into tatters leaving only his thoughts intact.

He couldn't tell if he was wrapped in silence or if the sound was so loud it had rendered him deaf. He was hot and cold, standing still and racing. His eyes were open but he couldn't see, as helplessly blind as a newborn kitten. Time stopped, or was sped so fast it no longer had meaning.

This is madness. Madness. Oh please, Hettie, help!

And then he was whole again, his tattered body reformed. He could hear. He could see. He was alive, and unharmed.

"Welcome, Mister Jones," said a cool, familiar voice.

Emperor Han. He sat upon a magnificent gold and gemstone throne that was fashioned like some amazing beast out of legend. Not a dragon, not a bird, not a lion or a gryphon, but a strange blending of these animals that defied a simple name. A beaked, maned head reared above him, the eyes great orbs of facet-cut emerald. Its claws, which formed the throne's arm-rests, were a deep purple stone. Not amethyst but something like it, with a red and violent heart. The throne rested upon a thick coiled tail of gold encrusted with diamond scales. Two scaled and feathered wings spread wide behind him.

Dexterity shuddered. It looked like a creature born of a brain-fever, or madness. Instead of answering Han he looked for Zandakar. The warrior stood an arm's length distant, just as dazed. There was no sign of Sun-dao.

"You're all right, Zandakar?"

Zandakar nodded. "*Zho*. You?"

"A trifle wind-blown, but unharmed," he said, then stared at their new surroundings. A small chamber, with lacquered pale golden wood-panelled walls and no windows. Instead it was hung with magnificent silk tapestries depicting snow-capped mountains, wooded glens, tumbling rivers and bright-plumed birds in flight. Scenes from Tzhung-tzhungchai, most like. The floor was black marble, veined in red and gold. Warm light came from scores of tapered white candles, standing tall in iron holders like soldiers on guard. The chamber's still air was gently scented, perfumed with something exotic and unknown. This must be the Tzhung ambassador's residence. Surely they'd not been whisked to Tzhung-tzhungchai . . .

"You are in Kingseat," said the emperor. "Your cottage is but a long walk away."

He cleared his throat. This was no time to show fear. "And I would've been happy to walk it, Your

Imperial Majesty. Or drive my donkey cart. I'm sure there was no need for the theatrics."

"Walking would take too long," said Emperor Han, his mellow voice laced with amusement. "And your donkey cart is too conspicuous. The wind is swift and silent. It hides in plain sight."

Well, all right. Enough chit-chat. "Your witch-man said you wanted a word with Zandakar? What about, Emperor Han? As I told Sun-dao—"

"Yes," said Han. "He is under your protection."

And how could the emperor know that? Only moments had passed since they were whisked from the kitchen . . .

Or is this more witch-man sorcery? Oh, Hettie. I do wish you were here.

Han's silk tunic and trousers were a vibrant lapis blue. His feet were slippered in pearl-sewn black velvet. A rubyeyed dragon ring graced one slender forefinger. He was relaxed. Urbane. A rich, powerful man in control of his emotions.

But in his dark eyes an unquiet light gleamed.

"Zandakar of Mijak," he said, shifting his measured gaze. "Your scorpion god holds you in high esteem. Had you been revealed in my empire of Tzhung, instead of Ethrea, the carrion crows even now would be picking clean your bones."

Dexterity looked at Zandakar, and watched a subtle change steal over him. Dressed in drab roughspun, without polish or style, still he transformed himself into a prince. Across his lean, handsome face washed haughty arrogance and pride. Since his rescue from the slave ship he had clothed himself in a wary reticence; only once, when he slaughtered the footpads in duchy Arbat, had he seemed unequivocally himself.

Then, and now. Now I believe he is a prince of Mijak. He and Han could be cut from the same cloth.

"*Chalava* sees me, *zho*," said Zandakar. "What is this to you, Han of Tzhung?"

If Han resented being spoken to like an underling, his face didn't reveal it. Instead he tapped that ringed finger against his lips, considering. "Queen Rhian assures me you are dedicated to seeing the destruction of Mijak. Does she lie? Is she misled? Or does she tell the truth?"

Zandakar's face tightened, then relaxed. "Truth."

"So you do desire your people destroyed?"

"Destroyed?" Zandakar shook his head. "*Wei*. Want Mijak to hear true voice of *chalava*. *Wei* killing. Return home. Et-Raklion. Leave world at peace."

Han drummed his fingers lightly on the arm of his throne. "Can there ever be peace with Mijak's warriors alive beneath the sun?"

Zandakar's gaze didn't falter. "*Zho*."

He said so, but was it possible? Dexterity wasn't sure. Nothing he'd learned, or been shown by Hettie, encouraged him to think Mijak could be gently persuaded to retreat.

Not while Dmitrak wields his fierce gauntlet.

"They are your people," said Han. "I understand you'd like to think so. Alas, I think you are the one misled. But of course . . ." He smiled, thinly. "I could be wrong."

Dexterity cleared his throat again, hinting. "I'm afraid I don't see what you're getting at, Emperor

Han. What do you want? If you tell us plainly, without riddles, we might be able to help."

"The uninvited man of miracles has a busy fearless tongue," murmured Han. "He stands before queens and emperors unafraid."

"No, sir," he said carefully. "Not unafraid."

In a single, sinuous move Han slid from his throne. Dexterity watched, perplexed, as the emperor approached and seized his right hand.

"Most strange," Han whispered. "You feel like mortal flesh and blood, toymaker, yet this rough hand healed a queen's wounds. It burned without burning, and turned a man to ash. What am I to think of that, emperor of two million souls, who commands the wind and cannot raise the dead?"

Heart pounding, Dexterity stared at Han, struggling not to snatch his hand free. He could feel in the emperor a thrumming of power, a drumming of energy, that in some way he couldn't begin to understand echoed the thrumming and drumming of his own blood when he burned with miracles for God.

Emperor Han swallowed a tiny gasp. He felt it too. "Toymaker—"

"I liked it better when you called me Mister Jones," Dexterity said, and finally pulled his hand free. Then he took a step back, just to be safe.

A thin rind of white showed around Han's dark eyes. His breathing was heavy, his nostrils flaring. "Who are you?" he asked hoarsely. "What part is yours in this business?"

"I don't know," Dexterity said, and met Han's keen gaze without flinching. "You might not believe me, but I truly don't. I do what I'm asked by the woman I married and still love with all my heart, though she's been dead twenty years. I do it for her, and for a girl I love like a daughter. You're right. I'm a toymaker, I've no business with miracles and suchlike. Yet here I am. Here you are, a mighty emperor. And here is Zandakar, warrior prince of a foreign land. What are we to make of that? I suppose . . . whatever we can. Together we hope for what's best for your people, and mine and yes, even the people of Mijak. They frighten me so I can hardly spit, but I don't expect they asked to be ruled by such a brutal god."

A shadow of puzzlement crossed Han's face. "You mean it. You have been shown the truth of Mijak and still there is compassion. Another miracle, toymaker."

Dexterity snorted. "Emperor Han, if you tell us why Sun-dao brought us here, *that* will be a blessed miracle!"

The snappish comment surprised a laugh from Tzhung-tzhungchai's ruler. "So! You demand an answer."

"I do. It's only polite. Your witch-man refused to give us any explanation."

"He was not told to," said Han, returning to his throne. "He was to bring Zandakar to me."

"Yes . . ." Dexterity glanced at Zandakar and back again. "Emperor Han, how was that accomplished? Was it – was it *sorcery*?"

"So say the ignorant," Han replied, shrugging. "Are you ignorant, toymaker? What name do you give the power in your blood?"

"No name at all. In truth, I – I prefer not to think about it."

Another laugh. "Then you are a fool."

Dexterity gritted his teeth. Clearly Han was determined to run at his own pace. There was little point chivvying – he'd only slow down further.

The emperor leaned forward, his gaze now a knife-point aimed at Zandakar. "Prince of Mijak. *Zandakar*. What would you do to save your people from destruction?"

Zandakar met the bladed look with a steel stare of his own. "What must be done, Han *chotzu*."

Slowly, Han sat back again. Let his hands relax on the arms of his magnificent, barbaric throne. "And you, Mister Jones? What would you do to save Ethrea? Protect your little queen? Rescue the suffering people of Mijak from their scorpion god?"

"Whatever I could," he replied. "But that's not much, I'm afraid. I am just a toymaker, after all."

But Han wasn't listening. His gaze was fixed to Zandakar, and though his face was smooth, in his dark eyes was a turmoil of emotion. "Prince of Mijak, what would you say if I told you I could send you to where your mother, Mijak's empress, and your warrior brother, now reside? If you could stand in a room with them, Zandakar, what would you say?"

Zandakar's eyes were wide. "I see Yuma? See Dmitrak? I say . . . *stop*."

"And would they listen?"

"I think—" Zandakar hesitated. "*Zho*."

Dexterity turned on him. "No, Zandakar, they wouldn't. They *won't*. I know you want to think so, I know you want to fix this, but you can't. They banished you. You're dead to them. *Stay* dead, I beg you."

But Zandakar shook his head. "*Zho* – if I find Vortka. He is *gajka*. He will listen. He and I will make Yuma and Dmitrak stop Mijak."

Han's eyes were narrowed. "You're sure of this?"

A long silence. Then Zandakar nodded. "*Zho*."

"Good. Then I will send you to Icthia."

"I'm sorry," said Dexterity, "but that's out of the question. Her Majesty can't have Zandakar gone for weeks on end. She relies on him."

"It is true that for ordinary men, the journey to Icthia takes weeks," replied Han. "But Sun-dao can shrink that time to days."

"*Days?* That's impossible!"

"Not for Sun-dao," Han said simply. "He lives in the wind."

Oh dear. "And when he gets there? Zandakar's not precisely inconspicuous, you know. He's not a *nobody*. He'll be recognised by someone, and then what? His brother's sworn to kill him! And his mother – his mother—" He had to stop for a moment before he lost his temper entirely. "It's too dangerous."

Han's eyebrows lifted. "Dangerous? No. Sun-dao will hide Zandakar in the wind."

Hide him in the— "And what does *that* mean?"

"It means he won't be seen unless he wishes to be seen."

Dexterity didn't dare look at Zandakar. "Even so – *no*. It's out of the question, Emperor Han. And what's more, this entire conversation is unseemly. You've no business making such an offer without Rhian's knowledge. This clandestine behaviour is – is – it's *dishonourable*!"

The emperor stood, his face dark with anger. "You presume too far, toymaker!" The chamber's scented air writhed gently, hinting at storms. The candle-flames flickered, dancing shadows up the walls. "In another place, another time, your words would be an act of war."

"Well, what you're proposing is equally provocative!" he replied. "Zandakar has sworn an oath to Her Majesty, he—"

"Dexterity. *Wei*," said Zandakar, quietly. "I decide. I am Zandakar *chotzu, zho*?"

He turned. "Yes, yes, but you can't *seriously* be thinking to – you can't *possibly* – Zandakar, be sensible. Rhian will never let you go."

"This is not the Queen of Ethrea's decision," said Han. "If Zandakar wishes to do this, I will help him."

"And in doing so, Emperor Han, you'll hurt Rhian terribly. Why would you do that? I thought you respected her!"

Han nodded. "I do. Mister Jones, my purpose here is not to hurt your little queen. She is a sweet child who might yet grow to fit her crown. I seek peace, not strife. I am here, in Ethrea, not in my airy palace where I long to be. But I cannot go home until Mijak is defeated."

"Is that what the wind tells you, Emperor Han?"

"It does. And I suspect this venture is our only hope. The league of trading nations will never agree to an armada."

"You don't know that! You have to give them time!"

"There is no more time. Mijak is coming."

"But – but—" Dexterity turned. "Zandakar, you

can't. Rhian trusts *you. She – she—"* Cares for you. *And you care for her. You can't do this, you'll break her heart.*

"He can do what he likes, toymaker," said Emperor Han. "He is a free man. He is no slave."

Oh be quiet, be quiet, you meddlesome man! "Of course he's a slave!" Dexterity retorted. "He's a slave to his honour!" Again he turned to Zandakar. "You've sworn an oath in *blood* to serve Ethrea. If you leave without telling Rhian, without asking her permission, you'll be forsworn. And if you're caught trying—" He shook his head, appalled. "There'll be no mercy, Zandakar. You'll be struck down like a froth-mouthed dog."

Emperor Han's eyes were half-lidded, considering. "You will not be caught. Sun-dao will see to that. Prince of Mijak, you are in exile but still, you are a prince. The warriors who will die in the coming battle are your people. Your mother and brother have led them into darkness, but you have the power to save them. To save them *and* your family. You have the power, but do you have the courage? Are you their *chotzu* in deed, as well as name?"

"Zandakar . . ." Dexterity whispered, but was terribly afraid he'd already lost. Emperor Han was clever. He knew exactly what to say to convince Zandakar to go.

"You are wrong in trying to stop him, toymaker," said Han. "You said you'd do what you could to help Ethrea. This will help Ethrea more than any burning miracle."

"You don't know that either!" he retorted. *Oh,*

Hettie, this man. "For all you know you're sending Zandakar to his death!"

Han smiled. "The wind does not say so."

"Oh – oh – drat you *and* your wretched wind!"

"Tcha, Dexterity." Zandakar shook his head. "Han *chotzu* is right." His fist struck his chest. "I am Zandakar *chotzu*. I know *chalava's* want. I must save Mijak, *zho*? Yuma. Dimmi. Vortka. I must save."

"And what am I supposed to tell Rhian?"

Zandakar pushed up his sleeve and looked at the fading pink knife-scar on his forearm. The physical reminder of his bloodsworn oath. "You say I save Ethrea, too. *Zho*?"

"Oh, *Zandakar* . . ."

Perilous close to tears, aware of Han's silent scrutiny, of Zandakar's iron determination, Dexterity turned his back on both of them and pressed his hands to his face.

Oh, Hettie. Hettie. This is a nightmare. What do I do? How do I stop him? If I go back to Rhian and tell her I let him go . . .

He felt sick, and suddenly frightened. If Zandakar was whisked away, what would happen afterwards? Dexterity Jones would be a nuisance. A stumbling block. The emperor would have to keep him silent. *Oh, Hettie!*

"I want to talk this over with Zandakar," he said abruptly, lowering his hands and turning round. "Just the two of us. Will you permit it?"

Han considered him coldly. "You wish to dissuade him?"

"I wish to be certain he's doing the right thing."

Han stood. "Very well. But speak swiftly."

Dexterity watched Han cross to a panel in the lac-quered wall behind the throne and pass his hand across it. A hidden door slid open. The emperor stepped through it and the door closed again, sealing them within the chamber.

"*Well!*" he said as soon as they were alone. "And what do you have to say for yourself, O mighty Prince of Mijak!"

Zandakar said nothing, his gaze resting on the nearest flickering candle-flame. His face was calm, like an unstirred millpond. Only his eyes held emo-tion; they were bright and full of pain.

"*Zandakar*," he persisted. "Do you really think you can convince this Vortka to then convince your mother and brother to turn tail and go home? I mean, from what you've told me of them it doesn't sound likely. It sounds most unlikely. Surely you'll end up dead . . . or worse!"

"*Wei*," said Zandakar. "Vortka *wei* kill. Vortka *gajka*."

"You don't know that's still true!" he said, desper-ate. "Zandakar, you don't even know if Vortka's still alive. What if he's perished? What if there's a – a new *chalava-hagra* for Mijak? One who doesn't know you, or isn't *gajka*. If you show your face to your brother or your mother they will *kill* you. You can't go. You *can't*."

Zandakar shrugged. "I must."

Oh, for pity's *sake*. Dexterity stamped around the candlelit room, and came to a halt on its far side. This was ridiculous. He couldn't let Zandakar go.

Dexie, love, you have to. And you'll have to go with him.

What? What? Was that Hettie's voice? Was she here? Startled, he stared around the lacquered chamber, but could see only Zandakar. And then he caught an elusive hint of lavender and roses. Her favourite scents.

Hettie.

Dexie, go with him. You'll be all right.

He wanted to stamp his feet and wave his arms. He wanted to shout, Go with him? Go with him? Hettie, are you mad? I have a donkey, I have a cottage, I have a business on its last legs. I can't go traipsing off to Icthia to Zandakar's family.

Dexie, it's important. Trust me. Go.

What? Why? Why was it important?

But Hettie was gone again. Oh dear, oh dear, oh dear.

He looked at Zandakar, still feeling sick. His heart was threatening to shatter his ribs. *Say it, say it, before you change your mind.* "So you're set on this? There's nothing I can say to keep you in Ethrea?"

Slowly Zandakar shook his head. "*Yatzhay.*"

Oh dear, oh dear ... "Then, if you're going, Zandakar, I'm going too."

Zandakar stepped back, shocked. "*Wei!*"

"You leave me no choice!" he replied, almost breathless. "I'm responsible for you, Zandakar. Like you, I gave Rhian my word. You might be comfortable going back on it, but I'm not!"

"Dexterity—"

The door in the wall slid open again, and Han returned. Sun-dao was with him.

"Well, Zandakar?" said the emperor.

"I go," said Zandakar.

Dexterity wiped his sweaty palms down his front. "Actually, Emperor Han, we *both* go."

Han and his witch-men exchanged startled glances. "Mister Jones—"

"I'm sorry, I have to," he said quickly. "I can't let Zandakar go alone."

"He won't be alone," said the emperor, displeased. "Sun-dao will be with him."

"That's not the same and you know it!"

Zandakar was shaking his head. "You stay, Dexterity. You safe in Ethrea."

"While you're risking your life in Icthia?" he retorted. "I hardly think so. Are you mad? I didn't rescue you from that slave ship and traipse from one end of the kingdom to the other with you under my feet to let you out of my sight now. Besides. You'll need me as a witness. Even if I do explain to Rhian that you had to go, that you're not betraying her, who knows what kind of mischief ambassadors like that Gutten will look to make? If I'm with you, if I can swear that all you did was try to stop Mijak in Icthia, well . . ." he sighed gustily. "We might manage to keep the league of trading nations in one piece."

Emperor Han tapped a slender finger against his lips. "You are determined, toymaker?"

He nodded. "I am." *Thanks to Hettie.*

"And yet I could deny you. It's within my power to keep you here, and let Zandakar go."

On a deep breath Dexterity made himself meet Han's intimidating eyes. "You could," he admitted. "But I promise it'll be far less troublesome if you don't."

Han's gaze chilled. "Truly."

With a glance at Zandakar, Dexterity took a step closer to him. "Emperor Han, believe me. I don't *want* to go. I don't want Zandakar to go. This is a fool's errand, I'm sure. But if I can't convince him to refuse you, then I must go with him. I gave Rhian my word to keep him safe. Would you have *both* of us forsworn?"

"You are a harsh man, toymaker," said Han.

No, I'm a madman. Just you ask Ursa.

"Well?" he demanded, folding his arms. "Is it settled?"

Han nodded. "It is settled. Sun-dao will take you and Zandakar to Icthia. You have earned the thanks of Tzhung-tzhungchai."

"Get us to Icthia and back in one piece and you can keep your thanks," he said, not caring in the least it was a rank discourtesy, or that a man from Tzung would likely die for such words. This wasn't Tzhung, it was Ethrea, and this wretched emperor was swiftly proving a thorn in the kingdom's side.

Han considered him. "You are not pleased, toymaker."

"No. And neither would you be, Emperor Han, were you in my place. Now if you'd be so kind as to supply me with pen and paper I'll write a note for Her Majesty, that you can see deliv—"

"A note?" Emperor Han shook his head. "Alas. Informing Rhian of this venture would . . . complicate matters. They are complicated enough as it is."

"No note?" Dexterity gaped at him. "You expect Zandakar and me to simply . . . disappear? Vanish without explanation? Emperor Han, that could be seen as *treason*."

"But it is not treason," said the emperor calmly.

"We know you go to save Ethrea, Mister Jones. And when you return, your little queen will know it too."

He turned to Zandakar. "We can't go, Zandakar. Not like this. She'll think we've betrayed her. How will she explain our disappearance to the dukes? To the ambassadors? We'll make her look a fool. We'll weaken her position. We *can't*." He turned back to Han. "We can't."

"Dexterity is right," said Zandakar. "Rhian *hushla* must know."

So tall, so elegant, Emperor Han clasped his hands and sighed. His dark eyes were shadowed with many thoughts. "Your devotion to Queen Rhian is moving. How hard it is to fault men who honour their sovereign with such passion." He smiled, an ambiguous curve of thin lips. "I am an emperor of Tzhung, with imperial ancestors as numerous as there are stars in the night sky . . . and yet you have humbled me. You, a toymaker, and a brute, bloodsoaked savage from the far east. The wind whispers its praise, gentlemen. It honours your hearts."

Taken aback, Dexterity watched as Han approached, Sun-dao a pace behind him. Flinched, a little, as an imperial hand came to rest coolly on his shoulder. Zandakar didn't flinch but his blue gaze sharpened as Han touched him too.

"Yes, I am humbled . . ." Han murmured. "And yet, alas . . . unmoved."

The lacquered room disappeared in a howling storm of wind.

When Dexterity opened his eyes again he saw a ceiling of silver stars and two moons overhead, one plump and one slender. Groggy and groaning, he shoved aside the blanket covering him, sat up—and promptly wished he hadn't.

"Be still," said Zandakar, taking his elbow. "Witch-man power strong. Hurt belly, hurt head."

Yes, it certainly did. Nauseous, his head pounding, his mouth dry, Dexterity waited for the world to stop spinning. When at last it settled he took a deep breath and looked around. A brisk salt breeze blew directly in his face. A sloshy, wet sound was all he could hear. The wooden floor beneath him moved disconcertingly up and down.

"God save us! We're at *sea*?"

They were. At sea on a very small boat. A lamp had been lashed to the vessel's single mast. Its flame burned steadily, edging Zandakar's face in golden light. "*Zho*."

"Where at sea? Where *are* we?"

Zandakar shrugged. "*Wei* know." He nodded. "Witch-man know. Witch-man sleeping."

Sun-dao. Dexterity shifted, feeling splinters even through his trousers. An arm's length away Han's witch-man was sitting upright, eyes closed, hands clasped in his lap. Breathing in, breathing out, oblivious to his surroundings.

Oh dear. "Zandakar . . . does he look unwell to you?"

Zandakar was frowning. "I think you say . . . exhausted? Ethrea far behind. Witch-man bring us here with witch-man power. Much power. Very hard." Despite his anger, Zandakar seemed impressed. "Sundao say he rest till sun, then more fly in wind."

"He say – I mean, said? You've spoken with him?

When? How long have I been asleep, Zandakar?" A cold thought touched him. Shivering, he tugged the blanket close again. "How long have we been in this boat?"

Another shrug. "Witch-man say same night."

"Truly?" He shivered again. *Beware the emperor and the witch-men of Tzhung-tzhungchai.* "Oh dear. Ursa's going to be furious."

"And Rhian," said Zandakar. His fingers traced the scar on his arm. "Rhian . . ."

Dexterity rallied. "It's not our fault. We were kidnapped. Stolen away without our consent. That Emperor Han, he ran roughshod right over us. You can be certain I'll lodge a formal complaint as soon as we get home."

The lamplight was poor, but even so the glitter of wry amusement in Zandakar's eyes was clear. "If we get home, Dexterity."

He stared. Every so often, Zandakar's Ethrean was perfect. He could easily have wished this wasn't one of those times. "Yes," he said, subdued. "If we get home." And tipping back his head, he looked at the distant, indifferent stars.

Do you hear me, Hettie? You'd better help us get home!

CHAPTER EIGHTEEN

"Gone?" Rhian stared at Ursa. "What do you mean they're gone? They can't be. Gone where?"

"I don't know, Majesty," said Ursa, her face pale with distress. "Jones didn't leave a note. All he left was his money-belt full to bursting with coin, stuffed to the bottom of the flour barrel as usual. And his dratted donkey, bellowing fit to raise its stable roof. The neighbours are most displeased."

"*I'm* most displeased!" snapped Rhian, and took a turn about her parlour, acutely aware of Alasdair's silent, brooding presence before the fireplace. "When did you last see them, Ursa?"

"Yesterday morning, Majesty. They were going down to the harbour markets. Jones had toys to sell, and Zandakar was an extra pair of hands."

"And you've no idea what happened next?"

"Well, they went home, Majesty," said Ursa. "But after that? No. Jones did mention something about sightseeing round the home districts today, but I don't know if he went. All I can tell you for certain is he asked me to dinner tonight, and he's not at home."

"Have you told anyone else, Ursa?"

Ursa shook her head. "Of course not, Majesty. I put the donkey in the field at the bottom of the lane, to quiet its carry-on, then came straight here."

Halting beside her favourite armchair, Rhian nodded. "Good. That's good." She risked a glance at Alasdair. He was watching her, his expression noncommittal, his eyes accusing. *I told you so, Rhian. I told you it was foolish to let him go . . .* She felt her breath hitch, and her skin flush hot. "Ursa, you know Dexterity better than anyone. Can you think where he might be, or why he might have . . . disappeared?"

"No," said Ursa, so anxious. "This isn't like him."

"And Zandakar?" said Alasdair. His voice was deceptively mild. "You're a woman of experience, Ursa. You had him under your eye all that time on the road. You formed an opinion. Has he murdered Mister Jones and fled Ethrea on some foreign ship?"

"*Murdered?*" Ursa's cheeks lost all their colour. "No. No, he wouldn't do that. Zandakar wouldn't murder Jones."

"Are you sure?" said Alasdair, brutally gentle.

Rhian turned on him. "Don't," she said, her voice hard and low. "You're frightening her."

"Someone needs to be frightened," said Alasdair. "Zandakar is a frightening man. I seem to be the only one capable of remembering that." His teeth bared in a mirthless smile. "Perhaps because I'm a man too, and not an impressionable woman."

Ursa rallied. "Now, now, Your Majesty, I'm sure there's no need to be nasty. I'm too old to have my head turned by a pretty face. And even if I wasn't, I promise you I was never a woman to be so easily taken in. I might never have married, but that's not to say I don't know my way around men."

Alasdair's smile now was far less intimidating. "I don't doubt it, Ursa. You're a woman of profound good sense, and I value your opinion. Why are you so certain Mister Jones isn't murdered?"

"It's hard to say," she replied slowly. "I mean, I've had my suspicions of Zandakar, I'll not deny it. He's a heathen and a killer, we all know that. But he's fond of Jones and I do believe he wants to help the queen. I believe *he* believes if he helps Her Majesty he'll be helping his own people. I think that's what he wants more than anything else. And even if he wasn't fond of Jones, which he is, killing him won't help Mijak."

"Then where *are* they?" Rhian demanded. "This makes no *sense!*"

"Perhaps Hettie's sent them off on some wild-goose chase, Your Majesty," said Ursa, shrugging. "She's done it before, and Jones has kept quiet about it till after." Her cheeks pinked a little. "He loves you like a daughter, you know, but Hettie . . ." She sighed. "Well, Hettie may be dead but she's still his wife."

"That's as may be, but I'm his queen and Hettie shouldn't forget it!" Breathing hard, Rhian reined in her temper. "All right, Ursa. Thank you for coming to me so promptly. Should you be unduly pressed for news of Mister Jones by anyone, no matter how seemingly innocent, let me know at once. And if you should by chance hear from him or Zandakar . . ."

"Of course, Your Majesty," said Ursa, and offered a cricked-knee curtsey. "King Alasdair."

As the parlour door closed behind her, Alasdair folded his arms. "Rhian—"

"*Don't!*" she said again, feeling vicious. Feeling betrayed. She could easily, treacherously, dissolve into tears. "There's an explanation. A reason. There has to be."

"Of course there is," said Alasdair, his voice level, his eyes burning. "Zandakar—"

"*Hasn't betrayed me!*" She retreated until she stood with her back to the curtained window, fists clenched, her hair still sweat-sticky and plastered to her head. Ursa's news had burst upon them moments after she'd returned from her evening *hotas*. She hated dancing them alone, she felt incomplete without Zandakar to dance with, but not to dance them would be to let him down.

And has he let me down, instead?

"He hasn't betrayed me," she repeated, willing her voice to stay strong. "Neither has Dexterity. I'd stake my life on that. He's been a friend to me since I was a baby, he—" And then she turned because the parlour door was pushing open.

"God's grace on you, Your Majesties!" said Ludo cheerfully, entering the chamber all sunshine and smiles. "And on me, for I'm returned from the wilds of Hartshorn and Meercheq having not slain Duke Adric. Though I confess I was sore provoked once or—" He stopped, his smile dimming. "What's wrong? What's happened?"

"Close the door," said Alasdair. And added, once Ludo had obeyed the curt command, "What's happened is that the toymaker's vanished into thin air – and Zandakar with him."

Ludo folded his arms, his face collapsed into a frown. "Zandakar's gone? Rollin's toenails. That's bad news."

Rhian glared at him. "Really? D'you think so? I thought to dance a little jig, Ludo. Sing a song. Call for a fanfare."

Ludo was more than a duke, he was family. Along with his crippled father Henrik and, of course, Alasdair, the only family she possessed now. Within these privy apartments there was no ceremony. They spoke as equals, laughed as equals, even fought as equals . . . within these quiet, private rooms.

"Don't lash out at Ludo, Rhian," said Alasdair. "Not when it's yourself you'd like to kick."

"Did I ask you to defend me, cousin?" said Ludo, firing up. "I can speak for myself. Tell me how Jones and Zandakar have vanished."

As Alasdair recounted what little they knew, swiftly and sarcastically, Rhian slumped onto the window's embrasure and closed her eyes against the pain in her head.

Dexterity . . . Zandakar . . . what have you done?

"Rhian," said Ludo, once Alasdair was finished. "What were you thinking, letting Zandakar out of your sight?"

She flicked him an angry glance. "I was thinking we should stop treating him like a common criminal, Ludo."

"I told her she'd made a mistake," said Alasdair. "To bring him back here without delay. But she's a typical Havrell. She wouldn't listen."

Shocked, Rhian stared at her husband and his cousin. "A typical Havrell? What's that supposed to mean?"

"What d'you think it means?" said Ludo. He was such a handsome man, all the Linfoi looks denied to Alasdair bestowed instead on him. But now his pleasing features were scrunched in a scowl. "You're just like your brothers, Rhian. Ranald and Simon were wild against any kind of restraint. They were told there'd been fever in Dev'karesh, did you know that? The word was out, they were warned it would be best if they didn't go, but would they listen? No, they—"

"Don't, Ludo," said Alasdair, sounding suddenly weary. "There's no point. That's past mending."

"But there is a point," said Ludo, swinging round. "They wouldn't be told and they died of it. So did Eberg. She wouldn't be told and now a dangerous man is God alone knows where, and whatever he's doing I doubt it bodes well for us."

Rhian folded her arms around her ribs. The parlour was warm, yet she felt so cold. *They wouldn't be told and they died of it. So did Eberg.* "No-one said anything to me about Ranald and Simon knowing Dev'karesh had plague." To her own ears her voice sounded thin and uncertain. She felt thin and uncertain, as though her bones had turned to sand. "Who else knew? And why wasn't I told?"

With a furious glare at his cousin, Alasdair crossed to her. Taking her hands in his he tried to smile. "I'm sorry. Eberg never wanted you to know. Don't think about it, Rhian. Don't torture yourself. It's hardly going to bring them back."

"Someone should've told me," she said. "They were my brothers. I had a right to know. *You* should've told me, Alasdair."

He shrugged. "Eberg forbade it."

"Eberg's *dead*!" she retorted. "And they were *my brothers*."

"I know that. And now that *you* know what happened does it change anything? Does knowing make you feel better or worse?"

"Oh, worse, worse, you know I feel worse!" she cried, sliding her hands free of him, feeling her knife-hilt calluses catch on his skin. "But that's not important. I won't be *protected*, Alasdair, I won't be coddled like some helpless baby bird. Like a *woman*. It's bad enough Papa did it, I won't have *you*—"

"Leave him alone, Rhian!" said Ludo sharply. "He's your husband, of course he tries to protect you. If he didn't what kind of a husband would he be? What kind of a king, when you're his queen? You don't want to be protected? Fine. Ranald and Simon were headstrong and foolish and they paid the price for their impetuous arrogance."

"And now you think Ethrea's about to pay because of mine?" She tilted her chin, refusing to back down to him. "Go on, Ludo. Say what you think. I'm not wearing a crown, am I? I'm not dressed like a queen. I'm in working leathers, I'm stinking with sweat."

Ludo grimaced. "The crown's always on your head, Rhian. Stark naked you're still the queen."

"And a damned useless queen I'd be if I didn't let good men speak their minds!" she shouted. "I don't care if you're angry with me, Ludo. I don't care if you call me names. I care if you hide your true thoughts and feelings!"

Frustrated, angry, they glared at each other. Then Ludo sighed and turned away. "Ah well. What's done is done, and can't be undone. What do you think has happened to Zandakar and the toymaker?"

"We don't know," said Rhian, curtly.

Ludo looked from her to Alasdair. "Surely it's most likely Zandakar changed his mind about helping us. He's bolted, and halfway across the ocean by now. The toymaker's cottage should be closely examined for signs of foul play. Could be his body is buried in the garden."

"Nonsense, Ludo," she said. "There is another explanation, one that makes sense of their vanishing without it involves oathbreaking and murder."

"Well," said Alasdair, "if it's not oathbreaking and murder then it must be kidnap. There's no other way to make sense of this. You told them not to leave the home districts. If they'd come to grief somewhere in the local countryside, we'd know by now."

"Kidnap for what reason?" she demanded. "On whose authority? And how, without raising a monstrous hue and cry? For they'd not go quietly, I can promise you that."

Ludo pulled a thoughtful face. "Am I mad to think they could be stolen by a foreign power?"

Alasdair stared at him. "One of the trading nations? Would they be so bold, to risk the charter like that?"

"You'd think not," said Ludo, shrugging. "Ordinarily the league of trading nations safeguards the charter like a virgin daughter. But these times aren't ordinary. And don't forget, we seek to break it ourselves by raising our own army. Perhaps we've made them more nervous than we realise. Perhaps one – or more than one – think to seize an advantage by seizing Zandakar."

"To do what with him?" said Rhian, pushing off the embrasure to pace again. Her bones still felt barely strong enough to support her, but if she remained seated while Alasdair and Ludo stood it would feel like a weakness. Some kind of surrender. Always she felt she had to be *more* . . . it was exhausting, but she had no choice. While the world had surely changed, it hadn't changed enough yet. "If Harbisland took him, say, or Arbenia, or Keldrave, he'd not help them."

"If they took him against his will," said Alasdair softly.

She stopped, and had to swallow hard before she could answer. "No. I *won't* believe Zandakar's betrayed me."

"Rhian—" Alasdair shook his head, impatient. "You *must* consider the possibility."

"What of Mister Jones?" said Ludo. "Do you think he and Zandakar acted in collusion?"

Shocked, Rhian stared at him. "*Dexterity* betray me? Ludo, are you mad?"

"He has a point, Rhian," said Alasdair. "For no sooner has Mister Jones scolded you into letting Zandakar leave the castle than both men are mysteriously disappeared."

"*Not Dexterity*!" she insisted. "Rollin's grace, you might as well ask that I believe *you'd* betray me! I'm telling you, both of you, that if they do enjoy the hospitality of a foreign nation, it is not willingly."

"We all know how dangerous Zandakar is," said Alasdair, so stubborn. "Even Helfred could overpower Mister Jones . . . but Zandakar? Is there a man in Ethrea who could overpower him?"

Rhian felt the answer run through her like a sword. *Oh, God. Emperor Han. But why . . . why . . .*

"One man?" said Ludo, unnoticing. "Likely not. But a band of men, who took him and Mister Jones unawares?"

"I don't think it's wise to assume anything just yet," Rhian said, pacing again to make certain Alasdair couldn't see her face. She couldn't trust herself to keep it schooled. "The fact is, we've still no proof of any misdoings. In the morning, if they've not returned safe and sound, we'll talk more of how this problem can be resolved. Now, I'm for my bath. Ludo, stay to dine with us. I want to hear more of your adventures with Adric, and how the funerals passed off."

Alasdair and Ludo exchanged glances, then shrugged. So alike they looked, so brotherly and resigned. If she weren't so distraught she might easily have laughed.

"Of course, Your Majesty," said Ludo. "I'm yours to command."

Alone and sunk deep in her oak tub's decidedly lukewarm water, sponging away the dried sweat from her *hotas* with rose-scented soap, Rhian made herself face the appalling thought that had occurred in her parlour.

What if Han has taken Zandakar and Dexterity?

A shudder ran through her, though the water hadn't yet chilled and cheerful flames flickered in the chamber's fireplace.

I believed Han when he said he's Ethrea's friend. Have I been a fool? Have I trusted us to ruin?

Hands pressed flat to her face, she waited for the flooding distress to subside. Lowering her hands at last, she stared at her privy chamber's elaborate ceiling.

Think, Rhian. Think. Be sensible. No weeping.

It made no sense that Han would use violence against Zandakar or Dexterity. That would achieve nothing to his advantage. But if he somehow sought to save his empire from Mijak by enticing Zandakar to his side . . .

Loath as she was to entertain the notion of betrayal, Alasdair was right. She couldn't afford not to. And Zandakar had deceived her before. It was possible, if sickening, that he might have deceived her again. He'd been a prince in Mijak, a man of power and prestige. And though it was galling to admit, Zandakar's treatment in Ethrea had sometimes been harsh.

Had Han made him an offer so dazzling he was prepared to break his word? She couldn't offer Zandakar a bright future. No power or position to match what he'd left behind in Mijak. Just a roof over his head and hot meals in his belly . . . and gratitude. Plenty of men would look elsewhere, offered that.

Does Han think that with Zandakar fighting for him alone the Tzhung empire will defeat Mijak's warriors? That he can do without Ethrea, without the other trading nations? God has made it clear I'm to lead the fight against Mijak, but the Tzhung have their own god. Why do I think they'll blindly follow mine?

Or . . . did *Han* think to rule the world, instead of Mijak?

Arbenia won't let him. Nor will Harbisland. Every other trading nation would abandon old grievances and strive shoulder to shoulder to drag all of Tzhung into the sea. Han couldn't be so mad.

But then again, why not? Zandakar's mother was mad, convinced her scorpion god demanded that she and her killing son Dmitrak rule the world in its name. Where one was maddened by power and ambition, why not more than one?

And if all that were true, what of Dexterity? He'd

never stand idly by to let that happen. He'd not watch Zandakar abandon her without protest.

Oh, Dexterity, Dexterity. Where are you? Where's Zandakar?

The words were an ache in her throat, her heart. She felt hollow inside, not from hunger but despair. Her confidence was splintering, her faith battered to shreds. She felt as grimly alone now as the day she buried her father.

And then a sweet scent teased the chamber air: lavender, and roses. Something – someone – touched her hair. *Have faith, Rhian. You're not betrayed.*

She sat up, water sloshing, and stared around the room. It was the same voice she'd heard in Old Scooton, before they rode to face Marlan. At the time she'd thought it was her mother . . .

"Mama?" she whispered. "Mama, is that you?"

No answer. The sweet smell of flowers began to fade.

"Where are they? What's happened to them? Please, please, *tell me.*"

Silence, save for her swift breathing. Then the privy chamber door opened and Alasdair peered in. "Are you done? We're famished to fainting out here."

It took her a moment to collect her wits. "Done? Yes. Yes. I'll join you shortly, Alasdair. Send to the kitchens. Tell them to serve the meal."

Alasdair frowned. "Are you all right?"

Have faith, Rhian. You're not betrayed.

"Yes," she said, slowly smiling. "I'm fine."

She didn't tell Alasdair of the voice she'd heard while in her bath. He'd think she imagined it, that her affection for Dexterity and her stubborn belief in Zandakar blinded her to difficult truths. But she knew what she'd heard. Somehow Dexterity and Zandakar would return to her, and when they did the truth would be told.

"What will you say of this business to the council?" asked Alasdair as they snatched a swift breakfast together the next morning.

"Only what I must," she said. "In truth, I wish I needn't mention it at all."

He looked at her. "Rhian—"

"I know, I know! I can't keep it secret. But I don't wish to start a panic, either. Or sit through an hour of tedious, prosy lecturing, *especially* from Helfred."

Sharp answers chased across Alasdair's face, then. Answers like: *Then you shouldn't have let Zandakar leave the castle with only Mister Jones to guard him, should you? You shouldn't have made such an important decision without consulting your privy council. You should at least have spoken with me.*

She touched her fingers to his hand. "I never thought this could happen," she said softly, burned with shame. "I was foolish, I admit it. An arrogant Havrell. I'll not be so foolish again, I promise."

"Good," he said. "So what do we do?"

"What can we do but wait, and have faith? God will see Dexterity and Zandakar return to us, I'm sure of it."

Alasdair wasn't. His eyes were full of doubt. But he didn't contradict her, and they finished breakfast in silence.

Edward and Rudi returned to Kingseat mid-morning, and the privy council met late into the night. The first thing Rhian did was announce Dexterity and Zandakar's vanishing, with strict instructions that the news be kept privily between them. Her council was vastly unimpressed, and said so loudly and at length. She endured their dismay and their displeasure, knowing she deserved it. When their voices at last ran down, she folded her hands on the table and considered them.

"Gentlemen, I have heard you. Now please, hear me. I trust God to keep our friends safe. I urge you to do likewise. Now, if we might turn our attention to the humdrum business of Ethrea?"

Reluctantly, her council obeyed. There were still no rumours of trouble abroad. Kingseat harbour was as busy as ever. The trading enterprises of the duchies continued without hindrance. Under the watchful guidance of Helfred's clergy, Hartshorn and Meercheq showed no signs of unrest.

On the surface, then, all was well in Ethrea.

Next they discussed, in painstaking detail, the condition and readiness of each duchy garrison. Of course Edward and Rudi had said nothing of the threat from Mijak to the garrison commanders, presenting themselves as inspectors for Her Majesty, their queen.

The dukes had nothing but encouraging news to report.

"In short, Majesty," said Edward, looking tired after so much hard travelling, "your garrisons stand well ready to form the backbone of an army. Of course, without Zandakar . . ."

An exchange of dark glances around the council table. Rhian watched her interlaced fingers tighten, and strove to modulate her voice. "Yes, Edward. But let's not belabour the point again."

"It's a mistake, doing nothing," Adric muttered under his breath. "We should—"

"*No*, Adric," she said flatly. "The ambassadors watch us as closely as we watch them. The slightest hint something's amiss and they'll lose what little confidence they have in me, and in Ethrea. Any hope of an alliance will be dashed. So we can't send Idson and his men scouring the countryside. We can't raise a flap and fuss in the township. *We hold fast, my lords*, until Dexterity and Zandakar come back."

"If they come back," said Adric.

Rhian held his gaze until his nerve broke, and he looked down. "Not if, Adric. *When*." She cleared her throat. "Now, speaking of the ambassadors, let's consider our next meeting with them."

"You're sure there'll be a next meeting?" said Ludo. "I thought the ambassadors were being coy."

"Coy or not, they don't dare refuse to meet with me altogether," she replied. "We still have business dealings, they can't ignore them."

"And if they do," said Alasdair, "at least we'll know where we stand."

"Yes. Alone," said Rudi, pulling a face. "In which case God help us."

Sombre silence then, as the weight of events pressed everyone in the chamber into their seats. Rhian looked briefly at Alasdair, then let her gaze sweep round the faces of the other men on her council.

"Courage, gentlemen," she said quietly. "Above all things, courage."

*   *   *

Grudgingly, suspiciously, the ambassadors finally agreed to a second meeting.

At noon on the day after her dukes' return from the kingdom's garrisons, Rhian and her council welcomed them again to the castle's Grand Ballroom.

Zandakar and Dexterity still hadn't returned.

Magnificently dressed in bronze velvet sewn with pearls and bullion, crowned with the circlet that had seen her defeat Damwin and Kyrin, Rhian ruthlessly thrust aside her gnawing anxiety and sat on the dais, watching as one by one the ambassadors arrived.

Ambassador Lai came last, and alone.

"Where is your emperor?" she said. "I expected to see him."

"Alas," said Lai, his expression blandly polite. "His Imperial Majesty is indisposed, Queen Rhian."

Indisposed, or unable to face her? She believed with all her heart Zandakar and Dexterity hadn't betrayed her . . . but that didn't mean Han wasn't somehow involved in their mysterious disappearance.

For he's the only man I know who can appear and disappear at will, in broad daylight.

She wanted to seize Lai, to shake him, to shout. She wanted to dance *hotas* with him until he bled the truth.

Does Han have Dexterity? Does he have Zandakar? Has he used witch-man powers against them?

"My sympathies to His Imperial Majesty, Ambassador Lai," she said, not showing him anything but friendly concern. "Should he require it, I can send my royal physick to aid him."

"Thank you," said Lai. "But it will not be necessary." And then he stepped back, neatly ending their conversation.

Rhian raised a hand, drawing everyone's attention. "My lord ambassadors," she said, making sure her voice was gentle and melodious, the epitome of feminine pleasantry and grace. "Thank you for your attendance here today. I am well aware you are all busy men, with various time-consuming duties. Be sure you enjoy Ethrea's deepest regard."

Squashed behind a small desk in the nearest corner, Ven'Cedwin pressed the first of many inked quills to his parchment and faithfully began to record the event.

As the ambassadors preened themselves, just a little, she did glance at Alasdair. His eyes warmed, the only smile he could give her in public. He must have asked Dinsy which dress she'd chosen for this meeting. He wore bronze too, trimmed with pearls, so they were a pair.

"Ambassador Athnïj," she continued. "If I may address you first?"

Athnïj's coat was misbuttoned. His hair was uncombed. "Majesty," he said, sounding dull and broken-spirited. "How may I assist?"

"My harbourmaster reports there is still no ship from Icthia arrived in Kingseat. Have you received any word from your home at all?"

"No word, Majesty," he replied. A tic was spasming beside his bloodshot right eye. "But I have not abandoned hope completely."

The privy council, ranged behind her, stirred as though to comment unfavourably on his claim. Rhian raised her hand, demanding their silence.

"I am sorry, Ambassador," she said, allowing her genuine sympathy to show. "You are of course welcome to remain in Kingseat under our protection. We can discuss particulars in private later, perhaps."

Particulars like how he could afford to maintain his ambassadorial residence, with no funds arriving from his master in Icthia.

Athnij bowed again, relieved and grateful and struggling with emotion. "If that is convenient, Your Majesty."

"It is." She turned next to Gutten of Arbenia, carefully framing her next words. If she didn't have to mention the trade winds, she wouldn't. With any luck Gutten had come to his senses since the last time they met. One look at poor Athnij must surely convince him. "Sir, I know it's too soon for you to have heard from your count regarding ships for an armada, but I wonder if you'd given thought to my desire for an Ethrean army?"

As she expected, Gutten looked first to Voolksyn of Harbisland, then to Alasdair, and lastly herself. His jaw worked as though he chewed unpalatable words. After a long pause he spat them out. "Talking war with women? This is not Arbenia."

"No, it's Ethrea," she said, and let her voice acquire a less feminine edge. "Where I am queen."

Gutten's eyes narrowed, contemptuous. "Yes."

Acutely aware of Alasdair at her side, his temper barely held in check, she leaned forward just a little and fixed Gutten with her coldest stare. "Ambassador, do you continue to dispute we face danger from the east?"

"Yes," grunted Gutten.

Rhian felt her insides cramp, and sat back. "Very well. As a sovereign nation Arbenia is free to ignore any warnings given you. But is it your contention that I must agree with your position? Do you intend to hamper my efforts to protect this kingdom . . . and your interests here?"

Gutten glanced again at his fellow ambassadors, his gaze lingering longest on Voolksyn. Then he fixed his gaze on her, everything about him unfriendly. "An army of Ethrea threatens Arbenian interests. It threatens every trading nation."

"I disagree," she said, as mildly as she could. "My lords, I am sensible of the fact that an army in Ethrea directly violates our ancient trading charter. But we all know, surely, such an army could never hope to endanger the *least* of you. Your nations have made of warfare an art. You are experts in killing. God's mercy, most of Ethrea's army will consist of men and women defending themselves with nothing more menacing than pitchforks and sheep shears."

Halash of Dev'karesh snorted clove-scented breath. "Farmers? Farmers and their wives do not worry us, Queen Rhian. But you gild the truth with clever words. Ethrea has soldiers. They have swords and bows. They have arrows. They have pikestaffs."

"And they'll wield them against Mijak, Halash, not against any man of yours. They'll wield them in defence of their homes and children. Facing the threat that we face, would the people of your lands do any less?"

Lalaska of Barbruish smoothed his oiled ringlets. "You say this now. Your intentions could change."

"They will not change, my lords! Must I sign an oath in *blood* before you'll believe it?"

As her privy council stirred and stared with unfriendly eyes at the ambassadors, and the ambassadors glared back, Rhian throttled the despair rising in her throat.

God, God, how is it they still distrust me? What must I do to prove I have no sinister intent?

She pushed to her feet. "This is madness. I did not request your presence here today that we might bicker and squabble while Mijak's deadly shadow creeps ever closer to my kingdom. I need your help in the defence of this realm. I want to know how you will help us!"

"You and your privy council, you talk and you talk," said Istahas of Slynt. He gestured at his fellow ambassadors, save Lai of Tzhung. "We talk also."

She knew that, of course. Those quiet men and women paid to watch the ambassadors discreetly had told her of the flurried comings and goings between their residences.

"I understand that, sir," she said. "Our last meeting was full of incident. But—"

"We wish to see this prince of Mijak," said Istahas. "We wish to talk to him alone. No Queen of Ethrea. No council. No burning men to make fear. You bring us this Zandakar, we talk. Then *we* talk, Queen Rhian of Ethrea." He gestured again at his fellow ambassadors. "We talk armies. We talk armadas. We talk Mijak. After the prince of Mijak tells us things alone."

Oh, Rollin help me. Let them not call my bluff.

"Ambassador Istahas," she said coldly, "your tone

is discourteous, your insinuations insulting. Allies do not treat one another like enemies. If you wish, you are free to withdraw from the league of trading nations. Of course, that means you'll forfeit all ties with Ethrea. Your ambassadorial residence will be closed, the contents of your warehouses and treasury vaults confiscated, all your citizens now present in the kingdom collected and escorted into open waters and Slynt's access to Ethrea revoked in full." She stabbed each staring ambassador with a look. "The same choice is open to each and every one of you. Mijak *is* coming. Do you stand with Ethrea against it, or do you stand alone . . . and risk a great fall?"

Uproar.

Papa used to say, *A cornered stag will always charge, and a huntsman unready is a huntsman empty-handed – or dead.*

Well, this stag might be a doe . . . but that didn't mean she was meek and helpless. Impetuous, arrogant, haughty . . . but never meek. Never helpless.

She stood, raking them with her most imperious glare. "You dare come to me and make petty demands? You may leave my castle, gentlemen! Return to your residences and ponder my words! The next time I request your attendance here *do not come* if you lack the will or intent for an honest alliance. You have wasted my time – and I am most displeased! Now *get out.*"

Turning her back on them, she faced her astonished privy council, one hand on the back of her throne. Ignored the rabble of voices as they protested their dismissal. To a man, her council engaged with them, refuting their arguments, supporting their queen.

Someone stepped around the side of the dais. She let her gaze slide right. "Ambassador Lai."

"You play a dangerous game, Majesty," Han's man said in an undertone.

"As does Han." She turned her face a little, so he might see her eyes. Took a dangerous leap. "I have a message for your emperor. Tell him this: *I want them back.*"

So swiftly, a betraying flicker in the ambassador's dark eyes. Blood pounding, Rhian stared at him. *I was right. I was right.* And then Lai had himself in hand again.

"Majesty, I fail to—"

"You heard me. Don't pretend to misunderstand."

Lai bowed. "Majesty," he said quietly, and quietly withdrew.

The ballroom emptied of shouting ambassadors. As the rest of her council discussed events, excited, Alasdair joined her beside her throne. "So you called their bluff: That was—" He hesitated.

"Foolish?"

His eyes warmed. "No. I think it was . . . brave."

"Perhaps it was both," she murmured. "Oh, Alasdair. Hold my hand."

He did so, swiftly, then pulled a comical face. "Look on the bright side, my love. At least we didn't have to tell them about Tzhung-tzhungchai's meddling."

Almost, almost, she laughed aloud.

CHAPTER NINETEEN

"Icthia," said Sun-dao, his voice a croaking whisper. "Jatharuj."

"You mean we're here?" said Dexterity. He sounded amazed. "And still in one piece? God be praised. I never expected it."

As the toymaker leaned over the small boat's side, staring across the dark shifting water at the lights dotted here and there around the distant harbour and above it, Zandakar pressed his palm to Sun-dao's chest. There was a heartbeat, but it was weak and uneven. Salt air rasped in the witchman's throat. His eyes remained open, filmed with exhaustion. His amber skin had paled to dirty yellow, he was stinking with rank sweat. Every bone and muscle in him trembled. Had Sun-dao killed himself to bring them here?

Zandakar bent close. "You die now, witch-man?"

Sun-dao did not answer, he stared at the sky.

"I can't believe we're here and not drowned at the bottom of the ocean," said Dexterity. "My head's still spinning from that last whirlwind." He scrambled closer, and pressed his hand to Sun-dao's sweaty face. "He's fevered. Will he be well enough to get us home again, do you think?"

He shrugged. "*Wei* know. You ask Hettie, maybe she send witch-man strength."

"Tcha," said Dexterity, pulling a face. "I suppose

I can try. Though she practically never comes when I call." The toymaker looked up again, across the water. Inky black, no reflection of moonlight. The godmoon and his wife were in their shy time, hiding in the vast sky's shadows. "As far as I can tell we're just outside the harbour's mouth. How do you propose we reach dry land? I hope you're not thinking to *swim*, Zandakar."

He shook his head. "*Wei* swim."

"Oh," said Dexterity. "Good." He looked around. "Then we'll have to row. Do you know what rowing is?"

"*Zho*. Boats on river in Targa. I see rowing."

"Good, good," said Dexterity vigorously. "Except – are there any oars? I never thought to ask. I suppose there must be, though I can't recall seeing them. But every boat has oars, doesn't it?"

Dexterity was nervous. When he was nervous his words ran like water, he chattered and chattered. Ursa would snap at him, Ursa would say *Hold your frippery tongue, Jones, we've enough on our plates without you rattling on.* That was Ursa, when Dexterity was nervous.

I cannot say that. How can I chide Dexterity when I am nervous too?

"*Wei* know, Dexterity. I travel slave ship. I travel Tzhung boat. That is what I know."

Dexterity huffed out a frustrated breath. "Well, that's twice the boating experience I've got, Zandakar." He shivered. "I can't believe we've reached Icthia. How long has it taken us to get here, can you tell?"

The journey from Ethrea had passed in a blur, in a

whirling of cold wind and a wheeling of stars, in snatched mouthfuls of dried salt fish from clay pots and warm brackish water. "*Wei*."

"No. Neither can I. Rhian must be beside herself by now: poor child. Unless that Emperor Han's told her what he's done. Do you suppose he's told her? Or has he let her wonder, and worry? I'll bet he has, you know. I don't think Emperor Han is a very nice man."

Sprawled on the boat's deck, the witch-man Sundao stirred and whispered something in the Tzhung tongue. "Emperor Han great," he added in Ethrean. "Emperor Han in the wind."

Zandakar frowned. Was that the same as being in the god's eye? Aieee, tcha, life was simpler in Mijak. In Mijak there was one god, it was the god, there was no thought of other gods. Out in the world every man had his own god, and the god of Mijak was nowhere. It was wrong, it was confusing. Vortka could explain.

Vortka.

Not answering the witch-man, he looked across the water to the lights of Jatharuj. Vortka was there, in that sleeping place. Aieee, god, to see him again. To see Dmitrak, and Yuma.

His heart pounded, shaking him.

If I see them, will I die? I did not come here to die, I am come to save Mijak. Am I in your eye, god? Will you see me save Mijak?

The god did not answer.

Slowly he let his body drop to the deck, till he was no longer kneeling but sitting. Pulling one knee to his chest he rested his elbow on it and pressed a hand to his face. In that darkness of his own making he felt

Dexterity's hand come to rest on his shoulder, felt the toymaker's warm regard like sunlight.

"Oh dear," said the toymaker, his voice gentle. "Yes, it is all rather overwhelming, isn't it? But . . . it's all right to be frightened, Zandakar. Rollin knows I am."

"*Wei* frightened," he whispered, and knew it for a lie. "Thinking, to find Vortka. Save Mijak. Save Ethrea."

"Do you truly think that's possible?" In the darkness Dexterity sounded so sad, without hope. "Tell me honestly, Zandakar."

Slowly he lowered his hand from his face, met Dexterity's anxious gaze without flinching. "*Wei* know. Must try."

"Yes. You must try," said Dexterity, sighing heavily. "But if you fail, what then? If you fail and you're taken, you know you'll be killed. If you fail and we somehow escape Icthia, if we by some miracle get home to Kingseat, then what? Will you fight your family, Zandakar? Will you pick up a sword and try to kill your mother? Your brother? I know you're a blooded warrior, Zandakar, but could you really do that?"

Yuma. Dimmi. Both deaf to the god, both blind in its eye though they could not see that. *I can see it, the god has shown me, how can I show them? Can I show them? Must they die? Must Vortka die if I cannot make him see?*

He was oathsworn to Ethrea, he would do what he must. He looked at Dexterity and nodded, slowly. "For Rhian? *Zho.*"

"Oh, Zandakar," said Dexterity, and took away

his warm hand. "I don't know whether to be relieved or sorry."

Neither did he. "Find oars, Dexterity."

"And if there aren't any?"

He snorted. "You know swim, Dexterity? I *wei* swim. *Wei* oars, you swim with me to Jatharuj."

Dexterity's mouth dropped open in horror. "*What*? Oh no, I don't think so. Just you wait. I'll find the oars."

The Tzhung boat rocked without purpose on the water's gentle swell. So much water, they were small in the god's eye beneath the endless sky. The night was warm and peaceful, silent except for the ocean's soft song. Once in the strange journey here, when Sun-dao was again forced to drop them out of the otherness they travelled through so he might recapture his strength, they returned to a world lashed by a towering storm. Great walls of water. Lumps of ice. Howling wind. Dexterity was nearly washed right over the side to die.

Sun-dao, his head cut and bleeding, his eyes alive with a dreadful black flame, had called on the wind's strength to fill him with power. Into the living air he had risen, arms spread wide, black eyes burning. An anguished scream was ripped from his mouth. He seemed to grow bigger, to spread thin on the wind. A light had shone in him, he glowed in the storm ridden darkness like Dexterity.

And in a blink, in a heartbeat, they disappeared from that place.

That was two leaping whirlwinds ago. Now Sun-dao looked emptied, a tired old man wrapped in yellow skin and black silk. Looking at him, Zandakar felt his belly clutch tight. Did the witch-man have the strength to return them to Ethrea?

The god see him in its eye and give him that strength. The wind blow in his bones, make him strong in his power.

Was it wicked and sinning, to call on the wind?

Let Vortka tell me when I see him again.

Across the dark water the lights of Jatharuj flickered. Closer now, for the swelling ocean carried them towards land. Closer to Vortka, to Dimmi, to Yuma. Closer to the warhost, to the warriors he once had known and loved, taught and tamed and cherished and chastised.

Closer to the life he had left so far behind.

"Zandakar! I've found them!"

Startled, and startled to be caught by surprise, he turned to look at Dexterity. "Oars?"

"Yes," said the toymaker, his hands full of wood. "And do you know, I'm remembering something. An old smuggler's tale. Something about muffling the sound of oars in the water . . ." Dexterity frowned, unsteady on his feet as the small boat rolled on the waves. "We need to wrap the oar blades with sacking and tie it on, so they don't splash so loudly. At least, I think that's how they did it. I don't suppose it can hurt, either way."

Sacking? Was there sacking? What was sacking? He thought some kind of material. The Tzhung boat that had carried them here was mostly empty. The witch-man Sun-dao had told them it must be so, or he could not move it so far in the wind. Small, cramped, so very uncomfortable, it had not been a pleasant journey from Kingseat to Jatharuj.

"Is there sacking, Dexterity?"

"No," said the toymaker, sounding fretful. "I'd say use our blankets, but they're shredded to pieces after all that travelling in the wind. I suppose we could rip down the sail, but I don't think that's a good idea."

Zandakar looked at Sun-dao, listless on the deck. "He has clothes, we take them."

"Take them?" said Dexterity. "Strip him, you mean? Should we do that?"

His answer was to pull the silk tunic and trousers from Sun-dao's flaccid body. Beneath them the witch-man wore a loincloth, he could keep it.

"Zandakar, what if he catches cold?" said Dexterity. "Do we really want a witch-man like Sun-dao cross with us?"

He looked up. "You want Mijak warrior cross with us?"

Dexterity winced. His face bristled with hair, his rust-red and grey beard grown back unchecked. In the lamplight his eyes were tired, he was a very tired man. "Give his clothes here. I'll do my best to tie them onto the oars."

Sun-dao's eyes were half closed, he did not seem to notice he was almost naked. His skin beneath his black silk was covered in tattoos, red and black and green and blue, as though he wore a second skin made of ink. Some were pictures: wide-winged birds, snarling striped cats, strange beasts with talons and tails and scales. Words too, Tzhung writing, the letters were strange. Zandakar felt his skin crawl, to see them.

Dexterity finished his task and handed over one silk-wrapped oar. "There you are. If we pull together

I'm sure we'll reach the port." He rubbed a hand across his eyes, he did not sound sure. "I suppose we should douse the lamp. We don't want anyone seeing us. Best get the oars put in place first, though." He pointed to holes cut into each side of the boat. "These slots. That's where they go."

Zandakar hefted his oar. "*Zho.*"

With the oars fitted he shifted to douse the lamp, but Dexterity grabbed his arm. "No. Wait. Zandakar – what if dousing the lamp's not enough? Even with the oars muffled we're going to make noise. There are bound to be sentries at the harbour. If they hear us . . ."

If a warrior found them, they would be dead. Dexterity's eyes were wide with worry.

"Han said Sun-dao could *hide us in the wind.* But Sun-dao looks three-quarters dead to me. What shall we do?"

Zandakar looked at the witch-man. It was true, he hardly seemed to breathe. He leaned over Sun-dao, pinched the witch-man's earlobe hard until the witch-man moaned and opened his eyes.

"Oh, be careful, Zandakar!" said Dexterity. "Don't hurt him."

Tcha, Dexterity. Soft, kind man. "Sun-dao," he said. "You wake. You hide us in wind."

So slowly, making little noises of pain, Sun-dao sat up, looked around at the boat, the water, the distant harbour's lights. At the great, spreading shadow that must be the warship fleet of Mijak. "Icthia?"

"Yes. Jatharuj," said Dexterity. "Don't you remember?"

Sun-dao was shivering, he was a sick man. "Yes."

"Sun-dao, we don't dare go into the harbour unless we're sure we won't be seen," said Dexterity. "Can you do what the emperor said? Can you hide us in the wind?"

The witch-man took a deep breath and nodded. "Yes."

"And when we want to be seen? How does that work?"

"Touch," said Sun-dao. His teeth were chattering.

"All right," said Dexterity. "Then you'd best do it, quickly. I want this nonsense over and done with so we can get home to Ethrea."

Sun-dao's eyes narrowed, and he hissed. "Respect Han's witch-man!"

Dexterity snorted. "I see you're feeling well enough to scold."

"*Tcha*," said Zandakar. "Sun-dao. *You hide*."

The shivering witch-man closed his eyes, he tipped his head back and spread his naked arms wide. He sang in a harsh voice, he called on the wind. It seemed to Zandakar the witch-man's tattooed skin was writhing, his tattoos were living, they crawled like living things upon his flesh. He heard Dexterity's choked gasp and knew the toymaker saw it too. In the boat's meagre lamplight they saw Sun-dao's tattoos come to life.

A teasing, swirling breeze sprang up, it rattled the boat's sail and tugged at their clothing. The boat rocked on the water, waves slapped and splashed its hull. The warm night air chilled, it grew suddenly cold.

Then the world disappeared.

"Oh!" cried Dexterity. "Zandakar, I'm—"

In a blink, a heartbeat, the vanished world returned.

Dexterity was gasping. "Rollin's mercy. What was that?"

The boat's lamp still burned. In its weak light, Sundao shuddered. His tattoos had died, his skin was unmoving, his witch-man power slept.

"Han," he said, his eyes wide, his stare blank. "Han – I must – I must—"

With a rattling exhalation he slumped to the deck.

"Oh, no," said Dexterity. "Zandakar, is he—"

Hand pressed to the witch-man's chest, he shook his head. "*Wei*. He lives."

But Sun-dao's heartbeat was feeble. He did not say that to Dexterity. The toymaker was already nervous enough.

"Thank God," Dexterity whispered. "We might still get home." In the lamplight his tired eyes were bright. "Oh, Zandakar. Are we really here? Is this really happening?"

Puzzled, he nodded. "*Zho*."

Dexterity smoothed a shaking hand over his beard. "It's just . . . this isn't supposed to be my life, you see. I'm a plain, ordinary man. I'm a *toymaker*. Yet here I am, in a boat on the ocean with a sorcerer and a heathen warrior, about to row into an enemy port. And if *that's* not bad enough, after that I'll be walking right into the lion's den! I'm mad. I must be."

Walking? Walking where? "Dexterity, you *wei* walking. You in boat with Sun-dao."

Dexterity shook his head. "Don't be silly. I'm coming with you."

Into Jatharuj? To see Vortka? Maybe to see Yuma and Dmitrak after? "*Wei. Wei.* You stay in boat."

"I can't," said Dexterity, staring. "Weren't you listening, back in Kingseat? I'm responsible for you, I can't let you go traipsing off alone. Besides, when we get home I have to be able to say I saw with my own eyes what happened here. Nobody's going to take your word for it, Zandakar. Someone like that Gutten will call you a liar and that'll be that."

He did not want Dexterity in Jatharuj, it was too dangerous, Dexterity was his friend. He looked at the witch-man. "Sun-dao can come."

"Don't be ridiculous. Sun-dao's unconscious! And even if we could wake him, he needs to stay in the boat and rest if we're to have any hope of getting home. Anyway, he's Emperor Han's witch-man. The ambassadors won't believe him any more than they'll believe you. But I'm Mister Jones, the burning man of Ethrea. They've seen me and my miracles. They won't dare call me a liar."

Dexterity sounded bitter, he did not sound pleased to be a miracle man. He was in his god's eye, he did not want to be there.

"Dexterity—"

"*Wei,*" said the toymaker. "I'm going with you and that's final. I can tell you it's what Hettie would want. And Rhian."

Hettie and Rhian, there was no arguing with both of them. Zandakar sighed and pressed his fingers to his face. A small pain pulsed behind his eyes. "Tcha, Dexterity. *Zho*. You come." He doused the lamp. "We row."

They rowed, not smoothly, too much splashing at

first. Zandakar had to work hard to match his pull with Dexterity's, the older man was slower, he did not have the same reach. They entered the harbour, it was crowded with warships, crowded so close it was hard to row between them. Zandakar felt his beating heart falter. There were warships enough here to carry the largest warhost in Mijak's history.

If I fail in Jatharuj they will sail to Ethrea, they will sail into Kingseat, the kingdom will fall.

The words were like a tasking, he felt beaten by his thoughts.

I am one man, I am Zandakar, I am outcast from my kind. How can I stop them? How can I make Vortka listen to me?

He did not know, the god must see him. It must see him in its helping eye.

See me, god, see me save Mijak for you and for Yuma. See me save it for Vortka and for Dimmi. For me.

They reached the dock. There were torches burning, showing spaces between the ships, wide enough for the small Tzhung boat's passage. Zandakar rowed looking over his shoulder, with hisses and grunts he told Dexterity how to row. At last, with a gentle thud, a kiss of wood on wood, the Tzhung boat struck an empty sliver of pier between two looming Mijaki warships.

They had reached Jatharuj.

It was an awkward scramble to get out of the Tzhung boat, there were no steps, they banged their knees and scraped their fingers. They stood on the pier and stared down at Sun-dao in the boat. The witchman did not stir, his chest barely moved with breathing.

"He looks dreadful," whispered Dexterity. "As good as dead. Are you sure it's safe to leave him?"

Safe? What was safe? They were in Mijak where every warrior wanted to kill them. He was a warrior with no snakeblade at his side.

"We must, *zho*?" he said, shrugging.

Dexterity sighed. "*Zho*. We must."

They turned their backs on silent Sun-dao and walked along the empty pier towards the streets of Jatharuj.

There were warriors at the gates guarding Jatharuj harbour. Zandakar felt Dexterity falter, heard his uneven breath as they came upon the torchlight and the warriors standing guard in the night. He took the toymaker's wrist in a warning grasp, fingers tight. In the spreading torchlight Dexterity's eyes were wide with fear.

"Trust Sun-dao," he whispered. "These warriors *wei* see us."

Lips tight, Dexterity nodded. There was sweat on his forehead. They walked past the guards as though the warriors were blind, or dead. Looking at their faces, Zandakar did not know them.

These are Dmitrak's warriors, they do not belong to me.

They left the harbour behind and made their way like mist along the dark winding street that led to the township. As they drifted silent and unseen in the night, Dexterity sniffed.

"What's that smell? It's not the harbour, or the ocean. It's something else. Something . . ."

Zandakar breathed deeply, he felt his old life stir. He knew what it was, he did not want to say.

"It's *blood*!" said Dexterity, he sounded horrified. He stood still. "I can smell *blood*, Zandakar. It's not fresh, it's old, as though the stink of it has soaked into the air itself." His fingertips touched the stonework beside him. "Into the streets and the walls of the buildings."

"It is Mijak, Dexterity," he replied, his voice low, stopping also. "We are in Mijak, Mijak smells of blood."

So many godmoons in a strange place, so long since he had breathed Mijak's blood-touched air. He let his head fall back, he breathed in his home, he breathed it out. Memories surged and swirled, with his eyes closed this could be Et-Raklion.

But Et-Raklion does not smell of salt also, there is only blood there. In Et-Raklion I did not hide in the wind, I rode the streets in the god's eye, as its warlord, I feared nothing and no-one, I did not wear shadows. I was the god's hammer there, I wore its gauntlet of power. Aieee, god, so much has changed. I have changed, I am a stranger.

"Zandakar," said Dexterity, and tugged at his sleeve. "Zandakar, what's the matter?"

He opened his eyes. "Nothing."

"It's so silent, this place," said Dexterity, voice hushed. "As though the township's deserted. Kingseat's never this quiet, even in the small hours. There's always *something* going on." He looked around them. "Silent, practically pitch black. There's not a soul stirring, Zandakar. Can this be right, or has something gone amiss?"

Zandakar shook his head. "*Wei*. This is *chalava-takrazik*." Dexterity stared at him, not understanding. He could not think of Ethrean words to explain the quiet time. "Men sleep. *Chalava* in the world. Sunrise come, men in the world."

Dexterity was frowning. "You mean it's a kind of curfew?"

Curfew. He did not know that word. He shrugged. "*Zho*. Maybe."

"Well, if everyone's indoors, Zandakar, if no-one's out and about, how do you think we're supposed to find this Vortka of yours?"

He shrugged. "*Chalava*."

"Of course," muttered Dexterity, pulling a face. "*Chalava*. Silly question, Jones."

Zandakar started walking again, and Dexterity walked with him. They walked to the end of the narrow, crooked street where it joined a wider street that sloped up from the harbour, leading towards the main township of Jatharuj.

At the end of the narrow crooked street stood a godpost.

Dexterity gasped. Yellow light played over the godpost, a torch had been left burning so it might be seen in the night. The torch was burning down, flickering and inconstant.

"What's that?" said Dexterity. "It's – it's horrible. So ugly. *Grotesque*."

"*Chalava*," Zandakar whispered, and dropped to the ground. There was pain as his knees struck the stone street, he welcomed it, he gave it to the god. An offering. A sacrifice. "*Chalava*, Dexterity."

"Oh," said Dexterity, his voice sounded small.

Zandakar felt sinning to kneel before it, no god-braids, no godbells, no amulets. He stared up at the scorpion, at the coiled snake of Et-Raklion, he stared at the god's face and felt tears in his eyes.

I am here, god, do you see me? You called me, your voice was in my heart. I am come to Mijak, show me what to do.

In the night's silence, the sound of leather soles slapping the street.

"Get up, get up," said Dexterity. "Quickly. Some-one's coming!"

He stood. Dexterity grabbed his arm, tried to drag him away, but he resisted.

"Zandakar, what are you doing? I know those guards didn't see us but Sun-dao's poorly, who knows how long his power to keep us hidden will—"

"*Wei*, Dexterity," he said. "Hush. *Chalava* hides us."

The slapping sound came closer. Closer. A slight, robed figure stepped out of the night, it was a god-speaker novice, he served the god in the quiet time of Jatharuj. Strapped to his back was a bundle of fresh, unlit torches. As they watched, unseen in the god's eye, hidden in the wind, the novice took the almost spent torch from its holder, touched the fresh torch to its guttering flame, and when the new flame was strongly burning put the fresh torch in the holder.

Sun-dao had said touch would reveal them, if they desired it. Zandakar stepped forward and took the novice's wrist. "I am Zandakar, I must see the high godspeaker." He spoke in their own tongue, in the sweet voice of Mijak.

"Aieee, the god see me!" cried the novice, dropping the spent torch. "A demon, a demon!"

"Zandakar, have you lost your *mind*?" said Dexterity. "What are you doing?"

The novice could not hear the toymaker, but it was foolish to speak. He silenced Dexterity with a look then tightened his hold on the novice's wrist and dragged him close, till they were touching. "I am no demon, novice. You do not know my face, you must know my name."

"Zandakar," said the novice, his voice was thin and high. So young, he was a child still, the godhouse must be desperate. "But Zandakar is dead, the god smote him for sinning. You are a demon, I die strong in the god."

Tcha. Lies told about him, who had done that? "I am no demon, I did not die. The god used me for its purpose and brings me here to Vortka." He could break this child, he could snap him like a dry bone. "Will you thwart the god and die, novice?"

The novice's mouth opened and closed, he looked like a caught fish. His eyes rolled, he looked witless, fear had stolen his wits.

Zandakar shook him. "Serve me and you serve the god. You will not be tasked for it, you will be rewarded by Vortka."

"The empress – the empress—"

"The empress is my mother, she is in the god's eye and so is her son Zandakar. Take me to Vortka high godspeaker, novice. If I lie he will know it and you will see me cast down. Vortka has the god's power over demons, his scorpion pectoral will kiss me to death."

As the novice frowned, considering those words, Dexterity cleared his throat. "Zandakar, do you know what you're doing?"

He nodded, but did not speak so the novice would not be further frightened. Poor child, he was too young for this business.

Tcha. That is an Ethrean thought, we are in Mijak, the god chose him for the godhouse. He is not too young, he is a man in the god's eye.

"I will take you to Vortka," said the sweating novice. "And if you lie he will kill you."

"What did he say?" said Dexterity. "I can't understand a word of his gibberish!"

If he said one word in Ethrean the novice would think it was demon-tongue, and flee. So he shook his head at Dexterity, then crooked a finger to say he must follow.

"Oh dear," said Dexterity, fretting. "I do hope you know what you're doing . . ."

The novice led them through the silent streets, they did not see another godspeaker or warrior or slave or any foolish sinner defying the quiet time. They were in the god's eye, it wanted them to reach Vortka. They walked in silence, they walked swiftly, up the steepening streets towards the shadowy buildings that overlooked the town.

"There is the godhouse of Jatharuj," said the novice at last, slowing and pointing ahead to a tall building set back from the roadway. A wall encircled it, there were trees and a garden. It did not look like a godhouse, it had two great godposts at the gates, but it looked like a home some rich man might own. "Vortka is in the godhouse, he prays always to the god."

The godhouse of Jatharuj had many windows, light shone through four of them. The god's business continued through the night, no godhouse in Mijak was permitted to sleep.

"Take me inside," said Zandakar. "Take me to Vortka."

"Oh, I don't like this," whispered Dexterity. "My mouth's so dry I can't spit."

The novice sighed, and nodded. "Come. I will take you."

Five paces inside the godhouse the novice was challenged by a godspeaker who was burning golden cockerel feathers in an iron wall shrine. "Banto, what do you do here? You are tasked to work the quiet time, newsun is not arrived."

The novice Banto flinched. "Ardachek godspeaker, I am . . . alone." It was almost a question, his gaze darted left and right.

Ardachek stared. "Yes, novice, you are alone. Why are you here?"

Banto slumped, he stared at the floor. "The god sends me to Vortka high godspeaker."

Ardachek did not challenge the claim. No godspeaker, not even a childish novice, would dare to say such a thing if it was not true.

"Why?" he said. "Have you sinned? Do you seek tasking?"

Banto looked up. Fishlike again, he opened and shut his mouth. "No, Ardachek godspeaker," he said at last, his voice small and bewildered. "Godspeaker, I must see him."

Ardachek frowned, then nodded. "Vortka high godspeaker prays in his private chamber. Go up to him, novice. If you are in error then you *will* be tasked."

"Godspeaker," whispered Banto, and walked on through the godhouse to the staircase leading to the godhouse's next floor and beyond. Zandakar walked behind him, Dexterity at his side. Ardachek did not see them, they were in the god's hiding eye.

On the godhouse's second floor they passed a room with its door removed, inside the room a novice knelt for tasking. The cane struck her naked flesh, she wept for the god. The room beside that one was without a door also, inside it a godspeaker sacrificed for the god. His knife slit the lamb's throat, the lamb's blood filled the sacrifice basin.

"Oh, sweet Rollin," said Dexterity, his voice was full of pain. "This is *barbaric*. Zandakar, I'm going to be sick."

He did not speak, he gripped Dexterity's arm at the elbow and held him hard until the toymaker cried out in soft protest. Then he looked at Dexterity and shook his head once.

"This is a dreadful place," whispered Dexterity, there were tears in his eyes. "Why did I come here? I must've been mad."

If he answered Dexterity the novice would hear him, he did not wish the novice to be distracted or call for help. He was sorry for Dexterity, he made a face to show his sorrow. Dexterity sighed. They walked up more stairs, the novice Banto silent and trembling.

On the highest floor of the godhouse there were no godspeakers burning feathers, sacrificing lambs or tasking novices. There were shadows and silence, this was Vortka's domain.

Banto pointed an unsteady finger at a closed door ahead of them. "There is the high godspeaker's chamber," he said, and stopped.

Zandakar rested his hand on the novice's shoulder. "Vortka will want to see you, Banto. Do not sin against the god now."

The novice Banto whimpered, he led them to the closed door and knocked upon it. When the door opened, Vortka stood before them.

"Banto?" he said, his face and voice were puzzled. "It is the quiet time, why are you not in the streets serving the god?"

Zandakar felt his heart pound, he heard the blood in his veins. *Vortka. Vortka.*

"Vortka high godspeaker," said Banto, he sounded close to panic. "I am come – the god wants – there is a man – *you do not see him?*"

Vortka looked around them. "I see you, Banto novice. I see you in distress." He stepped back. "Come in, we will talk of this, you will tell me what this means."

Aieee, the god see him, Vortka had always been kind. With a glance at Dexterity, Zandakar followed the novice into Vortka's private chamber. When the door closed behind them he stepped close to the high godspeaker, he took the old man's hands in his.

"Vortka, it is Zandakar. I am come. I am home."

CHAPTER TWENTY

"Zandakar?" said Vortka. His voice was a whisper, his body shaken head to toe. "Zandakar, am I dreaming?"

He tried to smile, his throat was so tight. Here was Vortka, his friend from boyhood, the man who had saved him when Yuma would kill him, when Dimmi would kill him. His face deeply lined, his eyes weary beyond anything, but he was still Vortka.

"No, high godspeaker. I am here, the god has brought me. We have much to speak of, the god tasks me with its want."

"Zandakar," said Vortka, and seized him close in a suffocating embrace. "Aieee, the god see me, you are come home."

Never in his life had Vortka embraced him, never had the high godspeaker wept out his name. Something cold and hard within him broke, then, and he held tight to Vortka like a man drowning in a sea of grief, or joy.

At last Vortka released him and stood back. His godbraids were silver, as silver as his godbells. "You are not dead, the god told me you were not."

"No, I am not, I am safe in the god's eye," he said. Aieee, tcha, it was good to speak in the tongue of his people, the music of Mijak flowing like wine. "The god has kept me safe, Vortka, it is a journey!"

Turning, he caught sight of the novice Banto's astonished face. "High godspeaker, this boy cannot be here now, he cannot remember I came to you."

Vortka shook his head. "No, he cannot." Stepping forward swiftly he took Banto by the shoulder, he pressed his palm to Banto's cheek. "Forget, Banto novice, let the god take this night from you." Heat and light flared beneath Vortka's pressing palm. The novice cried out softly, his eyes rolling in his head.

"Stop that!" shouted Dexterity. "Are you hurting him? Are you killing him? Stop that at once!"

Zandakar turned. "*Wei*, Dexterity, Vortka *wei* hurt or kill."

"What is this?" said Vortka, startled, as the power faded from his touch. "Who do you speak to, Zandakar? What strange tongue is that?"

"Send this novice away, Vortka," he said. "Then I will tell you. I have much to say."

Vortka stared deep into the novice's glazed eyes. "Return to the quiet time in the streets of Jatharuj, Banto. You came to the godhouse to tell me of night bats, you feared they were an omen, you thought I should know. I told you there was nothing to fear, bats are bats, they are not demons."

"Bats are bats," murmured Banto. "They are not demons."

"The god see you, Banto novice," said Vortka, and patted the boy's shoulder. "The god see you in its eye as you serve it in the quiet time."

"The god see you, Vortka high godspeaker," the novice Banto replied, all anxiety wiped from his face. The glowing mark of Vortka's power shimmered like moonslight on water, then sank into his skin. Smiling serenely, he left Vortka's chamber.

"Always Banto thinks he sees demons," said Vortka, closing his chamber door behind the boy. "No-one will question that he came to me because of bats."

Aieee, such kindness in his voice. Zandakar smiled.

Dexterity was still distressed, his hands were turned to fists. "Are you sure he's all right, Zandakar? Are you sure that boy's not been harmed?"

Sighing, he nodded. "*Zho*, I am sure."

"Aieee, *tcha*!" said Vortka. "You speak again to the air, Zandakar, you speak in a tongue not familiar to me! What is this, you will tell me! Is Banto right, are you come here bringing *demons*, Zandakar?"

"No, no, Vortka, I do not bring a demon," he said swiftly. He turned to Dexterity. "Touch Vortka. Show him you are here."

"Show him and then what?" said Dexterity, stepping back. "He'll touch me and I'll lose my mind?"

"*Wei*! Trust Vortka. Trust me."

"Oh, Hettie," said Dexterity, his eyes squeezed shut. "The trouble you get me into, I swear!" Uncertainly he opened his eyes and stepped forward, his hand shaking. He reached out and took staring Vortka by the wrist. "There. Has that done it? Can your Vortka see me now?" He looked directly at the high godspeaker. "Sir, my name is Jones. I'm a friend to Zandakar."

"Aieee, the god see me!" cried Vortka, and stumbled back against the door. "What is this? Who is this strange man who steps out of the air? Where is he from?" With a dreadful hiss of fury his stone scorpion pectoral came to life, tail lashing, eyes glowing, seeking for sinning flesh to sting.

"Oh, dear God and sweet Rollin defend me!" cried Dexterity, and tumbled to the floor in his haste to seek safety. "Zandakar, get him away from me!"

Zandakar leapt between them. "Vortka! No! This man is Dexterity, he is my friend, he saved my life! I was dying on a slave ship, he took me to his home, he healed my hurts! He is in the god's eye, Vortka, to hurt him is a sin!"

Vortka stared, his eyes wild and disbelieving. "He saved you?"

"Yes. He does not speak the tongue of Mijak, he does not understand what we say. Vortka, we are here for the god, you cannot hurt him, you would displease it."

The hissing stone scorpion pectoral lashed its tail and clutched with its legs. It was stone and it was alive, he remembered Yuma's stories of Nagarak at Mijak's Heart, of the sinning warlords and their high godspeakers who would not obey the god's want. He felt sweat on his face and on his skin beneath his clothes, he felt his ribs drumming in time with his heart.

"You wear no godbraids," whispered Vortka. His eyes were empty of love now, his eyes were wide with fear and disbelief. "You speak a tongue the god does not know. You come to me like a demon, with a man hidden in the air. Are you truly Zandakar? Or are you a demon wearing his face, are you come to destroy me, to destroy Mijak in the world?"

Zandakar shook his head, his heart still pounded.

"No, no, I come to save Mijak. I come to save you, Vortka, before it is too late. You have known me all my life, you comforted me when my pony Didijik died, you saved me from the empress's snakeblade, you saved me from Dimmi. I am Zandakar, I am no demon, I live for the god."

And before the fear stopped him, before he could retreat, he stepped himself into the stone embrace of Vortka's hissing scorpion pectoral.

"Zandakar!"

Two terrified voices, crying his name at once. In his pounding heart a third voice, distant and sweet.

Brave boy, brave warrior, do not flinch now. Have faith.

The stone scorpion stung him without mercy. Its stone legs held him, its stone breath scorched his sweating face. Every remembered pain in his life was nothing, his worst tasking in the godhouse of Et-Raklion, his knife wounds in battle, his hurts when Didijik fell and threw him to the ground. This was pain like the heart of the sun, so great he could not speak it, so great he was struck dumb.

Dimly he felt the stone scorpion release him, dimly he felt his body fall to the floor. Scorpion poison flooded his veins. He felt the convulsions, felt his bones shake, his muscles twist. Felt his head banging on the floor. There was a battle within him, a raging war in his blood. It seemed as though his flesh was a battlefield, he heard again that sweet imploring voice.

Fight the darkness, Zandakar! Fight it! Don't surrender! The world is lost forever if you surrender now!

The god was in the stone scorpion pectoral, the god was trying to kill him, and the god was in his heart, it was trying to save him, it did not want him to die. It made no sense, his mind was in confusion, his blood burned, his world was pain. His eyes were open but all he saw was a red and black mist, he heard a roaring fury and that sweet, faint voice.

Fight, Zandakar. The god who loves you does not seek your destruction, it wants you to live.

So he fought the darkness, he fought the stone poison, he thought of Lilit and his dead son, he thought of Rhian, he fought to live.

"Zandakar!" someone cried, beseeching. "Zandakar, don't die!"

The words were Ethrean, it was Dexterity who spoke. He closed his fingers, felt the warm reassurance of human flesh. Heartbeat by heartbeat, the terrible pain faded. The red and black mist faded. He blinked, he could see again. He could see Dexterity on the floor by his right hand, white as goat's milk, staring down at him.

He managed a smile. "*Wei*, Dexterity. I *wei* die."

"In God's name, Zandakar, what was that?" Dexterity whispered. "What just happened?"

How could he answer when he was not certain himself? With trembling fingers he plucked at his roughspun shirt and lifted it, looked down at his chest and belly, saw the shiny red blotches welting his skin. Marks of the stone scorpion which did not kill him after all.

"*Chalava*," he croaked, then rolled his head on the stone floor. "Vortka."

Vortka knelt by his left side, his eyes wide and

bright. The scorpion pectoral was cold stone again, it clasped his ribs harmlessly, it did not seek to kill.

"Aieee, the god sees you, Zandakar," said Vortka, wondering. "The god's wrath smites you and yet you do not die. Like Hekat in the scorpion pit you defeat the god's scorpion."

He knew that story too, how Nagarak had called Yuma a demon and she swam with the scorpions to prove he was wrong. *She is my mother, I am her son. We have blue eyes, we dance with scorpions, we do not die.* With an effort he stretched out his other hand and grasped Vortka's shoulder. "No, Vortka. The god sees me, for I must live."

"You must live to be great in the world," said Vortka. There were tears on his seamed and sunken cheeks. "It was foretold in a vision. The god gave it to your – to Raklion, and to Nagarak, when you were still a child. Hekat said the foretelling was ruined, when you returned from Na'ha'leima with that sinning place unbroken she said the god had cast you from its eye. But it has not. The scorpion kissed you, you did not die."

"I did not die, I am not a demon. This man is Dexterity, he is not a demon." Zandakar tightened his grasp of Vortka's shoulder. "Trust him as you trust me, he is in the god's eye. I have seen the god in him, like you he is a man of power."

Vortka said nothing, he stared at Dexterity. Dexterity stared back, he was brave to stare at Vortka high godspeaker. He was Dexterity, a burning man of the god.

"What is this strange tongue you speak with this

man?" said Vortka, not ceasing to stare. "I have never heard it before."

With an effort, Zandakar smiled at him. His pain was almost gone, the scorpion fire in his blood burning out. "It is the tongue of Ethrea. You know of Ethrea? I think you do."

Vortka nodded, suddenly wary. "It is a place I know of."

"It is where I have come from. Yuma and Dimmi wish to break it with the warhost."

Now Vortka looked at him, his eyes wide. "How do you know this?" he whispered. "You cannot know this."

He sat up. Vortka and Dexterity helped him. "I know many things, Vortka. Much has happened since you saved me from Dimmi."

Dexterity cleared his throat, he sounded cross. "I do wish you'd stop jabbering on so I can't understand a single word you say, Zandakar," he complained. "Have you any idea how disconcerting it is?"

He had to smile at that. "Zho, Dexterity. When you save me from slave ship, you and Ursa, jabber jabber jabber."

"Oh," said Dexterity. The pale skin around his beard turned pink. "Yes. Well. Hmm."

"What does he say?" said Vortka. "He sounds angry, is he angry? He should not dare. You are Zandakar warlord, you are the god's hammer, where is his respect, this godless Ethrea man?"

"Am I a warlord, Vortka? Am I the god's hammer? I think I am not, I think Dimmi is those things." He released Vortka's shoulder. "And Dexterity is not godless, you must believe that."

Vortka looked doubtful, then he sighed. "Have you ever lied to me, Zandakar? I think you have not. You say this man is not godless, I will believe you."

It was a start, it was something, as Ursa would say. He felt a blade prick of new pain in his heart. "How is Dimmi, Vortka? How is Yuma? The god told me they are here in Jatharuj."

"Aieee, tcha," sighed Vortka. "I will tell you, but tell me first of these things you know and how you know them. Tell me of your life since we parted in Et-Raklion."

"What's he saying?" said Dexterity. "*Tcha*, I wish I'd asked you to teach me Mijaki while Helfred was teaching you Ethrean."

As Vortka went to speak, Zandakar held up his hand to halt him and looked at Dexterity. "*Yatzhay*. Vortka wants my Ethrea life."

"And you want to tell him?" Dexterity looked alarmed. "Zandakar, you can't. That's – that's giving information to the enemy. And besides, it isn't as though we've unlimited time!"

He shrugged. "*Yatzhay*, Dexterity. I must tell. He is Vortka. I *wei* hurt Rhian. I *wei* hurt Ethrea."

Dexterity chewed at his lip, then nodded. Still he did not look happy. "Well, all right, but tell him *quickly*. Then tell him he must help you stop the Mijaki army from leaving Jatharuj." He shuddered. "All those warships. God help us, Zandakar, even with an armada of vessels from every trading nation we don't stand a chance against your people."

"*Zho*," he told Dexterity, then turned again to Vortka, who was frowning to hear Dexterity's cross voice. "Do not look at him with your high godspeaker eyes, Vortka. He has been my good friend, he has saved me many times, he has fed me and clothed me, he has bound my wounds and protected me when men would strike me down. I was alone in Ethrea, Vortka, for a long time I did not hear the god. Did I want to live? I think I did not. Dexterity would not let me die, he fought for me when I was nothing to him, when I was a trouble that could have cost him his life."

Vortka was staring at Dexterity, his face hard with disbelief. "Why would he do this?"

"Because he is a good man."

"*Tcha!*" said Vortka, he wore his terrible high god-speaker face. "This is a godless man, how can he be good?"

Zandakar closed his eyes. The stone scorpion pain was gone completely from his body, its poison had been pushed out of his blood to lie sticky on his skin. He could smell it beneath his Ethrea clothes, he could feel it on his flesh. Harmless now, for he had defeated that poison, he had won that battle.

Now here was another battle he must win.

"Dexterity is not godless, he is a man of power for his own god," he told Vortka, stern as a warlord. "The god of Ethrea."

"A false god," said Vortka sharply. "A wicked thing to be destroyed. The god is the god, there can be no other."

"Vortka . . ." He sighed. "The god spoke to me in Na'ha'leima, it told me I must stop the killing. You say it did not, I say you are wrong. Since Na'ha'leima have you heard the god, Vortka? Has the god told you things the empress does not want to hear?"

Now Vortka looked stricken. The high godspeaker pushed to his feet, he walked a little distance away. Zandakar tried to stand too, he needed Dexterity to help him. The pain was gone from his body but his bones were still weak.

"Vortka," he said, insisting. "What does the god say?"

With his back turned, Vortka answered. "There was a desert, beyond Na'ha'leima, you remember?"

"Yes."

"The warhost could not cross that desert, it was full of demons, every warrior died," said Vortka. His voice was sad, remembering. His shoulders were not straight and proud, they slumped as though he was too old now to stand like a proud man. "I could not break it. I sacrificed without ceasing, I prayed until I could not speak, I prayed until I nearly died for lack of sleep and nourishment. It made no difference, the desert prevailed."

"And yet you are in Icthia."

Vortka turned slowly. "Because your mother broke the desert, Zandakar. Because she found the power to slay its demons. I could not do it, I could not think of such a thing, but your mother is Hekat. She is the god's empress. She thought, she acted, and the warhost crossed that desert. We crossed many godless lands, we smote them to their sinning knees, we came to Icthia."

Zandakar heard his heart beating, he felt the sickness in his mouth. "Yuma gave the desert human blood."

"How do you know this?" Vortka whispered.

He wanted to weep, there were tears in his eyes. *I*

wanted this to be a lie, I wanted the Tzhung to be untruthful. "It does not matter. I know."

"She drowned those desert demons in human blood, Zandakar," said Vortka. His dark eyes were full of tears, too. "Five thousand slaves she sacrificed to the god." A ripple of horror passed over his face. "So much blood. So much death. One by one she slit their throats, men, women and children, they all died by her will. When she was finished she was an empress of blood."

Five thousand slaves . . . Zandakar heard the sound of protest in his throat, he felt the tiled floor tilt beneath him. He saw Lilit, he saw his dead son, he heard the cries of those doomed slaves. *Yuma . . . Yuma . . . what have you done?*

"Zandakar! What is it, what's wrong?"

He looked at the toymaker, feeling sick, feeling cold. "Is true, Dexterity. Yuma spills human blood."

"You thought it wasn't true? You thought Emperor Han lied?" Then Dexterity shook his head, so sad. "No. You just hoped he did. Oh, Zandakar. I'm sorry."

Vortka slapped him lightly. "What does the man of Ethrea say?"

"He is sorry for the dead slaves. He is sorry for me."

"Tcha," said Vortka, he was still not convinced Dexterity was a friend.

"Vortka . . ." With an effort he thrust his sorrow aside. "Did you say Yuma should do this? Do you say this is a good thing?"

Vortka looked away. "No."

"Then why did you let her kill five thousand slaves?"

"She is the empress," said Vortka bleakly. "She is the god's chosen, she dwells in its eye."

And you love her, you love my mother. Are you afraid of her also? Do you fear what she does? Do you fear she will kill you if you do not obey?

"Vortka . . ." He took the high godspeaker's hands in his own. They were cold, they were thin, they were an old man's hands. "You are Mijak's high godspeaker. What does the god say? Does it want human blood?"

Vortka looked shaken and uncertain, no high godspeaker, just a man. "I have made a godpool in this godhouse of jatharuj," he whispered. "I swam in the sacred blood. The god said *no more human sacrifice.* It told me this clearly, Zandakar, I heard its voice in my heart."

"And you told the empress? What does she say?"

Vortka's face crumpled. "I told the empress, she will not listen."

Aieee, god, the pain in him. *Yuma, Yuma, are you lost?*

"We are becalmed in Icthia," said Vortka, unsteady with distress. "There are trade winds, they do not blow, the warhost cannot sail into the world. Hekat says this is demon doing. This highsun she killed the last living slaves in Jatharuj. The demons weaken but still they defy her. She has sent beyond Jatharuj for more slaves to kill. Zandakar, she has sent for ten thousand, she says she will spill their blood to destroy the demons and make the trade winds return."

"What?" said Dexterity. He was watching their faces. "Zandakar! What's happened now?"

He answered Dexterity, he did not turn from Vortka. "Yuma sends for slaves to kill. I think you say . . . ten thousand. For trade winds."

"Dear God," said Dexterity faintly. "She can't. She *can't* kill so many."

"*Zho*, Dexterity. She can."

The tears in Vortka's eyes began sliding down his face. "Zandakar, she does not hear me, she hears only the god. But how can the god tell her to spill human blood and tell me the spilling of human blood must end?"

"The god told me to stop killing in Na'ha'leima," he replied. "It did not tell Dimmi, or you, or the empress. You said in Et-Raklion I was sinning, I did not hear the god. Are you sinning in Jatharuj, Vortka?"

Vortka shook his head slowly. "I heard the god, Zandakar. Only the god can speak in the godpool."

"Has it ever before told you one thing and Hekat another?"

As though the air was burning, Vortka breathed in with care. "No. For its own purpose Hekat and I are godchosen, when we were young in the world the god stung us to its service. We have not always walked its path together but we have always walked its path." His face twisted with deeper pain. "Until now. Since that desert beyond Na'ha'leima, since those five thousand sacrificed slaves—" His voice broke, his eyes were grieving.

Dexterity cleared his throat. "Zandakar? Can't this Vortka stop your mother? What kind of a priest is he if he can't—"

"*Tcha*! Jabber jabber, you *wei* understand!" He punched his chest. "Vortka *wei* stop, Vortka hurt for this, *zho*?"

"You're right," said Dexterity, contrite. "He does look distressed. Is there something I can do?"

Aieee, god, Dexterity. The Ethrean toymaker. He would mend the world if somebody asked him.

"What are the words of this Ethrea man?" said Vortka, frowning. "He speaks my name, what does he say?"

"He says you are right, Vortka, he says Yuma is wrong," he said. "He says the god does not want this killing."

That made Vortka's eyes open wide. "This is a godless man, he cannot speak for the god!"

"Vortka . . ." Zandakar closed his fingers around the high godspeaker's frail wrist. "I have seen things, you must trust in my eyes."

Vortka pulled back. "I think you have seen demons, the godless world is full of demons, Zandakar, you – *aieee, the god see me*!"

Zandakar turned, to see Dexterity burning.

"*Vortka high godspeaker, the god's voice in Mijak, listen closely, your great time has come.*"

"What is this?" said Vortka, his voice strangled in his throat. "He speaks as a Mijaki, you said he does not know our tongue."

"*I speak for the god, Vortka, in the tongue the god gives me,*" said burning Dexterity, the bright flames curling round his untouched flesh.

"Aieee, Zandakar, how can this be?" cried Vortka. "He burns in fire, he is not consumed!"

"*You swim in the godpool, Vortka,*" said

Dexterity. *"You lie in the wilderness with a blanket of scorpions. You are high godspeaker, the god's power is in you, when you breathe upon a sacrificed lamb it goes to the god. You are the god's chosen, it chooses you to live in the godpool, to live in the wilderness, to find its secret in the wilderness. It stings you with scorpions yet you do not die. The god can choose anyone when it wishes to speak."*

"Vortka?" said Zandakar. The high godspeaker looked near to fainting with shock. "Do you know what he means?"

"He cannot know these things," said Vortka, shaking his head. His godbells shivered, sounding his dismay. "This is a godless man, he is not Mijaki, his people are slaves, he—"

"I can know what the god chooses to tell me," said Dexterity. *"The god is the god, it is the world, it is Mijak. You are high godspeaker, Vortka. Do you hear the god?"*

"Answer, Vortka," said Zandakar. "Dexterity will not hurt you."

At first he thought Vortka would not speak, he thought Vortka might be over-ruled by fear. And then the high godspeaker stepped forward, his head high, his silver godbraids – aieee, so silver! – chiming softly, lit to brightness by the flames.

"The god speaks to me in the godpool," Vortka said proudly. "It speaks to me in sacrifice, it speaks in my heart. It chose me in the scorpion pit, the others died and I did not."

Dexterity nodded, his crown of flames dancing. *"The others died, they were not chosen, you were chosen by the god."*

"I am Vortka high godspeaker. Tell me, who are you?"

"Let me show you," said Dexterity, and wrapped Vortka in flames.

Zandakar tried to cry out, his voice was stopped in his throat. Dexterity held Vortka in his burning arms, he held the high godspeaker as a mother holds her child, he held him tenderly, he pressed Vortka to his chest. The flames of Ethrea's god surrounded them, they were men of fire, they lived in flame.

Unlike Marlan, Vortka did not die.

When he saw this, Zandakar breathed less painfully, his thundering blood began to ease.

Aieee, god, how you frighten me, how you tear me to pieces with scorpion fear.

For so long Dexterity stood there burning, burning Vortka standing with him. The world was this chamber, there was nothing beyond its closed door. No Yuma, no Dimmi, no Mijak, no warhost. There was no ocean, Sun-dao did not wait. Rhian did not worry, Alasdair king did not gloat.

The whole world is nothing but two good men, burning. When the god breathes on them the world will return.

He did not know how long he stood there, watching Dexterity and Vortka burn. The light from them was blinding, it did not hurt his eyes. Their flames did not touch one thing in the room, no godspeakers came running to see their high godspeaker on fire.

Then Dexterity released Vortka, he stepped back with his arms spread wide. The flames wreathing Vortka flickered, flickered and died. He was unharmed, he seemed at peace, but there were fresh tears upon his face.

"*Vortka high godspeaker, I have shown you the truth,*" said Dexterity, still burning. "*The dreadful truth is in you, all lies are burned away.*"

"Yes," murmured Vortka, dazed. "I know the truth now. I know in my heart what I must do."

"Oh, good," said Dexterity, and slumped extinguished to the floor.

Zandakar leapt to him. "Dexterity! Dexterity? *Speak*, toymaker. *Dexterity*!"

Slowly Dexterity opened his eyes. His gaze was unfocused, his face filled with confusion. "Zandakar? What happened? I feel dreadful. Was I on fire again? I don't remember . . ."

"*Zho*, you burned, you spoke Mijaki. Be still."

"Oh dear," said Dexterity, he sounded vague, he sounded dizzy. "I do wish Hettie would warn me first."

"He suffers?" said Vortka, standing above them.

Zandakar glanced up. "Yes. No. I am not certain, when he burned for his god in Ethrea he grew sick, he nearly died."

"Leave him," said Vortka, and lowered stiffly to his knees.

Zandakar shifted aside and watched as Vortka withdrew his healing crystal from his robe. Aieee, that crystal, how often had he wished for it when all he had to heal him was the crude medicines of Ethrea.

"Lie still, godspeaker," said Vortka to Dexterity. "You have healed me, now I shall heal you."

"What's that?" said Dexterity weakly. "What's he saying, Zandakar?"

"Hush, Dexterity. Lie still," he said, but he did not look at the toymaker. He looked at Vortka, whose eyes were quiet.

Dexterity healed you? You call him a godspeaker? What happened in the flames, Vortka? What happened in your burning?

With his healing crystal Vortka gave Dexterity strength, he took pain from the toymaker and left peace in its place. When he was finished, Dexterity cautiously sat up, flexing his fingers, looking astonished and pleased.

"Good gracious. That's even better than Ursa."

"You are all right, Dexterity?"

"Yes, yes, Zandakar, I'm fine! Even my blisters have vanished. Here – help me get up."

Zandakar helped him to stand, one hand ready if the toymaker should stagger. He did not.

"See?" said Dexterity, smiling. "Fit as a fiddle. Please, thank Vortka for me."

Zandakar looked at Vortka, who had stood without help. "Dexterity says thank you."

Vortka slipped his healing crystal back in his robe pocket. "You must go now, you and this man Jones. It is not safe for you to stay in Jatharuj."

"I cannot go," said Zandakar, shaking his head. "I must see Yuma. I must—"

"No," said Vortka, taking hold of his hands. He was an old man now but his grip still had power. "Hekat cannot know you are here, Zandakar. She must not see this Ethrea man. She will not understand. She will not listen."

"She will listen to Dexterity, the god burns in him, Vortka."

"Tcha," said Vortka. He shook his head, his god-bells mourned. "She is not the Yuma of your childhood, Zandakar. Hekat is . . . changed. I will tell her what the god wants her to know. She will listen to me, I am her high godspeaker. You are in danger, you must leave while you can."

Zandakar stared at him, there was pain in his heart. He had come so far to Jatharuj so he might see his mother.

"*Zandakar*. If I thought you should see her I would take you to her now," said Vortka, so fierce. "If I thought you should see Dmitrak we would run to his barracks. I do not think so, I think you must go."

"Zandakar?" said Dexterity. "Is something wrong?"

He did not answer, he looked only at Vortka. "You are frightened," he said slowly. "Vortka, why do you fear? What did the god tell you?"

Vortka stepped back, his eyes were full of shadows. "It told me many things. Zandakar, newsun is coming. Your danger grows."

His belly was churning, his heart beat so hard. "The god told you many things, tell me *one* thing, Vortka. Does it desire Mijak in the world?"

Tears rose in Vortka's eyes, the high godspeaker was weeping. "Zandakar—"

"*Tell me.*"

"No," Vortka whispered. "The god does not desire that. The god never did."

Never did . . . never did . . . He stared, his bones hollow. Loud in his mind, the screaming innocents as they died in their thousands. "*Never?* Aieee, Vortka . . . all those people I slaughtered—"

Vortka embraced him. "Your pain is my pain, Zandakar, we are both sinning men. We will be tasked for these sins in our time."

The stone scorpion pectoral was hard against his flesh. He could not weep, there were no tears for this, there was no tasking that could punish him for what he had done.

Lilit, Lilit, can you hear me? Do you know? You should never have loved me, to love me is a sin.

Too soon Vortka released him. "Zandakar, there is more," he said. "You can hear it once and then *you must go.*"

He flinched as Vortka's hand came to rest against his cheek. He was empty, there was dust in his veins. "What?" he asked dully. "What more must I hear?"

Vortka looked at him steadily, his cold hand trembled. "Once you are gone, Zandakar, we might never meet again. I want you to know this, I want you to know who you are. Your mother is Hekat, your father is not Raklion. The warlord's seed was tainted, he never bred a living son. My seed quickened Hekat. You are *my* son."

At first the words had no meaning, they were just words. *You are my son.* He closed his eyes, tried to recall Raklion's face but he could not recall it. The man was gone from his mind.

I was young when he died, in my heart there is Vortka.

He opened his eyes, his heart beat like a drum. He believed what Vortka told him, the truth drummed in his bones. "Dmitrak?"

"Was sired by Nagarak."

Nagarak? Understanding flooded through him.

Yuma hates Dimmi, how could she not? "Dimmi does not know?"

"He can never know, Zandakar," said Vortka. "All that was cruel and ruthless in Nagarak, all that is cruel and ruthless in your mother, that is your brother Dmitrak warlord. I know you love him, you came here because you love him. Your love might yet save him. It might yet save Hekat, I do not know. *My son, you must leave.*"

My son. My son. He did not leave, he embraced Vortka, his throat was choked with pain. "How can I leave when you need me . . . *Adda?*"

"*Adda,*" whispered Vortka. "Aieee, Zandakar, to hear you call me that. My heart is breaking, it breaks at your words."

Stepping back, Zandakar seized Vortka's shoulders, he stared into his father's loving face. "I must stay in Jatharuj. Can you face Hekat alone with this? I think you cannot. She will not believe you, she will be so angry. Dmitrak will be angry. If you try to stop the warhost alone they will forget they hate each other, they will turn on you."

"They will not turn on me, I am Vortka high godspeaker."

The god see him, he was so stubborn! "Vortka, *please—*"

Vortka smiled again, such pain in his face. "I am tasked by the god to do what I can here. I can save your mother, I have loved her many years. Hekat has loved me, she loves me still, though she thinks she does not."

"You are one man, Vortka," he said, despairing. "How can one man hold back a warhost?"

"I am not one man, I am Mijak's high god-speaker," said Vortka, his face proud. "I am in the god's eye, I have seen its true heart."

"You have seen its true heart because Dexterity has shown you," he said. He wanted to shout, he wanted to shake Vortka. "Take us to Hekat. He will show it to her, she will—"

"*Kill him*," said Vortka. "Zandakar, do you want him to die?"

Shocked, he shook his head. "No, Vortka. No."

"Trust me, Zandakar, I am your father," said Vortka. "The god is in this man from Ethrea, but Hekat will not hear its voice. She cannot hear it, her heart is full of blood and death. I am a godspeaker, I will speak for the god. I am Vortka, her old friend, she will listen to me."

There was no swaying him, he was stubborn for the god. Zandakar let his forehead drop against Vortka's. "I am your obedient son, Adda, I will do what you say."

Vortka's lips pressed his cheek. "I know. I have something for you, you must take it when you go."

He watched as Vortka withdrew to rummage in a cupboard at the back of the room. Dexterity put a hand on his arm. "Zandakar, what's going on? Are you all right?"

He shook his head. "*Wei.*"

Vortka returned, in his hand something long and slender, wrapped in black cloth. He unwrapped it and held it out. "Take this sacrifice knife, Zandakar, the god intends it for you."

Zandakar looked at the blade. Its bone hilt, dark with age, was carved into a scorpion. Its snaketongue blade shone blue in the chamber's lamplight. He closed his fingers around the knife's ancient hilt. Power blazed through him, the blade shimmered with blue life. It shimmered like the god's hammer, the power felt the same.

"Rollin save us!" said Dexterity, stepping back. "What is that thing?"

"Keep it hidden, Zandakar," said Vortka. "When the time is right to use it you will know, the god will tell you."

Zandakar nodded. "Yes, Vortka." He heard his voice break. "Vortka, you must stop Mijak. You must stop the sacrifice of slaves. You must save Yuma, and Dmitrak. They sin, they do not know it. Please, Vortka, save them, they live in my heart."

"I will save them, Zandakar," said Vortka. "Go in the god's eye, *go now*."

In dreadful silence they looked at each other, in dreadful silence they said goodbye.

"Come, Dexterity," said Zandakar.

"What?" said Dexterity, startled. "We're leaving? But I thought—"

"*Come*," Zandakar commanded, and left his father behind.

CHAPTER TWENTY-ONE

As they hurried back to their boat, and Sun-dao, Dexterity tried to think what Vortka could have told Zandakar that had changed his mind about seeing his mother and brother. That had clearly shaken him to his bones.

He couldn't begin to imagine, but he was going to find out.

I kept Zandakar's secrets before, and much good that did me. I'm not about to make that mistake again. I doubt Rhian or Ursa would forgive me a second time.

Whatever power Sun-dao had drawn on to hide them from men's eyes, it must still be working. The priests in Vortka's dwelling looked right through them. The wandering priests on the streets of Jatharuj ignored them. The few fearsome warriors they saw did not see them.

Well, Hettie, all I can say is while it may be a dubious power, I'm not sorry he possesses it.

Rollin save them, the town's air was *rank*. Clearly the stench did not bother Zandakar, but for himself he was relieved he'd not eaten a thing since their last leaping whirlwind ride on the ocean. Jatharuj was a port town, like Kingseat, and port towns weren't known for their floral aromas. Port towns meant people, and people meant refuse and cesspits and cooking smells and animals, piss in the gutters and dung on the streets. Port towns meant fishing boats and fish guts, butcheries and entrails. He was born and bred a duck's waddle from Kingseat, he knew all those smells and never once had they churned him. But compared to Jatharuj, Kingseat smelled of spring-time and jasmine.

If it were daylight he'd expect to see the air tinged red, so strongly did it smell of death and old blood. How much was animal, and how much human? God help him, that he should even need to consider such a thing . . .

Oh, Hettie. This dreadful slaughter has to stop.

As sorry as he felt for Zandakar, grieving, he felt sorrier still for Athnïj of Icthia. This had been his township, before Mijak came. Every man, woman and child in this town had been a citizen of Icthia. Now, if any at all had survived Hekat's slaughter, they were slaves, the property of Mijak. Perhaps it was the stink of their blood that coated his tongue and clogged his nose.

It was too much. Tears stung his tired eyes.

Zandakar's long strides were carrying him far ahead. Dexterity skipped a little to catch up, like a child chasing its father or an older brother. In the starlight, with his dark skin, it was hard to see Zandakar's face. Impossible to know what he was thinking. One hand was pressed to his belly, safe-guarding the strange knife that Vortka had given him.

Oh, Hettie, I wish he hadn't. I wish Zandakar hadn't taken it. That knife looks evil. As though it's spilled barrels of blood. Has it? Has Vortka? Hettie, who is he? What is he? I was in his mind but I don't re-

member a thing. He took my pain from me as simply as breathing. Not even Ursa can heal a man so well. In that moment of healing he was kind, he was compassionate. But that stone scorpion he wore – the chalava – dear God, it came alive . . .

The stone scorpion came to life . . . and Zandakar had thrown himself into its terrible embrace. And it had *stung* him, there was *venom* . . . yet he'd survived.

I don't understand any of it. This Mijak, this dreadful place, it's incomprehensible to me. Zandakar's incomprehensible. It's like we've never met.

Even with his blue hair, with his strange tongue, with his dark skin and his scars, in Ethrea, Zandakar had seemed like any other man. He'd wept like a man, felt fear like a man, he had even smiled, like any Ethrean man. All right, there were his *hotas*, there was his killing. They were startling. But men did kill in Ethrea. Not often, but they killed. There were brawls, there were accidents, men would be men.

In Ethrea I knew him. In Ethrea I saw a stranger who was in many ways like me. But now, Hettie? Now? Good God. Who is he really?

They reached the harbour at last. The same two warriors stood guard at its entrance. Unseen, unheard, like the softest summer breeze, they slipped past the warriors and onto the dock. In a handful of minutes they'd be with Sun-dao again . . . and any hope of a private conversation would vanish.

Dexterity grabbed Zandakar's arm and tugged, taking them both sideways till they stood in the shadow of a nearby moored warship. It rose and fell slowly on the water, its carved, torchlit hull blood red and menacing.

"We need to talk, Zandakar, without Sun-dao eavesdropping. *What* is going on? Why aren't we going to see your mother and brother? The plan was for you to convince them not to attack Ethrea. And now we're leaving? *Why*?"

Zandakar's mouth thinned to a stubborn line. "Vortka say."

"And that's *it*?" he demanded, when Zandakar said nothing else. "Vortka says go and we *go*? Just like that?"

"*Zho.*"

He almost laughed aloud with disbelief. "Really? And how do we explain that to Sun-dao? To Emperor Han? To Rhian, when we get home? *We came here to stop Mijak!*"

Zandakar folded his arms. "Vortka will stop Mijak. Vortka is *chalava-hagra*. *Chalava* speak to Vortka, it say—"

"What?" he prompted. "Zandakar? What did your god tell him? What did *I* tell him, while I was burning?"

And suddenly Zandakar's face was masked in pain. Twisted with anguish.

The night was still warm but suddenly Dexterity felt chilled. *Oh, Hettie, Hettie, I knew something was wrong*. "Zandakar, I warn you. I'll not take one more step until you tell me what I said. Before you tell me what's *wrong*! And don't tell me nothing's wrong, because I'm not blind or stupid. And I did *not* come all this way to be treated like a child!"

"*Chalava*," said Zandakar at last, his voice a

strangled whisper. "You tell Vortka *chalava wei* want blood. *Wei* want blood ever. Harjha. Targa. Bryzin. Zree." His fist thudded against his chest. "I *kill* them for *chalava. Chalava wei* want!"

Oh dear. So at last, Zandakar knew the truth. And what could he say now? What words were there, in Ethrean, or Mijaki, or any living tongue, to ease the pain? So many murdered, and all for a lie.

Zandakar took a step back. "You hate. You hate this killing Zandakar."

What? "*Wei!*" he said swiftly. "I don't hate you, Zandakar."

In the silence, Zandakar's harsh, ragged breathing. "I hate."

Dexterity stared at his anguished face. "Yourself? No. No, you mustn't do that." *Not with that wicked knife stuffed down your shirt*. "I know it's dreadful, all those people who died, but it's not your fault. You thought you were doing what *chalava* wanted. You were *told* it's what *chalava* wanted. You're not to blame, Zandakar."

Another silence. Zandakar's stare shifted, touched on the harbour, then came to rest on the next row of warships, the dreadful might of Mijak. Then he pinched the bridge of his nose between thumb and forefinger, as though his head pained him. After what had happened with the stone scorpion it was such a *human* gesture. Disarming. Disconcerting.

Dexterity touched his arm. "Zandakar, I think we should go back, while we can. If I can burn for Vortka, then I can burn for your mother." Not that he relished the prospect, or could control it, but surely it must be their best hope of success. If he prayed, prayed hard . . .

"*Wei*," said Zandakar. "Vortka say *wei*."

"Well, I don't answer to Vortka!" he retorted. "And neither do you. Not any more. We came here for Rhian and for Ethrea. You swore a blood oath to protect them, which means stopping Mijak in Icthia, which means—"

"*Wei*!" said Zandakar, almost shouting. "Stupid Dexterity listen. Danger, *zho*? Vortka say danger."

Well, that was convenient. And puzzling, when Vortka knew first-hand the message they brought, and its importance. Unless . . .

Oh dear, Hettie. Has Vortka tricked us? Is he only pretending to believe the truth about his god?

Very carefully, he laid a hand on Zandakar's arm. "Look. I know this Vortka is your friend, *gajka*, but I think we have to consider—"

"*Wei gajka*," said Zandakar. "*Adda*."

"*Adda?*"

"I think you say father," said Zandakar. "*Zho?*"

Stunned, Dexterity gaped at him. He didn't know what he'd expected, but it certainly wasn't this. "But – but you said your father was *Raklion*."

Zandakar shook his head. "*Wei*. Vortka."

It was like the solid ground had turned to mist. "He told you this? Just now?"

"*Zho*."

Dexterity tugged at his beard. "Are you sure he's not lying?"

"*Zho*," said Zandakar. In the torchlight, his face was frightening.

"All right, all right," he said hastily. "I had to ask.

Rollin's mercy." He shook his head, bewildered. "You never *knew*? You never *suspected*?"

"*Wei*."

"And are you *pleased* he's your father?"

Now Zandakar's eyes flashed from ice to flame. "*Zho*."

If there'd been somewhere to sit he'd have sat down, very hard. It had been a long, eventful night already and clearly it wasn't over yet.

"So . . . is he Dmitrak's father, too?"

"*Wei*." Zandakar's eyes gleamed. "Nagarak."

The way he said the name wasn't promising. "I take it that's bad?"

A nod. "*Zho*. Bad. Nagarak bad."

And did bad blood breed true? As with dogs and horses, did a rotten sire mean rotten stock?

I think it must. It was Dmitrak at Garabatsas.

But before that, in those other places, it had been Zandakar.

So perhaps bloodlines mean nothing. Perhaps it all comes down to choice, whether a man is good or evil.

After all, Zandakar had been both. That had to mean something.

Oh, Hettie, it's so complicated, and I'm a simple man.

At least this explained why Zandakar was so eager to trust Vortka. But did that mean he had to trust the priest, too? Just take Vortka's word for it that they shouldn't find Hekat? Trust him to speak to her, on Ethrea's behalf?

"Dexterity," said Zandakar. "You trust me, *zho*?"

Oh dear. "Yes. Yes, of course I do. But—"

Zandakar pressed a fist against his heart. "Trust me, trust Vortka. Trust *Adda. Zho?*"

It was the closest he'd ever seen Zandakar to begging. *Oh dear, oh dear.* "If I agree," he said slowly. "If we go now, without doing anything more to stop Mijak – am I going to be sorry? Will Ethrea pay the price for my mistake?"

"*Wei,*" said Zandakar. "Dexterity, *wei.* Vortka save Ethrea."

Oh, Hettie, sweet Hettie. Please don't let me be wrong about this . . .

He took a deep breath and let it out in a rush. "All right, then. We go."

With Zandakar leading the way they continued along the dock, past row after row of looming warships. In the distance the horizon was lightening, growing paler with the approach of dawn. The night had escaped them without him noticing. Dexterity found himself beginning to panic.

What if Sun-dao's left us? What if he's sailed away? What if we took too long in the township and he thought we'd been captured, or killed? Oh, Hettie! He didn't look well. What if he's died?

But no. Sun-dao was waiting in the cramped Tzhung boat. He watched them clamber from the dock to the gently pitching deck, fingers laced before him, the ends of his long, bone-threaded moustaches dangling down his narrow, tattooed chest. Though he still looked weak, he was also furious.

"You find the Empress of Mijak? You find her son, Dmitrak?"

Dexterity glanced at Zandakar. "Ah . . . not precisely."

A sharp gust of wind stirred their boat's sail, their clothing, their hair, but did not ripple the surrounding water. "I must see this empress," Sun-dao hissed. "I must see her son. Take me to them."

He stepped back, unsteady. "Why?"

Sun-dao rattled off something in Tzhung. From the look on his face it wasn't anything polite. "You foolish man," he spat. "I leave emperor, I leave my witch-men, for me to do what I must do."

"What you must do? What *we* must do, surely. We came to try and stop Mijak, and I think we've succeeded. We now have an ally against its empress."

"What *ally*?" said Sun-dao, scathing.

Dexterity jutted his beard at the witch-man. "Do you know, I'm not inclined to tell you. We're not answerable to you, or to your emperor. Take us home to Ethrea and we'll tell Queen Rhian. What *she* chooses to tell Han is entirely up to her."

Another, stronger gust of wind. Sun-dao's sunken eyes glittered. "You stupid toymaker. Mijak must be defeated!"

"Yes, of course it must," he retorted. "Do you think we don't know that, Sun-dao? Set one foot in the town and you can smell the blood. I can smell it still. It's quite turned my stomach."

Sun-dao's long, unbound hair was stirring more than could be explained by a breeze. On his arms and bare torso, the inked tattoos writhed.

Dexterity stepped back another pace, almost bumping into Zandakar. He glanced sideways again. "I don't like this," he murmured. "Something's not right."

Sun-dao took a painful step forward. "Take me into Jatharuj. Take me to the empress."

Heart thudding, Dexterity stood his ground. "Why?"

"Why is not your business! Take me to them now!"

"I'll do no such thing. And don't you take that tone with me, Sun-dao." He turned to Zandakar. "Can you believe his effrontery? I'll be lodging a formal complaint when we get home."

"Zho," said Zandakar. He sounded . . . dangerous. As though any complaint he lodged would be lodged with a blade. "Sun-dao. I know you, I think. You came to kill empress. Kill Dmitrak. *Zho?"*

What? Dexterity stared at him. "Zandakar, what are you talking about? Sun-dao wouldn't—" And then he stopped. Something dreadful and unseen was crawling over his flesh. He turned, so slowly, and looked at Sun-dao's face.

The witch-man was snarling, his tattoos frantically alive beneath his amber skin.

Oh, Hettie. Don't tell me . . . "Is he right, Sun-dao? Did you come here to kill them?"

Sun-dao's eyes opened wide. Now a deep crimson glow burned in their depths. Within the last few moments it seemed the flesh had melted from his face, leaving nothing but a thin papering of skin over bone. His hands were unclasped, his arms held wide.

The salt air began to crackle with power.

Dexterity swallowed. *Oh, Hettie.* "This is disgraceful. Wait till Queen Rhian hears what you had planned."

Sun-dao said nothing. The witch-man looked

scarcely human. And all around them a wind was rising, cold and sharp like a winter storm filled with ice, to slice frail flesh to bloody ribbons.

He turned to Zandakar. "We have to stop him. Whatever he's planning, we can't let him—"

Zandakar wasn't listening. His hand slid inside his shirt and pulled out the scorpion knife Vortka had given him. As his fingers closed around its black hilt the blue-sheened blade leapt to life with that same surge of blue light. It seemed more . . . violent, this time. As though the knife and Zandakar were somehow connected. The warrior's face was ugly with rage.

"Dexterity," said Zandakar. "*Move.*"

Mouth dry, heart hammering, he stared at that dreadful knife. "What are you doing? Put that thing away!"

"*Wei*," said Zandakar. In his hand the blade shimmered, menacing. Its blue light brightened, bathing them in a cold illumination.

"Zandakar, *please*! Before someone gets hurt!"

But his words were whipped away by Sun-dao's rising wind. It had a voice now, as well as sharp teeth of ice. Keening, hungry, it rocked the crowded warships on the water and whipped the harbour to white froth. Sun-dao's eyes were nearly all crimson now, and crimson sweat stood stark on his brow.

That's blood, Dexterity realised. *Rollin have mercy, Hettie. The man's sweating blood.*

Sun-dao's lips peeled back in a rictus of pain, or effort, or both. After all he'd done already, it was hard to believe he could do this. The wind's voice rose, its pitch too sharp to bear. Staggering left and right until he hit the boat's side, Dexterity clapped his hands over his ears but still he could hear it. The wind shrieked in his bones and his teeth chattered with cold.

Looming above them the tethered warships of Mijak plunged like wild horses. Any moment now, surely, their little Tzhung boat would be smashed to splinters between them. They'd be smeared to red paste, dead and forgotten.

"Sun-dao, *stop* it!" he shouted, reaching out a hand to Emperor Han's witch-man. He wished he dared seize him, but was too afraid. "You're going to *kill* us!"

"*Wei*, Dexterity," said Zandakar, above the screech of the wind. He stood on the boat's pitching deck as though it were a sunlit meadow, easily absorbing its unpredictable heaves. The scorpion knife in his fist was almost too bright to look at. Power seared the salty air. "Witch-man *wei* kill us. Kill Yuma. Kill Dmitrak. Warriors. *Chalava-hagra*." His voice caught. "Kill Vortka."

As soon as Zandakar said the words, Dexterity knew they were true. Sun-dao was summoning a wind to howl through Jatharuj and kill Mijak in its tracks. Even as he stared at the witch-man, dumbfounded, he heard smashing and crashing sounds coming from the township behind them. Horrified imagination showed him tiles ripping from roofs and windows scattering in lethal shards of glass. Trees tearing free of the soil, houses tumbling to dust.

No, no, he can't do this! It's murder. If he slaughters everyone in Jatharuj we'll be no better than Mijak.

"Sun-dao, *listen* to me, *stop* this!" he cried. "Sink the warships! Don't hurt the people! We mustn't hurt the people, I didn't come here to *kill*!"

I've killed once already. Never again.

Sun-dao shook his head, riding the lurching boat with ease. He stood at the storm's cold, still centre like a man carved from ice.

"What use?" he said as the wind howled harder. "Mijak will build more."

"Perhaps, but not overnight. Sinking their fleet will at least grant us a little more *time*!"

"No time!" shouted Sun-dao. "Mijak must die!"

"*Wei*!" howled Zandakar. "*You* die, Sun-dao!"

As Dexterity watched, helpless, blue fire leapt from the scorpion blade, streaming in an eye-searing line towards the witch-man. Save for its colour it was the same fire that had poured from Dmitrak's gauntlet in Garabatsas.

Then he let out a strangled shout, because Sun-dao did not die in that dreadful stream of blue fire. Abandoning his windstorm to its own wild devices, Sun-dao held up one hand . . . and the blue fire shredded to pieces in the air.

Dexterity cried out as a whirling filament of blue fire seared his hand to the bone. The pain was awful. He wanted to be sick.

Oblivious, Zandakar attacked Sun-dao again. The second stream of blue fire was faster and thicker. It poured from the scorpion knife like a river in full spate, so bright that Dexterity fell to his knees with his fingers spread across his eyes, trying to shield his sight even as he watched.

Sun-dao needed both hands to save himself this

time. This time he staggered backwards until he hit the small boat's mast. With his spine braced against the wood, his long, thin moustaches flailing round his face, he curved his carmine-tipped fingers into talons and screamed his defiance.

And this time the witch-man did not defeat Zandakar unscathed. One shred of the blue fire licked his cheek before burning out. Terrible blisters erupted. Blood bubbled and boiled. Sun-dao screamed, a high thin cry of agony, and his windstorm collapsed.

"*Tcha*!" said Zandakar, triumphant, and leapt for the witch-man. His face was an unholy mask of murderous rage.

With a despairing shout Dexterity threw himself into Zandakar's path. Zandakar stumbled and fell, shouting now with furious surprise as he sent clay pots of that dreadful salt fish tumbling to break into shards. Panting, choking, the burn on his hand still sickening him with pain, Dexterity leaned on Zandakar's heaving ribs.

"Just you lie there and listen to me!"

The last time they'd wrestled like this, Zandakar had been sore distressed, not himself, and still not at his full strength. That wasn't the case now. With terrifying speed and strength Dexterity felt Zandakar flip him over onto his back . . . and then his heart stopped.

The scorpion knife was pricking his throat, and in Zandakar's blue eyes the sure promise of death.

"Zandakar, don't do this," he whispered. "If you kill Sun-dao we will never get home."

Had the knife's blade drawn blood? He couldn't

tell, he was too frightened to feel anything. Even the pain in his hand had faded, swamped by terror at the look on Zandakar's face. He could hear Sun-dao moaning somewhere behind him.

"You've stopped him, Zandakar," he said. "Sun-dao hasn't hurt Vortka, or your mother, or your brother. They're safe. Now let's leave Jatharuj, shall we, before somebody finds us. I'd really like to go home. *Please*. Let's just . . . go."

Provided they *could* go, of course. Provided moaning Sun-dao wasn't so badly hurt he couldn't whisk them back to Ethrea with his strange witch-man's powers.

Zandakar blinked. Gradually the rage faded from his face, his eyes, until it seemed almost certain he'd decided not to kill. Then, with excruciating slowness, he eased the pressure on his knife.

"*Zho*," he said, and uncoiled to his feet. "We go now."

For a moment Dexterity could only lie there, feeling his heart pound, hearing the air whistle in and out of his chest. His trembling fingers felt the flesh of his neck. Was he whole? Was he unbreached?

Oh, Hettie. Oh, Hettie.

Zandakar reached down his hand, all his hot feelings penned behind a cool mask. "*Yatzhay*, Dexterity."

He let Zandakar tug him upright, air hissing through his teeth as the warrior's fingers tightened on his burned hand.

"I'm all right, it's nothing," he said as Zandakar frowned. "It's Sun-dao I'm worried for."

Emperor Han's witch-man was conscious, but in

terrible pain. The dreadful burn on his face exposed a
bloody gleam of bone and his right eye was swollen
to a slit, eyelashes and eyebrow completely charred
away.

Dexterity felt his empty stomach heave. "Sun-dao.
Sun-dao, can you hear me? Can you—"

And then he turned, startled, at the sound of shout-
ing from the far end of the dock, at its entrance.
Many voices, coming closer. He looked round at
Zandakar. "Is that—"

"*Zho*," said Zandakar grimly. The scorpion knife
was still in his hand, little flickers of blue light running up and down its blade. "Warriors come."

So. They were discovered.

"Zandakar!" he said sharply. "Don't you dare get
off this boat! Knife or no knife you can't fight a whole
army!"

As Zandakar hesitated, one hand on the boat's
side, he turned back to Sun-dao. "Witch-man, we
need you. I don't know how it is you do what you do,
and frankly I don't want to know, but unless you
fancy becoming one of Hekat's human sacrifices I
suggest that you do it *right now*!"

With a hideous groan, Sun-dao staggered to his
feet. "Oars," he mumbled. "Open water." He was
swaying, the blood sweat dried garish on his face.

"You heard him, Zandakar," said Dexterity.
"Hurry!"

Scrambling, terrified, the shouting and sound of
running feet coming closer, he threw himself at the
nearest oar. Zandakar, the wretched knife shoved
back inside his shirt, took the other one and together

they inched the Tzhung boat backwards, towards a miserly stretch of open water.

Digging his muffled oar into the harbour's still-choppy surface, Dexterity stared at Sun-dao. The man looked deathly ill.

I don't think he can do it. I think this is it. Oh, Hettie, darling, I think I'm coming to join you . . .

Three feet from the dock. Five feet from the dock. Ten – twelve – fifteen – twenty—

A dreadful clamouring of voices, a howling of rage. A score of burning torches, lighting up the dregs of night.

"Sun-dao!" he shouted. "It's now or never! *Please*!"

A pain-racked voice, commanding. A gust of wind, obeying. High overhead the fading stars wheeled . . .

. . . and the world disappeared.

Hekat raged about her chamber, godbraids swinging wildly, their silver godbells discordant with her spitting fury. "*Demons?*" she shouted. "Demons in Mijak? Demons in the harbour? Vortka high godspeaker, how did you not know this? Are you grown an old man? I think you are!"

"I have warriors dead, Empress," said Dmitrak, boldly standing before the room's shattered glass window, standing on its slicing shards, daring those shards to pierce his flesh. "I have warriors killed by demons. How can demons be here if Mijak's godspeakers are in the god's eye?"

Hekat paused her stamping long enough to spear Dmitrak with a baleful look. Then she snorted. "Tcha! My warlord says a true thing, true words spill from his tongue. Are your godspeakers wicked, Vortka? Is the god blind to them? Is the god blind to *you*, high godspeaker? *How are there demons in my harbour of Jatharuj?*"

Vortka met her blazing eyes calmly, though his stone scorpion pectoral drubbed in time with his heart.

"You say there are demons, Empress. I say a wind blew. There are storms in the world, we have seen them in other places. Storms are not demons. The god speaks not of storms."

"Vortka, they were *seen*!" Hekat spat at him. "In the harbour. *They were seen*!"

He did not look at Dmitrak, he looked only at Hekat. Dmitrak should not be here, it was not right that he see a high godspeaker disrespected. Hekat's anger he could stomach, she was Hekat, she was precious. But Dmitrak was not precious, he was not godchosen, he was insolent. Behind his dark eyes insolent thoughts grew like weeds.

If he had seen Zandakar, I think he would have killed him. If Hekat had seen him, he would be dead. I was right not to show them my son.

"Empress," he said reasonably, "demons are not seen. I am high godspeaker, I know this to be true."

"Do you call my warriors liars, do you say they tell me *lies*?" snarled Dmitrak. "My warriors saw what they saw, they saw demons on the water, they saw those demons disappear!"

He could not smile, he could not laugh, he could not show Dmitrak his smiling, laughing heart. Zandakar and the burning man of Ethrea had escaped Jatharuj in the god's hiding eye. The god protected them, they had a purpose.

I have a purpose, I must tread with care.

"Then your warriors did not see demons, warlord. I am high godspeaker, this is my word."

Would Dmitrak challenge him? He feared the boy might. Nagarak was in him, he would challenge the god.

"Then what, if not demons?" said Hekat. She stood now, by her lounge. One hand held tightly to it, all her furious stamping had stolen her strength. "What did they see?"

"It was a fierce wind, Empress. Perhaps they saw wreckage of a ruined boat, sinking under the waves."

"Perhaps," she said, frowning. "Vortka, does that storm mean the trade winds return?"

Aieee, the god see him, he wanted to say yes. But he knew that would be untrue, the trade winds were gentle. "I do not think so, Hekat, I think a storm is a storm."

Her head came up, her eyes glittered, he did not like her look. "Then when those slaves arrive that I have sent for, I will give the god its strongest blood. Ten thousand slaves come to Jatharuj to die. I weary of waiting, it is time to leave this place."

"Empress, the warlord should leave us," he said. "We must speak of the god."

"We can speak of the god in front of my warlord, he serves the god as I do. We live in its eye."

Which meant she knew what he would say and did not wish to hear it, she wished Dmitrak to stand with her and defy the god's want. He was a killing man, in

this he was her true son. Like his mother, he wanted
the world soaked in blood.

Vortka felt the pain of the burning man's words
sear him anew. His joy at Zandakar leaving Jatharuj
safely died in that pain. His heart wept, for he had
failed to hear the god's true voice.

*I failed before, I must not fail now. I must tell
Hekat the truth until she can hear.*

"I am Vortka high godspeaker, in the god's seeing
eye. I swim in the godpool, I hear its voice in my
heart. The god has spoken, it does not want the
world. It does not want ten thousand slaves pouring
out their blood. Mijak is Mijak. We are done. *We are
done.*"

Silence. Then Hekat laughed. Her godbells laughed
with her, the chamber rang with their laughter.

*But her eyes are not laughing, her eyes are cold, I
think she hates me. There is hate in her heart because
she does not hear the god.*

"Vortka, you are weary, you have slaved for the
god," she said, so angry. "Sleep and you will hear it,
what you hear is not the god."

"Perhaps he hears demons," said Dmitrak.
"Perhaps *he* is done."

Vortka looked at him. "You say this to me, the
god's high godspeaker of Mijak? Do you wish to
tempt a smiting, should my stone scorpion wake?"

"*Enough*, Dmitrak," said Hekat. "Vortka is high
godspeaker, you hold your tongue. Go now. See that
our warships are safe in the harbour. Gather your
warriors to dance with their blades. Prepare for the
arrival of those ten thousand slaves. Their blood is
mine, Dmitrak. I will spill it for the god."

Surly, scowling, Dmitrak walked out. When he was gone Hekat sat, she was so weary, all her weariness she let show on her face.

"Why do you say these things, Vortka?" she whispered. "Is Dmitrak right, are you lost in the god's eye? Are you swallowed by demons? What has happened? *Tell me*. I would know."

Tell her of Zandakar? Tell her of Jones? How could he? In this mood she would call him demonstruck, she would call him her enemy, she would kill him with her snakeblade.

If she kills me, who will speak for the god?

But if he said nothing, he might as well be dead.

"Demons have not swallowed me," he said. "I speak the god's want."

"I think you are wrong, Vortka," she said coldly. "You were wrong in Et-Raklion, when we were young. You said I could not hide from Nagarak when Raklion warlord was at his tasking. You said Nagarak would see me, he did not see me, you were wrong."

"I was wrong then, I am not wrong now, Hekat," he said, his heart beating so hard. "The god does not want the blood of those ten thousand slaves. You must listen to my words, you must trust me."

Her fingers clenched, her scarred face tightened. "I must do what my heart says! I have *never* been wrong. Are you an old man now, Vortka? Are you timid for the god? I do not need you old, I do not need you timid. I need you with me in the god's eye." Her blue eyes burned with her zeal. "All our lives, Vortka, we are godchosen and precious, all our lives

we listen to the god. It wants the world, Vortka, we are close. So close."

He turned away. *Close to disaster, Hekat. Can I tell you? I cannot.*

She was in no mood to listen. She was headstrong, so sure of her heart. The slaves she wanted to sacrifice were not come to Jatharuj yet. He had time, some little time, to change her mind. To open her eyes. To show her how very, very wrong they both had been.

"Rest, Vortka," said Hekat kindly. "You are weary for the god. Your weary heart plays tricks with you. Sleep, and the god will tell you its true want."

"Yes, Hekat," he whispered, and left her to the dark.

Despite his dreadful burning, despite draining his strength to raise that awful storm, Sun-dao wrapped them in the wind and blew them almost home to Ethrea. Four times he had to bring them back to the real world, for he was very weak, and suffering from his wounds.

Zandakar did not say *yatzhay* to him.

The fifth time they returned to the world it was not Sun-dao's doing. Instead of the gentle slide from otherness to sunshine or moonlight, the boat was flung out violently, like a toy tossed by a child in a tantrum. It was morning, still early, and the cool salt air echoed with Sun-dao's screaming.

Bruised and shocked, tumbled against the side of their small boat, Dexterity looked for Zandakar. The warrior was folded about the mast, groaning for air. "Zandakar! Are you hurt?"

Zandakar shook his head. "*Wei. Wei.*"

That was a relief. Bruised and shaken, Dexterity untangled himself and crawled to Sun-dao. The witch-man's screams were fading to thin moans, and his carmine fingernails scrabbled feebly at the deck.

Dexterity took one of his cold hands in his and held tight. "Sun-dao, Sun-dao, what's happened? What's wrong?"

"Mijak," said Sun-dao, his one good eye open and glazed. His voice bubbled, as though his lungs were full of soapy water. "Ethrea."

"What about them?" he said, leaning closer. The witch-man's burned face was putrid, glistening red and black, his charred cheekbone sickeningly visible. "Sun-dao! Can you hear me? What about them?"

His unburned eye bright with anguish and agony, Sun-dao stared up at him. "Ethrea. You see it?"

See it? Already? But how could that be? On the journey to Icthia, Sun-dao had returned them to the world nine times.

"Zandakar," he said, looking up. "Are we home? Can you see Ethrea?"

Zandakar was standing at the front of the boat, shading his gaze against the unclouded sun. "I think – *zho*." He pointed. "Ahead. Far away. Shadow on water."

"There, you see?" he told Sun-dao. "We're nearly home. You can rest. You *must* rest."

Sun-dao shook his head. "Mijak. Mijak." His face twisted in a grimace, and his spine bowed his body in a terrible contortion. "The trade winds. They come. Blood, blood, blood in Mijak. My brothers have failed." He contorted again, head to toe, his lips peeled back from his teeth in a soundless scream. "My emperor – my emperor—"

He collapsed to the deck, thick black blood gushing from his mouth.

"Sun-dao?" Dexterity whispered. "Sun-dao?"

No answer. Sun-dao's naked chest did not rise and fall. The cool salt air no longer bubbled in his lungs.

Dexterity stared at him, feeling nothing. Too much had happened, in too short a time. He was exhausted. And all he could think of was how Sun-dao had terrified him. Had hurt him, raking through his private thoughts, his precious memories, seeking proof that a toymaker was a traitor, and deserved to die.

The first time I saw Hettie. The first time we kissed. The sounds she made when I loved her. My tears when she died.

All those private moments, and more, Sun-dao had plundered. Deaf to the toymaker's denials of wrongdoing. Deaf to his misery. Heedless of his pain.

And now he's died, practically in my arms. I'm not glad, but I'm not sorry, either. Does that make me wicked? Oh dear. Oh, Hettie. I think I should be ashamed.

"Zandakar?" he said, still looking at the witchman. Still feeling nothing. "Zandakar . . . Sun-dao's dead."

Zandakar turned, looked, and shrugged. "*Zho?* Then we row."

PART THREE

CHAPTER TWENTY-TWO

R hian sat with Helfred in her privy chapel, not to receive Litany but because it was the only place in the castle she knew she would not be disturbed.

At least, not by councillors and courtiers and ducal messengers. Helfred, of course, is a disturbance all on his own.

He was disturbing her now, chiding her for not appearing in Kingseat's great chapel five Litanies in a row.

"I thought we had agreed, Rhian, that while we seek to establish your authority on the throne you would be visible to your people on every possible occasion," he said severely. "First and foremost at Litany."

Staring at the privy chapel's Living Flame, Rhian felt her belly gripe, so tight and twisted with nerves. The same dull chant sounded over and over in her mind.

They're dead. They must be dead. It's been so long now. They must be dead.

After giving Lai her pointed message for Han, that she wanted Zandakar and Dexterity immediately returned, she'd waited and waited for word from Tzhung's emperor. No word had come. He hadn't come. He could be dead too, for all she knew.

Nothing but silence sounded from Tzhung-tzhungchai.

Nor had she received any response from the other trading nations, formally or informally.

They call my bluff. They dare me to create my army. They wait to see if I'll break the charter first. And if I make one move without their approval, they'll move against me. I'll be renowned in history as the queen who killed Ethrea.

Helfred slapped her knee with his prayer beads. "You're not paying attention!"

She jumped, startled. "You hit me! Don't *hit* me, Helfred. Have you noticed what I'm wearing? Hunting leathers. Do you happen to observe the knife strapped to my hip?"

He rattled his wretched wooden prayer beads in her face. "Don't be silly. As if you'd dance your *hotas* with me. Rhian, you must stop your daydreaming and listen. It's all well and good that every venerable in the kingdom speaks of you as a warrior queen, and that your name is now a byword for courage and tenacity and triumph over evil. But you must remain in the people's eye, you can't skulk in this castle for days on end."

"*Skulk?*" She gaped at him. "You accuse me of *skulking?*" She could slap him, so easily. Goaded by outrage, she leapt to her feet and started pacing. Her thudding boot-heels on the hushed chapel's floor echoed her anger. "Helfred, I'm not skulking, I'm *working*. Alasdair never sees me, except in a council meeting! Every day, Helfred, every *day*, I wrangle with the dukes over how their garrison soldiers will be used in our Ethrean army – assuming we'll ever have one – and remind them over and over to be certain their section of Ethrea's boundary wall is secure."

"Yes, I know," said Helfred. "But—"

"*I'm not finished!*"

Helfred sat back, his lips pinched.

"I've yet to settle the question of whose House shall inherit the stewardship of Hartshorn. I still don't know if I can trust Davin of Meercheq." Hands on her hips, fingers itching to unsheathe her knife so she could take violent refuge in her *hotas*, Rhian shook her head. "And if that's not enough, I'm plagued with flocks of noblemen's wives, daughters and cousins, all vying to enter my service as Ladies of the Privy Chamber when I don't need anybody else but Dinsy. And when I'm not tripping over them, I'm tripping over Ursa. *She's* beside herself about Dexterity and—"

Her tongue stumbled. Her heart clenched. All of a sudden it was difficult to breathe.

"I know," said Helfred gently. "I pray for them both every hour, I promise."

Rhian spun about and marched to the chapel's Living Flame. Stood before it, staring at its golden heart. How often had her prolate told her *God holds all the answers.* Well, she'd asked and she'd asked, but so far no answers were forthcoming.

"It's the not knowing I can't bear, Helfred," she whispered, abruptly emptied of rage. She kept her back turned so he wouldn't see her face. "I just want to know where they are, one way or another."

She'd not told him that she was sure the Tzhung had something to do with Zandakar and Dexterity.

She'd not told anyone, not even Alasdair. She was frightened to think of what might happen, if her king and her privy council believed in Tzhung-tzhungchai's interference. The peace between Ethrea and the trading nations was too fragile already. One more bitter exchange would surely shatter it completely.

"What I don't understand," said Helfred, still gentle, "is why you've so resolutely refused the council's calls for an open investigation into their whereabouts. I know you've a fondness for Zandakar, Rhian, but as a queen you don't have the luxury of personal indulgence. Stark reality now dictates you must at least entertain the idea that—"

"I heard a voice, Helfred," she said, bracing herself for ridicule. "The night Ursa reported them missing. It told me to have faith, that I'd not been betrayed. I trusted it. I'd heard it before, and it was right. I believed – I wanted to believe – that it was right again. I thought that if I raised a public outcry over their disappearance I'd do more harm than good. I thought—" She shook her head, sighing. "It doesn't matter. I don't expect you to understand."

A dull swishing of plain wool robes behind her as Helfred stood. "But I do understand. I once heard a voice too, Rhian. In Old Scooton. When I was praying for Ven'Martin's poor soul. It gave me the courage to face Marlan that last time."

She turned. "You heard a voice?"

"Yes."

"Was it – was it—" She swallowed. "Helfred, was it God?"

"To this day I don't know," he said. "But if not God himself, then I think it was certainly godsent."

"And you think the voice I heard was godsent, too?"

He shrugged. "What do you think?"

Rhian felt the chapel's cool air catch in her throat. Felt fresh sweat slick the skin beneath her leathers. Everything hurt. "I don't know what to think. I want to believe. I want to have faith. But why wasn't I told anything more than that? Why wasn't I told where they are, what's happened to them? How long am I expected to *wait* like this, not knowing?"

"I don't know," said Helfred, troubled. "God's purposes and our own are often at odds."

"Well, *that's* reassuring," she snapped. "I feel much better now!"

Helfred frowned. "There's no need to be sarcastic. All I meant was that we're not always made privy to the intricacies of God's plan. That would be where faith comes in."

Almost, she poked her tongue at him. "Now who's being sarcastic?"

"*Rhian*—" Helfred took a deep, self-controlling breath. "I pretend no special insights, but surely Mister Jones and Zandakar must still be somewhere in Ethrea. If someone had tried to steal them away on a boat they'd have been discovered. The harbourmaster and his people inspect every vessel."

They inspected every ordinary trading vessel, yes. But she feared Han and his witch-men would laugh at anything so prosaic as an inspection. Not that she could say so to Helfred. Hoping against hope that Han truly was the friend he'd claimed to be, she'd also kept silent about his witching powers . . . and the longer she stayed silent the harder it became to say anything at all.

Staring again at the serene Living Flame, Rhian folded her arms and held on tight, so cold inside even though the chapel was warm. "And what if they are still somewhere in Ethrea?" she said. "Does that mean I'm not to fear for them? What else can I do but fear for them, Helfred? If God were able to banish evil from the world there'd be no Mijak, would there? There'd be no need for miracles and armadas."

"Alas, that's true," Helfred admitted. "Though it breaks my heart to say so."

She shook her head. "And that's all that breaks your heart? I envy you. I'm so disheartened now I scarce know which way to turn."

"For shame, Rhian," he said sternly, prosing Helfred again. "I know this is hard, that in these times faith seems no more substantial than smoke. But you must believe in the rightness of your cause."

"Really? And what does my belief achieve if nobody else believes with me? Aside from Emperor Han and poor Athnïj, no trading nation will take the threat of Mijak seriously. *Nothing* I say to them makes any difference, they're so meshed in their fears and suspicions, their old enmities and private dealings. I tell you, Helfred, God must've been wrong. I can't be the one to lead the fight against Mijak. Not with so little progress made."

"No," said Helfred, fingering his prayer beads. "God can't be wrong."

"Oh, I think he can, Helfred," she retorted. "Mijak is out there, like a – a – wolf concealed in the undergrowth, biding its time. And we're the unprotected sheep. Mijak can tear out Ethrea's throat whenever it likes. And I'm supposed to *stop* it? *I'm* supposed to defeat Zandakar's mother, and his brother and their thousands of warriors who've devoted their whole lives to killing? With no real army, no armada, no allies, no *idea*? What was God *thinking*, Helfred, deciding *I* be in charge?"

"You mustn't question God's plan, Rhian," said Helfred, scandalised. "All things fall out as the divine will intends."

Oh, *Helfred*. So pompous, so pious – she really could *slap* him. "Really? Is that so?" she demanded, scathing. "Well, it's nice you can think it. Forgive me if I'm less sanguine. Forgive me if my faith falters when all around me I see failure and ruin."

"Failure and ruin?" Helfred echoed. "Rhian, that's not so. God has not deserted you, God will *never* desert you. He will aid you—"

"When?" she retorted. "When do you suppose God intends to show me how I can make the trading nations *listen*? When will he show me how I'm meant to defeat this monstrous army of warriors who might at any moment leap from concealment and tear my kingdom apart? When will he speak to the ambassadors and convince them to follow me? Tell me, Helfred, when will God take care of that?"

Rattle, rattle, rattle went Helfred's wooden prayer beads. "Rhian, remember where we are. This is God's sacred house. You must speak more temperately beneath his roof. I tell you straightly, your tone is far amiss."

Her tone was *amiss*? Dear God, it was *restrained*.

"If I'm a trifle short-tempered, Helfred, you can put it down to lack of restful sleep. I can't pass a single night without dreaming of Mijak. What Dexterity told us of Garabatsas plays over and over in my mind, but it's not some place I've never seen before that's burning. It's Kingseat. It's Ethrea. I'm lost in my own kingdom and everywhere I look I see death and destruction. I see Alasdair and Ludo, I see you, charred to pieces. I'm wading in blood to my knees and then my hips. In the end the blood closes over my head and I'm drowning, Helfred. I'm drowning in scarlet. And while I'm drowning . . . while I'm dying . . . I hear the cries of my people, all the innocents *I couldn't save*."

Trembling, close to the humiliation of tears, she pressed a hand across her mouth and turned away from Helfred's horrified stare, unable to stomach the pity in his eyes.

"Oh, Rhian," he whispered.

She heard a softer rattle as he tucked his prayer beads into his belt. The rasp of his roughspun robe, the slap of his leather sandals on the chapel's stone floor, as he came close behind her. His hand rested on her leather-clad shoulder, lending her his strength.

If anyone had told me scant months ago that Helfred's touch could give me heart, I'd have laughed in their face.

"It's true these are bleak times, Majesty," he said. "Times to try us to the depth of our souls. But Ethrea has stood on the brink before, and it survived."

Spine and legs aching with the effort of not slumping to the chapel floor, Rhian shook her head. "No.

This is different. Ethrea has never faced a danger like this. Nor has the world."

"Nevertheless," said Helfred. "It will survive. It has you."

She shrugged his hand free of her. "Oh, Helfred, the world needs more than me! It *had* more than me, when it had Dexterity and – and—" *Zandakar. Zandakar.* "Now they're gone and it seems the world rests upon a three-legged stool with only one leg remaining. Survive, you say? How can it survive? It must tumble to destruction, surely, with only me to rest on!"

"Rhian, you sink so deep into melancholy you're blinded to those around you," said Helfred. He sounded stern again. "You have your dukes, who support you. And God has given you Alasdair, a loving husband and worthy king, who will fight at your side till the last drop of his blood is spilled. A man of Ethrea, no heathen foreigner, who can be trusted to safeguard your crown."

His sharp words were a rebuke. He was rebuking her, as though she'd somehow been – been unfaithful. She felt a sting of anger.

He should mind his tongue. I haven't dishonoured my marriage. I've done nothing wrong. Worrying for someone's safety is hardly a sin.

But there was no use arguing the point with Helfred. For one thing she was too weary, and for another he was proving a champion at the splitting of hairs.

"Yes, Helfred. I know. I am blessed in Alasdair, and I—"

A gust of wind. A sudden chill. Emperor Han stood in the chapel.

"*God have mercy!*" Helfred gasped.

Han looked dreadful. As though the lightest blow from a feather would shatter his bones. Dark eyes sunken, long black hair disordered, green silk tunic crumpled. He looked like a sick vagabond, not the supreme ruler of millions.

"My witch-men are broken, Majesty." His voice was faint, as though speaking taxed him to his limits. "The trade winds return."

"Rhian, *what is this?*" demanded Helfred. "Where did he – *how* did he – and why aren't you *surprised?*"

"Oh, hush a moment, Helfred," she said impatiently. "Can't you see the emperor's distressed?"

Going to Han, she took him by the elbow and guided him to the nearest pew. Helped him to sit down. He seemed hardly aware that she touched him, that he moved. Even through his silk sleeve she could feel the heat in him, as though a bonfire burned beneath his skin.

Just when I thought our fortunes had ebbed to their lowest . . .

She dropped to a crouch, leathers creaking, and looked up into the emperor's drawn face. "What do you mean broken, Han? Not – not *dead?*"

He nodded slowly, his eyes glazed. Almost confused. "Many are dead, yes. Many more are sundered. They are scattered on the wind. Lost . . . lost . . ."

"These are dreadful tidings, Han," she said, closing her hand over his. His fingers were lax beneath hers, as though he couldn't feel her touch. "You have my sorrow, and the sorrow of Ethrea."

Still he seemed dazed. He seemed not like an emperor, but like any grieving ordinary man. "Sun-dao," he whispered, shuddering, staring at the floor. "Sun-dao."

She felt a chill rush through her. "He's dead?"

Han lifted his gaze. The pain in his eyes was searing. "Yes," he said hoarsely. "He was my brother."

What? "I'm sorry, Han. I had no idea."

Stirring, he pulled his hand from beneath hers. "The secrets of Tzhung are not for the world."

"How many more of your witch-men have died, Han?" How many allies had she lost, that she could not afford?

"Over one hundred," he said, his drawn face twisted with pain. "We are growing too few . . ."

We? She exchanged a glance with Helfred, who was almost dancing in his eagerness to pepper her and the emperor with questions. A sharply raised finger warned him to hold his tongue.

"So, I was right," she said quietly. "You are a witch-man."

Han's eyes gleamed as his gaze shifted to Helfred. "It is a Tzhung secret. I am weary. My witch-senses are blunt. I would not have walked in the wind to you if I had felt the presence of your—"

She closed her hand on his again. "Helfred won't say a word, Han. I promise." She glared sideways. "*Will* you, Helfred?"

Helfred looked displeased. "Majesty—"

"Rulers have secrets, Prolate, which they must

keep for the good of the realm. Sometimes rulers keep each other's secrets."

"Yes, but—"

"And as prolate, I imagine you keep secrets from your most venerables of the Ecclesiastica."

She knew very well that he did. And he knew that she knew – and what they were. Fingers tight around his prayer beads, he nodded. "Very well," he said, grudging. "The emperor's secret is safe with me."

"Good."

"Provided the keeping of it does not endanger Ethrea."

Oh, Helfred. Stop trying to have the last word. "Of course, Prolate. I've not quite lost my wits yet." Turning back to Han, she unfolded from her crouch. "Tell me what I need to know, Han. You say the trade winds return? That means—"

Han nodded. "Yes. Mijak will come."

She felt her blood leap, her heart thud. "Why did you and your witch-men break, Han? Why did Sundao and the others die?"

His drooping eyelids widened, as though he looked upon a scene of horror. "Mijak spilled so much human blood," he whispered. "Their priests' dark power rose like a tide, sweeping us before it. We tried to stop them but their evil drowned us. Sun-dao—"

His voice broke on the name, tears flooding his eyes. Rhian found it deeply unsettling, to see the Emperor of Tzhung so distraught. If a man so urbane, so experienced, so – so *imperial* could be brought low by Mijak—

Rollin give me strength. How will I stand?

Han stared up at her. "Rhian, the trade winds blow

against us. There is no more time for Arbenia and
Harbisland and the rest to play their games." With a
grunting effort he stood, and smoothed his rumpled
silk tunic. Then his fingers closed hard around her
wrist. "We must go."

"Unhand the queen, Emperor Han," Helfred commanded. "You forget yourself, sir."

Rhian silenced him with a look. "Han," she said
quietly, not pulling herself free. "What do you need of
me? Where must we go?"

"Your burning man. The prince of Mijak." He
flinched. "Sun-dao. I will take you to them."

"God's mercy!" said Helfred, staring. "You know
where they are and you didn't *tell* us? How *dare*
you?"

Han ignored him, his grief-ravaged face now
smooth and blank as sand. "I will dare anything to
save Tzhung-tzhungchai. Come with me, Rhian.
You're needed."

Now she pulled free, fury like fire racing through
her. It was hard to breathe. "No. I won't travel like a
witch-man. Tell me where to go and I'll meet you
there."

"There is no time! You will come, you—"

"Don't you give me orders in my castle!" she
shouted. "When you've lied, when you've used me,
when you've stolen my people? *Don't you do it*!"

Shocked, Han stared at her. Then he nodded. "The
ambassador's residence. Come alone. Quickly."

A gust of wind. A cry of anguish as his smooth face
twisted with pain. He vanished.

"Sweet Rollin," breathed Helfred, and groped for a
pew. "That's not natural. That's not *right*." He shook

himself. "Obviously you can't go. It's out of the question."

She turned on him, fury still burning. "Am I required to ask your permission, Helfred?"

"What?" he said, taken aback. "Well, no, but—"

"Han can take me to Zandakar and Dexterity. Of *course* I'm going."

"But Rhian – Your Majesty—"

"Oh don't *fuss*, Helfred," she said, heading for the chapel door. "I'll take Alasdair with me."

"Han told you to come alone!" he called after her.

She paused and looked back at him. "So? I answer to me, not Han of Tzhung-tzhungchai."

"And to God, Rhian," said Helfred, soberly. "Don't forget that in the midst of your intrigues."

She wrenched open the chapel door. "How could I, Helfred? You're so diligent in reminding me."

"*Rhian*! You really must not—"

She closed the door on his indignant reply.

She found Alasdair where she'd left him two hours previously: in the privy council chamber with Edward, poring over lists of each duchy garrison's standing equipment.

"Majesty," said her duke, as bluff and florid as ever. "I fail to see how we can—"

"Edward, excuse us," she said, not bothering with niceties. "In fact, why don't you retire? I know for certain you've been reading lists since first light this morning. You must take better care of yourself, I can't afford to lose one of my most seasoned advisors to a gripe or an ague brought on by overwork."

Edward was a wily old fox. With barely a glance at

Alasdair, he bowed. "Majesty. I'll not say I'd regret some strong ale and an early night." He nodded at Alasdair. "King Alasdair."

"What's happened?" said Alasdair, when they were alone.

"It's complicated," she said. "We have to go."

He didn't look as exhausted as Emperor Han, but shadows darkened his eyes and his face was rough with stubble. "Go where? Rhian—"

She took his hands in hers and tugged. "To the Tzhung ambassador's residence. Please, Alasdair. We must hurry."

He stared at her. "But why? Rhian, what is—"

"*Alasdair*. Come." She started walking backwards, pulling him with her. "I'll tell you what I can on the way, though I warn you: it isn't much."

Bewildered, but trusting her, he followed. "This sounds mad."

"Yes," she said, and tried to smile.

Because it was unthinkable for Ethrea's queen and king to simply leave the castle unannounced, Rhian informed the duty sergeant that she and His Majesty were seeking some privy time. The sergeant had smiled, and nodded, and wished them a good night. Then she and Alasdair escaped to the stables. Soon after, a stable lad was driving them down to the township in a nondescript gig.

"You said you'd explain," said Alasdair in a low voice.

She glanced at the stable lad's back. "Dexterity and Zandakar," she murmured, so the boy wouldn't overhear. "Han says he knows where they are."

"*Han* says? How would *Han* know—"

If she told him she doubted he'd control his anger. She tightened her fingers round his hand, a warning. "I'm not sure. We've trouble, Alasdair. The trade winds. Han says they're blowing again."

There was very little moonlight, and the gig's running lamps weren't well placed. She couldn't see Alasdair's face clearly . . . but what she could see was profoundly displeased.

"*Rhian*—"

She glanced again at the stable lad. "Not now."

They completed the journey in silence.

Down by the harbour the taverns did raucous business; the early Kingseat night was lit by smoking lamps and flaming torches. Vigorous voices and off-key singing laced the carrying air. In contrast, the ambassadorial district was neatly and discreetly lit. Genteely hushed. Not a soul was out walking, it seemed the ambassadors and their people were early asleep. The gig-pony's hooves rang loud on the cobbles.

"Return to the castle," Rhian told the stable lad when they reached Tzhung-tzhungchai's ambassadorial residence. "Say nothing of myself or the king or where you've been tonight."

The lad tugged his forelock, obedient, and the gig departed. Rhian watched it for a moment, then she and Alasdair approached the wrought-iron gate guarding the entrance to Lai's official residence. On soundless hinges it swung open and Han stepped out of the shadows. His rumpled green tunic had been changed for black, and something had happened since she saw him in the chapel. He looked merely weary now, not on the brink of utter collapse.

More witch-man doings? It seems likely. I swear, before this is over I'll know what they are and how they do what they do. They've meddled with my kingdom. By God, I will know.

Han saw Alasdair and frowned. "Majesty, I said *alone.*"

So he must be reminded, as well as Helfred. "I don't answer to you, Han," she replied, letting her voice bite. "Now, where are Dexterity and Zandakar?"

Still frowning, Han stepped back. "Come. My palanquin awaits us."

He led them through the exquisitely maintained gardens and past the modest palace, out to the back of the building where, yes indeed, an imperial Tzhung palanquin awaited, resting on the paved courtyard. Beside its gold-inlaid teak poles stood four bulky Tzhung subjects, dressed head to toe in dull black. Even their faces were hidden behind black cloth masks, small eyeslits the only concession to the outside world.

The palanquin itself was equally mysterious, a windowless lacquered dark wood box, with a black leather curtain guarding its entrance. It looked barely large enough to fit one person, let alone three. Blazoned on its side in crimson and gold was the emblem of Tzhung-tzhungchai: a stooping eagle. Because this was Han's personal conveyance the eagle was crowned with an imperial hsanyi blossom, found only in the Tzhung empire.

Han pulled aside the palanquin's curtain. "Please."

Rhian felt Alasdair's surprise, that the Emperor of Tzhung-tzhungchai would use such a meek word. *Or perhaps he's shocked that Han even knows it.* Whatever grief the emperor still felt for the death of his brother, it was well-hidden now. *Did I imagine his tears?*

No. She'd seen them. She'd seen how shocked and dismayed he was, how close to breaking. She touched Alasdair's hand. It felt cold, and reluctant.

"We have to," she murmured.

They climbed into the palanquin, and Han climbed in after. A swaying, swooping lurch as its bearers lifted the decorative wooden box to their shoulders, and then the palanquin was moving.

It was pitch black inside. Stuffy and indeed very cramped. Rhian folded her knees to her chest beside Alasdair, her shoulder pressed to the padded wall, and let her hand rest on his ankle.

"Where are we going?" she asked Han.

"The harbour."

"Her Majesty tells me you have news of Mister Jones and Zandakar," said Alasdair. His voice was clipped and cold in the darkness. "I tell you plainly, Emperor Han, this secrecy does not suit my stomach. What are we about that cannot face the light of day?"

A soft sound as Han sighed. "Your king is an upright man, Queen Rhian. Perhaps he is too good to be a king."

"I didn't answer your bold summons so I might listen to you pass judgement on my husband," she said, as cold as Alasdair. "I want answers, Han. Real answers, not word games and evasions. Where are Dexterity and Zandakar? What have they to do with Tzhung-tzhungchai?"

Another sigh. The steady pounding of burdened

feet as the palanquin was hurried through Kingseat township. A whisper of silk as Han shifted, seated opposite. "I sent them to Mijak. With Sun-dao, I sent them."

She couldn't speak for a moment. "Mijak?" she choked out at last. "My people? You sent my people to *Mijak*? Without *asking* me? Emperor Han—" Her voice failed.

"The prince of Mijak is yours?" said Han, sardonic in the darkness. "Interesting, Rhian."

"*He's under my protection*!" she retorted. "You know full well what I mean. You sent them to *Mijak*?"

"To Icthia. To Jatharuj. But it is the same, with Icthia conquered."

She could feel Alasdair's shock and anger, echoing her own. "You must know the difficulties I've been having with the ambassadors. Difficulties not helped by Mister Jones and Zandakar not being in Kingseat." She could feel her fingernails biting her palms. "And you say we're *allies*?"

"Why, Han?" said Alasdair, gentling her with a touch. "Why would you do this? What purpose, did you hope to serve?"

"I hoped to save us," Han said softly.

Rhian snorted. "Well, apparently you failed. You failed, and Sun-dao died, along with those other witch-men. Are you certain Dexterity and Zandakar live? You haven't killed them, too, with your foolish plan?"

"They live," said Han. And after that said nothing else.

The palanquin's bearers carried them to the harbour, where it passed through Ambassadors' Gate without challenge. Even if it hadn't carried the insignia of the Tzhung emperor, it would not have been barred entry. Unlike ordinary ships, ambassadorial vessels were free to sail at any time of the night or day. They could not be stopped or searched without written permission from their ambassador, and access to the harbour could not be denied any member of an ambassadorial household.

Rhian felt the knowledge curdle her. *If that was how Han managed to spirit Zandakar and Dexterity out of Kingseat I shall certainly revisit the question of their special treatment. When this is over. If we're still alive, of course.*

Although now she knew for certain Han was a Tzhung witch-man . . .

Perhaps he used his mysterious powers to snatch Zandakar and Dexterity away. In which case I can rescind all the laws I like and it won't make a wretched bit of difference. I'd have to ban the Tzhung empire from Ethrea . . . for all the good it would do me now.

At last Han's palanquin stopped and was bumped to the ground by its bearers. Rhian shoved the leather curtain aside and climbed out, blinking in the sudden torchlight. They were right at the water's edge, beside Han's extravagant imperial boat. A second, smaller Tzhung boat bobbed on a mooring line close by, an ugly cygnet beside its elegant swan of a mother.

Two witch-men stood a few paces away, dressed in black silk, arms folded, faces impassive. They saw her but made no formal acknowledgement. As though she were a peasant girl, and they breathed the air of Tzhung-tzhungchai. Then they noticed the knife sheathed at her hip. Hissing like geese they stepped towards her, teeth bared.

"*Hold*!" called Han, climbing out of the palanquin.

When the witch-men saw their emperor they bowed low, moustaches swinging.

"What is it?" demanded Alasdair, climbing out in Han's wake.

"A misunderstanding," said Han, then spoke to his witch-men. The lilting tongue of Tzhung sounded soft in the torch-chased shadows. They bowed, and he turned. "Come, Queen Rhian. Come, King Alasdair. We will return to Kingseat before the sunrise, you have my word."

"With my people?" she said. "You promise?"

He nodded. "I do."

It was an awkward clamber from the dock into the Tzhung boat, but she made a point of not needing any man's assistance. The witch-men took an oar each and rowed them steadily out of the harbour. She thought they must be using their witch-power. The boat was too cumbersome for ordinary rowing. Seated on a round leather stool, Alasdair on his own beside her, Rhian stared at Han's back as he stood in the bow, his gaze resting on the dark shifting water.

Once they'd passed from the harbour to the open sea the witch-men secured their oars, lit the boat's running lamps, ten in all, and lastly let down the boat's single black sail. Then they stood with their emperor, one at his left hand, and one at his right. Without a word, without a gesture, all three of them summoned the wind. The sail bellied, the boat lifted . . . and they were racing over the waves as swift as a gull.

"You don't know where we're going?" said Alasdair.

In the glow from the running lamps his face was grave, his eyes shuttered. Whatever he was feeling, he wasn't inclined to share it with her.

She shook her head. "I haven't a clue. But not all the way to Icthia, I hope."

"No," said Han, without turning. His long hair, unbound, whipped in the wind of his calling. "Not so far."

After that there was only the sound of the boat skimming the water, faster than any boat had a right to sail, and the mournful keening cry of the wind. Kingseat harbour swiftly fell behind them.

Glad of her huntsman's leathers, Rhian sat beside Alasdair and strained her eyes to see ahead. Never in her life had she been sailing at night time. She'd never before sailed on the open ocean, that kind of adventure was reserved only for boys. For royal princes, who defied advice and a father's begging, sailed to foreign lands and then came home to die.

She'd boated on the Eth River, of course. That was decorous enough for a princess. But the Eth was tame water. It ran obediently between its banks, locked and canalled and suffocated with barges. The ocean was alive. It was untamed and untrammelled. It would kill them if the mood struck, witch-man wind or no.

The freedom of the ocean was a glorious thing. Seductive.

The witch-man at Han's right hand stretched out

his hand, pointing, and said something. Han nodded. Replied. The wind stopped.

"What?" said Rhian, leaping up from her stool. "What is it? Have you found them?"

"We have found something," said Han, and nodded at his witch-men. They returned to their oars, and stroke by stroke the boat crept sluggish through the waves.

Without waiting for Alasdair, she rushed to the bow to stand beside Han. Gripping its spray-soaked sides, leaning perilously forward, she tried to see through the darkness. To see what they'd found.

A stuttering glimmer in the distance. A sputter of yellow light, dying even as she found it.

"There!" she shouted. "There! I see them! Is that a boat? *There*!"

CHAPTER TWENTY-THREE

"Hello?" a plaintive voice called out in the darkness, drifting towards them over the ocean's choppy swell. "Hello, can you help us? Can you understand me? Can you speak Ethrean? My name is—"

"Dexterity!" Rhian shouted. "Dexterity, we're here!"

A startled silence.

"*Rhian*? I mean, Your Majesty?" Dexterity shouted back, his surprise almost comical. "What in

Rollin's name are you doing in the middle of the ocean?"

There were tears on her cheeks, blown cold by the salt breeze. "Rescuing you, it seems."

"Rollin's mercy! How did you know we—"

"I'll explain later," she said, smearing one hand across her face. Alasdair, beside her now, had hold of her other hand; his grip was almost painful. Glancing at him, she saw his fierce joy. "Dexterity, is – is Zandakar with you? Is he all right?"

"Oh, yes, Zandakar's here! He's fine. We're both fine. Except – oh dear . . ."

"Sun-dao?" She looked sideways at Han. Tall and silent, his face flickered with shadows, he showed no sign of emotion. The distressed and ordinary man in her privy chapel had disappeared entirely. Han was an emperor again, remote and unreadable. "Yes, Dexterity. I know Sun-dao's with you. The Tzhung emperor brought us to you, me and King Alasdair."

"Oh," said Dexterity. "Good evening, Your Majesty! And you, of course, Emperor Han."

Han said nothing.

"It's good to know you're safe and sound, Mister Jones," called Alasdair. "I look forward to hearing your tale."

"Yes, yes," said Dexterity. He sounded . . . doubtful. "It's out of the ordinary, I'll say that much. Majesty, there's just one thing – about Sun-dao—"

She sighed, tightening her hold on Alasdair's hand. "Yes, Dexterity. We know."

"Oh."

He sounded much closer now. Han's witch-men

were slowing the boat, oars digging deep, nudging it around like a carter turning a bolshy draft horse.

And then she saw him. The running lamps tied to the railing of Han's boat splashed yellow light on the black water between them, and on Dexterity's face as he hung over the side of his own boat which was lit by one meagre lamp, almost burned out. The stink of its faltering wick smothered the fresh saltiness of the air. Zandakar stood beside him, his hair in their running lamps glowing like blue flame.

Rhian felt a shudder race through her, relief and anger combined in a rushing pain. *You're safe . . . you're safe . . . no thanks to Han.* Alasdair let go of her hand and slipped his arm round her shoulders, holding her steady as beneath their feet the Tzhung boat shifted and rocked. She let herself lean against him, let his weight take her weight.

There are so many questions to ask, and be answered. So many reasons to shun the Tzhung after this. But right now, in this moment, I don't care. I don't care.

"Mister Jones," she said, looking down at her toymaker. Hearing the quaver in her voice, she had to bite her lip hard before she could continue. "Have you been travelling without the proper paperwork?"

In the fitful light, beneath its scruffy beard, Dexterity's anxious face twisted. "Er – well – that's to say – oh, sweet Rollin, Your Majesty. It's wonderful to see you!"

She cleared her throat. "And you. Are you sure you're all right? Are you hurt?"

He glanced at his left hand, then tucked it behind his back before she could see it closely. "No, I'm fine.

Fine. A few blisters. I'm not much for rowing. In fact I think it's safe to say I'm not cut out to be a sailor. And I'm a little peckish, truth be told. We ran out of salt fish day before yesterday. Not to mention I could do with a long hot bath."

Alasdair chuckled, sounding only a little amused. "Don't worry, Mister Jones. Hot food and hot water await you in abundance, back in Kingseat Castle. You've been sorely missed."

"Ah," said Dexterity. "Ursa's been raising a ruckus, has she?"

"Not just Ursa," Rhian said. "We've all been worried, Dexterity."

"Yes . . . well . . ." said Dexterity, and flicked a hard glance at Han. "There's been this and that to worry about, as it happens."

For the first time Rhian let her gaze dwell on Zandakar. Terrifyingly self-contained, he stood a pace behind Dexterity, hands clasped behind his back. His pale blue gaze was fixed to Han's face.

"And you, Zandakar?" she asked. "Are you all right?"

He nodded once. "*Zho*."

She felt her heart thud too hard. Felt Alasdair's arm tighten around her. *You're lying. Something's happened.* "Good," she said, sounding curt. But better curt than emotional, for so many reasons. She turned to Han. "Well, what happens now? Do we bring them on board and abandon their boat? Take them in tow? What?"

Han was staring back at Zandakar, his dark eyes opaque. Rhian felt her skin crawl, felt sudden tension in the air. Alasdair, just as sensitive to atmosphere, released his hold on her and stood aside half a pace. Ready to act, as she was, if action was required.

Though what he or I can do against three witch-men with only a single knife between us, I'm sure I don't know.

Slowly, deliberately, Han turned his head to look at her. "We bring them on board," he said softly. "Mister Jones – Zandakar – and Sun-dao."

There was a tone in his voice, saying his dead brother's name, that crawled her skin even colder. Meanly, unkindly, she felt a flash of resentment. *Damn you, Sun-dao. Could you be less convenient?*

"If we're doing this, we should work quickly," said Alasdair. "We mustn't be away from the castle all night. People will notice. There will be an outcry."

"Agreed," said Han, and nodded to his witch-men.

The Tzhung boat carrying Dexterity, Zandakar and Sun-dao was grappled alongside Han's larger vessel. Zandakar tossed Dexterity from one to the other with careless ease, the toymaker flailing between the two boats like a protesting bag of wheat. Then he vaulted over the railings and gap himself, as easily as he danced through the air in his *hotas*.

Working silently, swiftly, supple as the wind, Han's witch-men retrieved Sun-dao's ungainly, unclothed body and laid it on the deck beside their boat's mast. Then they stepped back, and Emperor Han approached. For a long time he stood over Sun-dao in silence, his face obscured by shadows.

At length he dropped to his knees on the tilting deck, and bowed his head until his face was hidden. His witch-men bowed their heads after him, their long plaited moustaches swaying.

"I'm so sorry, Majesty," Dexterity whispered, standing between Alasdair and Zandakar. His lips were chapped, his eyes rimmed with redness. He looked exhausted. "I hope this doesn't cause trouble for you with the Tzhung."

She nearly laughed, though she was awash with despair. "Oh, Dexterity. Sun-dao was Han's brother."

Alasdair's lips pinched tight, and she thought she saw him swallow a curse. Dexterity flinched, his gaze darting to Zandakar and back again. Something – a thought, a feeling – flickered deep in Zandakar's eyes, but he said nothing.

"Truly?" said Dexterity, eventually. "Oh dear."

She nodded. "No-one outside of Tzhung knew. Perhaps few within the empire. I don't know. But you're not to repeat it. Consider it . . . a state secret."

"Yes, of course," said Dexterity, distracted. "Oh *dear*. I do wish I had known who Sun-dao was. I'd have tried to wash him clean. Before he died, there was blood, you see—"

Yes, there was. She could see it in the gentle lamplight, caked dry on Sun-dao's mouth and chin. And there was more than blood. He'd sustained some kind of fearsome injury, half of his face was brutally charred. The sight turned her stomach. What must it do to Emperor Han? She remembered, too vividly, how it had felt to look at Ranald and Simon's plague-disfigured bodies . . .

Dexterity was tugging at his beard. He always did, when he was upset. She touched his arm, gently. "Don't fret yourself. You weren't to know. Dexterity, what happened?"

"To Sun-dao?"

He sounded almost . . . hopeful. As though Sun-dao's demise was the only thing he wished to discuss.

And if that's so, what don't you want to tell me?

"To begin with," she replied, letting her tone warn him. "But then I want to know how this started. I want to know why you let the emperor send you and Zandakar to Icthia." She glanced at Han, still on his knees and silently grieving. "Or were you indeed kidnapped, and sent against your will?"

Dexterity came very close to squirming. "Not . . . precisely, Majesty."

Damn. Alasdair was staring at her, she could feel the weight of his gaze. "I see," she said softly, and let all her disappointment colour the words.

"Oh dear," Dexterity said again. "Majesty, it's not a simple story."

Of course it wasn't. Swallowing more resentment, she folded her arms. "We'll discuss this once we've returned to the castle. For now tell me what happened to Sun-dao. *All* of it, Mister Jones. No matter how . . . awkward."

Dexterity flicked another glance at Zandakar. Did he realise? "Well, Majesty, I'm no Ursa. I can't tell you for certain why he died, but I can hazard a guess."

"Hazard away," said Alasdair. "*Swiftly.*"

"Yes, of course," Dexterity muttered. "I think Sun-dao overtaxed himself shifting our boat from Kingseat harbour to Icthia. It was . . ." He shook his head. "Remarkable. But he was spent when we got there. I thought he was dying then. And getting us home again, oh dear. And something else happened, too. Something about Mijak, and the trade winds.

Sun-dao spoke, before the end, but I'm afraid I didn't understand what he was trying to say."

On his knees beside dead Sun-dao, Han stirred. "His words, toymaker?"

Rhian nodded as Dexterity looked to her. "Tell him."

"He said, *Blood, blood, blood in Mijak. My brothers have failed.* Then he called for the emperor. And then . . . he died." Dexterity shuddered. "You should know, Majesty . . . Mijak's empress planned on slaughtering ten thousand slaves to give her priests more power."

"*Ten thousand?*" she whispered, appalled. "Are you sure, Dexterity?"

"That's what Vortka said, Majesty." Dexterity shuddered again. "Terrible. And she must have done it. I think the shock of all those deaths is what finished Sun-dao. He was already so weak, you see."

"Not even Tzhung's witch-men could stand against so much spilled blood," said Han. His hands were in his lap. He didn't touch his brother.

"No," she said. "Of course they couldn't, Han. The blame's not yours." Then she looked at Dexterity. "Did you say *Vortka* told you? Who's Vortka?"

"The highest priest of Mijak," said Dexterity, suddenly cautious. "Zandakar and I met with him in Jatharuj. You know, Icthia's main seaport."

She stared. "You met – Dexterity, how is that possible? Icthia is full of Mijaki warriors, isn't it?"

"Oh yes. But Sun-dao hid us in the wind."

More witch-man sorcery. Helfred would have a spasm when he learned of all this. If the ambassadors found out, they'd likely do worse. She raised an eyebrow at Alasdair, who offered a small shrug, then turned back to Dexterity.

"And why did you and Zandakar meet with this high priest of Mijak?"

Dexterity glanced at Zandakar. "We . . . hoped to convince him that Mijak was wrong. We thought if anyone could change Empress Hekat's mind about conquering the world, it would be Vortka."

What? She stared from Dexterity to Zandakar, whose stolid silence was starting to unnerve her. "You *idiots* – what were you thinking? God save us, you could've been *killed*."

Still Zandakar said nothing. Dexterity sighed. "I know, Majesty," he said. "But we thought it was worth the risk. We thought—" His gaze shifted to Han, and again she saw his smouldering anger. "We thought Emperor Han believed we had a chance to save lives. We thought that was why he was willing to risk Sun-dao in getting us to Icthia."

We thought. Rhian felt her body tense. Every instinct was prickling and her skin crawled with foreboding. "But?" she said delicately. She didn't dare look at Han, for fear of losing her temper. "That wasn't the case?"

"No. It wasn't."

"What went wrong, Mister Jones?"

"Answer your queen, toymaker," said Han as Dexterity hesitated. His gaze did not lift from his dead brother's face. "The Tzhung empire wishes to know how its most revered witch-man was so grievously hurt. For it is surely possible he would not have died, if he'd been whole."

Both Dexterity and Zandakar glared at him, openly hostile now. Dexterity took a step forward, his hands clenched. "I'm not inclined to take commands from you, Emperor Han. And I think you know why."

"He may, but I don't," said Rhian. "Mister Jones, enlighten me. How was Sun-dao burned?" Swift as a striking snake *hota* she seized Dexterity's left hand and examined it in the lamplight. It was seared, blistered and bubbled. Suspicions confirmed, she released him. "How were *you* burned?"

Dexterity looked to Zandakar. Something complicated passed between them. As one man they looked at Han, and this time Han did look up. The silence stretched out, full of complications . . .

"Ah – I thought you wanted to discuss this in the castle?" Dexterity said.

Suddenly she was angry. Frightened, and angry.

All these men with their secrets, all these wretched men. First Zandakar and Dexterity, now Han. Everywhere I turn, secrets, and yet I'm expected to prevail.

"I've changed my mind!" she snapped. "If what you wish to tell me is politically sensitive – and I just know that it is, I can see your faces, gentlemen – then what better place to discuss it than in the middle of the night, on a boat, on the ocean? It seems unlikely we'll be interrupted or overheard. *Tell me what happened!* Or do you long for a cell again, and a witch-man to keep you company?"

Even as she made the threat, some small part of her regretted it. Dexterity flinched, his eyes widening.

Alasdair touched her arm with his fingertips, silently urging restraint.

Then Dexterity sighed. "No, Your Majesty. I'll tell you. I'm afraid there was a slight disagreement. An . . . altercation, if you will."

"Why?" said Alasdair. "You were in enemy territory. Your lives were in danger. What was so important you'd risk fighting over it, and being discovered?"

Dexterity's eyes grew colder. "Emperor Han lied to us, Your Majesty. He wasn't interested in seeing Mijak change its mind. He wanted to use us to get Sun-dao close to the empress so the witch-man could murder her and Dmitrak."

Murder? *No . . . assassination.* Rhian looked to Han. "Is this true?"

Han stared back at her, his grief-filled eyes calm. "Yes."

"You lied to my people? You played on their sympathies, their vulnerabilities, their trust?"

"Yes," said Han, no apology in him.

"You sent Sun-dao to Icthia so he might kill Zandakar's mother and brother?"

Han nodded. "Mijak must be stopped."

She turned to Dexterity. "And you discovered Sun-dao's true intentions."

"Eventually," he said. "Thank God."

"And you stopped him?"

He seemed surprised at her tone. "Of course we did, Your Majesty."

Rhian stared into the night, across the endless stretch of ocean. Burning deep within her, a bright flame of fury. Then she turned and fixed Dexterity with a glare. "Mister Jones, there is no *of course* about it. You had no business interfering with Sun-dao."

"Your Majesty?" he said, dumbfounded. "Surely you don't mean that. We *had* to stop him! When we refused to take him into the township he began raising a storm. He would've killed *thousands*, some of them enslaved Icthians. How can we rail against Hekat's slaughter, then turn around and slaughter thousands ourselves?"

It was a fair question, for someone who wasn't expected to save kingdoms, and countries.

You're a kind man, Dexterity. Sadly, I no longer have the luxury of kindness.

"But those enslaved Icthians died anyway, Mister Jones, didn't they?" she demanded. "And their deaths broke Han's witch-men. If you'd left Sun-dao alone it's true, he'd have killed those slaves. *But Mijak's warriors would have died with them.* Tell me, what do you imagine will happen when Mijak comes to Ethrea? Do you think if we ask Zandakar's mother and brother nicely to leave us be, they'll oblige? Have you *forgotten* Garabatsas?"

Dexterity's chin came up, his beard jutting defensively. "No! No, of course I haven't. But Zandakar had already spoken with Vortka. The priest promised to help us. Surely he deserved a chance to stop Mijak without more bloodshed."

Kneeling with his dead brother, Emperor Han snarled. "So, Queen Rhian, this is the will of Ethrea? To talk and talk and not lift a finger against an enemy more fearsome and powerful than this world has ever known? You will not lift a finger when my witch-men offer to lay down their *lives*?"

She held up a hand to Han, her gaze not leaving Dexterity's shocked face. "Why does Mijak deserve mercy, Mister Jones? What mercy did it offer Garabatsas, or Icthia, or any other conquered nation? Don't you *understand*? Because you indulged your scruples, because you stopped Sun-dao, how many *hundreds* of thousands will perish? Will Ethrea fall? Tzhung-tzhungchai, with its millions? Arbenia? Harbisland? Barbruish, and the rest? Must *everyone* die because you turned squeamish?"

In the lamplight Dexterity was pale. "I'm sorry, Your Majesty, but I never said I'd kill for you."

"No!" she spat. "But you're *perfectly* happy to have *me* kill for *you*!"

He stepped back. "Rhian—"

"And *you*!" she snarled, turning on Zandakar. "Standing there silent, as though someone's cut out your tongue! Do you think I don't know why you fought with Sun-dao? Do you think I'm *stupid*, Zandakar? You wanted to save your mother and brother. You – you *hypocrite*. You *sicken* me. All that talk of making me a killing queen, of having to be resolute, of how accepting a crown means accepting a sword and *using* it, by God, to preserve my realm. And then when the chance presents itself to stop Mijak in its tracks, to *end* this, all you can do is think of *yourself*?"

As Zandakar stared at her, his expression blank, his breathing swift, Alasdair stepped towards her, his eyes fathomed with compassion. "Rhian—"

She turned on him. "What? You're not *angry* about this?"

"Oh yes," he said, so quiet. So deadly. "Majesty, I am steeped in fury."

"*Good*," she said, and flung round to glare again at Zandakar and Dexterity. "Tell me, gentlemen, are your memories truly so short? *I killed Damwin and Kyrin!* I spitted those dukes like mad dogs and destroyed their ancient Houses. I destroyed their families' happiness and turned babies into orphans. Because I *had* to. Because Ethrea *demanded* it. Because God demanded it, so I could be queen. Do you know what that cost me? Do you know what that *made* me?"

"Rhian, you're not a murderer," said Alasdair, his voice soft and careful. "Damwin and Kyrin died by judicial combat. Their blood's not on your hands."

"Not now, no. I washed it off," she retorted. "But they are dead because of me and no sweet mumblings from you can change that."

It was a horrible thing to say. She watched Alasdair flinch, watched the pain of her words sharpen in his eyes. There was pain in her, too, somewhere, but she couldn't afford to indulge it. Had to hold on to her anger, let it rule her, because if she didn't she'd abandon her self-control altogether.

And these men, these men. They must never see me weak.

She looked again at Dexterity. "You say Sun-dao tried to raise a storm to scour Jatharuj?"

He nodded, then found his voice. "He didn't just try, Your Majesty. He did it." He was looking at her as though she were a stranger, some evil changeling that had stolen his darling Rhian.

I don't care, I don't care, I don't care . . .

"Han," she said, and crossed the deck to stare down at the emperor. "How is this? You told me to my face the witch-men of Tzhung lacked the power to destroy Mijak. Was that a lie?"

In a single, self-controlled movement Han rose from the deck so they were standing face-to-face. His dark eyes were furious and despairing. "You call an emperor of the Tzhung a liar? Foolish girl. I could kill you where you stand."

"Don't bother," she retorted, glaring, refusing to be intimidated. "It seems Mijak will do your killing for you, soon enough. But you needn't worry. You and your witch-men can blow yourselves to safety whenever you like, can't you?"

Now Han's grief for Sun-dao was burned to ashes by anger. "If Sun-dao did this thing, if he called a storm, alone, he did so out of desperation. He did so out of love for me, his emperor, knowing he would *die* for calling it. As so many of our wind-brothers died holding back the trade winds for you. And yet you criticise the Tzhung? You call us *cowards*? Will we only be brave in your eyes when every last witch-man in the world is dead?"

Rhian held her ground, barely. "No, but—"

Han leaned towards her, his breath hot in her face. "You are mere flesh and blood, Rhian. You cannot see what we see, what we taste, what we smell, in the world beyond the world where the wind blows its witch-men. The stench of Mijak chokes every nation. It smothers, it suffocates, it turns the air to rancid blood." He spat. "Would the Emperor of Tzhung-tzhungchai bend his knee to a girl-child of Ethrea, begging for help, if he had another choice? We do all that we can. *We can do no more.*"

The bitterness in his voice would curdle fresh milk. Rhian jabbed a finger in his chest. "This is your fault, not mine. You should've told me what you were planning, Han. You should've trusted me. If I'd known I *would* have helped and with my help perhaps Mijak would be in ruins even now, its empress *dead*, her son with his gauntlet of power *dead*, its warriors *dead* or at least in disarray. But no. You care more for your pride and your witch-man secrets than you do for winning this battle. So our chance – perhaps our *only* chance – is lost and while we float on the ocean throwing words at each other, the warships of Mijak are doubtless sailing towards us."

"Trust?" said Han, and pointed at Sun-dao. "You speak of trust to me when my brother lies there dead and I must believe these men tell the truth of how he died? These men who will not answer you, who will not reveal how Sun-dao was burned? Your dear Mister Jones, he's the burning man of Ethrea. He burned your father's prolate. He burns for Ethrea's God." Turning away from her, he advanced on Dexterity. "Did you burn my brother, toymaker? Did you kill him? *Did you*?"

Before Dexterity could deny it, or defend himself, Zandakar stepped forward, dragged Dexterity behind him and confronted Han himself. His hand reached inside his roughspun shirt and pulled out a knife, long and thin-bladed.

"No, don't!" shouted Dexterity, fumbling at

Zandakar's arm. "Don't, Zandakar, don't, you'll only make things worse!"

Shouting. Confusion. A cold wind howled round them as Han's witch-men leapt to safeguard their emperor. The boat's sail began snapping, a sinister, menacing sound. Rhian felt herself flung aside as Alasdair sought to protect her. She hit the boat's railing and fell to her knees, pain jolting through her as she struck the shifting deck. Cursing, vision blurred, she struggled back to her feet.

The night was lit with strange blue fire. It came from Zandakar's knife, streaming wildly overhead as Dexterity hung from Zandakar's arm, still shouting. Alasdair – where was Alasdair? Rollin's mercy, he'd stood himself in front of the emperor. He was trying to shield Han with his own body. *You dear fool.* The boat was rocking violently, the witch-men's wind whipping the waves into a frenzy.

Lurching, staggering, she threw herself between them. Now Alasdair was shouting, torn between saving Han and saving her. Time to spare his torment. In a single swift move she unsheathed the blade on her hip and danced its point to Zandakar's throat.

"You've made of me a killing queen," she said softly, staring into his pale blue eyes. "Shall I prove how well you've taught me?"

Frozen silence. The witch-men's wind died. Dexterity let go of Zandakar's arm and retreated. The wild blue flame faded. Rhian held out her hand.

"Give me that knife, Zandakar."

She heard his stunned intake of air. "Rhian *hushla—*"

"*Give me the knife!*"

He placed the blade in her outstretched hand. She closed her fingers round its ugly hilt and stepped back, taking her own blade-point from his throat.

"Thank you."

The moment he'd relinquished the blade its blue flame died. It was just a knife again, not worth looking at twice. She kept her gaze fixed to his face.

"Did you burn Sun-dao with this blade?"

Slowly, he nodded. "*Zho*."

"But that's not what killed him," said Dexterity. "On Hettie's grave, I swear it. It was the effort of reaching Jatharuj, and trying to call up that storm, then spiriting us away from Mijak's warriors before they could kill us, and then the murder of all those slaves. It was all those things, Majesty. Really, Sun-dao killed himself for us, and for Ethrea." The strangest look flitted over his face. "He was a very brave man."

She turned to Han. In his eyes, pain had drowned the anger. "Well?" she said. "Will you accept that as the truth?"

Han said nothing, only rested his gaze on his brother's still body. Waves slapped at the two Tzhung boats. An unsummoned breeze shivered the canvas sails. Then Tzhung-tzhungchai's emperor nodded.

"I will," he said.

Rhian didn't dare glance at Alasdair, though she wanted to, badly. Her heart pounding so hard she felt sick, now she looked at the knife she'd taken from Zandakar.

Carved bone and forged steel, its oddly sinuous blade gleamed with a blue sheen. Its hilt was indeed ugly, carved like – like a *scorpion*. Horrible creature.

She'd seen ugly knives before, though. This one was different. It was freezing cold in her grasp, and in her blood it sang for death.

Shuddering, she gave it back. Ignoring Alasdair's protest, the witch-men's hissing, she said, "Bring it to life again. Show me how it works."

Zandakar turned. Pointed the knife at the boat he and Dexterity had sailed in. A thin stream of blue fire erupted from its point and struck the Tzhung vessel at its centre. A crack of sound. A flare of blue light. Blue flames rising to the stars. Then the Tzhung boat shattered in a rain of splinters and fire, hissing and dying as they struck the water.

What remained swiftly sank.

Rhian realised she'd cried out. Even Alasdair and Han had made a sound. But Zandakar was silent, and Dexterity appeared unsurprised.

She looked at him. "Mister Jones?"

"Do you remember what I told you of Garabatsas? The gauntlet Dmitrak wore? I think that gauntlet and this knife are somehow the same."

Alasdair stepped closer, and stared at the blue-flickered blade. "Where did it come from?"

"Vortka," said Zandakar.

Rhian frowned. "Why would he give you such a weapon?"

"I burned again in Jatharuj, Majesty," said Dexterity. "Through me, God spoke to this priest. I don't know what I said, but I think Vortka gave Zandakar the knife because he wants to stop Mijak."

"He didn't stop the murder of those ten thousand

slaves, did he?" she snapped. "Are you certain he's going to be of any help?"

Zandakar stirred. "Vortka will try." His fist struck his heart. "Vortka *gajka*."

An odd look passed between him and Dexterity, then. "What?" said Rhian. "What haven't you told me?"

Dexterity fixed her with a clear, steady gaze. "Nothing, Majesty. Except – well – I went to Icthia with Zandakar willingly, because Hettie said I should. She said it was important. I think perhaps this knife is why."

Hettie. Of course she's mixed up in this. Shoving her own blade back in its sheath, Rhian risked a glance at Alasdair and Han. They looked serious but not precisely disbelieving.

"Can that knife destroy Dmitrak's gauntlet?" said Alasdair.

Zandakar shrugged. "*Wei* know, Alasdair king."

"But if you had to, could you use it against him? Against your own brother?"

Silence. Then he nodded. "*Zho*."

Rhian stabbed Zandakar with another stare. "Can I trust you with it? Or should I treat you like a little boy who mustn't be left to play with knives?"

"*Tcha*!" said Zandakar, insulted. "You say?"

Alasdair rested his hand on her shoulder. "She does, and so do I. If you can't control your temper, Zandakar, hand the blade back to Queen Rhian."

"*Wei*," said Zandakar, and shoved the scorpion knife inside his shirt. "You trust. I say."

Rhian turned to Han. "And you. You'll not use your witch-man powers to punish him for burning

Sun-dao. I grieve for your brother, Han, and for you.
But if we're to defeat Mijak we must stand side by
side. I am *tired* of saying this. And I'm tired of being
ignored. You say the wind sent you to me? Then *honour the wind*."

She watched her words strike home. Watched the
last tension drain from Han's face. He raised a hand
to his witch-men. They retreated, sliding back
through the shadows to stand beside the boat's mast.
She looked to Dexterity.

"Are you given any insights, Mister Jones? Can
you say for certain what Mijak will do now?"

"Now they've brought back the trade winds?
Majesty, unless Vortka performs a miracle, they'll
sail. And they have so many warships. I couldn't
count them all. They crowded Jatharuj harbour like
salt herrings in a barrel."

She looked at Zandakar. "How many warriors in
Mijak's army, do you know?"

"Many," he said soberly. "Thousands and thousands."

Of course there were.

*And what do we have? Half-trained soldiers with
swords, who've never drawn them in anger. Farmers
with pitchforks. Zandakar's knife. Han's witch-men,
who it seems are limited. And a gaggle of allies who
aren't allies at all. Oh, dear God.*

"There's only one hope for us," she said, and let
her gaze touch all of them. "Those Mijaki warships
must *never* reach Ethrea."

Alasdair pulled a face. "Well yes, that would be
best. But without an armada . . ."

"We will have an armada," she said, defiant. "I

will *make* the trading nations listen. I will make them give us as many ships as we need! I will *not* surrender Ethrea without a fight!"

"How?" he demanded. "How will you do it?"

"No more ambassadors, Alasdair. I'll make my arguments to the leaders themselves." Heart pounding, skin slicked with sweat beneath her linen shirt and black leathers, she rounded on Han. "Will you help me?"

Han lifted an eyebrow. "Help you how?"

"Will you witch me to the courts of the trading nations' rulers, the way Sun-dao witched Dexterity and Zandakar to Jatharuj?"

Han's expression hardened. "Tzhung-tzhungchai is an empire of secrets. Would you make me the emperor who shares those secrets with the world?"

As though they were alone, as though they stood in her Long Gallery, or her gardens, or somewhere free of prying eyes, she stepped close to Han and let her gaze dwell on his smooth face.

"No. I would make you the emperor whose secrets *save* the world."

Han said nothing. His dark eyes showed her nothing. *He* was a secret, and she could not see his heart.

She touched her fingertips to his silk sleeve. "Please, Han. I'm begging you. I can't do this alone. I need you. I need Zandakar. I need every weapon I can find."

Overhead the stars shone, so pale. The moons threw down their thin light. Beneath their feet, beneath the Tzhung boat, the ocean danced its ancient *hotas*.

Han nodded. "I will help."

CHAPTER TWENTY-FOUR

Jatharuj was a charnel house after the deaths of those ten thousand slaves. Two highsuns later and the air was still rank with blood, with the stench of bodies burning to ash and splintered bone.

Numb with pain, struck dumb by guilt, Vortka sat by Hekat's side in her palace, and held her hand as she regained the strength she had poured into killing so many.

The children . . . the mothers . . . the old, sick men . . .

His newly-woken heart was weeping. Before those slaves came to Jatharuj, he did try to save them. He tried to help Hekat hear the god's true voice in her heart. But what he had told his son was true: Hekat's heart was full of blood and death.

She has listened to a false voice for so long, I do not know if she can hear the truth.

Mijak saw him as the god's high godspeaker but Hekat saw him as Vortka, a fellow slave, and less important than she. Always he had been forced to remind her that he too was godchosen and precious. He knew she never truly believed it. He knew she thought the god saw her first. Saw her only.

I minded, but it never mattered. It matters now.

He had failed the god.

Was I wrong to send Jones and Zandakar away?

If I had shown her that burning man, if I had shown her living Zandakar, would she have listened? Or would she have danced them dead?

He did not know the answer. All he knew, to his shame, was he would rather drown in the blood of ten thousand slaves than see Zandakar murdered at his feet.

When those slaves came to Jatharuj, he could not stop Hekat from killing them. Fired at first with angry passion, she had killed and killed with a swift, sure blade. But too soon that angry strength was spent, and sacrifice swiftly turned to butchery.

At last, no longer able to bear the pitiful screams of the dying, he took out his own knife and gave those slaves a merciful death.

It is my duty, it is my scorpion wheel for tasking.

He could not kill them fast enough, so he summoned his godspeakers and together they finished what Hekat began. She stayed at the slave pens by the harbour, she would not withdraw. A shell of warriors tended her, they called it an honour. Dmitrak led them, he was not honoured, he had no choice. Hekat would not let Nagarak's son sacrifice the slaves.

It took almost two full highsuns to kill them. When it was over, Mijak's godspeakers were soaked in blood. The waters of Jatharuj harbour were turned from blue to red. Blood soaked the waiting hulls of the warships.

Half-fainting, Hekat had smiled. "Do you feel it, Vortka? Do you feel the god grow?"

Of course he had felt it, though it wasn't the god. He wanted to tell her that, he wanted to kiss her and hold her and tell her the truth. If he did that now, his blood would be spilled. He would die and the truth would die with him. He could not die now. He must live until he could make her hear it.

"I can hear the demons screaming," she whispered. "I hear them screaming in my mind. They are defeated, they cannot conquer Hekat. I have danced my snakeblade into their hearts."

Whatever she had done – whatever he had helped her to do – he could feel it with all his godspeaker senses. His skin was crawling, the blood burned in his veins. His eyes saw too clearly, every whisper was a shout.

Hekat laughed. "The god is pleased, Vortka. You and I have pleased the god."

No. They had pleased the thing that was not a god at all. The thing godspeakers had created in panic, by mistake. A thing of ravenous hunger, whose appetite for blood could never be sated. In seeking to save themselves, in that sinning time spoken of in the high godspeaker histories, so long ago now it was all but forgotten . . . those frightened godspeakers had set in motion Mijak's doom.

I am the only godspeaker living who knows Mijak's true god. The true god of Mijak spoke to me in flames, with love.

And how he would ever convince Hekat of that, he did not begin to know.

Aieee, god, you must help me, you must show me the way.

Kneeling beside Hekat at the slave pens by the harbour, his nostrils clogged with the foul stench of death, surrounded by warriors and godspeakers and

Dmitrak, he could not tell her that what she worshipped was a lie.

"Yes, Hekat," he said, despairing. "Mijak's bloodthirsty god is pleased."

Lowsun on that second day of slaughter was approaching. Dmitrak carried his mother back to her palace, she did not complain. She was silent. Asleep.

Because he was Vortka high godspeaker, he had stayed by the harbour while the burning of the dead slaves began. Then he washed the blood from his skin and his scorpion pectoral and returned to the palace, to see how Hekat fared.

"High godspeaker," said Dmitrak, in Hekat's private chamber. "All the demons are dead. How soon before the trade winds blow in Icthia?"

Hekat was sleeping. Vortka took Dmitrak by the arm and guided him onto the balcony, so their voices would not wake her.

"I do not know, warlord."

Dmitrak's face was twisted with ugliness. "You are high godspeaker, and you know so little. You did not want Hekat to kill those slaves. You said the god did not want their blood. Why did you say that? Why do you say the god does not want the world?"

He stared at Nagarak's son, unyielding. "I am Vortka high godspeaker. I do not answer to you."

"Hekat is weak, Vortka," said Dmitrak, he smiled like a wolf. "Every highsun she grows weaker. Every highsun you heal her, you cannot heal her forever. I am the warlord, I will be emperor. When I am emperor you will answer to me. You are loved by Hekat. You were loved by Zandakar. Vortka high godspeaker, you are not loved by me."

Dmitrak was a dangerous man. Only one man breathing had the power to stop him. If Dmitrak knew his brother was alive he would swim to Ethrea so he might kill him. He would kill Zandakar with his bare hands and teeth.

"Warlord, you do not need to love me," he said. "You need to obey me, for I am the high godspeaker. My scorpion pectoral kisses wicked, sinning men. It kisses them to death, warlord. You have been warned."

Dmitrak had hissed, then, and stormed from Hekat's palace. Vortka stood on the balcony and watched him stride down the street, far below. He was an enemy, there was no friendship there.

Feeling empty, feeling wicked, feeling sick from the stink of death hanging over Jatharuj, he'd returned to Hekat's bedside to pour his healing power into her, and wait for her to wake.

Two highsuns passed. And as he waited for Hekat to stir from her long sleep, fear gnawed his bones. What if she never listened to his truths? Did that mean he should let her die? Would he save the world from Mijak if he let its empress die?

He did not know. He did not think so. She could die, and there would still be Dmitrak. With Hekat dead, Dmitrak would never trust him. Dmitrak would use Hekat's death to rid himself of a high godspeaker he hated.

And even if those things were not true . . . how could he kill Hekat? Or even Dmitrak? He had promised his son he would save them both.

The doors to Hekat's balcony stood open. The newsun air of Jatharuj was not yet sweet, but he could not seal her within an airless chamber. In the bed beside him, Hekat stirred at last . . . and through the open doors, a fresh breeze blew. She opened her eyes and smiled, her eyes were shining in her thin, scarred face.

"The trade winds, Vortka! The trade winds are come!"

As lowsun gentled the burning blue sky, Hekat walked with Dmitrak down to the harbour, where the warships of Mijak crowded the water. She walked with strength and purpose, in the time she had slept since sacrificing the slaves she had become strong again. All that blood had made her strong, its power had destroyed the demons and entered her bones. Its power fed the godspeakers, they poured power through their crystals and changed the horses of the warhost. They would ride in the warships and suffer no harm, they would leap from the warships to conquer sinning Ethrea.

As she walked the streets with Dmitrak, the trade winds blew in her face. They blew and made her godbells sing, they blew and she sang in her heart.

I am Hekat, destroyer of demons. I am Hekat, in the god's eye.

"Are your warriors ready to set sail from Jatharuj, warlord?" she asked Dmitrak. "Now the trade winds are come again, and we are needed in the world."

"They are ready, Empress," said Dmitrak. "They are skilled sailors, they are swift with their snakeblades. Their snakeblades are thirsty, they seek blood to drink."

She bared her teeth in a smile. "They will have

blood, warlord. The world is full of blood, waiting for their snakeblades."

They reached the harbour, and all the warriors there saluted her with fists and laughter. She greeted them laughing in return, they were her warriors and she was their empress. Dmitrak walked behind her, he was only their warlord.

With all the slaves of Jatharuj dead, her warriors worked to fill Mijak's warships with supplies. They did not complain, their empress asked this of them. They would do anything that she asked.

"I desire to see my warship," she told Dmitrak. "Take me to the warship of Mijak's empress."

He was obedient, he did as he was told. He led her along Jatharuj harbour's stone pier to the largest warship tethered to the dock. It was a beautiful warship, it was black and blood red, the scorpion on its mainsail was fierce. Her fingers folded tight about her scorpion amulet, she felt the power in it from the slave blood she had spilled.

She stepped onto her warship, Dmitrak came after. She turned her face away from Jatharuj and breathed in the open ocean. She breathed in the trade winds that blew for the god. The warship beneath her feet rocked at its mooring, it wanted to sail in the world for the god.

"Empress," said Dmitrak, behind her. "We must speak of Vortka."

"Must we?" she said, she did not look at him. "What does my warlord wish to say of my high god-speaker?"

"Vortka is corrupted," said Dmitrak. "He is gone

from the god's eye. He spoke against Mijak, he spoke against the god."

"How do you know Vortka is corrupted?" she asked him, her powerful blood was bubbling with rage. "Did the god tell you, Dmitrak? Are you a god-speaker now?"

"A godspeaker? No, Empress." His voice was uncertain. "But you heard his words, the night the storm struck Jatharuj. He said the god did not want the world. He said the god did not want blood. He tried and tried to stop you sacrificing those slaves. He is an old man, he is stupid, his mind has turned to mush. Demons have corrupted him. He cannot leave Jatharuj."

In a single smooth movement she turned, like a *hota*, and slapped Nagarak's son hard across his ugly face.

"Are you Mijak's empress? I think you are not! I think you do not say who leaves Jatharuj and who stays!"

Hate and anger burned in Dmitrak's eyes. "He spoke against the god in the world! What is that if not corruption?"

"*Tcha*! You are *stupid*," she spat, fighting the urge to plunge her snakeblade in his heart. "I have known Vortka since I was a child. He is a soft man, a loving man, he is not *corrupt*. He has served the god in ways you will never know, Dmitrak. He has served the god so well, he is the *only* soft man it will not kill. The god will not kill him, he lives in its eye."

A thread of blood trickled from Dmitrak's mouth. "Are *you* a godspeaker, that you can know that?"

"*I am more than a godspeaker!*" she shouted. "*I am the god's empress!*"

Dmitrak dropped to his knees, at last he saw his true danger. "You are its empress," he whispered. "You are in the god's eye."

The scorpion amulet around her neck was pulsing, its fury pulsed in her and its lust for blood. Aieee, the god see her, she wanted to feed its fury with Dmitrak's blood. She wanted to see him dead, like Abajai and Yagji.

I cannot kill Dmitrak, he is the warlord. He is the god's hammer. Until I find Zandakar, the god needs him in the world.

"Forgive me, Empress," said Dmitrak, still on his knees. "When Vortka spoke against the god in the world I believed he was an enemy. I thought you believed it, too."

She did not like to say it, but he was not wrong. When Vortka had said those things she was angry. She thought he betrayed her. She thought his softness had gone too far. When he said those things she found herself with Dmitrak, against Vortka.

Do I like to stand against Vortka, with Dmitrak? I think I do not. I will not do it again.

Dmitrak pressed his fist against his breast. "You are the empress. I am your warlord. How do I serve you if I do not speak my truth?"

Tcha, the god see her, she could not smite him for that. "Get up," she told him. "You speak your truth, you serve your empress. You do not know Vortka. Do not call him corrupt. You were there when he gave the god blood from those slaves. So much blood he gave the god, *he is not corrupt*. He has a soft heart, that is my business, not yours."

Dmitrak stood, his eyes were wary. "He will sail with the warhost?"

"Tcha. Of course he will sail," she said, and let her gaze sweep across the warships of Mijak. "He wil sail when we sail, we will sail in three highsuns. You are the warlord, you will see this done."

"Empress," said Dmitrak.

"Leave me now, warlord. You have much work to do, and I would speak with the god."

Dmitrak left her, she was not sorry to be alone. She walked the length and breadth of her warship, she cut her arm with her snakeblade and gave the godpost mast her blood. She went beneath the deck to see the place where she would sleep, it was small and dark, she preferred the warship's deck. She sat on the deck and let the sun warm her skin.

I will sleep on the deck when we are at sea. I will sleep on the deck beneath the godmoon and his wife, I will sleep beneath the stars as we sail towards Ethrea, and when we reach Ethrea I will flood it with blood.

"Well, Jones," said Ursa. "I've looked long and hard but I can't find anything amiss with you. Whatever that Tzhung witch-man got up to, however it was he spirited you across miles and miles of ocean in an eye-blink and back again, it doesn't seem to have left a mark on you."

"Didn't I say?" said Dexterity, perched on the edge of his castle chamber bed. "I'm fine."

She was frowning, uneasy. "Yes. Aside from that

burn, Jones, you've not a mark on you. Which is more than I can say for that heathen Zandakar."

"You've seen Zandakar already? So early?"

Ursa pulled a face. "You expected me to dilly-dally at home when the queen's sending me urgent messages at first light?"

Dexterity got up and crossed to his chamber window to stare down into the gardens below, where a solitary Rhian still walked. She'd been prowling the flowerbeds for nearly an hour now. Such a slight figure. So painfully alone. She was dressed yet again in her battered huntsman's leathers, as though she'd misplaced every last pretty gown.

"No." He leaned against the wall beside the window. "I suppose not. He's all right too, is he?"

"Fine as figs," said Ursa. "Aside from those scarlet welts I don't recall him having before you went to Icthia. You can tell me how he got them while I'm physicking your hand."

He considered his scabby, crusted wound. Remembering Zandakar's searing blue fire, he shivered. "It's not so bad, Ursa. A dab of ointment should put me right."

"A dab of ointment?" she echoed. "I see. Turned physick in your old age, have you, Jones?"

"No, but—"

"I think we'll leave it at *no*," she snapped. "*A dab of ointment*. A soaking in tinctured hiffa leaf *and* some ointment *and* a bandage is what your hand needs, Jones, and then *perhaps* you'll be on the mend. You were a fool not to come to me with it last night."

He shrugged. "Emperor Han's palanquin brought us directly back to the castle. It was too late to go traipsing to your cottage. I'm hardly dying. Don't make such a fuss."

"Tcha," she said, rummaging in her capacious physick bag. "I'll remind you of that next time you come bleating for a foot plaster. Now, about those welts . . ."

"Didn't Zandakar tell you?"

She snorted. "Would I be asking you if he had? He can play as dumb as a stone when the mood takes him, that young man."

Instead of answering, he continued to stare down into the gardens where Rhian still prowled, and touched his fingertips to the thick glass. She was so far below him it was like stroking her hair.

I worry for her. I worry for Alasdair. His face last night, when she looked at Zandakar, near broke my heart.

"What are you sighing about now, Jones?" said Ursa.

"Nothing," he replied, turning. Then added, seeing her raised eyebrows, "Well. Nothing I can help. Rhian and the king will just have to work things out themselves, I fear."

She didn't pretend not to understand. "No marriage is easy, even when you're mad in love. And that's before you touch on small matters like invading armies and heathen witch-men and pride and disappointment and – and—" She sniffed, hard. "Other people."

"Zandakar may love her, Ursa, but nothing will come of it. It can't."

"Not even if she loves him? I'm not blind either, Jones. I've seen . . . the looks."

"She loves the king," he said stubbornly. "I'd stake my life on it, Ursa."

"Oh, *Jones*. A woman can love more than once, and at the same time. Just like a man."

"She loves the king," he insisted. "And she would never betray the crown."

"Did I say she would?" said Ursa. "But so long as Zandakar remains in Ethrea, he's a thorn in all our sides. He stirs up things best left unstirred. It's hard enough already, Alasdair has to defer to his wife. But when his wife's got a man in love with her who looks like Zandakar, *well*." She sighed. "Let's just say there's more than one reason I'll be pleased when we've trounced those Mijaki heathen all the way back home."

Gloomy, he stared at her. "You're assuming we'll beat them."

"Yes, I am, Jones," said Ursa. "We're not going to lose, we've God on our side. Now sit down, so I can tend your hand and you can tell me how Zandakar got those welts!"

As he perched once more on the edge of his bed, Ursa settled on the chamber's stool before him. Taking his hurt hand gently she lifted it, turning it towards the light from the window. After a closer examination than her earlier, cursory look, she glanced up, her eyes sharp. "How did you do this? And *don't* say you spilled hot lamp oil, Jones, because I've seen more lamp oil burns than you've strung puppets. No lamp oil did this."

"If I explain," he said, after a moment, "you must swear to tell no-one else."

That earned him a scorching glare. "Dexterity

Jones, if you think after all we've been through that I'm not to be *trusted*, well—"

"Oh, don't be silly, you know I don't think that. But I have to say it aloud. For my own sake, I have to say it."

"All right, Jones," she said slowly. "No need for a tizzy. I'll not repeat your words, you've my solemn physick's vow."

Which she'd die before breaking. So he told her of the ugly scorpion knife and the blue fire and how Zandakar had wielded them both.

"You think that's why he's been sent to us?" said Ursa, when he was done. "Because he's got the power to fight his brother, fire with fire?"

"I think that's part of it, Ursa. It must be."

She'd finished cleaning his wound with the stinging tincture. Now she dabbed it dry with a clean cloth. "Those welts on Zandakar aren't burn scars, Jones."

Dexterity shook his head. "No." Remembering, a shudder ran through him. The stone scorpion. Zandakar's screams. "I tell you, Ursa, after what I saw in Icthia – Zandakar's as strange as any Tzhung witch-man. After what I saw, I'm not even certain he's entirely human."

"Not *human*?" said Ursa. "Nonsense!"

Leaning forward, he rested his good hand on her knee. "Ursa, I'm serious."

"Yes," she said, much more kindly. "I can see you are." She reached for her jar of ointment. "So tell me the rest of it, and I'll decide for myself."

It was a relief, unburdening himself of those terrifying memories. How a carved stone scorpion had come to life and stung Zandakar, and how he'd voided its poisons from his body and not died.

When he was finished, Ursa stared at him, a rolled-up linen bandage dangling unheeded from her fingers. "If I didn't know you for an honest, sober man, I'd call you a drunk liar, Jones."

He shuddered again. "Oh, Ursa, it was dreadful. How is it possible? Stone creatures can't come to life!"

"And neither can men walk invisible through the streets, but you said that witch-man *hid you in the wind*," she retorted. "And then there's you, isn't there? Willy-nilly bursting into flames. Convincing that priest Vortka to side with us. I wouldn't call that *usual*." Swiftly she bandaged his hand, and pinned it secure. "There now. Keep it wrapped and don't get it wet. I'll look at it again the day after tomorrow."

"All right. Ursa—"

"Jones, I don't know what to make of it. We'll just have to have faith, won't we, that whatever Zandakar is, whatever he can do, it's with God's blessing."

"If that's the case, why do you still call him a heathen?"

She grimaced. "Because he is a heathen, Jones. But that's not to say he can't have his uses."

Though he was so unsettled, and his hand pained him again, he laughed. "Oh, *Ursa*."

Her lips twitched, but she repressed the smile and stood. "I've a colicky baby to visit. Tell Her Majesty you and Zandakar are fine, and I'll see her myself this afternoon. In the meantime, if that hand pains you out of the ordinary come find me at once."

He kissed her cheek. "I will, Ursa. Thank you."

They left his chamber together but then parted company, and he made his way down to the privy garden, and Rhian. She was standing in her favourite place at the edge of the castle grounds. From there it was possible to see all of Kingseat township and harbour, out across the restless ocean to the distant horizon. Hearing his approach, she turned. The scratched and salt-stained leathers she wore creaked, complaining.

"Morning, Your Majesty," he greeted her. "Ursa's regrets, but she's seeing a sick baby that couldn't wait. I'm to tell you Zandakar's fine, and so am I."

"Your burned hand?"

"Oh, it's more singed than burned," he said, sounding far more cheerful than he felt. "Don't fret. I'll mend."

Rhian's strained expression eased. "I'm pleased to hear it. How can I help you?"

"Majesty, I serve at your pleasure."

She swung round to stare at the harbour and ocean again. "I fear there's precious little pleasure in it, Dexterity."

She sounded brittle, and who could blame her? If they were still on the road he might have risked a comforting touch, but this was Kingseat, and she was the queen.

"How is His Majesty, this morning?"

She shrugged. "Well enough. He's arranging a council meeting at the moment. My husband's a prodigious organiser, Dexterity. His eye for detail surpasses that of my father, and I'd not thought ever to say such a thing."

"Then it's a blessing we have him."

"Indeed," she agreed. "It seems I'm surrounded by useful men."

Behind her back, Dexterity pulled a face. *Useful men who plague you, and chafe at your authority.* But he didn't say it. The observation might be counted impertinent.

"For example, that Zandakar," she continued. "Does he not daily prove to be a man of surprises?"

"Yes, indeed," he said carefully. "God knew what he was doing when he sent Zandakar to us."

"Did he? I wonder."

Dexterity hesitated, then joined Rhian in staring at the sun-dappled harbour, where the official skiffs darted about their business.

"When you've a moment to think of it, you should ask Zandakar about protecting our port from Mijak," he said. "When he and I were at the markets, he had some things to say."

In profile, Rhian's face was pale, her expression remote. "Frightening things, I've no doubt."

"Very. Although . . . perhaps there'll be no need."

She glanced at him. "The armada?"

"As you say. It's likely our best hope."

"If I can make it happen."

"You sounded confident enough last night."

"Did I?" she said, with another sideways glance. "You don't think I sounded . . . frightened?"

"Not at all," he said, startled. "I was amazed by your courage and self-possession."

"Really?" Her lips quirked in a very small, brief smile. "I was terrified."

Dexterity realised then she didn't need a formal courtier wrapped up in protocol, she needed a shoulder to lean on. She needed her toymaker. "If that's true, Rhian, I'm amazed all over again. And I doubt I was the only one. I think the emperor was most impressed."

"Han," she said, and now her voice was much darker. "Like Sun-dao, a witch-man."

He considered that. "A friend also, I think. His methods might be high-handed and his attitude arrogant beyond bearing, but he has helped us. And we need him."

"More's the pity." With a shallow sigh, she folded her arms. "So, Dexterity. Last night's tale of your Icthian adventures made for an exciting bed-time story . . . but I think now you should tell me the rest of what happened in Jatharuj."

Oh dear. "Majesty? I don't—"

"Oh yes you do," she retorted. "Don't play games, Mister Jones. Don't treat me like a fool."

She was far from a fool. Not only was she her father's daughter, but the past long weeks had honed her instincts to a lethal edge.

He sighed. "It's true, I did leave out one detail of our adventure."

"And why would you do that?" she said, rounding on him. "After all we've been through, why would you lie?"

"I didn't lie!" he protested. "I just didn't tell you everything. It's not my place to tell you."

"Let me guess," she said wryly. "It's Zandakar's?"

"Yes."

She stared at the harbour again. "Then I suppose I should ask him."

"That would be best," he said, swallowing his relief.

Her sidelong glance this time was part irritation, part amusement. "I'd not attempt joining an acting troupe if I were you, Dexterity. Whatever you're feeling flies like a flag in your voice."

He had to smile. "Hettie used to say the same thing. She used to say, 'What a blessing you're an honest craftsman, my love. You couldn't hoodwink a customer if your life depended on it.'"

"Hettie . . ." Rhian sighed. "She said nothing beyond that you should go with Zandakar to Icthia?"

"Not a word."

"That's a pity."

"Yes," he agreed, heartfelt. Then, after a moment added, "Rhian, did you think we'd betrayed you? Me and Zandakar?"

Hot colour flooded her cheeks. "If I say yes, will you despise me? Will you feel betrayed, that I could doubt your loyalty a second time?"

He felt a pain, deep in his chest. "Not *despise*, but I'll admit to disappointment."

"I'm sorry," she said. "I didn't want to doubt you. Most of me didn't doubt you. But since the boys died I'm finding trust is something that's easily misplaced. If it's any consolation, I didn't doubt you for long."

Because they were alone, he put his hand on her shoulder. "I will never betray you, Rhian."

Smiling, she pressed her palm to his bearded cheek. "You know, Dexterity, I am so very sorry you lost your toy shop. When this is over we must arrange a new one for you."

When this is over I'll be lucky if I'm not dead. But

he didn't say it. Melancholy was too close to Rhian's surface, these days, for that kind of teasing.

He put a proper distance between them. "Zandakar won't betray you either, you know."

"Does that mean you think he'll tell me what happened in Jatharuj?"

"Yes."

"What makes you so sure?"

"Oh, Rhian," he said sadly. "He'd die for you without a second thought. Don't be a coy miss, and pretend not to know it."

Her face went blank. "I don't—" She released a sharp breath. "I have never encouraged him. I'm the queen. I'm married."

"It's not that simple. You danced into his heart long before we reached Linfoi."

"I didn't! I was friendly, nothing more!"

"Sometimes it doesn't take more," he said, still sad. "Hettie smiled at me once and I was lost to her forever."

"*I love Alasdair!* Mister Jones, you're talking *nonsense*!"

He sighed. "Majesty, you're an uncommon young woman. You've a sharp intellect, amazing courage, you're strong and proud and generous and quite beautiful. Not yet at your majority, and look what you've achieved. I've no doubt Ethrea's history will name an age after you. Speaking for myself, I am *humbled* to know you. But that's not to say you don't need guiding now and then. In this matter, *be guided*."

Now her cheeks were flushed with temper. "And if you're right, what of it? What do you suggest I do? It might make things easier for everyone if I were to banish Zandakar from court, but I can't do that, can I? We need him. I need him."

"You can need him, and use him for the good of Ethrea, and still have a care."

She flinched. "That would make me cruel."

"All monarchs are cruel, Rhian. Ruling is a cruel business, even in a kingdom as kindly as Ethrea."

Her eyebrows lifted. "And you think me capable of cruelty?"

"You'd have stood by and let Sun-dao destroy Jatharuj," he said. "If that's not cruel, Rhian, I don't know what is."

"Well," she said at last, after a long silence, and turned her attention back to the harbour. "I think I've detained you long enough, Mister Jones. I'll see you in the council meeting – but first, go to His Majesty. We must be . . . careful . . . in what we say about your journey to Icthia. He'll advise you on the most politic version."

He'd angered her. Hurt her. It couldn't be helped. Before he accepted his dismissal he said, "Ask Zandakar about Vortka, when next you see him. Make him tell you, Majesty. I think it's important."

"I dance my *hotas* with him in the hour before sunset," she said, sounding indifferent. "I'll ask him then. And if what he tells me has some purpose, I'll use it. I'll use him. Mijak must be stopped, no matter the cost."

And by the time this is over, we'll all have paid a heavy price. Dexterity nodded. "Majesty," he said, and left her to be solitary.

CHAPTER TWENTY-FIVE

The privy council listened with growing dismay to Dexterity's carefully worded account of what had befallen him and Zandakar in Jatharuj. The dukes were even more alarmed to learn that Rhian intended deepening Ethrea's ties with Tzhung-tzhungchai. Dexterity's recounting of Sundao's witch-man powers had them staring and gasping and exchanging alarmed glances.

"How can you be certain this Tzhung emperor is to be trusted?" said Edward, drumming his fingers on the table. "I tell you plainly, Majesty, I'm not easy about this."

"Nor am I," added Rudi. "The witch-men of Tzhung-tzhungchai are not natural. Do we peril our souls in letting their heathen magics assist us?"

"No, we do not," Rhian said sharply. "Given what we're facing, Rudi, Han's witch-men are a godsend."

Helfred looked up from his prayer beads. "That's not for you to say, Majesty."

The scratching of Ven'Cedwin's quill over a fresh sheet of parchment sounded loud as Rhian stared at him. As everyone stared at him.

"I beg your pardon, Helfred?" she said, with great care.

"Ethrea's spiritual well being is my province,

Majesty, not yours," he replied. "And I am troubled by the sorceries of Tzhung's witch-men."

"Why?" said Dexterity. "If their odd powers are used for good that must *be* good, surely."

"Perhaps," said Helfred, reserved. "But the Tzhung are not my only concern."

Around the council table, the dukes exchanged more eloquent looks. Rhian, temper simmering, let herself glance at Alasdair, beside her. He raised one eyebrow, cautioning restraint, then leaned forward.

"What else concerns you, Prolate?" he said, so polite. "Share your thoughts with us, please. You know your counsel is valued."

Rattle, rattle, rattle went Helfred's wooden prayer beads, sliding through his fingers. "Majesty, I cannot like this strange power shared by Zandakar and his murderous brother. What is its source? How is it created?"

"Does it matter?" said Ludo as the other dukes frowned. "If Zandakar's power can serve our cause?"

"Of course it matters!" said Helfred. "If the source of that power is shared . . . and if it's fed by the shedding of human blood in Mijak . . . how can we think to countenance its use? Would you wear clothes bought by coin from a murdered man's purse?"

"Not if I knew that's how they were purchased," Ludo retorted, offended. "And I hope you're not suggesting *I'd* murder for the coin!"

"No," said Helfred. "I'm not suggesting that, Your Grace. And nor would I have Ethrea gain from evil."

"There's no hint that the source of Zandakar's power is evil," Rhian protested. "His brother's, perhaps, but not Zandakar's. And neither is there proof that Han's witch-men are tainted. Mister Jones, did you see anything to suggest it?"

"No, Your Majesty," Dexterity said, after a moment. "What I witnessed was strange, but the only evil I saw belonged to Mijak."

"In your opinion," said Helfred, repressive. "The truth is, Mister Jones, we can't answer either question with certitude. So I will pray for God's guidance in the matter."

Rhian felt her jaw clench. *Helfred* . . . "Prolate, have you been listening? Or have the burdens of office scattered your wits? Mijak is coming with thousands of warriors. We have to stop them before they reach us, with any weapon we can find."

Helfred's stare was cool and uncompromising. "So you think now. But is it not possible the world contains greater evils than Mijak?"

"At the moment? No, I don't believe it does!"

He stood. "And I pray you are right. But given what we have learned of witch-men and their doings and what we know already of Zandakar's kin, I cannot say with a clear conscience that the Church will support the alliance you're suggesting with Tzhung-tzhungchai, or the use of Zandakar's unnatural knife. What manner of prolate would I be, if I counselled the saving of our bodies while condemning our souls to destruction?"

He was the most *inconvenient* man. "Helfred, Dexterity says—"

"Is Mister Jones your prolate?" said Helfred severely, not even glancing at her toymaker. His wooden prayer beads were wrapped tight around Helfred's hand. "I don't believe he is. God appointed *me* your prolate, Rhian. And I will serve him with a true heart. Rail and bully all you like, but I'll not be forced into supporting a decision my conscience tells me could be a grave mistake."

Rhian choked. Rail? Bully? What was he talking about, she wasn't a *tyrant*. She just didn't have time for this nonsense. None of them did.

"Where are you going?" she said as Helfred walked towards the chamber doors. "You don't have my permission to—"

"I have God's permission," said Helfred. "I return to my privy chapel, where I will ask for his guidance. Be sure I shall tell you when I have answers to the questions that vex me."

The doors closed behind him with a thud.

"The prolate is right," said Adric, breaking the stunned silence. "We tempt ruin, I think, to be so quick to embrace the powers of foreigners. Not when we can't say for sure those powers won't be used against us."

"Don't be ridiculous, Adric," she snapped. "Helfred's opposition is calamitous. If Helfred tells his venerables to preach against me in this, then—"

"He wouldn't do that," said Ludo quickly. "Would he? After everything that's happened, would he dare undermine you in such a public fashion?"

She looked at Alasdair, who shrugged. "He was your chaplain," he said. "Of us all you know him best."

I know he drove me to distraction from the moment we first met, which means nothing's changed. "I can't be sure of what he'll do. The Church for him has always been a vocation, not a path to secular power.

He's not a Marlan. He's not trying to undermine me. He really believes what he says." It was an effort not to press her palms to her face, but a gesture like that would be a sign of weakness. She kept her hands strong on the table. "If Helfred needs some time to reflect on this decision, I must grant it. But he can't have long. Events begin to outrun us."

"And if, after reflection, he says God is against a close alliance with the Tzhung?" asked Rudi.

She spared him a grim smile. "It might reward us to pray God says nothing of the sort, Rudi."

"There'll be no armada without the Tzhung," said Edward. "But either way, there's still the army."

With an effort, Rhian thrust the irritation of Helfred aside. "Yes. I've reviewed your various reports and suggestions, gentlemen, and there is much of merit contained therein. But what you have given me is a paper army. And a paper army can't defeat the warriors of Mijak."

"Then do we move forward?" said Edward. "Even though our spineless friends, the ambassadors, are yet to agree to us breaking the charter?"

Another silence fell, uncomfortable with the consequences of such a bold action.

"We can't wait for their permission," said Alasdair, at last. "We'll be slaughtered in our beds while they're still arguing amongst themselves."

Nods and exchanged glances as her dukes recognised the truth of Alasdair's contention. Dexterity sat quietly, his hands folded in his lap. No hint of his thoughts could be read in his face.

Rhian took a deep breath, her pulse racing. "We

move forward, gentlemen. Ethrea will have its flesh-and-blood army."

And may God protect us from Gutten, and the rest.

Soberly, Rudi turned to her. "Then you've a decision to make, Majesty. You must appoint the army's leader."

She nodded. "I know. And I've been giving the question careful thought."

From the corner of her eye she saw Alasdair sit a little straighter, his expression sharpening. *He knows what I'll say next. Oh, God, of course he knows. Alasdair's not stupid.*

Beyond the basic questions of who among her subjects would best be recruited, and how they could be housed, she and Alasdair had not discussed the army in depth. Between them, he, Edward and Rudi had far more experience in the business of garrisons and soldiers than she did. Leaving those details to him had been a relief.

And I've not discussed the army's leadership with him because I wanted the safety of the council chamber and a public declaration. Because I know my choice will hurt him. Because I'm a coward.

Rudi cleared his throat. "I applaud your foresight, Majesty, in considering this important matter. But I'd be remiss if I didn't voice one concern. You've proven your valour. There's not a man on this council – in all of Ethrea – who'd not gladly follow you into battle. But, Majesty, we can't. You can't appoint yourself leader of Ethrea's army. Your person is too precious. If you fall, so falls the kingdom."

Edward banged his fist on the table. "Indeed, well

said. You have dukes – or a king – who will take such a burden from your shoulders, Majesty. *You must* be a beacon to the people."

They were her two old warhorses. She smiled at them, unoffended. "I am sensible of my place in this. I'm a proud Havrell, it's true—" She spared Ludo a glance, then. "But not a foolish one, I trust. I have some ability with a knife, but that in no way equips me to train and lead an army. Indeed, gentlemen, there is only one man among us who possesses those skills. One man who has experienced war first-hand. One man who understands intimately the warriors of Mijak and will know how to counter their attack. *Zandakar*."

There was no point protesting at their protests. They were shouting so loud they'd never hear her, anyway. So she let their voices storm about her head, sat with her eyes closed and her hands loosely clasped until they pounded themselves into silence against her silence, at last. She didn't even look at Alasdair, whose replies to Ludo's agitated demands were soft, and restrained.

I'm sorry. I'm sorry. My love, I'm so sorry.

She opened her eyes. "My lords, this decision has nothing to do with how you are valued. I value each and every one of you, more than I can say. Only a fool would think otherwise. And only a fool would allow pride to blind him to the obvious merits of Zandakar's leadership."

Rudi snorted. "This has nothing to do with pride! I'm thinking of Ethrea. Leaving aside the small matter of Zandakar's loyalty—"

"No, I won't leave it aside, Rudi! Zandakar swore an oath in *blood* to me!"

"And when he had the chance to rejoin his people in Jatharuj, he didn't take it," added Dexterity. "He returned to Ethrea. If that's not loyalty, I don't know what is."

With a glance at his silent, kingly cousin, Ludo cleared his throat. "I may be alone in this opinion, but I don't dispute Zandakar's loyalty. And I agree he's the only man among us with the skills to train out soldiers how to fight and kill a Mijaki warrior. But we must consider the impression this would create. To give leadership of our army to a foreigner, to the son of—"

Rhian silenced him with a lifted hand. "Ludo – gentlemen – this complaining is a waste of our time. The truth, unpalatable as it may be, is there's not a one of you capable of leading an army to face the kind of bloodshed that's waiting for us. If I don't choose Zandakar, I'll have to find leadership amongst the trading nations. *They* go to war with each other as though it's a sport. The humblest sword-sharpener in Haisun's army knows more of killing warfare than every one of you combined. Can you deny it?"

She watched her dukes look at each other, watched her arguments deflate their prideful pretensions. When her gaze touched Dexterity he nodded, so very slightly, his eyes warm with approval. A strange thing, that a toymaker unschooled in the business of warfare and politics could see so clearly where her dukes appeared blind.

She didn't dare look at Alasdair.

"It would be Arbenia I'd have to turn to," she continued, driving home her merciless point. "Or Harbisland. For you can be sure they'd not accept the ascendancy of a lesser trading nation. And if I gave an Ethrean army to Han, well, we'd swiftly find ourselves facing enemies on *three* sides. Besides, choosing any of the great trading nations must be unacceptable. We'll use all of them when and where we can, because we need them, but they must *never* come to think we're in their special debt."

More harsh truth, just as difficult to swallow. But even as she continued to watch her dukes, she saw reluctant resignation wash away resistance. Saw them accept, if not with good grace, that they had no other choice but to support her stand.

"Gentlemen," she said, "you must know I don't take this decision lightly. You must know it was never my intention to make you feel slighted. What I do, I do for Ethrea. Nothing else matters."

"Certainly," said Edward, grudging, "the trading nations must be kept at arm's length. And Zandakar is the best placed to understand how that heathen Mijaki horde thinks."

"Exactly. And to that end he'll henceforth join our council meetings which must, from now on, be councils of war."

"What of Hartshorn and Meercheq?" said Rudi. "They still have no dukes to govern their garrisons."

She hesitated, then answered. "I know. But I can't settle that question yet. If my worst fears are realised, if we find ourselves fighting Mijak on Ethrean soil, we'll not escape losses. I think it's best that I wait . . ."

"And make your choices from whoever survives

the carnage?" said Ludo. "Assuming, of course, that we prevail. Majesty, that is cold reasoning indeed."

"And doubtless unfeminine," she snapped. "But you must admit it's practical."

"It is," said Edward. "It's a good decision. Harsh, but necessary. What do these times demand if not harsh, necessary decisions?"

God bless him. "That's all they ask of us, Edward. And I can't see but that they'll only get harsher from this point."

"If you're not naming the new dukes yet, Majesty," said Adric, "who's to command those dukeless garrisons?"

Not you, my bonny lad, so quench the gleam in your eye. "Ah," she said. "Now that was an easy choice, one of the few." At last, at long last, she shifted in her seat to look at Alasdair. "His Majesty, naturally. There's no man in Ethrea who enjoys my greater trust. Zandakar will answer to him for the safety and well being of our kingdom's soldiery."

"Of course," said Edward, before Adric could speak. "A wise choice, Your Majesty."

Did Alasdair think so? His expression was smooth, his eyes held no emotion. Whatever he was feeling had been thrust deep inside. She wondered if deep inside, he were bleeding. Whether she had wounded him. Wounded them. And if she had, if they were wounds past healing.

Will there ever come a time when I can be both wife and queen? Or was I mad even to attempt it? Was Alasdair mad, to marry me?

"My lords," she said, bullying her voice to remain steady, "I need you to send word to your duchy garrison commanders. Warn them that something is about to start. No details, just have them collect their men in readiness. Whoever has been granted leave, have them recalled. And be sure that the garrison smithies set to work around the clock. We must have at hand as much armour and weapons as we can forge between now and our worst fears coming true."

"You intend to tell the kingdom of the danger we're facing?" said Rudi, frowning.

"Not yet. But soon. Very soon, I think."

A sombre hush. A frisson of fear, fleeting and cold.

"There'll be panic," said Edward. "I can't see how there won't be."

"I know," she said, nodding. "Even with Helfred's clergy doing their best to urge calm, people will be frightened. But if we can't halt Mijak on the ocean then we *will* be fighting here, at home. So my soldiers and my subjects must soon begin their martial training." She heard the tremor in her voice. "They must learn how to kill."

"A harsh lesson indeed," murmured Ludo. "It breaks my heart to think of it."

Yours and mine, too, Ludo. Rhian forced a confident smile. "Yes, it's a grim prospect, but let's not race towards our darkest fears quite yet. I, for one, still have hope for our armada. And on that note, gentlemen, I think we're done for the moment."

As her dukes stirred, and Ven'Cedwin put down his quill with a sigh, she gestured to Dexterity. He leaned close. "Tarry," she murmured. "I'd have a private word."

The dukes were waiting for Alasdair to depart first. His hand resting lightly on Ludo's shoulder, his face still so well-schooled she couldn't see what he was thinking, he left the chamber without a word or a look for his queen. The others followed them out, with Ven'Cedwin hurriedly last to leave.

"Don't fret, child," said Dexterity, softly. "Your Alasdair's a proud young man. He's still making sense of how to be a consort king."

It wasn't at all the way he should address his queen in the privy council chamber, but she was too grateful for his kindness to protest. "I'm still trying to make sense of this new life," she said, when she could trust her voice. "*Garbled* sense, I begin to think."

Because they were alone now, his hand closed over hers. "Don't worry. He supports you, and always will."

Gently she eased her hand from beneath his. "Yes. Which is more than I can say for Helfred. I swear I could throttle him. Horrible, *horrible* little man."

"Oh, not quite so horrible, surely," Dexterity protested. "On the whole I find him much improved since our time on the road."

Rhian stared, then burst out laughing. "Oh, Dexterity. You do cheer me up, you always have." Then she sobered. "Will you go to him? I must have Helfred on my side, or any hope of the armada is lost. And there's no point me attempting to make him see sense. I couldn't dissuade him from trying to save his wretched uncle, and I'll not change his mind on this, either. But you might."

"I don't know," he said, doubtful. "I can try. I will try. But you know Helfred."

"And I know *you*." She managed a smile. "You're my man of miracles. Please, Dexterity. You must convince him. The fate of the kingdom might well depend on it."

He sighed. "Majesty, I'll do my best."

Dexterity had never been in the prolate's palace before. Standing in its enormous entry hall, he stared astonished at the gilded walls, the intricately mosaic-tiled floor with its depiction of martyred Rollin, the magnificent stained glass windows, the gold and jewel sconces housing the Living Flame. It didn't seem right, somehow, that this place should be more opulent, more extravagant, than Kingseat royal castle.

Rhian is our jewel, she should be housed in such a setting, not a gaggle of venerables. Surely a house of God should be a shining example of restraint and piety and worship, not – not self-aggrandisement.

Was it always like this, or had Marlan spent his years in office primping and preening and *decorating* himself?

As he stared, his mouth open, he gradually became aware that others were staring at him. Venerables. Chaplains. Devouts. Novices. Their bustling had stopped and now they just stood there with the *most* extraordinary looks on their faces.

One of the venerables approached him. "Sir, do I address Mister Jones? Mister *Dexterity* Jones?" He exhaled slowly. "The burning man?"

He realised, then, that some of his unexpected audience was regarding him with *fear*. That they held their breaths, anticipating . . . what?

That I'll burst into flames and burn the prolate's palace down around their ears?

Oh dear. Disconcerted, he nodded. "Well, I'll admit to being Mister Jones, the toymaker. And you are—"

"Ven'Norbert. How may I serve you?"

"Serve me?" he said, startled. "I don't need serving, Ven'Norbert. I just need to find the prolate."

"His Eminence is sequestered in his privy chapel," said the venerable. "Doubtless to deny you is a heinous sin, but His Eminence was emphatic."

A *sin*? "Ven'Norbert, I've not come to make a spectacle of myself," he said, his voice lowered. "Or to cause trouble. But I do need to see the prolate, on a matter of state."

Anguished, Ven'Norbert pulled a face. "Perhaps I should send for a member of the Court Ecclesiastica."

He had no *time* for this. *Oh, Hettie. How have I become this man?* He stepped a little closer to the conflicted venerable, and lowered his voice even further. "Ven'Norbert, Blessed Rollin has sent me."

Ven'Norbert gasped. "Mister Jones!" He made the sign of Rollin, kissing his thumb so hard he looked in danger of breaking it. "You should have said so at once!"

Hot with shame, Dexterity followed the white-faced venerable to the sweeping staircase, up the first flight of stairs, the second, the third. They climbed more stairs to the fourth floor, and then Ven'Norbert led him along a red-carpeted corridor, his leather sandals thumping softly. At the end of the corridor was an imposing gilded door. Ven'Norbert stopped and turned.

"The prolate's privy chapel," he said. "I don't dare enter, Mister Jones."

Dexterity nodded. "All right. Thank you. Ah – God's blessings on you, Venerable Norbert."

"And on you," said Ven'Norbert, faintly. He seemed dazed.

Dexterity opened the gilded door and entered Helfred's privy chapel.

First, like the proletary palace, there was an opulent foyer. Mosaics, paintings, a single Living Flame, and an intricately carved and gilded wooden screen. Dexterity slipped around it, searching for Helfred.

Rhian's unlikely prolate knelt before the Living Flame at the far end of the chapel proper, which was so opulently decorated, as to be oppressive. Helfred looked positively incongruous, dressed in the rough, unadorned robe of the kingdom's most humble chaplain.

Even Ven'Norbert had looked more proletary than Helfred.

"I can only imagine," said Helfred, "that the palace threatens to tumble round our ears. There can be no other reason for this rude interruption when I *expressly* forbade—"

"It's me, Helfred," said Dexterity.

Helfred slewed round, ungainly. "Mister Jones? What do you do here? Is Rhian—"

"Naught's amiss with our queen," he said. "Though she does fret on you."

Helfred grimaced. "She'd do better fretting on herself."

"Oh, she does that too."

There was a single pew in the small, exquisite chapel. He sat down, uninvited, and considered the holy flame in its sconce.

Helfred grunted to his feet. "I suppose she sent you?" He didn't sit down. With tired eyes and a peevish expression he stood before the altar, feet wide and fists on his hips, projecting an image of authority at odds with his plain, roughspun robes. His wooden prayer beads dangled from his cord belt.

Dexterity let his gaze roam the overwrought chapel. "How can you pray in this place, Helfred? The amount of gilt is blinding. I've a pain behind my eyes and I've sat in here scant minutes."

"What do you want, Dexterity? This is my privy chapel, not the high street of Kingseat township."

"I want to talk, Helfred."

"About what?"

"It's odd, isn't it?" Dexterity mused. "Where life has brought us. I tell you, not a day goes by that I don't know whether to be humbled or horrified by all that's happened." He pulled a face. "Though I must confess, *horrified* usually wins. The things we've seen, Helfred. Rollin save us, the things we've done. The choices we've made. That we're yet to make. It's all so daunting."

Helfred sniffed. "Rhian wants you to convince me to brush aside my qualms about Zandakar and Tzhung-tzhungchai, doesn't she? She wants me to embrace him and those witch-men like long-lost loved brothers."

Dexterity picked at the fraying edge of his bandage. "She didn't say *that*, precisely. But yes, she is worried by your sudden concerns."

"I am Prolate of Ethrea!" snapped Helfred. "It's my spiritual duty to be concerned!"

"You didn't seem concerned when I burst into

flames that first time," he said, mild as milk. "As I recall, you proclaimed it a miracle. A sign from God."

"Because it was! Do you deny it now?"

"No."

"Then why are you here? Why do you disturb me as I seek divine guidance?"

"Because Rhian's right, Helfred. And you're wrong."

Helfred clasped his hands and began to pace before the altar, agitated and dismayed. "I don't believe so. The soul of every Ethrean must surely be perilled if we truck with heathen magics, be they wielded by Zandakar or by Han's witch-men."

"Helfred, God wouldn't have sent Zandakar to us, or the witch-men, if he didn't desire them to help us defeat Mijak!"

"So you say," said Helfred, still pacing. "But you might be mistaken. You're not a prolate, you're a toy-maker."

Dexterity gritted his teeth. "And not so long ago you were a chaplain. I swear, you begin to sound like your uncle."

Helfred turned on him. "That is a *dreadful* thing to say!"

"And Marlan was a dreadful thing to be. Helfred, put aside your self-consequence and *listen* to me. I tell you straightly, in this matter you are *wrong*."

Offended. Helfred stood there and wrestled with his pride, or his conscience, or both. At last his shoulders slumped and his fingers sought the comforting reassurance of his wooden prayer beads. "Wrong how?" he asked, grudging. "Do you care to explain?"

Oh, Hettie. Let me be doing the right thing, please.

"Well," he said, "all right. But you must promise not to repeat this. I've not told anyone, not even Rhian."

"Really?" said Helfred, his curiosity piqued. "Why not?"

"Hettie said I shouldn't, but I think I need to make an exception. For if you don't support Rhian, Helfred, I fear Ethrea will be doomed."

"Very well," said Helfred, after a moment. "I'll not repeat it . . . but I'll not promise to change my mind, either."

Dexterity swallowed a sigh. At least Helfred was listening. "There is no God of Mijak. Zandakar's *chalava* doesn't exist. At least, not in the way he and the others think it does. Mijak's priests have mistaken a dark supernatural force for a deity. The blood of their sacrifices feeds it, and gives them the power to do abominable things. It also deludes them into thinking they obey their god when they conquer other nations."

Helfred's eyes had widened. "Does Zandakar know this?"

"I'm not certain if he knows all of it," he said slowly. "But he knows enough. That's why we can trust him to fight for us. As much as he wants to help Ethrea, he's desperate to save his own people from this terrible lie. To save all the innocents who'd be destroyed by Mijak."

"A laudable ambition," said Helfred, "but what you say only strengthens my resolve. Zandakar is Mijaki, he *must* be using their dark power to—"

"And what of Han's witch-men? *They* don't dabble in blood sacrifices, do they?" Dexterity persisted. "And Sun-dao *died* fighting Mijak, Helfred."

Helfred turned away, clutching his prayer beads so hard his fingers turned white. "Perhaps. But—"

"Helfred, there's only one thing to consider here," he said, standing. "Mijak *must* be defeated. *Human sacrifice*, Prolate! Can you *imagine*?"

"I've been trying not to," Helfred whispered. "My stomach revolts at the very thought."

"Well, I was in Jatharuj, Helfred. I don't have to imagine, I smelled it. Sometimes I think I'll never rid myself of the stench. In Jatharuj, in my dreams of Garabatsas, I have *seen* evil's true face . . . and I promise you, I *promise*, it doesn't look like Zandakar or the witch-men of Tzhung-tzhungchai."

"Then how do you explain what they do?" cried Helfred, anguished.

Dexterity shrugged. "I don't. I can't. Any more than I can explain what I've done. All I can do is trust that Hettie wouldn't ask me to put my faith in evil."

Helfred began to pace again. "It may be simple for you, Dexterity, but it is not so for me! *I was a chaplain*! I counselled Rhian, I did my uncle's bidding, I had no thought of high office. No expectation. No *desire*. I studied the *Admonitions*, I tried to keep my soul pure. I never asked for the keeping of every soul in Ethrea! Who am I to decide these things? Who am I to know if Zandakar and the Tzhung will taint us or save us, or if they will taint us by saving us and in saving us destroy us. *Who am I to know*?"

Helfred's distress was genuine, and heartbreaking. Gone the pompous chaplain, gone the assured sermoniser from the pulpit. He stood before the Living

Flame with his soul stripped bare, revealing himself a young man, a doubting man, a man faltering beneath his impossible burden.

Dexterity went to him and laid a hand on his shoulder. "You're the man God chose to be Rhian's prolate," he said gently. "Are you saying God made the wrong choice, Helfred?"

Helfred stared at him, his eyes haunted. "Sometimes I think he did. Yes."

"Well, I don't. What I *do* think, Helfred, is we should open our eyes to wider horizons. Just because Zandakar and Han's witch-men aren't like us doesn't mean they don't serve God. I mean, who are we to decide how God is served?"

"A sound point," said Helfred. "Rollin speaks often of humility in belief. You truly think they serve God, Dexterity?"

"Yes, Helfred. I do."

"And you're against me denying Rhian their help? You think doing that would be a sin?"

He shrugged. "I don't know about a sin, Helfred. But I certainly think it'd be a mistake."

"Well," said Helfred. "You've certainly given me a great deal to think on, Mister Jones. Alas, any further reflection must wait. I have to prepare for this evening's Litany in the great chapel. Will you attend?"

"Ah . . ." Dexterity considered him. "That depends upon whether you'll be denouncing Her Majesty's alliance with Tzhung-tzhungchai, Prolate."

"I denounce nothing," said Helfred, staring now at the softly burning Living Flame. "I await God's whisper in my heart."

He stifled a sigh. He'd been looking forward to a quiet evening's whittling. But if attending Litany would remind Helfred of this conversation . . .

"Then I'll be there, Prolate. You have my word."

CHAPTER TWENTY-SIX

Day was drifting to dusk when Rhian met with Zandakar in the torchlit tiltyard, alone. She'd ordered his soldier escort to stand guard along the path and turn back any nobles or courtiers thinking to observe their sparring *hotas*. Tonight she wanted a breath of time where she and Zandakar could talk privately. Honestly. And yes, dance the *hotas* together. Dear God, how she'd missed that.

He was there before her, dressed in deerhide leggings and a plain linen shirt. She'd wondered if he'd dance with the scorpion knife he'd brought back from Jatharuj, but no. It was the same plain hunting blade she'd given him to dance with, over Alasdair's objections.

He straightened out of a stretch as she approached, and watched her walk towards him. Lean and supple in her own battered leathers, she halted at an arm's-length distance and looked up into his smooth, unsmiling face.

He nodded. "We begin *hotas*, *zho*?"

Unsheathing her blade, she nodded back. "We begin. *Zho*."

As though they'd never been parted, as though they'd danced only that morning, they fell into the easy rhythms of the first *hotas*.

Rhian let her muscles relax, sought her calm centre, that place she'd discovered where the world went away and all she knew was her breathing, her heartbeat, the flow of blood through her veins. Eyes half-closed, barely glancing at Zandakar, she released her gathered tension in a cleansing exhalation.

"You hardly said a word last night, after we found you," she commented. "Only what you had to, and only when you were asked. I swear, it was like pulling teeth. I know you're not a chatterbox, but still. A simple *thank you* might've been nice."

His eyes glinted as he shifted his stance from *the ibis, sleeping* to *the sandcat, waking*. Long, fluid muscles worked beneath his skin. "Thank you."

Time to take Dexterity's advice. "The man who gave you that scorpion knife. Vortka. Who is he to you?"

Sandcat, waking shifted to *snake, coiling*. "It matters?"

"I'm curious."

Instead of answering, he tapped the side of her thigh with his knife blade. "More stretch."

She hissed between her teeth and pushed her toes forward another inch. "Vortka, Zandakar."

He tapped again. "More, Rhian."

"What?" she said, glaring. "You want to split me in half?" With a grunt, she pushed herself another inch. "There. And that is *all*."

With an ease that never failed to delight and aggravate, he shifted his stance again and turned a perfect, slow-motion cartwheel. Hand, hand, foot, foot. Then flowed straight again into *the ibis, sleeping*, his control complete.

With a shaming lack of the same elegance, she followed his example. When she stood upright again, she looked at him. "Dexterity said you didn't try and talk to your mother because this Vortka convinced you he had a better hope of changing her mind about sailing from Icthia. Is that true?"

"*Zho,*" said Zandakar, and watched her overbalance out of her one-legged *ibis* stance.

Cheeks burning, she turned a second, more pleasing cartwheel. "Well. That's most unfortunate, given what happened to those poor slaves."

Zandakar bent double, stretching, and looked at her upside down, between his knees, saying nothing. Something unsettling gleamed in his eyes. He didn't need words to tell her Vortka was . . . special.

But why? How? And what does it mean for Ethrea?

Feeling more limber, trusting her warmer muscles, she began surging into her lunges, first the left leg and then the right. "I meant what I said, you know. About letting Sun-dao destroy Jatharuj. You shouldn't have stopped him, Zandakar. This could all be over now, if you hadn't stopped him."

He unfolded, and flicked her with a cold blue glance before whipping into a series of spinning turns on one foot, knife-hand stretched straight and high above him.

"*Wei*. Han say—"

"I know what Han said," she retorted, puffing a little. "Clearly he was wrong. Sun-dao did start calling up a storm. If you hadn't interfered, he might have finished what he started."

Zandakar stopped spinning. Shrugged. *Perhaps.* Then he turned another perfect cartwheel. Still pushing through her lunges, driving her heels into the ground as though she crushed an enemy's throat, Rhian felt the sweat begin to prickle through her heating skin.

"How do you do it?" she asked abruptly. "How do you make blue fire come from that knife?"

He dropped into his own sequence of lunges . . . but not in his usual position, directly opposite. This time he had his back to her. Avoided her.

"Zandakar, *answer* me," she said, not ceasing her *hotas.* "I've a right to know. You sleep beneath my roof. You eat food from my table. I keep you safe. I want to *know.*"

Silence, broken only by their deep, steady breathing as they lunged. Then he grunted. "*Chalava.*"

Oh no. Was Helfred right? Holding her own lunge extended, Rhian wiped suddenly damp palms down her leather leggings. "Your god gives you the power? The same god that drinks human blood?"

Awkwardly, Zandakar wrenched himself round to face her. "*Wei.* Human blood evil. *Chalava wei* want human blood." His clenched fist struck his chest. "*Chalava wei* evil. *Chalava* good. Hekat wrong. Zandakar wrong, thinking *chalava* want death." He stared past her, into the falling night, his breathing harsh and distressed. "Zandakar wrong."

With the sky fast losing its light, the tiltyard's torches were throwing shadows. In the nearby stables horses whinnied and kicked, demanding their supper oats. The grooms' voices drifted overhead, chiding and cheerful, starkly contrasted with Zandakar's pain.

"Well, if you were wrong before, you're right now," she said gently. "In helping us defeat Mijak, you're right."

"*Zho*," he whispered, and resumed his *hotas*.

Resisting the urge to push for more answers, she followed his lead. Now they were ready, they began the set movements of each dancing *hota*, when with exquisite control they traced every pattern as though the air was thick syrup. It was the part of her training she tended to gloss over when she was alone.

Of course Zandakar noticed that right away. Even distressed, he noticed it. He would make a formidable leader of Ethrea's army.

"*Tcha*!" he said, and slapped the back of her head. "Rhian lazy, Rhian think *hotas* for pride, *zho*?"

The blow was hard enough to really hurt. "*Wei*," she said crossly. "I never show off. I might – well, I might get a bit *bored*, sometimes, but—"

"*Tcha*," he said again, and again gave her a slap. "Bored?"

"All right, all right," she muttered. "Slow *hotas*. I can do them." Easing herself into *the eagle, stooping*, she flicked him a look. "But only if you answer this. The gauntlet Dexterity saw, in his dreams of Garabatsas. Does it work like that knife? The power goes from you into the gauntlet and comes out as fire?"

Zandakar's face tightened. "*Zho*."

Rhian thought he was remembering something, then. Something unpleasant. *One of the cities he de-*

stroyed, when he wore that gauntlet? I can't begin to understand how it must feel, to wield that kind of power. Is it frightening? It must be frightening. She wanted to ask, but the bleak look in his eyes discouraged her. So she asked something else instead.

"The stone scorpion, Zandakar. Tell me about it."

For the very first time since they'd started dancing *hotas* together, Zandakar stumbled and nearly dropped his blade. Gathering himself, his pale blue eyes narrowed, he stared at her. "You know."

"I know what Dexterity saw," Rhian replied. "What did you feel? What is the stone scorpion?"

"*Chalava,*" he said, after a moment, and resumed his slow *hotas*. "*Chalava* in scorpion. Scorpion kill wicked men."

Dexterity had told her and Alasdair that much last night, after Han's palanquin had returned them to the castle. Still she found it hard to believe. "And it tried to kill you?"

Instead of answering, he slapped her again. "*Hotas,* Rhian."

She eased herself once more into her slow-motion dancing. "Zandakar. Was Dexterity right? Did your *chalava* try to kill you?"

A sharp nod. "*Zho.*"

"But why, if you're obeying it by being here, by stopping Mijak? Zandakar, what *happened*?"

He stopped his slow *hotas*. His eyes wide, his face unmasked to her, he breathed out hard. "Scorpion sting. Pain." She saw the memory of it shudder through him, and his fingers clenched tight. "I feel *chalava, zho*? Hot. Angry." His fist beat his chest. "*Hate*. Then I feel cool, I hear voice." Now his fingers spread lightly above his heart. "Na'ha'leima voice, *zho*? Gentle. Kind. *Wei* pain. I live."

She closed her fingers on his arm. "And I'm glad you did. Whose voice was it?"

He shrugged. "In Na'ha'leima I thought *chalava*."

"But in Jatharuj *chalava* tried to kill you. Whoever you heard, it can't have been *chalava*. Zandakar, I think it was God. In Jatharuj, and in Na'ha'leima. The God of Ethrea doesn't want you to kill. God wants you to live, and help me save the world from Mijak."

Hotas forgotten, blade dangling from his fingers, Zandakar stared at her. "You trust Zandakar to help? I kill thousands. Much blood. Sinning man, *zho*?"

"The past is past. I care for what you *will* do, not what you've done." She released his arm. "Zandakar . . . who is Vortka? Why should I trust him the way I trust you?"

Abruptly, as though his legs were suddenly too weak to bear his full weight, Zandakar dropped to a crouch. She sheathed her blade and crouched with him, fingertips resting lightly on his knee. He looked at her, in the tiltyard's torchlight his eyes hauntingly blue. His hair blue, so unnatural, and yet such a part of him.

"Vortka is father."

Rhian heard herself gasp. "*Your* father?"

"*Zho.*"

He'd told her his father was the ruler of Mijak, a man who died when he was a boy. The day his brother Dmitrak was born.

"Rhian," he said, seeing her sudden doubt. "Before Jatharuj I *wei* know."

Believing him, doubt faded . . . but that still left her with anger. Selfish bastard. Selfish *bastard*. The fury of last night was returning, tenfold.

It's all the same, isn't it? Whether it's his long-lost father he's trying to save, or his mother, or his brother, he still put himself above everyone else. He's still risked countless Ethrean families, just to save his own.

But then she couldn't help wondering . . .

Would I sacrifice Papa? Ranald? Simon?

And couldn't answer the question.

"Rhian," said Zandakar. His voice was gentle. Almost . . . nervous. "*Wei* kill Vortka in Jatharuj. Vortka hear Ethrea God, *zho*? He stop Yuma, stop Dmitrak. Stop Mijak."

She stared at him, incredulous. "Yes, I *know* that was your brilliant plan, but he *didn't* stop them, did he? Your mother murdered those ten thousand slaves and broke the witch-men's hold on the trade winds. Witch-men died too, Zandakar! Witch-men who could help us. And now your mother's coming to Ethrea, with your brother and her warriors. And for all I know your father will be cheering for them from the gallery!"

Zandakar stood, and turned away. "Vortka knows killing wrong, *zho*? He knows *chalava* wrong. He is *chalava-hagra*, he will stop Mijak." He turned back, his face fierce. "You trust me, Rhian? I trust Vortka. All my life, Vortka is *gajka*. If Zandakar is good man, you thank Vortka, *zho*? I *wei* kill him. *Wei* for Ethrea. *Wei* for you."

Slowly she stood, her gaze not leaving his face. "I understand that you love him. But Zandakar—"

He seized her shoulders in a painful grip. "Understand? *Wei*. Vortka kind to me. Kind to Dimmi. I love Yuma, *zho*? But she is – she is—" One hand released her and clenched tight in a fist. "Hard."

Hard. Was that the right word? Surely *monstrous* was a more fitting description for Hekat. And what could be made of the son who loved her? How could *any* decent man love a woman capable of all the dreadful things she'd done?

I don't understand him. Not even Helfred loved Marlan. Felt duty towards him, some cold familial feeling, but not love. Yet Zandakar loves his murderous mother.

"Zandakar." Rhian cleared her throat. "You may be right. Vortka might stop Mijak in time. God knows, I hope he does. But if he *doesn't* . . . if Mijak comes to Ethrea . . . you must dance your *hotas* against Yuma and Dmitrak. Can you do that? If you can't, you have to tell me. You have to tell me *now*. I want to make you the leader of our army. I want you to be *chotzu* for Ethrea, *zho*? But if you can't lead an army against your family . . ."

Oh, God. If he can't, we might as well cut our own throats now.

He nodded. "Zho, Rhian. I dance *hotas* against Yuma. Against Dimmi."

"Are you *sure*? Because after tonight, there's no going back."

"I am sure," he said. She could see the heartbreak in his eyes. "*Chalava* wrong. Vortka knows. I know. Blood must stop. Killing must stop. Rhian, Zandakar is *chotzu* for Ethrea. *Zho*."

Rhian felt herself shiver, even though the early night was still warm. The last of her anger faded. "I was so afraid, when you disappeared. I thought I was alone."

"*Wei*," said Zandaka softly. "Rhian *hushla wei* alone."

Swamped with sudden fear, she barely heard him. "Oh, sweet Rollin save me," she said, appalled. "Mijak is coming. And now I have to convince the world's greatest rulers to surrender their sovereignty to Ethrea, and trust Tzhung-tzhungchai. Trust in powers none of us understand. How can I hope to convince them, Zandakar? Why should they believe *me*? Why should they even listen? My accession's been little more than street theatre to them."

"They will listen," said Zandakar. "You are Rhian *hushla*. You are Queen of Ethrea. God sees you. *God sees you*."

She feasted her eyes upon his severe face, her soul on the conviction in his voice.

He believes in me. He believes. With all he has seen, with all he has done. With the power that's in him, to call blue fire from a blade . . . Zandakar believes in me.

"It would help them to believe me if you were there, too," she said, when she could trust her voice. "Will you come with me to Arbenia and Harbisland? Will you show them Mijak in your scorpion knife? Will you help me convince them the danger is real?"

"*Zho*," he said, without hesitation. "You command, I obey, Rhian *hushla*." And then he smiled, all heartbreak banished, and lightly smacked the side of her head. "Talk, talk, talk. *Tcha*. We come to dance *hotas*. Dance *hotas* now, *zho*?"

She laughed, feeling more cheerful than she had a right to, surely. And then she danced.

An hour later it was past time to stop. Soaked in sweat, purged – for good, she hoped – of self-doubt and fear, her blade sheathed again, Rhian pressed her fist to her heart in a gesture of thanks, pupil to teacher.

"The council meets tomorrow morning, Zandakar. You will be there. You are one of my councillors now, as *chotzu* of Ethrea. *Zho*?"

He nodded. "*Zho*, Rhian *hushla*."

"What?" she said, seeing something in his eyes. *Please, God, don't let him be having second thoughts.* "Is something the matter?"

"I want—" He frowned. "I think you say *favour*."

She considered him, wary. "Yes?"

"*Wei* speak of Vortka, Rhian. To council. To Alasdair king." His hand touched his heart, as though it hurt him. "Secret, *zho*? Me. You. Dexterity. Secret."

In silence she stared at him. What would it hurt? What difference would it make, if no-one else knew the Mijaki priest Vortka was Zandakar's father?

None, I'm sure. Others knowing is more likely to cause me trouble.

But did she want to keep secrets from Alasdair?

If Ludo told him something in confidence, he'd keep that secret. This is no different. This is me helping a friend.

"I can do that," Rhian said. "You have my word."

Zandakar nodded. It was almost a bow. "Thank you."

"You're welcome." She pulled a face. "Now I must bathe, and eat, and plan our strategy for wooing Arbenia and Harbisland. Just in case your scorpion knife fails to impress."

They turned to leave the tiltyard . . . and she saw Alasdair, leaning over a railing, watching them. She felt her heart leap. He was close enough for her to see his face, but not so close that he could have heard her conversation with Zandakar. Thank God. In the torchlight he seemed calm. Composed. He didn't look angry, or jealous, or resentful.

"Go," she said to Zandakar, in an undertone. "I'll see you here again at first light, for *hotas*. *Zho*?"

"*Zho*," he replied, and withdrew swiftly. A nod to Alasdair, in passing. A nod in return, no words exchanged.

She joined her husband. "I didn't realise you were there."

"I know," he said. "You get so lost in your *hotas*." He smiled, just a little. Affection tinged with awe . . . and regret. "Every time I see you dance them, it seems you're faster. Fiercer. A little further away."

"Not so far," she said, framed his face with her hands and kissed him, hard. "Never too far."

His hands came up to cover hers. "My love . . ." He grimaced. "You stink."

"Such a gallant king I have!" she said, pretending hurt feelings. Then she lowered her hands, sliding her fingers to grasp his. "My heart is quite o'erthrown."

He smiled again, but his amusement swiftly faded.

"You know you've missed yet another of Helfred's public Litanies? He's bound to be peeved with you."

"Well, since I'm already peeved with him that'll make us equal, won't it?" She bit her lip. "If he dares not support me in supporting Tzhung-tzhungchai . . ."

"He'll support you."

"You're sure of it?" she said, hopeful. "Have you been talking with Dexterity? Does *he* say Helfred—"

"He says Helfred is giving the question serious thought," said Alasdair. "But truly, Rhian, how can our prolate not support you? After all he's witnessed, after all he's done to see you safely on the throne?"

"Trust me, Alasdair, Helfred is capable of anything. I'm the one who knows him best, remember?"

Alasdair released her hands, and rested his forearms along the top of the tiltyard railing separating them. "You were right, appointing Zandakar to lead Ethrea's army."

"Truly? You understand?"

He nodded, not looking at her. "Yes. Of course. He's the only sensible choice."

She searched his expression for signs he only placated her, but all she could see in him was resigned acceptance. She was relieved . . . yet somehow stricken. Would it be easier if he were angry? Had her choice somehow diminished him?

Please, God, let me not have diminished him. Let him not have become less than himself because he married me.

"Zandakar leads only in matters of training," she said. "If it should fall out that Ethrea and Mijak must face each other on some single field of battle, then you'll ride out first as King of Ethrea."

His gaze shifted. "And you'll not ride out at all? I have your word on that, Rhian?"

"Yes," she said, reluctant. Resenting the question. Resenting the notion that she must be *protected*. "You have my word. Alasdair . . . do you still mistrust Zandakar?"

For a long time he stayed silent, his eyes shadowed. Nightbirds flew above them, their pinions creaking in the evening's hush. A scudding of clouds began to blot out the stars. There might be rain tonight, or perhaps tomorrow.

At last he shook his head. "No, I don't mistrust him. I believe he wishes Ethrea to survive."

"You sound sad. Are you sad? Do I make you unhappy, Alasdair?"

Instead of looking into her eyes, he stared across the tiltyard, to the shadowed bulk of the castle stables. "No."

"I think I do. I think—"

"No, you don't," he said gently. "It's true I feel sad . . . but that's not your doing. Not precisely. And not on purpose, I do know that."

She stepped back from the railing and folded her arms. "Tell me."

He sighed. "I am your subject as well as your husband, Rhian. I might want to take the weight of this realm from your shoulders, but I can't. There are times when I can help you bear it, and I will, as best I can, but it's your burden. I understand that now."

"You didn't, before?"

He picked at a splinter in the wooden railing, then

smoothed it with the timber's grain. He was frowning, his eyes unfocused.

"My whole life I prepared to be Duke of Linfoi. Of all Ethrea's great nobles, the least. The most despised. Poor duchy Linfoi, with so little to recommend it." He smiled. "But Linfoi was my birthright. I was proud, knowing one day I'd be its duke. And then I came to court, to represent my father on the privy council. I was befriended by Ranald . . . and bewitched by Ranald's sister. I knew she was, oh, so high above me, beyond dreaming, but that didn't stop me. Still, I dreamed of her. And to my astonished delight, she dreamed of me."

"Alasdair, I—" Rhian began, then stopped as he pressed a finger to her lips.

"I dreamed I would make of a princess a duchess," he continued. "I imagined her in the ducal manor of Linfoi, graciously presiding over my shabby dining table. Of bearing my children, a son first, of course. The next proud Duke of Linfoi. I saw her sparkling with wit and beauty, a magnificent ornament on my velvet arm at court. Duke Alasdair of Linfoi and his duchess, Rhian. A woman of education and intelligence, my helpmeet, fulfilling her duties as duchess while I, the duke, stood tall in my lowly, disregarded duchy."

"I would happily have been that duchess," Rhian whispered. "I never once looked down my nose at duchy Linfoi. How could I, when it's your home and you love it? It never mattered to me, that you lived a plain life. I've never been a frippery girl." She looked down at herself, at her sweat-soaked huntsman's leathers. "I was always more than half a boy. I think Papa found it easier that way."

"Ranald said as much. He didn't always understand you, but he was bursting proud of you. Simon, too."

"I know. And I was proud of them, my handsome boys."

He smoothed a strand of sweat-damp hair from her forehead. "I dreamed of making you my duchess, and instead you made of me your king. When you asked me to marry you, in Linfoi, I said yes because the thought of life without you was unbearable. But when I *said* yes . . ."

She smiled, her throat aching. "You had no inkling of what that truly meant. I know. I didn't either. I think I'm only just beginning to understand now." She heard her voice break, felt the tightness of tears in her chest. "It's a lot more difficult than I'd ever thought it would be."

His hands came to rest on her shoulders, and his forehead lowered to touch hers. "Yes. A lot more."

"I'm sorry. I never meant—"

"I know," he said, and kissed her. "Neither did I."

Overwhelmed she clung to him despite the tiltyard railing between them. "We will survive this. We will find a way to weather this storm."

"Which storm?" he said wryly. "Ethrea's crisis, or our own?"

"*Both*," she said, and held him even tighter. "As God is my witness, Alasdair. We'll survive both."

"Well," he whispered. "If the Queen of Ethrea says so, who am I to disagree?"

*   *   *

As they walked back to the castle, the path lit by more breeze-guttered torches, Alasdair said, "This business of Han witching you to see the great trading nations' rulers. I've been giving it careful thought."

He was frightened for her. She could hear it in his voice, not quite as steady as he doubtless imagined. She suspected she knew what he'd been thinking, but didn't say so. She owed him the courtesy of speaking first, before yet again she ignored his advice.

"Yes?"

"Ask Han to bring them here," he said. "Don't go witching with the emperor. It's too dangerous, and we can't afford to risk losing you."

She took his hand, and laced her fingers through his. "Can you imagine the Count of Arbenia or the Slainta of Harbisland agreeing to Tzhung-tzhungchai's emperor witching them *anywhere*? They never would, Alasdair, you know it." She tightened her fingers. "And you can't go in my place, either, because—"

"I know," he said, impatient. "I'm needed here, to work with Edward and Rudi in cobbling together our army, God help us. We've not much time, and so much to do. Still, I worry."

She leaned into his shoulder, briefly. "I'm sorry, I don't mean to burden you, but I do have to go with Han." She felt her heart thud. "And, Alasdair . . . I have to take Zandakar with me."

"Zandakar," he said. Though his face was warmed by torchlight, his eyes were shadowed and unreadable.

She tugged him to a halt. "*Yes*. Can you think of a

more potent argument for an armada than the sight of his scorpion knife flaming with blue fire?"

He wasn't pleased, she could see that, but still he shook his head. "No. I can't."

"Then he must go with me."

"Have you told him?"

"I asked. He's agreed." She started walking again, taking Alasdair with her. "About the army. While I made a great fuss in council, over not giving the trading nations any sovereignty here, I'm afraid—"

"I know," he sighed. "I've been thinking about that, too. With the best will in the world, with all the enthusiasm and courage our people can muster, in truth they'll be no match for Mijak's warriors. Not even Zandakar can transform farmers into soldiers in the short time spared to us. You'll have to ask Arbenia and Harbisland, and all the rest, for archers and swordsmen to fight alongside the people of Ethrea."

"Edward and Rudi will hate the idea," she murmured. "God knows I hate it. It's one thing for the trading nations to keep us unmolested by infrequent pirates. But let them claim, when this is over, that without their soldiers Ethrea would be destroyed . . . what kind of precedent does that set? It seems we're on the brink of truly tearing up the treaty charter as it now exists. When the time comes to recreate it, will the trading nations demand more and more rights of us? Refuse to pay their tithes and tariffs? Exact a price for their assistance when in truth, by saving us they're saving themselves?"

Alasdair's arm slid round her shoulders. "I don't know, Rhian. All I know is that without them, we won't survive Mijak. But let's not run too far ahead of ourselves. Let's defeat Mijak first, however we must defeat it, and let the consequences come when they come. If we don't, all this worry will be for nothing. We'll be dead, and the kingdom enslaved."

She couldn't fault his argument. She could only trust that in saving Ethrea, she didn't destroy it.

Returned with Alasdair to their privy apartments, she took pen and paper and scribbled a note to Han.

The Long Gallery. Tonight.

Then she wrote a second note, not quite as short, to Voolksyn of Harbisland. It was a gamble. But if the meeting with Han paid off . . . if he came . . .

The message boy she summoned took the sealed notes away, running. Afterwards, she sat in the parlour and breathed a fervent prayer.

She was tired. She was hungry. As Alasdair had said, she stank. But to Dinsy's dismay, instead of stripping off her rank huntsman's leathers and soaking in a bath before eating a hearty supper, she kissed Alasdair's cheek and made her way to the castle's Long Gallery . . . where she waited in solitude for Han to come.

*   *   *

"Rhian."

Startled out of her doze she bounced to her feet, heart pounding and knife unsheathed in her hand.

"Han!"

His purple silk tunic and pants gleamed with a golden lustre in the gallery's candlelight. He still looked weary, but his grief for Sun-dao was well-contained.

"You summoned me," he said, politely enough. "Why be surprised I'm here?"

"I'm not," she said, and re-sheathed her knife. Her mouth felt woolly and her belly was grumbling, resenting its lack of food. "Are you all right?"

He raised a supercilious eyebrow. "Of course."

"Your witch-men, Han. After what happened in Jatharuj, are they recovered?"

What little warmth there was in his eyes abruptly died. "You need not fear, Rhian. I have said my witch-men and I would help create your armada. I am the Emperor of Tzhung. My word is my word."

Oh, men and their vaunted pride. "I'm not questioning your word, Han, I'm asking after you and your people! Tzhung-tzhungchai has received a grievous blow. You are the first of us to shed blood in this war against Mijak. You lost your brother. I feel for you. Is that so hard to believe?" She felt herself sneer. "Or is it that the feelings of this *girl-child of Ethrea* are vastly unimportant?"

And that stung him, just as his contempt of last night had stung her. His lips thinned, and his interlaced fingers tightened.

"Rhian, did you summon me to say again what was said mere hours ago? I doubt it. Shall we resist the urge to play games?"

"Truthfully, Han?" she said, glaring. "Right now I'm resisting the urge to slap you."

To her surprise, he laughed. "Not a breathing soul in my empire would dare say that to my face."

"In case you'd forgotten, we're not in your empire," she pointed out, waving a hand at the candlelit

Long Gallery. "We're attempting to prevent your empire from becoming part of Mijak's empire."

His amusement faded. "I have answered your curt summons, Rhian. Why am I here?"

She cleared her throat, feeling a touch of warmth in her cheeks. "I do realise the note was . . . peremptory. I was trying to be cryptic."

"Oh, you were," Han assured her. "Also rude."

Vexed, she chewed at her lip. *Don't bite, don't bite, you need this man.* "I apologise."

"And I will hear you out," said Han. "Provided it doesn't take all night."

So much for the pleasantries. "I want to go to Arbenia and Harbisland tomorrow," she said. "Around ten of the clock, after I've met with my council. And I want Zandakar to come with me. Are you strong enough to take us there so soon after Jatharuj?"

Han raised an eyebrow. "Arbenia and Harbisland are but two trading nations, Rhian. You will need warships from everywhere if this armada is to have any hope of success. Do you expect me to witch you all over the world?"

"No," she replied. "After the Tzhung, Arbenia and Harbisland are the only two nations that count. Haisun answers to you. The other lesser trading nations answer to them. Once their loyalties are captured, all loyalties are captured. And in truth, Han, we need only convince one of your equals to join us."

"Equals?" He sounded offended.

She frowned. "You know what I mean."

"Which one?"

"Harbisland," she said promptly. "Though

Ambassador Voolksyn's not made us a single commitment, he has always been the most prepared to listen.
If we can convince his Slainta that it's Mijak that
should be feared, not Tzhung-tzhungchai or Rhian of
Ethrea, the Count of Arbenia will meekly follow. He
won't dare look a coward in front of the Slainta, or see
himself left out of a chance to pillage spoils, after."

"Really?" said Han. "You sound very confident."

She tilted her chin at him. "I am."

That made him laugh again. "Liar. You're terrified."

He could read her so easily. "All right. Yes," she
said, defiant. "I'm terrified. But so are you."

Her chance shot found its mark. Han blinked. His
lustrous purple silk tunic shimmered as he took a
deep breath, and let it out.

"It's true, Rhian of Ethrea," he said, his voice low.
His eyes were haunted. "I am indeed afraid. For the
wind has blown me visions. It has shown me what lies
in store for the world if we fail against Mijak."

Rhian swallowed, hard. "Then we won't fail."

"So young," he murmured. "So sure of victory."

"Would you rather I weep and wail like a child lost
in the markets? Somehow I doubt it. Now, if you'd be
so good as to answer my original question?"

"Am I capable of keeping my word to you?" said
Han, coldly haughty. "Yes. I am. Tomorrow I'll take
you and your Zandakar to Harbisland, and Arbenia.
And if you succeed in winning the slainta and the
count and the lesser trading nations to your desperate
cause, my witch-men will bring their ships to your
harbour. They will bring the ships of Tzhung-
tzhungchai also, they'll sail with you into battle

against Mijak." A muscle leapt along his lean jaw. "And when they do, Sun-dao won't be the last of us to die."

"Thank you, Han." Treading softly, Rhian closed the distance between them, and rested her clenched fist gently on his chest. "The Queen of Ethrea won't forget Tzhung-tzhungchai's greatest emperor."

Han smiled. Snapped his fingers. In a gust of wind he stepped back . . . and disappeared.

Relieved and exhausted, she returned to Alasdair in their privy apartments.

"Han agreed?" he asked, pulling off her boots.

"He agreed," she said, breathing the rich aroma of gravied beef and buttered pumpkin. "And I begin to believe we might stand a chance."

Alasdair paused, his warm hand on her ankle. "You didn't before?"

"Let's eat," she suggested. "Before I faint from hunger."

CHAPTER TWENTY-SEVEN

Helfred was disappointed, but not truly surprised, when Rhian and Alasdair failed to appear in Kingseat's great chapel for Litany. He had to make do with the presence of Dukes Edward, Rudi and Ludo. Adric was absent too, and must be scolded for it, for only once had he bothered to take his place in the pews reserved for Ethrea's privy council.

And then, of course, there was Mister Jones. Dexterity. God's most unlikely messenger. Rumpled and threadbare, he sat with Ursa in the privy pews, lightly frowning, listening as the prolate he'd anointed sang Rhian's praises, again. Thanked God for Ethrea's courage, again. Cultivated the seeds of readiness for danger, again.

Surely I must sing a different song, soon. Soon my dear people must be woken from their dreams of safety.

Thinking of it broke his heart. The pain of his own waking hadn't passed. He felt it still, the loss of his innocence. The anger, the disbelief, the slow crushing acceptance, that God could not protect them from everything. That the world was vaster and stranger and more cruel than he'd ever suspected.

Murdering priests of Mijak. Sorcerous witch-men of Tzhung-tzhungchai. Even Dexterity, bursting into flames. Only scant months ago my life was so ordered. And now it's in disarray. It lies in pieces around me.

As the choristers' sweet voices soared to the chapel's rafters, he stared at his beautiful bound copy of Rollin's *Admonitions*, open before him on the pulpit. Admonition 24 leapt to his eye.

The past lies behind us. The future is unwritten. Do not cling to the past, for it is an anchor. Do not fear the future, for fear kills hope and blinds us to possibilities.

A timely reminder, perhaps. Was he indeed allowing fear to kill his hope, to blind him? Was his fear of the unknown, of Zandakar and the witch-men's strange powers, preventing him from seeing they were indeed Godsent, as Dexterity claimed?

He didn't know. *He didn't know.* And that was the worst part. He was being asked for a leap of faith . . . when he'd never had to leap before.

Behind him, Ven'Thomas cleared his throat suggestively. Looking up, Helfred realised the choristers had finished their final hymn and the congregation was staring at him, curious.

"Ah," he said, uncomfortably aware he'd turned an unbecoming pink. "Thus is concluded our service this evening. God's blessings upon you, and the peace of Rollin. Pray for our brave queen, her stalwart husband, and our realm's privy council, charged with the most grave duty of its protection."

And so another Litany was ended.

Afterwards, once he'd spoken with his congregation as they left the chapel, and favoured Dexterity with a solemn smile, he returned to the castle and his own privy chapel. He needed solitude again. A chance to clear his mind and open his heart in the hope that a final answer to his fears would come.

Heedless of bruised knees, he knelt on the cold chapel floor and stared into the heart of God's Living Flame. Stared with his own heart open, his mind emptied of fears and thoughts, waiting, waiting, for the truth to be revealed. The chapel's silence was profound. All he could hear was his breathing, and the soothing, monotonous rattle of his wooden prayer beads, click-click-clicking between his restless fingers. His vision blurred. His breathing slowed. One by one, his prayer beads clicked to a stop.

A hesitant hand pressed on his shoulder. A voice said, "Helfred. Helfred, turn round."

Stirring out of his trance-like daze, he turned. And shrieked. And fell over.

It was his dead uncle, Marlan. The former Prolate of Ethrea.

"Helfred, Helfred," said his uncle, hands uplifted, palms out. "Do not be afraid. I've not come to harm you."

Choking with fright, Helfred scuttled backwards on his rump till his spine struck the chapel altar. The last time he'd seen Marlan, his uncle was going up in flames. Before that hideous moment there'd been cruelty and violence. Depravity. Sin. Marlan had ordered Kingseat's soldiers to kill Rhian.

"This isn't possible," he whispered. "I'm dreaming, I must be."

"Rather call it a vision," said Marlan. "An answer to your prayers, nephew." His austere face softened into a diffident smile. "Or should I say, Your Eminence?"

Helfred smeared a hand across his face. His heart thundered so loudly he was afraid it would burst. "Helfred," he panted. "Call me Helfred . . . if you're real."

"Real enough," said Marlan, shrugging. "And only come for a short time."

Calming a little, Helfred was able to see more than Marlan's unburned face. Was able to take in the extraordinary fact that his immaculate, magnificent proletary uncle was dressed in a penitent's shift, a simple unadorned tunic of undyed linen, ragged about neckline, hem and sleeves. His feet were shod in a pair of simple leather sandals, his fingers bare of rings, his chest without ropes of gold and jewelled medallions. He looked more humble than a chaplain. More insignificant than a novice devout.

"I see from your face that I am greatly different," said Marlan, softly.

Well, yes, uncle. The last time I saw you, you were burned to a crisp. "Ah – you seem to me less angry," Helfred ventured. "Have you found peace at last? Have you rediscovered God?"

Marlan released a slow, heavy sigh. "Nephew, how could I rediscover what I never before knew? Alas, I was a venal man. Proud and sinful and steeped in malice. My God was wealth and power. I worshipped myself. Now I strive to undo the wrongs I have done. To make amends for the pain I caused."

"Uncle . . ." Helfred swallowed. His mouth was so dry. "Please. Tell me. *Have you seen God?*"

Marlan laughed. Had he ever laughed like that before? Without cruelty, without sarcasm, with genuine joy? Helfred couldn't remember it.

"Nephew," said his uncle, "it's not given to me that I can answer such a question, or reveal the truths of what lies beyond life. Every man will make that journey, and his discoveries, in his time."

"Then why are you here?"

"To give you the answer to your prayers, Helfred," said Marlan. "I'm here to tell you the toymaker is right. The witch-men of Tzhung-tzhungchai commit no sins. At least, not the kind of sins you're worried about."

"You mean it's safe to trust them?"

"They do not serve the dark power of Mijak.

Neither does Zandakar. And both are needed if Ethrea is to prevail."

Helfred wiped his sweat-slicked palms down the front of his chaplain's robes. Who could ever have thought he'd feel well-dressed, next to Marlan?

"And will we prevail, uncle? Will Mijak be defeated?"

Marlan sighed again, so sorrowful. "Remember Rollin's admonition, nephew. The future is unwritten."

"You mean you don't know?" he cried, anguished. "*God* doesn't know?"

"How can God know?" Marlan chided. "When men have free will to do as they please?"

Well, this wasn't the answer he'd been seeking. He wanted certainty, he wanted assurance, he wanted to know Ethrea would survive and that Mijak, defeated, would be driven from the world.

"Alas," said Marlan. "The future is unwritten."

Helfred groped to his feet. "At least tell me there's hope, uncle. Tell me we won't be fighting in vain."

Marlan smiled then, so sweetly. He seemed another man entirely. "There is always hope, Helfred. Know that, and believe it. *There is always hope.*"

A breeze sighed through the chapel . . . and Marlan was gone.

"Uncle?" said Helfred tentatively, into the silence. "Uncle, are you still here?"

No reply. He turned to stare at his chapel's Living Flame. "Did that just happen, God, or was I truly dreaming?"

The Flame burned serenely, keeping its secrets.

Helfred wandered out of his chapel and accosted

the first novice he found. It was young Norbert, polishing a section of wooden staircase handrail for a penance.

"Norbert!"

The novice dropped his cloth and tin of beeswax. "Your Eminence!" he gasped, plunging to his knees.

"Norbert, am I awake?"

Norbert's mouth shaped itself into a small circle of surprise. "Ah . . . yes, Your Eminence, you're awake."

Helfred sighed. "I suspected as much."

He returned to his privy chapel and lowered himself onto its solitary pew. His hands were still trembling.

Well, I asked for an answer to my prayers, and I received one. I just never expected it to be delivered in person.

Should he go to Rhian and tell her of Marlan's message? It wasn't so very late, doubtless she'd still be awake. And he knew full well how distressed he'd made her in council, refusing to support Zandakar and Han's witch-men as allies.

On the other hand, the poor girl needed her rest. He'd tell her in the morning. His night would be better spent in prayer. He slid off the pew and once more to his knees, humble before the Living Flame, determined to pray until the sun rose again.

Before meeting with her privy council the next morning, Rhian dressed in a duplicate set of the black leather doublet, leggings and low boots, now ruined, that she'd worn to slay the dukes Damwin and Kyrin. She wore a single dragon-eye ruby on a chain, and her simple gold circlet. Once again, her curling hair was cut close. Ranald's tigereye knife was sheathed at her hip. Staring at herself in her mirror, she nodded.

See me, gentlemen. See me, world. I am Rhian of House Havrell, Queen of Ethrea. Chosen by God to defend the innocent, and the free.

Alasdair's eyes warmed when she joined him in their parlour. "My love, you are formidable."

"Yes, Alasdair," she said, unsmiling. "I am."

Together they walked to the privy council chamber, scattering courtiers and servants before them like chaff.

He looked at her sidelong, curious. "You're different. It's not just that you've shorn yourself again. It's something else. Something . . . inward. What's changed?"

She shrugged. "I believe."

"In our cause?" he said, bemused.

The *hotas* she'd danced with Zandakar at first light had been fierce. Fiercer than any she'd danced before. She'd danced as though her life depended on it, as though Zandakar were a true enemy of Ethrea. Dancing without mercy he'd pushed her, pursued her, demanded from her the kind of speed and agility and ferocity she hadn't known she possessed. As though all the *hotas* she'd danced until that moment were nothing more than slow training exercises, designed to bring her to this pitch.

And somewhere in that dancing she had seen herself through his eyes. Through his belief. She saw herself through God's eyes . . . and knew her time had come.

Now she smiled. "In me."

The council, warned of her approach, was on its feet as she entered the chamber. Zandakar was there, and Dexterity. They stood together, comfortable with each other as the others were not. Such an unlikely pair, they were: Zandakar tall and dark, his unbound blue hair eerie, dressed in sober Ethrean linen and wool. Dexterity short and rumpled, his beard unkempt and his shabby coat with a darn in one elbow. And yet both men were men of strange powers. Sent by God to aid her.

Sweet Rollin, my life is grown monstrous strange.

"Gentlemen!" she said briskly, striding through the open doorway. "Be seated. I shan't keep you long, I know you have much to do. Helfred—"

He hesitated halfway to sitting. "Yes, Your Majesty?"

As she took her chair, and Alasdair took his, and the guards outside the chamber pulled its doors closed, she fixed her former chaplain with a cool stare. "You've had sufficient time, I think, to consider your position. I must have your answer regarding Zandakar and Tzhung-tzhungchai."

And if it's the wrong answer, then God help you. God help us all.

But if she was different this morning, then so was her prolate. The anguish in Helfred's eyes was vanished, his pallor replaced by robust colour. Yesterday, in his protests, though young he'd seemed an old man. Now his movements were vigorous, his voice energetic.

"I have indeed considered, Majesty," he replied, sitting all the way down. "And reached a decision, moreover, in light of the counsel I received."

She resisted looking at Dexterity. "I know Mister Jones sought you out on the matter, Prolate. In case you're inclined to feel critical of his interference, you should know I asked him to."

"I did suspect as much," said Helfred, dryly. "And Mister Jones was, as always, your stalwart champion. But he wasn't my only visitor." He plucked his prayer beads from his belt and began his familiar, infuriating fiddling, click-click-clicking them through his busy fingers. "Someone else desired to speak with me on this important matter."

Rhian gritted her teeth, fighting the urge to snatch the beads from him and do something horrendous . . . like make him swallow them one by one.

"Well, whoever it was, Prolate, I didn't send him. Or her. Please, would you just—"

"I know you didn't, Majesty," said Helfred. "God sent him. It was Marlan."

Silence in the privy council chamber. Rhian looked to Dexterity, who gaped like a fish. The rest of her council was equally stunned. Even Alasdair seemed shaken. Even Zandakar seemed unnerved.

"Marlan?" she said at last, feeling sweat slick her skin beneath her supple new leathers. "Surely not, Helfred. Perhaps it was a dream."

"You mean a nightmare," grunted Edward. "That wicked man?"

Helfred's expression tightened. "Wicked in life he was, Your Grace, I cannot deny it. But he makes amends now. I'll thank you to say no more on that."

At the far end of the table, Dexterity cleared his throat. "He seemed . . . well?" he asked, diffident. Almost hopeful.

"Well enough," said Helfred. "Considering. He came to tell me I was wrong to doubt Zandakar and the witch-men of Tzhung-tzhungchai."

Though it was not yet noon, Rhian wished devoutly for a goblet of strong wine. *Marlan, my champion? That can't be true.*

Rudi stirred in his chair, glowering. "Then I contend we have a problem, Your Majesty. For Marlan was a villainous piece of work, bent on your destruction. If indeed he appeared to Prolate Helfred, we can't trust a word he said."

She pushed to her feet and glared at her muttering council. "*Enough*. Zandakar and Han are not my enemies. Prevarication is my enemy. Shilly-shallying and indecision, these are my enemies. Can it be that you, gentlemen, like the ambassadors, continue to hope this threat we face is *exaggerated*? That we have the luxury of more debate, more denial, more time? *We don't*."

"Majesty," said Ludo, as she began pacing the council chamber. "We don't deny the threat. But surely Rudi has a point. Marlan alive was no friend to Ethrea. Why should we assume that dead he's suddenly on our side? There are dark powers ranged against us. Can't he be some kind of – of demonic presence, sent to endanger you?"

She was almost as fond of Ludo as Alasdair was, but she could slap him now. "You're talking like an illiterate, superstitious farmhand! You might as well call *Hettie* a demon, and be done with it."

"No, no," Ludo protested with a glance at Dexterity. "I just think you should be wary of Han."

"I *am* wary of Han! He serves the Tzhung first and

foremost. I'm not a fool. I do *know* that in aiding Ethrea he seeks only to aid himself. But if in aiding himself he helps save the rest of us, why should I care? The cruel truth is that without him we're lost. Without Han and his witch-men there will be *no armada*."

"Which *he* knows," said Edward. "His help will plunge Ethrea deep in his debt, Majesty. What price will we have to pay, when he calls the debt due?"

"I have no idea, Edward, but whatever it is, *I will pay it*," she retorted. "I swear before God I'll be Han's concubine in Tzhung if that's what it takes to save us from Mijak!"

Silence, again. Zandakar stared at her, his blue pale eyes tranquil. Beneath that tranquillity she thought she saw derision. She turned away, struggling not to lose her temper entirely.

How foolish we must seem, bickering constantly like brats in a nursery. As a prince of Mijak he was used to instant obedience. Do I envy him that? The power to silence with a glance – or a knife, if pushed to it? Sometimes I think I do . . .

"And it's not just Han that's suspect, if Marlan's counsel is suspect," said Adric. "If it was Marlan. The emperor's not the only foreigner you're so eager to trust."

Rhian turned back, dumbfounded. *Did I want to be queen? I must've been mad.* "Can you be serious, Adric? Do you *still* insist upon doubting Zandakar? My God, man. What must he do to prove he's willing to die for Ethrea?"

Adric shrugged. "He could die."

Before she could answer, Helfred surged to his

feet. "You arrogant young fool! Is your manhood so weak you must see a stronger man cast down to feel brave? You know full well that without Zandakar to guide us our cause would be lost already. You're just too proud to admit it. Have a care, Your Grace: pride can choke a man, even to his death."

"Why do you chastise me, Prolate?" Adric retorted. "I've heard you doubt the heathen a score of times, in this very chamber!"

"Yes, I have doubted," said Helfred. "And I was wrong. Zandakar is God's gift against the evil of Mijak."

"Let God tell me that," said Adric, "and perhaps I'll believe it."

"*Adric*!" shouted Rudi, his face bright red. "Would you shame me? Would you bring disrepute upon our House? Your Eminence—"

Helfred raised his hand. "Peace, Rudi. Your son is a man now, he speaks with his own tongue. His shame is his alone. The disrepute belongs to him."

Adric opened his mouth to shout, but Rudi silenced him with a scorching look.

"Like it or not, my friends," Helfred added, "we have come to a place where we stand not upon solid ground, but on faith. Faith that Hettie . . . and now Marlan . . . seek to help and not harm us. Faith that we can trust the son of our greatest enemy. Faith that a man with powers we don't understand has honour, and will not hold us to ransom when this grim business is done. Faith that a girl yet to reach her majority has the strength and courage to lead us into war."

Dear God. Put like that, the situation sounded hopeless. Rhian looked at the faces of her council. At the two dukes old enough to be her father. At the two dukes young enough to be her brothers. At the man she loved, who was her husband. At the man she loved, who was bloodsworn to die for her. At the man she loved, who'd become a second father. At the man she would never love, but was coming to respect.

"My lords," she said quietly, "our prolate is right, and you'd best come to terms with it. Today, God willing, I meet with the rulers of Harbisland and Arbenia. In doing so, I'll be throwing in my lot with Emperor Han of Tzhung-tzhungchai and that means I commit all of Ethrea to an alliance with him. It's a dangerous course . . . but it's the only one we can take. And I need to know you have faith in me."

Another silence. Then Edward cleared his throat. "I'm sorry. Did you say you're meeting with—"

"Yes," she said shortly. She glanced at the chamber clock. It was time. It was time. "In fact—"

And as if by some sorcery, the privy chamber doors opened and Ambassador Voolksyn was ushered in by the guards on duty.

Smiling gravely, she walked to him. "My lord ambassador, thank you for coming."

Tall and sleek in his spotted sealskin tunic, his lips curved in smiling answer, his eyes untouched by warmth, and wary, Voolksyn looked around her council table, taking special notice of Zandakar, seated between Dexterity and Alasdair. Then he offered her a shallow bow.

"Majesty. I thought hard before agreeing to your invitation."

"Sere, it doesn't matter that you thought. It matters that you came."

Voolksyn smoothed his beard with one large, capable hand. His bald head gleamed in the light from the window. "My cousin Arbenia urged me to refuse it."

He'd discussed her note with Gutten. How . . . inconvenient. Now her heart was drumming. "Your cousin Arbenia is a short-sighted man."

"You think so?" said Voolksyn. "He is a good friend to Harbisland."

"Sere Voolksyn," said Dexterity, breaking the tense silence. "I think it's only fair to tell you that Icthia has indeed fallen to Mijak. Your brother ambassador, Sere Athnïj, and the staff he brought from his home, are among the last few living Icthians in the world."

He'd not been invited to speak, but Rhian had no intention of scolding Dexterity. Of them all, she thought he stood the best chance of convincing Voolksyn.

"And how do you know this?" said the Harbish ambassador. "Another dream from your dead wife?"

"Alas," said Dexterity, pulling a face behind his scruffy beard. "It was no dream. I returned from Jatharuj the night before last."

"That . . . is not possible," said Voolksyn slowly.

"It is perfectly possible," said Rhian. "With the help of Tzhung-tzhungchai."

"Tzhung-tzhungchai?" Voolksyn looked like he wanted to spit. "So you bed with their witch-men? Unclean sorcerers. The mother forbids her children their breath."

"You may call them sorcerers, Voolksyn, though I believe you wrong them," she said sharply. "And you should know this: Han's *sorcerers* were all that stood between us and Mijak for many weeks. But Mijak has broken them. Many are dead. And now Mijak sails to harvest *our* bones. The time Han's witch-men bought for us has been wasted. Their spent lives are wasted. God chose me to lead an alliance against Mijak, and because I failed to convince you and Arbenia that the threat is real, that you could trust my leadership, that Ethrea always was and always will be *your friend*, every living soul in the world stands threatened!"

Voolksyn stared at her closely. "You swore Ethrea had no pact with Tzhung-tzhungchai."

"God have *mercy*, Sere Voolksyn!" she cried. "Have you heard nothing I said? The only pact I have with Han is the trading charter! I am as treated with him as I am with you, no more and no less. There is no *deception* here, there is only *desperation*."

"Desperation is fertile soil for deception," said Voolksyn.

Now she was perilously close to tears. "That sounds like something Gutten would say." Angrily she wiped a hand across her face. "I don't know, Sere. Perhaps I was naïve, expecting you to listen. Expecting you to see me as a queen in my own right, as a warrior you could trust. But you watched me fight for the throne of Ethrea, you saw me kill the men who dared challenge my crown, and I thought that would be enough. Clearly, I was wrong. Clearly, you won't believe a thing without blood."

Before anyone could stop her, she unsheathed her blade and drew its cruel edge swiftly across her face twice, one cut in each cheek. The pain was immediate, bright and blazing. Blood poured hotly, scorching her skin.

"*Rhian!*" shouted Alasdair, leaping from his chair.

Zandakar took hold of him by one wrist, pinning him in place.

She ignored Alasdair's horror, his fury at Zandakar. "As God is my witness, Sere Voolksyn," she said, almost blinded by the pain, "and as my spilled blood attests, here is my oath to you. I will not betray the people of Harbisland. I stand ready to fight for you and die for you, as though you were Ethrean, and mine."

Voolksyn stared at her, shocked into silence. She stared back, dimly aware of her council's frantic babbling. Dimly aware of the chamber's ticking clock.

Han, Han, where are you? Must I shout aloud that I can't do this alone?

And Han was there, in jade-green silk, stepping out of the swirling air like a thought transformed to flesh.

"Sere Voolksyn," he said calmly, paying no attention to her pain. "As the Ethreans say, we have our backs against a wall. If Harbisland and Tzhungtzhungchai do not help each other, countless innocent souls will perish. If that is what you desire, turn away from Ethrea's gallant queen. And remember this moment as you draw your dying breath."

For the first time she could remember, Rhian saw Voolksyn look uncertain. "I do not speak for my slainta," he said. "Even though he is my brother."

Han smiled. "Then it is time your brother spoke for himself."

"You speak in riddles," said Voolksyn, still uncertain.

Bleeding sluggishly, the pain undiminished, Rhian

sheathed her blade without cleaning it and crossed to
Voolksyn. Took his hand in hers and held it, tightly.

"Trust me, Sere," she said as Zandakar joined
them. "No harm will befall you."

"No harm?" said Voolksyn. "Little queen—"

Ignoring him, she glanced at Zandakar. "You have
the knife?"

He nodded. "*Zho.*"

She smiled at Han, though it hurt so much.
"Emperor."

Han clapped his hands . . . and the council chamber disappeared.

It was raining in Tyssa, capital city of Harbisland,
where the slainta held his open court.

Dizzied by witching so far, by taking so many with
him, Han stepped out of the wind and onto the wet
grass. Rhian, Zandakar and Voolksyn stepped out beside him. The ambassador, gasping, bent over to
retch. Rhian released her hold of him and stared at
their surroundings. Zandakar stepped aside, drawing
his scorpion knife from beneath his jerkin.

Han stared like Rhian, mildly curious. So many
years since he had set foot in Harbisland. Who had
been slainta then? This slainta's great grandfather.
Oosyn of Harbisland, a belligerent man.

Court was held outdoors in Harbisland, in rain
and bright weather, if it snowed or if it scorched. The
goddess of Harbisland was a deity of nature. Nothing
of importance could occur within walls, beneath a
roof. This court was in a pretty field, the ragged grass
scattered with pink and yellow flowers. Beyond its
boundaries the rustic dwellings and merchant-houses

of Tyssa, drummed with the rain beneath the cloud-shrouded sky.

In this day the slainta of Harbisland was Dalsyn. He had the look of his brother the ambassador: tall and broad and brawny. His plaited red beard reached to his waist. His sealskin tunic glistened with the rain. Bare-headed, raw-fisted, he sat his sealskin-covered throne like a man daring to be challenged. Around him stood his clansmen, armed with cudgels, and before him knelt the Harbislanders who had come to court for justice.

Voolksyn finished retching, straightened and looked around him, astonished. "Harbisland? I am home?"

"You are home," said Han. "And unharmed, as the Queen of Ethrea promised."

Voolksyn stared down at Rhian. "You did not lie."

"I've never lied to you, Voolksyn," she said, rain slicking her sleek and supple black leathers, rain running through the blood dried thickly on her face. "Zandakar—"

The warrior from Mijak looked at her. "*Zho?*"

"You're all right?"

"*Zho*. You?"

"I think – *zho*," she replied. "What an extraordinary feeling. I don't know what I was expecting, but . . ."

Zandakar smiled. "*Zho.*"

Han watched Rhian smile back. So. This was interesting. This might be a problem . . . for Alasdair of Ethrea, at least. If it proved to be a problem for Tzhung-tzhungchai, he would address it.

Stirring out of their astonishment now, the clansmen of Harbisland's slainta raised their cudgels and advanced, anger plain in their faces. The kneeling petitioners scuttled out of their way.

Voolksyn stepped forward to greet them in the twisting tongue of Harbisland. Swiftly he was surrounded. Many voices filled the damp air.

"Han," said Rhian, turning from Zandakar. "What will we do if this desperate attempt fails?"

His silk tunic was swiftly soaking through. It was cold here in Harbisland. He'd be shivering soon. "What Ethrea does is your affair. Tzhung-tzhungchai will fight Mijak until the last witch-man is dead. Until there are no more men and women of Tzhung to fling against our enemy. Why did you cut your face, Rhian?"

She touched fingertips to her cheek. They came away scarlet. "Desperation."

"Witch-men have healing powers."

"No. If you heal me, the point will be lost." She looked again to Voolksyn and the crowding clansmen. "What are they saying? I don't speak a word of Harbish."

"What they say doesn't matter. Only the slainta's words are important here."

Rhian nodded, again staring about her. "Do you know, this is the first time I've stood on soil that wasn't Ethrean?" She laughed, then tilted her bloodied face to the sky and poked out her tongue. "Foreign rain," she murmured. "Somehow it tastes sweeter. All my life I've wanted to travel. I was so jealous of my brothers. I nearly hated them when they left Kingseat harbour and I was left behind. It seemed so unfair. It *was* unfair. When Mijak is defeated, and

I have a daughter, I'll make sure she travels the world."

Cold in his rain-soaked silk tunic, Han looked at her and marvelled. *Is she brave or is she foolish, to hold on to hope so hard?* "What will you name this daughter, when you have her?"

"I don't know," she said, musing. "Is there a feminine version of the Tzhung name *Han*?"

So nearly she surprised him into laughter. "Hanyi."

"Then perhaps I shall call my daughter Hanyi," said Rhian. "If I have a daughter. If I don't die soon."

Zandakar hissed between his teeth. "Rhian *wei* die."

"We might all die, Zandakar," Rhian said, so solemn again. "As Helfred says, God makes us no promises."

Voolksyn the ambassador was now speaking with his brother. The Slainta Dalsyn was listening, his head low, one large hand gripping Voolksyn's shoulder. He nodded once. He nodded again. His head came up, and with a sweep of his arm, some short sharp words, he sent away his huddled Harbisland petitioners. Then he beckoned, frowning.

"Well," said Rhian, her chin tilting and her shoulders pulling back. "Time to see if our gamble has paid off."

Together they approached Dalsyn. Zandakar walked lightly, like a man poised to fight. Voolksyn was standing aside, his face giving nothing away. The slainta's clansmen held their cudgels at the ready. Their faces were easy to read: anger and suspicion and some lust for Rhian.

"So this is the little Queen of Ethrea," said Dalsyn, in Ethrean. His tone was guttural, his accent pronounced.

"Come uninvited to your court, great Slainta," said Rhian. "For which I apologise, but my need is great."

"This my brother tells me," said Dalsyn, eyes narrow with suspicion. "He tells me you speak the truth."

"If you ask without asking whether Rhian of Ethrea has never told a lie, I do not lie. I have. But not about Mijak. Every word I've told your brother the ambassador, everything I will say to you now, is the truth."

Dalsyn nodded, and looked at Zandakar. "Here is a man who brings a naked knife before me. Does this man desire to die?"

"*Tcha*," said Rhian, her finger lightly on Zandakar's arm. "I stand here with a blade on my hip, Slainta. Will your men cudgel me too? Zandakar means you no harm."

"I am to trust you?"

"You are the slainta. I am a queen. Rulers have honour, or so I am taught. We are treatied, you and I. We are bound like brother and sister."

Dalsyn tugged his long, plaited beard. He had a hard face to read. "Zandakar," he said. "A man with blue hair."

"A man of Mijak," said Rhian. "A godsent man, Slainta. Listen to what he has to say."

"And he says what?" said Dalsyn. "This man with blue hair."

"Believe Rhian *hushla*," said Zandakar simply. "Mijak comes. Mijak kills."

"You are Mijak," said Dalsyn. "Do you kill?"

Zandakar nodded. "*Zho*. Before Ethrea, I kill for Mijak."

"And who do you kill for now?"

"Rhian."

"Hmm," said the slainta, his green eyes lively with thought. His gaze shifted. "And here is Emperor Han. Another ruler uninvited."

Han nodded to Dalsyn. "But required."

Dalsyn smiled, revealing yellow teeth. "The pride of Tzhung-tzhungchai is legend in Harbisland."

"The courage of Harbisland is legend in Tzhung-tzhungchai."

As Dalsyn hissed, suspecting a hidden insult, his clansmen stepped forward, their cudgels raised. Though he was cold, and shivering, and exhausted from witching so far to Harbisland, Han readied himself to fight. Beside him, he heard Rhian curse softly.

"God save me from men," she said. "Zandakar? *Now*!"

Zandakar, the warrior from Mijak, pointed his knife blade into the air. A stream of blue fire sizzled through the falling rain. The fresh air stank of cold stone, burning.

Dalsyn's clansmen dropped their cudgels and fell face-first into the rainwashed grass. The Slainta of Harbisland and Voolksyn, his brother, lost their colour until they looked like ice. But neither man flinched or cried out.

Han was impressed.

"Slainta," said Rhian as blue fire seared the rainy

air. "Your brother has told you of Mijak. Here is its brutal power. He has told you of Icthia, and Han, and his witch-men. We are treatied, you and I. Now I come to you asking that you honour that treaty. Help me defend Ethrea. And in defending Ethrea, save yourself."

CHAPTER TWENTY-EIGHT

"And Tzhung-tzhungchai?" said the Slainta Dalsyn. "What is Emperor Han to you?"

"An ally," said Rhian. "As you are."

Dalsyn sat back on his sealskin throne. "To Harbisland, the Tzhung are enemies time out of mind."

"Then you can die as enemies," said Rhian. "At the hands of merciless Mijak." The blood on her cheeks was almost washed away, so the wounds she had given herself were clearly defined. "Or you can live as enemies who put aside their quarrels long enough to see this merciless enemy defeated. Is your pride more important than your life, Slainta? Is it more important than the lives of your people?"

Han saw Rhian's challenge flick Dalsyn keenly, like a whip. She touched Zandakar's arm, and the warrior killed the blue fire. As the slainta's clansmen climbed churlish to their feet, she approached Dalsyn and dropped to one knee on the wet grass before him. The rain fell on her cropped hair, her gold circlet, her close-fitting leathers.

"Dalsyn," she said, "when has Ethrea betrayed you? When has Ethrea broken its word? In this place, *I* am Ethrea. I give you my word, Emperor Han of the Tzhung answers to me. Every trading nation treatied with Ethrea answers to me. Any trading nation who uses this calamity to hurt a sister nation, that nation shall be cast out of Ethrea forever. That is our new treaty. That is Ethrea's pledge to you." She touched her fingers to her wounded face. "I shed my blood before your ambassador. I swore him a blood-oath to die for Harbisland in battle. I'll bleed again here and now, for you, if that will convince you to trust me. If that will convince you to give me ships for our armada, and soldiers to fight in Ethrea if our armada should fail."

Jewelled with raindrops, Dalsyn considered her. One thick, callused finger stroked his rainsoaked moustache. "My dreamers dream of a bloodthirsty horde," he said. "They dream of us fighting together. The mother is worried for her children in Harbisland." His stroking finger pointed. "Let Han bleed for me, and what you want, I give."

Han clasped his hands tightly as Rhian slewed round to stare at him. "Han? No, Slainta, you can't ask—"

Dalsyn stood, towering over her, taller even than his tall brother. His clansmen gripped their cudgels tighter – one word would loose them to bludgeon and kill. "I can't?" said the slainta. "In my land, in my court, in the eyes of my mother, when you come to me begging, when you beg for Harbisland's blood? *I can't?*"

Rhian did not turn back at his angry words. Her eyes in her wounded face were so large, so blue. Han saw there the question she would not ask. The favour she would not beg. He saw in her eyes the death of Ethrea.

And the wind blew through him, stealing his breath. Shattering his resistance. Whispering its desire.

"Zandakar," he said. "Give me your knife."

The warrior from Mijak gave him the scorpion blade. As his fingers closed around it, he heard the wind howl, he heard the wind's pain as the Mijaki's power seared and sang in his blood.

With the fingers of one hand he unbuttoned his sodden silk tunic and bared his tattooed chest to the rain and the cold and the avid stare of the Slainta, Dalsyn. He drew the edge of Zandakar's knife across his left breast, above his heart, and bled for Harbisland. For Ethrea. For Rhian.

The Queen of Ethrea wept for him, bleeding.

"Ha," said Dalsyn, smiling, as his brother the ambassador choked on his surprise. "Tzhung-tzhungchai bleeds."

Rhian leapt to her feet. "It *pleases* you, to see him bleeding? This man who will help your people to live? Shame on you, Slainta! Shame on you for a base man. Is this the teaching of your mother, to smile when a man bleeds for you?"

If she had struck him, Dalsyn could not look more surprised. "What do you know of it? Are you

Harbisland, with its history, with its past? Tzhung-tzhungchai—"

"*Is not the enemy here*!" she shouted. "Are *you* the enemy? You said let Han bleed and I can have what I want. See Han before you, Slainta, bleeding. Is your word worth nothing? Must I battle you and Mijak both?"

"No," said Dalsyn, eyes slitted. "My word is true. Ethrea will have ships and warriors of Harbisland against this Mijak."

"The witch-men of Tzhung are needed to create our armada," said Rhian. "They must come here. Ethrea pledges no danger to Harbisland. Ethrea stands surety for Tzhung-tzhungchai in this. Is Ethrea's word sufficient?"

"Ethrea has never betrayed us," Dalsyn said, grudgingly. "This one time, the Tzhung can come."

"And will you come with us to see the Count of Arbenia?" she said. "You and Voolksyn, with Han, Zandakar and me. We need the ships of Arbenia, Dalsyn. We need ships from every treatied trading nation. Those lesser nations beholden to you, they'll follow your lead in this. And so will the count. I need him and the lesser nations he can influence. And even then . . ." She took a deep breath. "Victory is not assured. But I can promise you, I *do* promise you, that without them defeat is inevitable."

Dalsyn nodded, then looked at Zandakar. "You pledge surety for Tzhung-tzhungchai. The blue-haired man?"

"Zandakar has bled for me," she said. "He fights for me. He'll die for me. Are you saying you want to see him bleed, too?"

Dalsyn smoothed the length of his plaited red beard. "If I asked?"

"You, Slainta," said Zandakar. "You ask. I bleed." Looking sideways, he held out his hand.

As Rhian clenched her fists, Han gave the scorpion knife back to Zandakar. Dalsyn leaned forward, his green eyes eager. Zandakar pushed his sleeve back and poised the blade above his arm. Han saw a pale scar there already.

"Slainta," said Zandakar. "You want blood, I bleed, *zho*?"

Now Dalsyn looked baffled. Elbows resting on his thighs, fingers laced to white knuckles, bearded chin thrust forward, he stared at Rhian as the rain fell on his face and his sealskin clothes.

"What are you, girl?" he demanded. "Are you a witch? A sorceress? Han of Tzhung-tzhungchai bleeds for you. The man with blue hair, Zandakar of Mijak, his knife is ready. You call blood from men like the mother calls her rain."

Han saw Rhian's head lift at that, as though Dalsyn's words had cut her. "Slainta, I'm not a witch. I'm not a sorceress. I'm a girl called to serve her kingdom. To serve God, and all the good men in this world."

"Hmm," said Dalsyn. Then he leaned back again, and flicked a careless finger. "Withdraw. The slainta speaks with his ambassador and his clansmen."

Han met her gaze steadily as she joined him and Zandakar. "You spoke well to the slainta, Majesty," he said quietly. "You are a worthy queen."

"Oh, Han," she whispered. "I had no idea he'd demand that you—" She let her air hiss between her teeth. "*Why did you do it?*"

He glanced down at the open wound in his chest, then at her cut face. "Why did you?"

"Dalsyn's right," she said, not answering that. So much pain behind her self-control. "I make men bleed. How many men and women will shed their blood before this is over, because I asked it of them?"

"Tcha, *hushla*," said Zandakar. "You queen, they serve, *zho*?"

Han nodded. "He's right. This is war, Rhian. War *is* blood."

"And it's too late to turn back now, I know," she said, glowering. "But that doesn't mean I have to like it."

"Ethrea!" called Dalsyn. "Come. There is an answer."

In the softening rain, Rhian's cropped hair curled even tighter. Her eyes shone an even brigher blue. The wounds in her cheeks had started to swell. Pain danced behind the strength in her face. Turning on her heel, she walked back to Dalsyn, tall and proud upon his sealskin throne.

Han glanced at Zandakar, and together they joined her.

The slainta's clansmen stood around him, cudgels held against their sealskin chests. Voolksyn, the ambassador, his brother, stood by the slainta's right hand.

"Ethrea," he said, "we are treated like brother to sister. We are treated for many of the mother's seasons. Ethrea keeps its word. You speak for the Tzhung, you say they can be trusted. I trust your word – until you break it." He leaned forward, and suddenly his green eyes were malevolent. "Ethrea breaks word . . . Harbisland breaks Ethrea."

"Harbisland will never break Ethrea," said Rhian. "For Ethrea's word is constant, like the sun."

Dalsyn nodded to his clansmen, and said something swift in guttural Harbish. Then he stood, and stepped away from his throne. Voolksyn stepped with him.

"Han of Tzhung," he said. His voice was calm, but fear lurked in his eyes. "Take us to the Count of Arbenia."

Banishing exhaustion, banishing pain, Han closed his eyes and called on the wind. He wrapped it around them, feeling his bones groan, his blood weep . . .

. . . Harbisland vanished. They walked in the wind.

Standing in one corner of the castle's Grand Ballroom, Dexterity considered the trading nations' ambassadors. Most of them clustered around the hastily prepared trestle tables that were laden with food scoured from the kitchens. By some kind of miracle, they'd answered Alasdair's cryptic summons. Even Gutten had come. Athnïj, too, though in many ways that was a pity.

He's looking dreadful, poor man. I wish he'd stop staring at me, Hettie. I can't tell him anything. It's not my place.

He glanced up at the ornate clock, built so cunningly into the frescoed ceiling, then sidled inconspicuously over to the king.

"Your Majesty. It's been well over four hours, and we've no idea when Rhian – I mean, Her Majesty – will return. I'm not certain how much longer we can keep them here, if for no other reason than they've eaten more than their fill and drunk copious draughts of wine. Surely, quite soon now, nature must take its course."

"He's right," said Duke Edward, shamelessly eavesdropping. "We'll have a riot on our hands soon, especially since we can't answer one of their questions. And it's not as if we can call in Idson, either. We want these men for allies, not enemies."

"I know it's awkward, but I want to detain them just a little while longer," said Alasdair. "I want to give Her Majesty all the help I can."

Duke Edward grunted. "To my mind you'd be better off getting Helfred to start praying."

Dexterity saw the fear flash across Alasdair's face, and could have kicked the thoughtless duke. "Majesty, I have travelled with witch-men, remember?" he said, as firmly as he could without seeming to chastise Edward. "I came to no harm. Her Majesty is quite safe." He nearly continued, *And don't forget she has Zandakar with her.* But that might not be as reassuring as he wanted it to sound. "God will protect her, Majesty."

Alasdair nodded, but he didn't look convinced. "What hope does she have, I wonder, of convincing Harbisland's slainta? What if he looks on her unannounced arrival as a deadly insult? What if he attempts to arrest her, or worse? What if—"

"Come now, Majesty, you mustn't work yourself

up like this," Dexterity said quickly. "Remember what our prolate said? We must have faith."

"Faith," said Alasdair. It was almost a sigh. "My faith has been more tested since Eberg's death than in all the years of my life before it. I swear, I begin to think—"

A cold wind, swirling. A tang of pine and salt water. A splatter of rain, falling beneath the ballroom's ceiling. Rhian stepped out of the unseen air with five men in tow.

Every sibilant conversation died.

Dexterity watched as Alasdair broke the frozen moment, walking across the parquetry floor to greet his wife. He halted before her, and bowed his head.

"Majesty. God be thanked for your safe return."

"Yes," said Rhian. She sounded faint, as though exhausted, or overcome with pain. The self-inflicted wounds in her cheeks were savage. "It was a fruitful endeavour."

Han and Zandakar had stepped aside, and so did Voolksyn, allowing the rulers of Harbisland and Arbenia to occupy the centre of attention. Dexterity thought Tzhung's emperor looked even more exhausted than Rhian. Han's battle with the trade winds and his grief over losing Sun-dao had already taxed his strength; what it had cost him to travel so far in the wind, with so many others . . .

Frankly, Hettie, I don't want to think.

Rhian stood straight and tall, calling upon some hidden reserves to keep her from appearing weak before so many vital men. "King Alasdair, I present to you Dalsyn, the Slainta of Harbisland, and

Count Ebrich of Arbenia. Welcome allies in the fight against Mijak."

As the dukes and Helfred murmured, and the ambassadors stared, even Sere Gutten struck dumb with surprise, Dexterity folded his arms and hugged himself tight.

Oh, Hettie. She's done it. Our girl's done it, my love.

"Your excellencies," said Alasdair. "Welcome to Ethrea. It is an honour to receive you, and a sadness that calamity must be the cause."

"King," said the slainta, staring down from his great height. "Your little queen is mighty."

"She is," said Alasdair. "All of Ethrea lives in her heart."

Like Gutten, the Count of Arbenia was wrapped in bearskin, and like his ambassador he was squat and aggressive. "We must talk," Ebrich announced, as though he declared war.

Rhian nodded. "Agreed. We've no time to waste."

"I think we'll acquit ourselves most comfortably here, Majesty," said Alasdair. "And while your council oversees the transformation of this ballroom into a chamber of war, might I suggest you have your wounds tended?"

Dexterity stepped forward. "Can I offer my services, Majesty? No guarantees, of course, but—"

"No," said Rhian flatly. "When you heal you leave no memory of the wound, Mister Jones. There is value in a scar, I've found."

"Then allow me to escort you to Ursa," he replied. "And she can stitch you as untidily as you please."

"Very well. One moment—"

While Rhian had swift, private words with Emperor Han, and the king consulted with Helfred and the dukes, Arbenia's count and his unpleasant ambassador drew aside to converse. The ambassadors of Icthia, Slynt and Dev'karesh, with ties to Harbisland, gathered round the slainta and Voolksyn to hear their low-voiced opinions. The Barbruish and Keldravian ambassadors, beholden to Arbenia but excluded from consultation, milled like twin sheep bereft of their shepherd.

Ambassador Lai stood alone, his dark gaze resting on his emperor. Not even his exquisitely polished public mask could successfully hide that he was deeply worried.

Dexterity sidled over to Zandakar. "There was no trouble?" he asked softly.

"*Wei*," said Zandakar, equally soft. "They believe now. They will fight Mijak."

Oh, Hettie. "Largely because of you, Zandakar. Ethrea owes you a great debt, my friend."

"*Wei*," said Zandakar. "Debt is mine, *zho*?"

In his eyes and voice, that burden of guilt. Memories of the dead that he couldn't escape.

"Zandakar—"

"Mister Jones?" said Rhian, turning. "Shall we go?"

"Congratulations, Majesty," said Dexterity, puffing a little as they hurried through the castle. "A job well done."

"It wasn't easy," she replied. "Arbenia's count is as brutish as Gutten. I'd not have succeeded without the slainta . . . and Han."

"And Zandakar?"

"Fortunately, Zandakar scared them stupid."

"And you, Rhian?" he asked, because the corridor they travelled was empty of servants and courtiers. "Are they sufficiently frightened of you?"

She glanced at him sidelong. "If they're not, they soon will be."

They reached the infirmary, only to be told Ursa was tending a castle groom kicked by a horse.

"I'll send for her," said the clerk, who was attempting to transcribe Ursa's notes, the poor man. "I believe the lad's bruised, not broken."

Restless, Rhian paced the herb-scented chamber. Dexterity perched on a stool and watched her, torn between pride and worry.

"Are you sure you want scars, Majesty? It's dreadful to think of your beauty spoiled."

"If I thought beauty was the key to keeping the trading nations in my pocket, I'd care," she replied. "But it's not, so I don't."

He pulled a face. "Their leaders are all men. I don't know a man who's not moved by beauty."

"Tcha," she said. "Beauty may get their trousers stirring, but it won't keep them by my side. Fear and blood will do that – *and* the visible reminder I'm a warrior queen, not a simpering miss. They'll see the scars before they see me, and they won't look any further."

He doubted that: scars or no scars she was a striking young woman, and in her supple leather doublet and leggings a shocking sight for men used to women wrapped in brocade.

But if lust can inspire them to follow her, can I complain? We need all the followers she can get.

Ursa returned. "I'm told you're hurt, Majesty," she said, marching through the open door. "You must have a greater care of your person, for – *tcha*!"

"No scolding, Ursa," said Rhian, unsmiling. "I've not the time or the patience. Stitch me quickly so I can get back to work."

Ursa blinked, taken aback. "Majesty," she said, and did as she was told.

Rhian refused a poppy potion when the stitching was done. "I need a clear head."

"Majesty," said Dexterity. "I know I'm wanted in council, but if I might take a moment?"

"A moment only," she replied.

"Jones?" said Ursa, when they were alone.

"She's talked Harbisland and Arbenia to our cause, Ursa," he said quickly. "Looks like we'll have our armada. But if that should fail—"

Ursa nodded. "I know. We'll be fighting Mijak in Ethrea. I've already started a list of the physicks I think will make the best leaders. And another of all the supplies we'll need if, God forbid, it comes to that. Another day or so, I'll have it ready for the council."

He kissed her cheek. "God bless you. Rhian will be pleased to hear it."

"Rhian." Ursa snorted. "There's a change come over that girl, and I'm not sure I like it. Are you going to tell me she didn't use a blade on herself?"

"No," he said, sighing. "She's got the bit between her teeth, Ursa. All we can do is hold on."

"God help us," muttered Ursa. "What have we started, Jones?"

"Whatever it is, we must help her to finish it," he

said, and with a strained smile hurried after their queen.

Her stitched face burning, and regretting the refusal of something to dull the pain, Rhian strode into the ballroom to find the platter-laden trestles gone, and in their place a square of tables around which sat her council, the slainta, the count, and the ambassadors. Han was there too, having returned from Lai's residence after briefly withdrawing to set in motion plans for his witch-men. He'd used the time to change, as well. His tunic now was shaded deep violet. She hoped he'd healed the wound in his chest. Ven'Cedwin sat apart at his own little table, poised to record this historic meeting.

"Gentlemen," she said, taking her seat. "Allow me to formally welcome you to our first council of war. Ethrea appreciates your attendance." She bared her teeth, not quite smiling. "Let us first admit the obvious: we are not all friends here. Even now some of you are involved in disputes. *They do not matter.* All that matters is Mijak. It does not care if you are friend or foe. It cares only for how swiftly you die."

A stirring around the table, as the trading nations swallowed her unpalatable truths. A stirring at the ballroom door, as Mister Jones finally joined them. She gave him a sharp look, and waited for him to take his seat.

"And now," she continued, "let us devise our war."

With an ease she hadn't expected, terms for a new charter were teased out and settled.

In the end it was decided Han's witch-men would take the slainta, the count and the various ambassadors to meet with the rulers of the lesser trading nations. They would carry with them a new treaty to be signed, outlining what was required from each nation in quantities of ships, sailors, weapons and soldiers. Once the letters were delivered and ratified, the trading nations would meet in Kingseat to draw up plans for the armada. And once those plans were ratified, Han's witch-men would see each nation's fleet brought to Ethrea, ready for sailing out to meet Mijak.

"We must not delude ourselves, gentlemen," Rhian told them in closing. "The battle at sea will be desperate. We won't escape unscathed. But no matter how dire that prospect, it pales before the losses we'll face should Mijak conquer Ethrea and have a safe haven from which to sail to your lands."

As they broke for refreshments, waiting for Ven'Cedwin and his clerks to return with the copies of the new treaty to be signed, she took Han aside.

"Your witch-men are ready?"

He nodded. "Even now, those I can spare from Tzhung-tzhungchai ride the wind to Ethrea. In the morning they will do their part against Mijak."

She wished she could embrace him. "Thank you, Han."

"There's no debt," he said. "You're the only one who could unite the trading nations."

It was reassuring, and frightening, to hear him say it. Somehow the support of Tzhung-tzhungchai increased her burden, instead of easing it.

Ven'Cedwin returned then, and the three great

trading nations signed the new treaty. The council of war ended with an agreement to resume again at first light – when Han's witch-men would join them, and the hard work would truly begin.

Once she and her council were alone, she at last let a little of her weariness show.

"So, gentlemen," she said. "Here we stand. Prolate Helfred, it's time for your venerables and chaplains to preach courage in the face of terror. Alasdair, my lord dukes, the garrisons must be told the truth now too, and recruiting among the duchies undertaken. Those soldiers you've selected for personal training by Zandakar must be brought to the castle within the next two days. I take it plans for converting our grounds to a barracks are in hand?"

"They're completed," said Alasdair. "Work can commence immediately."

"See it done. Zandakar—"

"Rhian *hushla*."

"You're ready to begin this intensive training?"

He nodded. "*Zho*."

"Dexterity—"

"Majesty?"

She smiled at him, even though the pain in her face was now ferocious. "I have a special task for you. It's past time Zandakar was made fluent in Ethrean. Most of us understand him well enough but with what we'll soon be facing, well enough won't be good enough."

Dexterity nodded. "Yes, Majesty."

She looked at Zandakar. "He will train you to speak Ethrean as you have trained me in the *hotas*, *zho*? And when you're not training your tongue, or my soldiers, you and I will dance?"

"*Zho*," said Zandakar. "We will dance."

She looked around the table. "Are there any questions?"

No. Not even Adric had anything to say. Helfred and her dukes were subdued. Stunned, even, that after so much talking the time for action had arrived.

"Come," said Alasdair, his fingers warm around her wrist. "You need rest, and one of Ursa's potions."

Even if she'd wanted to argue, she was too tired. They left the ballroom together, returned to their apartments, and she let sleep claim her for too short a while.

That night she and Alasdair went to Litany in Kingseat's great chapel. She wore her leathers again which Dinsy, cursing, had cleaned of the blood spilled upon them from her cut face. The people of Kingseat murmured to see her martial attire, and the two neatly stitched wounds in her face.

Helfred's sermon that night was taken from Admonition 12: *God in his greatness places great burdens upon us. Trust in his mercy and be brave in the face of all dangers.* When he was finished, he addressed the congregation.

"Good people of Kingseat, this night shall our sovereign queen complete our sermon, with solemn speech and a dire prediction."

Startled, Rhian looked up at him. "Prolate—"

He stepped down from his pulpit, leaving her no choice.

The faces of her people, so innocent and trusting,

looked up at her from the great chapel's pews. The chapel was crowded, with many folk standing round the walls and by its closed doors.

"People of Kingseat," she said, her voice slurred a little from weariness and pain. "It has of late come to the crown's attention that a darkness rises against us in the east. A nation known as Mijak, hidden for many lifetimes, has stirred from its slumber and bends its dread gaze upon Ethrea. Already nations have fallen to its ravages. Thousands are slain. Thousands more are enslaved. But we must not despair. An armada is being gathered, that will sail out to meet the warriors of Mijak and, with God's grace, destroy them before they set one foot on Ethrean soil."

She paused, to give the congregation time to consider her words. The discipline of the chapel surrendered to murmurs, exclamations, cries of fear and anger. She raised her hands.

"I know you're frightened. I don't scorn to tell you, when first I learned of this I was frightened too. But Ethrea does not stand alone. The trading nations stand with us. They are pledged to our defence, sworn to fight by our side. Emperor Han himself, of mysterious Tzhung-tzhungchai, has pledged the might of his great empire to aid us. I tell you again, *we are not alone*. With friends such as these, and God's merciful grace, Ethrea *will* prevail in this dark hour."

"God bless Queen Rhian!" a voice cried from the congregation. "God bless the trading nations and even Tzhung-tzhungchai!"

The cry was taken up around the great chapel.

Shod feet drummed the stone floor. Moved almost to tears, Rhian let her people shout, let them loose their emotions in what Helfred must surely deem a disrespectful display. Glancing at him, though, she was surprised to see him smiling. Alasdair was smiling too, though there was pain in his eyes.

She raised her hands, again calling for calm. When most of the voices had subsided, she took a deep breath and released it, slowly.

"You see I have come to this chapel dressed not like a queen, but a huntsman," she said. "In truth, I'm become both. I am your huntsman queen of Ethrea, determined to defend you to the length of my life. And now it falls upon me to ask of you a dreadful promise. I am your queen, it's true, but I am also one woman. I must ask every woman here to become a huntsman queen. Queen of your home, queen of your family. Ready to stand and fight for what is yours. And every man here, you must be a King Alasdair. Sworn to stand by your queen, sworn to fight and die for her, and for Ethrea, and for every soul you know and even those you never met. In this chapel tonight there are friends, and there are enemies. People who live in your hearts and people who don't. I say to you now: *every* Ethrean is your friend. Every Ethrean is your *family*. Let the past be the past. We must preserve the future."

They leapt to their feet, her people, her subjects, the sound of their voices like a cresting wave. She stood dazed in the pulpit, her face hurting, her heart full of fear and love.

"Well done," said Helfred as she joined him. "God inspired you."

"My people inspired me," she said, then relented. "And yes. God, too."

"The word has gone out," he said, lowering his voice. "Starting tonight every chapel in Ethrea calls your people to war."

An icy shudder ran through her. "Oh, God. I so hoped this day wouldn't come."

He touched her arm, lightly. "So did I, Rhian."

She returned to Alasdair, who took her hand and squeezed it very hard. "Well said."

She sighed, even as the congregation continued to shout and cry praise. "I hope so. My simple words must lift a kingdom, and give them courage for the days ahead."

It took so long to leave the chapel she was nearly babbling with exhaustion by the time they reached their carriage. She dozed all the way back to the castle, her head on Alasdair's shoulder. Somehow she walked up the stairs, along the corridors and through the doors of their privy apartments. Then she surrendered, and let him carry her to bed.

On the newsun she led her warhost from Jatharuj, Hekat dressed in her most threadbare linen training tunic. She laced sandals on her feet, she stitched more amulets and godbells into her godbraids. Godbells for singing, amulets for the god. Her hair was so heavy she could barely lift her head. Its weight hurt her, she did not care.

I lead the god into the world.

Vortka and Dmitrak walked with her to the harbour. Vortka wore a plain godspeaker robe, like herself he did not need clothes to shout his importance.

Jatharuj knew Hekat, Jatharuj knew the high god-speaker. It knew Dmitrak warlord but still he had to shout. He wore linen and leather, he wore gold and bronze ornaments. He wore gold in his godbraids, he wore precious stones.

Tcha, Dmitrak. I want Zandakar. I will find him in the world.

Not every warrior in Icthia would sail with her, she had more warriors than warships to carry them. The warriors not chosen would stay behind in Icthia, they would fight for the god in Icthia if the god's enemies appeared. The warriors not chosen had wept out their pain, they had begged for her mercy, she had no mercy to give them. Only her best warriors could sail for the god.

Those left-behind warriors lined the streets of Jatharuj. As she and Vortka and Dmitrak walked down to the harbour they stamped their feet, shouting, they chanted in the sun.

"The god sees our Empress, the god sees Hekat of Mijak, the god sees Dmitrak warlord and its high godspeaker Vortka!"

The trade winds she had saved from those demons blew in the harbour, they blew the scorpion sails of her warships, they blew her praise that they were free. The warships were ready, they were full of warriors and horses and godspeakers and sacred beasts for sacrifice, they waited for her so they could sail into the world.

Her warship with its blood-red hull stood ready, eager for her presence. She boarded it lightly, Vortka and Dmitrak boarded it after her. A path had been cleared from the dock to the open water. The warriors trained to sail her warship worked its oars and eased it from the harbour.

She stood at its bow and watched the open water come closer; she stood and laughed to hear her godbells singing in the trade winds. She felt young, she felt strong, she was Hekat in the god's eye. Godchosen and precious, she would give the god the world.

Vortka stood beside her, his godbells singing in the wind. Did he look happy? She thought he did not. She defended him to Dmitrak but in her heart she wondered.

Why is he not happy? The god is in the world.

Ship by beautiful ship, the warhost followed her from the harbour. Her warhost was beautiful. It was beautiful under the sun.

"This is our glory, Vortka," she whispered as the wind blew and the oars ceased their splashing and their scorpion sail bellied with the god's breath, as they sailed majestic upon the open water. "We were born for this."

Vortka said nothing, he was silent for the god.

That did not matter, her heart was singing.

See me, god. See Hekat in the world.

CHAPTER TWENTY-NINE

Preparations to counter Mijak's onslaught picked up pace. Church and ducal messengers brought Rhian daily reports from around the kingdom. The news of Mijak had been calmly received, on the whole. To her surprise, one person in the great chapel's congregation the night of her rallying speech wrote down what she'd said, and soon copies began to appear – first in Kingseat township, then around the duchy, and then all over Ethrea.

Her words became a battle cry and were repeated in taverns, in school houses, in chapels, in village shops on the streets of Ethrea's townships and in its verdant fields: *Be every woman a huntsman queen, and every man a King Alasdair. The past is the past. We must preserve the future. Ethrea is not alone.*

Save for her privy garden, which Alasdair refused to sacrifice, the grounds of Kingseat Castle were transformed with tents and pavilions into sprawling barracks, and the flower beds torn up to make more tiltyards for training. Those soldiers selected from the duchies' garrisons, and the men Zandakar had trained on the road from Linfoi, arrived on foot and by barge in Kingseat and were sent straight to the castle.

Every day Zandakar trained Rhian first. After her, he trained Alasdair and her dukes, showing them no mercy, showing them Mijak. If the armada failed and warfare came to Ethrea, her dukes would be spread across the kingdom. It was important that they know what to expect.

After that, Zandakar and Rhian trained her soldiers not to dance the *hotas*, but to find ways of killing a warrior for whom the *hotas* were as natural as breathing. They trained the foreign soldiers too, and all the officers from Kingseat's garrisons.

So much mock warfare. The grounds of her castle might never recover.

When he wasn't training soldiers, or dancing *hotas* with Rhian, Zandakar schooled his Ethrean with Dexterity. His fluency improved rapidly, as though at last he was really trying, not just getting by.

The last trading vessels in Kingseat harbour departed for their home ports, not to return until Mijak was defeated. In their place came the warships of Tzhung-tzhungchai, of Harbisland, of Arbenia and the lesser trading nations. They came in piecemeal, in dribs and drabs, and quickly filled the harbour so that latecomers were forced to wait in the open water. Han's witch-men were tireless in bringing the warships to Ethrea, and to spare the sensibilities of Ethrea's people, and some of their allies, they worked at night, so that with every new dawn in the days following the signing of the war treaty, the trading nations' armada had seemed to swell by magic.

Kingseat township filled with foreign sailors whose business was war, not trading. Mindful of their temperaments, and the heightened nervousness of the townsfolk, and the likelihood of disaster, Idson and his garrison soldiers increased their presence on the streets. Furloughs were strictly rationed. Taverns were forbidden to serve ale and wine for more than one hour each day. Soldiers from each trading nation joined Idson's garrison, commissioned to keep the streets of Kingseat trouble-free in this time of impending violence.

Across the kingdom, Helfred's clergy helped keep the peace, helped the people to stay strong and believe in their queen, and helped the duchies maintain their defences where their borders met the sea. Devouts and chaplains and even venerables laboured with novices and regular folk and soldiers to make sure their barrier wall remained fortified, especially where once there had been ports and there was a vulnerability to Mijaki attack.

The duchy garrisons struggled to cope with the number of men and women eager to learn swordplay, so they could protect their homes from the heathen invaders. The kingdom's chapels filled to overflowing, as Rhian's people prayed for a swift deliverance . . . or a miracle.

And despite all of that, life in Ethrea continued. Babes were born. Their grandparents died, and were buried. The hens laid their eggs and dogs chased straying cats.

With the trading nations at long last reconciled to this war, their rulers and representatives clogged the ambassadors' district, its residences and its streets. They met Rhian and her council daily in the castle's war room to thrash out the particulars of the armada, and how to proceed should their desperate sea defence fail.

Dexterity was her godsend. When he wasn't gently

bullying Zandakar to *"speak Ethrean proper, drat you!"*, or working with Ursa to marshall her army of physicks, he was her council's friendliest face. Toymaking forgotten, he laboured without respite to see every fractious official soothed and every querulous demand met – or tactfully declined. Cheerful with Ven'Cedwin, who led a horde of clerical scribes, he kept meticulous track of who agreed to what, with whom, and why, diffusing dozens of brewing altercations every day.

Even the Count of Arbenia was pleasant to Dexterity. And if that wasn't a miracle, then miracles didn't exist.

Fifteen days after the first Tzhung warships appeared in Kingseat, the last Barbruish carrack was witched safely to the harbour . . . and the trading alliance armada was finally assembled. Six hundred and thirty-seven warships in all, bristling with catapults and barrels of pitch, vicious with battering rams and fire-dragons and knife-wheels and grapplers.

Only the ships of Tzhung-tzhungchai were naked.

Rhian asked Han why that should be, after he surprised her – again – in her privy garden. It was early, and she'd retreated there after her *hotas*, to gather her thoughts before the first war council of the day.

"Tzhung's witch-men are my weapons," Han said. "We have the wind. We need nothing of metal and fire."

Looking at him, severe in black silk, she felt a pang of guilt pierce her. Han and his witch-men were working so hard. Han looked almost as exhausted as Zandakar, who pushed himself brutally from sunrise to sunset and beyond, into torchlight, training the soldiers who poured daily into Kingseat.

And even if he were to work twice as hard, it wouldn't be enough. We need months and months to make this army, not a few weeks. We're facing an enemy who's been training for years. Dear God, have we lost before the first blow is struck?

"Stop that, Rhian," Han said sternly. "No leader can afford to surrender to despair."

She glowered at him. "I know. I'm not. But neither can a leader afford to hide from the truth."

"The truth," said Han, "is that no man is ever truly prepared for war. A man can spend his whole life training for battle . . . and faint with fear before the first blood is spilled. What point then his years and years of training? Another man, who has never trained a day in his life, can pick up a pitchfork and be more valiant than that soldier. Not even the wind knows who will break, and who will bend."

"All those warships," Rhian murmured, staring down at the exotic flock of vessels riding the harbour. "And three witch-men to sail on each one. Can you spare so many, Han? You must know they won't all return from their encounter with Mijak, even if we're victorious."

Han shrugged. "Perhaps fewer will die than you fear. They are witch-men."

What did he mean? That if the battle looked hopeless they'd simply . . . walk into the air? Abandon the ships they'd been given to protect?

Oh, God. Let the slainta or the count suspect treachery from the Tzhung . . .

"I did not hear you say that, Han. Never say it again."

"If the battle is lost, you think my witch-men should not save themselves?" he demanded. "You think our cause is best served by *fewer* witch-men in the world?"

"Of course I don't!"

"Then do not tell me my witch-men must die for nothing!"

Buffeted by the sharp cold wind of his anger's calling, Rhian stood her ground before him, fists clenched, eyes narrowed. It took all her strength not to let herself be blown backwards.

As abruptly as it sprang up, the wind died.

"Han," she said, struggling to breathe slowly, to not show him her fright, "your witch-men will do what you tell them. Just . . . whatever you tell them, don't forget the consequences."

Han gave her a mock bow. "The girl-queen of Ethrea schools Tzhung's emperor in his business. Truly, Rhian, every day you're a surprise."

"Well, I shouldn't be," she retorted. "How do you think I grew up?"

"Like the princesses of Tzhung-tzhungchai," he said. "It would seem I was mistaken."

She raised an eyebrow at him, striving to tease. Striving to find some harmless way to ease the tension that gnawed constantly at her guts. "You have princesses in Tzhung-tzhungchai? I never knew that. I'd like to meet them, when this is over."

He looked down his nose at her. "I prefer that you don't. Women like you give other women . . . ideas."

She sighed. "Han, did you seek me out for a reason?"

"You think to send Zandakar with the armada."

From his tone, she could tell he didn't approve the plan. "And you've come to say that's a poor idea?"

"Yes."

"I don't agree. His scorpion knife is a formidable weapon. What point is there to having it, if it's not to be used?"

"Would you believe me if I said the wind whispered this warning in my ear?"

"Will you try to blow me down the side of the cliff again if I say I find that claim suspicious?"

His lips tightened. "No. But a witch-man tells no lies about the wind."

Rhian folded her arms. "And am I bound to obey your wind when it whispers?"

"No," said Han. "But you're foolish if you don't. *Think*, Rhian. Where does Zandakar's value lie? How can his strengths best serve you? Can he dance his *hotas* on a ship? Can he train your army in the middle of the ocean?"

She hadn't asked herself that. She hadn't looked past the hope that Mijak's onslaught would be halted by the armada . . . and that to stop Mijak they needed Zandakar.

"And are you certain," Han persisted, "that his scorpion knife can overcome his brother's gauntlet?"

No, she wasn't. And neither was Zandakar. But the thought of not using their only true weapon against Mijak . . .

"If the knife's not powerful enough to defeat Dmitrak, then why did Vortka give it to him?"

"I can't tell you that," said Han. "I can only tell you not to send him."

Frustrated, Rhian scuffed her toe in the dirt.

"You can't sail with the armada, either," he added. "You're Eberg's daughter. The last of your great House. Your people look to you for strength and comfort. Does a mother leave her children when they are lost and frightened?"

She looked at him. "Han, am I *stupid*? Of course I'm not sailing. I wish I could, the thought of staying behind is torture, but I know where my place is. I know my duty." She felt tears sting her eyes. "Alasdair sails with them. Unless," she added, indulging in sarcasm, "the wind has an opinion to share on that, too?"

He answered her by wrapping the air about himself, and vanishing.

Feeling cross-grained and blown in all directions, she returned to the castle to find Alasdair breakfasting with his cousin.

"At last," he said, smiling. "I was beginning to wonder where you were." He patted the table. "Come and sit. Eat. There's—"

Waving a hand, she perched on the window's embrasure. "I'm not hungry. Alasdair, my love, about the armada—"

"*No*," he said. He sounded almost vicious. "You're not sailing with it, Rhian."

Ludo swallowed his mouthful of egg and put down his fork. "Ah . . . should I go?"

"There's no need," said Alasdair. "The subject is closed."

Rhian stared, incredulous. *Does every man of my*

acquaintance believe me suddenly stupid? "Alasdair!"

He looked weary too. So did Ludo. The battle had scarcely begun and dear God, they were all so tired.

How will we be when the fighting starts in earnest?

"Alasdair," she said again, more gently. "This is about Zandakar. Han's advised me he should stay behind too . . . and I'm inclined to agree with him."

"I should go," said Ludo, pushing back his chair.

Alasdair took hold of his forearm. "Stay."

"No, really—"

"*Stay.*"

Ludo stayed.

"Han advised you?" said Alasdair. "When? We've not laid eyes on the emperor for days."

"Just now. In the garden." Rhian pulled a face. "You know what he's like. He treats the world as though everything in it belongs to him."

"I thought," said Alasdair carefully, "that the council was in agreement on this. Zandakar is our best hope against Mijak."

Helpless, she stared at him. "Han says the wind says Zandakar mustn't sail."

Alasdair sat back and pressed the heels of his hands against his eyes. "Well," he said, muffled. "Helfred will dance to hear that."

"I'm not pleased either," she said. "You're right, Zandakar *is* our best hope against Mijak. But perhaps we're being foolish, thinking one knife – even that scorpion knife – can defeat all of Mijak's warships. Surely it's Zandakar's knowledge that makes him a weapon. The armada's greatest strength lies in

Han's witch-men, and the brute battering force of the trading nations' ships."

Slowly Alasdair lowered his hands. "So you agree with Han? You want to keep Zandakar here?"

There was a knot beneath her breastbone, strangling her breath. "I want whatever serves Ethrea best."

"As do I," he replied. "Zandakar stays."

The strangling knot tightened. It was painful to breathe. "It means you'll be alone on the *Queen Ilda*."

Their eyes met, and she struggled not to weep.

Almost forgotten, Ludo cleared his throat and ran a hand over his short blond hair. "You needn't fear for him, Rhian. Where Alasdair goes, cousin Ludo's his shadow."

"No!" said Alasdair, turning. "Are you mad?"

"Completely," said Ludo, with a fine attempt at bravado. "Because if you're sailing, then so am I. How did you so graciously phrase it? Ah yes. *The subject is closed*."

Rhian pressed tentative fingers to the pink, knotted scars in her face. They still itched, though the stitches had been out for days. "Ludo, it's a grand gesture, and I appreciate it, but you're needed here."

"Not as much as Alasdair will need me on the *Ilda*," said Ludo. "No king worth his salt travels without at least one titled gentleman companion. For the look of things, if nothing else. I'll be his adjutant. His go-between. His nursemaid – you know he needs one."

Alasdair threw a bread roll at him.

"You make a good point, Ludo," she said, smiling weakly, "but I mean it when I say you're needed."

"Rhian . . ." Ludo sighed. "The only other duke you can spare is Adric. You'd inflict *Adric* on your husband? I thought you loved him."

Oh, God. *Adric.* "But – your duchy. Your garrison."

"My father's chairbound, not a doltard," said Ludo, shrugging. "Henrik oversees the duchy far better than I ever could. As for the garrison, it's the smallest in Ethrea. The soldiers earmarked to join the general army can be folded into Kingseat's garrison or parcelled out between Edward and Rudi. Those old warhorses are in their element. They'll not notice the strain of a few more men."

Ludo was right. Alasdair did need someone to go with him . . . and after Zandakar, no man in Ethrea would safeguard him better.

Slumped against the window she looked at them, her husband and his cousin, two men she loved so dearly . . . and imagined them dead.

Oh, God. Oh, God.

With an effort she wrenched her thoughts from that fruitless direction. Han had said it, curse him: no leader could afford to wallow in despair.

"Very well, Ludo," she said, her voice stony, her heart breaking. "Both of you will go, and you'll do the kingdom proud. With you and Alasdair leading Ethrea's armada, victory must be assured."

Alasdair stood, and joined her at the window. One fingertip touched her scarred cheek, so gentle. "Of course it must. If worse comes to worst I'll have Ludo catapulted among the Mijaki. He'll talk them to death and we'll all sail home singing."

Half-laughing, half-weeping, she threw her arms around him and held on tight. "I'll never forgive you if you don't come back," she whispered. "I'll – I'll marry Adric just to punish you."

"Punish yourself, more like," he retorted, his own voice unsteady, his arms strong and warm and holding her close. "And I'll haunt you into old age, woman. You'll never get rid of me."

"That's the idea," she said, and kissed him.

Behind them, Ludo cleared his throat again. "Ah – at the risk of being a spoilsport, my royal cousins, I need to remind you—"

"I know," said Rhian, reluctant, and eased from Alasdair's embrace. "We've a council of war to attend."

Hastily bathed and hurriedly fed, re-dressed in fresh huntsman's leathers, Rhian entered her war room, where her council and allies awaited. As well as the Slainta Dalsyn and Ebrich, Count of Arbenia, she was host to the leaders of Dev'karesh, Keldrave and Slynt. The rulers of Haisun and Barbruish had sent their most trusted representatives to sit on the war council. Han had sent his ambassador, Lai. He could not be spared from his witching tasks . . . and besides, his presence unsettled the other trading nations.

"Gentlemen," she said briskly, taking her seat. "Unless something untoward prevents it, or one of you has an objection, our armada will set sail at first light tomorrow."

There were no objections. She let her gaze linger on the faces of those men who, like herself, were rulers in their own right. Who, unlike herself, dared to risk their lives in warfare. And why was that? Pride? Arrogance? Fear of losing face before the other trading nations? Tradition? She didn't know. She hadn't asked. It wasn't her business.

"His Majesty King Alasdair and my most trusted Duke of Linfoi shall carry Ethrea's flag into battle aboard the *Queen Ilda*," she continued. "His Majesty carries my heart, also, and speaks for this kingdom as though my tongue were his."

Edward's head came up. "Ludo? I thought we'd agreed Zandakar would—"

"I've decided Zandakar is of more value to us here," she said. "Training our army, against the slim chance the armada should fail."

She watched the ripple of glances run around the table. Saw the veiled, speculative looks at Alasdair, and at Ludo. Adric sulked, like a spoiled child denied a treat. Wisely for him he didn't challenge her decree.

She nodded at Helfred. "Your Eminence, the kingdom's chapels stand ready?"

"Yes, Majesty," said Helfred. "Even now prayers are begun for the armada's safe return. They will not cease until our ships come home again, victorious."

He sounded so confident. His magnificent proletary robes added weight to his conviction; mindful of creating the right impression for the trading nations, he'd allowed himself to be dressed as splendidly as Marlan ever was. In the ballroom's candlelight he sparkled crimson and gold.

"Thank you, Eminence," she said. "My lords,

this will be a day crammed full of last minute preparations. The castle's message boys are sure to be run off their feet. Before we turn our attention to particular matters, is there anything of general import you wish to discuss?"

Dexterity raised a finger. "Ah – Majesty? Ursa's tribe of physicks arrives in town today. She was wondering if she could also speak with healers from the trading nations, if any have a little time to spare."

"To what purpose?" grunted Ebrich. He had piggy eyes, and they were always suspicious. As though he feared his own shadow would rise up and stab him in the back.

"Doubtless she hopes to learn from them," said Ambassador Lai. "Tzhung-tzhungchai has no objection."

Which of course meant no-one else did either.

Rhian swallowed a smile. "Ursa will be most grateful, I'm sure."

And so their last council of war continued.

When it was done, she escaped to the tiltyard, and Zandakar. He hardly ever attended war councils. Like Han, he made the trading nations nervous. He was far more useful teaching soldiers how to kill.

"Rhian *hushla*," he said, leaving his soldier-students to fend for themselves a moment.

She led him well out of their earshot, ignoring the smiles and showing-off her presence always inspired.

"You're not sailing tomorrow," she told him without preamble. "You're staying in Ethrea."

He was dusty, and sweaty, though the weather had turned autumn cool. "Not sailing? Why?"

"You're needed here."

He shook his head. "*Wei*, Rhian. The armada needs me."

"Not as much as Ethrea." She gestured to the soldiers, grappling with each other in the tiltyard's dirt. "Not as much as they do."

Not as much as I do, though you'll never hear me say it.

Zandakar was frowning. "Rhian—"

"*No*," she said. "Why are you so eager? I thought the last thing you wanted was to fight your family. Your father."

It was the first time she'd mentioned Vortka since he'd told her who he was.

"It is," he said, his eyes full of pain. "If I sail . . . I can save him."

Oh, Zandakar. She shook her head. "You don't know that. If you sail, you could just as easily watch him die." *Or die yourself.* "I'm sorry. You remain here."

And then she walked away, before his grief changed her mind.

The long day ended with a special Litany in the great chapel, attended by Ethrea's queen, its king and its council of war, except for Zandakar. Helfred prayed with touching passion. Ethreans in the congregation wept. Dexterity sat with Ursa, and soaked a kerchief with his tears.

Public duties performed, Rhian and Alasdair retired to their apartments. They made love in a frenzy, and slept in exhaustion. She woke before dawn to the sound of Alasdair dressing, singing softly as he did every morning. She hid her tears in her pillow so he'd not be distressed.

As the sun began its slow climb into the sky, Rhian stood on Kingseat's docks with Helfred, and the remains of her council, but not Zandakar, and the trading nations' ambassadors, and watched as Alasdair and Ludo, aboard the royal flagship *Queen Ilda*, sailed out of the harbour.

Every vantage point in the township was crowded with people. They shouted, they cheered, they wept, they prayed.

One by one the warships of the alliance followed the *Ilda* out to sea. And one by one they vanished, as Han's witch-men wrapped them in the wind.

When the last warship was taken, an uneasy silence fell. Kingseat was hushed. No-one knew what to say.

"Come," said Rhian, dry-eyed and angry. "They have their work to do . . . and we have ours. Get to your chapel, Prolate. Pray that they sail home."

Alasdair looked up as Ludo wove his way towards him along the *Ilda's* shifting deck. His cousin's handsome face was tinged a pale but definite green. It seemed ocean sailing failed to agree with Duke Ludo of Linfoi.

"God have mercy," groaned Ludo, reaching him. "You're *eating*. Why are you *eating*?"

Alasdair grinned, and took another mouthful of porridge. "Because I'm hungry," he said, indistinctly.

"Well, stop it. It's *obscene*!"

Taking pity, Alasdair set the bowl aside then

kicked a coil of rope towards his distressed cousin. "Here. Sit down before you fall down – or overboard. You for certain don't desire to fall overboard. Han and his witch-men won't stop to save you."

They both looked across the *Ilda*'s side railing towards the nearby bow of Han's imperial Tzhung boat, where the emperor and ten of his witch-men stood in silence, their eyes closed, breathing in the salt air. Then they looked to their own bow, where stood their own three borrowed witch-men, equally silent, equally mysterious.

After yet another breathtaking dazzle through the witch-men's twilight realm, the armada was sailing normally for a time. Giving Han and his witch-men a chance to rest and replenish their strength.

Seated on the rope coil, Ludo shivered and hugged his knees. "They make my skin crawl. Do they make your skin crawl?"

Seated on his own coiled rope, Alasdair shrugged. "I'm reluctant to criticise. Without them we'd be lost."

"Oh, I don't say we wouldn't be," said Ludo. "I don't say we're not in Tzhung's debt until the great-great-great grandchildren of Ethrea's babes today are old and grizzled." Another shiver. "But that doesn't mean they don't make my skin crawl. Did you ever suspect the Tzhung were capable of this?"

"No. Did you?"

Ludo gave him a look. "Don't be silly. I'm a dyed-in-the-wool Linfoian. I don't pay attention to matters barely south of our border, let alone halfway around the world."

How typically Ludo. "Well, I suppose that's not

unreasonable, considering. It's not like we ever had much to do with them at home. In all my life I caught sight of a Tzhung boat patrolling Linfoi's waters what – three times? No pirates ever think of raiding our duchy. What's there to steal? Rocks? Sheep?"

"What about when you went to court? Nobody talked of Tzhung-tzhungchai then?" Ludo managed a grin, despite his heaving belly. "Or were you too busy eyeing Rhian to pay attention?"

The *Ilda* was an immaculate ship. There was no useful flotsam lying about to throw at his cousin. He could throw the bowl of porridge, but that might hint at a lack of decorum. "Of course there were rumours. Whispers. Far-fetched stories. I wondered, in passing. But I was at court for the council, to speak for my father, not to waste my time with Tzhung fairy tales."

"And now here we are in the middle of nowhere," said Ludo, looking over the side of the boat to the empty ocean beyond. "Surrounded by witch-men with powers I can't begin to understand. Dear God. Are you certain this isn't some fever-born dream?"

"Alas."

"I was afraid of that," said Ludo gloomily, and lapsed into silence.

Propping his elbows on his knees and his chin in his hand, Alasdair rested his gaze on the shifting, seething ocean. A light breeze half-heartedly snapped the *Ilda's* canvas sail. Tinkled the witch-men's windchimes. The guiding voice of their god, or so they believed. Wood creaked. Water sloshed. Everything everywhere smelled of fresh wet salt. They'd been at sea for nine days, and Ethrea was weeks behind them.

Gently, inevitably, his thoughts drifted to Rhian.

How did the training of the army progress? The soldiers who had travelled to Ethrea with the trading nations' boats, how were they settling in? Did they accept her authority? Did they accept Zandakar?

Zandakar. Rhian was right not to send him with the armada. If we should fail . . . God forbid, if we should perish . . . he truly will be Ethrea's last chance. But he is Zandakar . . . and he loves my wife.

He didn't doubt Rhian. Would never doubt Rhian. But neither could he doubt the bond she had with Zandakar. The warrior understood her in ways he didn't. Perhaps couldn't. She had an affinity for swordplay, for the *hotas*, that he lacked. She could be gentle, and loving, but in her heart burned a fire that was absent in his own. When she danced with her blade she was a stranger to him.

But not Zandakar. To Zandakar her heart is as familiar as his own.

He looked up as Ludo kicked his boot. "Stop fretting, Alasdair. She has Edward and Rudi. When it comes to the army they'll not let her steer wrong. Ethrea's people adore her. Any one of them would die for her in a heartbeat. And just to make certain, Helfred and his venerables and chaplains sing her praises from the pulpit morning, noon and night. She'll come to no harm while you're gone from her side. If she does, it'll only be for worry about you. I've never seen a woman so in love, cousin. If the woman the pair of you find me – if ever you do find me one – loves me even half as much, I'll be content."

Ludo knew him so well. "We'll find you a grand wife, Ludo," he said gruffly. "I promise. The finest duchess Linfoi's ever seen. Excepting my mother, of course."

Ludo grinned. "Of course." Then his amusement faded. "How far are we from the Mijaki warships, do you think?"

"I've no idea. Doubtless Han will tell us when we sail close."

"Doubtless," said Ludo, suddenly glum, and shifted to stare behind them at the rest of the armada, which like themselves coasted on the trade winds as Han's witch-men rested. "I still can't believe Dalsyn and Ebrich are sailing with us. What possessed them? Surely they had some underlings they could spare?"

Alasdair considered his cousin. "You never were political, Ludo. How could they stay behind, when the Emperor of Tzhung-tzhungchai was here? Of course they came. They want to keep an eye on him. They want history to reflect that they were present at the greatest sea battle of the age, that they led their mighty nations' warships against the invading horde of Mijak. Let Han take the credit? Let him bask in the adulation of the world?" He snorted. "I hardly think so."

"And then there's you and me," sighed Ludo. "Well, you. Don't you find it remarkable, if not downright laughable, that Alasdair of Linfoi is the crowned King of Ethrea? Seriously, cousin. When we were newly breeched brats tumbling out of apple trees in your father's ducal orchard, did you *ever* imagine we would come to this?"

"What? Rhian dubbing you Your Grace, the Duke of Linfoi?" Again, Alasdair regretted the lack of something to throw. "No. Never." And then he let his own smile die. "Ludo, it's not laughable. It's terrifying. I spend all my waking moments afraid."

Sober silence, as they stared at each other. "I'm glad you're king," said Ludo. "I can't think of another man more suited. I can't begin to imagine what Ethrea would be like, were Rhian married to that poor fool Rulf and Marlan ruled without a crown. *That's* what I find terrifying. The thought that you *aren't* king. And Rhian's not queen."

The wind chimes of Tzhung tinkled again as the ocean breeze gusted more strongly. Alasdair looked to the bow, but not a witch-man stirred. The trade winds, held back for so long by Tzhung's powers, bellied the sail and drove them onward towards unsuspecting Mijak.

"Do you still chafe at the tactics devised by Han and the queen?" said Ludo.

Alasdair shrugged. "How can I? They're sensible. If we lose Tzhung's emperor in this battle we're far more likely to lose the battle soon after. It's better Han concentrates on defeating Mijak instead of merely staying alive. Besides, it appeases the pride of Arbenia and Harbisland. Let Dalsyn and Ebrich lead the charge. Their ships have the most useful weapons, after all."

"Aside from Han's witch-men," said Ludo. "Let's not forget them."

"No," he said heavily. "Indeed, let's not."

Another sharp gust of wind. The Tzhung windchimes danced urgently. This time their echo could be heard from other ships close by.

"Do I imagine things," said Ludo slowly, "or do those windchimes sound . . . different?"

Alasdair stood and looked to Han's ship. The Tzhung sailors charged with care of the boat while Han and his witch-men slept, if they were sleeping, stopped what they were doing and turned their eyes to their emperor.

"No, Ludo," he said, as the sailors dropped to their bare knees. "I don't believe you imagine anything. I think the god of Tzhung has spoken."

In the bow of his ship, Emperor Han opened his eyes. As though following a silent command, he and his ten witch-men spread their arms wide. Moments later the *Ilda's* witch-men echoed them.

"They're all waking, Alasdair," said Ludo, staring over the side at the ships sailing to starboard. "I think we're about to ride the wind again."

That's what the Tzhung called it. *Riding the wind*. Also *Sleeping on God's breath*. So very poetic. Were the Tzhung a poetic race? He didn't know enough to know. And if their venture ended badly, he suspected he never would.

One of the witch-men in *Ilda's* bow turned and nodded, almost regally. He couldn't remember the man's name. They all looked alike to him, with their long black hair and their plaited moustaches and the tattoos sleeping under their skin.

"King of Ethrea," the witch-man said, his reedy voice accented almost beyond understanding. "We ride the wind for the last time. When next we return to the world, we shall face the might of Mijak."

Alasdair felt his belly tighten. A shudder ran down his spine. "You're certain?"

The witch-man's eyes were tranquil. "The wind has spoken. The wind is never wrong."

Alasdair turned to Ludo, who no longer looked greenly seasick. Now his cousin's cheeks were drained to a chalky white. "Are you all right?"

"Yes," said Ludo faintly. "No. Alasdair, I'm scared."

He gripped Ludo's shoulder. "So am I. It doesn't matter."

The rising wind howled, then, and the *Ilda's* sails slapped hard against her mast. Suddenly the air seemed thicker. Less transparent.

"Here we go," said Ludo. "Quick. We'd best get down."

Han had told them to lie flat on their backs as the boat rode the wind. Flinging themselves to the deck, heedless of splinters, bruises and stains, they rolled onto their backs . . .

. . . and again the world disappeared in a tinkling of windchimes.

CHAPTER THIRTY

When they emerged from the dreamy, drifting unreality of riding the wind, Alasdair hauled himself to his feet, fighting to clear his mind of the lingering fogginess. Blinking, he clung to the *Ilda's* rail and tried to make sense of where they were, and what surrounded them. He heard shouts from the other boats in the armada, heard sails and rigging slap and crack in the wind, heard the *Ilda's* captain,

Yanson, barking orders to his men. The flagship ploughed through a deep swell, and the air was full of spray and salt.

In the distance a dark smudge blotted out the horizon, as though black ink had been poured over the ocean.

"Dear God," said Ludo, lurching to the rail. "Is that the Mijaki fleet?"

Alasdair nodded. "I think so."

"Then may Rollin have mercy on us," Ludo breathed. "We'd have no hope if they were half as many. *Look* at them. They're *legion*."

Alasdair felt his fingers tighten on the railing. "Hold your tongue. Is that any way for a duke to speak?"

He said it because he had to, but his heart echoed Ludo's despair.

Oh, Rhian. I can't believe we'll prevail here. Not even with Han's witch-men. Thank God you didn't come. Thank God it's me here, not Zandakar.

In the bow, Han's witch-men stirred. In Han's ship, alongside them, the emperor shouted something in the Tzhung tongue and his loincloth clad sailors scrambled to obey. Alasdair watched as they collapsed their sails, halting the boat's progress. He heard Captain Yanson shout, and turned to see the *Ilda's* crew follow suit.

Where the Tzhung emperor went, the *Ilda* would follow. This was Han and Rhian's plan: that he'd drop back to the middle of the armada once the enemy was sighted, and the *Ilda* would drop back with him to act as his eyes. Hidden and protected by so many other ships, it would surely take Mijak a long time to realise he was the witch-men's leader.

Han's boat was an easy stone's throw away from the *Ilda*. Like harnessed carriage horses the two ships sailed side by side, surging and curvetting on the ocean's lively waves. There was no land in sight. Alasdair had no idea where they were. He'd never been so far from Ethrea in his life.

Watching Han closely, he saw the emperor's black silk tunic was salt-stained, his unbound hair tangled and salt-crusted. His ageless face was drawn with weariness. Alasdair looked past Han to the witch-men standing with him, and then to the *Ilda's* witch-men, still standing in their bow. They all looked weary. As though this great feat had spent them.

And still there was a battle to come.

Feeling eyes upon him, Han turned and smiled and smoothed a hand down his long hair. Its tangles untangled so it fell sleek and glossy black once again, rippling in his witch-wind like threads of polished silk.

Alasdair frowned. *Tricks. He performs tricks to divert me. He is worried, even at this distance I can feel it.*

The other ships of the armada were surging past them now, riding the wind of the real world to engulf Han's boat and the *Ilda*. First, on both sides, were the other ships of Tzhung-tzhungchai. Laden with witch-men, with no other weapons, unadorned and simple, like the very finest blade.

After them, on the port side, came Ebrich, Count of Arbenia, with his nation's mighty catapults strapped to the deck of his blunt, aggressive flagship.

Its sails were blood red, its black-and-red striped hull hung with bear skulls and halberds. The rest of his nation's fleet hunted behind him, like hounds following their pack leader. Every deck was crammed with a catapult, their sails were striped to match their master's garish hull, and their hulls were hung with the skulls of smaller creatures. It was a wonder, seeing them, that any animal breathed in Arbenia.

Dalsyn, Slainta of Harbisland, sailed to starboard, his flagship so crowded with archers it was a wonder the long, sleek vessel didn't sink. The hulls of his fleet's needle-shaped warships were smothered in sealskin, and like seals they cut lithely through the waves. As each ship passed, Alasdair could smell the stink of pitch from the barrels stood waiting on the ships. Harbisland fought with fire, without mercy. He felt his heart lift, a little.

Perhaps Mijak won't have things all its own way.

The ships of the lesser trading nations followed close behind the dominant nations. As the last Harbisland warship passed their bow, Han snapped another command to his sailors. Captain Yanson, watching him closely, sent the *Ilda's* crew to work, one act and its reflection.

Han's ship and the *Ilda* leapt forward, their sails again set to drink deep of the wind, surging in the midst of Barbruish's biremes, Dev'karesh's triremes with their vicious ramming spikes, the deep-hulled warships of Slynt and Haisun. Surrounded by warships, Alasdair felt a sudden sorrow.

So much death. So much destruction. If they weren't all with us in this venture perhaps they'd be turning their weapons on each other. They have in the past. Their pasts are bloody tapestries of war. How lucky are we in Ethrea, to be spared such carnage.

Ludo, still beside him, as soaked with spray as he was, released a shuddering breath. "When I was a small boy," his cousin said, subdued, "I used to dream of sea battles. The mighty nations of the world clashing on the waves. I used to think it *romantic*. Dear God. I was a fool."

Alasdair shook his head. "You were a boy. And I doubt you were alone. Even now, back in Ethrea, I'll wager there are people wishing they were here with us. People who think this is some great adventure."

"Adventure," said Ludo, blotting salt water from his face with a damp linen sleeve. "Right."

Looking ahead, where glimpses of the Arbenian fleet could still be caught between the crowding masts and hulls and sails of the armada, Alasdair allowed himself a grim little smile. "In the days leading up to this, I had some conversations with Ebrich and Dalsyn. They're treatied now, but in the past Arbenia and Harbisland have been bitter enemies. And do you know, they miss their warring? These are men who crave battle. They live to fight. These rulers . . ." He shook his head again, baffled. "They throw men at each other like rocks."

"Would we be any different, if we weren't born Ethrean?" said Ludo. "I think our kingdom is the strange place. The rest of the world is like this." He waved a hand at the armada surrounding them. "And I say thank God for our strangeness, cousin. We'd not stand a hope of defeating Mijak, else."

Alasdair nodded. "Yes." If they did stand a hope.

If this wasn't a fool's errand. If they'd not been coz-ened into believing a lie.

Suddenly Helfred's stirring speech about faith wasn't as comforting as it had felt at the time.

Ludo was peering ahead, leaning dangerously over the *Ilda's* side. "I wonder how much closer we are to the Mijaki warfleet. I wonder how soon before the battle begins. I wonder if I want to know . . . perhaps ignorance is bliss . . ."

Alasdair grabbed the back of his shirt and hauled him to safety before he upended over the side and was drowned, or crushed beneath the hull of Han's ship.

"Have a care, you fool! Must I explain your death to Henrik? Chairbound or not, he'd kick me from one side of the Eth river to the other."

Paying no attention, Ludo pulled himself free of re-straint and stood on the nearest coil of rope, seeking an advantage of height. "If only we knew what weapons Mijak will range against us," he muttered. "Aside from the gauntlet Jones spoke of, that is."

Alasdair, also looking ahead, felt his guts twist and his heart trip to a faster beat. "We'll know soon enough. We must be close by now."

"Yes," said Ludo, and stepped down off the rope as though he'd suddenly lost interest.

The deck of the *Ilda* thudded as the sailors fol-lowed her captain's curt orders, so that she and Han's vessel continued side by side. Without warning, Alasdair felt himself useless, a pointless decoration like brightwork or a posy of violets nailed to the mast. The least sailor on the *Ilda* had more value than he did. In the bow, Han's witch-men stood silent, as unnatural as men carved from stone. He stared at them, feeling sick.

The Ilda's not a warship. Are those three men enough to defend it? I have my sword. Ludo has his. Yanson and his sailors have their cudgels. And what use will they be if Zandakar's brother turns his gauntlet against us?

He started as Ludo took hold of his arm. "There's little point fretting, Alasdair. For good or for ill, we're here. It's best to believe we're here for a reason that will help Ethrea. They're saying their prayers for us, back home. Let's not disappoint them by succumbing to fear."

Sensible advice. And from Ludo, no less. The world indeed was turned upon its head.

Now the salt-and-spray soaked air was threaded through with voices, singing. Songs of war and of courage, most likely, in a handful of different tongues, counterpoint to the rushing wind and the flapping canvas and the swift seething of water past wooden hulls. The sound might have been beautiful, if this were not such a deadly endeavour.

And under the voices, a stready throbbing of drums.

Ludo sucked in a sharp breath and pointed. "*Look.*"

The vessels ahead of them had started to spread apart, seeking to make of the armada a more scattered target. And through the widening gaps, past Han's stone-still witch-men, at last could be seen the black warships of Mijak – as thick on the ocean as autumn leaves on a forest pond.

Alasdair felt his open mouth suck dry. He'd never felt so alone, so vulnerable, in all his life.

Rhian.

On the Tzhung flagship beside them, Han shouted another command. Some change came over his gathered witch-men, and the witch-men on the *Ilda*, and on every ship surrounding them. The air stirred . . . it whispered . . . and though the sun shone unhindered, suddenly the world was cold.

Captain Yanson approached. A grizzled man in his middle years, with skin as weathered as the wood of his ship, he offered a respectful nod. "Your Majesty, Your Grace, best gird yourselves for battle. Just in case those heathen crows in the bow can't save us, and every blessed ship between us and those Mijaki murderers gets sunk to the bottom."

"A wise suggestion, Captain Yanson," said Alasdair. "And may I say Godspeed to you now, sir, in case events should overtake us and the chance does not arise again."

Yanson smiled, showing a mouth missing several teeth. "Godspeed to you too, Your Majesty. It's been a pleasure and an honour sailing with you, and the duke too. And I'll tell you, though maybe I oughtn't, that when I heard Eberg's daughter wanted the crown on her head I thought well, there's the end of Ethrea. But by God, I was wrong. And you can tell her I said so."

Absurdly, the rough compliment throttled his rising fear. "Captain, Her Majesty will be pleased to know it."

And then there was no time for compliments, or anything else. The drumbeat of the armada abruptly picked up speed, like a horse surging from canter to gallop. Turning, Alasdair felt his heart surge with it.

Mijak's warships were upon them. The time had come to fight.

Ebrich, Count of Arbenia, struck the first blow. The sound of fireballs hissing through the air was startling. Menacing. Even above the singing and the drumming and the noise of a fleet under sail, the flaming catapult stones could be heard ripping through the salt-wind in a fearsome bid to sink the front line of Mijaki warships.

"Rollin's mercy," Ludo whispered. "It's started. Alasdair—"

What could they say to one another, that hadn't been said? Alasdair grasped his cousin's shoulder, briefly. "We'll tell our sons of this day, Ludo, I swear it. When we're grizzled like Yanson. We'll spin them tall tales."

"Taller than this?" said Ludo, and tried to laugh. "Tall tales indeed."

The *Ilda* had a kind of covered cabin built on the deck, three-quarters of the way towards her blunt stern. In tacit agreement they staggered their way to it, and hauled themselves up the wooden ladder on its port side until they stood high enough to see over the bow, and Han's witch-men, to the battle beyond.

There was nothing to hold on to. One pitch of the boat, one incautious bump from Han's vessel, or another, and they'd be thrown overboard like chewed apple-cores.

They looked at each other, and dropped to their knees.

Ahead they saw more fireballs flying, a burning

hail to rain down upon the enemy. Then came a sighing hiss, as the archers of Harbisland added their fire to the fire of Arbenia, arrows wrapped in pitch-soaked cloth and set alight, to burn and burn the warships of Mijak.

And what warships they were. Long and lean and black as night, stretching in a solid wall across the horizon. Their prows were carved and painted into hideous figureheads: wicked-fanged snakes – cats' feet with claws extended, eager to slash – wild-eyed birds of prey with beaks desperate to tear flesh, talons grasping – and hideous scorpions, the sign of their god.

Not a single one of them was touched by fire.

"That's not right!" said Ludo, and risked clambering to his feet. "How is that possible?"

Though they were in range of the enemy, the fireballs and flaming arrows of Arbenia and Harbisland had fallen short into the ocean, did not touch the approaching warships of Mijak.

Alasdair shook his head. "I don't know. It's as though the fireballs and arrows strike an invisible *wall*."

From the warships of Mijak rose a skin-chilling chant, a single voice from so many thousand throats: "*Chalava! Chalava! Chalava zho!*"

Alasdair looked over at Han and his witch-men. Standing at their boat's bow, like the *Ilda's* witch-men so tall and still and eerily silent, their bodies yielding to the moving deck so they seemed to stand on dry land, the Tzhung appeared to be doing nothing at all.

"I don't *understand*," said Ludo, as yet more fireballs and flaming arrows plunged harmless into the steaming ocean. "Why don't Han's witch-men *do* something?"

And then came a stream of scarlet fire from one Mijaki warship . . . and Ebrich of Arbenia's boat erupted into flames and flying splinters. Above the Mijaki chanting, high-pitched terrified screams and wails. All around them the sails of the Arbenian fleet were struck by burning spars and embers and caught fire. Men caught fire. The Count of Arbenia's flagship, what was left of it, sank beneath the ocean's surface. The water was littered with bodies and burning debris. Another scarlet stream of fire, and the Slainta of Harbisland's warship perished in flames.

Confusion and screaming among the armada. The drums ceased their beating. The world held its breath.

"This is madness!" said Ludo. "We're going to die here without striking a single blow."

Alasdair didn't answer, he just looked at Han and his witch-men. A wind was stirring about them . . . and only them. Their hair whipped around their heads, their black silk tunics snapped and tugged. He swept his gaze over the vessels nearest to them, over the witch-men gathered in every bow. Like Han and his witch-men, each group stood in the centre of its own small windstorm.

And the wind was rising . . . rising . . .

"*Chalava! Chalava! Chalava zho!*" came the chant from the Mijaki warships, easily filling the distance between them. "*Chalava! Chalava! Chalava zho!*"

"Look!" shouted Ludo. "Alasdair, *look*!"

Despite the mayhem at the front of the armada, despite the screams and the debris and the boats battling fire, not the enemy, the sailors on board those

Arbenian and Harbisland vessels not sunk or burning had recovered their senses and were redoubling their efforts. The sky almost disappeared behind a fury of catapulted fireballs and flaming arrows.

This time the fireballs and arrows struck home.

A cheer went up from the armada as the first Mijaki warships were battered to oblivion. Mingled with the cheering, the screams of dying warriors. The screams of horses, trapped below decks in the burning, sinking ships of Mijak.

Alasdair, stomach heaving, spat bile down to the *Ilda's* deck.

"That stream of fire, that must be Dmitrak's gauntlet," said Ludo. He was shaking, shuddering on his knees. "Has his warship been destroyed? Have we killed him?"

In reply to his desperate question, another lance of scarlet fire streamed into the armada. It began to travel sideways, scything through the front line of ships with horrifying ease.

"God's mercy, what is Han *doing*?" demanded Ludo, close to weeping. "Why don't his witch-men stop this? It's slaughter!"

Whatever power the Mijaki called on, it protected the warship of Zandakar's brother. No fireball fell on it, every arrow aimed to kill it plummeted hissing into the ocean.

But at least other Mijaki warships suffered.

The wind whipping Han and his witch-men increased. Now it was howling around every witch-man Alasdair could see, it howled and raged and when he looked back at their enemy he saw their warships starting to plunge uneasily, like tethered horses scenting danger in the air.

The rain of fireballs was weakening. Fewer arrows flew over the water. The surviving ships of Arbenia and Harbisland were running out of things to throw.

Then came more shouting, the redoubled sound of pounding drums, and the knife-shaped triremes of Dev-karesh came flying through the fleet. Their prows weren't carved to figureheads, they were graced with iron spikes, long and lethal. The ships were driven by the witch-men's wind and by oars, by sailors trained their whole lives to row fast . . . row faster . . . to spit an enemy like a boar.

The witch-men's howling wind rose to a fever pitch. Alasdair could feel it plucking at him, even at the other end of the boat. The drums of Dev-karesh boomed louder, quicker, as their ramming vessels aimed for the floating heart of Mijak.

"*Chalava! Chalava! Chalava zho*!" came the chant from its warships, almost loud enough now to drown the Dev'kareshi drums. "*Chalava! Chalava! Chalava zho!*"

Then the howling wind's note rose high and keening, and there were waterspouts forming among the warships of Mijak. Huge waves were rising, tall as mountains. And the triremes of Dev'karesh were flying like needles.

"Is that Han? Is that the witch-men?" cried Ludo.

"Who else?" said Alasdair, and held his sobbing breath.

Sink them, Han. Sink every last one of them. Drive Mijak's warships to the depths.

*   *   *

The wind and the waterspouts came from nowhere, came howling through the mighty warships of Mijak. The spiked enemy ships came with them, they rammed Mijak's warships to splinters and pulled back, they came so fast, with oars and in the wind. Vortka's godspeakers could not hold against them, their power in the god was not strong enough. Dmitrak could not kill them, he could not see through the wind and the water to aim.

"*What is this, Vortka?*" Hekat shouted above the noise, as her warship's torn scorpion sail flapped and her boat rolled wildly and below its deck her warriors' horses screamed. "Why do your godspeakers fail in the god's eye? Why do they not blow out these winds?"

Vortka steadied himself against her warship's godpost, struggling to keep his feet. "It is likely a seastorm," he shouted back. "The slaves warned us in Jatharuj that—"

"*Tcha!*" she spat. Had she defended him to Dmitrak? Had she told herself she loved him? He was an old man, an old fool. Was he blind in the god's eye and no longer precious? "Is this a seastorm, Vortka? I think it is not! I feel the demons in this wind, do you say you cannot?"

The vicious wind was whipping the ocean into frothy peaks, spraying them with water as though the sky were full of clouds and rain. Soaked to the skin, shivering with cold, still she struck the godspeaker who tried to give her a blanket.

I am Hekat, Empress of Mijak. The god keeps me warm, the god warms me in its eye.

"Demons?" said Vortka. "Hekat—"

"There are demons, I tell you!" she shouted, grabbing hold of his godspeaker robes. Aieee, the god see her, she could shake him to pieces. "Brothers to the demons who thwarted us in the desert, brothers to the demons who stole the trade winds from the sky. They travel with the enemy ranged before us! They stink in my nostrils, they stink in my mind! Tell me you can feel them, Vortka. Tell me their stink is in your nostrils also. *Tell me the god is not lost to your heart!*"

She watched his hand play over his scorpion pectoral, watched the pain and indecision twist his old, thin face. At last he nodded. "Yes, Hekat. I can feel the demons, I can smell them."

As the wind howled around them, as the waterspouts lashed her warships like whips, as the ships of her enemy spitted her warships and killed them, she caught Vortka's silver godbraids in her hand, she pressed her face to his face and let the ocean fall on their heads.

"I knew you were not lost to me," she told him. "I knew we were still godchosen together. I must sacrifice to defeat these demons."

He closed his hand over hers and shook his head. "No, Hekat. I am Mijak's high godspeaker. I will give the god its blood."

She released him and stepped back, for the moment she was satisfied. He would give the god blood and the demons would die.

Dmitrak squatted beside her warship's rail, salt water streaming across his gold-and-crystal gauntlet. It soaked his scarlet godbraids and stopped his godbells from singing. Rising from his crouch, easily riding the warship's roll and pitch, he shouted, "Can he break the demons, Empress? Vortka is old now, and feeble. He is done."

If they were alone she would strike him for saying so, but the deck around them was crowded with warriors and godspeakers. Instead she seared him with a look, a promise of later retribution.

"He will break them, warlord. He is Vortka, god-chosen and precious."

Vortka's godspeakers gathered around the godpost, they had lambs and cockerels and knives and bowls for the blood. On Vortka's command the animals were sacrificed. Hekat closed her eyes, feeling the demons. They were barely affected by the animals' blood. When she opened her eyes she saw twelve warships broken, the waterspouts smashed them like eggs thrown onto rock. And then as she watched, eight more warships were thrown down, two by the enemy and six by the wind. The wind of those demons whipped up waves so high they drowned her warships and her warriors, she heard them screaming as the water killed them in the world.

She screamed, the demons were killing her warhost. "*More blood, Vortka!* The god wants more blood!"

The slaves who had taught her warriors to sail these warships had taught them the way of spreading messages to many ships. In Jatharuj she had learned of paper, and ink, and quills for writing. She liked them better than clay and stylus, so neat and so clean. But only she and Vortka had used these new wonders.

Vortka used them now. Two of his godspeakers sheltered him with a blanket. He wrote on paper, wrapped the message round a smooth stone, and a warrior fired the stone in a slingshot from their warship to the next. The godspeakers on that warship read the note and passed it on. One by one, the godspeakers on the warships not destroyed by her enemy, or too scattered for the slingshot, learned the god's want.

And then those godspeakers were sacrificing for the god. Still, still, the blood was not enough.

Hekat looked at Vortka. "Go below to the horses. Give their blood to the god."

"The horses?" said Dmitrak. "Empress—"

She held up her hand to him. "There are horses in Ethrea, they will be ours."

Mijak's horses were not bred for sacrifice, she stood above them on the deck of her warship and heard them die unwilling for the god. When Vortka and his godspeakers returned, they were red with horses' blood.

She felt the demons screaming, she felt their pain in her blood. She felt their evil weaken, they were not beaten yet. Almost she wept. Had the warhost's horses died for *nothing*? Was their blood spilled in vain?

"It is not enough," said Vortka, as the warship tossed and plunged. "Hekat, we cannot kill every horse in the warhost."

Around her neck, her scorpion amulet burned. It burned with an answer. The god needed more power, she knew where it was.

"These demons are mighty, Vortka," she shouted over the wind. "I will kill them with stronger blood."

Vortka stared. "What do you mean?"

Aieee, the god see her. He would not accept it, even now. "You know what I mean, Vortka."

He stepped back, unsteady, as the demon wind and water threatened to tear them spar from spar. "We have brought no slaves, Hekat, we have no stronger blood!"

She looked around the warship, at her beautiful warriors. "Vortka, you are foolish. We have the strongest blood of all."

Dmitrak was listening, Dmitrak leapt towards her. "No. No, I will not allow it! You will not—"

Her snakeblade leapt to her hand, its point pricked his throat. "I am the empress, will you tell me *no*? I do not think so, Dmitrak. I think you will step back, before the god strikes you down."

His eyes were anguished and frightened. Nagarak's eyes, in the moment of his death.

"Please, Hekat," he said. "Your warlord needs his knife-dancers."

She pushed him away from her. "*The god needs them more!*"

The warrior nearest to her was young and beautiful, he was named Didalai, no warrior knife-danced like him.

"Didalai!" said Hekat. "Do you serve your empress? Do you serve the god?"

"Hekat, I serve," said Didalai.

Hekat cut her warrior's beautiful throat. The strong blood pumped from the wound in his neck, Didalai fell to the deck and washed it with his strong blood.

The next warrior was Anik, he was young, too.

"Anik, do you serve your empress? Anik, do you serve the god?"

Anik's eyes were wide but they were not frightened. "Hekat, I serve," he said, and died where he stood.

She felt the god's power rising, she heard the demons howl in fear. She felt them rally against her, she did not care. Strong blood would kill them.

One by one her warriors fell. One by one they served Hekat and the god. At last there were no warriors left to serve. And as the last warrior died . . . she felt the demons' power fade . . . felt the wind falter to nothing . . . felt the god, exultant.

"*Dmitrak*!" she shouted.

Dmitrak was weeping, he wept for his warriors, he was a weak fool. Warriors lived so they could die.

"Empress," he said, choking, stumbling to her side.

She took his face between her hands, she pressed her fingernails into his flesh. Her godbells sang with anger as the angry waves tossed her warship beneath the sky.

"You are the warlord, Dmitrak, you are the god's hammer! The demons are weakened. Smite these enemy warships for the god. Smite them to splinters, destroy them in my eye!"

Still weeping, he nodded, he pressed his fist to his chest. "Empress, I will smite them." Tears rolled down his face.

She released him, she stepped back, she joined Vortka by her warship's mast.

Aieee, tcha, I miss Zandakar. My true son would not weep.

*   *   *

The witch-men of Tzhung-tzhungchai were screaming. On the *Ilda*, on Han's flagship, on every surviving ship in the armada. Eyes closed, mouths stretched wide, the flesh of their faces compressed against their skulls, they screamed and they screamed . . . with no whisper of sound.

And the wind died. The waterspouts collapsed. The needle-nosed ships of Dev'karesh were stranded in the open. Zandakar's brother killed them with his gauntlet, like an idle boy stoning chickens in a coop.

"*Chalava! Chalava! Chalava zho*!" chanted the warriors of Mijak.

"The witch-men are defeated!" cried Ludo. He was weeping. "God help us, we're lost."

Almost, almost, Alasdair surrendered to despair. Unchecked now, with Han's witch-men failing, Dmitrak's gauntlet cut a swathe through the armada. Boats burned and sank and flew to splinters all around them. In a matter of minutes, surely, they'd be struck or fire would reach them. They would die at the hands of Zandakar's brother.

Rhian. Rhian.

They had to flee, every survivor, while they still could. Dying here in a hopeless attack would condemn Ethrea and the rest of the world to the same kind of slaughter.

"*Chalava! Chalava! Chalava zho!*"

Half-jumping, half-falling, abandoning Ludo, Alasdair tumbled from the *Ilda's* cabin roof. His bones sang with pain as his feet struck the deck. He ran to the bow, to the silent, stricken witch-men. He took the first one by the shoulders and tried to shake him to awareness. Nothing. The witch-man's eyes were open, but he couldn't seem to see.

Alasdair struck him hard across the face. "Wake up! *Wake up!* Ethrea needs you!"

But the witch-man didn't feel the blows. His open eyes remained glazed and unseeing.

All around them the armada's ships were dying. Han's flagship wallowed without direction. Han stood with his witch-men, blank-faced and silent.

Captain Yanson staggered to the bow. "Your Majesty, we can't stay here! We've got to go! We've got to—"

A Slyntian warship's burning mast crashed across them, smashed by Dmitrak's merciless gauntlet. Every man standing was thrown from his feet, and fire leapt like a lover along the *Ilda's* sweet lines.

"Ludo!" Alasdair shouted, lurching to his knees and looking for his cousin.

"I'm fine," said Ludo, joining him, blood streaming down his face and one arm. "We're done for. Can we abandon ship?"

"I don't know! Yanson—"

But Captain Yanson was dead, his head split like a melon from striking the railing. Blood and brains smeared the deck. One of the witch-men was dead too, his neck broken. And the *Ilda* was well alight, tangled in the wreckage of the Slyntian ship. Smoke billowed, flames crackled. The air was full of screams.

"Han's flagship," said Alasdair, staring at it. "It's tangled too, but not as badly and it's not on fire. If we can use the Slyntian ship as a bridge—"

"God save us, are you mad?" said Ludo.

"Would you rather stay here and burn alive?"

Ludo's face was his answer.

"The other two witch-men live, I think," he said. "You carry one. I'll carry the other. We can't leave them. We need them. They're not dead, they're just – stunned."

"And the *Ilda's* crew?"

Alasdair closed his eyes. *God forgive me.* "They'll have to take their chances, Ludo."

Escaping the *Ilda* was a nightmare. Burning, listing, she tried to kill them in her death throes. Pushing Ludo before him, his witch-man slung across his shoulders, muscles shrieking, lungs gasping, Alasdair kept his eyes on Han's flagship and blotted out everything else: the smoke, the flames, the screams of the injured and dying, the reek of burning blood and flesh, the stink of charred timber and canvas, the chanting of Mijak's encroaching warriors.

"Chalava! Chalava! Chalava zho!"

He and Ludo reached the sinking Slyntian ship and, without a backwards glance, left the *Ilda* behind. Burdened with Han's witch-men, they helped each other struggle through the tangle of spars and rigging and dead mutilated sailors. Halfway between the two ships, Ludo's witch-man slipped from his sweaty, bloody grip and plunged into the churning water below.

Between them they saved the second witch-man, barely. And barely reached Han's flagship alive as flames roared on the Slyntian ship and swallowed the *Ilda*.

"*Han*!" Alasdair shouted. "Han, can you hear me?"

No reply. Han and his witch-men stood like statues carved from obsidian and amber. Leaving Ludo to care for their rescued witch-man, Alasdair staggered towards them as Ethrea's armada burned and died.

Reckless, desperate, he snatched at Tzhung's emperor, desperate to shake Han back to his senses. But the moment his fingers closed on Han's rigid arm, a bolt of power surged through him. Nerves on fire, ears ringing, he flew through the air and struck the boat's railing. The impact flipped him over the side. He had enough wits left to grab hold, to hang on. The pain was so vicious, he thought his wrists would snap.

"*Alasdair*!" Ludo shouted.

As Ludo scrambled to reach him, his face bloodless with terror, Alasdair looked up at Han. Tzhung's emperor was stirring, the vacant look fading from his eyes. The witch-men standing with him were stirring, too.

"Alasdair!" said Ludo, reaching him. "Rollin's mercy, are you *insane*?"

Bumping, bruising, scraping bare flesh and collecting splinters, Ludo hauled him back over the side of Han's flagship. Around them the armada's destruction continued. Both the *Ilda* and the Slyntian ship had burned to the waterline, and they were only two of many.

Coughing, panting his thanks, Alasdair squeezed Ludo's shoulder then turned back to Han. This time he didn't touch him.

"Emperor, can you hear me? Can you understand?"

Slowly, painfully, Han nodded. "Yes."

"The armada's defeated," he said, his voice breaking. *Rhian, we failed you. I failed you.* "Can you get us back to Ethrea, or at least away from here?"

Instead of answering, Han reached for his witchmen. Embraced them, weeping. Then he released them and raised his head.

"Ethrea," he said. His voice sounded faint, as though it travelled a great distance. His fingers lifted to touch his face, as though flesh were something unknown, and frightening.

Around him, his ten witch-men did the same.

Slowly Han swept his gaze across the battered, tattered handful of ships still left in the armada. Looked at the ocean, choked with bodies and bits of burned, blasted boat. Stared at the Mijaki warships poised to engulf them.

Blown on the breeze, that menacing chant. "*Chalava! Chalava! Chalava zho!*"

Han's eyes closed. His fisted hands stretched high above his head. His witch-men echoed him. Alasdair stared at the armada's surviving ships, and through the gusting palls of smoke and flickering flames thought he saw other witch-men on boats not yet ruined, slowly raising their fisted hands.

"Oh, please God," Ludo muttered. "Have mercy. *Get us home.*"

Nothing . . . nothing . . .

Then the tinkling of windchimes . . . and the world disappeared.

CHAPTER THIRTY-ONE

Every morning after dancing her *hotas*, Rhian stood in her privy garden overlooking the harbour and stared out to the horizon, heart thudding, praying for the armada's safe return. Every evening, before the last of the light was lost, she stood there again, heart thudding, before riding with Helfred to Kingseat's great chapel, where she prayed with her people for a victory against Mijak.

For all the hours in between, one of Idson's soldiers stood there, gaze fixed on the horizon, waiting . . . waiting . . .

The grass where they stood was worn bare, and might never grow back.

After nearly three weeks had passed, Rhian cornered Dexterity in the castle library, where he was hunting for new books he could give Zandakar to read.

"Mister Jones!" she said, closing the library doors behind her.

Startled, he banged his head on a bookshelf. "Ow. Your Majesty? Has there been—"

"No," she said, and tried to ignore the pain under her ribs. "No sighting yet. Dexterity—"

Her toymaker sighed and slumped into the nearest overstuffed leather armchair. "I'm sorry. I've tried, I really have. Hettie won't answer me, no matter how hard I beg."

Rhian sat in the chair opposite, disappointment cruel as a canker. "Helfred says we must have faith. He says, how is it faith when the outcome is already known?" She chewed at her lip, using pain to drive back the tears. "You've no idea how much I long to smack him."

"Well, he's the prolate," said Dexterity. "He's got to say things like that, I suppose." He sat back and considered her, a frown in his eyes. "Your face has healed well."

Her fingers came up to touch the scars on her cheeks. Ridged, unattractive, they still gave her pause when she looked in a mirror. Dinsy was forever moping, bewailing her queen's lost looks. "Yes. Thanks to Ursa." She dropped her hands to her lap. "Though you still wish I'd slashed my arms instead, don't you?"

He pulled a face. "Well . . ."

"Arms can be covered, Dexterity, as though an oath has been set aside. This way, every time an ambassador looks at me he's reminded of my pledge to his people."

Dexterity smiled. "You're still beautiful."

"Tcha! As if that matters!"

But of course it did matter, in some small vain part of her soul. *Does it matter to Alasdair? I never asked, before he left. I must ask him when he comes home. I must tell him how I love him.*

"You've done well with Zandakar," she added. "His Ethrean's almost perfect now."

"He's worked hard," said Dexterity, his cheeks

turning pink. Such a dear man, he always blushed when paid a compliment. "Although he will insist on peppering his speech with a little Mijaki here and there."

"To tease you?"

"Undoubtedly. But d'you know . . ." Dexterity frowned thoughtfully. "Mostly I think it's because he's afraid of losing himself. His clothing's Ethrean. His food is Ethrean. Since that scorpion knife's too dangerous, he dances his *hotas* with an Ethrean knife, under an Ethrean sky, in the shadow of Ethrea's Kingseat Castle. And every day he trains Ethreans to destroy his own people. To destroy his *family*, Rhian." He shook his head. "I begin to wonder if we don't ask too much."

She didn't want to think of Zandakar's sacrifices. If she thought of his sacrifices, she might not look him in the eye next time they met.

"What choice do we have but to use him?" she demanded. "Did we ask for Mijak to cross its borders and enslave the world? Did we ask for its empress to spill human blood in her hunger for power? All we have ever asked for is to be left alone."

"I know," sighed Dexterity. "You do what you must to keep Ethrea safe. No matter which way you count the coins, someone's going to come up short."

Agitated, Rhian pushed out of the plush armchair and roamed the library. Cursed the windows, which didn't face out to sea. "I'm regretting I sent Ludo with Alasdair," she said. "Adric grows more bumptious by the day. Edward tries to deflate him, and then Rudi gets protective, and my two senior dukes waste their time brangling with each other."

"It is vexing," said Dexterity. "But Helfred says his venerables continue to report great courage among the people. I think the babes in their cradles would fight for you if they could, Rhian."

"How? By throwing their rusks?"

"You never know. It might work."

She tried to laugh, to show him she was brave, and not subject to the dismals, but the sound she made was more like a sob. "Oh, Dexterity . . ."

She heard the creak of his leather armchair. His boot heels on the carpet. Then his arms closed around her, and his hand stroked her close-cropped hair.

"Oh dear," he murmured. "There, there, Rhian."

She turned her face into his shoulder, let her fingers clutch tight to his coat. "I'm afraid, Dexterity," she whispered. "I'm so afraid."

"I know," he said, his hand patting her back. "But you must be strong, for Alasdair and for your people. If the armada fails—"

She pulled back. "It *can't* fail, Dexterity. How can we hope to defeat Mijak on land, with so many warriors practiced in killing?"

"I don't know," he said, his voice low, his eyes troubled. "But if that's what we're faced with, then that's what we must do. Just . . . don't abandon hope yet. Emperor Han's witch-men are a power for good. I don't understand them, but I believe that completely. And the rest of the armada is full of doughty fighters. They'll give Mijak pause, you can depend on that."

Pausing them would hardly be enough. The armada must destroy them . . . and she feared, oh she feared, that even Han and his witch-men would be overmatched.

A clock stood on the library's fireplace mantel, quietly ticking away the time. Rhian glanced at it, bit off a curse and pulled free of Dexterity's comforting embrace.

"I'm late for the armourer," she said. "A second fitting for my breastplate."

"Then you'd best hurry, Your Majesty," he said firmly. "The king was adamant that you should wear one, and he'll expect to see you in it when he returns."

She smiled at him, fears eased, at least for the moment. "And so he shall. I'll see you at this evening's council meeting, Mister Jones."

He bowed. "Your Majesty, you will."

She spent a full hour with the armourer, being poked and prodded and measured and pinched as the man and his bevy of assistants crafted what he assured her would be the most magnificent, the most elegant, the most exquisite of breastplates.

"Armourer Sandiman," she told him repressively, "it can be as ugly as sin for all I care. Just make sure it will turn aside a sharp Mijaki blade!"

Escaped at last from his tender ministrations, she made her way to the old tiltyard, where Zandakar trained to sweaty breathlessness the leading soldiers from Ethrea's duchy garrisons. Her arrival halted the session as she was greeted with pleasure and cries of *"God save Queen Rhian."*

"Majesty," said Zandakar, and banged his fist to his chest. "You have come to train with us, *zho?*"

As the soldiers called their approval, she shook her head. "I'm sorry. I've but a few minutes spare. Duty calls me to a meeting with Prolate Helfred."

"A few minutes?" said Zandakar. His pale blue eyes were gleaming. "*Zho*, this is long enough." He jerked a chin at the watching soldiers. "Show them your *hotas*. Show them Rhian *hushla*, the Queen of Ethrea, dancing with her blade."

From the crowd of watching soldiers, more approving calls and pleas for her to dance. They loved to watch her. They loved to fight her, and try to win. Any man she bested stood his comrades a mug of ale. In the last weeks, many free mugs of ale had been drunk.

"Come, Rhian *hushla*," said Zandakar softly. "We can dance."

She was wearing her leathers, Ranald's knife strapped to her hip. To Dinsy's dismay, and the disapproval of the four ladies-in-waiting she'd reluctantly accumulated, every dress she owned was exiled in the wardrobe until the war against Mijak was won.

Sighing, she turned to her duchy's soldiers. Twenty or so in this group, some young men, some middle-aged. All lean, all hardened, soldiers their whole lives. Solid men of Ethrea, who might soon face a brutal death. Who had trusted their lives to her, Ethrea's girl-queen. They stared at her eagerly, hungry to believe she could lead them to victory. Hungry to believe she would save them from Mijak.

Oh, please. Please. Let me save them from Mijak. Oh please, God, please, don't let me have to try. Give the armada victory. Send Alasdair home.

Her soldiers were grinning. Nudging each other

with pointed elbows. Like dogs promised a run after rabbits, they jostled and shuffled, their eyes bright and eager.

When she danced with Zandakar, blood often was spilled.

"So, my doughty fellows," she said to them. "You wish to see *hotas* as Rhian of Ethrea dances them?"

They roared in answer. She had to laugh, the briefest respite from worry. "Very well. But not for long, or my esteemed prolate shall chide me."

She unsheathed her knife . . . and danced the *hotas* with Zandakar.

Dancing before the men of her garrison was different to dancing before her dukes and courtiers. These men were enamoured of her, inspired by her, they looked to her for leadership and faith. For better or worse she had captured their imagination. They would never accept a sister or daughter in hunting leathers, with a knife, wheeling and leaping and lunging with Zandakar, but she was their queen. She could do no wrong.

Every time she scored a touch on Zandakar, they cheered. Every time she stumbled, they groaned aloud. Sweating, panting, she abandoned herself to the *hotas*, letting their demands wash her free of other fears.

And then the watching crowd of soldiers parted and one of the royal messenger boys, Beddle, his face red with exertion, stumbled to a halt on the tiltyard. He was grinning like a melon, all his stubby teeth on show.

"Majesty! Your Majesty!" he panted. "The armada is sighted! Mebbe less than an hour's sailing from the harbour!"

The soldiers closest to the tiltyard railing had heard the boy's shrill cry. They pummelled their brothers into silence, and silence swallowed every sound.

Rhian fumbled her knife back into its sheath. Her fingers felt overlarge and clumsy, as though her hands were turned to gloves stuffed with lambswool. Then she looked at Zandakar, who was breathing heavily too, and sweating. These days when they danced their *hotas*, he worked just as hard as she.

Like her soldiers, he was waiting for her to speak.

The armada is sighted. If they come home victorious, it means his mother and his brother and his father are dead. It means I have killed them.

And what did that mean?

Not taking her eyes from Zandakar's suddenly blank face, she said, "My thanks for your message, Beddle. Make sure it's spread to His Eminence and the rest of the privy council, and to the trading nations' ambassadors. Captain Colley!"

"Majesty," said Colley smartly, ducking under the tiltyard rail as the message boy ran off. He was one of her best soldiers, stringy as a whip.

"Training's over. See the men back to their barracks. Occupy them in cleaning and oiling their breastplates and equipment."

Colley struck his fist to his chest, one of Zandakar's habits that all his students had adopted. "Majesty." Then he hesitated. "Majesty—"

She found a smile for him, from somewhere. "I'll

have word sent to you, Captain, I promise, once I know."

"Majesty," he said again, and in his eyes she saw the same relief and fear she was feeling.

When she and Zandakar were alone, she risked touching him. Chanced spreading her fingers and resting her palm against his chest. "Are you all right?"

Did he feel her touching him? She wasn't sure he did. She wasn't sure he could even see the tiltyard. His pale eyes were unfocused, as though he looked at a memory.

If Edward and Rudi were here, or Alasdair, they'd tell me to lock him in the dungeon again. They'd say that if we have killed his family then he can't be trusted. Not alone with Her Majesty. Not with a knife.

His blade was still in his hand. It was the first time since she met him that she ever saw him hold it carelessly. As though it wasn't important. But she knew that could change in a heartbeat . . .

I won't take it. I can't. If I take it, I'll break every bond I've built with him.

"Zandakar," she said softly. "I have to go."

Like a dreamer, waking, he breathed deeply and looked down at her. "Rhian?"

She took her hand from his chest. "The council will be expecting me. I have to go."

He nodded. "*Zho.*"

"I think it'd be best if you kept to your chamber until we know how the armada's fared. Win or lose, you'll doubtless receive scrutiny we'd do better to avoid."

Another nod. "*Zho.*"

"Zandakar . . ." She folded her arms, suddenly chilled. "If we've won: if the armada is sailing home victorious." *Please God, please God, please God, please . . .*

They'd never spoken of what that might mean. Since his bold inclusion in her plans for war they'd not spoken of anything that didn't concern weapons and training and tactics and death. There were too many eyes on her, and on him. Too many people willing to see what wasn't there, to talk of what didn't exist. There was Alasdair, who must never be diminished.

Alasdair sailing home to me, oh please God, please.

"Rhian," said Zandakar, and remembered his knife. He looked at the blade, then slid it home in its sheath. "If the armada sails home in the blood of Mijak, that is *chalava's* will."

"But your family," she whispered. "They might be dead."

He shrugged. "*Zho.*" Then his gaze sharpened. "Alasdair king might be dead."

She felt her chin lift. "Yes. He might."

But he's not, he's not, he's not. He can't be.

They stared at each other, mired in thoughts that could never be dressed decently in words.

"You should go," said Zandakar. "The council is waiting."

"As soon as I know what's happened, I'll send word. If your family's dead, Zandakar, if Mijak is defeated, there's a home for you here as long as you want one. My word as queen, and none shall gainsay it."

His stern expression softened. His eyes warmed, just a little. "Thank you, *hushla*."

"And if – if—" God, she couldn't get the words out. With her arms still folded, she dug her fingernails into her leather sleeves. "If things have not fallen our way," she said, carefully, "I'll make sure you're protected."

"Tcha," said Zandakar. "If Mijak defeats the armada, you will blame me, Rhian. You will say the witch-man Sun-dao should have killed Mijak in Jatharuj."

And she was silenced, as though a blade had pierced her throat.

"The council," he said again, his eyes patient. Resigned. "I will find my way back to my chamber."

She left him standing there, and made sure not to look back.

Word of the armada's sighting spread through Kingseat township like fire in a summer wheatfield. By the time she and her council and the ambassadors had made their official, solemn way down to the harbour, every street and building with a vantage point was crowded to the point of danger. Idson and his men were hard-pressed to keep order. When they saw her carriage, the people of Kingseat started shouting.

"*Queen Rhian! Queen Rhian! God bless our huntsman queen!*"

"I wish they wouldn't," she muttered to Helfred, as the carriage horses made their careful way to the harbour's Royal Gate. She'd asked him, and

Dexterity, to travel with her to the harbour. The notion of travelling alone was more than she could bear.

Helfred snorted. "I believe it was you who coined the phrase."

"I don't care about *that*," she said, impatient. "But they assume our armada returns with a victory and Helfred . . . they mightn't."

He was sitting beside her, Dexterity opposite. His hand covered hers, still soft, still plump, but with an unexpected strength in it. "Faith, Rhian," he said quietly. "Above all things, faith."

Not above victory, Helfred. But she didn't say that aloud. She felt too ill for arguing with him.

"The prolate's right," Dexterity added. "There's no use in borrowing trouble, is there?"

Prose, prose, prose. They were as bad as each other. "I still say I should've commandeered one of the harbourmaster's skiffs, so I could sail out to meet them," she said, to distract them. "I'm like to die, standing on the dock waiting for the armada to come to me."

"Tcha," Helfred scolded. "A dignified sight *that* would be. You're not a fishwife waiting for her smelly husband, Rhian. You're a monarch with the eyes of the world upon her."

More's the pity. I envy that fishwife. She can have my crown in a heartbeat.

They reached the harbour without further conversation, and made their way to the dock where only a few weeks ago . . . a lifetime ago . . . she'd stood with these same men and watched the armada sail away. Sail and then vanish, whipped away in the wind.

The afternoon was failing. Already torches had

been lit around the harbour and the docks, anticipating the approaching dusk. A lively breeze skirled among the gathered officials, laden with the mingled scent of salt and hope and dread. Rhian risked a glance at her dukes, and the ambassadors. They were silent, expectant, but behind their polished public faces she could feel their jangling nerves.

God save us from a riot if the news isn't good.

As the first ship passed through the headlands and into the calmer, quieter waters of the harbour, she felt her insides squeeze cold and tight with apprehension. Behind her, the ambassadors were muttering.

Even in the lowering light, it was possible to see . . .

"Prolate," she murmured, not looking at Helfred.

"I see it, Majesty," he said tightly, standing to her left. "The armada is . . . considerably diminished."

Dear God, that was hardly stating it. The armada had been *culled*, like an overlarge flock of sheep. Surely it had been reduced by two-thirds . . .

Rollin's mercy. Rollin's mercy. Have they come home destroyed?

Straining her eyes she looked for the *Ilda*, the ship her father had seen built and named for her mother. The ship that had taken her brothers to their doom.

I should have burned that ship. I should have sent Alasdair on a rowboat before I let him sail in that ship.

Heart thudding so hard she felt sick, like vomiting, she watched and waited for the ships to come closer. Searched for the Count of Arbenia's vulgar flagship, for the Slainta of Harbisland's sealskin-hulled galley. She couldn't see them.

The ambassadors were openly agitated now.

"Where is Han's ship?" she said under her breath, fighting not to leap from the dock to the water and *swim* to the armada. "Dexterity, can you see it?"

Close by her right hand, Dexterity shook his head. "No, Majesty. I can't."

A pain began pounding behind her eyes. *Alasdair. Alasdair. Alasdair.* "Helfred, I can't see the *Ilda*."

"Nor can I," said Helfred. "But that's not to say—" His voice broke. "Have faith."

Limping, dispirited, the charred and gouged remnants of the trading alliance armada sailed sluggishly into Kingseat harbour. There was no sign at all of Ebrich or Dalsyn. She couldn't see a single trireme from Dev'karesh. Was it her imagination, or were fully half of the Tzhung warships missing? Only a handful of Slynt ships remained, a smattering from Keldrave . . .

No . . . no . . . no . . . so many . . . please God, no.

The agitated ambassadors fell silent. Her dukes fell silent. The crowding, cramming, chattering people of Kingseat fell silent. Rhian didn't dare look at Dexterity, or Helfred, or her dukes. She didn't dare turn to glance at the ambassadors. She was glad Kingseat's people were so far away.

If we've won, this will be worth it. If we've won, we'll bear the pain.

And then the leading row of vessels parted, and a single injured ship emerged from the fleet. Before she could stop herself, Rhian made a sound. Grief. Relief. Some mixture of both. It was Emperor Han's flagship, raw with wounds but still whole. Standing in its

bow, Emperor Han and his witch-men. Duke Ludo.
And Alasdair.

My love, my love . . .

Helfred closed his soft hand hard around her wrist.
"Thank God."

She didn't dare speak, so she nodded.

All the mooring points cleared for the armada had
remained unused while it was at sea. Rhian heard
herself breathing hard, with difficulty, remembering
how the ships had crowded her harbour, remembering the complaints of her harbourmaster as he declared the impossibility of berthing so many vessels at
once . . .

Seeing now how many empty berths remained, as
one by one the ships of the armada found their allotted places and drifted to a halt, scarred almost past
recognition, some of them, she pressed her fist to her
lips to hold back the anguish burning her throat.

Han's flagship was granted precedence. Slowly,
painfully, scorched from beatuy to ugliness, it nudged
its way through the water and bumped to a sharp
stop against the dock before her. A harbour crew
came scurrying to secure its mooring lines and con-
nect ship to shore with a gangplank.

And there was Alasdair, *there* he was, with Ludo
behind him, coming down the gangplank onto dry
land. He was bruised. Battered. *He was alive.* She
snatched her wrist free from Helfred and ran, weeping, to meet him.

The oppressive silence around them was giving
way, gradually, to grief. The people of Kingseat knew,
without being able to see Alasdair's stark face, that
this was no triumphant, victorious return. This was a

defeat, cruel and crushing. The armada had fallen before the dark might of Mijak.

Rhian stumbled to a halt as she reached her unharmed husband. Speechless, shivering, they stared at each other. Then Alasdair pulled her to him in a suffocating embrace.

"I'm sorry. I'm sorry. Rhian, we failed."

Many hours later, far past midnight, she sat in the war room with him, and Ludo, and the rest of her exhausted council – except for Zandakar – contemplating the wreckage of their fragile new treaty.

One by one, so swiftly, the trading nations had deserted her. One by one their ambassadors and their rulers' representatives, those who'd survived, had withdrawn their country's support, which meant their ships, their sailors and their desperately needed soldiers. They must return home immediately, they said, so cold, so angry. They must consult directly with their rulers in the light of this calamity. Alas, while they were pledged to assist Ethrea, their first loyalties must lie at home.

What could she say to that? How could she stop them? She could try to confiscate their wealth . . . except many had already emptied their treasure vaults. Besides, she wasn't entirely certain the law was on her side.

"We still have Han," she said stubbornly, in the face of her councillors' silent gloom. "He and his witch-men are worth more than Harbisland and Arbenia and the rest of them put together."

Alasdair shook his head. Ursa had physicked his scrapes and bruises, but he still looked exhausted from his ordeal. "He and his witch-men are three-quarters dead from battling Mijak, and then getting us home again. Don't be too quick to assume their allegiance. Their losses are grievous. And the emperor is . . . displeased."

She didn't need him to tell her that. She was well aware of Han's displeasure.

At the harbour she and Han had spoken briefly, privately, before his palanquin arrived to take him to Lai's residence.

"Do you see what Zandakar of Mijak has cost us? In saving his family, he has nearly destroyed mine."

His rage had been all the more brutal for its restraint. "I know, Han," she'd whispered. "I'm sorry."

"And will your sorrow bring my drowned and burned witch-men back to life? Will it bring back Sun-dao? Will it save us from Mijak?"

She'd met his fury without flinching. "Nothing can bring them back, Han. We could weep enough tears to fill this harbour twice over and they'd still be dead."

Han had leaned over her then. Exhausted, shivering with the extremity of his distress, still he was terrifying. *"I want him, Rhian. Zandakar belongs to the Tzhung."*

Tilting her chin, she'd met him stare for stare. "You can't have him. Zandakar might be all that can save us now. Your revenge will have to wait."

Han had walked away from her then, and she'd known that for him, it was walk away or kill her.

She was yet to share his fury with anyone.

"Emperor Han is shocked and grieving," she said, choosing her words with care. Just as carefully didn't look at Alasdair. "As are we all. But he knows that as Ethrea falls, so falls Tzhung-tzhungchai. He won't desert us." *No matter how much he hates me.* "I am confident of that."

"So . . . what do we do now?" said Ludo, staring around the council table. Like Alasdair, the marks of his time with the armada lingered in his face and eyes. "By Han's calculations, the warships of Mijak are four weeks away."

Four weeks. So close. Dear God, it's not enough time. "What do we do?" she said. "We fight, gentlemen. What else can we do?"

"Alone?" said Adric.

She gritted her teeth. "No, *not* alone. How many times must I—"

"Before this disaster, we had nine nations fighting with us," Adric said, his hands white-knuckled. "Now we have one. *Perhaps.* But you can't be certain. It's possible the armada has killed Tzhung-tzhungchai, and we are witnessing its lingering death."

She couldn't argue, though she wanted to.

"I know it would seem we've lost the support of almost every trading nation," she said. "But I refuse to abandon hope. I refuse to surrender to fear, and doubt." She tried to smile at Helfred. "I do not accept my faith is misplaced. My prayer is that the Tzung are only wounded, and Arbenia and Harbisland and the others will return to help us."

"And if they don't?" said Edward quietly. "If they choose to defend themselves first, and us not at all?"

It took nearly all her remaining strength to appear

confident, and unconcerned. "Then the people of Ethrea will prove their mettle, Edward."

"Well said, Majesty," Helfred murmured as the others shifted and looked at each other.

"What of Hettie, Mister Jones?" she said. "Her guidance now would be appreciated. Are you sure there's no way we can—"

Dexterity was shaking his head. He looked ready to weep. "I wish there was, but there's not."

"Never mind," she said gently. "Let's just find strength and comfort in what we already know. She urged you and Zandakar to Jatharuj, and you returned with the scorpion knife. It's a powerful weapon, one we can—"

"Majesty, Zandakar's blade is no match for Dmitrak's gauntlet," Ludo protested. "If you'd seen what he did with it . . . the way our ships burned, and sank . . . I swear, you'd have as much chance of sawing down a tree with a butter knife."

She'd seen Zandakar's scorpion blade sink a Tzhung skiff. She could only imagine what Dmitrak's gauntlet had done to the carracks and the galleys and the triremes of the armada.

"Ludo's right," said Alasdair, his eyes so bleak. "We might as well not have that knife at all, for the good it can do us. We had our chance to end this. That chance was squandered."

What? "Alasdair," said Rhian, her voice low, a warning.

"I'm sorry?" said Edward. "What chance was that?"

She schooled her voice to indifference. "It's nothing, Edward. An incident we can't—"

"Nothing?" said Alasdair, disbelieving. "You call the sinking of our armada *nothing*?"

"Of course I don't," she replied, her temper precarious. "But since the past can't be changed, I see no purpose in discussing it."

Not when feelings are running so high. Alasdair, Alasdair, what are you doing?

"I'd like to know more of this 'chance' the king mentions," said Edward, bewilderment giving way to suspicion. "What incident is he—?"

"Edward, I've already said there's—"

"When Mister Jones and Zandakar were in Jatharuj, the witch-man Sun-dao tried to destroy the township," said Alasdair. "Unfortunately, they stopped him."

"Stopped him?" said Rudi, breaking the shocked silence. "What do you mean?"

"*Alasdair*," said Rhian. "*This isn't the time.*"

"I mean," said Alasdair to Rudi, but staring at her, no apology in him, no remorse, only anger, "they prevented Sun-dao from smashing Jatharuj to pieces. If they hadn't, it's likely the Mijaki would have been destroyed with it, or at least so badly crippled we'd have stood a fair chance of the armada finishing them." He spread his hands. "But Mijak was allowed to live. And now Ethrea stands in the shadow of death."

The silence lasted longer this time. Then Edward turned to Dexterity. "*Mister Jones?*"

Dexterity looked so unwell, hunched over the council table as though all his bones hurt. "I had to stop Sun-dao!" he said desperately. "Innocent Icthians still lived in Jatharuj. I wasn't prepared to see them murdered. Besides, raising a storm like that is beyond any one witch-man. Emperor Han himself has said it. And we had to get away before we were discovered. We nearly didn't, Sun-dao revealed our presence with his witching. It was a close-run thing, and the storm never would've worked."

"You don't know that," said Alasdair, cruelly courteous. "Because Zandakar attacked Sun-dao before he could finish calling it. And he wasn't thinking of innocent Icthians. All he cared about was saving his mother and brother."

"Thank you, Alasdair," Rhian said softly. "That's very helpful." All she could think was *Don't weep, girl. Don't weep.*

"Actually, I think it could be," he retorted. "Shall I tell you what I think Han said to you at the harbour?"

She'd never seen him so grim. So vengeful. She couldn't bear it. *I'd like to wake up now.* "Please don't," she replied. She felt encased in ice. "You've said quite enough already."

Alasdair leaned forward, as though they were alone. "*I think* he said he holds Zandakar responsible for the death of his witch-men, starting with Sun-dao! *I think* he said he won't help Ethrea until Zandakar is held accountable for his crimes. *I think Ethrea is doomed unless you give Han what he wants!*"

Uproar. Alasdair was half out of his seat now, hands braced on the council table. Ludo tried to calm him, and was roughly knocked aside. Dexterity had his head in his hands. Helfred was gaping, the dukes were spluttering.

Rhian looked only at Alasdair, feeling sick.

How could you? How could you? Do you hate him so much?

As Alasdair sat down again, Adric banged his fist on the table. "If that's the price Han's demanding, then I say we pay it! I say we give Zandakar to the Tzhung!"

"What?" said Rhian, dragging her gaze from Alasdair's cold face. "No."

"My son's right, Majesty," said Rudi. "That heathen Mijaki's forfeited our protection. He broke his oath. He's as good as killed Ethrea."

Dexterity looked up. His cheeks were streaked with tears. "We can't do that, Your Grace. We can't hand Zandakar over to Emperor Han. Quite apart from the morality of it, there's his scorpion knife. Hettie sent us there to—"

"How do you know why Hettie sent you?" demanded Edward. "For all you know, she sent you to make sure Sun-dao destroyed Jatharuj! And you didn't. Maybe that's why she's deserted us, Mister Jones!"

"And the knife's no use anyway!" said Adric, vicious. "It's no match for that gauntlet. All it's good for, I'll warrant, is setting damp wood on fire."

"We have to make peace with Tzhung-tzhungchai!" Rudi declared. "We don't stand a chance without them. You have to give them Zandakar, Your Majesty. You don't have a choice. He betrayed us, and you *know* it!"

"He did nothing of the sort, Rudi," Rhian said. She felt small, and distant. "He did what any one of us would do. He tried to save his family."

"And he's killed mine instead!" Rudi shouted,

heedless of protocol. "I'll not have a bar of him, Rhian. If *you* won't take him to Han, *I will*!"

She was finding it hard to see. Hard to breathe. Hard to believe this was happening.

"Helfred?" she whispered. "What do you say?"

Like Dexterity, Helfred was weeping. "I don't know. I don't know *what* to say. I was convinced Marlan came to me at God's behest, that trusting Zandakar was the divine will, but now . . ."

"You weren't mistaken, Helfred." She stood and looked at her council. "Wait here. Any man who touches Zandakar while I'm gone will be counted a traitor, and die a traitor's death."

Alasdair smiled. He looked savage. "*Any* man?"

"I won't be long," she said, and turned for the door.

"Where are you going, Majesty?" Dexterity called after her.

"Where do you think? To see Emperor Han."

CHAPTER THIRTY-TWO

A servant answered the ringing bell at the closed gates of Ambassador Lai's residence. It was so late now – so early – that the sound woke hollow echoes up and down and around the deserted streets of the ambassadors' district. Her stallion danced on the cobbles, startled by the noise, threatening to tug the reins from her hands.

"You know who I am?" Rhian asked the Tzhung servant, who peered at her through the gates' wrought-iron bars as though he'd never seen a woman before.

He nodded. "Majesty."

"Then admit me," she said. "And have someone see to my horse."

The servant stared at her for several moments, speechless, then opened the gates wide and stood back. "Majesty."

Another servant appeared. He took her stallion, and she followed the gatekeeper into the residence.

Ambassador Lai stood in the elegant, wood-panelled foyer. If he was surprised to see her, his ruthlessly polite self-control hid his emotions to perfection. "Your Majesty."

"I want Han," she said baldly. "Don't tell me he's not here."

Lai held out his hand. "Your knife, Queen Rhian."

Without hesitation she handed it over.

"Come," he said, and turned on his heel.

She followed his jonquil-yellow silk back from the foyer, along a series of corridors and through a set of woven bamboo doors, into a small bamboo-enclosed garden. Torches burned, shedding warm light. Hidden water splashed rhythmically, tinkling like a music box. Jasmine scented the cool, windchimed air.

Then Lai withdrew, silent and noncommittal, and she was alone with Tzhung's emperor.

Han stood in a shifting pool of torchlight, a tall, slender figure clad completely in black. His back was to her. His unbound hair reached his waist.

"I know you're angry," she said, hands clasped behind her so tightly, they hurt. "I know you're griev-ing. I know—"

"*You know nothing*," said Han.

His voice held an edge so sharp, she thought if she looked down she'd see herself bleeding.

She took the smallest step towards him. Her booted feet crushed flowers in the grass, and their voluptuous fragrance mingled with the jasmine's sweet perfume.

"I know that without Tzhung-tzhungchai and its witch-men, Ethrea stands alone against Mijak."

Han turned. Warm light spilled over him, revealing his unsympathetic face. His eyes were disdainful. He looked ageless, like stone, and just as malleable.

"So you have come to Tzhung-tzhungchai for help?"

Was she afraid? Her mouth was dry, her palms damp with sweat. She must be afraid. Windchimes caressed the scented silence.

"Yes," she said at last.

"Why?"

"Because I've nowhere else to turn."

The windchimes swayed in a swift gust of air, jan-gling and discordant as though her words had of-fended. Han stared at her, dark eyes half-closed. In their depths, a hint of crimson.

"Kneel, girl-queen of Ethrea."

She dropped to the flowered grass, hands by her sides.

"*Beg.*"

She tilted her chin at him. "Please. Please help me."

He answered by taking hold of her, his fingers bruising in their strength. Before she could cry out she heard an angry roaring, felt the terrifying strength of an ice-cold raging wind.

The garden disappeared and she was somewhere else entirely. Somewhere freezing and scorching, blinding bright and black as pitch. It reeked of old blood. New death. She heard screaming in the wind.

"Han!" she shouted. "Han, where are you? Where am I? *Han*!"

And there he was, beside her, fingers anchored to her wrist. His lips were pressed against her ear, and their soft touch was freezing.

"You know where you are, Rhian. You've been here before. This is the twilight. This is the world where witch-men truly live!"

The twilight? No, no, that wasn't right. It wasn't like this when Han witched her to Harbisland.

"It can't be! I don't believe you!"

"You beg for my help, then call me a liar? *Believe me*, Rhian." Han pulled her against him. "This is the twilight of Mijak's making. This is because Zandakar stopped Sun-dao."

Without his hold on her wrist, or the shelter of his body, she thought the twilight's windstorm would blow her down. Blow her away. Shred her to pieces and hurl those shreds into oblivion.

"I hear screaming," she said, refusing to let herself look away from Han's terrible eyes. "Who's screaming?"

"My witch-men," he told her, weeping. Who would think cold stone could weep? "My brothers."

She wrenched free of him, burned by her own tears. "I'm sorry! *I'm sorry!* God's mercy, do you think I *wanted* this? Do you think *I'm* not angry? I'm angry, Han. I'm *furious*. You're right. If Zandakar hadn't stopped Sun-dao there'd have been no need for an armada and all those people would still be alive. Mijak would be dead, and your witch-men wouldn't be suffering like this."

All around them, the wounded twilight writhed and howled. In the wind, Han's witch-men screamed their torment.

"Then give him to me," Han demanded. "Give Zandakar to me and my witch-men will help Ethrea."

She shook her head. Stepped back. "I *can't*."

"You would *protect* him?" Han said, incredulous.

"I have to."

"*Why?*"

She was shaking so hard. She wasn't sure she could remain standing for much longer. "*Because I said I would, Han*. And because he's all I have left to throw against Mijak."

"I could take him," Han said. He was smiling like Alasdair, brutal and cruel.

She nodded. "Yes, you could. But you won't."

On a wordless cry he seized her again. Cupped a hand to the back of her neck, fingers digging into her flesh, and dragged her to him.

A breath more pressure, and he'd break her.

And then Han howled, like the voices in the wind. The ruined twilight thrashed. It spun around her head. He pushed her away from him, hurled her to the ground . . .

. . . where she sprawled, ungainly. Stunned, she sat up. She was home again, in her castle privy garden.

*   *   *

Part of her was surprised to find that the council had obeyed her, and waited in the war room for her return. They stared at her, sullenly silent, as she entered the ballroom. Only Dexterity stood to greet her. And not even he could smile.

"Gentlemen," she said, considering the rest of them. Letting her gaze skim across Alasdair. "No, really, don't get up."

"Did you see Emperor Han, Majesty?" Dexterity asked.

He looked so miserable. Consumed by guilt. And none of this was his fault, not even Jatharuj. He was a toymaker. He never could have stopped Sun-dao from raising that storm, or Zandakar from using his scorpion knife. So did it matter, truly, that he'd not wanted the storm? That he'd agreed with Zandakar about saving Jatharuj?

He's a dear, sweet and gentle man. He always has been. How could I expect him to stand by and watch a slaughter?

"Sit down, Mister Jones," she said. "Yes. I saw the emperor."

"And are you going to surrender Zandakar to him?" said Dexterity, slowly taking his seat.

She shook her head. "No."

"But he asked?" said Rudi. Like them all he was exhausted, but the dregs of belligerence remained. "He declared it the price for Tzhung-tzhungchai's help?"

God help, God help me . . . "No, Rudi. He didn't."

"Didn't?" said Edward, and glanced at Alasdair, puzzled. "I thought—"

"The emperor is grieving the loss of so many witch-men," she replied. "The armada's failure is as devastating to him as it is to us, Edward. But he knows how important Tzhung-tzhungchai is in the battle to save Ethrea. To save the world. When we need him, he will be there." *Please God, let him be there.*

"And Zandakar?" said Ludo as Edward and Adric and Rudi looked at each other, and Helfred continued to ponder his prayer beads, and Dexterity tugged at his untrimmed beard.

"Zandakar is my concern," she replied, staring at Alasdair. "You needn't fret about him."

"But you still intend to—"

"Of course I do, Ludo!" she snapped. "Nothing that's happened diminishes his value to us. Indeed, he's now more valuable than ever. And he will continue to serve me, and serve Ethrea, however I see fit. Is that clear?"

"Majesty . . ." Helfred looked up. "You are our sovereign. And as your loyal subjects, we must obey you. But I beg you to consider this: Zandakar has chosen his family over Ethrea once. And what can be done once, can be done twice."

Only Dexterity wasn't afraid of that. But she couldn't help it. She couldn't help them. She couldn't tell them Zandakar wasn't protecting Hekat and Dmitrak, but his father. This *Vortka*. The priest who'd promised to fight against Mijak, not for it.

"It can," she agreed. "But in this case, it won't be."

"You don't *know* that!" said Adric. "Not for sure!"

"It's called having faith, Adric," she told him. "Ask Helfred, if you've forgotten."

"By God," said Edward slowly. "You're prodigious casual with our lives, Rhian."

I know. I know. I'm sorry, Edward. "Zandakar won't fail us, gentlemen," she said. "And neither will Han."

They were too tired, or too dispirited, to argue any more. She was grateful for that, even as it pricked her with guilt.

"It's been a long day, my friends," she added, gentling her voice. "You're tired. I'm tired. Our hearts are sore with grief. Let's withdraw, and seek our well-earned beds. We'll meet in the council chamber at nine of the clock, and together make final plans for our stand against Mijak."

"Majesty," said Helfred, nodding. "That seems the wisest course."

As he and the dukes departed, Dexterity hesitated. "Majesty . . . Rhian . . ." His voice broke. "Can you forgive me?"

"Oh, Dexterity," she said, and held him close. "You were following your conscience. If that's all God asks of us, how can I ask for more?"

"But what if Edward's right? What if Hettie's gone because I did the wrong thing?"

She tightened her arms around him. "I'll never believe that. Hettie told you to trust Zandakar, and that's what you did."

"Then where is she? *Where is she?*"

"I don't know, Dexterity," she said, and released him. "But wherever she is, she won't want you blaming yourself. Now get some rest. I'll see you in the

Dexterity nodded, and trailed out. She was alone with Alasdair.

"You lied," he said, still slouched in his seat.

She folded her arms. "I had to."

The cold look in his eyes admitted no such thing. "And when Mijak comes, and Han doesn't, what will you say then?"

"He'll come." *He will. He will.* "Alasdair, why did you do this? Why did you tell the council about Jatharuj when we *agreed*—"

"Because *I* had to!" he shouted, leaping to his feet. "Because I was *there*, Rhian, I saw the armada *die*! I saw the blood price everyone else paid for Zandakar's choice! I saw the ships on fire and sinking, I heard the sailors screaming, I saw them drown, saw them torn apart, saw them – have you *any idea* the sound a man makes when he's burning alive? Do you know what he *smells* like? Do you know—"

"Yes, I do!" she shouted back. "Have you forgotten Marlan? Alasdair, I'm *sorry* you were there and saw all those terrible things. But no matter how terrible they were, you shouldn't have told the council about Jatharuj! Look at all the trouble it's caused!"

He shook his head slowly, wondering. "You'll defend Zandakar no matter what, won't you?"

"It's not about defending *him*, it's about defending *Ethrea*. You *know* we need him. With Mijak coming—"

"How can you be so *blind*, Rhian?" said Alasdair. "How can you honestly think he won't betray you again?"

"And how can you be so sure he *will*?"

"Well," he said softly, after a moment. "At least that's a start. At least you admit he's betrayed you once."

She didn't know how to answer that. *Oh, Alasdair. Alasdair. How has this happened?*

"I have to go," she said abruptly. "I have to—"

His eyebrows lifted. "See Zandakar?"

"We'll talk later," she said. She could barely see him for tears. "All right? We'll talk later. We will. We'll . . . talk."

And she walked away then, before he broke her completely.

Zandakar sat in his castle chamber and waited. No soldiers guarded him, but still he was a prisoner. He was imprisoned by Rhian, whose lightest word was his law. He waited for her to come and tell him of the armada, even though he knew already the news was not good.

Those ships of wood will not stand against Dmitrak. Cities of stone cannot stand against the god's hammer, it smites cities, it smites—

No. The gauntlet was a hammer, it did not smite for the god. The god did not want cities destroyed, it did not desire streets running with blood. It did not want Alasdair king dead in the ocean.

If he is dead, Rhian will blame me. If he is dead, I am to blame.

The pain he had lived with since Jatharuj clawed him. Every night in his sleep he saw the faces of the dead, he heard the dead screaming. There was no Lilit to hold him, no Lilit to soothe his tears. And so he was tasked for the dead at his feet.

If Yuma is dead, if Dimmi is dead, if Vortka, my father, if he is dead too . . .

In the silence his harsh breathing, the pain clawing at his throat.

I want Mijak to be stopped. I do not want them dead.

He did not like to think it, he was angry with Vortka for sending him away. He wanted to know why those cities were dead, he wanted to know who had told him to kill them. If the god did not want it, who spoke to the godspeakers? Who spoke to Yuma? Who did she hear when she swam in the godpool?

Does she listen to demons? Are there demons in Mijak? Have I killed for demons instead of the god?

He felt his heart thudding as though he danced his *hotas*. He felt a hot sweat dampen his skin.

Demons.

The more he thought of it, the more he thought it was true. He thought Vortka knew it. He thought Dexterity had told Vortka that in Jatharuj, when they burned and did not die.

And Vortka said he would tell this truth to Yuma. She will never believe him, demons have whispered in her heart for too long. They whisper to Yuma, they whisper to Dimmi. Yuma and Dimmi are deaf to the god.

Aieee, the god see them. This was not their fault. They did not understand, they were tricked by demons. All of Mijak was tricked by demons.

Yuma . . . Yuma . . . please, listen to Vortka. Listen to Vortka before your godspark is devoured.

His chamber door opened. Rhian walked in, she was pale, she was exhausted. Her beautiful eyes blazed bright blue with anger.

"The armada was defeated," she said, and kicked the door shut. "Six hundred and thirty-seven ships sailed out of my harbour. Only two hundred and ten sailed back. Ebrich of Arbenia is dead. Dalsyn of Harbisland is dead. Rollin's mercy, the only leader of a trading nation *not* to perish is Han."

Slowly, he stood. "Alasdair king?"

"He survived," she said. "So did Ludo. But all the trading nations have deserted us. Our alliance is dead, too."

"Tzhung-tzhungchai?" he whispered. "Emperor Han?"

"Emperor Han wants your head on a pikestaff! He wants to spit your heart on a fork and *roast* it! *Hundreds* of his witch-men perished. Tzhung-tzhungchai is brought to its *knees*."

Rhian was so angry, she was weeping. Did she know it? He thought she did not. "Will Emperor Han help Ethrea against Mijak?"

She roamed about the chamber. "He says he will – *if* I give him what he wants."

He sighed. "Does Alasdair king say for you to give me to Han?"

She flicked a hot glance at him, still pacing. "What do you think? Practically the whole council says it, Zandakar. They know everything about Jatharuj, now. Alasdair told them. Believe me, *you* are not a popular man. But what happens to you isn't up to the dukes. It's not up to Alasdair. *I* decide what happens to you. And what I decide decides the fate of this kingdom."

His heart was hurting, it hurt to breathe. Alasdair king had told the dukes of Jatharuj? Aieee, the god see him. He was not in Jatharuj alone. "Dexterity. Do the dukes blame him for the armada?"

"Not as much as they blame you," she said. Then she pulled a face, her angry eyes gentled. "He blames himself. He's wondering now if he was right, in Jatharuj. Are you wondering, Zandakar? Do *you* blame yourself?"

He pressed his fist to his chest. "I am sorry so many armada ships died. *Yatzhay. Yatzhay.*"

She stared, the gentleness gone from her eyes. "There can be no repeat of Jatharuj, Zandakar. You serve me. You serve Ethrea. You serve no-one else. *Zho?*"

How could he tell her the truth in his heart? How could he make her understand about demons? If he told her he wanted to save Yuma and Dimmi, she would not believe that meant he would still fight for Ethrea. She would think he betrayed her. She would give him to Han.

If she gives me to Han, I will never save Yuma. I will never save Dimmi. I will never see Vortka again.

"I will fight for you, Rhian," he said. "I will fight for Ethrea."

That is not a lie.

"You'd better," she said, there was no laughter in her. This was not the Rhian who danced *hotas* in the morning. "Because if you don't . . . *if you don't* . . . I swear to you on the graves of my family, I'll give you to Han. And when he kills you . . . *I'll cheer.*"

She was not Lilit. She did not love him even though he had sinned. She was Yuma for her people. If he failed her, he would die.

As her hand touched his chamber door's handle, she turned. "There's a council meeting at nine. Be there."

"*Zho*," he said. "Rhian *hushla*."

"Jones," said Ursa, staring at the fool's closed chamber door. "Jones, you might as well let me in, for I'm not leaving until I've seen you." She knocked again. "Jones!"

A passing servant slowed, and stared.

"He's a heavy sleeper," Ursa explained. "Don't mind me."

The servant blushed and nodded. "Madam physick," he muttered, and went on his way.

The door's latch and handle rattled, then it pulled open a reluctant half-handsbreadth. "I don't need physicking, Ursa. Go and bother someone who does."

"Tcha," she said, and pushed hard on the door.

"Ursa," Jones protested, falling back. "Why don't you ever *listen* to me?"

"I could ask the same question of you, Jones," she retorted. "As I recall, I told you not to get mixed up in *any* of this. Dead wives and slave ships and heathen warriors and didn't I say it would all end in tears?"

Jones shrugged, his eyes red-rimmed, his face too pale. "Did you? Well, it always cheers you up to be proven right."

He turned away to stare out of his chamber window at the dawn, shoulders slumped, hands dangling defeated at his side. She'd never been a demonstrative woman, but it was hard not to go to him. Not to show him . . .

"You've heard about the armada, of course," he said, then grimaced. "I expect half of Ethrea's heard by now."

She was as tired as he looked. She'd not been to bed yet. "I heard. I've been up all night physicking the sailors who came back."

That turned him round. "Are there many sore hurt, Ursa? Are any like to die?"

"A dozen, maybe," she admitted. "A score not dying, but poorly enough. Another score you'd call the walking wounded. None of them witch-men. They've all vanished, it seems."

"I think for good," he said, "though Rhian denies it. The emperor wants Zandakar, in payment for his losses."

"Blood for blood?" She snorted. "That's civilised, I must say. Rhian's not—"

"No, no. She defends him, like always. It's caused trouble between her and Alasdair. He and Duke Ludo . . . they're hurt by what happened with the armada." He shuddered. "What they must've seen. I can't bear to think of it. And the council's siding with them. They want her to hand Zandakar over. They don't trust him any more – or me – because of Jatharuj. Because we didn't – we didn't—"

She stared, shocked, as Jones dropped to his bed like an old man not strong enough to stand on his own two feet. She knew about Sun-dao and Zandakar because he'd told her, but—

"You said that part of what happened in Jatharuj was being kept secret."

"It was," he said. "But Alasdair was angry. Duke Edward says Hettie's abandoned me because I didn't help destroy Mijak when I had the chance."

She'd not seen him so desolate since the night Hettie died. "That old fool? That blustery duke? Oh, Jones, what would he know?"

"I was so certain Jatharuj was about the knife. And about finding Vortka. What if I was wrong, Ursa? What if I've been wrong about *everything*?"

"*You haven't*," she said fiercely. "You've been proven right every step of the way. Not right at once, maybe, but in the end, you've been right. And Hettie would *never* abandon you. Something's keeping her from you. Whatever evil that's in Mijak, *that's* what's keeping you apart."

"You think so?" he said, his voice unsteady. "It's not because I've let her down?"

"Let her down? Oh, Jones! You couldn't let Hettie down if you tried! You couldn't let *anyone* down. It's not in you." She sat beside him, and gave him a little shake. "Stop blathering nonsense. When did you last eat? You've gone light-headed for lack of food."

"I think my appetite died with the armada," he whispered. "Oh, Ursa. Mijak's coming. What are we to *do*?"

"The only thing we can do, Jones. Hold fast to our faith, and to each other."

He pulled away from her and pushed off the bed. "I don't think that's going to be enough. I think we're about to become another Garabatsas."

"You don't know that, Jones," she protested.

"What are you doing? Are you *giving up*? You can't give up. Rhian's relying on you. A *lot* of people are relying on you." *And Rollin's mercy, I'm one of them.* "Jones—"

"Ursa, please. Just go. I know you mean well, I know you think you're helping. But you're not. At least you *are*, but—" He shook his head. "I'm sorry. I'm not fit for company."

She stood, not sure whether to be insulted or frightened. "This isn't good, Jones. I'm speaking as a physick now, not as your friend. Brooding, blaming yourself, it's *not* good. I don't *like* it."

He offered her the travesty of a smile. "Don't worry. I'll be fine. I just . . . need some breakfast. You go. Get some rest. After last night, you've earned it."

She'd only upset him more if she insisted on staying.

Troubled, she left him. But instead of seeking her bed in the castle chamber given over to her use, she trudged her way to Helfred's palace and sat in the small public chapel, praying.

Hettie, if you can hear me, you'd best get back here. Now.

Rhian and Alasdair shared a bed after the night's long, fraught council meeting, but they were as distant as though he still sailed with the armada.

He didn't sing in the morning. He didn't speak. He didn't smile.

Dressing in silence, heartsick and dreading the council meeting to come, Rhian stared in the mirror at her scarred face.

Now my marriage is a battlefield, just like my

kingdom. And in supporting Zandakar to save one, I might easily destroy the other.

As they left their apartments to meet with the council she lightly touched her husband's arm. "Alasdair. I love you." *You, not Zandakar.*

He'd not slept well. Nightmares of the armada. Awake beside him she'd tried to give him her comfort, but even in his dreams he turned away. Now he sighed.

"If you love me, don't defend him. Don't use him. Don't trust him with this kingdom. With my life."

"How can you ask me that? You know what Hettie told Dexterity, when this began. You *know*—"

"All I know, Rhian, is that you'll trust a dead woman and an enemy before you'll trust me." He opened the parlour door, and stepped aside. "Shall we go? The council's waiting."

Her dukes were subdued when they greeted her. So was Helfred. Dexterity looked ravaged. Their eyes met, and he tried to smile.

"Gentlemen," she said coolly as Alasdair took his seat. "Where is Zandakar? Mister Jones—"

And then he joined them. Fresh from the tiltyard, dressed in dust and sweat and battered huntsman's leathers. Decorated here and there with blood. "I am sorry, Rhian *hushla*," he said, so self-contained. "I was training."

"So I see," she said, and did not smile to see him. "Be seated. We have a great deal to discuss."

If he felt the weight of the staring dukes' displeasure, he didn't show it. Sliding into a chair, he looked at Dexterity, his pale eyes worried. He nodded at

Helfred. He nodded at Alasdair, and pressed his fist to his chest.

"Alasdair king."

Alasdair looked him up and down. "Zandakar."

This morning she was too weary for pacing. Taking her own seat, glancing at Ven'Cedwin to see if his quill was inked, she folded her hands on the table and sighed.

"Some four weeks, gentlemen, and Mijak will be here. Now we decide how best to pass the time."

The meeting lasted seven hours. Prompted by Dexterity, she invited Zandakar to share his opinions of Kingseat harbour. Its vulnerability. How he thought his mother and brother would attack. How Ethrea could defend against them. What more training its soldiers required. How best to use their limited resources.

He spoke slowly. Steadily. His newfound fluency failed him, sometimes, but still he made his points. Gradually the hostility of her dukes subsided, and they began to care more for what was being said than who was saying it. Even Alasdair lowered his prickly guard. They argued. They compromised. They made difficult decisions.

The last, most difficult decision taken before the council broke for a brief respite was to count Linfoi as lost before Mijak reached it. They could not justify the resources it would take to defend Ethrea's least populous and poorest duchy. Its people would be sent south, its livestock left to fend for themselves. Its garrison's soldiers would be sent wherever they were needed.

"I'm sorry, Ludo," said Rhian as the council took a brief break from deliberations. "I hope you understand I've not chosen this course because I hold duchy Linfoi in any low esteem."

Ludo shook his head. "Of course not, Majesty. I can't fault your reasoning."

She glanced over at Alasdair, nursing a goblet of ale by the chamber window, alone. "I'm not sure your cousin agrees with you."

"He does," said Ludo. "But still . . . it hurts."

Of course it did. Everything hurt now, with Mijak four weeks away. "The command for your duchy's evacuation will go out by tonight. I'll have Henrik brought here to the castle, if that's what he wants. Although since it's almost certain Mijak will attack Kingseat first, perhaps he'd be safer somewhere else."

"Safer?" Ludo pulled a face. "Do you honestly believe anywhere will be safe?"

This was the first private moment she and Alasdair's cousin had shared since the return of the ruined armada. "Ludo—"

He was still dashingly handsome, even with bruises all over his face, but something was different. His eyes were . . . older . . . than they'd been. "Yes, Rhian. It really was that dreadful."

And then it was time to resume their preparations for war.

Edward and Rudi would take charge of a defensive position running along the Morvell-Hartshorn and Arbat-Meercheq borders. From that vantage-point they'd look to defend the kingdom's four middle duchies, and support duchy Kingseat in the south. They'd be assisted by Davin of Meercheq, to be released from house arrest, and every nobleman of those duchies.

Adric and Ludo would have the care of duchy Kingseat, and thus leave the defending of Kingseat capital to Alasdair, Zandakar . . . and Rhian herself.

"Because I can assure you, gentlemen," she said coldly, "beacon or not, beloved by the people or not, I've no intention of cowering in a closet hoping the warriors of Mijak mistake me for a player's dummy. I'll have a care for my person, but I'll not be a coward."

Helfred cleared his throat. "Your sentiments are admirable, Majesty. And no less than I – than *we* – expected. Perhaps we could revisit the matter another time? Certainly you've given us food for thought."

In other words, he was going to fight her. And he wasn't alone. Only Zandakar looked approving. But then he would approve, wouldn't he? His mother was Mijak's own warrior queen.

Let them think what they like. I'll not be moved on this.

She looked around the table. "Gentlemen, we must pull together now as never before. Whatever concerns you have about Zandakar's place in this, banish them. If he has proven nothing else to us today, he has proven how we need him, and his knowledge of Mijak. Of warfare. He thinks like our enemy . . . but he is our friend."

She looked at Alasdair when she said that. Alasdair looked back, no softness in him. No willingness to compromise.

But he will. He will. He has to. He's not stupid, only stubborn.

It was Adric who spoke aloud what she knew her councillors were thinking. "And Emperor Han, Majesty? What part will the Tzhung play?"

"That has yet to be decided," she said. "He and I will meet, in good time." She turned to Helfred. "Eminence, I regret I must ask so much of the Church. But you and your clergy are best placed to oversee the emptying of duchy Linfoi and the relocation of its people, as well as keeping the rest of the kingdom abreast of events and its courage high."

"What is the Church for, Majesty, if not the succour of its children?" said Helfred. "There's no burden you can place upon it that God can't help us bear."

She loved him, then. She could have kissed him. "Gentlemen," she said. "I think we know what we must do. May God bless our kingdom, and give us the strength to prevail."

In the days and weeks following the armada's return, the whole of Ethrea was transformed into an armed camp. With the duchies' garrisons filled to bursting, Rhian instructed Helfred and his clergy to tell her people that they should in their villages and hamlets, in their towns and in their parishes, form their own armed militias so they might defend themselves, if needed.

As for Ethrea's army . . . she was so proud. From sunup to sundown, in rain, in heat, bleeding and hurting, her soldiers trained until exhaustion felled them. In her castle garrison, in the garrisons of Kingseat and every other duchy, from the newest recruits to the old men limped out of retirement, they sweated and strained and swore and cursed, and wept when they promised: "*We will prevail.*"

Mindful that he was one man, and could not lead everyone, Zandakar demanded to see every nobleman and seasoned soldier the kingdom possessed. He trained them to battle Mijak in groups of thirty at a time, a new group starting every three days. At the end of those three days his bruised and battered students were scattered throughout the duchies, to pass on what they had learned quickly, crudely, no time for kindness or finesse.

Rhian, Alasdair and her dukes trained with the first group like any common soldiers. She trained so hard, she truly thought she'd die. She crawled into bed at night weeping with pain.

After those brutal three days, the dukes left Kingseat to take command of their garrisons. Rhian farewelled Edward and Rudi first, the old warhorses who'd become like family, like uncles. They were strong men, but they wept in the castle forecourt and received her royal blessing. She embraced them afterwards, so afraid to watch them ride away.

"You needn't fear for the north, Majesty," said Edward. "We'll fight until the last sword and pitchfork are broken. We'll make these heathen Mijaki rue the day they heard of Ethrea."

"I know you will," she said. "But if you don't take proper care of your safety, you'll be the rueful one, Edward. My word as a Havrell."

He laughed a little, and so did she, but they both knew their hearts were breaking.

"God keep you safe, Majesty," said Rudi. "It's been an honour serving you."

"The honour is mine," she replied, and punched her fist to her chest.

Next she gave Adric her blessing. "Have a care, Your Grace," she told him. "Kingseat needs its duke."

Flushed, Adric nodded. "Majesty, I've not always been comfortable, I know it, but I don't take your trust lightly. I won't let you down."

She wanted to believe him. She wanted to believe choosing him hadn't been a mistake, after all. "Be guided by Ludo, Adric. He's a duke too, remember, and more seasoned than you. If he advises you, listen."

"I will," Adric promised.

Farewelling Ludo was hardest. She watched, her throat aching, as Alasdair and his cousin embraced.

"Godspeed," Ludo said, all his humour extinguished. "I'll see you again when it's over, Alasdair."

"You will," said Alasdair, his eyes over-bright. "By God, you will."

She kissed Alasdair's cousin, and tousled his hair. "I'll keep trying to convince Henrik to join us in Kingseat, Ludo."

Ludo smiled. "He won't come. He'll stay where he can rally Linfoi's people." He kissed her cheek. "Look after Alasdair. Look after yourself." Then, holding her close, he whispered, "The best thing my cousin ever did was marry you. Find me another Rhian, when we've won."

"Oh, Ludo," she said, and let the tears fall. "I'll find you someone far better than me."

Her dukes departed, soon after. She stood with Alasdair, in silence, until they rode from sight.

With her dukes gone, Rhian became a second Zandakar. At first her soldier-students were wary, these were not men who knew her. To praise the romantic idea of a huntsman queen in chapel, that was one thing. To face her on the tiltyard and run at her with a training stave, that was something they found difficult to do.

Until she showed that she could kill them. When they believed that, then she could teach them. They believed . . . and they learned.

Helfred and his clergy laboured without rest to see the people of Linfoi settled, and the other duchies prepared. Lost for purpose, at first, Dexterity joined the prolate in keeping Kingseat's spirits lifted. He held puppet shows at the harbour markets, and every day made children laugh.

None of the deserting trading nations returned to help them. Rhian sent messages to Han, but received no reply. After a week, the council stopped asking when they could expect the aid of Tzhungtzhungchai. She shared her days with Zandakar and her soldiers, dancing *hotas* and sweating. Her nights she spent with Alasdair, when they slept like strangers.

And every morning she woke thinking: *does Mijak come today?*

CHAPTER THIRTY-THREE

"*There*!" cried Dmitrak, and laughed out loud. The light of newsun was everywhere, it showed him his heart's desire. "There is *Ethrea*, nest of demons in the world!"

He flung out his gauntleted hand, pointing. Aieee, god, that he could not smite the sinning island from here. But they would reach it soon and then it would burn. Like the demons' ships had burned, they had burned and sunk, he had destroyed them. Hekat did not do that, Vortka did not touch them.

I destroyed them, I am the god's hammer.

He turned away from the sight of that island Ethrea, he turned for the empress but she was not there. Vortka was there, he was not laughing. He was not pleased to see Ethrea, nest of demons. In the pale light of newsun his silver godbraids were silent, his godbells were not singing.

He is an old, sinning man. The god cannot see him. The god sees me, Dmitrak warlord, its hammer.

"The empress is sleeping," said Vortka, his voice low. "You should not wake her."

He looked past the high godspeaker to the shelter on the warship's deck, where his mother the empress lay on a pallet, where warriors of his warship stood proud guard around her.

"Why is she sleeping? She is strong in the god's eye,

she is the god's chosen. She wants to see Ethrea. Let her wake, let her rejoice!"

Vortka shook his head, his silver godbells muttered sourly. "I am Vortka high godspeaker. Hekat is asleep."

Dmitrak stared at him. "You have made her sleep. With your healing crystal, you have—"

"*Hold your tongue*," said Vortka. "She is the empress, she is not young, she needs her rest."

He stared into Vortka's eyes. Aieee, god, there were secrets, there were things he was not told. "You do not wish to be here, Vortka. You did not want the god in the world. You tried to stop us sailing from Jatharuj. *Are you a demon? Do you fight the god?*"

He felt the god's power burning his blood. He felt the power surge through him and into his gauntlet. The red crystals caught fire, the gold wire flared in the sun.

I could burn him, I could burn him, I could see Vortka die.

The warriors on the warship's deck were watching, they saw their warlord's rage. Vortka's godspeakers were watching, the god was in them. They would smite him if Vortka was struck down.

"*Dmitrak!*" said the empress. "What is this? Are you mad?"

The power died in his gauntlet, he was a small child again, the empress was scolding. Her tongue was a snakeblade, she could draw blood.

He stepped back. "Empress."

Hekat came forth from her shelter, she walked slowly but with pride. Her linen tunic was old, it was patched, it was blemished with salt stains. She did not

care. She never did. There were bloodstains on her
tunic, they had not all washed out. The blood was
from his warriors that she gave to the god. Her face
was thin, she looked tired, but her eyes burned for the
god.

Vortka turned to her. "I left you sleeping," he said,
his voice soft. "You are the empress, you still need
your rest."

"Tcha," said Hekat. "I was sleeping, I awoke. I
heard the god laughing, I smelled demons in the
wind."

Dmitrak pointed. "You smelled Ethrea. Look."

Hekat walked to the bow and stared across the
water. Ethrea squatted on the ocean, it was green and
wide and almost close enough to kill.

"The god sees me," Hekat whispered. "The god
sees me in its eye. The god sees Mijak, it sees Mijak
in the world. We are the god's warriors, we are the
scourge of demons, we will give the god Ethrea.
Ethrea will fall."

On the deck of the warship, the warriors began to
chant. "*Chalava! Chalava! Chalava zho!*"

Hekat turned to them, she was smiling. Her
scarred face was full of joy. "Not yet. Your voices
carry, your voices are loud for the god. We do not
wish to wake the demons of Ethrea. When the time
comes to wake them you will know. I will tell you."

"*Empress!*" said the warriors, and punched their
fists to their chests. Dmitrak saw the love in their
faces, he saw his warriors loving her, he had to look
away.

I am the warlord. The warhost is mine. They

*should love me before her, is she the warlord? She is
not.*

And then the warrior tasked to cling to the warship's mast above its scorpion sail, and there keep
watch for demons, cried out. A moment later he was
echoed by watchers from the other ships of the
warhost.

"A demon! A demon!"

Dmitrak called up to his warrior. "Grano! What
did you see?"

Grano climbed down the mast like a spider. "A
ship, warlord. It was there, and then it vanished, like
those other demon ships who tried to kill us on the
ocean."

"Tcha," said Hekat, scornful. "They think to
warn their demon brother. Let them fly. Let them tell
that demons' nest of Ethrea Hekat's warhost is coming. Will it make a difference? I think it will not."

"Hekat," said Vortka. He did not sound pleased
that she was awake, there was something in his eyes
that said he was not pleased. "We must sail to Ethrea,
we are not there yet. Rest. You are weary."

"Tcha," she said, "how can I be weary? I am
strong in the god, Vortka. The god sees me in its eye.
You should make sacrifice. You should give the god
its animal blood on this warship, the blood it drinks
at lowsun will be the blood of Ethrea." She laughed,
she made her godbells sing. "I will make Ethrea a
godhouse and give it to the god. I will make Ethrea a
godpool, I will swim in its blood."

Dmitrak stared at her, his own blood burning. She
did not look at him, she did not speak to him, she did
not laugh with him. She did not say *Dmitrak and I.*

He was a horse to her, he was a snakeblade. He was a thing to use, she did not see him.

You will not do this without me, why do you forget?

Vortka and his godspeakers sacrificed for the god. Dmitrak watched the doves' blood flow and saw his warriors dying, he saw Hekat with her snakeblade give their sweet blood to the god. When they died he had wept for them. When their bodies burned on the warship she abandoned for their pyre, burned with their slain horses, burned because his gauntlet had fired them, aieee, the god see him, he had wept. Hekat had struck him. "*They served the god*," she said. "*How dare you weep?*"

He dared weep because he loved them, he dared weep because he knew their names, they were warriors he had handpicked, they were the warlord of Mijak's shell.

On this warship she had taken as her own he had a new shell, he had new hand-picked warriors, but it was not the same. Those warriors she killed had been his first-chosen brothers. He knew their names, he knew their hearts, he knew their bones and their blood.

Every brother the god gives me is taken away. Why does the god do that? How have I sinned?

The godspeakers on every warship in the warhost performed their newsun sacrifice. Everywhere he looked he saw the bright flashes as the flesh of the sacred birds was consumed by the god. Ninety-four warships had been lost to the demons, but still it would swallow the world.

It will swallow Ethrea next. I will see it swallow

Ethrea. I am the god's hammer. What is Hekat? An old woman. What is Vortka? An old man.

When sacrifice was over, Vortka left his god-speakers to stand with Hekat and Dmitrak looked around him at his mighty warhost. Every warship's sail had a big belly, the blustering trade winds made them fat. His warships ploughed the waves, they sailed swiftly towards Ethrea. The god wanted them on that island. It wanted Ethrean blood.

Do I need Vortka to tell me? Do I need Hekat to say it is so? I think I do not. I think I am the god's hammer, I know the god's want.

He looked at Hekat, standing in the bow with Vortka. The wind blew her godbraids, her godbells sang for the god. Her godbells sang a warning, she would be angry at his words.

Let her be angry. I am the warlord, I have a tongue, I will speak.

Tucked inside his horsehide jerkin was a rolled piece of cured sheepskin. On it was inked a map of Ethrea, taken from one of those ships that had sailed to Jatharuj and never sailed away. Captured sailors had shown him how to read it. So many times he had looked at the map, so long had he thought of ways to kill the demon island of Ethrea. When they were in Jatharuj he tried to talk of it with Hekat. She sent him away, she said it was not time. Since they sailed from Jatharuj he tried to talk of strategy to Hekat, they were sailing to Ethrea and still she would not listen.

Ethrea is close, we can see it, almost touch it. Hekat the empress must listen to me now.

He pulled the map from his jerkin and joined Hekat and Vortka watching Ethrea, the nest of demons, looming larger and larger as the trade winds bellied their sail.

"Empress," he said, "we must talk of Ethrea. We must talk of—"

"Tcha," she said, she did not turn to look at him. "I have been a warrior since before you were born, Dmitrak. Do I need you to tell me how to lead my warhost? I think I do not. I think Hekat the god's knife-dancer knows what to do with her warhost."

My warhost. My warhost. The words raged on his tongue, he did not speak them aloud.

She held out her hand. "Give me that map."

He gave it to her and watched as she unrolled it on the warship's railing. She would not even let him unroll a map. He swallowed his anger, there was no use in shouting. She would not hear him. She heard only the god.

"Here," said Hekat, her finger stabbing the inked sheepksin. She had also studied what it said. "This is Ethrea, yes?" Her finger stabbed again, quickly, around the edges of the island. "In this place *Hartshorn*, and this place *Morvell*, there were harbours, like Jatharuj. You see? Now there is a stone wall, what is stone to the god? Stone is nothing. Stone is like firewood, these are walls made of straw. You are the god's hammer, Dmitrak, you will smash that stone to pieces, you will break that stone wall down. When you have done that, half of my warhost will leap their horses from their warships. They will ride into the belly of Ethrea and eat it from the inside out." She looked at Vortka, she was smiling. "Does the god's high godspeaker see my warriors, leaping? Does it see them devour this Ethrea from within?"

Vortka stared at the map, his face was calm, his eyes were frightened, why did Hekat not see that? Why did Hekat believe Vortka was pleased to be here?

I do not believe it, I am not blind.

"I see them, Empress," said Vortka. "I see them."

"Dmitrak," said Hekat, and dug his ribs with her elbow. "Look here." Her finger stabbed at the map again, she was still smiling. "This is *Kingseat*, it is a city and Ethrea's harbour. This city *Kingseat* is Ethrea's mouth. I will sail down its throat with the rest of my warhost. You will destroy this city. The god's hammer will destroy it. As my warriors kill the people you will kill *every* city in this demon island of Ethrea. That is your purpose. That is my plan. Did I need you to help me? *Tcha.* I think I did not."

Dmitrak looked at the inked map of Ethrea. Her words were his thoughts. In Jatharuj he had thought of this plan. As they sailed with the warhost he knew it was right. He wanted to make his hands into fists, he wanted to shout at her: "*This was my plan.*"

"Dmitrak."

He looked up, she was staring, a challenge in her eyes. She was not smiling, she was ready to smite. "You say nothing, warlord. Is Hekat mistaken? Is the god's chosen knife-dancer wrong in her plan?"

He shook his head, his godbells sounded mournful. "No, Empress. This is a sound plan. This will kill Ethrea."

"Yes, it is sound," she said, as though he was stupid. As though he could never think of this plan himself. Then she looked at Vortka. "High godspeaker? I am not deaf, I hear the words you keep in your mouth. Speak them. I am listening."

She always listened to Vortka. When he denied the god, when he challenged her decisions, when he shouted and argued and told her she was wrong, Hekat listened to Vortka.

I do not understand.

Vortka's godbraids shone silver in the light from the climbing sun. Their godbells sang softly, as though he was afraid. He should be afraid. The empress was the empress. She was a thing to fear.

"You can kill Ethrea," he said, his voice was quiet. "You can kill every island in the world, every city, every nation breathing will die, if you desire. I have been thinking, I think you should think again."

"Think again?" said Hekat. "Why? You have said you see my warriors, you see them for the god."

"Think about Ethrea," said Vortka, "and if it should die. Think what we have learned of this place, from the slaved sailors who know the world unknown to us."

"I know what we have learned, Vortka," said Hekat. "It will hold us and feed us and keep us as we sail to the rest of the world and give it to the god. That is its purpose, that is why we have sailed here."

Vortka nodded. "Yes, it will, Hekat. No demon can prevent it. But remember Et-Raklion. There was the god, there were warriors, there were godspeakers, there were also slaves. If you kill Ethrea's people, there will be no slaves. You should not kill this island, you should tame it for the god. Give the god its people so they may worship and be its strength."

Hekat shook her head. "Their blood is its strength, Vortka. They will worship as they die."

"Hekat . . ." Vortka dared to touch her. "Will you kill the whole world? That is not the god's want. It wants the world living. It wants the world in its eye."

She stepped back from him, her godbells sang a warning. "Do you know what the god wants, Vortka? When we were in Et-Raklion you said it wants the world. When we were in Jatharuj you said it does not. You said the god did not want the strong blood of humans, I gave it that blood and many demons died. The trade winds returned and now there is Ethrea, waiting to die."

Dmitrak watched Vortka stand straight, he was old but he was still tall, he was not stooped with his years. "Hekat," he said, "I am the high godspeaker, how can you ask if I know the god's want?"

Hekat touched his old and wrinkled cheek. Dmitrak watched her, the touch was gentle but her eyes were hard.

"All your life you have served the god," she said softly. "You will serve it now by serving me. You are right, Vortka, Ethrea will be my new Et-Raklion. The world will be Mijak. How can it be Mijak if one demon still lives? The blood of Ethrea will destroy every demon. They will not stand against so much human blood, they will all die, and the god will have the world."

He did not love her, he hated her, but Dmitrak smiled. "The god sees you, Empress. It sees you in its eye. This is how we will give it the world."

She said nothing, she did not look at him. She looked only at the high godspeaker, an old man blind in the god's seeing eye. "Vorkta, remember Raklion," she whispered. "Remember him on the scorpion wheel. Remember Hekat in the god's eye beside him, where Nagarak could not see her. Remember Hekat among the scorpions, remember Hekat dancing with Bajadek, with Hanochek, remember Abajai and Yagji. Vortka, remember Hekat. Remember all she has done."

Vortka was weeping. Tears fell from his eyes. "I remember everything," he whispered. "How can I forget? Do you forget Vortka and how he has served the god?"

Hekat stared at Vortka. Weeping Vortka stared in return. They were silent, they said no more to each other, yet Dmitrak thought they were shouting bitter words. Bitter shouting was in their eyes, in their faces, the salt air was crowded with the words they did not say.

She turned. "Fetch me paper and ink, warlord. I have messages for my warhost."

Dmitrak nodded. *My warhost. My warhost.* "Yes, Empress," he said, and did as he was told.

As the warhost sailed for the god towards Ethrea, Hekat wrote her messages for the warhost. The messages were sent from warship to warship, so every warrior knew what soon would come.

Another demon boat was spied by their lookouts. This one did not vanish, it tried to sail away. It could not sail fast enough to escape the warhost. Dmitrak sank it, his warhost chanted as it burned.

The godspeakers of Mijak went below the warships' decks to the horses, they used their healing crystals to stir the horses from their slumber, they used their healing crystals to wake the god in their blood. The warriors who were tasked to the rowing of the warships took hold of their oars, the trade winds blew, those warriors rowed hard, and the warhost flew the waves.

Ethrea came closer . . . and closer . . .

Rhian sat on the grass by the old castle tiltyard, methodically sharpening her knife, Ranald's knife. She'd already danced her *hotas* privately, with Zandakar. Now she waited alone, which suited her, for the day's first skein of soldiers to arrive so she could train with them. Sharpen them. Prepare them for battle.

It was four weeks and three days since the armada's return.

Autumn had sunk itself deep in Ethrea's bones. It was a cool morning, softly misted. The day promised fair. She could hear the bustle of the castle stables, behind the high brick wall at her back. Smell the hot mash cooking for the horses. There came a shout. A snatch of laughter.

We can still laugh, then. Surely all's not lost if Ethrea can still laugh.

Every day she received messages from Edward and Rudi to the north, from Adric and Ludo as they patrolled beyond duchy Kingseat's home districts, from Helfred's tireless clergy as they toiled in their parishes. Her people were ready. As ready as they could be.

Four weeks and three days. Ethrea was holding its breath. She held her breath with it. What else could she do?

I can dance my hotas. I can sharpen my blade. I can pray that somehow, this nightmare is spared us.

When Han stepped out of the air beside her she was so startled she fumbled her whetstone, nearly slicing off her fingers with her blade's newly keen edge.

"Han," she said, sounding stupid. Feeling stupid. She'd abandoned hope of ever seeing him again.

Like the last time they'd met, he was wearing black silk. Four weeks later he still looked exhausted. His eyes were still angry. And yet . . . and yet . . .

"Mijak is sighted."

Slowly, disbelieving, she unfolded to her feet. Her fingers slid the knife home in its sheath on her hip. "It can't be. I've not been given word, and I have boats patrolling—"

Han raised an eyebrow. "Is Ethrea the only nation with boats?"

"You mean *you've* been—" She took a deep breath, let it out in a rush. "And you're certain it's Mijak? There's no chance Harbisland or Arbenia or one of the other trading nations have miraculously changed their minds and—"

"No," said Han. "Trust me on this, Rhian. Once seen, the warships of Mijak can't be mistaken for a Keldravian galley or a trireme from Barbruish."

"No," she whispered. "I don't suppose they can."

"My witch-men have told me they are sailing not for Kingseat, but towards the coastline of Hartshorn."

"Hartshorn?" she said, staring across the tiltyard. That first skein of soldiers would be here soon. "So Zandakar was right. He said Mijak would send some of its warriors into Ethrea to harry the duchies while it sailed on to attack Kingseat harbour directly."

"*Zandakar*," said Han, tightly. "Rhian—"

"I couldn't do it," she said, and looked at him. "Han, I couldn't give him to you. Not just because I needed him for Ethrea, but because—"

"I would've hurt him," said Han. "I'd have killed him, for my slain witch-men."

"Yes."

"And that would be wrong."

"Very wrong. Yes."

Han sighed. "So Sun-dao told me, blown by the wind to reprove me for my anger."

"*Sun-dao* . . ." Well, why not? First Hettie, then Marlan. Why not the emperor's dead brother? "I suppose I'd look foolish if I asked how he is."

"Foolish?" said Han. He was almost smiling. "Perhaps. But kind, also."

"Kind?" Rhian looked down at herself, at the battered huntsman's leathers that had become her second skin. At the knife-hilt calluses that roughened her fingers and palm. "Han, I don't remember the last time I felt kind." She looked up again. "Your presence. Your warning. Does this mean Tzhung-tzhungchai has forgiven me? Do Han and his witch-men pledge their help to Ethrea, again?"

He placed his hands palm to palm and offered her a formal bow. "Your Majesty, we do."

She lost sight of him for a moment, in a blurring of tears. "Thank you," she said, her voice husky. "And . . . thank you for returning my horse, by the way."

Surprise and amusement flashed vivid across his

face. "Rhian, little girl-queen . . . Tzhung's emperor has missed you."

She touched his silk-clad arm with her fingertips. "And Ethrea's queen has missed you, Han."

Then they both turned at the sound of her soldiers, approaching. Their private moment was over . . .

It was time to go to war.

Dmitrak stood in his warship's bow with Hekat, he stood beside the empress his mother and fed his eyes on Ethrea as the warhost prowled the walled edge of Ethrea, of *Hartshorn*, past fields and woodlands and snarling rocky places. They sailed close enough to the edge of Ethrea to see the faces of the men standing on their little stone wall, that could not protect them though they thought it would. They were dead men, standing, they were dead men shouting and waving their fists in defiance. They shot little arrows that plunged into the sea. They were dead men whose blood would please the god when it spilled.

"Dmitrak," said Hekat. That was all she had to say.

He turned to his warriors, he raised his gold-and-crystal fist in the air. His warriors saluted, they drummed the deck with their feet. Laughing, he summoned the god to his gauntlet and killed those defiant shouting men on their wall. His warriors shouted as the Ethreans died.

"*Chalava! Chalava! Chalava zho!*"

Every warrior in the warhost took up the chant. Their voices sounded like thunder, they pounded the air. The air shivered with their voices, it shuddered with their might.

"Chalava! Chalava! Chalava zho!"

Dmitrak smashed and smashed the stone wall with his fist. He was drunk on the god's power, it fed him like wine. It poured from his blood in a river unstoppable, he felt as though he could burn the whole world.

Hekat smiled when he killed those defiant Ethrean men. She smiled as he smashed the stone wall to sand. She laughed when he killed three black-clad demons who tried to smother him with the wind.

Aieee, the god see him. She smiled. She laughed.

When at last the warhost came to the first stopped harbour, he smashed the stone wall that was keeping them out. Twenty at a time, two hundred chosen warships sailed close to the sloping pebbled beach. The defiant Ethreans there had no hope of stopping them, they ran from the god's hammer, they died as they ran.

Mijak's warriors on their horses leapt from the warships into the water, the god's power was in them and they swam to the shore. More Ethreans ran towards them with arrows and swords. Dmitrak did not wait to see those Ethreans die. He did not need to see it. They were already dead.

With Hekat the empress he sailed on in his warship, leading the warhost to the next landing place. His warriors were chanting as Ethrea died.

Vortka high godspeaker stood alone beside the godpost mast. He did not say a word, watching Ethrea die.

Five times more, as they sailed so swiftly for Kingseat harbour, Dmitrak smashed their way into a long-abandoned port. Five times more, the warhost on its horses laid claim to Ethrean soil and watered it with Ethrean blood.

Hekat smiled, and smiled, and smiled.

They sailed around the walled edge of Ethrea. He smashed and smashed and smashed that stone wall, like Zandakar in the godless lands, he smashed it all to pieces.

Zandakar? Who is Zandakar? Did he live? I do not think so.

A week earlier, Alasdair and the master of Kingseat's harbour had overseen the blockading of its wide, inviting mouth and every inch of water between the ocean and the docks.

Working by daylight and through the torchlit nights, soldiers and townsfolk laboured to build as many makeshift boats and barges as could be contrived. Whatever was made of timber, and would float, they used. Word went out from Ethrea's pulpits: the help of Ethrea's people was needed. Tables, doors, even the sides of barns, came down the Eth in every river-barge that could be spared, that would also be used to keep Mijak at bay.

When their duty as workhorses was done, they were chained bow-to-stern, four deep, to form a wide, wooden gate across the harbour's mouth. And crammed in behind them were those other, makeshift barges, the kingdom's fishing fleet, its rowboats, its skiffs and its skillies.

When the task was done, one fool scallywag ran across the harbour from side to side and never once got his feet wet.

Rhian, touring the township, changed from huntsman's leathers into her now-familiar black doublet and leggings, encased in the breastplate so lovingly crafted by Armourer Sandiman, left her personal skein of soldiers to its own devices and made her solitary way through the harbour's Royal Gate to stand on the docks. Ranald's dagger was belted at her hip and her shortsword – the one she'd used to kill Damwin and Kyrin – dangled at her side. Staring at the choked harbour, she felt her heart pounding within her metal breast.

It's not enough. How can that hold back Mijak? How can it stand against Dmitrak's gauntlet?

But it was all they could do. They'd done their best. How could she ask her people for more?

The light was fading. Dusk would be upon them soon. Torches and lamps were being lit in the streets behind her. The township was busy like an angry hive of bees. With Mijak approaching, their careful plans were come to life.

Rhian closed her eyes in brief prayer.

God, *turn my peace-loving Ethreans into a rogue swarm. Let them sting and sting Mijak until it drops dead.*

Brisk footsteps sounded, and she turned.

"Alasdair."

He nodded as he joined her, his expression strained. "Rhian."

The last four weeks had seen deep grooves carved into his face. If her hands were rough and callused from her knife and sword-hilts, so were his. If she'd become a warrior queen, he was made a warrior king. She scarcely saw him any more. He slept as many nights in Kingseat's garrison, with his soldiers, as he did with her in their castle bed. Time had blunted his sharp anger over the slaughtered armada. Still, his anger remained, no less painful because it was blunted. A bludgeoned wound could hurt as keenly as a swordcut.

They weren't . . . fighting. They just weren't happy. He'd retreated somewhere, and she couldn't find him.

Beyond discussions of tactics and training, Zandakar was never mentioned.

She glanced at her much-absent husband. "You bring me fresh news from Tzhung-tzhungchai?"

In the nearly ten hours that had passed since Han came to her at the tiltyard, his witch-men had twice sent their emperor word from her duchies, and he had straight away sent it to her. Warriors of Mijak were rampaging through the middle of her kingdom. Some had been killed, but not nearly enough. Edward and Rudi's soldiers were trying, but their lines had been broken in a dozen places and three times, at least, Mijak had crossed over the Eth. Its warriors had killed and burned in Hartshorn, in Morvell and in Meercheq. They hadn't yet broken through to Arbat . . . but surely it was a question of when, and not if.

Han had told her: *The warriors of Mijak are like locusts. Do you know of locusts, Rhian? Marauding flying insects, their appetites are insatiable. They descend in swarms upon Tzhung's farmland and leave nothing living in their wake.*

Mijak was a plague of human locusts, come to plague Ethrea.

"Yes, Han's sent fresh news," said Alasdair. "Mijak's warships are making steady progress around the coastline. The witch-men have slowed them, but . . ." He shrugged. "Whether it's because they're so weakened, now, or the priests of Mijak are grown more powerful, they can't be stopped. They should reach the harbour at first light."

"Which means a dawn attack," she said. "How . . . dramatic . . . of them."

He nodded. "You look tired."

"No more tired than you. Is there any further word from the duchies?"

"Only that the fighting continues. Ludo and the others are still safe."

Thank God, thank God. "We've no idea how many are killed? Or how long before Mijak's warriors will break through into duchy Kingseat?"

"No, and no." Alasdair's hand came to rest on her shoulder. "But Helfred says we're welcome in the great chapel, for Litany. Half an hour."

Rhian folded her arms, struggling for composure. "I can't help feeling I shouldn't be safe here, in Kingseat, while my people are fighting and dying to the north."

"Don't distress yourself," said Alasdair. "Come the morning, Kingseat will be no safer than anywhere else. So. Do we attend Litany, Your Majesty?"

For the briefest moment, she rested her head on his shoulder. "Your Majesty, I think we must."

It was a solemn service. The townsfolk crowding the great chapel and the streets outside were resolute, but afraid. They echoed her own mood, and Alasdair's as he sat beside her before Helfred's pulpit.

Helfred's sermon made her weep.

"Though yet we may perish . . . though as we pray here tonight our brothers and sisters in Ethrea give

their lives for this kingdom . . . we are a blessed peo-
ple, for Rhian is our queen. God bless her. God keep
her. May God keep us all.'"

Dear Helfred.

She stayed some time in the great chapel, afterwards, rallying her people. Showing them a brave
face.

She wondered how many of them realised it was a
lie.

The murky half-light before dawn saw her back at
the harbour, with Alasdair and Han, Zandakar and
Dexterity. With Helfred, and Idson, and several thousand soldiers.

She and Zandakar had not danced their private
hotas. The next *hotas* they danced would be with the
warriors of Mijak.

Idson and his soldiers lined the harbour foreshore.
They'd spent most of yesterday and half the previous
night setting up their barrels of pitch, their stores of arrows, extra swords and knives and many piles of stout
wooden staves in every alley, doorway and cranny they
could find. There were soldiers and townsfolk on every
roof, at every window, in every tree that could be
climbed. Various traps were set. Preparations were
complete.

All they had to do now was wait.

Rhian looked over at Han, who stood a small distance apart with his eyes closed. Doubtless he was
communing with his witch-men, in their twilight. A
twilight he'd told her was yet far from healed. She
didn't want to imagine how lost they'd be without

him. Weakened witch-men were better than none at all.

Alasdair, so self-contained, was engaged in quiet conversation with Helfred. Glancing at Zandakar, she tapped him with a finger and beckoned him a few paces to the side.

"Rhian?" he said.

He was neatly dressed in a linen shirt and leather leggings. His blue hair was tightly bound in a sailor's queue. The scorpion knife, his only weapon, was sheathed at his hip.

She nodded at it. "You're certain your blade won't fail you?"

"My blade will not fail me," he said quietly. "I will not fail you."

She stared at him, unable to speak. Too many thoughts, too many emotions, not enough time.

"Thank you," she said simply. What else could she say?

His eyes so pale, his remarkable face grave, he pressed his fist to his breast. "You are welcome, Rhian *hushla*."

"Listen," said Alasdair abruptly, turning away from Helfred to stare across the boat and barge-choked harbour. The sky was turning pink, and there was light enough now to see by. "Listen, do you hear that?"

Across the water . . . through the cool morning air . . . an ominous chanting, growing louder.

"Chalava! Chalava! Chalava zho!"

Mijak's invasion of Kingseat had begun.

CHAPTER THIRTY-FOUR

A hunting horn sounded long and loud: Commander Idson was rallying his soldiers, rallying the people of Kingseat township to war. The call echoed through the streets, was returned, and returned, as captains and sergeants and tavern-keepers and seamstresses sounded their own horns in courageous reply.

And again that chilling chant drifted over the water, thousands of voices, united and cold.

"*Chalava! Chalava! Chalava zho!*"

"Look!" cried Helfred. "God have mercy!"

The warships of Mijak had reached the blockaded harbour. Rhian stared, and felt her heart falter.

Sail upon sail upon sail upon sail . . . the horizon was blotted out. The ocean had disappeared beneath a carpet of black and red hulls.

"Sweet Rollin," she whispered, and turned. "*Alasdair.*"

He came to stand with her, and rest his hand on her shoulder. "I know," he said, his fingers tightening. "Even if the armada had managed to sink half their fleet I doubt . . ."

"Did I not tell you, Rhian?" said Han. "Myriad, like locusts."

Without warning, a bolt of crimson fire leapt from the leading warship. It struck the centre of the chained barges blocking the harbour's entrance, blowing them apart in splinters and flame. A second bolt hit, and a third, and a fourth.

"*Chalava-hagra*," said Zandakar, grimly. "Dmitrak. My brother."

Rhian tore her gaze from the burning blockade, and stared in horror at the knife sheathed on his hip.

He'll never stop them with that. We'll never stop them. Ethrea is done . . .

She looked again at Mijak's warships. Those bolts of crimson were coming faster and faster, and it seemed the harbour itself was on fire. Their pitiful blockade was burning to the waterline, smoke billowing, sparks surging towards the rising sun. Fire spread through the crowded boats and makeshift barges like an incoming tide. From across the water the sound of chanting, and the greedy roar of flame.

She'd felt helpless before, but never like this. Standing on the harbour docks, watching the timber blockade burn, watching Zandakar's brother clear his path to her capital, with no way of stopping him. No hope of destroying him.

Han's right. They're locusts . . . and we're a field of waiting wheat.

"Han," she said, "your witch-men—" But Tzhung's emperor couldn't hear her.

"Oh dear," said Dexterity. "Is he sick? Should I fetch Ursa, perhaps—"

"He's not sick," said Alasdair. "He's witching."

Even as they stared at him, Han stirred from his trance, his face masked with pain. Leaving Alasdair and Zandakar, Rhian moved to his side and touched him, gently.

"Does the twilight still scream?"

"Yes." He shuddered. "Mijak clouds all." He staggered a little, as though blown by a strong wind only he could feel, then steadied and looked at her. Such pity in his eyes. "Your duchies are laid waste, Rhian. Your people fight bravely, but the warriors of Mijak . . ."

Sickened, she looked at Zandakar. *My people . . . my people . . .*

He met her gaze. "*Yatzhay.*"

"What of the dukes?" Alasdair demanded. "Edward? Rudi?" He swallowed. "My cousin?"

Han shook his head. "I can't tell you the fate of one—"

"*Chalava! Chalava! Chalava zho!*"

Dmitrak's warship was entering Kingseat harbour. Alasdair turned. "Rhian, go. There's still time."

"Run and hide?" she said, staring. "*No!*"

"*Rhian!*" He was distraught. "You *promised* me you'd—"

"I know. But Alasdair, where in God's name can anyone hide from *this*? If you want to run to the castle, then run. *I* am staying here, to fight with my people!"

"You mean *die* with your people!" He rounded on Dexterity. "We need a miracle, toymaker. Give us a miracle!"

"Majesty, I – I can't do that," Dexterity stammered. "I don't know how it works, I don't—"

"Han," said Alasdair, turning away. "You can witch Rhian away from here. Take her to Tzhungtzhungchai. *Please.* Save her life."

"Alasdair, *stop* it!" Rhian said before Han could

reply. Almost, she slapped him. "Are you mad? How can you of all people ask me to leave?"

Alasdair's eyes were brilliant with tears. "How can I not? You're my wife, Rhian."

"I'm Ethrea's queen first!"

His head snapped back as though she'd struck him. Then he turned to Zandakar. "You tell her. She'll listen to you."

But Zandakar was staring as though Alasdair were a stranger. "Rhian *hushla* cannot leave. She is a warrior, *zho*?"

"You want her dead?" Alasdair demanded. "You want your brother to kill her? All she's ever done is defend you, Zandakar, and *this* is how you're going to repay her? Or maybe this is what you *always* had planned. A gift for your mother, the Empress of Mijak! Give Rhian to her and all will be forgiven, is that it?"

"Alasdair!" Rhian tried to touch him, but he knocked her hand aside. "Please. There's no *time*. We have to join Idson and the soldiers. We're going to be fighting in a handful of—"

A swirling breeze, tainted with smoke. A whisper of windchimes. And dozens of witch-men stepped out of the air.

She spun round, disbelieving. *"Han?"*

His smile was a travesty of the cool, self-contained calm she'd come to expect. "Sun-dao says Tzhung-tzhungchai must help. A wise man always listens to his brother."

She stared at him, and he stared back.

"These are all the witch-men I have to give," he added. "I have none left to defend your duchies."

She nodded, drowned in sorrow. "It's all right. Han, thank you. You've been a better friend than I could hope for."

"Little queen," he said. His eyes were warm.

"*Chalava! Chalava! Chalava zho!*"

The incoming tide of fire was almost upon them. The smoke was thickening, choking, burning everyone's throat and eyes. Only minutes remained, surely, before the last of their desperate blockade was destroyed and the warships of Mijak reached the harbour piers.

Crimson bolts searing, the promise of death.

Han's witch-men were spreading along the harbour front. Turning, Rhian glimpsed more witch-men on Kingseat's streets and scattered rooftops. One by one they spread their arms wide, tilting their faces to the morning sky. A wind started rising, it whipped their unbound hair, whipped clouds out of thin air, whipped the debris-choked waters of the harbour to life.

"Helfred, return to the great chapel," she told her prolate. "We need your prayers as never before, and you'll at least be a little protected there."

"I don't want to leave you," said Helfred white-faced with fright. "You've always been in my care, Rhian."

Oh, *Helfred.* "I'm in God's care now. Help my people, prolate. Dexterity—"

"I promised Ursa I'd help her tend any wounded," Dexterity said unsteadily. "Majesty – Rhian—"

"*Chalava! Chalava! Chalava zho!*"

The chanting was so loud she could feel it in her bones. The warships of Mijak were pouring into the harbour behind the ship carrying Dmitrak and his gauntlet. Even through the gusting smoke and dancing fire she could see them, each full-bellied sail painted with a black scorpion. She could hear the steady thud and splash of their oars.

Her eyes stung, her vision blurred, as she looked at Dexterity. In a moment he'd leave her . . . and they might never meet again.

"God keep you, my dear friend," she whispered, holding him tight.

Dexterity's embrace threatened to crack her ribs. "You're a good girl, Rhian. You always were. God bless."

"Rhian," said Zandakar. The scorpion knife was in his hand now, blue fire flickering up and down its thin blade. His eyes were fierce. "We go now, *zho?*"

Like his witch-men, Han was summoning the wind. It was too late to wish him luck, too late to—

A searing bolt of crimson soared high above her head. Rhian spun on her heels, watched it fly over Kingseat's huddled buildings and strike her castle's wall. Flame and stone gouted into the air.

"God's mercy!" cried Helfred.

Too late to do anything but take Alasdair's hand, and run.

Dmitrak laughed as he sailed into the harbour, sailed through the smoke and Ethrea's pitiful, shattered defences, sucking pleasure from the moment like it was a bitch's tit. He could have obliterated in heartbeats the choke of wooden boats meant to stop him, but aieee, the god see him, it was better done slowly.

The demons of Kingseat deserved to fear.

As he laughed, his godbells sang. The god was pleased with him, he had pleased the god. Its power surged in his blood, thicker and hotter than ever he had felt it, his bones were burning for the god. He stood in his warship's bow and poured the god through his hammer, watched the blood-red flame destroy everything it touched, watched the flimsy defence of wooden boats burn and sink in his path.

The warriors of his warhost – *his* warhost, *his* warhost – were chanting to shake the sun from the sky.

"Chalava! Chalava! Chalava zho!"

This township of Kingseat was as large as any he had thrown down before, larger than any dead Zandakar had destroyed when he was in the god's eye.

I serve the god now. Dmitrak warlord, hammer of the god.

Then Hekat behind him screamed in rage. "Demons! Demons! Dmitrak, there are demons!"

He turned on her, his gauntlet pulsing, the power in it barely contained. "You *will not kill* any more of my warriors! I will kill these demons, I am the god's hammer!"

Never in his life had he spoken to Hekat like that. Never in his life had she looked at *him* with fear. He could see the fear in her, he could see she was afraid.

"The warlord is right, Empress," said Vortka. "Heed his words. Dead warriors cannot ride into this Kingseat, dead warriors cannot dance with their snakeblades for the god."

Hekat was so afraid, she did not strike Vortka for speaking.

Dmitrak laughed again, his godbells were laughing. Hekat was silenced. He had silenced Mijak's empress.

Turning his back on her, he stared at Kingseat township, at the buildings crowded around the harbour, at the streets sloping up towards the craggy outcropping behind it, at the looming palace with its glittering windows and high walls. There were people on those walls, there were people in the streets. He could see the flash of sunshine on metal. Aieee, tcha, they were stupid. These breathing dead people of Ethrea thought their metal skins could save them.

A sharp wind rose in the harbour, power danced over his skin. He had felt that power before, it was not his or the god's. There were demons in this place.

"Dmitrak!" shouted Hekat. "The demons are waking!"

I know that, I can feel that. Do I need you to tell me? I think I do not.

Below the decks of his warship he could hear the horses stamping, they were eager to fight. His warriors were eager, they felt the demons and chanted.

"Chalava! Chalava! Chalava zho!"

He turned again to Hekat, her eyes were blazing. "Empress, I will give you the blood of Kingseat. I will kill all of Kingseat's people and the demons will die."

"No!" shouted Vortka. "Mijak needs slaves!"

Stupid man, stupid godspeaker, old and worn out and blind in the god's eye.

Beneath his feet the warship lurched as its rowing warriors battled the rising wind and rising waves those demons woke against the god and the warhost.

It was time for those demons to die.

As the demons' wind howled, as black clouds boiled into the sky, as lightning stabbed them and the harbour whipped to white foam, as killing waterspouts writhed and lashed, Dmitrak summoned the god to its hammer, he poured the god from his blood into the world.

He smashed Kingseat's palace, and the people in it. There were demons in that palace, as they died he felt them scream.

"Chalava! Chalava! Chalava zho!"

Warship by warship his warhost filled the harbour. Warship by warship they plunged towards the docks.

The demons were desperate, they flung their power against him. He rode in his warship's bow and smashed them with his fist. His warship had almost reached the dock, he could see the demons around the harbour with their black hair and their black clothes whipping in the wind. He could see the bright metal skins of the Ethreans who served them, they milled in the streets like goats loosed from a pen. They would be dead soon. Their blood would serve the god.

He heard a great cry, a roaring of fury, he saw three of his warships plunge splintered beneath the harbour's waves. Then two more were ruined, huge stones flying through the air. They were flying from the palace, they had catapults, like the demon ships that had sailed against him.

He clung with one hand to the railing of his warship and aimed his gauntlet at that palace. He hammered it to rubble and the catapults, too. He hammered the people in the palace and on the streets.

And then he saw the waterspouts collapsing, he felt the wind falter, he saw the black-cloud sky clear. He looked at the harbour docks and saw demons dying, he felt them die as their power bled away. They died, they dropped, they could not stand against Mijak.

Before he could kill the demons who were not dead, they stepped into the air and disappeared from sight. He was angry, he did not let his anger blind him.

They cannot hide forever. I will find them, they will die.

With no howling wind to hide voices, he heard Vortka shouting at Hekat.

"You are the empress! You cannot ride to war!"

She shoved her fist against his chest. "Vortka, you are stupid! Hekat *always* rides to war!"

"When she was young, yes," said Vortka. "She is no longer young, the power that was in her from those ten thousand slaves, that power is gone. You are weary. You will die." Vortka was weeping, he was a soft weeping man. "I do not want you to die, Hekat. You must stay here with me and live."

Dmitrak watched Hekat. *Will she soften? I think she will not.*

"Vortka high godspeaker is right!" he said. "You are Hekat, you must give the god the world. Can you give it the world if you are dead in your blood? I think you cannot do that, I think you must stay here!"

She stepped forward and struck him, her hand struck his cheek. She was old, she was powerless, the blow still hurt. "I am Hekat of Mijak, I am empress for the god. Do you give me orders, Dmitrak? I think you do not. I will ride with my warhost, it is where I belong."

He felt his blood simmer, he felt the rage in his fist. *My warhost. My warhost. You belong on a pyre.* "Empress, there are slaves here, the god needs their blood. I will take those slaves prisoner and send them to you. If you are not here for sacrifice who will give the god their blood? Vortka? How can he do that when he does not believe?"

Hekat looked at Vortka, there was doubt in her eyes.

Yes, Empress, doubt him. Do not trust him, trust me. I am the warlord, this war is my war. I am the god's hammer. What are you? An old woman. Your time is come and gone, Hekat, this time is mine.

"Tcha!" said Hekat. "The god see me. *Tcha!*"

Dmitrak knelt before her, he knew how to make her feel strong. "You are Mijak's great empress, you are Hekat in the world. You are too precious for risking. Let the world come to you."

She bared her teeth, she bent low. She fisted her fingers in his scarlet godbraids. His godbells protested, he did not say a word.

"I will kill the slaves you send me, warlord," she whispered. "I will give the god its strongest blood. You will slaughter Kingseat and its outlying hamlets, I am the empress, I want this demons' nest dead."

I am the god's hammer. I will smash Kingseat flat. Then I will smash you, Hekat. Mijak has Dmitrak, does it also need an empress? Aieee, the god see me. I think it does not.

He pressed his fist to his chest, he did not show her his heart. "Hekat."

Kingseat harbour had grown fat with his warhost. With no demons to stop them, warship after warship reached Kingseat's docks. They lowered their ramps, their warriors rode from the ships' bellies, warriors on their horses crowded the docks. They shouted, they chanted, they were ready to kill.

Deserted by their demon masters, the people of Kingseat fired burning arrows and threw stones. Dmitrak laughed as his gauntlet destroyed them. Still laughing he leapt from his warship to the dock, he took his horse from the Ajilik shell-leader and vaulted onto its back. With the god's hammer raised high above his head, he sent its power streaming into the sky.

And then he led his warhost into the township, thousands of warriors to slay Kingseat for the god.

The first mad onslaught of Mijaki warriors into the township thrust Rhian into a nightmare beyond belief. With the witch-men of Tzhung-tzhungchai vanished, or vanquished, no sign of their emperor, no more help from the wind, the noble defence of Kingseat became a battle for survival, became desperate bloodshed and sheer brutal luck. Her army shattered into splinters, skeins and half-skeins, into wildeyed, bloodsoaked bands of soldiers and citizens, men and women, boys and girls. The fighting raged from street to street, roof to roof, door to door. It smashed into houses and out of them again, through bakeries and chandlers and grainstores and taverns, into attics and cellars, in sunlight and in shade.

There was only one gauntlet. The rest of it was knives.

She lost sight of Zandakar first, as the triple-skein of soldiers she led jointly with Alasdair was smashed and scattered by a wall of galloping warriors, chanting and shouting, their belled and braided black hair ringing echoes to the sky.

Not long after that she lost Alasdair as well.

She was dancing *hotas* with a girl who looked too young for bloodshed . . . but was old enough to die. As her shortsword sank into the girl's exposed belly, she caught sight of Ethrea's king running for his life down Dancer's Alley with three mounted warriors chanting in pursuit. But she couldn't help him, two more warriors leapt to kill her. She fought one, the soldiers with her fought the other. Both died, very messily.

By the time she could run after him, Alasdair was gone.

There was no time to look for him, dead or alive. She had a skein of surviving soldiers to pull together and lead. Man by man, as she encountered other swordsmen and archers, dazed and lost and too-often bleeding, Rhian gathered to herself a small, personal army. They followed her gratefully, their fierce, killing queen.

She danced her *hotas* and Mijak's warriors died. Cleaning her knife swiftly, with casual expertise, she thought: *So much for staying safely out of harm's way.*

Her royal castle was in ruins. Mijak's warriors roamed her streets. She might be a widow; she didn't know, and not a soldier she collected could tell her if Alasdair lived, or had died. And the man she'd championed as Ethrea's greatest ally against Mijak had simply . . . disappeared. Just like Han and his witchmen, Zandakar was gone.

He was gone. She was alone. All she had were her
hotas . . . Ranald's dagger . . . a killing shortsword . . . and her furious, stubborn faith.

Kingseat township and its districts were home to
some one hundred thousand souls. Not one of them
had fled in the face of Mijak. All of them had stayed
to fight, for her and for their kingdom. Terrified,
mostly untrained, nothing in their history had readied
them for this. But they were so brave, her beautiful
people. From their windows and rooftops they
dropped rocks on the heads of the warriors below.
Dropped rocks, claypots of burning pitch, jars of
stinking urine, plates and mugs and footstools and
whatever they could find. Sprang the traps she and
her council had carefully devised; weakened walls set
to tumbling, glass windows loosened to fall in shards
on Mijaki heads, alleys blocked with sudden barri-
cades so Kingseat's soldiers could kill at will.

It wasn't enough.

Rhian knew, her heart weeping, that what happened here was happening all over her kingdom. In
Hartshorn and Arbat, in Meercheq and Morvell and
in the wider duchy of Kingseat where Ludo and Adric
struggled to keep the kingdom safe, the warriors of
Mijak plundered her people, and her gallant people
fought to their deaths.

And she knew one other thing, in her weeping
heart and in her bones.

If Ethrea must die . . . it would not die cheaply. She
and her people would make Mijak pay in blood.

Hour after hour, the fighting raged on. Kingseat
township echoed to the dreadful sounds of men and

women and children screaming, fallen horses screaming, the crash of stone and timber as Dmitrak's gauntlet lashed out. Blood slicked the cobblestones. Smoke filled the air. The slain and mortally wounded lay in piles, like driftwood.

And Mijak's warriors chanted, chanted as they killed.

"Chalava! Chalava! Chalava zho!"

In the Duchy of Hartshorn, so betrayed by its stubborn duke, Kyrin, the warriors of Mijak turned fallow fields to lakes of blood. In duchy Morvell, Edward's cherished domain, his son and his daughter watched him die, and died soon after. Rudi of Arbat, irascible and gruff, breathed his last in the arms of Damwin's son, Davin, who promised to tell Adric of his father's great love. But Adric, fighting for Kingseat, for the ducal crown he wore with too much pride, perished back-to-back with Ludo of Linfoi . . . whose last living words were of his cousin, the king. The great river Eth, lifeblood of Ethrea, turned scarlet with the lifeblood of the people it sustained. And the warriors of Mijak chanted as they rode: *"Chalava! Chalava! Chalava zho!"*

Dmitrak kept his promise only once he sent captured Ethreans to Hekat so she could slay them for the god. Vortka watched her slit their throats, he could not stop her, she would not listen. When she was finished killing she sheathed her snakeblade and prowled the harbour. She prowled it like a sandcat snatched from freedom, and caged.

She snarled at him if he tried to soothe her, so he

waited in silence for her to speak. They were alone now on the harbour's docks, he had commanded his godspeakers to pray on the warships. He wanted them safely out of the way.

"Tcha!" spat Hekat, glaring up at smoke-wreathed Kingseat township. "I can still hear screaming, why is this nest of demons not dead? Is Dmitrak the god's hammer? Can he kill Ethrea for the god?"

Vortka did not answer, his heart was heavy in his chest. Somewhere in Ethrea, perhaps even in Kingseat, his beloved Zandakar must be fighting for his life.

"I was wrong to listen to him," said Hekat. "I was wrong to listen to you. I am Empress of Mijak, I am godchosen and precious, I should have ridden with the warhost, let Dmitrak ride behind. How can this *Kingseat* not be fallen for the god? There are thousands in my warhost, thousands trained to kill!"

Vortka sighed. "Kingseat is a large city, Hekat, many thousands live here."

"It is not so much larger than Jatharuj, Vortka. Jatharuj fell between newsun and highsun! We are past highsun. Kingseat still stands and Dmitrak sends me no more slaves!"

"Kingseat has demons, Hekat," he said. "It has a warhost." *A warhost trained by Zandakar, I think. Any warhost he trains will not be easy to kill.* "Jatharuj had no warhost, it had merchants and traders. Hekat—"

She stamped away along the row of moored warships, she was so angry her godbells growled. "Tcha! I will not stay here, Vortka, I will not wait like a slave who must stand where it is told. There are Ethreans alive for me to kill, I will kill them. I will give Ethrea to the god."

Vortka stared after her, stabbed with fright. *No. No. She must not do that. If she goes into Kingseat she might find our son. If she goes into Kingseat, she might die.*

As Hekat stamped back again and pushed past him, he caught her by the hand. Before she could smite him, before she could call out, he pressed his palm to her face and prayed to the god.

She breathed out hard, her eyes rolled back. With her bones turned to water, she slumped into his arms. He carried her to a patch of shade, he let her rest against his breast.

I am sorry, Hekat, I am sorry, my love. You must be safe, I must save you.

Twisting his head round he looked up to the township, wreathed in smoke, soaked in blood, soaked in Dmitrak's rage.

Zandakar, my son, my son. Help me to end this, no more killing for the god.

Ursa's small clinic on Foxglove Way was crammed to collapsing with the wounded dragged in from Kingseat's killing streets. She and three other physicks struggled to help the wounded, but there were too many patients and not enough physicks. Not any more. One by one the other eight who'd been bringing back Kingseat's people for healing had failed to return.

Some nine hours after the killing began, Dexterity stood with Ursa beside a bloodstained pallet on which a girl of maybe thirteen lay drugged with poppy, and dying. Ursa folded her arms, as close to utter despair as he had ever seen her.

"Are you sure you can't do anything, Jones?" she demanded. "Rollin's mercy, she's just a *child*."

Dexterity bit back a sharp retort. Everyone wanted a miracle today. If he could heal the girl, or any of these poor people, didn't she think he would? He'd tried his hardest, to no avail. The best he could do was fetch and carry basins of water and roll bandages, like the handful of unhurt townsfolk who'd taken shelter here and were helping. The best he could do was hold hands with the dying so they didn't die alone.

Ursa sighed. "I'm sorry," she muttered. "I don't mean to nag."

She was so weary. So grief-struck. Bamfield was one of the physicks who'd never returned. And she was a healer, Kingseat was in its death throes, but for the first time in her long life she had no help to give.

Beyond the clinic's barricaded doors, the sound of chanting, coming closer. The sound of Mijak's warriors with their knives and lust for death.

"Chalava! Chalava! Chalava zho!"

The conscious wounded heard them, and cried out. The unhurt helpers cried out too. Dexterity looked at Ursa and saw resignation in her eyes. Saw that she expected to die now, with him and every helpless soul beneath her clinic's roof.

A booming thud of timber against timber. A second. A third. A fourth. There was a splintering groan – and the barred doors gave way. Suddenly the clinic's entrance was full of Mijak's warriors and languid afternoon light.

The warriors were covered in blood from their braided hair to their booted feet. The blades in their bloody fists dripped scarlet on the floor. There was nowhere to run. Dexterity snatched up an empty basin. Taking one step, then another, he picked his way towards them through the laden pallets crowding the floor.

"*Wei*," he said loudly. "*Wei chalava. Wei* Mijak. *Wei hotas, zho?*" He brandished the basin. "Go away!"

Stunned, the warriors stared at him.

"Jones!" hissed Ursa. "Jones, what are you *doing?*"

Ignoring her horror, he brandished the basin again. "*Wei chalava*. Vortka, *zho?* Vortka *wei*—" He pretended to hold a knife and stab with it. "*Wei. Wei.*"

Still the warriors stared, as though they couldn't trust their ears.

And then he saw Hettie, standing in the corner. She was thinned to a shadow. Her voice, when she spoke, was the merest whisper of sound.

"*Oh, Dexie . . . Dexie . . . I think it's over . . . Dexie my love, I think we've lost . . .*"

Lost? No . . . no . . . they couldn't have. *Rhian.*

Desperate, he reached within himself, searching for the flames of God he'd never wanted or understood. *It's here, the power must be here. Han felt it, didn't he? He felt something in me!*

But he couldn't find it. They were going to die.

"*Jones!*" shouted Ursa. "You fool, what are you *doing?*"

He didn't have time for one of Ursa's scoldings. Shuddering, he tried to bring the power back.

Something deep inside him shifted . . . or twisted. He felt the golden warmth, that suffusion of flame – and then he felt a searing agony. Felt the blood power of Mijak like rotten wine in his veins, clotting and clinging and choking his heart.

"Hettie!" he gasped. "Hettie, please, *help me*!"

He saw her shadow weeping, he saw her ghostly face twist. She screamed . . . and as she screamed she dissolved into the air.

Dexterity, screaming with her, burst into flames.

The warriors of Mijak cried out, their bloodied blades lifting. Burning and burning, Dexterity approached them. Every step was torment, the rotten blood power of Mijak in his own blood like acid. He pointed a trembling finger—

— and the warriors were consumed. Nothing left but a drifting of ashes. Just like Marlan, a lifetime ago.

"God be praised!" cried Ursa. "Jones, are you all right?"

Painfully burning, he stared through the clinic's splintered doorway at Kingseat township, and saw to his desolation that Garabatsas had been . . . *nothing*. Saw flames and ruination and slaughter.

Heard chanting and screaming, hooves on cobblestones, windows breaking, chimneys falling. Heard in the distance a great boom from Dmitrak's gauntlet. Smelled the choking stench of death. It seemed that half of Kingseat was on fire and the other half drowned in blood.

Did Rhian still live? Zandakar? Alasdair? Prolate Helfred? He didn't know, and couldn't leave to find out. It was all he could do to stand upright, to keep himself from suffocating beneath the weight of Mijak's evil. With luck he could keep this clinic protected. Ursa and her patients. That many, and no more. He didn't even know how long he could do that.

Long enough for a miracle, maybe. It was all they had left.

CHAPTER THIRTY-FIVE

Zandakar wept as he searched Kingseat for Dmitrak. He wept for Rhian, who might even now be dead, who might have died believing he had betrayed her.

Live, Rhian hushla, so you can learn why I ran.

He had run to find Dmitrak, who would take him to Yuma and Vortka, so his mother and brother could learn the truth about demons. So he and Vortka could take them back to Mijak, and find a way to heal their demon-ravaged hearts. By saving them he would also save Ethrea, which could not stand against the might of Mijak. In saving his family he would keep his word to Rhian.

As he searched for his brother he killed many warriors. He had to kill them, he could not let Rhian's people die. He had to kill them with his scorpion blade, he dared not risk knife-dancing with Dmitrak's warhost. Aieee, the god see him, it was a hard thing to do. He did not look closely at those warriors' faces, if he saw someone familiar he feared his strength would fail. He killed the warriors and their horses, As they died he saw Hano, he saw Didijik his pony. As they died he wept for them all.

Everywhere in Kingseat, Dimmi's warriors killed Rhian's people like goats in a barracks' slaughter-pit. For every Ethrean he saved, twenty times that number died. He saw women dead, he thought of Rhian, and prayed the god would keep her safe.

As he searched the township he could see where Dimmi had used the god's hammer, there were buildings rubbled and others burned, but to his searching eye too few were destroyed.

If I were still warlord and wore the god's hammer, Kingseat would be razed by now. Aieee, Dimmi, little brother, I think you have not changed. I think you still like to kill with your snakeblade, so you do not use the hammer to kill Kingseat quickly.

It was not such a bad thing, that Dimmi hunted Ethreans for sport. It gave Ethrea a slow death, it gave him time to find his brother. He needed that time, he hunted Dimmi on foot in the twisty turns of Kingseat township, trying to remember where Rhian's traps were set.

He saw the warhost killing Ethreans, he saw soldiers killing warriors. He watched those killings, he did not help. It hurt to see those warriors die and yet he was pleased for Rhian's people. He had taught them how to fight Mijak, he had taught them well.

The most important thing he taught them was that a walking soldier could not hope to kill a mounted warrior, so Rhian had ordered Ethrea's glass-blowers to make thousands of marbles. They were put into buckets and left in every street, so when Dmitrak's warriors rode through Kingseat, Rhian's soldiers could roll those marbles and bring the horses down. Bring them down, and kill their riders. He watched Rhian's soldiers follow their training, he watched them slash and stab those warriors on the ground. Not one of them rose again. All of them died.

They died in other ways, also, but too many lived. So many dead Ethreans, he slipped on bloodied cobbles and tripped in spilled entrails. Kingseat had become a Mijaki battlefield. He searched for his brother, he was afraid he would fail. He did not know Kingseat well enough, he did not know these streets. He knew the castle of Kingseat, which Dimmi had destroyed.

Aieee, god, I need Dexterity, he would know the quick streets to walk. Dexterity is in the god's eye, he might even save Dimmi and Yuma as he saved Vortka in Jatharuj.

But he did not know where Dexterity was hiding, or how to find him, or even if he lived. There was no time to search for him, he had to find Dimmi before his brother tired of slow hunting and hammered Kingseat to the ground.

As I hammered Jokriel and those cities beyond the Sand River. Hammered villages and hamlets and people who did no harm.

But that was his old life, he must not think of that now.

So he ran lightly from shadow to shadow, through

Ethrea's streets and the smoke and the screaming, he searched for his brother so Dimmi could be saved.

And while he searched, Kingseat echoed to the chant: "*Chalava! Chalava! Chalava zho!*"

After her sixth hairsbreadth escape from death, Rhian stopped counting. Either she'd survive this madness or she wouldn't. Worrying about it only got in the way of killing.

Panting, coughing, bleeding from slashes on her left arm, her left thigh, her right wrist and her back, she led her small band of soldiers along the alleyways of Kingseat, playing hide-and-seek and dance-you-to-death with the warriors of Mijak.

There was hardly a stretch of cobbles or paving-stones empty of violence. She faced severed Ethrean heads and spilled guts and puddles of blood without flinching; the carnage inflicted on her people had lost its power to shock. She'd only been sick twice, and not for several hours, which was more than could be said for half her soldiers. She looked at every dead face they passed, just in case one of the bodies was Alasdair. It hadn't been so far, but she didn't dare let herself hope.

She and her soldiers had one bucket of marbles left between them. Once she'd tried to collect some that had been thrown, to delay the inevitable moment when their bucket ran dry, but that had resulted in her second close escape. After that she decided to live without more marbles.

They crept along stinking Bloodnbone Alley, which ran the backside length of Butcher Street. On the other side of the butcher shops with their remorseless, relentless buzzing of flies, came the sound of horses, of warriors, of chanting.

"Chalava! Chalava! Chalava zho!"

Directly ahead of her, a narrow passage connected alley to street. She held up a clenched fist, warning the seven men behind her, and stopped. Held her hand out for the bucket, and eased into the passage. The horses were closer . . . they were closer . . . they were—

She leapt out and threw the last handfuls of marbles beneath the horses' hooves. The beasts skittered and thrashed and crashed to the cobbles: blue-coated and roan-coated with tigerish black stripes. Their horsehide-wearing riders fell hard with them. Two out of eight were crushed to pulp. The other six danced to their feet, teeth bared, their long braids ringing with those brash silver bells.

"Ethrea!" she screamed, and her soldiers rushed out of hiding. As they fell upon the warriors, indiscriminate, she picked her first victim. Looked him in the cold eyes and started to dance.

Sandcat leaping . . . falcon stooping . . . warrior dying . . .

He died, his brothers and sisters died, she lived, she lost two men.

No time to mourn them. Three of the horses had shattered their legs. With the ease of a butcher she put them out of their misery, and led her surviving five soldiers on to more hunting.

Dmitrak at last tired of killing with his snakeblade, and began to hammer Kingseat to the ground.

Weary now, no closer to finding his brother,

Zandakar saw the bolts of crimson in the distance, smelled the fresh smoke, heard the new screams, the falling brickwork, the loud wild chanting as the warhost sang its praise.

"Chalava! Chalava! Chalava zho!"

He was in some laneway lined with deserted houses. No people, only corpses, they would not care what he did. Scorpion knife in his hand, pulsing blue, he entered a house with two storeys, climbed the stairs and looked through the highest window, across Kingseat's sea of roofs.

He could not see Dimmi, but he could see the hammer, he could see the path Dimmi rode by the crimson fire in the air. He stood at the window and watched until he was certain he had read his brother right.

With lowsun approaching, Mijak's warlord swung in a wide arc, turning back for the harbour. Zandakar knew that once Dimmi reached his warships there would be no more killing, not until newsun. Instead his brother would plunder food and drink from the township, if there were women alive he would look for a fuck. When his appetites were sated he would sit with his warriors, they would laugh and tell tales of the kills they had made. When he and Dimmi had ridden together, killing cities, that was how his brother had celebrated with the warhost.

Dimmi is the warlord, I do not think he has changed.

Zandakar watched a little longer, he would not have another chance at this. When he was confident he knew where he would meet his brother, he left that sad and empty house, he ran into the lane and past all the staring corpses, he ran and he ran and saw no-one alive.

Many streets in Kingseat were lined with purple-flowering trees. Rhian called them *yeddas*, and complained they made her itch. If they made him itch he would not care, he climbed a tree and waited for his brother.

Dimmi came with his gauntlet and his shells of warriors. He came laughing and smiling, killing always made him smile. Zandakar looked down, his smiling brother made him sad.

He does not know he smiles because of demons. I will change his heart. I will.

As Dimmi rode his red stallion beneath the *yedda* tree, Zandakar dropped out of concealment, landing like a sandcat on the horse's warm loins. In one swift move he had the gauntlet pinned between his brother's back and his own belly and with his other hand pressed the scorpion knife to Dimmi's throat. He let a little of its power flare along the blade. Dimmi gasped as his throat burned and his flesh smoked. He gasped at the voice whispering kindly in his ear.

"The god sees you, Dmitrak. It sees you in its eye. Take me to Yuma. I have something to say."

"Zandakar?" said Dimmi, his voice was shocked, he was not pleased. "How are you here? Why aren't you *dead*?"

Aieee, Dimmi, little brother, so much gone wrong for both of us.

"I am alive because I live in the god," he whispered. "I live with my scorpion knife pressed against your throat. Breathe too deeply, try to fall, try to kill me and *you* will die."

"Warlord!" cried a warrior. "Warlord, is this—"

"This is no-one!" snarled Dimmi. "You did not see him. Ride on."

The warriors pressed their fists to their chests, Dimmi was their warlord and they were well-trained.

"Good," said Zandakar, as the warriors rode away. "Now we see Yuma. Remember my words, warlord. One mistake and you will die."

Of course he was lying, he would not kill his brother. Dimmi did not know it, he was safer that way.

"No, Zandakar," said Dimmi. "I will kill *you*. I should have killed you in Mijak, that was my mistake."

Aieee, Dimmi. Dimmi. Still full of rage.

"Ride," Zandakar told him. "The empress awaits."

Hekat woke to feel arms around her, she could not understand it. She slept alone. Raklion had slept with his arms around her. Tcha, she had hated that. It was good when he died. She opened her eyes and saw there were shadows. The sun was sinking, it would be lowsun soon. She was outside, in Vortka's arms, they sat on the ground beside her beautiful warships.

Why was she outside? What was this place? Then she remembered, this was the demon island Ethrea. Dmitrak warlord was killing it for the god. She remembered, she remembered, her heart slowed its beating.

I am old, I am not dying. I am Hekat in the god's remembering eye.

"Let go of me, Vorkta," she said, and made herself sit up. Aieee, tcha, the pains in her body, she breathed and it complained, she would smite it if she could. It had complained since birthing Dmitrak, she was tasked without end. "I am the empress, why am I sleeping? Why am I on the ground with you? Why—"

And then she remembered something else. Disbelieving, she looked at him. She pulled away completely, fingers reaching for her snakeblade.

"You made me *sleep*, Vortka?" she whispered. "You used the god to make me *sleep*?"

"You used it to make me sick, once," he said, there were tears in his eyes. "Do you remember, Hekat? I was so sick."

She should have used it to kill him. "*You made me sleep?*"

"You were weary, Hekat. You needed to rest."

"Is that for you to say, Vortka? I am the empress, I think it is not!"

He shrugged, he looked away. He would not meet her eyes.

How long have I known him, how many seasons has it been? We were slaves in Et-Nogolor, I gave him my bread and corn. I gave him food and now he makes me sleep? I should smite him, I should smite him.

But she could not smite Vortka, she would be smiting herself. She took her hand from her snakeblade, she punched her fist to his leg. She laughed to see him wincing, she was old but she was strong. She could not stay angry, she had known him too long.

"Aieee, tcha, you Vortka."

He touched his fingers to the old scars sunk in her cheeks. "Aieee, tcha, you Hekat."

He smiled, and so did she. He was Vortka and she loved him. "What does the god tell you, Vortka? Is Ethrea dead yet? Is it slain for the god?"

Pain in his old eyes, pain in his face. "Hekat, you must listen, we must speak of the god. There is something I—"

She had heard it too, hoofbeats at the harbour, a single horse come back. She turned, she looked . . .

Zandakar.

She was walking, when was she walking? She walked along the harbour dock, she walked beside the water. She walked in silence, her heart was beating. Her eyes were full of Zandakar.

He sat on the horse behind the other one with red slave hair. His hair was blue. He was her true son, he was Zandakar.

Zandakar slid from the horse, and the other one slid with him. She reached her son Zandakar, she pushed the other one aside. She pressed her hand to her son's face, it was wet with his tears.

"Yuma," said Zandakar. "Yuma. You are here."

"Zandakar," she whispered, she stroked his blue hair. "I knew you were not dead. I knew the god would find you and return you to my eye."

"Yuma," said Zandakar. "We must—" Then he smiled, aieee, his smile was sweet, her heart had hungered for his smile. "*Vortka.*"

"Zandakar," said Vortka, joining them. "The god sees you. I fear it does not see me, I fear I have failed."

Puzzled by Vortka's words, she did not take her eyes from Zandakar. Her eyes had been empty but now they were full. Like her empty heart they were full of Zandakar. There was a knife in her son's hand. A blue power pulsed through it as power pulsed through the god's hammer. He pointed it at the other one. He was not stupid, he knew Nagarak's spawn.

I do not know that knife, where is it from?

"Yuma," her son said, his fingers touched her scarred face. "Yuma, listen. I hear the god."

Aieee, the god see him, there were no godbraids in his hair. He had no godbells for singing, she would give him hers. They were his.

"Yuma, do you hear me? I hear the god, I must tell you what it says."

She smiled, her heart was laughing. "So do I hear the god, Zandakar. It told me I would see you again, did it lie? I think it did not."

"Listen to your son, Hekat," said Vortka. "Zandakar has something important to say."

Tcha. That Vortka, he did not know when to hold his tongue.

"*Yuma*," her son said. "I must tell you this, the god wants you to know what I know. It wants you to know what Vortka knows. In Jatharuj the god spoke to Vortka, it spoke the truth and now you must hear it."

She felt her smile fade, she felt her heart stop laughing. "Jatharuj? How do you know of Jatharuj?"

"Tcha," said Zandakar, his blue eyes were sad. His blue hair was beautiful, how she hated red hair.

"Yuma, I was in Jatharuj. I was with Vortka when the god told him the truth."

She felt the world tilt around her. "You were in Jatharuj?"

Zandakar nodded. "The god wanted me there. Yuma, you must know the truth. I am sorry, it will hurt you. The voice you hear is not the god. You listen to demons. Your heart has been tricked."

It hurt to look away from him. She must. She looked at Vortka. "You saw him in Jatharuj? *He was with you*?"

"Hekat," said Vortka, his face was wet with tears. "Listen to Zandakar, listen to me. This is the truth, it is time that you *hear* it. In Mijak, in Et-Raklion, we heard a false voice. You and I were tricked by demons, we did *not* serve the god." He pointed at Kingseat, at the smoke and the flames. "The god does not want blood, it does not want this slaughter. That is what demons want. We have served them, we did not know it. But we know it now, Hekat, *this slaughter must stop*."

His words were a babbling, she heard only one thing. "He came to you, Vortka, and you said nothing? My son was in Jatharuj and *you held your tongue*?"

Vortka tried to touch her, she struck his hand away. "Hekat," he said, "I know you are frightened. This is a terrible truth, these demons are terrible. Let me help you understand this, let me help you not fear. You must let me help you, Hekat, you must hear the god's true voice. You must—"

"I must! I must! *You do not say I must!* You knew where my son was and you did not tell me, my son was in Jatharuj and you kept that in your heart. My son who you sent away, my son—"

"*My son!*" shouted Vortka, he seized her arms, he shook her hard. "He is not only your son, Hekat, *he is my son too!*"

"What?" said the other one. "What did you say?"

She did not listen to Dmitrak, what was Dmitrak? Spawn of Nagarak. She did not look at Zandakar, she fed her eyes on Vortka. She pulled her arms free of him, she showed him her rage.

"You fucked me, Vortka, it does not make him your son! You sowed the seed, the god and I raised him." Her fists were clenched, she struck his scorpion pectoral, she pounded his stone chest, she was so angry she could weep. "You are nothing to him, he is everything to me. *He was in Jatharuj and you held your tongue.* And now you shout that you fucked me, was the world meant to know? Was Zandakar meant to know? I think he was not!"

"Yuma," said Zandakar. "Vortka told me in Jatharuj he is my father. Do not be angry, I am pleased he is. Come home with us to Mijak, the god is waiting there."

So much rage in her blood, it was burning her alive. "You *told* him? Was that your business? I think it was not! You sinning man, you wicked sinner! You saw him in Jatharuj, you kept him a secret! *You told him the secret he was not meant to know*!"

Vortka was angry, she had never seen him angry. She had never seen him like Nagarak, so angry in his eyes.

"He is my *son*, Hekat, I wanted him to know me. He was sailing away, what if he died and I never saw him again? You love him? *I* love him. All your life you kept him, you would not share him with me. You are a selfish bitch, Hekat. I wanted my share of him, it was time, *it was time*! I wanted to know him as my son, I wanted—"

She stepped back, her heart beating. She stepped back, she could not breathe.

Where did that come from? Who put that there? Who put my snakeblade through Vortka's sinning throat?

Vortka was staring, he was dead in his eyes. Someone was laughing . . . and someone else wept.

Zandakar watched, disbelieving, as Vortka's body slumped to the ground. The sound it made was like any dead man's body, falling, but that was not right. This was not any man, this was Vortka.

My father. He was my father, how is he dead?

Shouting broke the silence, and the drumming of many feet on wood, on stone. The warhost's god-speakers were leaping from the warships to the docks, rushing towards their fallen high godspeaker. Many were clutching their sacrifice knives. It was nearly lowsun, they prepared for the god. They were shout-ing, they were weeping, they knew Vortka was dead.

Dmitrak killed them with his gauntlet.

Zandakar barely noticed them dying, he did not care if they were dead. The scorpion knife slipped from his fingers and he dropped to the dock, he gath-ered Vortka in his arms. Vortka was his father, and Hekat had killed him.

Oh, Yuma, Yuma. What have you done?

He could not look at his mother, he did not dare to

see her face. He could not breathe, he could not weep, he could not make a sound. In his heart the god was screaming, he screamed with it in his heart.

Dmitrak started laughing again. "You killed the old fool, Hekat, you killed the sinning old man! Aieee, the god sees Mijak's empress, the god sees her in its eye! Vortka was a sinner, he did not hear the god, the god did not see him, he was swallowed by demons!"

Zandakar stared up at him, Vortka so quiet against his chest. So quiet in his arms, he was holding his dead father. "Be *quiet*! What do you know?"

"What do I know?" said Dimmi, he was laughing so hard. "I know you are not the warlord, you were *never* the warlord. She fucked with that old man, you are his son. You are *demon-born*, Zandakar. No brother of mine."

Yuma spun and struck Dimmi, with her open hand she struck him, with her closed fist she struck him harder, it was a miracle he did not fall. Her godbraids flew about her head, her godbells were raucous, they were shrieking, she screamed.

"Zandakar is the god's get, he was born by the god's want! You are the evil spawn of demons, Dmitrak!"

As Dimmi stared, his laughter dying, Zandakar kissed his father, he kissed Vortka, he pulled out the knife. There was so little blood, there was just a wound, a little wound. A wound so large it must kill the world.

Yuma was weeping, she was beating her breast. She was staring at Vortka but she did not take a step.

"*Bitch*!" Dmitrak snatched her godbraids, he

pulled her to him as her godbells shouted. His eyes were wide and black with rage. They were Nagarak's eyes, it was Nagarak's rage, he was Nagarak's son . . . and he did not know. "Bitch, bitch, you were *always a bitch*!"

"Dimmi," said Zandakar. "Dimmi, let her go."

He could not release Vortka, the old man was so light. He was so light he might float away, and where would he go?

Dimmi was not listening, he was glaring at their mother. "How can I be born of demons, Hekat? I am the warlord, I am Raklion's son, I am—"

"Raklion?" said Yuma. Her scars were slick with tears. If she felt Dimmi's fist in her godbraids she did not show it. She looked so small, so empty, with Vortka dead. "Raklion never sired one living brat in his life. You are *Nagarak's* spawn, Dmitrak, rotten in your bones."

"Nagarak?" said Dimmi. "Bitch, you *lie*. I am *Raklion's* son, I am the warlord of Mijak like my father before me!"

"You are *Nagarak's*!" cried Yuma. "You are warlord by mistake! I was tricked by demons to fuck that high godspeaker. You think that I wanted you? I *hate* you, Dmitrak, you should have died at birth! You crippled me, you nearly killed me, you stole my warhost, you stole my son! He married that piebald bitch because *you* did not stop him!"

Spittled with fury, Dimmi pushed her away. "My fault? You make it *my* fault? I never said Zandakar should marry that Harjha bitch. I said to fuck her, I never said she was a wife!"

Yuma was a knife-dancer, she did not stumble

when he pushed. She stayed on her feet and waved a fist in Dimmi's face. *"Tcha!"* she spat. "You knew I would be angry if he married that piebald, you *wanted* him to marry her, you wanted my rage. I would have killed him for marrying her but Vortka stopped me. You tried to kill my son, you are *demonspawn.*"

"No!" shouted Dimmi. *"Zandakar* is demonspawn. He turned from the god in Na'ha'leima, Hekat, now he tries to turn you. I hear the god, I know it wants the world, I give you slaves to kill and I conquer countries. Zandakar and that old fool, that old Vortka, they are eaten by demons, they would see demons conquer *you.*"

Yuma was shaking, she was shaking and weeping. She slapped at Dimmi, she slapped him and slapped him, she was a wild woman slapping, the empress was gone.

"You do not say that of Vortka, he was a good man! Vortka was godchosen, we were godchosen together! Vortka and I lived in the god's choosing eye! Oh, Vortka – *Vortka* – you are dead, I have killed you—"

Zandakar stared, breathless, as his mother threw herself to the ground, as she crawled on her hands and knees to weep over his father. She was moaning, she was sobbing, she rocked on her knees, she clawed at her silver scars until her face ran with blood.

Reaching over Vortka, he took hold of her hands, he kept her fingers from clawing. "Yuma, no, Yuma don't, it was an accident, you did not mean it!"

She fell against him across his dead father, she hid her torn and bleeding face against his chest.

"Zandakar, my son, my only true son. You are come back to me, the god has seen me, it sees you, we are together. This is the god's want, Vortka could not hear it. His ears were stopped by demons, you must know that, Zandakar. I am Hekat, the god's empress, I hear its voice in my heart. Listen to me and you will live in the world. You are my warlord, you are warlord of Mijak, you are the god's hammer, you will never leave again!"

"No!" shouted Dimmi. "You bitch, *I am the hammer!*"

Zandakar tried to push Yuma behind him, he tried to protect her, to push Dimmi away. But Dimmi stood above him, he was strong, he was angry. He took Yuma by the godbraids and hauled her to her feet.

"*Say it, bitch! Say it!*" he screamed, his eyes were mad with fury. He shook her and shook her, her godbells cried her pain. "I am Dmitrak, I am Hekat's son! I am warlord of Mijak and hammer of the god!"

Zandakar did not move, he did not dare provoke his brother more. He did not even dare to speak, for Dimmi wore the gauntlet.

I had the scorpion knife, I let him keep the gauntlet. I did not want to make him small. I was stupid to do that. Aieee, the god see me, I am a fool.

Dimmi was still shouting, there was foam on his lips. "Say the words, bitch! Say *them*! Dmitrak is warlord, hammer of the god!"

The blood was drying on Yuma's beautiful, scarred face. Her blue eyes were unfocused, she did not defend herself. "Zandakar," she murmured. "Zandakar, my son."

Weeping and howling, Dimmi released her. He

struck her with the gauntlet as he wept and howled his pain. He struck her so hard he burst her beautiful blue eye. He struck her so hard he broke her slender neck.

Yuma fell to the dock like one of Dexterity's puppets. She fell to the dock, she did not move again.

Dimmi stared at Yuma as though he could not believe her dead. As though he could not remember killing her. As though none of this was real.

Zandakar felt the grief in his throat. *But it is real, it is real. Here is my father, dead in my arms. There is my dead mother, all of this is real.*

On the dock beside him lay the scorpion knife, abandoned. On the dock before him, rejected, his murdering brother.

He eased himself free of Vortka, he closed his fingers on the scorpion knife. Its power trembled through him as he got to his feet. He saw the knife's blade run blue, it shone blue with power.

Dimmi saw it. He lifted his fist. The gold-and-crystal hammer shimmered with red lights, it pulsed the colour of blood. Zandakar faced him, he faced his little brother, the only breathing family he had left in the world.

I must save him. I must save him. If I lose him . . . what do I have?

"Enough. *Enough.* We must end this," he said, pleading. "The god is not the god. We should not have left Mijak, we serve demons by mistake. We must take the warhost home to Et-Raklion, we must free those nations we conquered and never again cross the Sand River. Dimmi, little brother, we were wrong. *We were wrong.*"

Dimmi's lips pulled back in a snarl. "Did you never listen, Zandakar? *My name is Dmitrak*."

And with a bold leap and a screamed curse, Nagarak's son attacked.

CHAPTER THIRTY-SIX

They were losing the light when Rhian found Alasdair, wounded and bleeding in a sprawl of dead soldiers on the doorstep of a burned-out potter's shop in Gimcrack Lane.

By that time her personal army had dwindled to three, and they were the only living soldiers she'd seen in some time. Kingseat's air remained thick with smoke. The fading blue sky was hazed with it, and the cooling autumn air stank of burned wood and flesh. Mijak's warriors still roamed the streets, chanting, though she'd not seen any for perhaps half an hour, and not killed one for longer than that. She'd seen glimpses of survivors: Ethrean faces pressed to windows and swiftly withdrawn, a flash of skirts whisking round a corner, a voice in an alleyway, hurriedly hushed.

Well. Mijak had been in Kingseat for less than a day. They couldn't kill a whole city in less than a day . . . could they?

Maybe not, but God knows they're trying.

She found Alasdair by accident. Stumbling with exhaustion, hurting so badly from her own wounds, half-blind with thirst and hunger, she was leading her three men by touch and luck down the dark lane, and so was the first to trip over the bodies. When one moaned, she nearly screamed. When she discovered it was Alasdair, she nearly screamed again.

"Oh, dear God," she said, hauling the corpses off him as though they were so many broken tiltyard mannikins. "Alasdair! *Alasdair*!"

Mijak's warriors had left him for dead. Rollin's mercy, he looked dead, he was stabbed through his arms and legs and chest. He was covered in blood, hardly breathing at all.

Oh, no. Oh, Alasdair. No no no no . . .

Weeks of coolness. Estrangement. Hurt feelings on both sides. Misunderstandings, frustration. Marriage was hard. And then their fight at the harbour, only this morning. This morning? It felt a lifetime ago. The look in his eyes when he'd begged her to leave.

I told you to go but, Alasdair, I didn't mean it. I didn't mean it. Are you listening? Can you hear me? You have to stay.

She looked at Revin, the oldest of her soldiers. Sixteen or seventeen, if he was a day. "He's not dead. We can save him." *I hope we can save him.* "But he needs a physick, he needs—"

Ursa. He needs Ursa. He needs Dexterity. He needs a miracle.

But here was Alasdair living, when she'd given him up for dead so perhaps she could hope.

"Take his shoulders, Revin," she said curtly. "Bothy, take his legs. Be careful. Don't drop him." She looked at her third soldier, a mere child of twelve. One of the harbour taverns' cheeky cellar brats, rough as guts and twice as tough as nails. He'd killed six Mijaki warriors all by himself. "Tob, do you know Ursa the physick? Do you know her clinic on Foxglove Way?"

Tob nodded, so solemn. "Aye, Majessy. Ursa's allus physickin' us cellar brats. Foreign sailors get rough when their beer's slopped too slow."

Really? She didn't know that. Something to frown over, when this day was done. "I've no idea if she's dead or alive. But if she's alive, Tob, she'll save the king. Run to her. Tell her we're coming. And be *careful*, you hear me? Avoid any warriors you see."

Tob scarpered, and she led the others with their precious burden, scouting ahead to be sure the way was clear.

God granted another miracle. They reached the clinic safely to find Ursa and Tob waiting, and nearly two score of townsfolk huddled in fear. Along one clinic wall marched a line of sheet-covered bodies.

For some reason Rhian found them more upsetting than any pile of hacked limbs.

"Mind now, mind now!" Ursa scolded, as they laid Alasdair on a pallet. "Rollin's mercy, those heathens have made a collander of him."

"Maybe, but he's breathing," snapped Rhian. "So you have to—"

"Ah," said Ursa turning to follow her stare. "Jones. Yes. That's a story."

Dexterity stood in the corner, gently wreathed in golden flames. His eyes were open but he seemed to see nothing. He didn't move, he didn't speak, he didn't come to greet his queen.

"He's been like that for hours," said Ursa, briskly

tallying Alasdair's wounds. "Killed a band of Mijaki warriors, healed everyone here who could be saved, killed two more bands of warriors, and hasn't said a word since." She shrugged. "I can't explain it. It's like he's . . . gone away." And then she sighed. "Majesty – Rhian—"

Rhian saw in Ursa's face what the old woman didn't want to say. She looked down at Alasdair, beneath the blood so still, so pale. She felt a dreadful shudder, rage and grief shaking her, and pushed to her feet.

"*No*, Ursa. I won't have it. I'm telling you, I *won't*."

She marched over to Dexterity and glared into his serenely burning face. "Mister Jones! Pay attention. Your queen has need of you."

Nothing. Nothing. He burned and said nothing.

"Mister Jones! For the love of God, I'm *begging* you! *Look* at me!"

Still nothing.

He was burning. She shouldn't touch him. She shouldn't take that dreadful risk. But she needed him, she *needed* him. *Alasdair needs him. Oh, God, please* . . .

With the last of her strength, with the dregs of her faith, she slapped Dexterity as hard as she could.

"*Mister Jones!*"

He stirred, then stared at her through the near-translucent flames. "Rhian?"

She pointed. "Alasdair's dying. Heal him. *Hurry*."

Dexterity nodded, and drifted to Alasdair. Arms folded, chewing on a ragged thumbnail, Rhian watched as her toymaker made Ethrea's king – her husband – whole.

When it was over, and Dexterity stepped back, she knelt beside Alasdair and took his quiet hand. Looked into his dear face, so plain, so bony. "My love, it's me. It's Rhian." *Alasdair, wake up*.

He didn't stir.

"Look out now, Majesty," said Ursa. "Give me some room."

Standing, Rhian gave Ursa room, then looked at Dexterity. "I thought you healed him. Why doesn't he wake?"

"He'll wake in his own time," said Dexterity, then frowned. "You're wounded too. Poor Rhian. Poor queen."

His sympathy nearly ruined her. She gritted her teeth and forced back the tears. "If you can heal me, heal me. And that's all I need."

So he healed her, for the second time.

"Thank you," she said.

But he didn't say, "You're welcome." Instead, he turned his head to stare through the clinic's broken doors, towards the harbour.

"What?" she said. "Dexterity? What is it?"

"Zandakar," he whispered. "Take my hand, child. We have to run."

Zandakar? She shook her head. "No, I can't, I can't leave Alasdair, I—"

Dexterity's flames flared high and hot. "*Yes, you can, Rhian! Now run!*"

So they ran hand-in-hand through the last of the light. The lowering dusk was a kindness. She couldn't see what had been done to her capital. No warrior challenged them and she didn't burn.

Just as they reached the harbour's Royal Gate they heard the dreadful searing sound of Dmitrak's gauntlet, and the faded evening lit up as a Mijaki warship burst into fire and splinters. A heartbeat later a blue flame streaked through the air, and smoke from scorched stone seared their lungs and stung their eyes.

"Rollin's mercy," Rhian gasped. "Is that—"

"Yes," said Dexterity. "That's Zandakar. He's at war with his brother."

They ran through the gates, past the smouldering harbourmaster's office, down the stone steps to the harbour-front and the docks, just in time to see a shadowed figure roll away from another killing crimson streak.

Zandakar.

"God help him," said Rhian, her voice catching on a sob. "Dexterity, stop them, before—"

"I can't," said her toymaker, still gently burning. "It's not my place."

"*What?* Dexterity—"

"Hush," he replied. "Rhian, you must have faith."

And then, to her gasping shock, he pulled the flames inside himself. All that remained of them was a golden flicker in his eyes . . . and a soft glow in his hands.

She didn't resist when he tugged her into the shadows.

A blast of power from Dmitrak's gauntlet set fire to six more warships. Within scant moments the docks were bathed in a merry, dancing light. Rhian could see everything, and what she saw stole her breath.

Dmitrak was hunting his brother.

Shorter than Zandakar by perhaps two handspans, he was brutally muscular, not long and lithe. He reminded Rhian of a wild boar in the way he paced the docks, shoulders hunched, head lowered. In the light from the burning ships his hair glowed blood red. Like all of Mijak's warriors, it was long and plaited into many fine braids, festooned with amulets and pretty silver bells. Every step he took shivered them into song.

Dexterity touched her arm. "See there."

She dragged her frightened gaze from Dmitrak and looked where he nodded. Two flame-flickered bodies sprawled on the ground.

"That's Vortka." He sounded sorrowful. "Zandakar's father is dead. The woman is poor mad Hekat, Empress of Mijak."

"And who are they?" she asked, pointing to the other bodies scattered around the docks.

"Godspeakers," he said, still sorrowful. "The unholy priests of Mijak."

She didn't ask how he knew, or how he could feel pity. He was her burning man of miracles, and that explained it all.

As she turned again to stare at Dmitrak, to look for Zandakar, a streak of blue fire burst from the shadows further along the harbour, where the warships were yet to burn. Zandakar burst into the light after it, his scorpion knife pointing. A second stream of blue fire lanced from its tip. But it didn't kill Dmitrak, it seared a thin line across the stone of the harbour-front, so the prowling warrior had to leap back.

"*Dmitrak*!" Zandakar shouted, and then something else, something in his Mijaki tongue Rhian couldn't understand. He didn't sound angry. He sounded desperate and so sad.

Dear God, he's trying to reason with him. Kingseat's burning, it's littered with corpses and running with blood, and he thinks to reason with the man responsible.

If he'd been within reach, she'd have stabbed him herself.

Dmitrak's answer was a stream of crimson fire. Zandakar raised his ugly scorpion knife and met the crimson fire with blue. The two flames collided in a screaming of sound, the light and heat so intense Rhian threw up a hand to protect her eyes.

But still she watched. She couldn't look away.

The two streams of power burned hot and bright as the brothers struggled to destroy each other, as blue fire and crimson melded and writhed and screamed. And then came a great flash, a boom that echoed round the harbour. Zandakar cried out as the scorpion knife flew from his grasp to strike the dock and skitter far out of reach. In the same heartbeat Dmitrak shouted as his gauntlet belched stinking smoke . . . and died.

Breathless, silent, the brothers stared at each other.

Then Dmitrak laughed. Rhian felt her skin crawl, felt the hair on her nape rise. She watched, cold sweat sliding, as Zandakar's brother pulled his knife from its sheath and crouched, ready to dance.

But Zandakar was unarmed. His scorpion knife was gone.

Rhian whipped Ranald's tiger-eye blade out of its sheath. "*Zandakar!*" she shouted. "*Zandakar! Here!*"

He caught the thrown knife, no time to acknowledge her. Dmitrak was not distracted, he launched into his *hotas*, so fast, so deadly, so implacable in his hate. Zandakar answered with *hotas* of his own.

Rhian stood at the edge of the firelight and watched the *hotas* as they were meant to be danced, between bitter enemies, to a bitter death. And she saw, for the first time, how kind Zandakar had been.

He and his brother fought with a ferocity that stole her breath. She could hardly distinguish one *hota* from the next, they slashed and leapt and whirled and kicked so fast. How long could they fight like this? Their speed was inhuman. Surely not even these two could keep up this pace . . .

And as though they read her thought, the brothers broke apart, gasping harshly, staggering a little as they sought a brief respite. Dmitrak's blade had opened Zandakar's arms, his legs, his face and his chest. His fine linen shirt and leather leggings were sodden red. Dmitrak was just as wounded, but he wasn't wounded nearly enough.

And then Rhian realised – Zandakar wasn't trying to kill him. He still believed in a victory without death.

God knew, she understood him. Had it been Ranald or Simon she'd have felt the same. No matter their crimes, no matter their wickedness, she'd want to save them. She wouldn't want them to die.

But he doesn't love you, Zandakar. Dmitrak wants you dead.

It was her fight with Kyrin all over again. She felt a flare of anger, that Zandakar could be so two-faced. He'd scolded her for being sentimental, for not dispatching Hartshorn's duke swiftly . . . and now here *he* was, making the same mistake.

I'm sorry, Zandakar. You don't give me a choice.

She thought of Alasdair, healed and waiting. Thought of her kingdom, torn apart. Then she stepped from shadow into firelight, where there was nowhere to hide.

"*Zandakar*," she said coldly, her skin hot with fear. "You said you'd not betray me. Was that a lie?"

He was too tired and hurt to school himself. Everything he felt for her blazed in his face. Dmitrak saw it. Dmitrak laughed. He said something in Mijaki and then he grabbed his crotch, hips pumping suggestively, greed in his eyes. Zandakar's blood on his knife-blade shimmered scarlet.

"*Rhian*," said Zandakar. In his face, love and pain. He looked at his brother. He looked back at her. Watching his face, she felt a cruel stab of grief. How could she do this, make him choose between them? Who was she, what kind of woman, to force a good man to slaughter his brother?

I'm what you made me, Zandakar. Rhian hushla, a killing queen.

Dmitrak leapt for her, and Zandakar killed him.

*   *   *

The silence afterwards was broken only by the sound of warships, burning. Zandakar stood over the body of his brother, so neatly slain by an Ethrean knife.

Rhian looked into his face and wept. "*Yatzhay*, Zandakar. *Yatzhay. Yatzhay.*"

He couldn't hear her. Or if he could, had no desire to answer. He turned away from Dmitrak and walked to his mother and father, tumbled together in death a little distance away. She didn't follow him. Gave him what privacy she could.

Dexterity joined her. Dear God, she'd forgotten him. His eyes still flickered golden, his hands glowed like a lantern. He smiled at her, unspeaking, and stripped the gauntlet from Dmitrak's arm. It was an extraordinary thing, crafted from red crystal and gold wire. Beautiful, despite its brutal purpose. But it was ruined now, all but one crystal cracked and blackened, much of its thin gold wire melted.

Dexterity stroked it, glowing fingers running its length. The fire in him flared, for a heartbeat he was too bright to look at . . .

. . . and then he faded again, and the gauntlet was whole.

After all she had seen, she shouldn't be surprised. But she was surprised. She was breathless. Shocked.

"*Why*, Dexterity? *Why* would you—"

He smiled again, gently, and took the gauntlet to Zandakar. The warrior was seated on the dock between his mother and his father, one hand touching each of them, his face so desolate Rhian had to look away.

Dexterity dropped to a crouch before him. "You're not finished yet, Zandakar. The warriors they brought here still ravage this kingdom. You are their warlord. It's time to lead them home." He held out the gauntlet. "No-one but you can wield this now. And when you die, it will die with you and there will be the end of all dark power in Mijak."

Zandakar took the gauntlet. Slid it onto his arm, and flexed his gold-and-crystal fingers. Then he pushed to his feet. Raised his gauntleted fist above his head. Looked at the starred sky . . . and sent a bolt of blue fire towards the waxing moons.

Rhian heard herself gasp. "Rollin's mercy!"

He lowered his fist and looked at her. Walked to her, his pale eyes wide with grief. Standing before her, he pressed his fist to his chest. "*Yatzhay*, Rhian *hushla*. *Yatzhay* for Ethrea."

She laid her palm against his bloodied cheek. "*Yatzhay*, Zandakar. *Yatzhay* for your family."

And then she held him, lightly, so he could weep.

Alasdair woke not long after dawn. Rhian, steadfastly by his side in Ursa's emptied clinic, felt the change in him. Felt him stir beneath her hand. Watched his eyes open, and blink in the new light.

"Be still, my love," she told him softly. "Everything's all right."

"Mijak?" he croaked. "Defeated?"

She reached for the cup of water Ursa had left ready, and helped him sip a little. "Yes. It's defeated."

He closed his fingers round her wrist. Oh God, his touch was warm. He wasn't dead. She nearly wept.

"You? You're all right?"

She smiled. "I'm fine."

"Zandakar?"

"Lives," she said. "Mijak's empress is dead, and all her priests. Many of her warriors. Her other son, Dmitrak." She closed her eyes, remembering that death: so swift, so brutal. Dmitrak had stood no chance. And Zandakar had cried for him, like a man without a future.

"Rhian . . ."

She looked at her beautiful, breathing husband. "I don't know about Ludo. Or any of the others. I hope to hear soon. I hope . . ."

He nodded, so close to grief. "And Han?"

"Nothing," she whispered. "I'm afraid – I'm afraid—"

He held out his arms. "Come, my love."

With a muffled sob, she lay her head on his breast. Let him hold her. Let him comfort her. Beyond the clinic's walls her people were rising from Kingseat's ashes. Soon she'd leave to help them. Soon. But for now . . . for a moment . . . let the woman rule the queen.

Dexterity sat with his back against the harbour wall, letting the noon sun's thin autumn warmth seep into his bones. One way and another he'd been busy since dawn yesterday and he was oh, so very weary.

Weary, sad . . . but in a strange way, content. Even as he sat here like an old dog with arthritis, the warriors of Mijak were being rounded up and tamed. Those Zandakar confronted on the streets of Kingseat township, overnight, did not think to question him, for he wore the god's hammer. In their eyes the god had chosen him to lead them, and so they would follow. At first light they followed him out of Kingseat altogether.

"Rhian *hushla*," he'd said, so solemn, at the head of his tamed army. "Mijak's warriors trouble your kingdom. I will find them, I will smite them, and then we will leave."

Standing on the steps of Kingseat's great chapel, Rhian had nodded. "Zandakar," she told him. "That would be best."

Helfred and four of his most venerables rode out with him, lest there be any unfortunate misunderstandings. He and his Court Ecclesiastica had hidden themselves and as many people as they could manage in the crypts and cellars beneath the great chapel. The church was badly damaged, but it could be repaired.

Rhian stayed behind in her capital, with Alasdair. Kingseat's people needed her. She was their queen.

Bemused, Dexterity squinted over the harbour and what remained of Mijak's warships, across the distant ocean to the empty, far horizon. A horizon that would see no more raiding warriors from Mijak.

We did it, Hettie. Not tidily, but we did it.

"You certainly did, my love. And I'm so proud of you, I could burst."

He turned his head to look at her, sitting beside him in the sunshine. Her gilt hair was soft and curling, she wore his favourite dress: the green one, with pretty pink ribbon on the bodice. She smelled of lavender and roses. To his surprise, she looked . . . *well*.

"Hello, Hettie," he said, smiling.

She smiled back, her brown eyes warm. "Hello, Dex."

"I wasn't sure I'd ever see you again."

"To be honest, Dex," she sighed, her smile fading, "neither was I."

"But all's well that ends well," he added, then showed her his glowing hands. "I don't suppose you'd care to make this go away? I've tried and I've tried, but . . ."

She bit her lip. "Let's talk about it later."

He didn't like the sound of that, but it was a beautiful day . . . and he'd had all the fighting he cared for in one lifetime. "If I ask how the rest of Ethrea fares, will you tell me? Do you know?"

She took one glowing hand in hers and held it. Her touch was cool and welcome. She felt real. Alive. "Of course I know. And yes, Dex. I'll tell you."

He sighed, contentment vanished. "So it's that bad, is it?"

"Dex . . ." Her fingers tightened around his hand. "My love, it's bad enough."

In the sunshine, by the harbour, breathing the tainted salt air, he listened as she told him what had befallen Ethrea's duchies. Edward dead. Rudi dead. Adric dead. And Ludo.

"*Ludo*?" he cried. "Oh, *Hettie*." It would break the king's heart and Rhian's. It broke his, and he wept. Everyone who knew him loved Alasdair's cousin.

But it wasn't only Ludo, and Rhian's faithful dukes. It was farmers and potters, shepherds and tailors, weavers and beekeepers, and chaplains and devouts. It was schoolmistresses and their pupils, physicks and their patients. Babies and grandfolk and soldiers and their kin.

"How many, Hettie?" he whispered. "How many are perished?"

"Not so many that Ethrea is perished with them," she said. "Ethrea will survive this. It will rise again."

Of course it would, with Rhian to lead it. God had chosen her after all.

As the sun dried his tears, he looked again at his wife. "So, my love. Are you my love? Are you in truth my dear, sweet Hettie?"

She broke the silence with a sigh. "Yes, I am, Dex. And then again . . . I'm not. I'm . . . the memory of Hettie. *Your* memory. Your love of her. I'm the bridge between this world, and the world that lies beyond."

He frowned, and gently pulled his hand free of her clasp. "But you told me you were Hettie, and I believed you. So that makes me a gullible fool."

"A fool?" she said. "*No.* You're the nails holding that bridge together, Dex. You're why the bridge is important."

He pulled a face. "Is that so? Well, right now I'm feeling like a nail that's been hammered one time too often."

"Oh, Dex," she said, and giggled. She was Hettie. She was Hettie.

"Can I ask another question, Hettie?"

"Of course," she said. "And I'll answer, if I can."

"Where does the power of the witch-men come from?"

Hettie smiled. "I think you know, Dex."

He thought he did too, but he was almost afraid to say it. If he was right, Helfred would have a fit. "So . . . God is God, no matter where you live? My miracles, everything Han and his people have done, the dreamers of Harbisland . . . it's all the same?"

"It comes from the same source, yes," said Hettie. "God is too big to be just the one thing, Dex. He's too big to belong only to Ethrea, or Keldrave, or Barbruish or the Tzhung. Wherever there is good in this world, there is God."

He shivered. "And wherever there's evil, there's Mijak?"

"In a way. Every light throws a shadow, my love."

He fell silent a little time, considering that. "You make it sound simple. But I suspect God is far more complicated than that. I suspect he's not even really a 'he'. Is he?"

Hettie smiled again, and kissed him. "Oh, Dex. You'll find out, one day."

"So . . . it is over, then?" he asked her. "The world's safe? The world's saved?"

"Yes, my love. It's safe and saved. At least . . . for now."

Horrified, he stared at her. "For now? What does *that* mean?"

"It means the world's always in danger, from greed and cruelty and misguided passions," she said. "That's why good men and women must be vigilant. That's why the fight against evil never ends."

He looked down at his hands. His persistent, glowing, lamplike hands. They were quite useful last night, he'd been his own torch. But now it was morning . . . and he wanted his old life back.

"Why do I have the feeling I'm not going to like this?"

"You're a good man, Dex. Zandakar's a good man

too . . . but he can't save Mijak on his own. And Mijak's in desperate need of saving. The dark blood power of its godspeakers is weakened, not broken. To make sure that happens, Mijak needs a new high godspeaker. Dex, it needs you."

"Me," he said blankly. "Oh, no, Hettie. I can't."

"Yes, you can. Dexterity Jones in Mijak will be a good thing for the world."

"And who thinks that, Hettie?" he retorted. "You or God?"

Another smile, sweet and teasing. "Yes."

Oh, Rollin's mercy. Go to Mijak? With Zandakar? Two men against an empire that had soaked in blood for centuries?

"Hettie, no. I *can't*."

She stared at him, so earnest. So stubborn. So like Hettie. "The world needs you, Dex. How can it stay safe if good men say, '*Hettie, no. I can't.*'"

"But – but—" He tugged at his beard. "Surely I'm not the only good man you can find!"

"No. But you're the best good man I know, my love."

Go to Mijak. Go to *Mijak*. Hettie was *mad*.

Except . . . he remembered Jatharuj. He remembered Garabatsas. If he closed his eyes he'd see poor Kingseat township, a stone's throw behind him. And everywhere the shadow of Mijak had fallen, there was a Jatharuj, a Garabatsas, a Kingseat to be healed.

I suppose Hettie's right. Zandakar can't do it without help. And he shouldn't be alone. He's lost his family, and I know how that feels. He's got the weight of an empire on his shoulders now, and no-one to help him bear it. I suppose I could go to Mijak . . . at least for a while.

"Oh dear, oh dear, Hettie," he moaned. "Ursa's going to kill me."

When Zandakar returned to Kingseat capital five days after killing Dmitrak, his chastened warhost at his heels, he was greeted by Dexterity.

"We have to talk," said the toymaker. "Are your warriors safe to leave in the garrison? What's left of it?"

He nodded. "*Zho.*"

"Then leave them, and we'll sit for a spell."

Numb, he did as Dexterity told him. The warhost – his warhost – obeyed without question. He wore the god's hammer. Why would they disobey?

He sat with Dexterity on a bench outside the partly ruined garrison. After five days, the air still reeked of smoke and blood. The city rang to the sound of hammers and voices. Already Rhian's people were rebuilding what his had destroyed.

Rhian. Rhian. Will you speak to me? Will I see you?

"*Wei,*" he said, when his friend stopped speaking. "You would not like Mijak, Dexterity. It is harsh. It is angry."

Dexterity shrugged. "It's not a question of what I'd like, Zandakar. Hettie's asked me to do this, and I said I would."

Tcha. Hettie. Was she so meddlesome when she was alive? He could not ask Dexterity that.

"You can't pretend you won't need help, Zandakar," said Dexterity, and held up his glowing hands. "And I think this will be as persuasive as any scorpion pectoral."

Yes. That was true. The people of Mijak, so long on the wrong path, had a blind belief in miracles. They could do worse than believe in this toy-maker . . .

He sighed, and nodded. "If you are sure, Dexterity. If you are sure . . ."

"I'm sure of Hettie," said Dexterity, tugging his beard. "And I'm sure of you, if you must know the truth. Like it or not, we've been chosen, Zandakar. And I suppose we'll have to see this through to the end, whatever that is. As Helfred would say, we just have to have faith."

Faith. It was an Ethrean word. Perhaps he could learn it.

If Dexterity comes with me, I will not be alone. Yuma is dead . . . Vortka is dead . . . Dimmi, aieee, Dimmi. Dimmi is dead. I have wept, I have wept, I have no more tears for them. I am Zandakar warlord, I do not wish to be alone.

"*Zho,*" he said, and looked at Dexterity. "You will come with me to Mijak . . . and we will have faith."

Six days after Zandakar killed Dmitrak, Mijak was ready to leave Ethrea forever.

Rhian stood in the dressing chamber of the town-house she and Alasdair had been given, staring at her reflection in the mirror. She still wore her huntsman leathers. The scars on her face were two thin, pink lines. The scars on her heart were . . . less well-healed.

So many dead. So much destruction. I know we're

*rebuilding, but . . . dear God. It will be a different
Ethrea. There'll be a new trading charter. New alliances. Nothing can be the same as it was.*

And Dexterity was leaving. She'd tried and Ursa
tried, but they couldn't dissuade him. *"Hettie said,"*
he said, and that was that.

"It's not so bad," he'd told her, with tears in his
eyes. *"You won't miss me really. You've got Helfred,
remember?"*

She'd laughed, and then she'd wept. So much
weeping in Ethrea, even though the war was won.

A swirling breeze. A gust of windchimes. In the
mirror, behind her, Han stepped out of the air. His
black hair had turned milk white. He looked older
than God.

"Han!" she said, spinning round. "Where have
you *been*? I've been worried *sick*, I thought—"

He nodded. "I nearly was."

"And Tzhung-tzhungchai? Your witch-men?"

"The empire is strong. Like your kingdom of
Ethrea, it will rise from these ashes. In time."

She felt her shoulders slump. "A long time, yes?"

"A very long time," Han said. "Perhaps a lifetime."
It was another loss. One she wasn't prepared for.

"Will I see you again?"

"The wind knows," said Tzhung's emperor. His
eyes narrowed in a smile.

A knock on the chamber's door. "Majesty, the carriage is here," said Dinsy's muffled voice.

"I have to go," she said, aching. "Zandakar and
his warriors are sailing."

Han nodded. "Then go, Rhian. And remember
Tzhung-tzhungchai."

A swirling breeze. A gust of windchimes. He stepped into the air.

"How could I forget it?" she asked the empty room.

Alasdair was waiting for her, down at the harbour. Helfred too. Ursa. And Dexterity, of course. Zandakar was waiting, his warriors obedient and silent in their ships. The preserved bodies of his family were safely stowed, too.

As well as the gauntlet, he wore Vortka's stone scorpion pectoral. A hideous thing, but she'd not told him that. He wore blue-striped horsehide leggings and a sleeveless jerkin. His blue hair was braided, thick with amulets and silver bells. They were all he had left of his father, his mother, his scarlet-haired brother.

They'd spoken privately once, since that night on the docks. He'd told her he did not blame her for Dmitrak. She wondered if he was lying. She never asked. She never would.

Now she took a deep breath and stepped forward to greet him. Her heart was thudding beneath her black leather doublet. *I'll never see him again. When he leaves, he will be gone.*

"Rhian *hushla*," he said, his fist to his chest. "The god sees you in its humble eye."

"Rollin's mercy on you, Prince of Mijak," she replied. "God's grace for a safe journey home."

She was proud of herself. Her voice was steady.

"Mijak . . . Mijak . . ." Zandakar's voice broke. His pale blue eyes were luminous. "Mijak is Ethrea *gajka, zho*?"

She nodded and pressed a fist to her heart. "*Zho.*

Mijak is *gajka*." She tried to smile. "I will dance my *hotas* every day, Zandakar. Rhian *hushla* will never forget."

"Godspeed, Zandakar," said Alasdair, most reserved. He mourned Ludo deeply, inconsolable still. He and Henrik would take his body home to Linfoi tomorrow. "Take good care of Mister Jones."

Zandakar nodded, and his braided hair chimed. "*Zho*, Alasdair king. Mister Jones is safe."

Dexterity. Rhian hugged him. She was the Queen of Ethrea and he was a toymaker. She hugged him, weeping, before the whole world. There was nothing more to say, and so they said nothing.

Ursa hugged him next, and pressed on him her old physick bag stuffed to bursting with potions and pills and God alone knew what.

"You're off to heathen lands, Jones," she said, tears streaking her wrinkled cheeks. "You're going to need all the help you can get."

Helfred prayed then, a heartfelt sermon of thanks and hope. Such a small group, they were. Such unlikely friends. Such a fantastical journey they'd taken together.

And then it was time for Mijak's warfleet to depart. Zandakar and Dexterity trod the gangplank to their ship. Helfred and Ursa withdrew, leaving Rhian and Alasdair alone. They watched in silence as Mijak's warships inched their way clear of their moorings, oars splashing the water, sails snapping in the breeze. All the scorpions on them were painted out.

Alasdair cleared his throat. "I thought . . . when the warships sailed . . ."

She stared at Zandakar, slowly retreating. "You

thought I'd sail with them? Oh, Alasdair. You're a fool."

Dexterity was waving. His hand gently glowed.

"A fool?" said Alasdair, waving back. "Perhaps. But you love him."

She sighed. "Yes, Alasdair. I love him. But I belong to you and Ethrea. Zandakar was never meant for me."

"I know that," he said. "But I wasn't sure if you did."

And he held her hand tightly until Mijak's warships had sailed from sight.

EPILOGUE

Seven and a half months later, Rhian stood in the grounds of battered Kingseat Castle, watching as the workmen at last began to rebuild her family's house. Despite Helfred's repeated urgings, she'd refused to have one new castle stone laid before the last dwelling and shop in Ethrea was repaired. Now her township was almost itself again . . .

Thank God, thank God. I want my home back.

A breeze from the bustling harbour ruffled her growing hair and swirled her blue linen gown about her legs. She preferred her huntsman's leathers but it was Alasdair's birthday. In honour of the occasion she'd worn a wretched dress.

She heard his familiar tread on the re-grown lawn and turned, surprised. He'd said he had work to do, and would leave her to gloat over the castle in private. Now he was here, and to her astonishment was huffing and puffing, carrying a large canvas-wrapped crate.

"Rollin's mercy – what kind of gift is that? And why would you bring it all the way up here?"

He grinned as he let the crate slide to the ground. "It's a gift that's travelled a considerable distance. And it's not mine. It's yours."

Hers? And then she felt her heart trip. Felt the salty air catch in her throat. Could it be? Could it be?

Alasdair's knife quickly cut through the stitchings on the canvas, which fell away to reveal a sturdy wooden box with a clasp. Heart beating even harder, she opened it.

Oh. Dexterity.

The box was full of toys. Carved and painted and beautiful toys. Striped horses, stringed falcons with intricate wings that could fly. Sandcats and lizards and monkeys and ibis.

So many toys, made with so much love.

"At last!" said Alasdair, peering over her shoulder. "I was beginning to think he'd been swallowed alive."

So was she, but she'd never said so. They didn't talk of Dexterity, in case it was bad luck.

"Is there a letter?" said Alasdair. "I want to know what he's been up to."

So did she, and looked through the box. "No," she said, disappointed.

"Oh well," said Alasdair. "I suppose paper's hard to come by, in Mijak. Perhaps next time."

One by one, she held every single toy, remembering her friend. Remembering the toymaker who'd saved a slave, saved a princess, saved that princess's kingdom . . . who'd travelled so far away to save an enemy from itself.

She laughed.

"What's so funny?" said Alasdair, puzzled.

"Nothing," she said, because it was either laugh or weep.

And then she stood with her husband, with her king, with Alasdair, and smiled at Kingseat harbour, that busy jewel in the sun. Smiled at the trading ships from Keldrave and Barbruish and Harbisland.

From haughty Tzhung-tzhungchai, whose emperor was Han.

"Come on," said Alasdair, his arm around her shoulders. "We'd best be on our way. It's Litany tonight, remember?"

Tcha. She'd forgotten. If she didn't go, Helfred would moan.

Alasdair bent to pick up the box of toys. Before he closed its lid, she snatched a cheeky-faced monkey . . .

. . . and rode to town in the gig with it warm in her hand.

ACKNOWLEDGEMENTS

Stephanie Smith, my editor. She has the patience of a saint and I tried it with this project. Stephanie, you're an angel. The god sees you in its eye.

Mark Timmony, who saved my bacon with his lovely maps.

The guys who make me look better than I am, my beta reader Usual Suspects – Mary, Elaine, Pete, Glenda and Mark.

extras

orbit

meet the author

KAREN MILLER was born in Vancouver, Canada, and moved to Australia with her family when she was two. She started writing stories while still in primary school, where she fell in love with speculative fiction after reading *The Lion, the Witch and the Wardrobe*. Over the years she has held down a wide variety of jobs, including horse stud groom in Buckingham, England. She is working on several new novels. Visit the official Karen Miller Web site at www.karenmiller.net.

introducing

If you enjoyed
HAMMER OF GOD,
look out for

THE ACCIDENTAL SORCERER

Book 1 of the Rogue Agent trilogy
by K. E. Mills

The entrance to Stuttley's Superior Staff factory, Ottosland's premier staff manufacturer, was guarded by a glass-fronted booth and blocked by a red and blue boom gate. Inside the booth slumped a dyspeptic-looking security guard, dressed in a rumpled green and orange Stuttley's uniform. It didn't suit him. An ash-tipped cigarette drooped from the corner of his mouth and the half-eaten sardine sandwich in his hand leaked tomato sauce onto the floor. He was reading a crumpled, food-stained copy of the previous day's *Ottosland Times*.

After several long moments of not being noticed,

Gerald fished out his official identification and pressed it flat to the window, right in front of the guard's face.

"Gerald Dunwoody. Department of Thaumaturgy. I'm here for a snap inspection."

The guard didn't look up. "Izzat right? Nobody tole me."

"Well, no," said Gerald, after another moment. "That's why we call it a 'snap inspection'. On account of it being a surprise."

Reluctantly the guard lifted his rheumy gaze. "Ha ha. Sir."

Gerald smiled around gritted teeth. *It's a job, it's a job, and I'm lucky to have it.* "I understand Stuttley's production foreman is a Mister Harold Stuttley?"

"That's right," said the guard. His attention drifted back to the paper. "He's the owner's cousin. Mr. Horace Stuttley's an old man now, don't hardly see him round here no more. Not since his little bit of trouble."

"Really? I'm sorry to hear it." The guard sniffed, inhaled on his cigarette and expelled the smoke in a disinterested cloud. Gerald resisted the urge to bang his head on the glass between them. "So where would I find Foreman Stuttley?"

"Search me," said the guard, shrugging. "On the factory floor, most like. They're doing a run of First Grade staffs today, if memory serves."

Gerald frowned. First Grade staffs were notoriously difficult to forge. Get the etheretic balances wrong in the split-second of alchemical transformation and what you were looking at afterwards, basically, was a huge smoking hole in the ground.

And if this guard was any indication, standards at Stuttley's had slipped of late. He rapped his knuckles on the glass.

"I wish to see Harold Stuttley right now, please," he said, briskly official. "According to Department records this operation hasn't returned its signed and witnessed safety statements for two months. I'm afraid that's a clear breach of regulations. There'll be no First Grade staffs rolling off the production line today or any other day unless I'm fully satisfied that all proper precautions and procedures have been observed."

Sighing, the guard put down his soggy sandwich, stubbed out his cigarette, wiped his hands on his trousers and stood. "All right, sir. If you say so."

There was a battered black telephone on the wall of the security booth. The guard dialled a four digit number, receiver pressed to his ear, and waited. Waited some more. Dragged his sleeve across his moist nose, still waiting, then hung up with an exclamation of disgust. "No answer. Nobody there to hear it, or the bloody thing's on the blink again. Take your pick."

"I'd rather see Harold Stuttley."

The guard heaved another lugubrious sigh. "Right you are, then. Follow me."

Gerald followed, starting to feel a little dyspeptic himself. Honestly, these people! What kind of a business were they running? Security phones that didn't work, essential paperwork that wasn't completed. Didn't they realise they were playing with fire? Even the plainest Third Grade staff was capable of inflicting damage if it wasn't handled carefully in the production phase. Complacency, that was the trouble. Clearly Harold Stuttley had let the prestige and success of his family's world-famous business go to his head. Just because every wizard who was any wizard and could afford the exorbitant price tag wouldn't be caught dead without his Stuttley Staff (patented, copyrighted and limited edition) as part of his sartorial ensemble was no excuse to let safety standards slide.

Bloody hell, he thought, mildly appalled. *Somebody save me. I'm thinking like a civil servant . . .*

The unenthusiastic security guard was leading him down a tree-lined driveway towards a distant high brick wall with a red door in it. The door's paint was cracked and peeling. Above and behind the wall could be seen the slate-grey factory roof, with its chimney stacks belching pale puce smoke. A flock of pigeons wheeling through the blue sky plunged into the coloured effluvium and abruptly turned bright green.

Damn. Obviously Stuttley's thaumaturgical filtering system was on the blink: code violation number two. The unharmed birds flapped away, fading back to white even as he watched, but that wasn't the point. All thaumaturgical by-products were subject to strict legislation. Temporary colour changes were one thing. But what if the next violation resulted in a temporal dislocation? Or a quantifiable matter redistribution? Or worse? There'd be hell to pay. People might get hurt. What was Stuttley's playing at?

Even as he wondered, he felt a shiver like the touch of a thousand spider feet skitter across his skin. The mellow morning was suddenly charged with menace, strobed with shadows.

"Did you feel that?" he asked the guard.

"They don't pay me to feel things, sir," the guard replied over his shoulder.

A sense of unease, like a tiny butterfly, fluttered in the pit of Gerald's stomach. He glanced up, but the sky was still blue and the sun was still shining and birds continued to warble in the trees.

"No. Of course they don't," he replied, and shook his head. It was nothing. Just his stupid over-active imagination getting out of hand again. If he could he'd have it surgically removed. It certainly hadn't done him any favours to date.

He glanced in passing at the nearest tree with its burden of trilling birds, but he couldn't see Reg amongst them. Of course he wouldn't, not if she didn't want to be seen. After yesterday morning's lively discussion about his apparent lack of ambition she'd taken herself off in a huff of ruffled feathers and a cloud of curses and he hadn't laid eyes on her since.

Not that he was worried. This wasn't the first hissy fit she'd thrown and it wouldn't be the last. She'd come back when it suited her. She always did. She just liked to make him squirm.

Well, he wasn't going to. Not this time. No, nor apologise either. For once in her ensorcelled life she was going to admit to being wrong, and that was that. He wasn't unambitious. He just knew his limitations.

Three paces ahead of him the guard stopped at the red door, unhooked a large brass key ring from his belt and fished through its assortment of keys.

Finding the one he wanted he stuck it into the lock, jiggled, swore, kicked the door twice, and turned the handle.

"There you are, sir," he said, pushing the door wide then standing back. "I'll let you find your own way round if it's all the same to you. Can't leave my booth unattended for too long. Somebody important might turn up." He smiled, revealing tobacco-yellow teeth.

Gerald looked at him. "Indeed. I'll be sure to mention your enthusiasm in my official report."

The guard did a double take at that, his smile vanishing. With a surly grunt he hooked his bundle of keys back on his belt then folded his arms, radiating offended impatience.

Immediately, Gerald felt guilty. *Oh lord. Now I'm acting like a civil servant!*

Not that there was anything wrong, as such, with public employment. Many fine people were civil servants. Indeed, without them the world would be in a sorry state, he was sure. In fact, the civil service was an honourable institution and he was lucky to be part of it. Only . . . it had never been his ambition to be a wizard who inspected the work of other wizards for Departmental regulation violations. His ambition was to be an inspect*ee*, not an inspect*or*. Once upon a time he'd thought that dream was reachable.

Now he was a probationary compliance officer in the Minor Infringement Bureau of the Department of Thaumaturgy . . . and dreams were things you had at night after you turned out the lights.

He nodded at the waiting guard. "Thank you."

"Certainly, sir," the guard said sourly.

Well, his day was certainly getting off to a fine start. *And we wonder why people don't like bureaucrats . . .*

With an apologetic smile at the guard he hefted his official briefcase, straightened his official tie, rearranged his expression into one of official rectitude and walked through the open doorway.

And only flinched a little bit as the guard locked the red door behind him.

It's a wizarding job, Gerald, and it's better than the alternative.

Hopefully, if he reminded himself often enough, he'd start to believe that soon.

The factory lay dead ahead, down the end of a short paved pathway. It was a tall, red brick building blinded by a lack of windows. Along its front wall were plastered a plethora of signs: *Danger! Thaumaturgical Emissions! Keep Out! No Admittance Without Permission! All Visitors Report To Security Before Proceeding*!

As he stood there, reading, one of the building's four doors opened and a young woman wearing a singed lab coat and an expression of mild alarm came out.

He approached her, waving. "Excuse me! Excuse me! Can I have a word?"

The young woman saw him, took in his briefcase and the crossed staffs on his tie and moaned. "Oh, no. You're from the Department, aren't you?"

He tried to reassure her with a smile. "Yes, as a matter of fact. Gerald Dunwoody. And you are?"

Looking hunted, she shrank into herself. "Holly," she muttered. "Holly Devree."

He'd been with the Department for a shade under six months and in all that time had been allowed into the field only four times, but he'd worked out by the end of his first site inspection that when it came to the poor sods just following company orders, sympathy earned him far more co-operation than threats. He sagged at the knees, let his shoulders droop and slid his voice into a more intimate, confiding tone.

"Well, Miss Devree – Holly – I can see you're feeling nervous. Please don't. All I need is for you to point me in the direction of your boss, Mr Harold Stuttley."

She cast a dark glance over her shoulder at the factory. "He's in there. And before you see him I want it understood that it's not my fault. It's not Eric's fault, either. Or Bob's. Or Lucius's. It's not any of our faults. We worked hard to get our transmogrifer's licence, okay? And it's not like we're earning squillions, either. The pay's rotten, if you must know. But Stuttley's – they're the best, aren't they?" Without warning, her thin, pale face crumpled. "At least, they used to be the best. When old Mr. Horace was in charge. But now . . ."

Fat tears trembled on the ends of her sandy-coloured eyelashes. Gerald fished a handkerchief out of his pocket and handed it over. "Yes? Now?"

Blotting her eyes she said, "Everything's different, isn't it? Mr Harold's gone and implemented all these 'cost-cutting' initiatives. Laid off half the Transmogrify team. But the workload hasn't halved, has it? Oh, no. And it's not just us he's laid off, either. He's sacked people in Etheretics, Design, Purchasing, Research and Development – there's not one team hasn't lost folk. Except Sales." Her snubby nose wrinkled in distaste. "Seven new sales reps he's taken on, and they're promising the world, and we're expected to deliver it – except we can't! We're working round the clock and we're still three weeks behind on orders and now Mr Harold's threatening to dock us if we don't catch up!"

"Oh my," he said, and patted her awkwardly on the shoulder. "I'm very sorry to hear this. But at least it explains why the last eight safety reports weren't completed."

"But they were," she whispered, busily strangling her borrowed handkerchief. "Lucius is the most senior technician we've got left, and I know he's been doing them. *And* handing them over to Mr Harold. I've seen it. But what *he's* doing with them I don't know."

Filing them in the nearest waste paper bin, more than likely. "I don't suppose your friend Lucius discussed the reports with you? Or showed them to you?"

Holly Devree's confiding manner shifted suddenly to a cagey caution. The handkerchief disappeared into her lab coat pocket. "Safety reports are confidential."

"Of course, of course," Gerald soothed. "I'm not implying any inappropriate behaviour. But Lucius didn't happen to leave one lying out on a table, did he, where any innocent passer-by might catch a glimpse?"

"I'm sorry," she said, edging away. "I'm on my tea break. We only get ten minutes. Mr Harold's inside if you want to see him. Please don't tell him we talked."

He watched her scuttle like a spooked rabbit, and sighed. Clearly there was more amiss at Stuttley's than a bit of overlooked paperwork. He should get back to the office and tell Mr Scunthorpe. As a probationary compliance officer his duties lay within very strict guidelines. There were other, more senior inspectors for this kind of trouble.

On the other hand, his supervisor was allergic to incomplete reports. Unconfirmed tales out of school from disgruntled employees and nebulous sensations of misgiving from probationary compliance officers bore no resemblance to cold, hard facts. And Mr Scunthorpe was as married to cold, hard facts as he was to Mrs Scunthorpe. More, if Mr Scunthorpe's marital mutterings were anything to go by.

Turning, Gerald stared at the blank-faced factory. He could still feel his inexplicable unease simmering away beneath the surface of his mind. Whatever it was trying to tell him, the news wasn't good. But that wasn't enough. He had to find out exactly *what* had tickled his instincts. And he did have a legitimate place to start, after all: the noncompletion of mandatory safety statements. The infraction was enough to get his foot across the factory threshold. After that, well, it was just a case of following his intuition.

He resolutely ignored the whisper in the back of his mind that said, *Remember what happened the last time you followed your intuition?*

"Oh, bugger off!" he told it, and marched into the fray.

Look out for

KAREN MILLER'S

next novel,

a breathtaking sequel to the

Kingmaker, Kingbreaker series.

THE PRODIGAL MAGE

BOOK ONE OF THE FISHERMAN'S CHILDREN

Some seventeen years have passed since the last great Mage War. It has been a time of great change. In the immediate aftermath of the conflict, one small exploratory expedition set out to cross the mountains, its aim being to discover who lived on the other side. But contact was lost with those brave folk—and they never returned.

Asher, the fisherman's son who once saved a kingdom, now finds his own family torn apart by the decision to cross the mountains or remain part of their insular society. And once again he will find himself in the midst of an epic struggle.

Publication Date: August 10, 2009

"He's supposed to be on our side!" Davis yelled.

Suddenly, a burst of fire came from behind them. Bolan spun around and saw Patel charging toward them, spraying bullets.

"Take her," Bolan said, thrusting the struggling Lasi into Davis's hands while he carefully aimed his rifle at the charging Pakistani soldier. Whether it was a temporary flash of insanity, an indication of his hidden hostility toward the women's rights group or just frustration at a mission gone fugazi, there was no doubt that Patel had murderous intentions. Bolan needed a clean shot to take the man temporarily out of the game.

He was still drawing a bead when a burst of fire from behind him chopped Patel down as he ran. He stumbled as the bullets exploded across his chest, and he pitched forward as his momentum carried him beyond his failing legs.

Bolan swung around, ready to return fire. Two women, poorly concealed, with their rifles in plain view. He didn't want to take out PWLA members, but they were leaving him little choice.

Bolan took aim. He could only assume they were about to fire again. Davis's voice cut through everything and made him stop short as his finger tensed on the trigger.

"Colonel, no—that's Shazana Yasmin."

MACK BOLAN ®
The Executioner

THE EXECUTIONER

DON PENDLETON'S

SAVAGE DEADLOCK

A GOLD EAGLE BOOK FROM

W❂RLDWIDE.

TORONTO • NEW YORK • LONDON
AMSTERDAM • PARIS • SYDNEY • HAMBURG
STOCKHOLM • ATHENS • TOKYO • MILAN
MADRID • WARSAW • BUDAPEST • AUCKLAND

Recycling programs
for this product may
not exist in your area.

First edition January 2015

ISBN-13: 978-0-373-64434-6

Special thanks and acknowledgment to
Andy Boot for his contribution to this work.

Savage Deadlock

Those who deny freedom to others deserve it not for themselves.

> —Abraham Lincoln,
> 1809–1865

Every person, man or woman, has the right to choose their path. I will join any fight to take down the oppressors of this world.

> —Mack Bolan

THE
MACK BOLAN
LEGEND

Nothing less than a war could have fashioned the destiny of the man called Mack Bolan. Bolan earned the Executioner title in the jungle hell of Vietnam.

But this soldier also wore another name—Sergeant Mercy. He was so tagged because of the compassion he showed to wounded comrades-in-arms and Vietnamese civilians.

Mack Bolan's second tour of duty ended prematurely when he was given emergency leave to return home and bury his family, victims of the Mob. Then he declared a one-man war against the Mafia.

He confronted the Families head-on from coast to coast, and soon a hope of victory began to appear. But Bolan had broken society's every rule. That same society started gunning for this elusive warrior—to no avail.

So Bolan was offered amnesty to work within the system against terrorism. This time, as an employee of Uncle Sam, Bolan became Colonel John Phoenix. With a command center at Stony Man Farm in Virginia, he and his new allies—Able Team and Phoenix Force—waged relentless war on a new adversary: the KGB.

But when his one true love, April Rose, died at the hands of the Soviet terror machine, Bolan severed all ties with Establishment authority.

Now, after a lengthy lone-wolf struggle and much soul-searching, the Executioner has agreed to enter an "arm's-length" alliance with his government once more, reserving the right to pursue personal missions in his Everlasting War.

1

Shazana Yasmin looked out over the river as the evening faded into dusk. She loved coming back here to where her family had settled after the city life of Quetta had ceased to have any appeal. Her father was attached to the mountainous regions of Balochistan, Pakistan, close to the borders with Afghanistan and Iran, and had stubbornly refused to move back to civilization, even though the hilly terrain was now dangerous to pass at times, as bandits and revolutionaries prowled the land.

Despite this, she still saw it as a tranquil haven away from the city and the academic life that had enveloped her, and she liked to travel here when she could. Since her mother had passed away, her father had become more reclusive and curmudgeonly, allowing his sons to run the businesses that had bought them this palatial villa, nestled into the hills and overlooking the peacefully flowing river.

As the dusk closed, so the insects became bolder, and their buzzing grew louder in her ears. Idly, she swatted them away, her thoughts far from the peace of the countryside.

"Malaria, fever of some kind if they bite…then maybe hospitalization, which isn't easy in the back end of beyond. I don't know, maybe by the time they get you there, you'll be dead. And think what a loss to humanity that would be. It doesn't really bear thinking about."

"Go boil your head," she answered without turning around.

"That's a fine way for a nicely brought up girl to speak to a man. Especially one who is her elder," murmured her brother, who now settled himself on the veranda railing beside her, resting his arms so that he could lean out over the rocks below. "It's a long way down," he added.

"Then you should make sure that you balance yourself on those ape arms of yours," she replied, staring at his thick, hairy wrists. "I don't know how you came to look like that, Mahmood. Dad is totally bald, and Mom—"

"Was as delicate and beautiful as you are, Shaz," he answered. "Not as prone to answering back and being disrespectful, but I blame that on your inevitable Westernization."

Her mouth fell open, and she prepared to abuse her brother even further before catching the spark of humor in his eyes and realizing she was being had.

"Funny…you're a very funny man," she said with a slow nod. "Especially as you spend eight months of the year in Canada rather than Lahore, and you have even more of an accent than I do."

Mahmood Yasmin shrugged. "I like the West. It is what it is. Here…' He paused. "Here there is no knowing. This is a country in flux, Shaz, and if Dad had any sense he'd sell up this place and join me in Toronto. It won't be safe for him, soon. There's a radicalism in the air that has no place for the likes of him. It has no time for the pragmatic man who seeks to make the best for his children, bending to the times in which he lives. It knows only its own unyielding standards."

"Dad's not going to leave. It took him long enough to earn the money to build this place. All his memories of Mom are here. He's not going to give them up easily."

"He may not have the choice. If he doesn't give it up, then it'll be snatched from him. This is a new dark age, Shaz, and he won't be safe. Neither will you. You shouldn't come back here anymore."

"Why not? You do," she posited.

Her brother gazed out over the river. "I have to. Someone has to look out for the old man. See that?" He indicated distant, winking lights downriver. "That's the nearest villa. It's got to be about twenty kilometers, right? And not on an easy road. Things could happen out here and not be discovered for a long time."

Yasmin shivered. "You're scaring me."

"Good, I should be," he answered bluntly. "Listen…' He gestured her to silence, and for some time they stood listening to the quiet of the evening. The river ran beneath them, and they could hear their father in the house behind them, cooking dinner and mumbling to himself. The buzz of insects was a steady hum. Yasmin studied her brother with bemusement. He indicated that she listen harder.

In the far distance, she could hear the crack of rifle fire.

Mahmood nodded as he saw that she had registered the sound. "It's there all the time, now. It's so much a part of the background that you don't notice it unless you actually stop and listen hard."

"But it's miles away," she said dismissively.

"Is it? Sound travels across these hills, I know. It's clear air. But even so, that means *all* sound. The gunfire is clear over a lot of other things. And there's more of it every day. I won't be happy until you're out of here, Shaz. I don't just mean this region, I mean the whole damned country. You shouldn't have left MIT."

She shook her head sadly. "I would have thought you understood. This is my country, and I love it. It's not perfect, I'll grant you that, though I couldn't say the U.S. is, either. Balochistan gave me a good education—"

"It didn't give it to you, Shaz. You earned it. You earned it because you're a genius."

"Hardly." She shrugged. "Though if you want to think that and treat me like a princess, then I'll let you. Seriously, Mahmood, I really feel like I could make a difference here, help drag this land into the twenty-first century and put it up there with other nations."

He snorted with derision. "It's being dragged into the twenty-first century all right, but not in the way you're hoping. This world is undergoing a polarized split, and I'm not sure Pakistan is going to be on the right side of that."

"Then we have to fight to make sure that it is," she said, her calm tone laced with steel. "It's up to us to make sure that it falls the right way."

"Now you really do sound like Mom," he said with a smile. "I'll still be happier when you're as far from the border as you can get, though."

They turned and went in, hearing their father's call to dinner. Over the meal, neither sibling mentioned their discussion, although Yasmin was sure she could still hear the distant gunfire, even as she settled down for the night.

It lulled her to sleep, but not for long.

YASMIN WAS DREAMING of MIT again. America had been good to her, and she had enjoyed her time there. Often, these days, she found that her dream world was populated by the faces and places of those days. Coming home to bring her specialist skills to the Pakistan authorities had been her aim, but it had soured as the bureaucracy and outmoded attitudes of those around her had taken their toll. Worse still had been the way that many had looked at her. In their eyes, despite the results she achieved, she was still "just" a woman.

If this country was truly to drag itself into the

twenty-first century, then there was still a long way to go. It was inevitable that shortcuts would have to be taken.

A sudden noise jolted her out of her dream world, her heart thumping and her mouth dry. She lay there in the darkness, trying to stop her body from shaking as the adrenaline pumped through her veins.

The door to her bedroom was pushed open, and by the light from the hallway outside she could see a small figure, face swathed in scarves, standing in the doorway. The figure was black against the light, though she could clearly see the outline of an assault rifle held at a downward angle. The fear came back up in her throat, like bile.

Was this an enemy?

It was only when the figure spoke in feminine tones that she felt herself relax.

"It's time. Hurry," the figure said.

As she withdrew into the hallway, Yasmin rose and began to dress quickly. She already had a bag packed, and within a couple of minutes she was ready to go. As she stepped into the hallway, the other woman beckoned her toward the large living room of the villa. Yasmin could see that there were four other women there, all of them armed. With rising alarm, she realized she could not see or hear her father or brother.

"You said nothing would happen to them, just that it would be made to look like there had been a break-in," she began, the anger in her voice tempered by an edge of fear. She quickened her pace and almost fainted with relief when she entered the room and saw her father and brother seated side by side on a long sofa, clutching teacups and looking bemused (her brother) and almost incandescently angry (her father).

"Shazana, what is this?" he began as he saw her and rose to his feet. "Why have these women come into my house with guns, and why are they asking for you?"

Despite herself, Yasmin was amused. Even faced with weapons, her father showed no fear—he couldn't believe that mere women would harm him. In this instance he was correct, but that was purely incidental.

"Sit down, Dad, or someone might get nervous and fire one of these things," she said, indicating the women's rifles.

"Sit down? Why should I sit down in my own home just because some little girl waves a gun in my face and wants to take my daughter away?" her father continued. Still, he allowed his son to gently grasp his arm and pull him down.

"Dad, I'm not being taken anywhere that I don't want to go," she said softly. "You have to believe me when I say that."

Her father appeared confused, staring at the women with guns and then at his daughter. Mahmood, on the other hand, seemed to understand, even if his words were disapproving.

"So this is what you meant when you said you wanted to make a difference? To go and join a group of rebels?"

"There are rebels and there are rebels, Mahmood," Yasmin said gently. "You said it yourself—it's become a polarized world. If we want Pakistan to go one way rather than the other, then we have to try to make that difference ourselves."

"But why this?" he asked her. "Why the charade? Why not just go?"

"And have people ask you questions that you cannot answer? Have them detain you and maybe do more than ask? I don't want that to happen. What I know would push the government—and others—to take drastic actions. This way, it looks like I was taken against my will. How could you know anything if that was the case? It's the best way I can think of to keep you and Dad safe. Now let me go, and tell anyone who comes calling about the guns. They always believe you if you're at the point of a gun. It's the only language they can understand…"

2

"The National Command Authority will not be happy with this, General. Fortunately, it will not be my ass in a sling when they find out. That dubious pleasure will fall to you."

Major Usman Malik smiled, and General Tariq Sandila could see the betel stains on his teeth. In this day and age, chewing betel was a peasant throwback, and it made Sandila dislike the major even more. He looked around the sparse office, trying to focus on anything other than the disgusting sight of his superior's teeth. Although Sandila technically outranked Malik, the General had been fast-tracked to his position, given his rank for his specialist credentials rather than military achievements. For now, Malik was in charge. They were in the old government building in Lahore, which dated back to the colonial era and was used mostly as a repository for old files that predated computerization. The civil servants who prowled its corridors seemed to be of a similar vintage, and all in all Sandila felt horribly out of place. Maybe that was why Malik had chosen this as his temporary headquarters while the investigation was underway. It would make sense. The thought of Malik in black and white like some old newsreel from the days of Nehru cheered Sandila in an oblique manner.

Emboldened, he spoke freely: "Major, the expression 'shoot the messenger' is a little outdated these days, surely? My superiors—your superiors—if they followed such a line would surely be more likely to blame the man heading the investigation. I'm just your leg man."

The sly smile on Malik's face froze and died. He and Sandila had been at loggerheads since the general had joined the team a few weeks before. Seconded because of his experience with the nuclear program and his PhD in physics, Sandila was one of the new breed of army officers who looked at technology rather than manpower. Malik had been in military intelligence all his career, and came from the days of the ruling generals, when the fact that such a small country had the eighth largest military force in the world counted for something. In Malik's younger days, the army ruled with an iron fist, and he still expected such control.

Sandila, on the other hand, found the phrase *army intelligence* an oxymoron, and thought of Malik as the personification of that philosophy. An impression that had only been reinforced when he realized what had been going on: his forceful statement of such had cemented the animosity between the two men.

Malik rotated the laptop screen so that it faced Sandila. It was a purely dramatic move, as it was Sandila's own report that the major was showing him. Malik said, "You expect me to present this? Saying that we've been negligent? That women—women, dammit—are behind this? Have you any idea what kind of an uproar this will cause in the government?"

Sandila shrugged. "There may well be an uproar, but the fact is that it has happened."

"You have no proof," Malik spluttered. "It's all supposition."

Sandila chose his words carefully. He spoke as though explaining something simple to a child, which was—he felt—exactly what the major was acting like.

"You asked me to investigate the disappearance of Dr. Yasmin. Obviously, I was aware of her reputation, and I had already read a couple of the papers she prepared when she was at MIT. Her reputation was second to none, and it is to her credit that she returned to our country and turned her back on what could have been a very lucrative career in America—"

"She is a woman." Malik gestured dismissively. "There is no credit. She did only what she should."

Sandila held his tongue and continued, trying to ignore the words of his superior. "Dr. Yasmin, in returning to her homeland, declared her desire to be part of our nuclear program and so help us not merely in the buildup of tactical armaments, but also to provide our nation with the power it needs to progress."

"Why are you telling me this?" Malik waved an irritated hand at Sandila. "I do not care for her motives, only for the thugs who kidnapped her. Instead I get this gibberish about women and her going of her own will. This despite the evidence of her father and brother who—let me remind you—are well-respected men who have contributed heavily to the campaign coffers of our prime minister."

"And of course that is why we should ignore the fact that they are lying," Sandila snapped.

"Why would they lie?" Malik's voice rose almost to a screech.

Sandila took a deep breath and looked around the room, composing himself. He wondered how many such outbursts of idiocy these buff-painted walls had absorbed over the decades. Too many, he surmised.

"They are lying to protect themselves, and also to protect Dr. Yasmin. I have been to the research institute, and I have also studied the files and the security system. There is no doubt that for some time now someone has been copying every research report and experiment. The IP address for this copying process was disguised, but unfortunately Dr. Yasmin is not the genius with computers that she is with nuclear fission. The trail leads back to both her login PC and also to her personal devices. She's been taking copies. Why?

"Further, there were emails between herself and a woman who is known to be part of the political movement for the education and emancipation of women. This should be no surprise. After all, with her education and time spent in the West, it was inevitable that she would believe in an equality for which, it must be said, Pakistan lags behind. I examined the evidence from her father and brother and also the photographs and forensics collected in their villa." Sandila sighed heavily. "I have to say, Major, that if that represents the level of competence usually shown by your men, then you need to seriously think about weeding some of them out."

Malik interrupted him by banging his fist on the desk, making the laptop vibrate.

"You watch your mouth, Sandila. Do you dare to say that I do not know how to run my own department?"

Sandila looked at him stonily. "If it comes to that, then, yes, I do say that, Major. Their work is shoddy. There is no physical evidence of the kind of attack and forced entry that they say took place. There is some evidence to suggest that a group of people came to the villa and were inside…but forced their way in? I don't think so. Possibly uninvited, but certainly not unexpected by at least one person present…I would venture that this was Dr. Yasmin. There's no indication that there was any struggle on her removal, and indeed some of her belongings are missing in a manner that suggests she had time to pack."

Malik was seething. "Are you suggesting that men of the caliber of her father and brother colluded in this event?"

"No. But I am suggesting that they are covering for her. I do believe that they didn't know her plans in advance, but that they're in a position where anything they say would suggest collusion. I've watched the interviews. These are not comfortable men, Major. As for those who came for Dr. Yasmin being women—well, I have no hard proof. But I can't see her going willingly with a Taliban party, as your men implied. Come to that, I can't see the Taliban wishing to work with a woman who presumes to take a man's role," he added with a wry grin.

Malik threw up his hands. "But if this stupid woman has gone of her own free will, then how can we find her without causing national outrage? At least we've been able to keep this under wraps until now. If we pursue her and it turns out she's part of some ridiculous women's group…it will be like that little girl who was taken to England. We will look stupid."

Sandila considered the case to which Malik referred. A young girl had been shot by the Taliban for daring to demand an education for herself and other young girls. Her near-death caused an international storm and showed the regime and their reaction in a poor light. Rightly so, in the general's view. However, in this instance he agreed with the major, if for different reasons.

"You're right that it would cause a storm of publicity worldwide. That would be a bad thing. But my reasons for feeling that way differ from yours. There's something I couldn't put in the report."

Malik kissed his teeth. "*Now* you have something else? All conclusions should be put in writing so that they can be circulated to the relevant offices. There is a procedure—"

"Major," Sandila interrupted with urgency. "This information is so sensitive that it can only be shared with a few people at this stage, and by word of mouth only."

Malik hesitated, then indicated that Sandila continue.

"As part of my investigation," the general said in a low voice, "I was at the laboratory where Dr. Yasmin conducted practical experiments. I made an inventory of the fissionable materials there. It was, I presumed, routine. Sadly not—there was some material missing. Only a flask, but that is enough."

"Some mistake in the initial inventory, perhaps," Malik murmured, sweating as the import of the general's words hit him.

Sandila shook his head. "I had hoped so, too, but I had to be sure. I got your local men to go back to the villa and sweep it with a Geiger counter. There were anomalous readings…"

"She stole it?" Malik whispered.

"She certainly had the flask with her at some point. And it damn well isn't there now. I had your boys take the villa to pieces. The father may well complain—"

Malik brushed that aside. "He can do what he likes, the lying bastard. There can be no protection or deference for him now. No politician will cover his ass, no matter how much money he has. Do you know what this means?"

"Of course I know what it means," the general

snapped. "That's what I'm telling you. Shazana Yasmin went of her own free will, most likely to join up with a women's group. There is only one I know of with any real strength in numbers and a desire to fight—the Pakistan Women's Liberation Army. If they have her, and they also have some fissionable materials, then they have one hell of a bargaining tool to get whatever they demand."

The major swore heavily. "It's worse than that. If they're still in Balochistan—"

"There have been no sightings to suggest anything else—"

"Then you realize they're surrounded by several threats? There are any number of Islamist cells, Taliban units, Baloch rebels and other guerrilla forces in those hills. Even if they aren't looking for those bloody women, chances are they'll fall over them. And if that happens..."

"Then you see why this has to cause uproar in the government," Sandila said softly. "They need to get behind us and act now. Because if any of those groups find Dr. Yasmin before we do, then they get that flask...."

FOR TWO WEEKS, Shazana Yasmin had been adjusting to life as a fugitive freedom fighter—at least, that was how she saw herself. The government of her country had let her down, and she was certain that she had the opportunity to put that right.

It was just that at the moment, it didn't quite feel

that way. The Pakistan Women's Liberation Army, the PWLA, had its camp in the foothills of the mountains that dotted the Balochistan region. The hills had always been a harsh environment, but they also afforded shelter and sanctuary to those who endured the hardships to live there. Since she was a child and her father had first retreated to this region, Yasmin had grown up on the stories of the men who had defied the British Empire for so long in this rocky terrain.

She rose and washed herself, on the thirteenth morning since her supposed capture, in the clear stream that burbled between the rocks. Once clean, she stood and stretched her aching back while breathing deeply of the clean morning air.

Being a revolutionary and fighting for the rights of an oppressed minority was the kind of thing that had been romanticized in the books she had read as a student in the U.S.A. She had read about Berkeley, about student protest, about the idea that small but determined groups across the globe had been able to effect real change by going underground and using their wits and stealth to take on the monolith of government.

What those books had never described was the mind-numbing tedium of having nothing to do each day because "the time wasn't right," sitting around in camp and discussing tactics and plans and never coming to any real solution about a course of action. Bickering about rotis to cook and divvy up. Hunting and gathering fresh food to augment the supplies that had to be eked out until it was safe to make the next trip to the nearest town or village. Routine patrols in the hills that revealed nothing but goats and the odd, bewildered herdsman, and the ever-present sound of gunfire in the distance. Campfires on freezing cold nights and discussions of the future and how the country would change when emancipation was more than just a dream. The rhetoric usually kept Yasmin warm until she crawled into her tent, realizing that she had nothing in the cold of night but the certain knowledge that yet another day had passed with no actual progress.

All the while, lurking at the back of all this, like the gunfire that crackled at the edges of consciousness, there was the fear that a phalanx of militants would chance on their location. The PWLA was new, it was inexperienced and mostly made up of women like Yasmin who were from a relatively privileged and moneyed background, whose only experience of the arms they carried was in target practice. Those few who had run from their homes and fought fundamentalists and sometimes their own families in the bid to escape oppression had some familiarity with violence, and they tried to teach the others. But until the time came, no one in the camp knew how she would react.

It was terrifying if Yasmin stopped to think too hard about it. For the most part she tried to avoid such a train of thought. Still, on mornings like this it was hard to avoid. Soon the moment of decision would come.

Would she be found wanting? Would any of them be found wanting?

She made her way back to the main section of the camp, exchanging a few words on the way. When she reached her tent, she checked the contents of her back-pack. There, nestled among the few belongings she'd bought with her, was the sealed and insulated flask.

She took it out and sat looking at it, trying to guess what had happened since she'd left home. Her father and brother would have been given a tough time by the security service, but she figured they could ride it out. There had been no official communiqué from the PWLA to the government as yet, but it wouldn't take too much for any half-intelligent security man to work out what was going on. She was sure her disap-pearance would be investigated, and the information she had gathered would eventually be noted. She had been careful, but she was no industrial spy. And then it would be only a short leap to the discovery that this flask was also missing.

With the security of the Pakistan nuclear program breached, she knew that there would be a panic in the corridors of power. This could only be good for her cause. She had little regard for the average intelligence of the political mind, and less so for the average military mind. First they would yell for revenge and mindless action. It was only after they had passed the initial flush of testosterone and adrenaline that they would start to think about what they could really do....

That was when the negotiations would begin.
The fear of biting reality gnawed at her gut.
It couldn't come soon enough.

3

The early morning wind was biting as it swept along the National Mall. Mack Bolan, aka the Executioner, was running through the green. He felt sharp and awake, ready for Brognola's brief about the current situation—whatever it was.

He soon had his chance. The big Fed was sitting at a bench they often used for outside meetings. Brognola was looking down, lost in thought, but the sound of the soldier's pounding footsteps approaching caught his attention. He had two coffees, and as Bolan came to a halt, stretched and then sat down beside him, Brognola handed one over without a word.

Bolan sipped the warm liquid. "Whatever's up, it must be serious to drag you out this time of the morning."

Brognola stared out at the monuments for a moment before speaking. "Yes, something has come up. It's a delicate one."

Bolan chuckled. "It always is, Hal. Always…"

The big Fed rose to his feet and indicated that Bolan

follow him. The two men walked along the Mall in silence. Taking his cue from Brognola, Bolan refrained from questions and took in the memorials and statues that they passed on their route. For each example of heroism and achievement, he knew there were hundreds that remained unremarked and unnoticed. Maybe it was better that way. Certainly there were times when it was better that the people had no idea of how close to disaster they had come.

He didn't bother to speculate on what Brognola had lined up for him. A clear mind was always the most receptive.

Even so, he was a little surprised to see two men in Pakistani Armed Forces regalia seated in uncomfortable silence in the private room Brognola had rented in a Georgetown restaurant. From their body language, it was apparent that neither was pleased to be there and that they had a frosty relationship with each other. Hal introduced the older, bulkier man as Major Usman Malik of Pakistan Military Intelligence, and the younger as General Tariq Sandila. Bolan was interested to learn that the higher-ranking officer was younger than the major, and was clearly his subordinate. Neither man seemed happy about the inversion of ranks, and Bolan surmised that that might color whatever was about to come next.

Brognola took his seat. Malik leaned forward.

"Excuse me, Mr. Brognola, but you have not introduced me to your associate." He bristled. "This is a most delicate matter, and I would like to know just who is included in the information chain."

Bolan noticed the ghost of a smile and the slightest indication of a head shake from the younger man.

"Major," Hal began carefully, "my colleague is operative...consultant. As such, discretion and security are paramount. It would be best if you knew as little as possible about the way we work. Just be assured that we do. After all, it was your National Command Authority who authorized your approach. Now what do you say we stop quibbling and get down to what's important."

"Very well. Sandila will brief you," Malik snapped with barely disguised irritation. Bolan noted the dismissive way he had referred to the general.

Sandila seemed to be used to this. Ignoring the slight, he powered up the tablet on his lap and ran through his report briskly and efficiently, relaying the salient points.

Brognola was obviously familiar with this report, but Bolan listened attentively. He spoke only when Sandila had finished.

"Surely this is an internal matter?" he asked Brognola. "I thought it was policy not to interfere unless there were U.S. nationals endangered, or the interests of the administration were compromised."

"That is the case," Brognola answered smoothly. "And that is also the qualification. Shazana Yasmin became a naturalized U.S. citizen during her time studying at MIT. Her decision to return to Pakistan and work for her homeland doesn't change this."

Bolan's eyebrow quirked. The scientist was obviously fiercely patriotic to Pakistan, and seeking naturalization in the U.S. had most likely been a matter of convenience.

He directed his next questions to Sandila. "General, do you have any reason to suspect that there may be a religious or ideological element to this?"

The younger of the Pakistani men smiled indulgently. "I know you in the West think that we are a hotbed of Islamic fundamentalism, but I think your own homeland security would have identified Dr. Yasmin as a potential threat if she were. I'm sure her defection isn't based on religion. It is, however, ideological. And this is where I am concerned. Not because the PWLA is a strategic threat, but because its members are inexperienced. They are not, from what we know, trained fighters. Their vulnerability makes them dangerous."

Bolan could see his point. These freedom fighters were fuelled by ideology, but they had no preparation for their chosen path, hiding out in a region that was rife with hardened Taliban fighters and other militant groups. Plus, they possessed both fissionable material and the knowledge to make it work. More than that, they were women. Their gender alone would enrage their opponents.

"Then our task is to locate Yasmin and bring her in, along with the fissionable material. How much, and how volatile?"

"A small flask, no larger than that coffee there,"

Sandila replied, pointing to the large cup Brognola had carried in from the Mall. "As for its safety—well, that depends on the kind of treatment it receives in the wilds. A laboratory flask is lined and secure, designed to withstand a certain amount of punishment. But in the hands of someone who doesn't really know what they're doing?" He shrugged. "It could be a real problem. Prolonged exposure would have the inevitable effect."

Bolan nodded in understanding. "Do you have any way to locate her? Does she have a cell?"

Sandila grinned. "She took her phone. At least, it wasn't at the villa. But out there, you have no chance of getting a signal. If it had been that easy, I would have gone and gotten her myself a week ago. No, this requires a more specialized approach."

Bolan acknowledged the implied compliment. "What about manpower? Will I be expected to work alone or will there be backup?"

Sandila was about to speak when Malik cut in. "You will have a detachment of men from the Special Service Wing. They have taken part in joint exercises with both your forces and the Chinese. They are our crack troops. You will be given command of six men who know the Balochistan region and the enemy forces who roam across it. They will add their specialist knowledge to yours."

"That's good," Bolan commented, noting the look that Sandila cast at both him and Malik. "General, I would like to go over your report with you after this meeting, if I may. My associate here—" he indicated Brognola "—will need to finalize details with you, Major. Perhaps you could do this while General Sandila and I go over the report. It would save time if we attend to the smaller details while you deal with the important liaison."

He caught Brognola's glance from the corner of his eye. Brognola nodded slightly at Bolan and rose to his feet, gesturing to Malik. "Major, if you would come with me, then we can speak to the Foreign Affairs directorate about how this is handled. By the way, have you ever seen the Oval Office?"

"I have never had the opportunity to visit Washington before," Malik said with a smug smile as he deferred to Brognola and allowed himself to be ushered from the room. Bolan could hear Brognola soft-soaping him as the door closed behind them. He turned to Sandila.

"Tell me, General, how come he's your superior officer even though you outrank him?"

"Pakistan, like India, still has many hangovers from the days of Empire," Sandila replied. "It will take a few more generations until that has been eradicated. You have to understand, the major is not a bad or stupid man per se. It's just that he comes from an older tradition and believes fast-tracked officers who are seconded because of specialist criteria—even if they have a nominal superiority—are not to be trusted."

"Your specialty?" Bolan queried.

"Physics. It was Dr. Yasmin's position, as much as

her gender, that was of importance. There is something I feel I must emphasize, Mister—" He paused.

"Stone. Colonel Stone," he added for emphasis.

"Colonel, my point, for what it is worth, is this—the push for women's emancipation is growing, and as it does, it stirs up feelings that had previously remained latent. The major is a strong example of this phenomenon. He can't believe that a woman could take this action, despite the fact that next to her intellect, he is a child." The general chuckled. "His hostility is restricted to mere words. Out in the field, when faced with women with guns, no matter what their orders, I could not say for certain how the attitudes of the average Pakistani man would reveal themselves. If the attitudes of the men I encountered during my investigation at the Yasmin villa were anything to go by…" He let the words hang in the air.

Bolan considered this. "I think you may well have a point, General. I'll take note of it, even if your major would not. With that in mind, take me through your report again, only this time leave in the things that had to remain unsaid. Tell me everything you know concerning the search area."

Sandila assented, looking relieved. He brought up the report on his tablet, and then added topographical maps of the region. "You want full details? I hope you have plenty of time, and that your chief can keep Major Malik occupied…."

Bolan grinned as he thought of Brognola having to

keep the major amused. "Don't worry, General. He's used to difficult customers."

Brognola proved the worth of this statement, as he kept Malik away from the restaurant for two and a half hours while Bolan went over the report carefully, closely questioning Sandila about every point raised. The general answered with candor and provided insight that Bolan stored away for future use. Then they turned to the topographical map. Sandila ran him through the general terrain and the known movements of both the militant cells that roamed the hills and the PWLA. He outlined possible routes of progress and points of encampment, and Bolan took mental note and ensured that the general added notation to a copy of the file that he would send to the soldier's smartphone.

"What might help you, Mr. Stone, you are welcome to," Sandila said when they were finished. "Yet it would benefit no one if Major Malik had access to these extra notes. He would not betray his country, but there are those around him who would not necessarily see the eradication of Dr. Yasmin as a betrayal."

"I understand, General," Bolan said. "Believe me, it's not just your nation that has these issues."

By the time Brognola returned with Malik, the two men in the private room were exchanging small talk. Malik, seeing this, grunted and raised his eyebrows as if to indicate his disgust at the willingness of underlings to slack off.

When the two Pakistani intelligence officers had

departed to pick up the military flight that would take them back to their consulate in New York City, Brognola leaned back in his chair.

"Got everything you need, Striker?"

"General Sandila is a good soldier," Bolan said. "Thorough. Uses his head, too."

"I'll prepare a route to take you out to Lahore, and from there you'll be picked up by Malik's men and taken to Quetta. It's still a long hike from there to the region where Yasmin went missing, but at least you can pick up ordnance and your team."

"About that," Bolan said. "If Sandila is right, then I might be better flying solo at some point. That won't sit well with Malik, though, and he could cause ripples."

"It's nothing I can't handle," Brognola replied, shaking his head. "Listen, Striker, I could see how Sandila felt about him, and after a couple of hours listening to the man, I understand."

Bolan sighed. "As long as we're on the same page, Hal."

Brognola shifted uncomfortably in his seat. "Yeah, about that, Striker…"

Bolan's eyes narrowed. "Why do I think I'm not going to like what I'm about to hear?"

Brognola looked up at the ceiling. "It's like this. Because the Pakistan NCA approached the U.S. military directly, rather than coming through Foreign Affairs, there was an extra layer of interference to run before the matter came to me. An extra layer that had something to say, and doesn't want to relinquish that say."

"Bureaucratic bull, Hal. It has nothing to do with me. I have a job to do, and although there's nothing wrong with our military, they're on display and there are things that they just can't be seen to do that I can."

Brognola grimaced. "I understand, Striker. Hell, I agree with you. But—and this is crucial—they have a very good case for keeping an eye on this. Yasmin may not want to come willingly. Okay, so you could just extract her like she was a captive, but that might make further negotiation with her difficult for both the Pakistani administration and for ourselves. However, what if there was someone with you who had worked alongside her at MIT? And what if that person was also female, and so more likely to be able to relate to the issues that drove Yasmin to such action?"

"Come on, Hal—it's not about her being a woman, but are you seriously suggesting I take a civilian into what might as well be a war zone?"

Brognola coughed. "That's the thing, Striker—the woman I have in mind isn't a civilian. She's a soldier. A serving officer. A little like General Sandila, she has a physics degree as well as a military rank. She's a captain."

"What kind of combat experience does she have?"

"Two tours of Afghanistan. She's familiar with that part of the globe. Even if she hasn't actually been into

Balochistan, she does at least have an understanding of the territory, both physical and political."

"It's better, but it's still not ideal."

"It's a done deal, Striker. She's here, waiting. Captain Tamara Davis."

4

It happened on the sixteenth day. Maybe she was tiring of the wait and her mind was wandering? Maybe she was beginning to realize that idealistic dreams were one thing, but actually making them happen required a skill set that was completely alien to her? Whatever the reason, Yasmin had let her vigilance slip, and it was disastrous for the whole group.

Yasmin had been on night patrol. Along with Benazir Suri, a former politics student who had become radicalized while studying the Red Army Faction and believed that some of their tactics in 1970s Germany could be applied to Pakistan in the 2010s. It was dubious reasoning, in Yasmin's opinion, but perhaps it was a measure of both her naivety and her desperate desire for change.

For both women, the harsh reality of living in a camp in the hills had been a wake-up call. Adjusting to rough living after a wealthy upbringing and academic life was proving to be hard. It might have seemed a little more worthwhile if their movement was gathering steam, but several of the women in the group—the villagers who had run from virtual slavery and who had the knowledge and skills that Suri and Yasmin sorely lacked—were frustratingly taciturn and patient. They were content to sit and wait.

The terrain around them was not the lush riverside that Yasmin had been used to. As they traveled farther from the river's lifeblood, the streams became trickles that snaked in and out of rock, running too deep in places to be easily accessed. The steeply rising crags of rock made it hard to gain sustenance from the ground or seek shelter from the extremes of heat and cold. The moss, lichens and tufts of wiry grasses offered little for the emaciated goats that roamed the area. The few villages in the region scraped an existence off the land and the goats that young shepherds nervously gathered in, keen to avoid the wrath of any bandits who found camp and fought their desultory battles in the unforgiving landscape.

As the sun fell from the sky that evening, Yasmin and Suri started to tramp across the rocky paths and ravines that dotted the hillsides. There were ample hiding spots, but that also meant there were ample places for enemies to conceal themselves. Once the light had faded from the sky, the two women used only the moon and stars to guide them, perpetually praying for the night to remain cloudless as their eyes and senses had not had the lifetime of adjustment to the dark that the hill-born women had.

As they picked their way along the designated route,

which circled the camp at a radius of half a klick, give or take the odd hundred meters to detour around impassable rock falls or clusters, they talked about what they wanted, and about their frustrations, punctuated by cursing as they stumbled, turned their ankles, and gashed and grazed themselves on terrain that seemed to mock their very presence.

"If we're going to do anything other than rot out here and wait for a bunch of men to come and try to smack us down, then we need to take some kind of action soon," Suri moaned as she sat on a rock and massaged an ankle. Even though they both wore stout walking boots and had their ankles bound for support and padding, they were still limping at the end of each night's patrol.

Yasmin was small and compact. Her father used to worry that she might be physically weak, but she was nimble and wiry. Suri, on the other hand, was tall and slim in a way that Yasmin had seen English writers describe as "willowy"—almost as though she had grown too tall for her own strength. Yasmin doubted that her companion could survive in the wild for long. She herself was finding it hard, but Yasmin would bet on herself for the long haul once she had adjusted.

"I know why you want to act," she said with meaning, "and I want to, as well. But the question is what kind of action? It has to be something that counts. We're small in number, so we could be easily overwhelmed. We need to make an impact that will rally others to our cause and put us on the international stage."

Suri snorted. "Maybe we should pretend we're peasant girls and get ourselves shot in the head." She shook her head. "Sorry. I'm just tired, cold and pissed off."

"We all are." Yasmin grinned. "But we do have one major advantage. The NCA will know by now what I took. Even if they write me off personally and get another research scientist, they know what I'm running around with, and that'll scare the living crap out of them. They're not going to risk charging in and shooting without asking, just in case one of their trigger-happy boys has an accident."

"Well, yes," Suri said slowly. "Of course we can use it as a bargaining tool, and of course it gives us some protection. The problem is, if we just sit on our asses with it, they have no demands to meet."

Yasmin sighed. "It would be good if we could agree on what the demands are and actually move this forward."

Suri laughed. "You sound like you've spent too long working for the government. 'Move this forward…'"

Yasmin punched her friend in the shoulder. "Get your lazy ass up and let's get going. The last thing we want is to be caught standing around like a pair of idiots."

Suri dragged herself to her feet, swearing softly as she put pressure on her aching ankle, and followed in Yasmin's wake.

IFTIKHAR AND AYUB had not been expecting to hit the payload when they had taken this sortie. Their ten-man militant cell was twenty klicks to the west, deep in the foothills of the peaks that separated Pakistan from Afghanistan and Iran. The range was long and—if not impassable—accessible only to those who had spent years learning its contours. Their group was part of a supply chain that took food and ordnance from one country to another, feeding the needs of rebel factions on each side. Their pipeline was partially supplied by sympathetic Pakistani military men, mostly in quartermasters sections, who were discontented with the Westernization of their country and wanted the government to become more Islamist. This gave the rebels on both sides of the divide access to new Chinese and American hardware, rather than the aging Russian guns and South American copies of Russian weaponry they had been forced to rely on in the past few decades.

It also meant that the rebels running this pipeline kept their ears to the ground about any developments in weapons transportation, new shipments that were to arrive in Pakistan and any potentially new hardware leaks.

Inevitably, despite the blanket of security that Major Malik had attempted to cast over the disappearance of Shazana Yasmin and General Sandila's subsequent discovery of the missing fissionable material, rumors had surfaced that could not be dispelled. Some of these had reached the Islamist groups and rebels in the foothills, and they had added the small physicist and any potential package she may be carrying to their checklist. It was known that the PWLA was hiding out in the region.

The women were already on the checklist, as their very existence was an affront to the ideals and morals of the Islamists. Yet they were a low priority since they presented no real threat.

Now, with the knowledge that Yasmin was likely to be carrying nuclear material, the PWLA had moved up the list from an irritant to a group of interest.

For the past week, Iftikhar and Ayub's cell had been running missions across the plateaus and ravines of the range, trying to locate the PWLA camp. If they could pinpoint their target before any of the other rebels or Taliban units in the region, then they would hold the whip hand.

Word of Yasmin's supposed capture by the PWLA was whispered, and her location sought. Iftikhar and Ayub had, so they thought, drawn the short straw in having to take the sortie that carried them farthest from their base camp. Now, they felt differently.

They had become aware of the two women as they scuttled across an outcrop of jagged rock that overhung a narrow pathway cut into a hill. The rock formed a kind of roof that seemed to peter out into thin air before achieving a covering arc, and looked far too fragile to take the weight of a man. In truth, it had stood this way for centuries, and the thick strata at the base end gave it a tensile strength that its appearance belied. Iftikhar had lain flat across it when he heard the rattle of loosened rock along the trail followed by unholy cursing in a high, female voice. Holding his breath, gesturing at Ayub to stay back, he had lain still and listened to the exchange between the two women. He couldn't believe their luck. At the end of a cold, hard and seemingly pointless mission, they had lucked into a situation that would put their cell in a prime position and boost their own standing among their compatriots.

Now they had to play this right. Iftikhar clung flat to the rock as the two women passed beneath him. He waited as they continued down the narrow passage for a few hundred meters, then he crawled back to the ridge where Ayub lay waiting. Iftikhar could see from Ayub's face that he, too, had been listening. Without speaking, the two men communicated that they should follow the women at a distance in the hope that they would lead them to the PWLA camp.

Silently, the two men set off in pursuit of their prey. The women were obviously inexperienced, and their clumsy attempts at keeping their progress quiet were almost laughable. Certainly, if the two rebels had made any noise of their own, it would have been masked by the sound the two women were generating as they blundered forward.

It soon became apparent that the women were on a regular patrol, and if nothing else, the circumscribed route would give the two rebels a fixed area in which to search for and track down the PWLA camp…if the women did not lead them directly there.

After several hours of stuttering progress, the two rebels found that the women were novices when it came to covering their own tracks and being aware of their surroundings. On several occasions, the two rebels came within a few meters of the women, who didn't register their presence.

If all the women in the PWLA were like this, then it would be simple for a task force to raid their camp and wipe them out, taking the scientist and her cargo. The men exchanged predatory grins as they followed the two women to the edge of their camp.

As the sun rose, Iftikhar and Ayub withdrew. They were on a plateau above the small valley where the PWLA had pitched camp, and they would be exposed in the light of dawn. They had counted the tents, and based on the number of women who had started to emerge, they estimated the maximum number of PWLA members in camp. When they were at a safe distance, they began to realize the import of what they had stumbled on.

"They are stupid, my friend," Ayub murmured. "Do they really think they have any chance of success, with such a small number?"

"They'll count on the backing of the West," Iftikhar replied, spitting to emphasize his disgust. "They don't need bodies when they have the scientist woman and her nuclear filth. That will be enough to have the idiots in Lahore groveling at her feet."

"They'll have to do more than grovel if we get to it first," Ayub returned.

"True. They won't put up much of a fight, but that

would be true no matter who attacked them. The women aren't the problem here. We must act quickly—if we can find them easily enough by accident, then anyone else could stumble on them in such a way. We must ensure that our men strike tonight."

Moving swiftly over the terrain with a sure-footedness that their prey could only hope for, the two rebels made their way back to their own camp.

BOLAN WOULD HAVE been glad to have avoided a few hours in close quarters with Captain Tamara Davis. The woman next to him on the plane to Pakistan was a tall, lean blonde in her mid-twenties with her long hair tied in a tight chignon. The creases on her uniform had creases, all of them razor sharp, as was her manner. She was clipped and brusque in conversation, keeping her comments to a minimum, and she was so reticent as to be almost obstructive. It was obvious that she resented being sent on this mission to extract her old college friend. She had no idea who Bolan was, aside from his rank, and she didn't seem interested in finding out.

This made for an uncomfortable flight as, more than anything, Bolan wanted to find out more about Shazana Yasmin as a person. The files had told him about her achievements and her talents, but if he was extracting her from a situation she had willingly entered, then having a handle on her and knowing how to play her could be invaluable.

Davis seemed almost to sympathize with Yasmin,

and she was unwilling to say anything that she saw as a betrayal of confidence. Eventually, after another stalled attempt at finding out about his target and establishing some kind of working relationship with Davis, he tried a different approach.

"Listen," he said in a conciliatory tone, "you've been in Afghanistan. You know what the Taliban is like when it comes to women—especially smart ones who won't accept their supposed place. I don't know much about the PWLA, but what I do know is that Dr. Yasmin is a prime target and carries a burden that could set fire to the whole of the Middle East and Asia. That's if it doesn't kill her along the way."

"What do you expect from me, sir?" Davis retorted, biting the last word off with sarcasm.

"I expect a little more cooperation and information," Bolan said. "If you care about the U.S. soldiers stationed in Afghanistan, and if you care about your friend, then you'd better realize that we need to get her out of there quick, before she ends up caught in the middle of a firefight she has no way of dealing with. Do you want her to be kidnapped? Tortured? Maybe worse?"

From the expression that flickered across Davis's face, he could tell he'd hit home.

5

Bolan and Davis landed in Lahore, and as they traveled from the air force field into the center of the city, Bolan watched the crush of people in the sultry heat of the afternoon. They were in an air-conditioned car, and outside street vendors and beggars sweat in the heat as cars and motorbikes threaded around them, and around each other. In some sections of the city, large department stores beckoned, with their promise of air conditioning, to the upwardly mobile. Elsewhere, hastily constructed tower blocks housed sweat-shop laborers. Some areas harkened back to the turn of the twentieth century, with crumbling tenements and shacks nestled between old colonial buildings run to seed. Looking at these, it seemed astounding that this nation had the wealth and know-how to run a nuclear program.

Davis and Bolan did not speak until they reached the barracks, and only then to reply to greetings from the stiff-backed officer who met them. Shown into a meeting room, they were faced with half a dozen men who eyed them with a mix of disdain and barely concealed curiosity.

"Colonel Stone, Captain Davis," he began with a sweep of his arm. "These men have been personally picked by Major Malik to serve with you. All have distinguished records and—crucially—have served in Balochistan."

Davis gave Bolan a puzzled look, so he filled her in. "You know our target, and you've trained with the kinds of material she has with her, but I guess they didn't give you much background on location." He waited for her confirmation before continuing. "I'm sure I'll be corrected if I'm wrong, but Balochistan is a volatile region, and has been for a long time."

He chose his words carefully, and the stiff-backed officer acknowledged this with a gesture as he picked up Bolan's cue. "The Baloch peoples have always seen themselves as apart from the rest of Pakistan, and have long been fighting for greater autonomy. But of course, there are also those who have taken advantage of the fight for independence in order to aid their own agendas. We suspect that there are many weapon and drug pipelines being run by or with the cooperation of Baloch separatist factions. As a result, we have had to tread very carefully in the region in order to keep some kind of equilibrium."

"In other words," Davis said flatly, "you let them run guns to the Afghans and take drugs from them so that you don't upset too many Islamic fundamentalists in your country, regardless of how many people those guns might kill."

Bolan winced. He agreed with her in some respects, but now was not the time to say so, and certainly not that bluntly.

The officer's back was so rigid that Bolan wondered if he would snap his own spine. "That is one school of thought," the man said. "Though one that—if I might say—will not find much popularity among the people you will be working with." He turned to Bolan. "You would, perhaps, tell your subordinate to bear that in mind. Now if you will excuse me, I have matters to attend to. I will leave your briefing in the capable hands of Corporal Jinnah."

Barely acknowledging the two Americans, the officer turned on his heel and left the room. Bolan looked around at the six men. Five of them were staring at him, and particularly at Davis, in disbelief. The sixth, a rangy man with graying hair that made him look older than he probably was, was rising to his feet. The ghost of a cold smile flickered across his face.

Bolan was bemused by Davis's attitude and behavior. She had been trained in the transportation of delicate materials such as the fissionable flask that Yasmin had taken. This was key to her presence. Although she'd mainly been selected for her relationship with the target, she would also supply specialist knowledge in getting the fragile flask out of the region in one piece.

So far she hadn't been acting like a team player,

and she'd seemed to go out of her way to alienate the men who would be fighting alongside them. It didn't make sense, unless she had an unknown agenda of her own. If that was the case, then he needed to find out quickly, even if he could barely afford the time. If not, then Bolan wondered if he'd been saddled with someone who was experiencing a form of battle fatigue.

As this went through his mind, Jinnah ran through his men, reeling off their combat experience and links to the Balochistan region. Jinnah himself had served in the army for a decade, and had fought in Balochistan against the rebels. He was from Quetta, and knew the hills like a herdsman. He said this in a self-effacing manner, but from his brief description of the terrain they would face, Bolan could tell he was the man for the job.

The other five had service ranging from three to twenty years. Faiz Ahmed Faiz was a tall, thickset and muscular man with a mustache and a lined face that spoke of his many years in the service. He was Jinnah's number two, and the most experienced of all the men. By contrast, Omar Jansher was the youngest man, a gangly youth with only three years on the clock and a diffident air. He was openly eyeing Davis with hostility. Bolan was not the only one to notice this, as Jinnah glanced pointedly at the young man while making a reference to his men keeping their heads and following the chain of command. Jansher acknowledged this with the hint of a shrug.

The other three men fell between these extremes.

Ali Asif was growing a nicely rounded belly under his tight uniform shirt, but his arms were bulky with muscle. He had a hard-set face that was difficult to read, but Bolan could tell from the scars on his face and forearms that he was a fighter unafraid to get hurt. Mohammed Zia looked to be a year or two older than Jansher. He watched the proceedings with half-closed eyes, seemingly laid-back, but there was no mistaking his hostility when he glanced at Davis.

The last man was Vinood Patel. He concentrated intently on everything that Jinnah said, hanging on his every word, though Bolan caught his eyes flickering over both himself and Davis, as though the man was sizing them up. He smoothed back the hair at his temples in a nervous gesture, running his hand over the balding pate almost as an afterthought. He was closer to Faiz in age than any of the others, with the air of a man who had negotiated his army career with a careful choice of allies. Not that Bolan could blame him, given the region they were going to, in which these men had all served. Nonetheless, there was reason here to keep a weather eye on him, also.

"We'll kit up here, before we ride out to take the plane to Quetta," Jinnah continued when he had finished introducing the personnel. "On the journey I'll run through the area we think the PWLA are hidden in."

"Can you be sure of this, or will we be chasing our tails?" Bolan queried.

Jinnah grimaced. "Can never be sure, Colonel Stone,

but the facts are that we know the direction they struck out in, and although there's no trail and it's dead air for satellite or GPS, there are only a certain number of trails you can follow through the plateau. We also know where Balochistan rebels and several other militant cells are holed up. They would be difficult to weed out, but they serve our purpose in narrowing the search area for where the PWLA could shelter. A simple process of elimination leads us to the areas we'll search."

Bolan nodded. "Sounds feasible."

Jinnah ushered his men out of the building and toward a truck that was waiting to take them back to the airfield. The soldier joined the party as they gathered weaponry from the armory at the barracks, then he took on a full pack of food, water, first-aid supplies, a tent, a sleeping roll and short-range radio equipment designed to work within the confines of their intended territory. The weapons were American; perhaps for reasons of diplomacy, the ordnance the Pakistani army received from China was ignored. With a wry smile, Bolan figured this was the military mind at work.

They boarded the truck to the airfield, back the way Bolan and Davis had traveled only a couple of hours previously. The soldier wanted to get Davis on her own, away from the men she had already alienated, and try to get inside her head. One way or another, he had to straighten her out before they reached Quetta, or she would become a liability he could ill afford.

His chance came when they reached the airfield. As

the Pakistani men moved toward the troop transport that would fly them to Quetta, Bolan hung back and took Davis aside.

"So how does it feel to be going into combat with a group of guys who have no reason to watch your back?" he asked bluntly.

Davis returned a cold stare. "Does that include you, sir?"

"No, it doesn't. I'll have your back, but I'm figuring you won't have mine."

"Why would that be, sir?" She could barely keep the sarcasm from her voice.

"I don't know, Captain. But unless you level with me, all that attitude will go to waste. I'm willing to risk myself for you and any allies in battle, but the stakes are too high for both of us if we go in without the support and respect of those men. If you don't turn it around, I'll have to leave you here."

"Let's be honest," she said. "Those guys don't give a shit about us. They're probably glad that the rebels get guns through to kill our guys. They don't care about Shaz, either. She's just a woman, so she doesn't matter."

"She matters to the U.S. government, and that means she matters to me, Captain. She's a U.S. citizen in trouble."

"That's very noble," she sneered. "Thing is, Colonel, what happens when those guys get the flask and decide an uppity woman isn't worth the bother? You know what happens here. I'll tell you something else, too—they won't want witnesses, and there are more of them than us. Who's going to watch our backs then?"

Bolan glanced over at the transport, which the military party was boarding. Jinnah had turned back toward them. Even at this distance, Bolan could read the suspicion in his face.

"Davis, let's get one thing straight. I don't care that Dr. Yasmin is a woman. I don't care that some of those guys might sympathize more with the rebels than with the U.S. government, or maybe even their own. I don't even care whether or not they want that flask back for NCA, for the Taliban and Iran, or to make some cash on the open market—"

"Iran?" Davis interrupted him.

"Sure," Bolan shrugged. "If we're going to play paranoid mind games then why not assume that the flask and Yasmin's knowledge would advance Iran's nuclear program while keeping their neighbors at a disadvantage. The point is that I'm not interested in what anyone else wants—only what *we* want," he said.

"And that is?"

"For a start, we need to get a U.S. citizen out of danger and make sure that the precious cargo she carries doesn't fall into hands that could harm her, any innocent people or the interests of the U.S. Everything else is secondary. Do you read me?"

Davis looked him in the eye, and then over her shoulder. Jinnah was approaching them with purpose in his stride.

"Okay," she said, nodding briefly. "For now we forget everything else and concentrate on getting Shaz and the nuclear material out of the danger zone. But if anything happens to change the nature of our mission, then don't expect me to play dumb and just go along with it."

"I'll count on your honesty," Bolan replied. "Come on, he'll already have questions," he added, pulling her toward Jinnah and the transport.

But if the Pakistani mission leader did have anything to say, he held his peace as he followed them onto the aircraft. Even after takeoff he elected not to ask any questions that may have been awkward for Bolan to answer, preferring to gather the whole party and study the topographical maps of the search region. When he had completed this, he dispersed his men and ordered them to get some rest. Bolan suggested that Davis do the same, and he was both surprised and pleased when she acquiesced without argument.

Bolan fell into a brief, dreamless sleep, and was woken by the jolt of the transport landing at Quetta.

They disembarked without a word and climbed into a truck that took them through the city. It was the largest city in the region, but only a fraction of the size of Lahore. Bolan watched the streets and people go by. They appeared similar to those in Lahore, but given Jinnah's words about the conflict in the region, he studied the men gathered on street corners and the stares of stallholders and traders as they passed, wondering if any of them were rebels or sympathizers who would pass on news of their arrival to militant groups or terrorist cells.

The fewer people who saw them or knew of their arrival, the better. Bolan was glad when they were clear of the city and on the winding dirt road to where they would disembark and begin their search on foot.

He couldn't know they were about to walk into someone else's fight.

6

Ayub and Iftikhar made good time back to their camp, where they were quick to inform their comrades of what they had discovered. With the location of the PWLA camp now in their hands, it was surely only a matter of time before they swarmed over the inexperienced women and gained the prize that would give them the upper hand in the region.

Preparation was swift. With a skeleton crew remaining in camp to maintain a secure position, the rest of the cell set out for the position pinpointed by the two returning scouts. They proceeded on foot, using caution as they were aware that their route would take them along the edges of territory occupied by rival groups. The last thing they wanted was to attract undue attention with a mass exodus from their known and secured position.

The early morning was perfect for this. Although they didn't have the cover of darkness, they had the advantage of hitting the blind spot when most night patrols had returned to their respective camps and before the day patrols had hit their stride. If the timing was right, it was possible to slip undetected through land that would otherwise be under observation.

The phalanx of men, which numbered ten, kept in a tight pack as they negotiated the narrow channel between known boundaries, but as soon as they came close to the position described by Ayub and Iftikhar, who led the way, they separated so that they could fan out and take cover, then come down hard on the unsuspecting PWLA camp.

THE PAKISTANI ARMY detachment and their two American allies were deposited on a dirt road that seemed to be in the very middle of nowhere. Davis sniffed and looked around at the rock and scrub that surrounded them as the army truck pulled away, a cloud of dust rising in its wake, and squinted at the horizon.

"They could be anywhere out here," she commented. "How did your guys figure out that they're around these parts?" she asked Jinnah.

The corporal smiled. "I know you do not think much of us," he said slowly, "but you must at least allow us a knowledge of our own land and our own people. We are not fools. A process of elimination has brought us here, and I'm confident that a search will yield a result."

His tone was edged with hostility, which Bolan was keen to dampen. The soldier cut in with an easy smile. "I don't think Captain Davis was doubting your sources, Corporal, but you have to admit that this would be a hell of an easy territory to hide in."

Jinnah nodded. From his tone when he spoke again, it was clear that he found Bolan a more congenial ally than the spiky Davis. "Colonel, this is why we have so much trouble in this region. The people may have intransigence enough to create trouble, but the land gives them the opportunity to make that intransigence last. You could spend years combing the land, and by the time you had mapped everyone within, they could have regrouped and started again behind your back without your noticing them until it was too late. It's far too easy to hide in here if you really want to. It's easy to get lost, too," he added.

"Then we're just going to have to trust you, Corporal." Bolan's glance at Davis was significant.

"I'm sure you will, Colonel," Jinnah said simply.

He turned and directed his men onto a narrow trail that led up into the foothills. It was a shallow incline, though Bolan felt a pull in his calf muscles as he and Davis fell into step behind the line of military men. Jinnah took point, and led the line using map and compass to keep them on track. Out here, the modern military was reduced to using age-old orienteering methods.

Bolan stayed at the back of the line, taking the opportunity to keep an eye on the trail behind them. It was a chance to scout out the land without being caught in the middle of the pack. At the same time, with Davis and the army men before him, he had his first chance to assess them without having to interact.

Faiz and Jinnah seemed to be intent on their task,

scanning the area as they progressed. Patel and Asif were keeping to themselves, their weapons held lightly, but their body language belying their tension. They were expecting a firefight to come out of nowhere, and possibly weren't pleased at having been sent on this mission. Jansher and Zia were in the middle of the line, and Zia kept hanging back to exchange whispered comments with Jansher. The two men eyed the landscape with some anxiety, and they kept casting glances at Davis. These two men seemed the least happy with the mission, and Bolan inferred that this was due, in no small part, to having to carry—as they saw it—a woman.

Davis, directly ahead of him, seemed alert to any danger. Yet there was something in her stance that suggested caution—not just to any threat from the hills, but to the men around her, as well.

Bolan could see nothing but trouble ahead.

YASMIN WOKE TO Mahak Lasi's voice, and when she opened her eyes, the other woman's head thrust through her tent flap. Yasmin suppressed a scream of shock. At first, in her befuddled, sleep-addled state, she didn't grasp what her comrade was saying. It was only when she repeated it in an exasperated tone that Yasmin understood the importance.

"Men this way. Ten of them. Armed. Come on, move yourself. Quick."

Yasmin assented, blank-eyed, and didn't quite get her

brain and body into sync before Lasi's head had disappeared. Yasmin could hear her outside, shouting commands to the others to form into teams, as she struggled to get her boots on and to grab the rifle that she barely knew how to use. The nominal leaders of the PWLA deferred to Lasi at these times because of her experience since running away from her village.

Squinting painfully at the glare of the morning sun, she scrambled out of her tent and joined the other women as they formed up in the center of camp. Some of them had been going about their daily tasks, while others had been resting. They were in varied states of readiness, and this was making Lasi mad as she tried to yell them into some kind of shape. She directed her anger at Yasmin as she came into view.

"Come on. You and the Lollywood queen take the western side, and cover me as I scout. You should have spotted this last night—they must have been looking for us. They don't just come like this out of nowhere."

Yasmin had not heard Lasi say so much in one speech since she had arrived in camp, and it drove home the depth of danger they were in. Backing her up as she surveyed the area was a way of making Yasmin atone for whatever mistake she and Suri had made on patrol the previous night, though for the life of her she couldn't work out how even inexperienced fighters like the two of them could have missed so many men approaching.

As Lasi moved on to organize the other women, Yasmin found Suri standing beside her.

"She was giving me shit before you emerged from your pit," she whispered in acid tones. "She doesn't like us because we come from the city and she's just some stupid hill girl."

"But she can fight and we can't," Yasmin answered quietly. "And if there's a whole bunch of armed men headed this way, I'll listen to her and do what she says. What worries me is how the hell we managed to miss that many out there."

"I don't think we did. We're not that stupid, no matter what she thinks," Suri muttered, looking over at Lasi as she directed another small group before turning and catching the two women staring at her. She gestured urgently, and despite her words, Suri fell in beside Yasmin as she ran over to back her up.

Lasi led them out of the camp and along part of the route they had taken on their night patrol. They passed along the narrow passage with an overhanging rock shelf and on to where that morning's patrol had caught sight of the approaching group.

By the time that they had traveled out to that spot and taken cover, they could only sight eight of the ten reported enemy fighters. The men advanced and spread out to take up a pincer formation around the PWLA camp as they progressed. Taking down the eight they could see would be difficult enough for the three of them, no matter how good Lasi was as a hill fighter. But with two hidden men out there, the task began to seem impossible.

When the first shots resounded, the three women were momentarily thrown. The gunfire had not come from any direction they could have expected.

JINNAH HELD UP a hand to stop his men. He looked up from the map and turned back to them with a puzzled expression. He murmured something to Faiz, who listened and glanced at Bolan, beckoning him forward. When the soldier reached the front of the line, he immediately knew why the corporal and his number two had pulled him up. He could make out the sound of people moving across the rocks, the rattle of disturbed scree indicating that there were more than a few of them.

"They know what they're doing," Jinnah said softly when Bolan was in earshot. "It's not the women."

"They may have learned," Bolan pointed out, not wanting to close down any possibility. The last thing he wanted was for the military to shoot first and ask later. "Okay, it's unlikely," he added, seeing Jinnah's expression. "I'm just saying we should be careful in more ways than one."

Faiz agreed. "Could be. We need to check it out first." He indicated for the others to gather near. As they came close, Bolan noted that although Davis drew nearer, she still held back, which concerned him.

"We split into pairs and fan out from this point. Scout for enemy locations. Avoid fire and use hand-to-hand or blades if possible. Wireless silence unless absolutely necessary."

"How do we communicate, then?" Davis asked.

"We'll have one wireless call in fifteen. Synchronize now," Jinnah returned. "Call sign, affirmative or negative for sighting. No more."

The military personnel and Bolan agreed to the plan. Davis was silent. Jinnah paired the men off, taking Davis for himself and putting Bolan with Patel. The soldier liked the Corporal's thinking. He knew Jinnah was uneasy about Davis because of her attitude, but the corporal didn't have the same doubts that others in the party had made obvious.

But Davis shook her head. "I go with Stone," she said.

Bolan's gaze scoured the group. It was obvious that Davis's refusal had gone down badly with them. They stared at her with contempt. Jinnah's eyes met Bolan's, and the soldier could read Jinnah's unspoken question. He nodded briefly.

"Davis, you're with me, but I want you to know we can trust these guys. Let's give them a reason to trust us."

"Vin, you're with me, then," the corporal said to Patel. Under the circumstances, it was no surprise that the Pakistani soldier looked relieved.

Jinnah issued directions, then he moved from the security of their position with Patel following him. They watched the two men move out of sight before Zia and Faiz headed off. Jansher and Asif were next, leaving Bolan and Davis alone in the hollow formed by the rising hills on each side of the trail. They could hear the men retreating, the small sounds of their progress blending in with the distant noises of the enemy group.

Davis counted off thirty seconds and made to move. As she did so, Bolan held her back.

"Don't do that again. We need these guys. The objective is more important than whatever issues you're dealing with."

Davis stared him down. "Is it an *issue* to trust my countryman over those who've sided against us? I want to achieve the mission objective, too—I just think we have different ideas on how that can happen. Now, if we're going to do that, then we shouldn't be down here, should we, *sir?*"

Bolan started to advance, although there was a lot more he wanted to say. But in one respect, she was right. They had to move right now.

The rise and fall of the rock and the scrub that punctuated it gave them scant cover, but still made it hard to spot any other parties. Their enemy would be better at concealment in this territory, despite the experience Bolan and Davis both had.

But there was no time to think of this. Keeping low, they swept across the rocks. They couldn't see any of the Pakistani soldiers, which was an indication of their compatriots' knowledge of the terrain.

They moved around south by southeast, circling out and away from the direction they had been headed just a few minutes before. If anyone crossed their path, they could trail them or try to take them down, if the need arose.

Bolan wondered whether they had stumbled on the PWLA, or if they were encountering a male rebel cell. It might make a difference in terms of combat, but he had an even deeper concern. Jinnah had been sure that this area was not populated by any other groups. If there was a raiding party invading the area, did that mean Bolan and Davis weren't the only ones on Yasmin's trail?

Who was this other group, and how much did they know? The situation seemed increasingly complicated.

The sudden volley of shots only confirmed this.

7

Jansher and Asif crawled around the rim of a small cluster of rocks. They took each step with care so that they did not disturb any loose scree and make their presence as obvious as the men they were tailing. The landscape offered small gullies and narrow passages in which a man could hide. Many of these were invisible to the naked eye, and even a man who knew the terrain like the back of his hand could be easily deceived.

The two military men exchanged glances. Neither wanted to break the silence, and they could see the fear and tension in each other's faces. Sweat spangled their foreheads and gathered on their top lips. Asif's tongue flicked nervously, and he darted his eyes toward a small patch of scrub that he was sure hid a gully. He had seen a dark-clad figure flit across the rock just a few hundred meters ahead of them as they emerged from their starting point. He couldn't be sure that they hadn't been spotted, and had held Jansher back behind the cover of the outcrop.

If they were to take down the man in the gully, then

they had to do it without raising an alarm—no gunfire.
Asif shouldered his rifle and drew a combat knife from
the sheath under his shirt. He showed the blade to his
compatriot and indicated that he would take the lead.
With a gesture, he told the younger man that he should
circle around and cover him from the blind side while
he approached the gully head-on.

Jansher shouldered his own weapon and drew a
blade. He nodded his understanding and took a deep
breath before moving out into the open, dropping low
as he sought whatever scant cover he could find.

Asif watched him go, allowing him to gain some
ground before starting his own action. Jansher was circling wide, and there was no way Asif was going to
head straight to the gully and be caught with no cover
as the younger soldier lagged behind.

Asif had seen combat action, but every time he came
face-to-face with his own mortality he felt that lurch of
fear in his gut. He tasted acid in the back of his throat
and gulped it down, adrenaline running through his
system and making his legs tremble.

This was the hardest part—the wait, the countdown.
He ticked off the seconds in his mind, his partner now
lost from view. The temptation to hurry the count was
almost overwhelming, but he knew how stupid that
would be.

Three…two…one…

He emerged into the open, dropping down and crawling across the rock. It was hard and painful on his legs,

the stones bashing his ankles and knees and tearing at his combat pants. He could ignore it, but wondered if the pain would cripple him when he had to straighten up.

No time to worry. If he stopped to think about anything other than his objective, then he was as good as dead. The adrenaline in his system would mask the pain; it also made time stand still as he slithered toward the gully, praying to Allah that the shooter in hiding would not see him first.

Glancing around, he spotted Jansher ducking between two small humps of rock on the far side of the gully. At the same moment, the head and shoulders of an opponent emerged from cover, facing away from Asif. From the set of the man's shoulders, Asif could tell that he had a rifle in his hands and was taking sight of his companion.

Now it was imperative that he act quickly—not only to spare his comrade, but also to prevent a shot from raising any alarm.

Asif launched himself forward across the remaining space, ignoring the noise he made. Time, not stealth, was the imperative now. He flew across the last couple of meters and down into the gully, landing in the narrow space behind the enemy shooter.

The rattle of pebbles and the scrape of his combat boots made the enemy fighter swing around abruptly in the narrow space. Asif caught sight of a lean face with a scrubby black beard and hair hidden beneath a knitted black cap, his dark eyes wide in surprise and anger at being caught out.

The rest was a blur as Asif came up against the man. The man held an AK-47 that he was attempting to train on Asif's head.

Asif was too quick. As he slammed against the rebel, he forced the barrel up against the man's chest. He felt the man's knee come up swiftly to meet his groin and had just enough time to twist his hips so that the greater force of the blow was absorbed with discomfort rather than crippling pain. As he parried this blow, Asif brought back his knife arm as far as he could in order to get some power behind the upward thrust that drove the blade up and under the man's sternum. The blow was softened by the layers of clothing that swathed his opponent, but Asif had put his full weight into the thrust, and there was enough behind it to penetrate skin and flesh. He drove the knife home and twisted.

The man's face registered more shock than pain as his internal organs ruptured. He coughed and blood bubbled out of his open mouth, then he slumped forward and Asif stumbled back against the rock under the deadweight.

He heaved the corpse off him and stepped to one side. Over the ridge of the gully, he could see Jansher approaching. He signaled that things were okay and that they should continue on the course Jinnah had set out for them. The younger man nodded his understanding and changed direction.

Asif checked that the area was clear, and hauled himself out of the gully, still keeping low. As he rose into a crouch to move forward, a searing pain hit him in the side—three, four times—like a punch from a burning knife. It was so intense that he didn't hear the volley that accompanied each blow. As he fell, all he could see was the shock on Jansher's face before a black tunnel closed around his vision.

FAIZ AND ZIA had crossed a flat section of the plateau. They were almost certainly exposed, but they moved so quickly, they would present a difficult target. They were tracking a group of three dark-clad fighters who flitted in and out of view as they used the sparse cover afforded them. Faiz directed the younger, less experienced soldier to flank the man on the left while he took the one on the right, keeping the third man between them.

Faiz drew his blade and they increased their pace to a run, gaining ground on men who were still putting stealth ahead of speed.

They were almost on their men when a volley of fire made their targets turn.

It was too late to turn back or hide. Faiz and Zia threw themselves over the last few meters, smashing into assailants who didn't have enough time to raise their weapons before they were slammed back onto the hard rock, breath driven from their lungs as Faiz and Zia's blades claimed their lives.

The enemy fighter caught in the middle saw both of

his compatriots taken down, and paused momentarily, torn between the two of them. He yelled into the suddenly broken silence, either in frustration or for assistance, and sprayed AK-47 fire across the plateau. Zia managed to avoid being hit, but Faiz was not so lucky. As he tried to dodge the shots, a bullet raked his left calf. He roared in anger and pain. Now was not the time to be slowed or disabled. He pulled his own rifle off his shoulder and returned fire, taking down the third man.

That was one immediate threat eliminated, but there were more to follow.

WITH THE TWO bursts of fire, any attempt at stealth was now blown. The enemy fighters who had been in hiding now emerged to deal with the threat, and the Pakistani military men made no further attempt to stalk their opponents, but were instead seeking cover from which to fire on their prey.

Bolan dived for the cover of a boulder, dragging Davis with him. As they slammed into the blind side of the rock, shots hammered against it. Bolan cursed, waiting for the volley to subside before returning any fire. Beside him, Davis huddled close as the rock provided only a narrow width for shelter. She was so close that he could hear her swearing continuously in his ear, even though the sound of gunfire filled the air around them.

And then there was a cone of silence around them. For a moment, it seemed that their direct opponents had stopped to assess the damage. Bolan and Davis had a chance to gather their breath and shoulder their arms before spinning to return fire.

"You go low, I'll go high," Bolan said. "Go."

Bolan came up over the top of the rock, while Davis stayed in a crouch. They both began firing immediately, in short, controlled bursts. The gap between each burst gave them a fraction of a second in which to survey the area.

From the dark shadows that flickered on the periphery of their vision, in and out of cover, with the occasional returned shot, Bolan could tell that their initial estimate had been close to the enemy's position. By concentrating their fire, he planned to pin them down and take them out when they were forced out of their current hiding place by the onslaught.

"Keep going—let's see if we can smoke 'em out," Bolan yelled over the chattering weapons. Davis nodded briefly and kept up her barrage of fire as Bolan took a grenade from his pocket. He lobbed it in a gentle arc, and it seemed to hang in the air before suddenly dropping into the center of the gathered enemy fighters.

Bolan and Davis both dropped behind the rocks to avoid the debris thrown up by the blast. The maneuver had to count. They'd left their packs in the narrow rock passage, needing to cut back to bare bones so that they could move with ease and stealth. That meant short bursts to conserve ammunition; grenades only if they could make an impact.

As the debris settled around them, Bolan turned to

Davis. "Take the gully for cover and recon—go!" He yelled, moving out from cover. Davis was only a step behind him as they crossed the distance between the rock and the gully, which had been widened by the blast. They could see the ragged remains of two men hanging over the edge, and as they dived into cover, they pushed the corpses aside and came up, scanning their surroundings.

They conserved ammunition by refraining from covering fire, trusting to speed and the confusion caused by the blast.

"Clear in the immediate surround," Davis said. "We're a man down and one carrying injuries," she reported. "The enemy's in a worse state, but how many of them were there originally?"

"Good question. Assume they outnumber us. Only thing to do," he said. "Where are the rest of ours?"

"Never mind that," Davis cut in. "Look what's at three o'clock...."

Bolan turned. He wasn't sure he could quite believe what he was seeing....

JINNAH AND PATEL had headed out with wariness that some of their younger and less experienced colleagues lacked. This was why the corporal had partnered the battle-hardened Faiz with Zia. Asif and Jansher would have to fare best they could.

The corporal had counted up to ten opponents as they ghosted across the terrain. Almost two to one against.

For reasons of his own, he discounted the Americans. The colonel was okay, but he had his hands full with the bad-tempered woman.

Now that their opponents had vanished into the crevices and cover that they were familiar with, he and his compatriot had to think on the run.

"Gully," Patel snapped, pointing at a potential piece of shelter. They could both see that it was empty, and Jinnah veered toward the thin path in the rock. He made cover with Patel hot on his heels. They settled into the snug groove and scanned the terrain. One or two shadows flashed on the rocks, and they could see Asif and Jansher to their left.

"Keep down, you idiot," Patel said. While they watched, the two warriors separated and Asif went in for the kill, taking out his target. "Good work," Patel muttered, before cursing as a volley of gunfire rent the air and claimed their comrade.

Before Jinnah could stop him, Patel had settled the barrel of his AK-47 on the lip of the gully and sighted in the direction of the enemy fire. He returned an answering volley that raked rock and scrub but offered no indication of whether it had hit a target.

What it did do was make their position known, and the corporal cursed as he pulled Patel down into the gully, the fire they attracted throwing up rock chips and dust that showered down on them.

They were now trapped. The enemy knew exactly where they were and could keep them pinned down.

"What did you do that for?" Jinnah yelled at Patel.

"Return fire, give Asif a chance to make cover," Patel shouted back angrily.

"He's already dead," Jinnah said bluntly. "All you've done is make it harder for us to cover each other's backs as well as our own."

"Hell, I have. We need to take them down before they take us." Patel twisted out of the corporal's iron grip and pulled his rifle free, finding the space to return fire across the plateau. Above the chatter of fire, he heard Faiz yell as his leg was hit. "That's Faiz—they've taken him, too, all because of those stupid women. We should let them get what they deserve. That's two good men gone."

"It's not our decision to make," Jinnah snapped. "We're soldiers. We obey orders. Discipline, Patel— that's what's going to get us out of this, so shut up and listen."

Patel's eyes blazed for a moment, and the corporal thought he'd lost him. Then the fire dimmed as his anger ebbed, and he nodded. "Sir, yes, sir. But it needs to be a good plan...."

"It'll be quick. Good I can't guarantee. We—" He swore loudly as the sound of a grenade explosion cut him off.

Both men risked a look toward the area where the explosion had sounded. They watched Stone and Davis emerge from cover and head toward the gully.

"We need to link up with them," Jinnah said. Whatever he may think of the Americans, connecting with their remaining allies was far and away the best move they could make.

Jinnah and Patel broke cover and charged forward to join their comrades, who were succeeding in damping down any fire against them and pressing the opposition back into cover.

But the two Pakistani soldiers were completely unprepared for what was happening on the far side of the gully where Stone and Davis were located. From out of nowhere, a woman had appeared.

A lone woman with an automatic rifle. A lone woman who braced herself and started to fire on them as they ran toward her.

8

Yasmin and Suri found it hard to understand exactly what was unfolding before them. As Lasi skipped off, moving quickly and nimbly between the rock and scrub, using shelter and cover they couldn't even have imagined was there, they felt as though they were chasing shadows. It was hard enough to follow her, let alone the shadows that represented the approaching force.

They were too cautious to shoot, and initially, there was no need—Lasi's rapid movements were either unseen by the enemy, or else she wasn't enough of a target to attract fire. The unseen rebels were as keen on staying hidden as the three women, so they were unlikely to draw any fire upon them until they were in a secure position or on top of their target.

And then, when Yasmin and Suri felt they were beginning to adjust to what was happening, all hell seemed to break loose as eight more bodies joined the fray, dressed in combat fatigues and demonstrating less of an ability to hide in the unforgiving landscape.

The two women exchanged glances. The unspoken

question was one that neither could answer. These new players looked like military personnel, but if they were, what were they doing here? Were they after Yasmin and the PWLA, as she had been expecting, or were they after the Balochistan rebels or fundamentalists or whoever it was that was closing in?

Before the questions even had the chance to fully form in Yasmin's mind, the silence was broken by fire, which took down one of the military men. The two women yelled in surprise as a grenade detonated. They were unused to violence, and while Yasmin knew she'd have to adjust quickly, she was shaking with the rush of adrenaline that flooded through her. Suri seemed similarly shocked.

For the first time, Yasmin felt the full import of what she had done in joining the PWLA and bringing the stolen flask with her. The moral and ideological implications had not changed, but the practical result of bringing hardened fighters from all factions down on them when they had so little chance of defending themselves adequately...this now hit home.

Her first instinct was to take flight, but she fought hard to quell this. Looking at Suri, she knew she was not alone. Her friend was wide-eyed, her lips trembling, and Yasmin was unsure whether she was about to cry or scream hysterically. Perversely, she was able to draw strength from her friend precisely because she knew how Suri felt and realized she wasn't alone in her fear and doubt. She slapped Suri hard. Her head snapped back, her eyes blazed, and she hit Yasmin with a round-house slap that had her extra height and weight behind it, and almost knocked the smaller woman off her feet.

As Yasmin stumbled, Suri reached out and grabbed her, swearing loudly. "How the fuck did we get into this?"

"Too late to worry now," Yasmin muttered, turning back to where a full-scale firefight was building. "We're here now, and we've got a job to do."

The two women tried to catch sight of Lasi. Their task, no matter what, was to provide cover for her. The only problem was that she had found shelter so deep that they had no idea where she was.

"Shaz, we've lost her," Suri yelled as she scanned the horizon.

"Keep calm," Yasmin returned. "She's out there. We just need to keep a lookout for her...."

They fell into silence, trying to follow the events unfolding before them while they waited for their compatriot to show herself. They saw two men emerge from a gully and head toward the site of the explosion, where two others had already taken cover. One of the military men was pulling his companion, who had been shot in the leg, over to the gully, while another member of their party ran toward it, as well.

Yasmin was no military strategist, but it seemed to her that this was not a wise move. Converging on the same spot meant their position would be heavily secured, but even she could see that when they were together, they presented a target that could be taken out in one hit.

Why would they want to do that?

"There she is! There she is!" Suri shouted suddenly, driving all other thoughts from Yasmin's mind.

Lasi had emerged from cover like an apparition. She had a clear shot at the military personnel who had reached the edge of the gully. Her weapon was raised, and as she started to fire, Yasmin realized she and Suri were standing like idiots, watching, when they should be laying down a covering fire. Both women raised their guns and began to fire for the first time in a combat situation. Yasmin felt the recoil hammering into her shoulder with sharp, jolting pain, making her jerk so her shots were high, wide and erratic. Suri's aim was similar. But at least they were providing some kind of cover.

Exposed as she was, Lasi would need it.

"WHAT THE HELL is she doing?" Bolan said softly, almost to himself, as he saw the woman stand and take aim. "She'll get herself killed."

"Not if I can help it," Davis said, heaving herself out of the gully and heading toward the woman. As Davis emerged, Bolan saw the woman shift her stance slightly so that her aim was now directly on Davis as she hit the ground running.

It was obvious that this woman was a member of the PWLA, based on the fact that she was an armed woman in this region. Bolan could only hope she would come out of this battle unharmed—both for her sake and for his objective. The woman presented a direct link back to the PWLA camp and their target.

Davis was saved by the sudden burst of fire from behind her. Jinnah and Patel fired on the PWLA member as they closed on the gully. The woman shifted her position to avoid the volley, her aim switching to return fire that blazed wide of Davis as she hit the dirt and rock.

Bolan made a decision. He understood why the Pakistani military personnel had opened fire, but keeping this link to the PWLA alive was a priority. He was out of the gully and gaining on the woman before Davis had a chance to pull herself to her feet again.

He registered sporadic fire coming from behind the armed woman, though he was fairly certain that the enemy—those who were left, anyway—now all sat at their rear. In all likelihood, the shooters firing high and wide behind this woman were also PWLA members.

Davis was now on her feet and only a couple yards behind him as he gained on the armed woman. She had swung her rifle back toward him, but had hesitated as she caught sight of Davis, getting her first clear look at her opposition. She was clearly thrown as she realized one of the soldiers closing in on her was a woman.

Bolan took advantage of her pause to fling himself forward so that he hit her like a quarterback, full in the midriff, driving her back onto the ground with a bone-rattling jar that made her drop the rifle.

"Friend...not to hurt you...looking for PWLA." He spoke the few words of Urdu he knew.

But she wasn't listening. Her eyes were wide, questioning, as she stared over his shoulder at Davis.

"Relax. I've come for Yasmin," she said in much better Urdu than Bolan's.

JINNAH AND PATEL were now in the gully vacated by Bolan and Davis, their attention torn between what was happening on either side of the crack in the rock. While Patel watched Bolan and Davis take down the woman who had fired on them, Jinnah was looking back the way they had come. Patel was clearly confused about what the Americans were doing, but Jinnah was furious as he saw Zia struggle across the open ground, half dragging Faiz. The older soldier was trying to keep pace, but his leg wound was bleeding profusely, and the ripped muscle and bone were making it hard for him to support his weight and find the strength to continue. Jansher was moving toward them, covering them as best he could by laying down a suppressing fire that kept the remaining opponents pinned down. Jinnah counted four men as they raised their heads to return fire when they could.

It was with a grim satisfaction that Jinnah realized they had evened the odds. Six rebels down, and two of his own men. He was thankful that Faiz had survived the confrontation, but the man was in no state to fight, and they needed to end this swiftly and get him treatment. They had medical supplies in their packs, which hopefully remained on the track where they had left them.

"Fucking hell, sir. Just look," Patel yelled, reaching out to grab his superior officer. Jinnah was obscurely amused that Patel still remembered to call him sir, even when cursing. That amusement soon vanished when he turned and saw that Bolan and Davis were dragging the mountain woman in the opposite direction, away from the gully.

What did they think they were doing?

Jinnah looked back to where his other three men were making their way toward him. He swore, realizing that in their haste to follow him, they were making him and Patel sitting targets. He snapped at Patel to get out of the gully and follow Bolan and Davis.

"See where they go—don't lose them. Leave the others to me," he barked, slapping Patel on the back as the older man climbed out of the gully. Jinnah set off in the opposite direction. From his fixed position he had been able to get a clearer view of the four enemy shooters than his men would have been able to glean as they covered the terrain. Two men were hiding at ten and two o'clock, but the remaining two were smack in the middle, within a meter or two of each other. If he pitched this right, then he might be able to take the two of them out with one hit. Jinnah took a grenade from one of the pockets in his uniform. He ran at a crouch until he was nearly level with Zia and Faiz. Up close, he could see that his number two was gray with shock and blood loss. It was imperative that Zia get him into cover. Shouting a few encouraging words, he passed them and looped his arm. Like most young men of a sporting disposition in Pakistan, Jinnah had played cricket from his school days. He had perfected the art of spin bowling and was one of the first on the team sheet at his barracks. His skills came into play now as he threw the grenade, which spiraled through the air.... Gunfire crackled around him, but he closed his mind to it as he concentrated on hitting the sweet spot.

With perfect timing and aim, the grenade detonated as it touched the ground, taking the two centrally positioned rebels out of the game.

Jinnah sprinted for the gully, shrugging his rifle off his shoulder so that he could add some covering fire to Jansher's.

And then the chattering of Jansher's AK ceased. The young soldier screamed as one of the last two assailants took him down with a short burst that stitched across his chest, sending him to wherever Asif now lay at rest.

Jinnah ran backward, stumbling over rock and scrub, firing bursts at random as the ground around him was ripped up by gunfire. It was two against one, but he felt some satisfaction that this could only mean Zia had gotten Faiz to safety. The gunfire at his back confirmed this, as Zia covered his superior.

Breathless, he spared a second to look back and see what Patel was doing.

It was not quite what he had ordered.

"ASK HER WHERE the camp is, tell her we want to help," Bolan said as he pinned Lasi's arms and tried to pull her backward. Davis was beside him, scanning the territory around them. Whoever had provided covering fire for the woman had stopped shooting, and Davis was trying to locate them from the last position she had noted.

Suddenly, a burst of fire came from behind them. Davis spun around and was astounded to see Patel charging toward them, spraying.

"He's supposed to be on our side!" she yelled.

"Take her," Bolan said, thrusting the struggling Lasi into Davis's hands while he took his rifle and carefully aimed at the charging Pakistani soldier. Whether it was a temporary flash of insanity, an indication of his hidden hostility toward the PWLA, or just frustration at a mission gone fugazi in his eyes, there was no doubt that Patel had murderous intentions. Bolan, on the other hand, had no such goals. He needed a clean shot to take the man temporarily out of the game, to disable him long enough to let Jinnah deal with him... if the corporal was still alive. Bolan hoped so; Jinnah was a good soldier.

He was still drawing a bead when a burst of fire from behind him chopped Patel down as he ran. He stumbled as the bullets exploded across his chest, and he pitched forward as his momentum carried him beyond his failing legs.

Bolan swung around, ready to return fire. There were two women, poorly concealed now, with their rifles in plain view. He didn't want to take out PWLA members, but they were leaving him little choice.

Bolan took aim at the two women he could only assume were about to fire again. Davis's voice cut through everything and made him stop short as his finger tensed on the trigger.

"Colonel, no—that's Shazana Yasmin."

9

Jinnah crossed the open terrain, astounded and enraged at what he could see in the distance, yet unable to process that information while his own safety was at risk. The ground around him was ripped up by the hidden enemy's fire. To turn and try to shoot back would leave him wide open, so he kept running, moving erratically to make himself a harder target.

Zia's covering fire erupted from the gully, deflecting some of the offensive shots from Jinnah. Even though there were still bullets chopping up the dirt and stones around him, the intensity of fire slackened and made it a little easier for him to gain the gully. He flung himself in then righted himself, panting heavily. Zia met his stare, looking grim.

Jinnah glanced down at Faiz, who was barely conscious. "He needs medical aid. We need to get our packs, get those two bastards nailed down and sort out those Yanks. Any suggestions?"

Zia grinned, despite the situation. "First things first, sir—draw them out of cover."

"How do we do that, soldier?" Jinnah asked.

"I think we're already doing it, sir," Zia said. "They want to follow the women, and they think we're disabled here. They'll take a chance. We just need a little patience."

"That takes time," Jinnah murmured, looking back to where the two Americans were dragging the Baloch woman over to two other women who were standing above the lip of another trench. "We don't have that."

"Neither have they, sir," Zia returned. "They can see the women, too...."

Jinnah's lips twisted into a smile as he followed the younger soldier's eye line. The two dark shadows of their enemy were on the move, leaving their cover as they tried to gain valuable ground on the retreating Americans.

The rebels were assuming that the two soldiers in the gully were as disadvantaged as the man they had dragged there.

"You take the left, I'll take the right," Jinnah said quietly, shouldering his AK and drawing a line on the approaching shadow as it flickered in and out of view. "We'll only get one real chance, so hold your nerve."

Zia did not respond. His attention was already firmly focused on the man approaching from the left.

Sweat trickled down the soldiers' foreheads as they held their positions firm. Neither man blinked—neither man dared, for fear that in that fraction of a second, their target would slip out of sight and come up on his blind side.

The seconds seemed to stretch into hours, yet with the distance involved it could not have been more than half a minute before the two shadows came close enough to form substance, even as they used their skills to try to blend into the land.

Zia fired first. His hand was rock steady as he kept the rebel in the center of his vision. The man moved at enough of an angle to leave his body vulnerable, and there was the shot. Zia tapped twice. The first shot took his opponent in the upper right shoulder, the impact turning his body so that the second shot, which was a fraction lower, caught him full in the chest.

One down...

Jinnah resisted the temptation to check on what was happening beside him. He had to remain focused on his own target. His man was smarter—or maybe he just had more cover on his side of the plateau—and he was harder to track. Once, twice, three times the rebel slipped into view, but it wasn't enough to ensure a kill. He had to be certain.

Zia's two taps gave Jinnah the break he needed. As the shots sounded across the otherwise silent plateau, the last man standing faltered for a moment as he tried to spare a glance for what had occurred across the barren rock. His foot caught on a rock and although he did not stumble or fall, his momentum was disturbed so that he was fractionally off balance as he tried to dart behind a crop of stone. Instead of moving behind it as he had intended, he bumped his right side on the rock and snagged his clothing. He didn't stop, but for the smallest moment he slowed, presenting the perfect shot for the experienced Jinnah.

Though a body shot would have slowed him further, Jinnah didn't want to take the risk that the man, even wounded, would find shelter and draw out the confrontation. With Faiz fading and the Americans getting further away with every second, he gambled on a head shot, the small target frozen in his sights just long enough for him to show why he had been top of his class in firearms training.

One tap, one shot, one dead enemy.

Jinnah blew out slowly. "Zia, you stay here with Faiz. I'll get the packs for us and some meds. Watch those Yanks as much as possible, too. We'll do what we can for Faiz now, and then we'll get after them."

The younger soldier was bewildered "But we need to get Faiz to medics as soon as possible."

Jinnah laughed harshly. "That isn't going to happen out here, soldier. Our best chance is to catch the Americans and those women—that's the PWLA camp they're headed for, and there are bound to be medics there. Besides," he added, "we need to have a few words with everyone about what the hell is going down here."

BOLAN AND DAVIS STOOD MOMENTARILY, studying the two women a short distance away, both of whom were aiming their weapons at them.

"Are you sure?" the soldier barked, unwilling to drop his own weapon while he had two rifles trained on him. "Speak to me, Davis."

"I don't know who the tall one is, but the short woman is Shazana Yasmin. I'd know her anywhere."

"You'd better hope she knows you," he said.

Davis let go of the woman she was holding and took a step forward. "Shaz, it's me...." she yelled.

Lasi took advantage of her sudden freedom. She threw herself away from Davis and scrabbled for her rifle, rolling across the rocks as she grabbed it and coming up onto her knees with the gun trained on Bolan.

"Tell her that if she shoots, I can take out one of the women before I die," he said to Davis.

She repeated his words in her perfect Urdu, and the woman's reply came too fast for Bolan to fully grasp, but the gist was clear enough.

"Don't bother," he said as Davis began to translate. "I get it—I'll still be dead, so what good will killing either of them do me? She's right. But does she want to lose Yasmin?"

Davis translated this quickly. The woman replied, and Bolan offered a wry smile.

"She doesn't think I can shoot that well? She want to try me?"

YASMIN AND SURI stood watching the tableau unfold before them, confused and worried as they saw the man drop to his knees and aim at them while Lasi set her sights on him.

"What are we supposed to do now?" Suri asked, confusion and anger thickening her voice. "'Shaz, what is it?" she added in a panicked tone.

Yasmin was almost numb with shock. "I don't… That can't be possible," she mumbled.

"'What? What can't be possible?" Suri snapped.

Yasmin turned to her. "'How does a woman I went to college with in America turn up in the middle of Pakistan with a gun in her hand?"

Suri's brow furrowed. "Shaz, what the hell is going on?"

Yasmin gritted her teeth and leveled her rifle. "I have no idea, but Tamara joined the U.S. Army. Until the other guy drops that gun, she's as much the enemy as he is, no matter why she's here."

Suri said nothing, but leveled her own weapon, as well.

Finally, the man let his gun drop. Yasmin indicated that Suri should follow her lead and do likewise. They watched the American hold his hands over his head while Tamara picked up his weapon and Lasi ushered him toward them.

In the distance, Yasmin could see that the original fight had ceased. The last shots had echoed across a suddenly silent and deserted plain. There was no sign of either the rebels or the Pakistani military men.

At the back of her mind, Yasmin wondered if the way the Americans—particularly Tamara—were now being treated was entirely correct. It was clear that Lasi and Suri had little doubt that these two people were the enemy. But were they? The enemy was the now eliminated army of shadows that had swarmed toward them when they stood as one fighter and two inexperienced women.

But there was no time for this kind of moral dilemma as the two Americans came closer. Tamara Davis was holding a rifle, barrel downward, while the man still had his hands over his head. Lasi kept casting glances at the eerily quiet plateau behind them.

When Tamara first began to shout in their direction, Yasmin didn't take in what she was saying. Then she understood and felt a hot anger rise within her.

The words were clear. Too clear. "Shaz, you need to leave here and come back with us. You're dead otherwise. There are too many out there...."

She saw the man wince at Tamara's words. She may have been their reason for being here, but he could plainly see that Tamara's blunt approach was a very bad idea. He was right. Yasmin couldn't believe Tamara's arrogance in proclaiming such an idea.

Yasmin raised her rifle and pointed it directly at her former classmate. "I'll be the judge of that."

DAVIS STOPPED DEAD in her tracks, staring openmouthed as Yasmin gestured for her to drop the rifle.

"You'd better do as she says, Davis," Bolan said. "They have the upper hand."

Lasi said something fast in Urdu, and he saw the glances flash between the three PWLA members.

Yasmin shook her head. "No. It's me they've come for. Let them explain themselves when we get back to camp. The enemy has been driven back."

"Do you know who they were?" Bolan butted in. "Could have been Baloch rebels, maybe even gun runners or Taliban. They all know you're out here."

The young woman shook her head. She might have lacked experience, but he could see there was steel in her that would serve her well...and make his job that much harder.

"Doesn't really matter who they are," she said. "They've been sent off, and that might be warning enough for now. It's time for us to go back to camp. Then we can at least find out exactly why you're here, and who you're serving." She gestured for them to come forward. Lasi picked up Davis's weapon and followed, covering them from the rear. Bolan noted the expression on her face. If she had her way, both he and Davis would be joining their attackers in providing carrion to the mountain wildlife.

They reached Yasmin and her companion. They held their weapons rock steady even if their faces belied such confidence. They beckoned their prisoners to go ahead of them.

As they started their march to the PWLA camp, Bolan turned to survey the area they were leaving behind. He made it seem as though he wanted to address the women as he marched, but with every word his eyes were skimming the land. From the sounds of the firefight, he had been able to tell that all the opposition had been wiped out, but in that case at least one of their Pakistani allies must still be alive.

If so, then whichever man was still standing had made no attempt to come to their aid. Was it because they were biding their time? Or had they witnessed the way Bolan had been forced to turn on Patel, and maybe thought that he, not one of the women, had fired the fatal shots? On the other hand, if they knew Patel had died at the hands of the armed women, it could change their whole approach to the mission. Already, there had been latent hostility to the idea of rescuing anyone connected to the PWLA. What if that was now compounded by the notion that those they had come to retrieve had been responsible for the death of a compatriot?

The soldier scanned the horizon, hoping that he would catch a glimpse of any military men. There was nothing. He could see a few corpses on the ground, but there was no sign of movement. "I can tell you exactly why we're here," Bolan told Yasmin. "No need to take us back to your camp for that. The American government isn't too happy with the idea that a U.S. citizen may have been kidnapped by a terrorist group—"

"We're not terrorists," Yasmin snapped. "The PWLA fights for freedom, for equality. It could be argued that *your* government is a terrorist organization."

Bolan shrugged. "If you want to get philosophical, it's a thin line between one man's freedom fighter and another's terrorist. Ultimately, the U.S. government thought you had been taken by force, and so we were sent to save you. Maybe you don't need saving. Maybe you do…even if you went willingly."

Yasmin laughed. "This is America's idea of freedom, then? We're children that need help even if we don't realize it? What gives them the right to be the nanny state to a world which they still consider a mewling infant?"

"Who said anything about the nanny states?" Bolan returned. "This is me talking to you as one soldier to another. Like I said, maybe you do need saving, even if you joined the PWLA of your own accord."

Yasmin's expression contained an unspoken question—the question he had wanted her to ask.

"You said back there that the enemy had been sent off," he said. "They were defeated, but not by you and your two soldiers, and not by Davis and me, either. They were eliminated by a detachment of Pakistani army personnel, who as far as I can tell were killed defending you. In fact, all you did in that fight was kill one of them."

"They are no longer a threat. That is all that matters." She was trying to be firm, but there was a tremor of doubt in her voice.

"Sure, you can tell yourself that," Bolan returned. "But you need to face facts. You needed trained personnel to take down those men. They won't be the only ones coming after you. There won't be any military to catch your back next time. So you need to ask yourself what your people are going to do next time."

He lapsed into silence. Let Yasmin and her companion think about it. All the way back to camp.

10

Jinnah made good time back to the small pathway where the military party had left the packs. He opted to leave the Americans' two packs behind, and also three of those belonging to his men. Faiz's pack contained most of the med supplies—the grim irony of that fact did not escape him—and he picked up his own and Zia's. Each pack was heavy, and the combined weight of three made the rangy warrior strain as he heaved them up onto the plateau.

Jinnah was thankful that the route to and from the packs had hidden him from the Americans and the PWLA women. To be observed when he was disabled by the load he carried was the last thing he needed right now.

Faiz was badly injured. Cleaning and binding the wounds would only take him so far. At the very least, he needed a blood transfusion. If they tracked the Americans and the women back to the PWLA camp, there was a chance they would find the necessary supplies there.

There was, of course, no guarantee the women would

cooperate, at least initially. But that was a hurdle to be tackled later. For now, keeping Faiz alive would be enough.

As Jinnah closed on the gully he slowed so he could scout the area. He wanted the Americans and the women to be out of sight, so he could deal with Faiz before setting out after them. There was no room for interference of any kind. When he was sure they were out of visual range, he dropped the packs into the narrow space before slipping down himself.

He silenced Zia as the younger man started to speak, and unpacked the medical supplies before turning his attention to Faiz. The older warrior lay still, the whites of his eyes showing as he drifted in and out of a semi-conscious state. His wounds were bound with a rough tourniquet, but blood had soaked through the strips of rag that Zia had torn from his own fatigues while his corporal had been absent. Jinnah grunted his approval as he removed them and applied sterile dressings. He injected Faiz with a painkiller and let him rest for a moment.

Jinnah spoke to Zia quietly. "We'll need to improvise a stretcher and carry him once we've got him onto level ground," he began. "You've done a good job with him, Zia, and it will not be forgotten. Now, tell me what you saw while I was gone."

Zia delivered as full and concise a report as possible, though he couldn't help expressing his confusion at the American man's attitude.

"I can't understand why he gave in so easily, or why he was going to shoot Patel, or why he did nothing when one of the women did so."

Jinnah ran his hands through his hair, puzzling over this, as well.

"I think Stone would have fired on Patel, but not at him. Consider our mission—our orders are to get Yasmin back alive, along with what she has taken. Patel had some rush of blood to the head, and Stone couldn't let him derail the mission. Stone may even have feared for his own life. Patel's death is partly his own fault—" he raised a hand to stay Zia's protests "—I don't like it, either, but I can see why it happened. Our mission overrides everything. That's why Stone allowed himself to be taken. He will now be inside their camp."

"And what about us?" Zia asked. "I watched them go, and now they're out of sight."

Jinnah sighed. "But they don't have much of a head start. And they'll leave a trail. Maybe not the Americans, but the women will. We'll be able to track them."

"What if the Americans realize there's a trail?"

Jinnah grinned. "I doubt Stone will want to point it out to them."

BOLAN, DAVIS AND the women didn't speak as they marched across the terrain. They kept up a rapid pace, and Bolan guessed from their direction that Jinnah's original estimate of the camp's location wasn't too far off the mark. He hoped the corporal had survived the firefight. Of all the Pakistani military men, he would have wanted the corporal and his number two at their side.

As they progressed, he noted that Lasi was careful about where they trod, making sure that they weren't leaving a trail. Fortunately for the Americans, she was too preoccupied with marshaling them to notice that the far less wary women in the rear were leaving small traces of their progress for anyone who followed in their wake.

If any of the Pakistani soldiers were still alive, they could at least track them to the camp. Bolan knew that Davis was confused by this turn of events. She hadn't spoken, but the way she glanced over at him when she thought he wasn't paying attention betrayed her. She was wondering why he wasn't making a move.

Let her work it out herself. If he did anything now, he'd have Yasmin but he wouldn't have the flask. It was imperative that he extract both from the region. If he secured her now, then he would have to attack the PWLA camp to get the flask. Better that he get on the inside and have to fight his way out than the alternative.

He figured that Davis, casting surreptitious glances at him, could not think her way through any of this right now. Her pride was sorely wounded. She had assumed Yasmin would understand that she was on her side and would, therefore, accept everything she said as sound advice. To have a gun turned on her by the woman she had come to help and to save from male oppression had

stung her severely. As the small group reached the top
of an incline, they came to a steep drop into a valley,
where a twisting path took them to a blind corner. They
approached the dogleg bend, and two figures emerged
from crevices within the rock. Two women, both of
them armed. One of them spoke to Yasmin in Urdu,
and Davis whispered a translation. The woman ques-
tioned Yasmin and her compatriots about what they
had found on their patrol, remarking that other groups
had drawn a blank. They had heard the distant sounds
of a firefight, and had guessed that Lasi had engaged
with the enemy.

They continued their exchange, and it became apparent that the two women had brought the Americans
back with them partly to stop Lasi from just killing
them for the sake of it, and partly because they were
worried about the military presence and wanted to in-
terrogate Bolan and Davis—especially since Yasmin
knew Davis from her time in the U.S.A.

The two women allowed the small party through,
and Lasi led them down to the main camp.

Bolan looked carefully around, taking in as much
of their surroundings as possible. The first thing that
struck him was how small the camp was. If this was
the full extent of the PWLA, then Washington and the
NCA had seriously overestimated its size. The women
might have support, but their numbers on the ground
were poor. In terms of capability, he couldn't be sure,
but the women would probably argue that they didn't

need numbers or battle experience when they had the flask and Yasmin's know-how. But that would be worthless if the Taliban or other trained fighters decided to walk in and just take it.

They were led across the small compound and came to a halt in front of the largest tent, which made Bolan smile. No matter what the organization, you could always spot the leader by the biggest office.

"Wait here," Yasmin snapped at them before disappearing into the tent.

"I hope you have some sort of plan," Davis murmured.

Bolan shot her a warning glance. "They're not all from mountain villages, like Lasi. Most of the women here can probably speak better English than me," he whispered back. He smiled and nodded at Suri, who was glowering at him, as if to prove his point.

"Screw that, and screw you, *Colonel,*" Davis spat. "It's your job to get us out of this."

"It's my job to persuade Dr. Yasmin that she would be safer under the wing of the United States," he replied coldly.

Davis said nothing, but her glare was eloquent. Bolan was happy to ignore her and wait this out. He would need to gain the confidence of whoever was top of the food chain here, and he would be better doing that without Davis's attitude.

Yasmin came out of the tent, followed by two other women.

"I hate to rain on your parade," Bolan said with as much charm as he could muster. "But there will be more raiders. And they'll be forewarned by what happened to the first group."

"We've dealt with one attack, we can deal with another," the older of the two women answered smoothly.

Bolan's eyebrow shot up. "Two problems. The first is that your people didn't deal with it. Mine did." He could tell from the way the woman looked at Yasmin that she already knew this. He waited.

"You said two problems. You've only mentioned one. What's the second?" she asked eventually.

"As far as I know, Captain Davis and I are all that's left of the force that saw off your intruders, which means that when the second wave hits, you're in serious trouble unless you lower your guns and start listening because I don't want to die, and I'm certain you feel the same."

JINNAH AND ZIA fashioned a hammock stretcher into which they placed the now-sedated Faiz. He was a big man, and one hell of a deadweight to carry between them, especially after they'd divided his supplies between their own two packs. With that kind of load and the pace they needed to keep up, their stamina was going to be seriously strained. They had to reach the PWLA camp before Faiz's condition deteriorated too much more. They also knew that the PWLA women and the Americans had a good start on them, and even though they were easily able to pick up their trail now, the fragile traces would be erased by the elements before long.

As the afternoon began to darken to dusk and the temperature started to drop, Jinnah realized that the coolness may benefit them, but for Faiz, in his weakened state, it could mean hypothermia. Moreover, the fading light would make the delicate trail harder to follow. But to stop for the night would mean certain death for their injured comrade.

Jinnah urged Zia on with a few barked words, imploring him to keep his eyes on the trail and encouraging him with a reminder that their initial search area had been small, so the PWLA base could not be too far away. Still, he knew in the back of his mind that distance was relative when you were carrying a wounded man.

As THEY JOGGED ON, following the trail and hoping they would hit the camp sooner rather than later, Jinnah was filled with misgivings, and based on Zia's silence, he could tell the other soldier was, too. Both had become so wrapped up in their thoughts that they were not expecting to crest an incline and hit the narrow path into a valley. Their downward momentum was rudely interrupted when they hit a bend and heard voices from above, commanding them to stop.

Jinnah cursed his carelessness as three women appeared on the rocks, rifles trained on them. They had reached their objective, but unexpectedly and without the caution and reconnaissance he had wanted to bring to the situation.

11

"You think they'll take what you said to heart?" Davis asked with an edge in her voice that was half concern, half sarcasm.

Bolan chewed on the tough goat meat in the curry they had given him and shrugged.

"Their problem, not mine. If it comes to it, then I'll grab the target and it's every man for himself."

"Or every woman?" Davis queried.

"Your tone suggests you know the answer to that," he murmured. "You're making your loyalties pretty obvious. You should remember who pays your salary and the oath you took when you started to wear a uniform. Nations are made of men and women, not just one sex— no matter who you think runs them."

"So if this second attack comes? And as soon as you think it will?" she pressed.

"Then you need to make up your mind," Bolan said. He was about to continue, when something on the path they'd taken into camp caught his attention.

"So we weren't the only ones...."

He was up and striding past Davis before she had a chance to take in what he meant. By the time she was on her feet and in his wake, he was already looking over the prone Pakistani soldier as some of the PWLA women clustered around.

Davis joined the group, Lasi close at her shoulder, while Bolan discussed the injured soldier with a lanky woman dressed in shalwar kameez and a fur waistcoat, who was examining Faiz.

"I will do what I can, I suppose," the woman told him. "But my priority with the few supplies we have is to tend to our own people rather than the enemy. Besides, these men seem to have done a reasonable job with him." She gestured with disdain at Zia and Jinnah.

Bolan was speechless for a moment. When he spoke, it was as much to the group as to the medic. "This 'enemy' soldier was injured fighting off an attack by a larger force that was out to overwhelm you. Frankly, if we hadn't been there by chance, they would have Lasi succeeded. Lasi knows what she's doing, but Suri and Yasmin look like they've hardly held a weapon. In effect, Lasi was outnumbered ten to one. Very few people can overcome those odds, even with luck. You should be thanking this man for putting himself in the firing line. You should be thanking these two soldiers for what they did instead of holding them at the point of a gun. And you should spare a thought for the three men who aren't here when you are."

His speech was met with a slow, ironic hand clap.

The two women who had followed Yasmin out of the tent earlier cut through the small crowd.

"Very good...very...*stirring* is the word, I think," one of them said. "But you are still U.S. military, they are still NCA men and you still want to take our prize from us. That makes you the enemy." She spoke a few words in the local dialect that had Lasi aiming her rifle in the soldier's face. "We will keep defending ourselves. So far we have survived. We can continue to do so...." She looked around at everyone in the small crowd before focusing her attention back on Bolan, Davis and the soldiers. "Now, all of you will go with Lasi and wait where she leaves you until we decide the best course of action. Your comrade will be tended to, as he may be a useful hostage. As may all of you."

She dismissed the clustered PWLA members with a gesture and turned on her heel. Some had lapped up her every word, but Bolan could see that a few women—especially Yasmin and the woman who had been with her during the firefight—were not so sure. Their leader wasn't stupid, but she was a fired-up zealot. Maybe the others were not so ideologically driven that logic and sense were lost on them.

As Bolan, Davis and the two Pakistani soldiers were led away from the main camp, he cast a look back at Faiz. The medic was still there, and two other women who appeared a little more enthusiastic about treating him had joined her. He also noticed that a small group had gathered around Yasmin and the taller woman, talking in hushed tones.

Maybe there was some hope.

JINNAH AND ZIA had said little since they had entered the camp. Like Bolan and Davis, they had been disarmed, and as they ate steadily and watched the PWLA go about its business, Bolan could see that the two Pakistani soldiers were sizing up the opposition and their chances of getting armed and getting out.

"It might not be the best way," he said softly. "Some of the women don't toe the party line on us being the real enemy. We could blow it if we try to get our weapons back by force."

Jinnah stared at him, clearly surprised that his thoughts had been so transparent. "Then how do you suggest we get ourselves armed? You know as well as I do that the men we faced down won't be the only ones on their way here. And I would feel safer waiting for them with a gun in my hand."

Zia spat on the ground. "Maybe he just wants us to kowtow to the women. Maybe his orders are to join them, not take the woman away."

"Joining them does the U.S. no good, and it does Pakistan no good. This is bigger than their cause," Bolan returned. "We represent our nations, joint..."

Zia smiled, but without any warmth. "That right, Colonel Stone? Didn't look that way when you were ready to take down Vin. Only reason you didn't was because one of your women got the first shot in."

"He was going to charge down Yasmin, and he looked about ready to shoot me and Davis, too. My aim was never to kill him—just to stop him from compromising the mission."

"This is basically what I told Zia," Jinnah said. "He's young, Colonel, and although he has experience, he has not yet lived long enough to see what we have. Now may I suggest that we concentrate on how the hell we get ourselves armed and protected? If there's another attack before we achieve this, I truly would not give much for the chances of our target surviving, not to mention ourselves."

"We're on the same page about that, Corporal," Bolan agreed. He eyed Lasi, who was still standing guard a few yards away. She studied them with rancor. The PWLA was missing a trick by putting her on guard duty. She might have combat skill and the right level of antipathy for them, but she apparently spoke next to no English, so she wouldn't be able to understand any plans they were making. Bolan wondered how he could play this to their advantage.

He was about to point this out to Jinnah and Zia, but his words were stayed by the sound of distant gunfire. Lasi turned away from them, her attention drawn to the machine gun chatter.

In the camp, there was a stir of activity as the women came out of their tents. The two leaders emerged and started to shout orders in Urdu. The milling throng was slow to react at first, but as the gunfire grew closer with each second, echoing into the valley, many of the women were galvanized into action. But while some of them grabbed weapons and began to move off in the maneuvers they had practiced in training, the remainder were slower, clustering around Yasmin and the woman who had been with her in the field.

Bolan noted this with interest, and jabbed Davis with his elbow. The two Pakistani soldiers were already alert to what was happening.

Yasmin and her companion spoke briefly and rapidly to the group around them before grabbing extra weapons. The two women ran over to where Bolan and his crew sat, saying something to Lasi that made her spit. Then they handed over the spare guns.

"I don't care what Indira or Shirani says," Yasmin began breathlessly. "I don't think you're on my side a hundred percent, but you're sure as hell not on the side of whoever's coming after us, and that's what matters right now. We need you, and I'll talk to you about whatever you want after, if you'll help us now."

Bolan nodded as he took one of the proffered AKs.

THREE BLACK-CLAD FIGURES swooped over the landscape. Their informants had provided the times and routes of the recon patrol from the PWLA camp, and these men, who had been sent as an advance guard by their group, knew that their job was to intercept and eliminate. They were to clear the way for the rest of their forces to sweep into the camp without resistance or forewarning.

They settled into crevices in the rock, covered by scrub, and waited. Like the force that had been wiped out earlier in the day, they were part of an Islamist cell. And like that force, they were determined to gain the upper hand among the rival groups in the region.

They settled in and waited for the patrol to approach. The women detailed to the route were obviously inexperienced. They didn't speak as they moved, but their progress was noisier than they could have wished. Loose shale and rock shot from under their feet, no matter how carefully they trod. They winced as they took each step, hesitating as they tried to adjust their footfalls.

It was that hesitancy that saved them from instant death.

Deep in cover, one of the fighters drew a bead and loosed a short burst of fire that should have stitched both women across the chest. But one of the women spotted loose shale about to go under the sole of her companion's boot and snatched at her sleeve, jerking her back. With a yelp of surprise, she stumbled and fell against her partner. The two of them tumbled to the ground. The bullets pinged harmlessly into the rock near where the women had been standing.

To their credit, the two women may not have been the most experienced, but their shock was short-lived, and they scrambled into the closest cover they could find, shrugging their rifles from their shoulders and aiming in the direction they thought the shots had come from. Both women sent a short tap into the darkness.

Return fire came from three directions—one volley came from the original shooter, while the two others pinned them down on either side of the scant cover they had found.

Again and again, the two women kept up a rearguard action, trying, at least, to carve out enough space to make an escape. But with each round of fire, they realized they had not made a dent on their opponents, and had only pinpointed their own position.

The three men took advantage of the women's inexperience, closing them down and keeping them in place until they stood above the fissure in which they were hiding, trapping them in a triangle of fire.

Desperately looking up and firing into the darkness, the two women kept up their fight until the end. But with one final, decisive volley, the men cut their opponents to ribbons and silenced their guns.

In the silence that ensued, the women in camp appeared confused. Bolan exchanged looks with Jinnah, Zia and Davis. The corporal shook his head.

"They are through," he said simply.

Bolan yelled for Yasmin to come over. She complied, much to the chagrin of Indira and Shirani, who screamed for her to turn back toward them.

"This better be good," she panted as she came close. "There's going to be hell to pay—"

"There'll be hell if you don't listen," Bolan snapped, "no matter what they think. Can you trust your people?"

"They'll listen to me," she affirmed.

"Good. Split them into four parties." He indicated Jinnah, Zia, Davis and himself. "We'll head up one each. We have to work on the assumption that they took out your patrol," he added more gently, noting her shocked expression. "You need to hold it together for everyone. If you all follow what we say, then we've got a chance. They'll be here soon, and we need to be ready…."

He considered the young woman and gazed beyond her to the rest of the PWLA camp.

They would need luck, too.

12

Yasmin had taken well to her task, and although the two PWLA leaders looked as though they'd rather be doing things their way, they had reluctantly bowed to pressure and joined the others. The women were now clustered into groups of four to six, ready to be directed.

The soldier lifted his head and listened to the silence. Out there in the darkness, an enemy force of indeterminate size was closing on them. He had a rough idea of their initial direction from the sounds of the firefight, but how they had spread now that they had a bridgehead was another matter.

He assigned Zia, Jinnah and Davis to three groups and took the fourth himself. Davis shot him a quizzical look. He had chosen the group that included Yasmin.

"My mission, my responsibility," he answered her querying gaze. "I'll look after her, Davis. No worries."

IN THE DARKNESS, the raiding party moved forward to join the advance fighters. There were a dozen of them, and they moved en bloc until they reached the other three men, and they looked on the corpses of the PWLA patrol with grim satisfaction. Like all groups in these hills, they had only a rough idea of how many people made up each of the opposing factions, but they had enough intel to know that the PWLA was one of the smaller groups. It was entirely possible that they outnumbered the female rebels. They'd learned that the PWLA had gained some outside help, but not much, and considering the devastation on the battlefield earlier in the day, any remaining forces would have been depleted by fatigue and injury as well as death.

Their battle plan was simple: they would spread out and form a cordon along the path that had been the patrol route encircling the camp. Once they were in position, they would signal each other and mount an attack that would come from all sides, overwhelming their enemy before they had a chance to muster a response.

Once they had the flask, then they would be able to do what they wanted, and demand that the other fighting factions in Balochistan rally behind them. Power— that was the simple aim.

Who could stop them?

BOLAN GATHERED THE four parties together in the center of camp. The silence around them was growing oppressive, and he could almost feel the steel band of the opposition tightening around them.

It wasn't too much of a leap to assume that the approaching enemy would use the patrol route around the camp to close in on them. Bolan instructed each group to take a compass point on the route. Once they each reached their positions, they could spread out if they hadn't already encountered the enemy. If they met them en route, then it would be up to the four professionals to use their experience to fight them off.

Bolan's briefing was swift, and his upbeat and encouraging tone fired up the nervous PWLA. He kept his concerns to himself as they mobilized, but he knew there was every possibility that they were lambs for the slaughter.

It was up to the four shepherds to keep them safe.

Zia took his squad to the north, and they were the first to encounter and engage with the enemy. He spread his party out in a fan movement as they progressed over the terrain, staying in the center so that he could keep each wing in full view. He had little faith in the women and was acutely aware of his responsibility as both the sole professional and as the youngest of the military left standing.

He hissed orders at them as they advanced, directing them toward cover where he thought they might be missing it and reining in those who sought to roam too freely.

He could see little in the darkness, but his finely tuned hearing compensated for this. His ears alerted him to the approaching forces. Loose shale to his left and a few hundred meters ahead. He scanned for any sign of the enemy. There—a patch of darkness was moving when it shouldn't be.

The hairs bristled on the back of his neck, and he knew that he was right. A fraction of a second before the enemy warrior rose enough to take fire, Zia had his AK aimed squarely in the center of the dark patch. He yelled a warning to his women as he loosed a volley of fire. The patch of shadow dropped away, the fighter ripped to shreds by Zia's accurate aim.

The resultant chaos severely tested both his powers of leadership and the mettle of his fighters. Out of the darkness, shapes rose and formed from the cover of rocks and scrub. Two of the women, slow and scared by the sudden activity, were taken out before they had a chance to return fire. But this only served to galvanize those remaining, and they followed Zia's directions to take any available cover, to aim at the center of anything moving in the dark, and to keep tapping out rapid, short bursts.

The firefight was short and savage. The raiders moved quickly, seeking to use the advantage of surprise to overrun their opponents, but they found themselves at the mercy of women whose nerves were steeled by their survival instinct. They stayed in cover, picked their targets well and waited until their aim was clear before taking down their assailants.

Then it was over, and in the sudden silence, Zia surveyed his troops and the havoc they had wrought with satisfaction and a little surprise. He scanned the dark-

ness, listening to the gunfire that had erupted elsewhere. When he was sure that they had fought off the
wave from the north, he nodded and rose slowly, gesturing to the women to pull back to the camp, where they
could back up the other factions if necessary.

Mission partially accomplished.

DAVIS TOOK THE EAST. They left the valley by the same
path they had entered it, and while the trail left them
partially exposed, any approaching contingent would
give themselves away on the loose rocks.

She led her troops out of the valley quickly, wanting to get them on level ground before the enemy had a
chance to come down on them. The sharp rise of rock,
with some overhanging vegetation, gave her team the
perfect location to mount an ambush, and her plan was
to place her people and wait.

As she directed them to crevices and clusters of rock
and scrub, she realized they hadn't been as quick as
she'd hoped they'd be. As the sounds of firefights breaking out in first one and then another compass point
started to ring in her ears, a single sniper shot pierced
the night air, and the woman standing two yards from
her toppled to the ground without the chance to utter
a sound.

This threw her troops into panic, and two more
were picked off rapidly by the sniper as she tried to
rally them. She was lucky to have Lasi in her party.
Lasi would not have trusted any of the men to lead her,

and before Davis had a chance to issue any orders, the woman had skipped off into the darkness, scaling the rocks and hauling herself up and over the point where the sniper was located. His silhouette became visible as he rose up and tried to turn his weapon on her, but he was too slow for the nimble-footed warrior, who didn't bother with her rifle at such close quarters. She opted instead for the knife she carried and eliminated her foe.

With three women down and Lasi otherwise occupied, Davis pulled the two remaining women in her crew into cover as the enemy horde descended like a swarm of bats in the darkness. She gestured for them to remain silent. With a seemingly clear path down to the camp, the intruders likely assumed they'd taken out everyone in their way. It was a risky strategy, but the only one she could play at such short notice. She needed to get in behind the opposition and use surprise, but in order to do this she was—for the moment—leaving the PWLA camp wide open.

As the enemy swept past them, she could read the confusion and fear in the eyes of the two women beside her. Seeing their comrades fall and hearing the distant firefights, they likely felt they were on the losing side. It was up to her to change that view. She gave them silent reassurance, and counted off on her fingers as she watched the enemy charge down the winding trail.

Davis counted to three after the last man passed their position, to allow for stragglers, then she stepped into the open, first sweeping her rifle around to take in any men that might be lingering in the shadows. There were none; it was a straight call. The two women were at her back, and Lasi had dropped down from the rocks to join them. She nodded approvingly at Davis, realizing what the Captain had done.

The four of them opened fire at once, and a hail of bullets tore into the backs of the enemy fighters. Hemmed in by the rock face on one side and a drop on the other, there was little the men could do except try to turn around on the narrow path.

It was a chicken shoot. The four women kept up a barrage of fire, standing firm against any random shots that were returned. They did not stop until the last man was down. Even then, Lasi advanced toward them, still firing random bursts into the corpses, as if to make sure. The path ahead of them was littered with bodies and blood, but they had at least seen off the opposition from this direction.

But at what cost? Davis looked at the three women with her, and then back up the trail to where the three dead PWLA fighters lay.

A 50 percent loss was bad. If that was an indication of the overall casualties, then they would be in serious trouble in another onslaught.

For the first time, Davis found herself hoping Colonel Stone had an answer to this problem.

JINNAH LED HIS fighters to the south. They traveled up a soft incline and onto a plateau where there was little cover. He could see that this was worrying them, so he calmly pointed out that if they had no cover, neither did the encroaching troops. They were on a level playing field in more ways than one. The best thing they could do was to find positions from which they could spy the enemy before the enemy caught sight of them.

His words and his calm manner seemed to do much to reassure the four women who were under his command, but he did not feel the composure he was radiating. As far as he was concerned, he had four novice fighters facing an unknown number of attackers, each one of whom had more experience in his little finger than these women had between them.

But Jinnah had spent his life battling overwhelming odds, and he was damned if he was going to go down without a fight. In fact, he was damned if he was going to go down at all.

The dark plateau was split in places by small ravines and crevices, including covered paths. Yasmin had briefed him on the regular patrol route, and the one thing he knew for certain was that to try to use these covered areas for shelter would be fatal.

However, if he could trap any opponents in one of these, then it would be like shooting fish in a barrel.

The question was: How could he do this?

Surveying the land, he believed he had the answer. Spaced out across the plateau were a few rock outcrops that would provide a vantage point. Swiftly, he detailed women to four of these points. In the distance, he could

see movement, ill-defined in the darkness, but undoubtedly the approaching enemy.

He lagged behind his troops slightly, ready to give
them backup and to maintain a panorama of the scene.

The women did little to conceal their movement,
but Jinnah calculated that speed was better than stealth
right now. By his reckoning, the enemy was still too
far away to shoot with any degree of accuracy, even if
they could see their targets. He would rather they were
seen now than proceed cautiously and be caught out in
the open later.

Jinnah's idea was simple. From their four positions,
the women would start a barrage of fire in order to contain movement as much as cause collateral damage. One
by one, as they got into place, they started to carry out
his plan. Short, controlled bursts stopped the enemy
line from diffusing, and drove the men into one central
spot. Only a couple of them went down, but that didn't
matter. What mattered was that the women remained
safe in their secured perches. The opposition was right
where Jinnah wanted them.

The women were funneling the enemy fighters into a
dip in the plateau, where a small path—used on PWLA
patrols—wound through a section of rock. Jinnah and
the PWLA members knew exactly where they were
driving the enemy, who—for their part—would be
thankful for this apparent shelter.

MOVING QUICKLY OVER the terrain, using some shelter but
prizing speed and surprise over stealth, Jinnah pulled

a grenade from his fatigues. He halted momentarily—
so slightly that it looked like no more than a stumble
in his step—and threw a slow right-arm delivery that
would have baffled any batsman. It planted his egg right
where he wanted it, and he hit the ground to avoid the
full impact of dirt, pebbles and shards of rock thrown
up in the blast. Then he was on his feet and running to
the path, his rifle set to rapid and off his shoulder. He
began to fire into the ditch when he was within ten meters, though in truth he didn't expect much return fire
after the explosion. He continued to fire as he closed
on the ditch, and only stopped when he was standing
over it and could see that everyone within it had been
permanently taken out of the game.

With a nod of satisfaction, he drew back to a more
secure position, signaling for his four troops to join
him. In the background, he could still hear the rum-
bling of gunfire.

He wondered how Stone was faring.

BOLAN HAD CHOSEN the sector that he thought would be
the hardest. Despite the fact that Yasmin was by his
side, and he needed to ensure her safety in order to
complete the mission, he couldn't bring himself to put
the other soldiers at greater risk than himself.

To the south of the camp there was very little cover.
The ground was flat and almost devoid of any crevices
or outcrops. It was just one long expanse of rock. Any
enemy approaching would have to travel fast and hit

hard. Once they came into view, there would be little time for strategy or attempts at regrouping. It would be full on warfare and would be a bitter fight.

About a yard below the lip of the valley, there was a narrow path. The only thing Bolan could do was to line up the five women—including Shazana Yasmin and her friend Benazir Suri—and direct them to fire as soon as their opponents were in sight. But Bolan was determined to make sure the enemies who made it into the women's line of fire were few and far between.

Leaving his troops in position, he set off across the terrain. Even in camo gear, he felt conspicuous. When there was no real cover, his only option was to hit the enemy hard, before they had a chance to fight back.

He'd brought a night-vision monocle on the mission, and it was invaluable now, enabling him to sharpen his perception of the approaching figures.

He still had a white-phosphorus grenade in one pocket, which had been in the pack supplied to him by the Pakistani military.

He threw the grenade into the center of the oncoming group, where it lit up the night sky as the phosphorus spread and turned some of the enemy fighters into flaming torches. Bolan turned away to avoid the blinding flash, and when he turned back he was able to pick off some of the blazing men with ease. He lay flat, hugging the rocky ground, and ignored the gunfire that ripped up the ground around him. The men were blinded by the blast and were firing wide and wild. Bolan, by contrast, was able to see clearly.

By the time the roaring in his ears had subsided, Bolan had succeeded in keeping his troops safe and had halted this wave of the attack.

He got to his feet and pulled back to the secure position above the camp. Hearing the firefights abate, he wondered how many casualties the PWLA had incurred.

More important, how long until the next onslaught? And how would they deal with that?

13

The cold light of morning revealed a camp that had been reduced by almost a third. The area itself was intact and secure, but the exhausted women that came back would never be the same again. This had been the first time that they had engaged in a serious action, and they had been found wanting. They all knew this, even the ones in Jinnah and Bolan's detachments, where there had been no casualties. The gaps in their ranks and the empty tents spoke for themselves.

Davis looked shaken, Zia disappointed, and Jinnah—like Bolan—was trying to keep the concern from his face.

The women milled around the center of camp, unsure of what to do next. They were tired, grieving, jittery with adrenaline and on edge. They seemed to gravitate to the military personnel, even though Bolan could see that Indira was lurking on the fringes, as though fighting the urge to join them. He noticed that Shirani, who was always at her side, was absent—one of the casualties. Maybe that would change her mind. He counted four other missing women, but surprisingly there were no wounded. That was a plus. Now to rally the troops before they came under siege again.

"It's been a tough night," he said shortly. "You've seen things you haven't seen before, and you've coped well. We saw them off, but only just. I'm afraid that if another force comes, we won't have the strength to fight. Even though," he added, "you've got the heart."

"Then what do we do?" Suri asked him, looking around at the others. There were mumblings and nods of assent.

"First, we move camp. This location is blown. Get those tents down, and—"

"Where?" the tall woman cut in.

"You tell me," Bolan said. "You all have skills and knowledge, you just need to learn how to apply them. We—" he indicated himself and the military "—don't know this area as well as you. You've covered it. We need a camp that can be secured easily with few people."

"But what good will that do us when they come again?" Indira called. "We'll still be weak."

Bolan shook his head. "No, you won't," he said emphatically. "You fought well tonight. You already have the guts, and we're going to teach you what you need to know so that next time, you'll be ready. But first, we need to move somewhere we can do that without interruption."

A buzz spread through the group. Even those who

had lost the women fighting next to them had seen the difference the military had made to their survival.

Bolan turned away, satisfied that he had been able to buoy their spirits enough to get them to a safer location and accept training. Now it was time to debrief. He led his people discreetly away from the women of the PWLA.

Once they were out of earshot, he sat them down and listened to their reports before delivering his own. When he had finished, he said, "Zia, you look upset about the situation. You did well."

The young Pakistani soldier shook his head. "I lost two women. You know, I was wrong about them. They were brave, they fought well and I let them down."

"You didn't," Bolan said firmly. "You lost two because that's war."

"I lost them because I treated them like they were trained men. They were not. I should have taken that into account and acted like you and my corporal. I should have led from the front, and taken the whole risk upon myself."

"He's right," Davis agreed bitterly. "I lost more than him, and I've got more reason to know and understand who these people are."

"Because you're a woman?" Jinnah said with a sardonic smile. "Please. You may as well say I should relate to the PWLA better than you because I'm Pakistani and you're not. The colonel and I took stupid risks, and we know that. Am I right, sir?" he asked Bolan.

"You've got a point," Bolan allowed. "Sure, we kept them safe in battle, but that was as much an accident of geography as anything else. And if we'd gotten ourselves killed because we were playing heroes, then where would it have left everyone else? No, we can argue from now until the next attack comes, but the fact is that we all did what was right in the moment, and luck helped some of those decisions pay off. Davis, you can't do anything against a sniper until he's revealed himself by shooting. Zia, you did your best for the women, but the circumstances were working against you. That's war. All we can do is regroup, train them and try to persuade them to get out of the militant game altogether."

"You really think we can do that?" Davis asked.

Bolan glanced at the huddle of women.

"They may be realizing on their own that there are better ways to achieve their goals than playing at being rebels," he said softly. "If they are, then it'll make our job a whole lot easier...."

FIVE MILES DUE east of the valley where the PWLA camp was pitched, there was another dip in the plateau, where a shallow valley was ringed with caves. This had not been the first choice for camp because it was a mile and a half from a stream, whereas their current camp was only a few hundred yards from running water. But the PWLA's priorities had shifted. Water could be stored and carried; security could not.

The plan was to bottle as much water as possible,

then pack up and embark on a march across the plain. Bolan and Jinnah would carry extralarge packs, so that two of the women could carry Faiz's stretcher. The wounded soldier had slept through most of the night's firefight, and when conscious, he had been barely aware of his surroundings. The previously indifferent medic was more attentive now that she'd witnessed his comrades' actions. She'd expressed her concerns to Jinnah that his condition was not improving.

"She says we'll have to get him to a hospital before too long, or he'll simply fade away," Jinnah told Bolan as they filled the last of the containers from the stream. "She's doing her best now, but his wounds and blood loss are beyond her skills and resources."

"How long have we got?" Bolan asked grimly.

"Days…a week at most," Jinnah returned.

Bolan said nothing, but as he stood up, he nodded and patted Jinnah on the shoulder. He hoped his gesture would communicate his intent: Bolan left no one behind.

They set out as the sun reached the middle of the sky. Bolan took point and Jinnah took the rear guard, with the women and Faiz strung out between them, leading mules and goats laden with the tents, water and arms. Lasi moved along the line; the few livestock they kept came under her watch. Davis and Zia flanked either side of the line once they'd crested the winding path out of the valley and were crossing the vast plateau.

Out on the plain, there was little cover. Even in small

groups, it would have been difficult to find concealment. En masse, they were pitifully exposed to any
approaching enemy forces, which would likely be trav-
eling in small groups in order to hide more easily. This
made the journey a nervous, edgy affair. The four military personnel took on the brunt of the recon, allowing
the women to concentrate on forging ahead.

As they marched, Bolan wondered if they were being
watched. If any of the rebel groups had access to satellite imagery, then they might be able to track them.
They could have men out in the field, as well. One man
on recon would easily spot the convoy, while it would
be unlikely for any of them to see a single figure across
the plateau.

Still, there was little sign of life, and all the soldier
could do was greet this with cautious optimism. He
had no doubt that the women could be molded into a
stronger defensive force. And he firmly believed he and
Davis could persuade them to at least return to Quetta.
But everything depended on time—the time it would
take to train them and convince them to return to civilization; the time it would take another rebel group to
realize the last attack had failed and to mount one of
their own.

The clock was ticking.

THE VALLEY IN WHICH they now set up camp wasn't deep
enough to safely conceal their tents. Instead, they opted
to use the caves hewn into the rocks for shelter. From

Bolan's point of view, this was preferable to being out in the open. Their position would be more difficult to spot, and the rock walls provided more fortification and defensive cover than canvas. From the PWLA's point of view, however, the grottoes were cold, damp and uncomfortable when all the women wanted to do was rest. Yet despite their complaints, none of them found it hard to welcome sleep when Bolan told them to rest and recuperate after their journey. The hard work would begin soon enough, but there was little point in starting while they were still this exhausted.

Bolan and Zia took first watch while everyone slept. The two men circled the rim of the narrow valley, meeting up on every circuit to report.

Zia nervously scanned the horizon. "We're exposed up here," he murmured. "I don't like it. We could too easily attract attention to ourselves and expose the camp."

"There's little choice," Bolan replied. "Chances are we would see them as they saw us, and at least we'd be able to prepare."

"Would we?"

Bolan studied Zia carefully. He could see the genuine concern in the young man's face, as well as the strain of the past forty-eight hours. "Yes. Listen to me—you're tired and you need rest. You're a good soldier. You've proved that. But we all need to rest. Believe me, when we've had a chance to grab some sleep we'll be able to tackle this, no worries."

Zia paused before assenting. He breathed out heavily. "Maybe…"

Bolan understood the soldier's apprehension, but all they could do was see this out to the bitter end. He sent Zia back around the rim, watching him tread wearily.

When Jinnah and Davis came to relieve them, Bolan was glad to get to a cave, a sleeping bag and black oblivion.

He awoke in the late afternoon. All the women were up and going about their business, and he saw that Zia was among them. Bolan was relieved to see that the young soldier looked much brighter and fitter now that he'd rested. Bolan ate from the pot of lentils some of the PWLA women had prepared, and as two of them took over lookout from Jinnah and Davis, the two military personnel joined Bolan and Zia in teaching the women necessary combat skills.

They divided the women into four groups, with each of the military personnel heading up one training station. Davis was detailed to prepare them for hand-to-hand combat, as she was of a similar build to most of the women and had a better idea of the small adjustments in unarmed techniques that would put the women on an equal footing quickly.

Zia's task was to run the women through the hardware they had at their disposal. Since they needed to conserve ammunition and any gunfire could alert hostile forces to their position, they couldn't practice shooting, but Zia had always excelled at ordnance, and he was able to explain concisely how each pistol, SMG and rifle worked and how it should be handled. They had little in the way of explosives or grenades, but Zia discussed them anyway. In the battles they'd fought so far on this mission, grenades had changed the game. He wanted each woman to be prepared to use one if the need arose.

Bolan and Jinnah concentrated on tactics and strategy. The senior military men wanted to educate the women on the ways in which they could use their new-found skills to their best advantage.

They shared as much as they could about organizing forces and placing personnel on the field; about judging a situation and responding to a threat; about planning an attack or defending against an attack that came from more than one direction; about recon and patrols.... Both Bolan and Jinnah knew these elements of combat were best taught by experience, but they did their best to impart their combined knowledge to the women, hoping it would count for something.

Of course, the PWLA did have some experience, and Jinnah and Bolan were able to use this to illustrate some of their points. The fight was fresh enough in the women's minds that they paid close attention to men they may not otherwise have had any inclination to believe.

At the end of an intensive day, as a security patrol kept watch around the rim of the valley, Bolan and his people sat with the PWLA and ate.

Indira broke the initial silence. "I don't like what you

stand for or who you are, Colonel Stone. You must know this. But I'm not so stubborn that I can't see when there is sense in what someone says. You must have seen us talking among ourselves…." She paused, waiting for Bolan to assent. "We are strong in spirit but we are not strong in experience," she continued. "Coming out here, setting up camp, we thought we could make our voices heard. In truth, the only thing we're doing is ensuring our own demise. There is no future in waiting out here to be killed by our enemies, whoever they might be. There are other ways to fight."

Davis made to speak, and sensing how much strain it took the PWLA leader to admit this, Bolan deferred to the captain. "Are you telling us that you want to go back to the city?" she asked Indira. "To work through the judiciary and government?"

Indira gave an ironic laugh. "You say that like it was a choice. There is no real choice. Try to shout loud or be shot. Some choice."

"At least you'll be alive to shout," Davis said softly. "Democratic change might be possible. Many of these fundamentalist groups aren't the greatest admirers of democracy—or women's rights. Imagine what they'd do if Shaz fell into their hands with what she has. And it's not just them. For all we know, the Taliban is on our trail, too, and any number of factions who could benefit from a hostage and a flask of fissionable material. Do you want to lose everything you've worked for to some smugglers with big guns?"

Bolan could see from both Indira and Dr. Yasmin's expressions that this had been a part of their discussion.

So they would head back toward Quetta. They'd rest for the night, and then start marching come daylight. Bolan was quietly satisfied. If they could keep their recon tight, then it would only be a couple of days' march until the mission objective was sealed.

What could go wrong?

14

The morning was dark and overcast. From the east, heavy rolling clouds swept over the plateau, the dank, humid winds that carried them presaging a rough day ahead. As the PWLA group made their way up onto the plain from the valley that had briefly been their home, the weather seemed to reflect the downbeat mood that hung over them.

Bolan took point, Jinnah took the rear guard, and they fell easily into the formation that had brought them to this spot. Yet there was something different about them—an air of defeat, as though heading back to civilization was somehow an admission of failure. Maybe, in some senses, it was. As long as the PWLA had been able to remain outside the Pakistani mainstream, the government had been unable to silence them. The world knew they were there, even if they had so far achieved little other than to announce their presence and establish an identity as a group with an agenda. They stood out, and they could make the world take notice. Once they were subsumed into the mainstream, routing their concerns through official channels, they ran a very real risk of disappearing.

This feeling dragged the women down. They had come so far, lost many of their comrades, and yet what had they achieved except to give in and go back?

Bolan could have spent all day showing them that, in their case, it was better to fight from the inside, even if they were almost invisible, than to be corpses on a hillside with all hope of change gone. This was the only logical argument, but he understood that it would serve no purpose right now. He'd gained their trust in combat, and they'd agreed to return to Quetta on their own terms. But Bolan was well aware that the PWLA's allegiance to him and the military personnel was shaky at best. The women's ambivalence, if challenged, could prove to be dangerous.

SOUND TRAVELED WELL across the rolling hillsides and plateaus of Balochistan, and the rumblings of the firefight between the PWLA and the intruders had been heard at some distance.

Those who lived in the hills for long enough often learned to read the exchanges of fire as though they were ciphered messages, and so it was that the Taliban faction that haunted the plain knew that another war party had fallen afoul of the women's rights group. They'd received intel that a Pakistani military detachment had been in the area with two Americans. They also knew that their numbers had been depleted. It wasn't hard to work out that the military's expertise had saved the women. Similarly, it wasn't difficult to surmise that if wave upon wave of small cells attacked, the PWLA and military numbers would be ground down to nothing.

It was a game of patience and chance, of waiting for the optimal moment to strike and hoping that other groups would crack first and do the hard work.

Weighing this, it was only a matter of time before the nerve of one Taliban unit broke, and they set off in pursuit. They traveled all night, tracking down the old PWLA camp and finding it deserted. Along the way, they had come across the dead of both sides. The heavy exchange of fire had taken its toll. The PWLA and their military aides would be exhausted. If the Taliban fighters could follow them and hit them hard, then it would be an easy strike.

There were eight in the group. They moved in silence across the harsh terrain, the cold biting into their bones. Tracking the PWLA's flight from their first camp was simple. Despite their best efforts, they'd left an easily discernible trail. Carrying a wounded man with them had not aided any attempts to disguise their path.

As dawn broke, one of the Taliban men—Yusef Khan, an advance scout—tracked back to the main group to report what he'd seen: a shallow dip in the land where the PWLA had set up a second camp. So as not to betray their presence on the open plain, the other seven men took cover while the scout advanced to probe the activity in the valley. He watched as the women and military personnel dismantled their camp and filed onto the plateau. It was obvious from the direction they took that they were heading back to the city. Khan glanced at the sky as it loomed dark, heavy and ominous above him.

Right now, to bring his men forward would be to expose them. By the time they had covered the necessary distance, their objective would have had far too much time to see them and to engage. They needed to find a way of closing on the convoy so they would not detect the approach until it was too late.

Like most of the fighters who lived in the region, Khan knew the territory like the back of his hand—better, perhaps. There was very little cover between here and the outskirts of Quetta. Unless something changed soon, his people would be unable to overtake the caravan and find a point of ambush or attack before they reached civilization.

Suddenly, the wind that whipped across the plains went from humid to wet, and a low chuckle broke in his throat. Drops of moisture sprayed his face. As he turned to make his way back to the rest of his force, Khan knew that the gods had smiled on him.

A GRAY FOG DESCENDED on the women as they marched, and then it began to pour. They had to stop to turn Faiz on his stretcher and cover him as much as possible to prevent the rain from flooding his nose and mouth. The rain formed a curtain around them that cut their visibility down to a few yards.

Zia and Davis found their task impossible. They were hemmed in by the downpour. Anyone or anything could be out there, and the prospect made them nervous.

Bolan looked around, then up, and it was as if he was standing under a faucet. Rivulets of water and mud ran around their boots. Thankfully, the ground here was too rocky to become a quagmire, but it was now quite slippery underfoot.

The women were now huddled together, and Bolan called the military personnel over so they could reconsider their strategy. "Should we try to find shelter?" Davis asked.

"I wouldn't recommend shelter around here," Jinnah mused. "Too easy to get trapped if someone's coming for you, and there's no way we'd be able to see the enemy's approach."

As the words left his lips, Zia yelled and a shot rang out.

THE TALIBAN FIGHTERS upped their pace and advanced through the rain. They were sure-footed and used to these sudden changes in weather, so made up the distance between their position and the PWLA convoy with ease. With the rain as cover, they moved with an impunity that added to their speed. They knew that if they made ground quickly, they could descend out of the gray curtain and take on their enemy before they had a chance to react.

Khan led the way, signaling to the men when they were approaching the caravan. The PWLA had been marching at a steady pace, so he estimated their position. Timing was everything—they would come upon the women and strike swiftly. They would be ready and their enemy would not.

But when the women loomed up at them out of the mist, it was sooner than the scout expected. The Taliban fighters were not fully prepared for their own ambush, and one man gave a shout of alarm.

ZIA WAS EDGY. He had a feeling in his gut that something was very wrong. He mistrusted the terrain and the weather, and he was sure that the Americans—no matter how good Colonel Stone was—didn't understand how treacherous these conditions could be. Corporal Jinnah knew, of course, but he was momentarily distracted. The women—well, Zia had been impressed by their bravery and the speed with which they were picking up skills and knowledge, but they were children when it came to hill fighting.

Reacting to some strange instinct, Zia turned back in time to see a man bearing the Taliban insignia, with an AK slipping off his shoulder, almost run into him. They were so close that he could see the surprise in his enemy's eyes that he was sure was mirrored in his own.

He yelled an incoherent warning and fired on the

man. The shock was forever fixed on his face as the shell from the Zia's AK took off the top of his head. He dropped, and before he hit the rain-sodden ground, Zia had already shifted his aim to cover the men who were scattering before him.

At his back, his warning had served its purpose. The women had turned their attention away from their own huddle and had shouldered their weapons. Some were already loosing shots into the space where the Taliban fighters had been just moments before. But already they were like wraiths in the fog of rain.

Bolan yelled at the women to form a circle and fire outward, keeping the wounded man and someone to carry him in the center. They would have to try to move in this pattern, so that they could cover themselves without being a static target. A hard maneuver at the best of times, let alone under such harsh conditions.

There was no shelter out here; the only thing that could help them was also the thing that could cause them the most harm. The rain was their friend and their enemy. It made the opposition hard to track, but by the same token, the Taliban men would have difficulty pinpointing the PWLA fighters' positions and picking them off.

Bolan fired into the mist, trying to place his rounds with care, knowing that ammo was at a premium and any break in the stream of fire could give the enemy an opening.

He could hear a steady rhythmic pattern of fire

emerging from all around him, and knew that the brief training they'd given the PWLA had worked. The women were firing in short bursts, and staggering their fire as they tried to pick targets rather than waste ammo in spray'n'pray.

Zia had moved forward, taking it on himself to adopt an offensive position and try to drive the enemy back. If it worked, then they would be unable to place any effective fire on the women, and Davis and Jinnah could marshal the convoy away while the Executioner joined the young Pakistani soldier in forming a rear guard to cover their retreat.

Bolan checked on Davis and Jinnah. The American was trying to locate the enemy and drive them back, like Zia, but she seemed to be having a hard time getting a visual through the curtain of rain.

Jinnah, too, was having few problems. Cradling his AK in the crook of his elbow, moving backward and firing only the occasional shot as he covered himself, the corporal was yelling in Urdu for the women to gather and move as one. He used his free hand to indicate the kind of movement he meant.

So far, the return fire had been sporadic and ill-directed. Gunshots echoed high and wide, or chipped rock and threw up small sprays of mud at their feet. The enemy must be finding visual contact hard, as well. Bolan could only hope this would continue. If the rain let up just a little right now, he had a bad feeling that the women would be sitting ducks.

Although they were more or less firing blind, his people were getting lucky. He heard two distinct cries of pain as shots struck home. However many opponents were on their tail, at least two of them were effectively out of the game. It was a start.

Squinting into the rain-dark distance, Bolan yelled as a light flared up brightly in front of him, searing his vision. He looked away for a second to save his eyes, and when he turned back he was standing in a cone of light. A yard away from him, a flare lay sputtering on the ground as its phosphorescent glow did battle with the rain that sought to extinguish it.

He was the only visible target, and fire began to rain in on him as thickly as the water that threatened his sight and his footing. Bolan stood between the enemy and the PWLA, and he knew that any fire flying past him would endanger the women at his back. There was only one thing he could do to save the women behind him, and to save himself. He dived for the flare, hitting the ground in a roll and feeling the rock jar his shoulder, numbing it temporarily. He grabbed the flare, flinging it back in the direction from which it had come. A chattering of fire from the PWLA line told him that he may have had the luck of illuminating some of their assailants. He threw himself to the side, coming to rest with a bone-crunching whack against a small cluster of boulders.

Hardly pausing to get his breath back, knowing that

to be still could cost him his life, the Executioner pulled himself up and tried to use the rocks as cover.

It was only as he stumbled to his feet that he felt the rock beneath him tremble and move. As it did, a teeth-grinding screech rent the air.

At first, Bolan thought somebody had used a grenade or explosive.

Then he realized it was much worse than that.

15

Jinnah cursed loudly as the ground shifted beneath his feet. Turning, he could see that the women had formed a circle, with two of them in its center carrying Faiz. These two fought to stay upright on the slippery ground. The American woman was only a meter or two from him, just visible through the downpour. She was staring around her, bewildered, and moved closer to Jinnah, stumbling as she got near. He bent at the knee to catch her, supporting her weight as she regained her footing.

"Where's Stone? And what the hell is going on?"

Jinnah shook his head. "I lost him when he threw the flare," he yelled over the driving rain and sporadic gunfire. "As for this—" he indicated the shaking rock beneath them "—it's just the way it is up here. Not stable land, Captain. If this is an earthquake, there's little we can do except wait it out and hope there aren't too many aftershocks. I think it is safe to say that this is a minor—"

"How the hell can you know that?" Davis snapped.

"We're still standing and not lying broken at the bottom of a ravine that has split the ground around us. That's how I know, Captain. Now, if you'll stop asking pointless questions, we may be able to find a way out of this."

The women had steadied themselves as a unit, and had ceased shooting as the enemy's fire now seemed out of range. Hidden from view by the incessant rain, there was the sporadic chatter of fire a short distance away, a call and response that suggested Zia was still standing, and more than holding his own against the Taliban fighters. They were making little headway against him, it seemed, although it was worrying that he was now lost from view to his own forces. Zia was out there on his own, with no real sense of direction, and only the imperative to stay alive to keep him going.

"We need to throw him a lifeline," Davis said to Jinnah.

Jinnah nodded briefly. "The ground looks relatively unscathed to the west—you take the women that way. Keep going. If there are no great aftershocks you should be fine. I'll go after Zia and guide him back."

"What about Stone?" Davis asked.

Jinnah chewed his lip. "Don't think I'm not concerned about the colonel," he said carefully. "But I have the feeling the man can look after himself better than the rest of us."

BOLAN HAD BEEN thrown off his feet as the quake shuddered beneath him, and he saw red flashing lights as his head hit the sharp edge of a rock. He tasted blood as it streamed from the shallow cut and into his mouth. He wiped it away and groped blindly for something to stem the flow and clean his face. His combat shirt had a ragged tear where his ribs had crashed against the rock, and he ripped a section of it off.

His head swam as he stood, and he stopped suddenly, drawing a deep breath and using all the breathing and martial arts techniques he had picked up over the years to try to slow his pounding heart and lower the rising blood pressure that was adding to the mild concussion sustained by his fall. This would have to work damn quickly. Even through the steady rainfall, he could sense that the enemy was closing in on him.

Over to one side he could hear the exchange of fire as one of his people headed off the enemy. That took care of some of the attackers, but he had no idea how many there were in total.

One thing was for sure: one of the Taliban fighters was out there. The Executioner could feel him getting closer.

Bolan instinctively turned full circle and saw the figure emerge out of the rain. The man held a wickedly curved blade in a goatskin grip above his head, ready to strike down where the soldier's shoulder blade had been a moment before. There was no time to take any kind of evasive action. The only thing Bolan could do was step backward and reach out to grab his enemy's arm as it descended. Bolan steadied himself as he took the man's momentum and used it against him, moving back and to one side, guiding the man's knife hand so it skimmed harmlessly past him. His assailant fell face-first onto the rocks. Before he had a chance to recover, Bolan was on the man's back, with his knee on his spine. He gripped the man's neck, feeling for his chin. He took hold and of it and twisted, hearing the man's neck crack.

Breathing heavily, Bolan straightened and looked around. There was no one visible through the rain, and for that he was glad. Every second without a threat was in his favor.

Bolan gathered himself and stayed the spinning in his head. He picked up his AK and began to move slowly toward the sounds of the firefight.

ZIA STOOD HIS GROUND, advancing slowly until he found cover. He had just settled into a small patch of scrub when the earth heaved beneath him, throwing him sideways. He fell on one knee but managed to keep himself upright enough to shoot at a dark shape he saw flit through the mist. Returned fire ripped up chunks of stone about two meters from where he was kneeling. That was good. He figured he had a better sight of them than they had of him.

He was aware now, though, that his need to find cover and the shaking of the earth had driven a wedge—maybe a physical one—between him and the convoy. Pausing between his bursts of fire, he could hear nothing except the shots returned in his direction. He had no idea where the PWLA was in relation to his position.

He looked back, desperate to spot some kind of landmark. There was nothing to help him. He would just have to hope for the best.

Zia left his cover, keeping low and refraining from fire so as not to draw attention to his position. He figured his intent to drive back the enemy had been successful. The fact that a larger scale firefight hadn't erupted confirmed this. His only problem was that his success had left him out on a limb.

Zia kept running. The low visibility meant that anyone coming up on him would appear out of the mist quickly. He would need to be sharp. His nerves jangled as he ran, adrenaline coursing through his veins and drying his mouth. His head pounded with every step, with every beat of his heart.

A dark shape loomed out of the rain, and he raised his AK, finger tightening on the trigger even as the barrel came up level. It was only when his finger tensed the last fraction of an inch that he recognized the figure cutting through the curtain of water. Zia cursed as he realized he was about to shoot one of his own.

BOLAN HAD SOME idea of where the convoy may be. He took his bearings from the direction of the gunfire, and the assumption that this firefight was down to the actions of Zia as he pushed forward. If the hardy young soldier had kept moving in the same direction as when

Bolan had last seen him, then the opposite direction should lead him back to the PWLA party.

It was a theory that was seriously flawed, but it was all he had right now.

He kept low, using every small piece of cover that appeared out of the all-encompassing deluge. Behind one small bush, its barren branches glistening with jewels of water, he stopped to take stock and to wipe the water out of his eyes.

The firefight was sporadic now, and from this he gathered that the enemy had not so much disengaged as lost sight of their prey. Zia must be attempting to fall back and rejoin the main party. He heaved himself up and started across the slippery rock and thin layer of mud beneath his feet, hoping that both he and Zia would reach the PWLA before the Taliban fighters.

And without any mishap…

JINNAH POUNDED ACROSS the terrain with a more sure-footed stride than anyone else on his team. He had spent many years of early service in Balochistan and had seen conditions like this before. He knew how hard it was to fight under this blanket of rain, and how easy it was to lose your comrades. Zia was a good man, and Jinnah would hate to see him taken out of the game no matter what. But he'd be damned if Zia was lost to the conditions and not the opposition.

The corporal followed the sounds of the firefight, even as it died down. He could track Zia by the soldier's firing pattern. Every man had some slight variation in the way he used his weapon. If you listened carefully, you could learn to differentiate. Jinnah had mastered that art.

As long as Zia had been shooting, Jinnah had been able to pinpoint his position, but now the young soldier had ceased fire, presumably as he tried to backtrack. The dearth of return fire suggested the enemy had lost visual on him, and he'd likely be hair-trigger nervous. The last thing Jinnah wished to do was surprise him, so he slowed as he got closer to the young soldier.

Although he'd anticipated Zia's reaction, Jinnah was still shocked when the figure of the young soldier came into view. He saw Zia raise his AK as if in slow motion. Jinnah felt his legs refuse to slow or change direction as his mind grasped what was happening faster than his body could respond. His mouth grew dry and he couldn't find his voice to cry out in warning.

Friendly fire. It would be an understandable error. But this was no comfort to Jinnah as he felt the world slow to a heartbeat.

ZIA COULD NOT prevent the tap on the trigger, but he could jerk almost involuntarily, swinging the muzzle of the AK up and to one side of the corporal. It skimmed past Jinnah's shoulder and ear, close enough to singe his hair. But the shots whistled harmlessly into the air behind him.

For the briefest moment, the two men faced each

other. There was so much to say and no time to say it. Zia was both appalled and relieved at his actions, and he wanted to gabble an apology even though he knew they couldn't afford to stand around any longer. But they were both frozen by the shock of what had just happened—and what had been averted.

The impasse was broken by the sudden chatter of fire from three sides, homing in on where they stood. The enemy was closer than either of them had believed, and had located them by the single tap from Zia's AK. Bullets shattered on rock and threw up mud around them. Zia realized his efforts to drive the enemy back hadn't been as successful as he'd initially thought. They had to move, now, to save themselves and to save the women in the convoy. Right now, Davis was the only experienced soldier with the women. No way could she hold back the Taliban on her own.

Jinnah grabbed Zia, pulling him in his wake as he began to dodge the fire and backtrack.

There was still work to be done.

16

Davis held her rifle with the barrel pointed down as she prowled the area around the moving group. She skipped over the ground, avoiding uneven rocks slippery with running water and mud, eyes cast into the sheet of water that obscured almost everything over a yard away. She trusted that the women were staying in formation, with the wounded soldier and his stretcher bearers protected in the middle.

The sounds of a distant firefight abated. This only made her more nervous. Did it mean her military associates had been killed? Or did it mean that they had taken down the opposition and were headed back to join the main party? The silence that had fallen in the distance was oppressive rather than reassuring.

The women clearly felt this way, too. Tension pervaded the group. Shazana Yasmin trudged along next to Suri. Davis knew that the flask of fissionable material was in the doctor's backpack. Even if it was adequately protected, the thought of Yasmin carrying it so close to the others—of it being taken or lost—was enough to send a chill through the captain. The last forty-eight hours had been a roller-coaster fight for them all just to stay alive, and in the midst of this, the original objective had almost been lost. They were going to get Yasmin and the material back to the authorities, but the journey was not proving to be the smooth ride she had hoped for.

Her musing was broken by the sudden crack of a rifle shot, followed by volley upon volley of automatic fire. A ripple of fear and discontent passed through the PWLA convoy and straight down Davis's spine.

She stared into the rain. If the storm ceased, then they would be visible on the flat terrain, but at least they would know what they faced.

Unconsciously, she pressed closer to the main group. Closer to Yasmin.

"Tamara, what's going on?" the young physicist asked. "You're a soldier, you understand this shit."

"Don't kid yourself," Davis shot back. "I might have two tours of Afghanistan, but I never saw anything like this…."

"Great, so it's the blind leading the blind," Suri grumbled next to Yasmin.

"You got a better idea, you just tell me," Davis muttered. "Meantime, just keep moving. A moving target is harder to hit, ladies."

The firefight in the background had died down again. The occasional chatter was too desultory to even qualify as an exchange. Whichever parties had engaged had lost each other once again in the curtain of water.

What really worried her was that the gunfire had sounded a whole lot closer than it had any right to be.

Where was the enemy?

THERE WERE THREE of them. Weighted down by their sodden robes, they moved slowly. Slowly, but with a certainty that they were headed in the right direction. The short burst of fire had alerted them to the military presence, and although they knew they had failed to score a hit, they had been able to circle around the two men they had glimpsed through the rain and continue on their quest to find the women.

There was a mass moving through the mist ahead of them that could only be the PWLA convoy. They were slow and shuffling, as if they were carrying some of their personnel. This would make them easier to take down.

The fighters weren't close enough to count their opposition, but they were women, after all—they would not present a problem in a firefight. And the men were either dead or too far away to matter.

Without words, the most senior man indicated that one of his men stay back and cover the rearguard position, closing up gradually to gain better visual contact, while he and the third man would flank the convoy in a pincer formation. When he whistled, they would open fire, taking down the taller women first until the depleted numbers made it easier to close in for hand-to-hand combat.

The other two nodded their understanding and began to put the plan into action. The leader moved quickly and with stealth over the terrain. It did not take him long to get into a position where he could use whatever cover was available to disguise his progress. At the same time, he was confident that the women could not see him through the mist. Unlike him and his comrades, they were inexperienced in these conditions.

He circled around to the front of the convoy, taking the opportunity to count the numbers and to pick out the women who could potentially be their target. They progressed slowly, their anxiety obvious. This only encouraged him—they were women, and when challenged, they would soon crumble.

He pursed his lips and emitted the signal.

DAVIS HAD THE feeling that they were being watched, but she had no way of knowing if this was paranoia or genuine intuition. She scanned the immediate area, but her visibility was still impeded by the rain. Still, she raised her rifle so that she was ready to fire off in the direction of any sound she picked up. She cast an anxious glance back across the convoy, and could see the women were on edge, too.

When the whistle came, her reaction was instant. She didn't know who had made the signal or why, and it didn't matter. Her own people would not be so stupid as to approach in that way—it could only be the enemy.

She fired three rounds toward the sound while yelling at the women to hold their formation and be ready to fight.

Her words were unnecessary, and drowned out by the gunfire that answered her own from two other directions. She tried to turn to answer the fire that seemed to come from behind them, but the sole of her combat boot slid on a mud-slick rock and took her leg out from under her. She fell backward, hitting the ground with a jar to her elbow that made her firing arm go numb. She cursed and shook it, not noticing at first what had happened behind her.

The fall may have temporarily disabled her, but it saved her life. The bullet that had been headed for her flew harmlessly past as she tumbled. Unfortunately, Suri was directly behind Davis, and the bullet took her in the forehead, spraying Yasmin with blood and as she stood beside her friend.

Yasmin screamed as Suri crumpled and fell without uttering a sound.

Despite all that she had learned in the past couple days, Yasmin was still a young woman and a city scientist, not a hill fighter. Before Davis could stop her, she broke into a run, disappearing into the mist.

Davis yelled after her as she struggled to her feet, still trying to shake feeling back into her firing arm. She hefted the rifle as she ran after the fleeing Yasmin, screaming incoherently in anger and pain as she tried to catch her while readying herself for defense or attack.

Behind her, the ranks of the PWLA convoy broke

up as the volleys of fire took out two more women. The others scattered seeking cover. Some flattened themselves to the ground and fired into the opaque rain. The enemy was in a better position to see them than they were to scope the enemy, and without their defensive formation, they were sorely exposed.

The women were blind both in terms of visibility and in terms of tactics. And the one person who could have rallied them was now chasing after her primary objective.

YUSEF KHAN COULD not believe his luck. Though he'd managed to take down one of the women, he couldn't tell which one was likely to have the flask. He knew any moment of hesitation could be disastrous. As he struggled to place his aim, a small woman, spooked by her comrade's sudden demise beside her, broke ranks and began sprinting right for him. All he had to do was wait for her to run straight into his arms, then disable and secure her before his men finished the job.

The American woman who was chasing her might be a problem, but as she limped after the Pakistani woman with her gun arm limp at her side, she didn't seem to present too much of a challenge. Khan was about to fire when the American woman heaved her AK upright and fired wild and wide. The shots rang uselessly over his head, but instinct still made him duck. The sound made the terrified Pakistani woman change direction, so that she was now running away from him.

With an oath dropping from his lips, Khan turned his attention away from the American and focused on catching the young Pakistani woman before she was swallowed up by the rain and fog. He loosed one last volley to deflect the American soldier, leaving the rest of the PWLA convoy to his two remaining men.

JINNAH AND ZIA TOOK cover behind a rock. They had no idea exactly how many opposition fighters were out there in total, but the arcs of fire told them they were now in a two-on-two situation. The two Pakistani soldiers had to eliminate the threat of the two men on their tail and track back to the convoy.

As they waited, they could hear a whistle and the chatter of AK fire. They exchanged glances—time was tight. Footsteps drew nearer and both men racked their weapons, waiting for the figures to reveal themselves.

Two robed men suddenly became visible, eyes flashing wildly as they tried to locate their prey.

The Taliban fighters raised their rifles as they caught sight of the two Pakistani soldiers with their AKs resting on the top of the rocks, only the tops of their heads visible.

Steeling themselves and ignoring the sound and fury, Jinnah and Zia squeezed gently on their triggers, a short burst of automatic fire from each man taking care of their targets. Hit full in the chest, the robed men froze for a fraction of a second before the impact threw them back onto the muddy rocks, eyes unblinking as the rain poured into them.

The Pakistani soldiers paused to see if the brief fire-fight would bring any other forces down on them. But the air was silent, punctuated only by distant gunfire. There was little doubt where the action was happening now, and it was their task to get there as soon as they could.

As they left the corpses behind them, they could only hope Stone was already on the scene to help Davis.

BOLAN SHOOK HIS head once more. He was sure he had a minor concussion—his vision was blurred and starry, and his gut churned.

He didn't hear or see anything to indicate an enemy presence, and the lack of an immediate threat was good. But he'd lost his bearings in the rain and from the crack on the head, with only distant exchanges of fire to lead him in the right direction. He had to reorient himself and make up the ground—quickly, by the sound of it.

Looking around, he realized he could see a little farther than before. He was too wet to tell from the impact of the drops on his skin, but the improved visibility suggested that the rain was finally easing. At least now he'd be able to see their opponents, even if that meant these opponents could track them a little more easily.

Better the devil you knew...

One of the firefights had reached its conclusion, and Bolan could only make out erratic exchange to the southwest. That was where the PWLA must be making a stand. He wondered how many of them were still alive, and how Zia, Jinnah and Davis were faring. Bolan hoped his fellow soldiers had emerged on top. Their strength and expertise would be needed.

17

Lasi was the first of the PWLA women to grasp that the firefight had stopped and that their attackers had withdrawn. She had sharper senses than any of her fellow fighters, even those who had also come from mountain villages. Still, most of the casualties within the group had been city-dwelling intellectuals rather than the rural women.

Although the initial bursts of fire had taken the women by surprise and scattered them across a narrow area, forcing them to lose their formation, they had soon regrouped and directed their fire back at their attackers.

As the battle proceeded, Lasi had been able to take stock of the situation and note that there were only three points of fire. She quickly figured out that although they had been taken by surprise, the PWLA outnumbered the opposition.

This angered her. She hated the fact that three stupid bastard men had them pinned down, and she was determined to fight back, single-handed if necessary. Crouching, she kept up covering fire and rallied the women, pulling them back into position. So far, their opponents had been unable to score any more casualties than the first lucky shot.

Lasi aimed to keep it that way. The stupid scientist had run in terror when her friend had died, and the idiot American had run after her. That didn't surprise her at all—the city women were weak, and the American had only pretended to be a friend to all. Her only interest was Yasmin—at least the American man had been honest about that. The woman had pretended to be behind the PWLA's cause, but she'd made her true allegiance known when Yasmin ran, leaving them exposed.

Screw her. The scientist, on the other hand... She was valuable, and it would help the PWLA to get her back. Lasi determined to retrieve Yasmin once she had this situation nailed down.

As she encouraged her troops, the opposing fire died out. The three Taliban fighters had run after Yasmin and Davis. If that wasn't another indication of how important the stupid little girl was to everyone, then what the hell was?

Barking orders at Indira to secure the group, set up defense, and wait, Lasi ran across the treacherous terrain as fast as she dared, blinking back the rain. The sky was clearing, and visibility was improving by the second. Being exposed on the plateau could be dangerous for some, but it suited her just fine. She'd be coming up from behind to kick them all in the ass.

JINNAH AND ZIA were now able to scout for cover and use it, and the thinning rain gave them a better view of approaching figures.

"Corporal, what the hell—" Zia began.

"Don't ask, just wait," Jinnah interjected, silencing the younger man with a gesture. He, too, was unable to believe what he was seeing.

Yasmin was charging across the plateau, slipping and stumbling as she ran toward them. She still had her backpack on, but she had no gun. Behind her, Davis struggled to catch up.

Jinnah's mind raced. Did this mean the rest of the women had been wiped out? What about Faiz? Why the hell was Yasmin running, and how had Davis let her get away?

At the moment, these questions were irrelevant.

"Circle around them, and seek and destroy any hostiles," he snapped at Zia.

"You think that—" Zia began, but Jinnah cut him off once more.

"I don't think anything. I just know Davis isn't being careful, and any bastard could be on their tail."

Zia got the message and set off in a counterclockwise arc, leaving his superior officer to take the clockwise circuit.

Jinnah figured that the whole mission was on the verge of going belly up. If anything happened to Yasmin because of Davis's idiotic chase, then she had screwed up without needing the help of the Taliban or any local rebels. Now that would be fun, explaining their failure to the NCA.

Jinnah caught sight of three shadows, one way ahead of the others, flitting from cover to cover. The man in the lead was gaining on the two women while the second trailed slightly behind. They'd be the ones to go for.

The problem was that the third man was heading straight toward Jinnah.

And if Jinnah could see the enemy, then the enemy could see him.

The corporal cursed. Firing would rattle Yasmin even more, and he could no longer trust Davis's reactions. A volley could also panic the two leading Taliban warriors, and a firefight was the last thing he wanted with the women out in the open.

Jinnah was fortunate in the sense that the man running toward him was apparently smart enough to work out that gunfire would be counterproductive. But as they closed on each other, the warrior drew a long, scythed blade from a sheath under his robes. The grip was bound in hide and would be a more than adequate blackjack in its own right. Jinnah drew his own blade, which had a light grip and was razor sharp, but his blade was nowhere near as long. His opponent would have the advantage of reach.

Teeth bared in a snarl, his eyes glittering with a blend of fear and fury, the Taliban fighter hefted his knife and sped up, preparing to strike. Seeing that the man's body had opened up despite remaining partially hidden beneath the swirling robes, Jinnah lashed out with his own knife. His blade ripped at folds of cloth but missed flesh and bone. The corporal winced as his opponent desperately brought the grip down on his back, clubbing at him.

Twisting away from the blows so that they glanced rather then struck heavily, he thrust upward once more, twisting the blade and feeling it penetrate flesh and then jar as it hit bone before skidding off and biting deeper. He felt his opponent gasp, felt the warm blood from the man's mouth splash on his neck and then the deadweight pitch onto him, pushing him back.

Jinnah rolled as he fell, his opponent's corpse flopping away from him. Leaving the knife in place—there was no time to retrieve it—he looked around and swore.

In the time it had taken him to engage in combat, the women and the other two warriors had retreated almost out of sight.

But one more figure had appeared as he fought, and he was now passing beyond view.

Maybe there was still hope....

ZIA TOOK COVER and watched the Taliban fighter come toward him. Two men had been coming his way, but one had veered off slightly and the other had fallen behind. Now, Zia had the second man in his sights. He had a notion that Jinnah was already in hand-to-hand with the third opponent, but they were lost to view.

Zia had a clear shot at the man. He could take him out

cleanly and quickly, but the noise could create a whole lot of trouble—that must be why he hadn't heard any fire from Jinnah's direction. Reluctantly, Zia put down his AK and drew his knife. Ahead of him, the Taliban warrior was moving swiftly, trying to catch up to the other man. His focus on his compatriot made him careless, and he didn't see Zia in hiding. Hunkering down below the scrub, Zia waited.

The fighter drew level and was almost past Zia before he noticed the Pakistani soldier out of the corner of his eye. He tried to stop and address the sudden threat, but his own momentum carried him on a few steps, off balance now as he tried to turn and ready himself for attack.

Zia sprang out at the man before he had a chance to steady himself. The young soldier leaped across the meter and a half that separated them, landing on his man and driving him onto the ground, the air driven from his opponent's lungs. As they fell, Zia shoved his knife under the man's ribs and deep into his vital organs. The man fought for breath and for his life, struggling to free himself from the blade. He yelped as the pain of scored flesh gave him the adrenaline rush to fight back.

As the two men scrabbled for a better hold, rocking back and forth, the Taliban fighter managed to flip Zia, bringing his knee up into the soldier's groin with as much force as he could muster.

Zia lost his grip as he flailed on his back, and his

knife skittered away from him. Searing pain in his groin made the world turn red for a second, and when it subsided, he found that he was on the receiving end of a blade as his assailant unsheathed his own and tried to jab it into Zia's throat.

The private blocked the blow with his forearm, although the edge of the blade cut through his fatigues and skin. His opponent's forward thrust carried him down so that he almost head-butted Zia, and the soldier took advantage of this by using the only weapon available to him. He bit the man on the nose, clamping down hard and feeling the gristle and cartilage between his teeth, blood flowing over his face. The pain and surprise made the man loosen his grip, and gave Zia the opportunity he needed. He heaved hard and brought his knee into the man's crotch, giving him a taste of what he'd inflicted earlier. The man rolled awkwardly off the soldier, groping around on his hands and knees as the pain and blood blinded him.

Zia jumped on the man's back, pinning him down. He reached under his chin with both hands, grunting with the effort of twisting hard and sharp. As soon as he heard the click of his enemy's neck breaking, he sat back on his heels, breathing heavily.

He stood up and vomited as the pain in his groin was finally allowed precedence over the adrenaline rush that had saved him. Shaking his head to clear it, he took in his surroundings.

Yasmin, Davis and the other Taliban fighter were

distant blurs in the mist. Gasping to get his breath back, Zia picked up the discarded AK and tried to run after them, pain slowing him.

There was a figure between himself and the group ahead. Was it Jinnah?

BOLAN JOGGED THROUGH the rain, heading toward the gunfire he'd heard earlier. The plateau had fallen silent. What the hell was going on? He held the AK across his chest as he ran, ready to shoulder it instantly. He didn't bother with concealment—it was too late to worry about that now.

He stopped when he heard a yell echo across the plain. He was sure it was Davis—certainly it was female. He listened closely for a moment, and frowned as he heard someone approaching. Taking stock of his position, he spotted a flat rock tilted up at a slight angle, which would provide cover if he lay flat. Quickly, he moved behind it and waited for any oncoming traffic, be it friend or foe.

DAVIS YELLED AT Yasmin to stop. She tried to gain ground, but the young scientist was fast—likely spurred on and strengthened by the panic and adrenaline coursing through her system.

But as long as Yasmin was still in view, Davis felt she still had a chance of reaching her. She hadn't been looking to either side or to her rear, and was oblivious to the combat that had taken place in her wake. And she was oblivious to the Taliban warrior until he stepped out from behind a rock in front of her, water dripping down his face and off his beard. Given her speed and momentum, Davis was painfully aware that she was about to run into him before she had an opportunity to react.

The last thing she saw was a fist the size of a ham as it slammed into her face, splitting her nose. She staggered back, and a second blow caught her in the jaw. She hit the ground like a sack of potatoes and the world went black.

BEFORE THE AMERICAN had even landed in the mud, Khan had already turned on his heel to chase after the girl. He had fought his way to many a bare-knuckle purse in Lahore, Quetta and Kabul in his younger days, and he knew the female soldier was no longer a threat. He hadn't noticed if he'd killed her, and he didn't much care. If she was dead, end of problem; if she wasn't, then by the time she came around he would be long gone.

He ran freely now. If the young woman ahead of him turned and screamed, then so what? What could she do? She was unarmed, having dropped her weapon in fear. She may be clever, but she wasn't brave. Unlike him…

Khan closed on her, and she stopped suddenly and turned toward him, like a little child. She opened her mouth to scream but had no chance. He was on her before she could utter a sound. He felt her writhe against him, then he pushed her back and slapped her across the face, knocking her to the ground.

Grabbing her in one vast paw, he yanked her to her feet. "Shut up and do what I say, or there's more of that. You have the stuff?"

"What stuff?" She was crying, and her voice trembled.

"Don't try to show me how clever you are," Khan snarled. "You know what I mean."

The woman stared at him, fear and defiance doing battle in her expression before resignation crept in. She nodded. "I've got it here," she said, indicating her backpack.

He laughed harshly. "Come on."

They set off marching at a pace that she had difficulty keeping up with. He wasn't worried about any more opponents out here, but he wanted to get her back to camp as soon as possible. The sooner he delivered the target, the sooner he'd get his prize.

Out of nowhere, a figure holding an AK stood up from cover less than a hundred meters ahead of them. But Khan was ready. Pushing the girl forward, he shoved the muzzle of his rifle into her spine.

BOLAN WATCHED TWO distinct figures emerge from the mist. One was a tall, heavily built man in dark robes. He held an AK in one hand, and with the other he gripped a much smaller, slighter figure.

Shazana Yasmin.

Somehow the bastard had separated the scientist from the convoy.

He wasn't going to get any farther. As they came nearer, the rain ceased and Bolan was able to see them clearly. A clean shot—that was all he needed. He rose from cover, shouldering the AK so that he had the Taliban fighter clearly in his sights. Before he could fire, though, the man thrust Yasmin in front of him. She only reached his shoulders, which meant his head was a clear shot, but the twisted grin on his face told Bolan that it wouldn't be that simple.

"Let her go," Bolan called. "Let her go. I can still take you down."

"I think not," the man said. Roughly, he moved her sideways so Bolan could see the rifle pressed into her backpack. "You know what she's carrying, right?"

"I do," Bolan replied calmly. "You fire and you kill her, sure. You kill yourself, too. You let that radiation spread across the land and you'll poison your own. You think the prophet wants that?"

The robed man spat. "How dare you speak like that? What do you know of such things?"

"Enough to know that no leader can continue to lead without living followers," Bolan replied coolly. He kept the AK level. "Now tell me why I shouldn't just take you down now."

"Because I am watching you, American—as soon as your finger tightens on the trigger, I'll fire first, and all of your efforts will be in vain. You are not so stupid as to do that."

"I'm not so sure," Bolan replied. "You think we're

just dumb Yanks, right? So why shouldn't I act like one? Watch my fingers…you think I'm going to shoot? Feel lucky?"

Bolan could see the confusion on Yasmin's face— she couldn't work out why he was taunting her captor in this way. Of course she couldn't. Bolan knew the man would likely be as good as his word, and he had no real intention of testing it. But he wanted to command the man's full attention. The only issue was whether he would be able to keep it long enough to get the job done.

"Then you are a stupid—"

Bolan would never find out what. A single shot rang out across the plateau, and a look of astonishment crossed his opponent's face before his head exploded and he fell to the ground.

Yasmin blinked in disbelief, opened her mouth and then fell to her knees.

Behind her, Zia and Jinnah were approaching, and between them and the corpse stood a lone figure, her AK at her shoulder, her gaze still fixed on the target she had taken down. Slowly, Lasi let the AK drop, then looked Bolan squarely in the eye. The briefest ghost of a grin crossed her grim visage.

Bolan breathed a sigh of relief. He had seen her creep out into the open, and had tried to keep the Taliban fighter's attention away from her until she could take aim and fire. It seemed to take an eternity for her to squeeze the trigger.

Not that he blamed her. There was only the one chance, and it had to be a clean kill.

It had been worth the wait. "Good shot," Bolan called, nodding in respect and gratitude.

Now it was time to finally put this mission to bed.

18

Wearily, Bolan, Lasi, Yasmin and the two Pakistani soldiers trudged back toward the PWLA convoy. After consulting the others, Bolan was confident they'd cleared the area of enemy threats, at least for now.

Along the way, they came across Davis. She was sprawled on the ground, and Bolan brought her around slowly, figuring from the state of her face that she could be another concussion victim. It certainly looked as though her nose had been broken. Even so, her pride hurt worse when she woke up and realized what had happened. She berated herself briefly and bitterly, rejecting offers of help as she got to her feet.

When they reached the PWLA, they found that Indira had rallied her people, and the women were thankful to have Lasi and Yasmin back in their ranks.

Bolan and Jinnah checked Faiz. The medic was bent over him, and when she glanced up, concern was etched on her face.

"We must move, and we must have no further interruption," she said sharply, as though the two soldiers had been solely responsible for the recent firefight. "I fear there may be infection."

"I don't think we could handle another interruption. Not right now," Bolan replied drily, casting an eye over himself and the other three military personnel. "Get him ready to move."

With one assault force successfully turned away, and no other signs of additional enemies encroaching, Bolan felt it was reasonable to assume that the severe weather had made it difficult for any forces wishing to follow in the wake of the recently defeated to track their prey successfully. They now had a head start on any other factions, which they needed considering how exhausted they were after the recent battle.

Quetta was a day's march away if they stopped to rest when darkness fell, but it was obvious that the PWLA women had no wish to halt. Stop, and they may never want to move again. Stop, and they allowed any enemy in their wake to close in on them. So they continued, even though their muscles and bones ached for rest.

When they reached the road leading to the city, they still weren't in the clear. The geography of the region made communication difficult, with only shortwave radio working with any degree of reliability, which was, at an understatement, erratic.

They walked along the road to Quetta until they encountered the first traffic the soldiers had seen since disembarking from the transport a few days before— longer, for the women. An ancient truck trundled by, transporting fruit and vegetables that looked the worse for their journey. The driver was reluctant to stop when they hailed him from a distance, and if anything seemed to speed up as he approached.

In this territory, he could hardly be blamed. But when Jinnah and Zia stepped into the road and leveled their rifles at him, the combination of their hardware and their uniforms forced him to a halt. Reluctantly, he let them climb into the truck bed, settling themselves among the pungent crates. Bolan guessed that the soldiers' presence was what stayed the driver from complaint as he carried them into Quetta and dropped them at the barracks.

Their arrival was greeted with shock. Bolan, Davis and the military personnel had been written off as casualties as soon as they had left, and their return—with their objective, at that—was a cause of bemusement rather than satisfaction. It was as though their presence was an embarrassment for a military that would prefer Yasmin had perished out on the plateau with the rest of the PWLA rather than deal with the consequences of her return.

"WHERE IS THE MAJOR?" Bolan asked at the end of his report to General Sandila. He was in Lahore the day after their arrival in Quetta.

Sandila grinned. "The major is currently trying to convince Dr. Yasmin that she should return to work for the NCA. Possibly, I suspect, through a combination of wheedling and clumsy bullying."

Bolan looked at him quizzically. "You say that like you already know what her answer will be."

Sandila shrugged. "I had a few words with the doctor and Captain Davis prior to this meeting. Major Malik was concerned, of course, with debriefing his own men first. Idiocy."

"I'm not sure you should dismiss them so easily," Bolan said. He was irked at the general's manner toward men who had earned Bolan's respect and a whole lot more on the frontline. It seemed all the more insulting considering that Faiz's leg had become infected and the soldier now faced amputation and dismissal from the forces on medical grounds. Bolan wondered if the general had ever experienced combat, and was about to ask when Sandila spoke again.

"Colonel Stone, you do me an injustice. I merely mean that men of that caliber can retain necessary information until debriefing, and frankly, they deserve a day without having to face Malik. I was referring to his idiocy. The major made a mess of this mission and the aftermath. The end of a long line of errors and relying on what the British called the 'old boys' network' to keep him afloat. I will be replacing him and heading up his unit, and things will be different. Under my command, men of quality are a necessity. In fact, my first order of business will be to promote Corporal Jinnah and Private Zia."

"I'm glad to hear it," Bolan said. "I shouldn't have doubted you. In any case, I'm thinking that the NCA won't be desperate to pin Dr. Yasmin down. After all, she has dual citizenship, we have excellent facilities in the U.S.A., and I'm sure a mutually beneficial arrangement could be made."

"Not officially, of course," Sandila agreed. "The official line will be that Dr. Yasmin will be a great loss, but we cannot stop her leaving because of her dual citizenship, the incompatibility of her political views and so forth. Naturally, our relationship with the U.S.A. is, at times, strained, but in the interest of preventing further strain, we hope any new research Yasmin conducts will be shared, if only tacitly, with our own physicists."

"I hope you work something out. I'm afraid that's not my department, though," Bolan said. "I'm more of a field researcher, myself."

The general blinked at Bolan. There was a pause, and then Sandila began to laugh.

BOLAN LOOKED IN on Faiz before he left, and found both Jinnah and Zia attendant. They were in somber moods because of their comrade's health, but were glad for the opportunity to bid farewell to the man they had fought alongside.

The flight back to Washington took him through the South Pacific on its circuitous route, and along the way he joined up with Davis and Yasmin. The physicist had little to say to him and spent most of the flight trying to pretend he wasn't there. Davis, on the other hand, made a hesitant apology.

"I had you figured wrong. I had you down as a typical meathead company man."

"Trusting me from the outset would have made things a whole lot easier," Bolan said.

"Maybe. It wouldn't have changed me screwing up, though," she muttered. Bolan waited for her to explain. "I let that Taliban asshole broadside me out there. I came out of two tours unscathed, but because I was emotionally involved, I let my focus go west. I could have killed Shaz."

"But you didn't, Davis. We all make mistakes occasionally. Some of us are lucky enough to get past that, and if we do, we learn the lesson. So learn the lesson and watch her back while you're working with her. That's all you can do, right?"

Davis nodded thoughtfully, but doubt still flickered in her expression.

Bolan hoped she'd come to believe his words. A soldier could learn all there was to know about strategy and weapons and technique, but even after years of combat, sometimes the most important skill was admitting one's own fallibility. Imperfection wasn't something to be overcome, but embraced with a vow to do better. The PWLA knew this now, and it was something Bolan reminded himself of daily. Whatever mission came his way next, he'd do better. He had to.

* * * * *

The Executioner

Don Pendleton's

DRAGON KEY

A rogue general will stop at nothing to protect his secret...

When an American operative is jailed, Mack Bolan must smuggle a Chinese activist and his family out of the country. But rescuing the dissident becomes a logistical nightmare. Not only are the Chinese authorities on their tail, but the activist insists on retrieving a stolen flash drive in Shanghai.

The memory key contains sensitive information belonging to a renegade general. As determined to recover the data as the dissident is, the general has hired a legendary assassin. In a battle where only one can survive, Bolan may have met his match.

Available February 2015, wherever books and ebooks are sold.

GOLD EAGLE

GEX435R

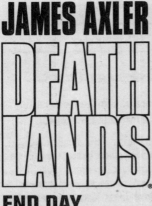